PAUL AUSTER – COLLECTED NOVELS
Volume 3

PAUL AUSTER

Collected Novels

faber and faber

First published in 2008
by Faber and Faber Limited
3 Queen Square London WC1N 3AU

Typeset by Faber and Faber Limited
Printed and bound in the UK by CPI Mackays, Chatham ME5 8TD
Chatham, Kent

A CIP record for this book is
available from the British Library

ISBN 978–0–571–24304–4

2 4 6 8 10 9 7 5 3 1

Contents

TIMBUKTU

for Robert McCrum

Mr. Bones knew that Willy wasn't long for this world. The cough had been inside him for over six months, and by now there wasn't a chance in hell that he would ever get rid of it. Slowly and inexorably, without once taking a turn for the better, the thing had assumed a life of its own, advancing from a faint, phlegm-filled rattle in the lungs on February third to the wheezy sputum-jigs and gobby convulsions of high summer. All that was bad enough, but in the past two weeks a new tonality had crept into the bronchial music – something tight and flinty and percussive – and the attacks came so often now as to be almost constant. Every time one of them started, Mr. Bones half expected Willy's body to explode from the rockets of pressure bursting against his rib cage. He figured that blood would be the next step, and when that fatal moment finally occurred on Saturday afternoon, it was as if all the angels in heaven had opened their mouths and started to sing. Mr. Bones saw it happen with his own eyes, standing by the edge of the road between Washington and Baltimore as Willy hawked up a few miserable clots of red matter into his handkerchief, and right then and there he knew that every ounce of hope was gone. The smell of death had settled upon Willy G. Christmas, and as surely as the sun was a lamp in the clouds that went off and on every day, the end was drawing near.

What was a poor dog to do? Mr. Bones had been with Willy since his earliest days as a pup, and by now it was next to impossible for him to imagine a world that did not have his master in it. Every thought, every memory, every particle of the earth and air was saturated with Willy's presence. Habits die hard, and no doubt there's some truth to the adage about old dogs and new tricks, but it was more than just love or devotion that caused Mr. Bones to dread what was coming. It was pure ontological terror. Subtract Willy from the world, and the odds were that the world itself would cease to exist.

Such was the quandary Mr. Bones faced that August morning as he shuffled through the streets of Baltimore with his ailing master. A dog alone was no better than a dead dog, and once Willy breathed his last, he'd have nothing to look forward to but his own imminent demise.

Willy had been cautioning him about this for many days now, and Mr. Bones knew the drill by heart: how to avoid the dogcatchers and constables, the paddy wagons and unmarked cars, the hypocrites from the so-called humane societies. No matter how sweetly they talked to you, the word *shelter* meant trouble. It would begin with nets and tranquilizer guns, devolve into a nightmare of cages and fluorescent lights, and end with a lethal injection or a dose of poison gas. If Mr. Bones had belonged to some recognizable breed, he might have stood a chance in the daily beauty contests for prospective owners, but Willy's sidekick was a hodgepodge of genetic strains – part collie, part Labrador, part spaniel, part canine puzzle – and to make matters worse, there were burrs protruding from his ragged coat, bad smells emanating from his mouth, and a perpetual bloodshot sadness lurking in his eyes. No one was going to want to rescue him. As the homeless bard was fond of putting it, the outcome was written in stone. Unless Mr. Bones found another master in one quick hurry, he was a pooch primed for oblivion.

'And if the stun guns don't get you,' Willy continued, clinging to a lamppost that foggy morning in Baltimore to prevent himself from falling, 'there's a thousand other things that will. I'm warning you, kemo sabe. You get yourself some new gig, or your days are numbered. Just look around this dreary burg. There's a Chinese restaurant on every block, and if you think mouths won't water when you come strolling by, then you don't know squat about Oriental cuisine. They prize the taste of dog, friend. The chefs round up strays and slaughter them in the alley right behind the kitchen – ten, twenty, thirty dogs a week. They might pass them off as ducks and pigs on the menu, but the in-crowd knows what's what, the gourmets aren't fooled for a second. Unless you want to wind up in a platter of moo goo gai pan, you'll think twice before you wag your tail in front of one of those Chink beaneries. Do you catch my drift, Mr. Bones? Know thine enemy – and then keep a wide berth.'

Mr. Bones understood. He always understood what Willy said to him. This had been the case for as long as he could remember, and by now his grasp of Ingloosh was as good as any other immigrant who had spent seven years on American soil. It was his second language, of course, and quite different from the one his mother had taught him, but even though his pronunciation left something to be desired, he had thoroughly mastered the ins and outs of its syntax and grammar. None of this should be seen as strange or unusual for an animal of Mr. Bones's intelligence. Most dogs acquire a good working knowledge of two-

6

legged speech, but in Mr. Bones's case there was the advantage of being blessed with a master who did not treat him as an inferior. They had been boon companions from the start, and when you added in the fact that Mr. Bones was not just Willy's best friend but his only friend, and then further considered that Willy was a man in love with the sound of his own voice, a genuine, dyed-in-the-wool logomaniac who scarcely stopped talking from the instant he opened his eyes in the morning until he passed out drunk at night, it made perfect sense that Mr. Bones should have felt so at home in the native lingo. When all was said and done, the only surprise was that he hadn't learned to talk better himself. It wasn't for lack of earnest effort, but biology was against him, and what with the configuration of muzzle, teeth, and tongue that fate had saddled him with, the best he could do was emit a series of yaps and yawns and yowls, a mooning, muddled sort of discourse. He was painfully aware of how far from fluency these noises fell, but Willy always let him have his say, and in the end that was all that mattered. Mr. Bones was free to put in his two cents, and whenever he did so his master would give him his full attention, and to look at Willy's face as he watched his friend struggle to make like a member of the human tribe, you would have sworn that he was hanging on every word.

That gloomy Sunday in Baltimore, however, Mr. Bones kept his mouth shut. They were down to their last days together, perhaps even their last hours, and this was no time to indulge in long speeches and loopy contortions, no time for the old shenanigans. Certain situations called for tact and discipline, and in their present dire straits it would be far better to hold his tongue and behave like a good, loyal dog. He let Willy snap the leash on to his collar without protest. He didn't whine about not having eaten in the past thirty-six hours; he didn't sniff the air for female scents; he didn't stop to pee on every lamppost and fire hydrant. He simply ambled along beside Willy, following his master as they searched the empty avenues for 316 Calvert Street.

Mr. Bones had nothing against Baltimore per se. It smelled no worse than any other city they'd camped in over the years, but even though he understood the purpose of the trip, it grieved him to think that a man could choose to spend his last moments on earth in a place he'd never been to before. A dog would never commit such a blunder. He would make his peace with the world and then see to it that he gave up the ghost on familiar ground. But Willy still had two things to accomplish before he died, and with characteristic stubbornness he'd gotten it into his head that there was only one person who could help him. The name of that person was Bea Swanson, and since said Bea Swanson was last known to be living in Baltimore, they had come to Baltimore to find her. All well and good, but unless Willy's plan did what it was supposed to do, Mr. Bones would be marooned in this city of crab cakes and marble steps, and what was he going to do then? A phone call would have done the job in half a minute, but Willy had a philosophical aversion to using the telephone for important business. He would rather walk for days on end than pick up one of those contraptions and talk to someone he couldn't see. So here they were two hundred miles later, wandering around the streets of Baltimore without a map, looking for an address that might or might not exist.

Of the two things Willy still hoped to accomplish before he died, neither one took precedence over the other. Each was all important to him, and since time had grown too short to think of tackling them separately, he had come up with what he referred to as the Chesapeake Gambit: an eleventh-hour ploy to kill both birds with one stone. The first has already been discussed in the previous paragraphs: to find new digs for his furry companion. The second was to wrap up his own affairs and make sure that his manuscripts were left in good hands. At that moment, his life's work was crammed into a rental locker at the Greyhound bus terminal on Fayette Street, two and a half blocks north of where he and Mr. Bones were standing. The key was in his pocket, and unless he found someone worthy enough to entrust with that key, every word he had ever written would be destroyed, disposed of as so much unclaimed baggage.

In the twenty-three years since he'd taken on the surname of Christmas, Willy had filled the pages of seventy-four notebooks with his writings. These included poems, stories, essays, diary entries, epigrams, autobiographical musings, and the first eighteen hundred lines of an epic-in-progress, *Vagabond Days*. The majority of these works had been composed at the kitchen table of his mother's apartment in Brooklyn, but since her death four years ago he'd been forced to write in the open air, often battling the elements in public parks and dusty alleyways as he struggled to get his thoughts down on paper. In his secret heart of hearts, Willy had no delusions about himself. He knew that he was a troubled soul and not fit for this world, but he also knew that much good work was buried in those notebooks, and on that score at least he could hold his head high. Maybe if he had been more scrupulous about taking his medication, or maybe if his body had been a bit stronger, or maybe if he hadn't been so fond of malts and spirits and the hubbub of bars, he might have done even more good work. That was perfectly possible, but it was too late to dwell on regrets and errors now. Willy had written the last sentence he would ever write, and there were no more than a few ticks left in the clock. The words in the locker were all he had to show for himself. If the words vanished, it would be as if he had never lived.

That was where Bea Swanson entered the picture. Willy knew it was a stab in the dark, but if and when he managed to find her, he was convinced that she would move heaven and earth to help him. Once upon a time, back when the world was still young, Mrs. Swanson had been his high-school English teacher, and if not for her it was doubtful that he ever would have found the courage to think of himself as a writer. He was still William Gurevitch in those days, a scrawny sixteen-year-old boy with a passion for books and beebop jazz, and she had taken him under her wing and lavished his early work with praise that was so excessive, so far out of proportion to its true merit, that he began to think of himself as the next great hope of American literature. Whether she was right or wrong to do so is not the question, for results are less important at that stage than promise, and Mrs. Swanson had recognized his talent, she'd seen the spark in his fledgling soul, and no one can ever amount to anything in this life without someone else to believe in him. That's a proven fact, and while the rest of the junior class at Midwood High saw Mrs. Swanson as a squat, fortyish woman with blubbery arms that bounced and wiggled whenever she wrote on the blackboard, Willy thought she was beautiful, an angel who had come down from heaven and taken on a human form.

By the time school started again in the fall, however, Mrs. Swanson was gone. Her husband had been offered a new job in Baltimore, and since Mrs. Swanson was not only a teacher but a wife, what choice did she have but to leave Brooklyn and go where Mr. Swanson went? It was a tough blow for Willy to absorb, but it could have been worse, for even though his mentor was far away, she did not forget him. Over the next several years, Mrs. Swanson kept up a lively correspondence with her young friend, continuing to read and comment on the manuscripts he sent her, to remember his birthday with gifts of old Charlie Parker records, and to suggest little magazines where he could begin submitting his work. The gushing, rhapsodic letter of recommendation she wrote for him in his senior year helped clinch a full scholarship for Willy at Columbia. Mrs. Swanson was his muse, his protector, and good-luck charm all rolled into one, and at that point in Willy's life, the sky was definitely the limit. But then came the schizo flip-out of 1968, the mad fandango of truth or consequences on a high-voltage tension wire. They shut him up in a hospital, and after six months of shock treatment and psychopharmacological therapy, he was never quite the same again. Willy had joined the ranks of the walking wounded, and even though he continued to churn out his poems and stories, to go on writing in both sickness and in health, he rarely got around to answering Mrs. Swanson's letters. The reasons were unimportant. Perhaps Willy was embarrassed to stay in touch with her. Perhaps he was distracted, preoccupied with other business. Perhaps he had lost faith in the US Postal Service and no longer trusted the mail carriers not to snoop inside the letters they delivered. One way or the other, his once voluminous exchanges with Mrs. Swanson dwindled to almost nothing. For a year or two, they consisted of the odd, desultory postcard, then the store-bought Christmas greeting, and then, by 1976, they had stopped altogether. Since that time, not one syllable of communication had passed between them.

Mr. Bones knew all this, and that was precisely what worried him. Seventeen years had gone by. Gerald Ford had been President back then, for Chrissakes, and he himself would not be whelped for another decade. Who was Willy trying to kid? Think of all the things that can happen in that time. Think of the changes that can occur in seventeen hours or seventeen minutes – let alone in seventeen years. At the very least, Mrs. Swanson had probably moved to another address. The old girl would be pushing seventy by now, and if she wasn't senile or living in a trailer park in Florida, there was a better than even chance that she was dead. Willy had admitted as much when they hit the streets of Baltimore that morning, but what the fuck, he'd said, it was their one and only shot, and since life was a gamble anyway, why not go for broke?

Ah, Willy. He had told so many stories, had talked in so many different voices, had spoken out of so many sides of his mouth at once that Mr. Bones had no idea what to believe anymore. What was true, what was false? It was difficult to know when dealing with a character as complex and fanciful as Willy G. Christmas. Mr. Bones could vouch for the things he'd seen with his own eyes, the events he'd experienced in

10

his own flesh, but he and Willy had been together for only seven years, and the facts concerning the previous thirty-eight were more or less up for grabs. If Mr. Bones hadn't spent his puppyhood living under the same roof with Willy's mother, the whole story would have been shrouded in darkness, but by listening to Mrs. Gurevitch and measuring her statements against her son's, Mr. Bones had managed to stitch together a reasonably coherent portrait of what Willy's world had looked like before he came into it. A thousand details were lacking. A thousand others were muddled in confusion, but Mr. Bones had a sense of the drift, a feeling for what its shape both was and wasn't.

It wasn't rich, for example, and it wasn't cheerful, and more often than not the air in the apartment had been tinged with sourness and desperation. Considering what the family had been through before it landed in America, it was probably a miracle that David Gurevitch and Ida Perlmutter managed to produce a son in the first place. Of the seven children born to Willy's grandparents in Warsaw and Lodz between 1910 and 1921, they were the only two to survive the war. They alone did not have numbers tattooed on their forearms, they alone were granted the luck to escape. But that didn't mean they had an easy time of it, and Mr. Bones had heard enough stories to make his fur tingle. There were the ten days they spent hiding in an attic crawl space in Warsaw. There was the month-long walk from Paris to the Free Zone in the south, sleeping in haylofts and stealing eggs to stay alive. There was the refugee internment camp in Mende, the money spent on bribes for safe conducts, the four months of bureaucratic hell in Marseille as they waited for their Spanish transit visas. Then came the long coma of immobility in Lisbon, the stillborn son Ida delivered in 1944, the two years of looking out at the Atlantic as the war dragged on and their money ebbed away. By the time Willy's parents arrived in Brooklyn in 1946, it wasn't a new life they were starting so much as a posthumous life, an interval between two deaths. Willy's father, once a clever young lawyer in Poland, begged a job from a distant cousin and spent the next thirteen years riding the Seventh Avenue IRT to a button-manufacturing firm on West Twenty-eighth Street. For the first year, Willy's mother supplemented their income by giving piano lessons to young Jewish brats in the apartment, but that ended one morning in November of 1947 when Willy poked his little face out from between her legs and unexpectedly refused to stop breathing.

He grew up American, a Brooklyn boy who played stickball in the streets, read *Mad Magazine* under the covers at night, and listened to Buddy Holly and the Big Bopper. Neither one of his parents could fathom such things, but that was just as well as far as Willy was concerned, since his great goal in life at that stage was to convince himself that his mother and father were not his real parents. He found them alien, wholly embarrassing creatures, a pair of sore thumbs with their Polish accents and stilted foreign ways, and without really having to think about it he understood that his only hope of survival lay in resisting them at every turn. When his father dropped dead from a heart attack at forty-nine, Willy's sorrow was mitigated by a secret sense of relief. Already at twelve, just barely on the brink of adolescence, he had formulated his lifelong philosophy of embracing trouble wherever he could find it. The more wretched your life was, the closer you were to the truth, to the gritty nub of existence, and what could be more terrible than losing your old man six weeks after your twelfth birthday? It marked you as a tragic figure, disqualified you from the rat race of vain hopes and sentimental illusions, bestowed on you an aura of legitimate suffering. But the fact was that Willy didn't suffer much. His father had always been a riddle to him, a man prone to weeklong silences and sudden outbursts of rage, and more than once he had slapped down Willy for the smallest, most trifling infraction. No, it wasn't hard to adjust to life without that bag of explosives. It didn't take any effort at all.

Or so reckoned the good Herr Doktor Bones. Ignore his opinion if you will, but who else are you prepared to trust? After listening to these stories for the past seven years, had he not earned the right to be called the world's leading authority on the subject?

That left Willy alone with his mother. She was hardly anyone's idea of a good time, but at least she kept her hands to herself and showed him considerable amounts of affection, enough warmth of heart to counterbalance the periods when she nagged him and harangued him and got on his nerves. By and large, Willy tried to be a good son. At those rare moments when he was able to stop thinking about himself, he even made a conscious effort to be nice to her. If they had their differences, they were less a result of personal animosity than of starkly opposing world views. From hard-won experience, Mrs. Gurevitch knew that the world was out to get her, and she lived her life accordingly, doing everything in her power to stay clear of harm's way. Willy also knew that the world was out to get him, but unlike his mother he had no qualms about fighting back. The difference was not that one was a pessimist and the other an optimist, it was that one's pessimism had led to an ethos of fear, and the other's pessimism had led to a noisy, fractious disdain for Everything-That-Was. One shrank, the other flailed. One toed the line, the other crossed it out. Much of the time they were at loggerheads, and because Willy found it so easy to shock his mother, he rarely wasted an opportunity to provoke an argument. If only she'd had the wit to back off a little, he probably wouldn't have been so insistent about making his points. Her antagonism inspired him, pushed him into ever more extreme positions, and by the time he was ready to leave the house and go off to college, he had indelibly cast himself in his chosen role: as malcontent, as rebel, as outlaw poet prowling the gutters of a ruined world.

Lord knows how many drugs that boy ingested in the two and a half years he spent on Morningside Heights. Name an illegal substance, and Willy either smoked it or snorted it or shot it into his veins. It's one thing to walk around pretending you're the second coming of François Villon, but feed an unstable young man enough toxic confections to fill a dump site in the Jersey Meadowlands, and his body chemistry is bound to be altered. Sooner or later, Willy might have cracked up anyway, but who would argue that the psychedelic free-for-all of his student days didn't accelerate the process? When his roommate walked in on him one afternoon in the middle of his junior year and found Willy buck naked on the floor – chanting names from the Manhattan phone book and eating a bowl of his own excrement – the academic career of Mr. Bones's future master came to an abrupt and permanent end.

The loony bin followed, and then Willy returned to his mother's apartment on Glenwood Avenue. It wasn't the ideal place for him to live, perhaps, but where else could a burnout like poor Willy go? For the first six months, not much good came of the arrangement. Other than Willy's switch from drugs to alcohol, things were essentially the same as they had been. The same tensions, the same conflicts, the same misunderstandings. Then, out of the blue, in late December 1969, Willy had the vision that changed everything, the mystical encounter with blessedness that turned him inside out and set his life on an entirely different course.

It was two-thirty in the morning. His mother had gone to bed several hours before, and Willy was parked on the living-room sofa with a pack of Luckies and a bottle of bourbon, watching television out of the corner of one eye. Television was a new habit for him, a by-product of his

13

recent stay in the hospital. He wasn't particularly interested in the images on the screen, but he enjoyed having the hum and glow of the tube in the background and found comfort in the gray-blue shadows it cast on the walls. The *Late Late Show* was on just then (something to do with gigantic grasshoppers devouring the citizens of Sacramento, California), but most of the airtime had been given over to chintzy exhortations on behalf of miracle breakthrough products: knives that never went dull, lightbulbs that never burned out, secret-formula lotions that removed the curse of baldness. Yak yak yak, Willy muttered to himself, it's the same old suds and blather. Just as he was about to stand up and turn off the television, however, a new commercial came on, and there was Santa Claus popping out of someone's fireplace in what looked like a suburban living room in Massapequa, Long Island. Given that Christmas was just around the corner, Willy had grown used to commercials that featured actors dressed up as Santa Claus. But this one was better than most – a roly-poly guy with rosy cheeks and an honest-to-goodness white beard. Willy paused to watch the beginning of the spiel, fully expecting to hear something about rug shampoos or burglar alarms, when all of a sudden Santa uttered the words that would change his destiny.

'William Gurevitch,' Santa said. 'Yes, William Gurevitch of Brooklyn, New York, I'm talking to you.'

Willy had drunk only half a bottle that night, and it had been eight months since his last full-blown hallucination. Nobody was going to trick him into swallowing this garbage. He knew the difference between reality and make-believe, and if Santa Claus was talking to him from his mother's television set, that could only mean he was a lot drunker than he supposed.

'Fuck you, mister,' Willy said, and without giving the matter another thought, he clicked off the machine.

Unfortunately, he wasn't able to leave things as they were. Because he was curious, or because he wanted to make sure he wasn't having another breakdown, Willy decided it would be all right if he turned the television back on – just for a peek, a last little peek. It wasn't going to hurt anyone, was it? Better to learn the truth now than to walk around with that sack of Yuletide shit preying on his mind for the next forty years.

And lo and behold, there he was again. There was Santa bloody Claus, wagging his finger at Willy and shaking his head with a sad, dis-

14

appointed look in his eyes. When he opened his mouth and started to talk (picking up precisely where he had left off ten seconds earlier), Willy didn't know whether he should burst out laughing or jump through the window. It was happening, folks. What could not happen was happening, and right then and there Willy knew that nothing in the world would ever look the same to him again.

'That wasn't nice, William,' Santa said. 'I'm here to help you, but we're never going to get anywhere if you don't give me a chance to talk. Do you follow me, son?'

The question seemed to call for a response, but Willy hesitated. Listening to this clown was bad enough. Did he really want to make things worse by talking back to him?

'William!' Santa said. His voice was stern and reproachful, and it contained the power of a personality that was not to be trifled with. If Willy was ever going to squirm out of this nightmare, his only hope would be to play along.

'Yeah, boss,' he mumbled, 'I read you loud and clear.'

The fat man smiled. Then, very slowly, the camera moved in on him for a close-up. For the next several seconds Santa stood there stroking his beard, apparently lost in thought.

'Do you know who I am?' he finally said.

'I know who you look like,' Willy said, 'but that doesn't mean I know who you are. At first I thought you were some asshole actor. Then I thought maybe you were that genie in the bottle. Now I don't have a clue.'

'The thing I look like is the thing I am.'

'Sure, pal, and I'm Haile Selassie's brother-in-law.'

'Santa Claus, William. A.k.a. Saint Nick. Father Christmas himself. The only force for good left in the world.'

'Santa, huh? And you wouldn't happen to spell that S–A–N–T–A, would you?'

'Yes, I would. That's exactly how I'd spell it.'

'That's what I figured. Now rearrange the letters a little bit, and what do you have? S–A–T–A–N, that's what. You're the goddamn devil, grandpa, and the only place you exist is in my mind.'

Notice how Willy struggled against the apparition, how determined he was to thwart its charms. He wasn't some pea-brained psycho who let figments and specters push him around. He wanted no part of this one, and the disgust he felt, the downright hostility he expressed whenever he recalled the first moments of the encounter, was precisely what convinced Mr. Bones that it was true, that Willy had experienced an authentic vision and was not making the story up. To hear him tell it, the situation was a scandal, an insult to his intelligence, and merely having to look at that bovine lump of clichés brought his blood to a boil. Let someone else make with the ho-ho stuff. Christmas was a fraud, a season for quick bucks and ringing cash registers, and as the symbol of that season, as the very essence of the whole consumerist shebang, Santa was the biggest fake of them all.

But this Santa was no fake, and he was no devil in disguise. He was the true Father Christmas, the one and only Lord of the Elves and Spirits, and the message he'd come to preach was one of goodness, generosity, and self-sacrifice. This unlikeliest of fictions, this contradiction of everything Willy stood for, this absurd display of hokum in the red jacket and the fur-fringed boots – yes, Santa Claus in all his Madison Avenue glory – had sprung forth from the depths of Television Land to debunk the certitudes of Willy's skepticism and put his soul back together again. It was as simple as that. If anyone was a fraud, Santa said, it was Willy, and then he let him have it in no uncertain terms, lecturing the frightened and bewildered boy for the better part of an hour. He called him a sham, a poseur, and a no-talent hack. Then he upped the ante and called him a zero, a douche bag, a dunderhead, and little by little he broke down the wall of Willy's defenses and made him see the light. Willy was on the floor by then, weeping his eyes out as he begged for mercy and promised to mend his ways. Christmas was real, he learned, and there would be no truth or happiness for him until he began to embrace its spirit. That would be his mission in life from now on: to embody the message of Christmas every day of the year, to ask nothing from the world and give it only love in return.

In other words, Willy decided to turn himself into a saint.

And so it happened that William Gurevitch concluded his business on this earth, and from his flesh a new man named Willy G. Christmas was born. To celebrate the event, Willy scuttled off to Manhattan the next morning and had himself tattooed with a picture of Santa Claus on his right arm. It was a painful ordeal, but Willy suffered the needles gladly, triumphant in the knowledge that he now bore a visible sign of his transformation and would carry its mark with him for ever.

Alas, when he returned to Brooklyn and proudly showed his mother this new ornament, Mrs. Gurevitch went wild, erupting in a tantrum of tears and angry disbelief. It wasn't just the idea of the tattoo that bent her out of shape (although that was part of it, given that tattooing was proscribed by Jewish law – and given what role the tattooing of Jewish skin had played in her life-time), it was what *this particular tattoo* represented, and in that Mrs. Gurevitch saw the three-color Santa Claus on Willy's arm as a token of betrayal and incurable madness, her outburst at that moment was perhaps understandable. Until then, she had managed to delude herself into thinking that her son would make a full recovery. She blamed his condition on the drugs, and once the noxious residues were flushed out of his system and his blood count returned to normal, she felt it would only be a matter of time before he turned off the television set and went back to college. But not any more. One glance at the tattoo, and all those vain hopes and false expectations shattered at her feet like so much glass. Santa Claus was from the other side. He'belonged to the Presbyterians and the Roman Catholics, to the Jesus-worshippers and Jew-haters, to Hitler and all the rest of them. The *goyim* had taken hold of Willy's brain, and once they crawled inside you, they never let go. Christmas was only the first step. Easter was just a few months down the road, and then they'd drag out those crosses of theirs and start talking about murder, and before long the storm troopers would be breaking down the door. She saw the picture of Santa Claus emblazoned on her son's arm, but as far as she was concerned, it might just as well have been a swastika.

Willy was frankly perplexed. He hadn't meant any harm, and in his present blissful state of remorse and conversion, the last thing he wanted was to offend his mother. But talk and explain as he did, she refused to listen. She shrieked at him and called him a Nazi, and when he persisted in trying to make her understand that Santa Claus was an incarnation of the Buddha, a holy being whose message to the world was one of merciful love and compassion, she threatened to send him back to the hospital that very afternoon. This brought to mind a sentence that Willy had heard from a fellow patient at Saint Luke's – 'I'd rather have a bottle in front of me than a frontal lobotomy' – and suddenly he knew what was in store for him if he let his mother have her way. So, rather than go on beating a dead horse, he climbed into his overcoat and left the apartment, heading in a beeline for God knows where.

Thus began a pattern that continued for the next umpteen years. Willy would stay with his mother for several months, then leave for several months, then come back. The first departure was probably the most dramatic, if only because Willy still had everything to learn about the wandering life. He was gone for just a short spell, and although Mr. Bones was never quite certain what Willy meant by *short*, whatever happened to his master during the weeks or months he was away proved to him that he had found his true calling. 'Don't tell me that two and two is four,' Willy said to his mother when he returned to Brooklyn. 'How do we know that two is two? That's the real question.'

The next day, he sat down and started writing again. It was the first time he'd picked up a pen since before the hospital, and the words poured out of him like water gushing from a broken pipe. Willy G. Christmas proved to be a better and more inspired poet than William Gurevitch had ever been, and what his early efforts lacked in originality, they made up for in hell-bent enthusiasm. *Thirty-three Rules to Live By* was a good example. Its opening lines read as follows:

> *Throw yourself into the arms of the world*
> *And the air will hold you. Hold back*
> *And the world will jump you from behind.*
> *Go for broke down the highway of bones.*
> *Follow the music of your steps, and when the lights go out*
> *Don't whistle – sing.*
> *If you keep your eyes open, you'll always be lost.*
> *Give away your shirt, give away your gold,*
> *Give away your shoes to the first stranger you see.*
> *Much will come of nothing*
> *If you dance the jitterbug waltz . . .*

Literary pursuits were one thing, but how you conducted yourself in the world was quite another. Willy's poems might have changed, but that still didn't answer the question about whether Willy himself had changed. Did he actually become a new person, or was the plunge into sainthood no more than a passing impulse? Had he boondoggled himself into an untenable position, or was there something more to be said about his rebirth than the tattoo on his right biceps and the ridiculous moniker he took such pleasure in using? An honest answer would be yes and no, perhaps, a little of both. For Willy was weak, and Willy was often belligerent, and Willy was prone to forget things. Mental mishaps dogged him, and whenever the pinball machine in his head speeded up and went tilt, all bets were off. How could a man of his ilk propose to don the mantle of purity? Not only was he an incipient lush, and not only was he a bred-in-the-bone liar with a strong paranoiac bent, he was too damn funny for his own good. Once Willy started in with the jokes, Santa Claus burst into flames, and the whole hearts-and-flowers act burned to the ground with him.

Still and all, it would be wrong to say that he didn't try, and in that trying hung a large part of the story. Even if Willy didn't always live up to his expectations for himself, at least he had a model for how he wanted to behave. At those rare moments when he was able to focus his thoughts and curb his excesses in the beverage department, Willy demonstrated that no act of courage or generosity was beyond him. In 1972, for example, at no small risk to himself, he rescued a four-year-old girl from drowning. In 1976, he came to the defense of an eighty-one-year-old man who was being mugged on West Forty-third Street in New York – and for his pains received a knife wound in his shoulder and a bullet in his leg. More than once he gave his last dollar to a friend down on his luck, he let the lovelorn and the heartsick cry on his shoulder, and over the years he talked one man and two women out of suicide. There were fine things in Willy's soul, and whenever he let them come out, you forgot the other things that were in there as well. Yes, he was a bedraggled, demented pain in the ass, but when all was right in his head, Willy was one in a million, and everyone who crossed paths with him knew it.

Whenever he talked to Mr. Bones about those early years, Willy tended to dwell on the good memories and ignore the bad. But who could blame him for sentimentalizing the past? We all do it, dogs and people alike, and in 1970 Willy had been nowhere if not in the pink of youth. His health was as robust as it would ever be, his teeth were intact, and to top it off he had money in the bank. A small sum had been set aside for him from his father's life-insurance policy, and when he came into this money on his twenty-first birthday, he was kept in pocket change for close to a decade. But above and beyond the boon of money and youth, there was the historical moment, the times themselves, the spirit abroad in the land when Willy set forth on his career of vagabondage. The country was crawling with dropouts and runaway children, with long-haired neo-visionaries, dysfunctional anarchists, and doped-up misfits. For all the oddness he demonstrated in his own right, Willy hardly stood out among them. He was just one more weirdo on the Amerikan scene, and wherever his travels happened to take him

– be it Pittsburgh or Plattsburgh, Pocatello or Boca Raton – he managed to latch on to like-minded souls for company. Or so he said, and in the long run Mr. Bones saw no reason to doubt him.

Not that it would have made any difference if he had. The dog had lived long enough to know that good stories were not necessarily true stories, and whether he chose to believe the stories Willy told about himself or not was less important than the fact that Willy had done what he had done, and the years had passed. That was the essential thing, wasn't it? The years, the number of years it took to go from being young to not-so-young, and all the while to watch the world change around you. By the time Mr. Bones crept forth from his mother's womb, Willy's salad days were but a dim memory, a pile of compost moldering in a vacant lot. The runaways had crawled back home to mom and dad; the potheads had traded in their love beads for paisley ties; the war was over. But Willy was still Willy, the boffo rhymester and self-appointed bearer of Santa's message, your basic sorry excuse rigged out in the filthy duds of tramphood. The passage of time had not treated the poet kindly, and he didn't blend in so well anymore. He stank and drooled, he rubbed people the wrong way, and what with the bullet wounds and the knife wounds and the general deterioration of his physical self, he'd lost his quickness, his heretofore astonishing knack for slithering out of trouble. Strangers robbed him and beat him up. They kicked him while he slept, they set his books on fire, they took advantage of his aches and pains. After one such encounter landed him in the hospital with blurred vision and a fractured arm, he realized that he couldn't go on without some kind of protection. He thought of a gun, but weapons were abhorrent to him, and so he settled on the next best thing known to man: a bodyguard with four legs.

Mrs. Gurevitch was less than thrilled, but Willy put his foot down and got his way. So the young Mr. Bones was torn from his mother and five siblings at the North Shore Animal Shelter and moved to Glenwood Avenue in Brooklyn. To be perfectly honest, he didn't remember much about those early days. Ingloosh was still virgin territory to him back then, and what with Mrs. Gurevitch's bizarrely mangled locutions and Willy's penchant for talking in different voices (Gabby Hayes one minute, Louis Armstrong the next; Groucho Marx in the morning, Maurice Chevalier at night), it took several months to get the hang of it. In the meantime, there were the agonies of puppyhood: the struggles with bladder and bowel control, the newspapers on the kitchen floor, the snout-whacks from Mrs. Gurevitch every time the pee dribbled out of him. She was a crotchety old complainer, that one, and if not for Willy's gentle hands and soothing endearments, life in that apartment would have been no picnic. Winter was upon them, and with everything ice and stinging salt pellets on the streets below, he spent ninety-eight percent of his time indoors, either sitting at Willy's feet as the poet cranked out his latest masterpiece or exploring the nooks and crevices of his new home. The apartment consisted of four and a half rooms, and by the time spring came Mr. Bones was familiar with every stick of furniture, every blot on the rugs, every gash in the linoleum. He knew the smell of Mrs. Gurevitch's slippers and the smell of Willy's underpants. He knew the difference between the doorbell and the telephone, could distinguish between the sound of jangling keys and the clatter of pills in a plastic vial, and before long he was on a first-name basis with every cockroach who lived in the cupboard under the kitchen sink. It was a dull, circumscribed routine, but how was Mr. Bones to know that? He was no more than a lame-brained pup, a nincompoop with floppy paws who ran after his own tail and chomped on his own shit, and if this was the only life he'd ever tasted, who was he to judge whether it was rich or poor in the stuff that makes life worth living?

Was that little mutt in for a surprise! When the weather at last turned warm and the flowers unfurled their buds, he learned that Willy was more than just a pencil-pushing homebody and professional jerk-off artist. His master was a man with the heart of a dog. He was a rambler, a rough-and-ready soldier of fortune, a one-of-a-kind two-leg who improvised the rules as he went along. They simply upped and left one morning in the middle of April, launched out into the great beyond, and saw neither hide nor hair of Brooklyn until the day before Halloween. Could a dog ask for more than that? As far as Mr. Bones was concerned, he was the luckiest creature on the face of the earth.

There were the winter hibernations, of course, the returns to the ancestral home, and with them the inevitable drawbacks to life indoors: the long months of hissing steam radiators, the infernal ruckus of vacuum cleaners and Waring blenders, the tedium of canned food. Once Mr. Bones caught on to the rhythm, however, he had little cause for complaint. It was cold out there, after all, and the apartment had Willy in it, and how bad could life be if he and his master were together? Even Mrs. Gurevitch eventually seemed to come round. Once the house-breaking issue was resolved, he noticed a distinct softening in her attitude toward him, and though she continued to grumble about the hairs he deposited throughout her domain, he understood that her heart was not fully in it. Sometimes she would even let him sit beside her on the living-room sofa, softly stroking his head with one hand as she flipped through her magazine with the other, and more than once she actually confided in him, unburdening herself of assorted worries in regard to her wayward, benighted son. What a sorrow he was to her, and what a sad thing it was that such a fine boy should be so screwed up in the head. But half a son was better than no son, *farshtaist?*, and what choice did she have but to go on loving him and hope that things turned out for the best? They'd never allow him to be buried in a Jewish cemetery – not with that funny business on his arm, they wouldn't – and just knowing that he wouldn't be laid to rest beside his mother and father was another sorrow, another torment that preyed on her mind, but life was for the living, wasn't it?, and thank God they were both in good health – touch wood – or at least not so bad, all things considered, and that in itself was a blessing, something to be thankful for, and you couldn't buy that at the five-and-dime, could you?, they didn't have commercials for that on TV. Color, black-and-white, it didn't matter what kind of set you had. Life wasn't for sale, and once you found yourself at death's door, all the noodles in China weren't going to stop that door from opening.

As Mr. Bones discovered, the differences between Mrs. Gurevitch and her son were much smaller than he had at first supposed. It was true that they often disagreed, and it was true that their smells had nothing in common – the one being all dirt and male sweat, the other a mélange of lilac soaps, Pond's facial cream, and spearmint denture paste – but when it came to talking, this sixty-eight-year-old *Mom-san* could hold her own with anyone, and once she let fly with one of her interminable monologues, you quickly understood why her offspring had turned into such a champion chatterbox. The subjects they talked about might have been different, but their styles were essentially the same: lurching, nonstop runs of free association, numerous asides and parenthetical remarks, and a full repertoire of extraverbal effects, replete with every-thing from clicks to chortles to deep glottal gasps. From Willy, Mr. Bones learned about humor, irony, and metaphorical abundance. From *Mom-san*, he learned important lessons about what it meant to be alive. She taught him about anxiety and tsuris, about bearing the weight of the world on your shoulders, and – most important of all – about the bene-fits of an occasional good cry.

As he trudged along beside his master that dreary Sunday in Baltimore, Mr. Bones found it odd that he should be thinking about these things now. Why hark back to Mrs. Gurevitch?, he wondered. Why recall the tedium of the Brooklyn winters when there were so many fuller and more buoyant memories to contemplate? Albuquerque, for example, and their blissful sojourn in that abandoned bed factory two years ago. Or Greta, the voluptuous she-hound he'd romped with for ten nights running in a cornfield outside of Iowa City. Or that nutty afternoon in Berkeley four summers ago when Willy had sold eighty-six xeroxed copies of a single poem on Telegraph Avenue for a dollar a piece. It would have done him a world of good to be able to relive some of those things now, to be back somewhere with his master before the cough began – even last year, even nine or ten months ago, yes, maybe even hanging out with that tubby broad Willy had shacked up with for a while – Wanda, Wendy, whatever her name was – the girl who lived out of the back of her station wagon in Denver and liked to feed him hard-boiled eggs. She was a pistol, that one, a bawdy sack of blubber and booze, always laughing too much, always tickling him on the soft part of his belly and then, whenever his pink doggy dick came popping out of its sheath (not that Mr. Bones objected, mind you), roaring with even more laughter, so much laughter that her face would turn fifteen shades of purple, and so often was this little comedy repeated during the short time they spent with her that he had only to hear the word *Denver* now for Wanda's laugh to start ringing in his ears again. That was *Denver* for him, just as *Chicago* was a bus splashing through a rain puddle on Michigan Avenue. Just as *Tampa* was a wall of light shimmering up from the asphalt one August afternoon. Just as *Tucson* was a hot wind blowing off the desert, bearing with it the scent of juniper leaves and sagebrush, the sudden, unearthly plenitude of the vacant air.

One by one, he tried to attach himself to these memories, to inhabit them for a few more moments as they flitted past him, but it was no use. He kept going back to the Brooklyn apartment, to the languors of those cold-weather confinements, to *Mom-san* padding around the rooms in her fluffy white slippers. There was nothing to do but stay there, he realized, and as he finally gave in to the force of those endless days and night, he understood that he had returned to Glenwood Avenue because Mrs. Gurevitch was dead. She had left this world, just as her son was about to leave it, and by rehearsing that earlier death, he was no doubt preparing himself for the next one, the death of deaths, which was destined to turn the world upside down, perhaps even destroy it entirely.

Winter had always been the season of poetic labor. Willy kept nocturnal hours when he was at home, and most often he would start his day's work just after his mother went to bed. Life on the road did not allow for the rigors of composition. The pace was too hurried, the spirit too peripatetic, the distractions too continuous for anything but an infrequent jotting, the odd note or phrase dashed off on a paper napkin. During the months he spent in Brooklyn, however, Willy generally put in three or four hours a night at the kitchen table, scratching out his verses into $8^{1}/_{2}''$ by $11''$ spiral notebooks. At least that was the case when he wasn't off on a binge somewhere, or too down in the dumps, or stymied by a lack of inspiration. He sometimes muttered to himself as he wrote, sounding out the words as he put them down on paper, and sometimes he even went so far as to laugh or growl or pound his fist on the table. At first, Mr. Bones assumed these noises were directed at him, but once he learned that carryings-on of this sort were part of the creative process, he would content himself with curling up under the table and dozing at his master's feet, waiting for the moment when the night's work was done and he would be taken outside to empty his bladder.

Still, it hadn't been all slump and torpor, had it? Even in Brooklyn there had been some bright spots, some deviations from the literary grind. Go back thirty-eight years on the dog calendar, for example, and there was the Symphony of Smells, that unique and shining chapter in the annals of Willydom, when for one whole winter there were no words at all. Yes, that surely was a time, Mr. Bones said to himself, a most beautiful and crazy time, and to recollect it now sent a warm glow of nostalgia coursing through his blood. Had he been capable of smiling, he would have smiled at that moment. Had he been capable of shedding tears, he would have shed tears. Indeed, if such a thing were possible, he would have been laughing and crying at the same time – both celebrating and mourning his beloved master, who was soon to be no more.

The Symphony went back to the early days of their life together. They had left Brooklyn twice, had returned to Brooklyn twice, and in that time Willy had developed the keenest, most ardent affection for his four-legged friend. Not only did he feel protected now, and not only was he glad to have someone to talk to, and not only did it comfort him to have a warm body to curl up against at night, but after living with the dog at such close quarters for so many months, Willy had judged him to be wholly and incorruptibly good. It wasn't just that he knew that Mr. Bones had a soul. He knew that soul to be better than other souls, and the more he saw of it, the more refinement and nobility of spirit he found there. Was Mr. Bones an angel trapped in the flesh of a dog? Willy thought so. After eighteen months of the most intimate, clear-eyed observations, he felt certain of it. How else to interpret the celestial pun that echoed in his mind night and day? To decode the message, all you had to do was hold it up to a mirror. Could anything be more obvious? Just turn around the letters of the word *dog*, and what did you have? The truth, that's what. The lowest being contained within his name the power of the highest being, the almighty artificer of all things. Was that why the dog had been sent to him? Was Mr. Bones, in fact, the second coming of the force that had delivered Santa Claus to him on that December night in 1969? Perhaps. And then again, perhaps not. To anyone else, the matter would have been open to debate. To Willy – precisely because he was Willy – it wasn't.

Still and all, Mr. Bones was a dog. From the tip of his tail to the end of his snout, he was a pure example of *Canis familiaris*, and whatever divine presence he might have harbored within his skin, he was first and foremost the thing he appeared to be. Mr. Bow Wow, Monsieur Woof Woof, Sir Cur. As one wag neatly put it to Willy in a Chicago bar four or five summers back: 'You want to know what a dog's philosophy of life is, pal? I'll tell you what it is. Just one sentence: "If you can't eat it or screw it, piss on it."'

Willy had no problem with that. Who knew what theological mysteries were at work in a case like this? If God had sent his son down to earth in the form of a man, why shouldn't an angel come down to earth in the form of a dog? Mr. Bones was a dog, and the truth was that Willy took pleasure in that dogness, found no end of delight in watching the spectacle of his confrère's canine habits. Willy had never kept company with an animal before. As a boy, his parents had turned him down every time he'd asked for a pet. Cats, turtles, parakeets, hamsters, goldfish – they would have nothing to do with them. The apartment was too small, they said, or animals stank, or they cost money, or Willy wasn't responsible enough. As a result, until Mr. Bones came into his life, he had never had the opportunity to observe a dog's behavior at close hand, had never even bothered to give the subject much thought. Dogs were no more than dim presences to him, shadowy figures hovering at the edge of consciousness. You avoided the ones who barked at you, you patted the ones who licked you. That was the extent of his knowledge. Two months after his thirty-eighth birthday, all that suddenly changed.

There was so much to absorb, so much evidence to assimilate, decipher, and make sense of that Willy hardly knew where to begin. The wagging tail as opposed to the tail between the legs. The pricked ears as opposed to the flaccid ears. The rolling onto the back, the running in circles, the anus-sniffs and growls, the kangaroo-hops and midair turns, the stalking crouch, the bared teeth, the cocked head, and a hundred other minute particulars, each one an expression of a thought, a feeling, a plan, an urge. It was like learning how to speak a new language, Willy found, like stumbling onto a long-lost tribe of primitive men and having to figure out their impenetrable mores and customs. Once he had surmounted the initial barriers, what intrigued him most was the conundrum he referred to as the Eye–Nose Paradox, or the Senses Census. Willy was a man, and therefore he relied chiefly on sight to form his understanding of the world. Mr. Bones was a dog, and therefore he was next to blind. His eyes were useful to him only in that they helped to distinguish shapes, to make out the broad outlines of things, to tell him whether the object or being that loomed up before him was a hazard to be shunned or an ally to be kissed. For true knowledge, for a genuine grasp of reality in all its manifold configurations, only the nose was of any value. Whatever Mr. Bones knew of the world, whatever he had discovered in the way of insights or passions or ideas, he had been led to by his sense of smell. At first, Willy could scarcely believe his eyes. The dog's avidity for smells seemed boundless, and once he had found an odor that interested him, he would clamp his nose over it with such determination, such whole-hog enthusiasm, that everything else in the world would cease to exist. His nostrils were turned into suction tubes, sniffing up scents in the way a vacuum cleaner inhales bits of broken glass, and there were times, many times in fact, when Willy marveled that the sidewalk did not crack apart from the force and fury of Mr. Bones's snout work. Normally the most obliging of creatures, the dog would grow stubborn, distracted, seem to forget his master entirely, and if Willy happened to tug on the leash before Mr. Bones was ready to move on, before he had ingested the full savor of the turd or urine puddle under scrutiny, he would plant his legs to resist the yank, and so unbudgeable did he become, so firmly did he anchor himself to the spot, that Willy often wondered if there wasn't a sac hidden somewhere in his paws that could secrete glue on command.

How not to be fascinated by all this? A dog had roughly two hundred and twenty million scent receptors, whereas a man had but five million, and with a disparity as great as that, it was logical to assume that the world perceived by a dog was quite different from the one perceived by a man. Logic had never been Willy's strength, but in this case he was driven by love as much as by intellectual curiosity, and therefore he stuck with the question with more persistence than usual. What did Mr. Bones experience when he smelled something? And, just as important, why did he smell what he smelled? Close observation had led Willy to conclude that there were essentially three categories of interest to Mr. Bones: food, sex, and information about other dogs. A man opens the morning paper to find out what his fellow creatures have been up to; a dog does the same thing with his nose, sniffing trees and lampposts and fireboxes to learn about the doings of the local dog population. Rex, the sharp-fanged Rottweiler, has left his mark on that bush; Molly, the cute cocker spaniel, is in heat; Roger the mutt ate something that didn't agree with him. That much was clear to Willy, a matter beyond dispute. Where things grew complicated was when you tried to understand what the dog was feeling. Was he merely looking out for himself, digesting information in order to keep a leg up on the other dogs, or was there something more to these frantic sniff-fests than simple military tactics? Could pleasure be involved as well? Could a dog with his head buried in a garbage can experience something akin, say, to the heady swoon that comes over a man when he presses his nose against a woman's neck and breathes in a whiff of ninety-dollar-an-ounce French perfume?

It was impossible to know for sure, but Willy tended to think that he did. Why else would it have been so difficult to wrench Mr. Bones away from the site of certain smells? The dog was enjoying himself, that's why. He was in a state of intoxication, lost in a nasal paradise he could not bear to leave. And if, as has already been established, Willy was convinced that Mr. Bones had a soul, did it not stand to reason that a dog of such spiritual inclinations would aspire to loftier things – things not necessarily related to the needs and urgencies of his body, but spiritual things, artistic things, the immaterial hungers of the soul? And if, as all philosophers on the subject have noted, art is a human activity that relies on the senses to reach that soul, did it not also stand to reason that dogs – at least dogs of Mr. Bones's caliber – would have it in them to feel a similar aesthetic impulse? Would they not, in other words, be able to appreciate art? As far as Willy knew, no one had ever thought of this before. Did that make him the first man in recorded history to believe that such a thing was possible? No matter. It was an idea whose time had come. If dogs were beyond the pull of oil paintings and string quartets, who was to say they wouldn't respond to an art based on the sense of smell? Why not an olfactory art? Why not an art for dogs that dealt with the world as dogs knew it?

Thus began the lunatic winter of 1988. Mr. Bones had never seen Willy so excited, so calm, so filled with steadfast energy. For three and a half months he worked on the project to the exclusion of everything else, scarcely bothering to smoke or drink anymore, sleeping only when absolutely compelled to, all but forgetting to write, read, or pick his nose. He drew up plans, made lists, experimented with smells, traced diagrams, built structures out of wood, canvas, cardboard, and plastic. There were so many calculations to be made, so many tests to be run, so many daunting questions to be answered. What was the ideal sequence of smells? How long should a symphony last, and how many smells should it contain? What was the proper shape of the symphony hall? Should it be constructed as a labyrinth, or was a progression of boxes within boxes better suited to a dog's sensibility? Should the dog do the work alone, or should the dog's owner be there to guide him from one stage of the performance to the next? Should each symphony revolve around a single subject – food, for example, or female scents – or should various elements be mixed together? One by one, Willy talked out these problems with Mr. Bones, asked for his opinions, solicited his advice, and begged his indulgence to serve as guinea pig for the numerous trials and errors that followed. The dog had rarely felt so honored, so implicated in the throb of human affairs. Not only did Willy need him, but that need had been inspired by Mr. Bones himself. From his humble origins as a mutt of no particular worth or distinction, he had been turned into the dog of dogs, an exemplar of the whole canine race. Of course he was happy to do his bit, to play along with whatever Willy asked of him. What difference did it make if he didn't fully understand? He was a dog, wasn't he?, and why should he object to sniffing a pile of urine-soaked rags, to pushing his body through a narrow trapdoor, or to crawling through a tunnel whose walls had been smeared with the traces of a meatball-and-spaghetti dinner? It might not have served any purpose, but the truth was that it was fun.

That was what came back to him now: the fun of it, the ongoing rush of Willy's excitement. Forget *Mom-san* and her sarcastic comments. Forget the fact that their laboratory was in the sub-basement of the building, next to the furnace and the sewage pipes, and that they worked on a cold dirt floor. They were collaborating on something important, enduring hardships together in the name of scientific progress. If there was anything to regret sometimes, it was simply the depth of Willy's commitment to what they were doing. He was so consumed by it, so wrapped up in the nuts and bolts of the project, that it became increasingly hard for him to keep things in perspective. One day, he would talk about his invention as if it were a major discovery, a breakthrough on a par with the lightbulb, the airplane, or the computer chip. It would rake in bags of money, he said, turn them into millionaires many times over, and they would never have to worry about anything again. On other days, however, suddenly filled with doubts and uncertainties, he would present arguments to Mr. Bones that were so finely parsed, so hair-splitting in their exactitude, that the dog began to fear for his master's health. Was it perhaps pushing things too far, Willy asked one evening, to include female scents in the orchestration of the symphonies? Wouldn't those smells induce lust in the dog who inhaled them, and wouldn't that undermine their aesthetic aspirations, turning the piece into something pornographic, a kind of smut for dogs? Immediately following that statement, Willy started bending words again, which happened whenever his mind was working at top speed. 'Cure porn with corn,' he muttered to himself, pacing back and forth across the dirt floor, 'pure corn will cure porn.' Once Mr. Bones had untangled the knots of the spoonerism, he understood Willy to mean that sentimentality was preferable to sex, at least as far as the symphonies were concerned, and that to remain faithful to the endeavor of bringing aesthetic pleasure to dogs, spiritual longings would have to be emphasized over physical ones. So, after two straight weeks of rubbing his nose in towels and sponges saturated with the aromas of bitches in heat, Mr. Bones was offered a whole new set of instruments: Willy himself, in all his vaporous guises. Dirty socks, undershirts, shoes, handkerchiefs, pants, scarves, hats – anything and everything that bore the scent of his master. Mr. Bones enjoyed these things, just as he had enjoyed the other things. For the fact was that Mr. Bones was a dog, and dogs enjoyed smelling whatever they were given to smell. It was in their nature; it was what they were born to do; it was, as Willy had correctly observed, their calling in life. For once, Mr. Bones was glad that he had not been endowed with the power of human speech. If he had, he would have been forced to tell Willy the truth, and that would have caused him much pain. For a dog, he would have said, for a dog, dear master, the fact is that the whole world is a symphony of smells. Every hour, every minute, every second of his waking life is at once a physical and a spiritual experience. There is no difference between the inner and the outer, nothing to separate the high from the low. It's as if, as if . . .

Just as Mr. Bones was beginning to unfurl this imaginary speech in his head, he was interrupted by the sound of Willy's voice. *Damn*, he heard him say. *Damn, damn*, and *double damn*. Mr. Bones jerked up his head to see what the trouble was. A light rain had begun to fall, a drizzle so faint that Mr. Bones hadn't even felt it landing on his fluffy coat. But little beads of wetness were glistening in Willy's beard, and the master's black T-shirt had already absorbed enough moisture to be showing a fine polka-dotted pattern. This wasn't good. The last thing Willy needed was to get drenched, but if the sky delivered what it seemed to have promised, that's exactly what was going to happen. Mr. Bones perused the clouds overhead. Barring a sudden change of wind, in less than an hour the present feeble raindrops would develop into a full-blown, lusty downpour. Damn, he thought. How much farther to go before they found Calvert Street? They had been stumbling around for the past twenty or thirty minutes, and Bea Swanson's house was still nowhere in sight. If they didn't get there soon, they weren't going to make it. They weren't going to make it, because Willy wouldn't have the strength to go on.

Given their predicament, the last thing Mr. Bones was expecting just then was that his master would start to laugh. But there it was, rumbling up from the depths of his stomach and bursting forth into the Sunday stillness: the old familiar *haw*. For a moment he thought that maybe Willy was trying to clear his throat, but when the first *haw* was followed by another *haw*, and then another, and still another after that, he could no longer doubt what his ears were telling him.

'Lookee here, ol' bud,' Willy said, launching into his best cowboy twang. This was a voice reserved for special occasions, an accent that Willy called upon only when he found himself in the presence of life's grandest, most dizzying ironies. Baffled though he was to hear it now,

Mr. Bones tried to take heart from this sudden shift in the emotional weather.

Willy had come to a full stop on the sidewalk. The neighborhood all around them stank of poverty and uncollected garbage, and yet where should they be standing but in front of the loveliest little house Mr. Bones had ever seen, a toy-sized edifice made of red bricks and adorned with slatted green shutters, three green steps, and a brightly painted white door? A plaque was affixed to the wall, and Willy was squinting forward to read what it said, sounding more and more like a Texas ranch hand with each passing second.

'Two-oh-three North Amity Street,' he recited. 'Residence of Edgar Allan Poe, eighteen-thirty-two to eighteen-thirty-five. Open to the public April to December, Wednesday through Saturday, noon to three forty-five p.m.'

It sounded like pretty dull stuff to Mr. Bones, but who was he to grumble about his master's enthusiasms? Willy sounded more inspired than at any moment in the past two weeks, and even though his recitation was followed by another brutal coughing fit (more sputum, more gasping, more foot-stomping as he clung to the downspout for dear life), he quickly rebounded once the spasm was over.

'We done hit pay dirt, little pard,' Willy said, spitting out the last bits of mucus and pulmonary tissue. 'It ain't Miss Bea's house, that's for sure, but give me my druthers, and there's no place on earth I'd rather be than here. This Poe fella was my grandpa, the great forebear and daddy of all us Yankee scribes. Without him, there wouldn't have been no me, no them, no nobody. We've wound up in Poe-land, and if you say it quick enough, that's the same country my own dead ma was born in. An angel's led us to this spot, and I aim to sit here awhile and pay my respects. Seein' as how I can't take another step anyway, I'd be much obliged if you joined me, Mr. Bones. That's right, take a seat beside me while I rest my pins. Never mind the rain. It's just a few drops is all, and it don't mean us no harm.'

Willy let out a long, laboring grunt and then eased himself to the ground. It was a painful thing for Mr. Bones to observe – all that effort to travel just a few inches – and the dog's heart welled up with pity to see his master in such a sorrowful state. He could never be certain exactly how he knew it, but as he watched Willy lower himself to the sidewalk and lean his back against the wall, he knew that he would never get up again. This was the end of their life together. The last moments were upon them, and there was nothing to do now but sit there until the light faded from Willy's eyes.

Still, the trip hadn't worked out so badly. They'd come here looking for one thing and had found another, and in the end Mr. Bones much preferred the thing they'd found to the thing they hadn't. They weren't in Baltimore, they were in Poland. By some miracle of luck or fate or divine justice, Willy had managed to get himself home again. He had returned to the place of his ancestors, and now he could die in peace.

Mr. Bones raised his left hind paw and began working on an itch behind his ear. In the distance, he saw a man and a little girl walking slowly in the opposite direction, but he didn't trouble himself about them. They would come, they would go, and it made no difference who they were. The rain was coming down harder now, and a small breeze was beginning to kick around the candy wrappers and paper bags in the street. He sniffed the air once, twice, then yawned for no particular reason. After a moment, he curled up on the ground beside Willy, exhaled deeply, and waited for whatever was going to happen next.

2

Nothing did. For the longest time, it was as if the entire neighborhood
had stopped breathing. No one walked by, no cars passed, not a single
person went in or out of a house. The rain poured down, just as Mr.
Bones had predicted it would, but then it slackened, gradually turned
into a drizzle again, and at last made a quiet departure from the scene.
Willy stirred not a muscle during these skyward agitations. He lay
sprawled out against the brick building as before, his eyes shut and his
mouth partly open, and if not for the rusty, creaking noise that intermittently emerged from his lungs, Mr. Bones might well have assumed that
his master had already slipped into the next world.

That was where people went after they died. Once your soul had been
separated from your body, your body was buried in the ground and
your soul lit out for the next world. Willy had been harping on this subject for the past several weeks, and by now there was no doubt in the
dog's mind that the next world was a real place. It was called Timbuktu,
and from everything Mr. Bones could gather, it was located in the middle of a desert somewhere, far from New York or Baltimore, far from
Poland or any other city they had visited in the course of their travels.
At one point, Willy described it as 'an oasis of spirits.' At another point
he said: 'Where the map of this world ends, that's where the map of
Timbuktu begins.' In order to get there, you apparently had to walk
across an immense kingdom of sand and heat, a realm of eternal nothingness. It struck Mr. Bones as a most difficult and unpleasant journey,
but Willy assured him that it wasn't, that it took no more than a blink of
an eye to cover the whole distance. And once you were there, he said,
once you had crossed the boundaries of that refuge, you no longer had
to worry about eating food or sleeping at night or emptying your bladder. You were at one with the universe, a speck of anti-matter lodged in
the brain of God. Mr. Bones had trouble imagining what life would be
like in such a place, but Willy talked about it with such longing, with
such pangs of tenderness reverberating in his voice, that the dog eventually gave up his qualms. *Tim-buk-tu*. By now, even the sound of the
word was enough to make him happy. The blunt combination of vowels

and consonants rarely failed to stir him in the deepest parts of his soul, and whenever those three syllables came rolling off his master's tongue, a wave of blissful well-being would wash through the entire length of his body – as if the word alone were a promise, a guarantee of better days ahead.

It didn't matter how hot it was there. It didn't matter that there was nothing to eat or drink or smell. If that's where Willy was going, that's where he wanted to go too. When the moment came for him to part company with this world, it seemed only right that he should be allowed to dwell in the hereafter with the same person he had loved in the here-before. Wild beasts no doubt had their own Timbuktu, giant forests in which they were free to roam without threat from two-legged hunters and trappers, but lions and tigers were different from dogs, and it made no sense to throw the tamed and untamed together in the after-life. The strong would devour the weak, and in no time flat every dog in the place would be dead, dispatched to yet another afterlife, a beyond beyond the beyond, and what would be the point of arranging things like that? If there was any justice in the world, if the dog god had any influence on what happened to his creatures, then man's best friend would stay by the side of man after said man and said best friend had both kicked the bucket. More than that, in Timbuktu dogs would be able to speak man's language and converse with him as an equal. That was what logic dictated, but who knew if justice or logic had any more impact on the next world than they did on this one? Willy had somehow forgotten to mention the matter, and because Mr. Bones's name had not come up once, *not once* in all their conversations about Timbuktu, the dog was still in the dark as to where he was headed after his own demise. What if Timbuktu turned out to be one of those places with fancy carpets and expensive antiques? What if no pets were allowed? It didn't seem possible, and yet Mr. Bones had lived long enough to know that anything was possible, that impossible things happened all the time. Perhaps this was one of them, and in that *perhaps* hung a thousand dreads and agonies, an unthinkable horror that gripped him every time he thought about it.

Then, against all odds, just as he was about to fall into another one of his funks, the sky began to brighten. Not only had the rain stopped, but the bulked-up clouds overhead were slowly breaking apart, and whereas just an hour before everything had been gray and gloom, now the sky was tinged with color, a motley jumble of pink and yellow streaks that bore down from the west and steadily advanced across the breadth of the city.

Mr. Bones lifted his head. A moment later, as if the two actions were secretly connected, a shaft of light came slanting through the clouds. It struck the sidewalk an inch or two from the dog's left paw, and then, almost immediately, another beam landed just to his right. A crisscross of light and shadow began to form on the pavement in front of him, and it was a beautiful thing to behold, he felt, a small, unexpected gift on the heels of so much sadness and pain. He looked back at Willy then, and just as he was turning his head, a great bucketful of light poured down on the poet's face, and so intense was the light as it crashed against the sleeping man's eyelids that his eyes involuntarily opened – and there was Willy, all but defunct a moment ago, back in the land of the living, dusting off the cobwebs and trying to wake up.

He coughed once, then again, and then a third time before lapsing into a prolonged seizure. Mr. Bones stood by helplessly as globules of phlegm came flying from his master's mouth. Some landed on Willy's shirt, others on the pavement. Still others, the looser and more slithery ones, dribbled weakly down his chin. There they remained, dangling from his beard like noodles, and as the fit wore on, punctuated by violent jolts, lurches, and doublings over, they bobbed back and forth in a crazy, syncopated dance. Mr. Bones was stunned by the ferocity of the attack. Surely this was the end, he said to himself, surely this was the limit of what a man could take. But Willy still had some fight left in him, and once he wiped his face with the sleeve of his jacket and managed to recover his breath, he surprised Mr. Bones by breaking into a broad, almost beatific smile. With much difficulty, he maneuvered himself into a more comfortable position, leaning his back against the wall of the house and stretching out his legs before him. Once his master was still again, Mr. Bones lowered his head onto his right thigh. When Willy reached out and started stroking the top of that head, a measure of calm returned to the dog's broken heart. It was only temporary, of course, and only an illusion, but that didn't mean it wasn't good medicine.

'Lend an ear, Citizen Mutt,' Willy said. 'It's starting. Things are falling away now. One by one they're falling away, and only strange things are left, tiny long-ago things, not at all the things I was expecting. I can't say I'm scared, though. A little sorry, maybe, a little miffed at having to make this early exit, but not crapping my drawers the way I thought I might be. Pack up your bags, amigo. We're on the road to Splitsville,

35

and there's no turning back. You follow, Mr. Bones? Are you with me so far?'

Mr. Bones followed, and Mr. Bones was with him.

'I wish I could boil it down to a few choice words for you,' the dying man continued, 'but I can't. Punchy epigrams, succinct pearls of wisdom, Polonius delivering his parting shots. I don't have it in me to do that. Neither a borrower nor a lender be; a stitch in time saves nine. There's too much mayhem in the attic, Bonesy, and you'll just have to bear with me as I ramble and digress. It seems to be in the nature of things for me to be confused. Even now, as I enter the valley of the shadow of death, my thoughts bog down in the gunk of yore. There's the rub, signore. All this clutter in my head, this dust and bric-a-brac, these useless knickknacks spilling off the shelves. Indeed, sir, the sad truth is that I am a bear of but little brain.

'By way of proof, I offer you the return of O'Dell's Hair Trainer. The stuff disappeared from my life forty years ago, and now, on the last day of my life, it suddenly comes back. I yearn for profundities, and what I get is this no-account factoid, this microblip on the screen of memory. My mother used to rub it into my hair when I was just a wee thing, a mere mite of a lad. They sold it in the local barber shops, and it came in a clear glass bottle about yea big. The spout was black, I believe, and on the label there was a picture of some grinning idiot boy. A wholesome, idealized numskull with perfectly groomed hair. No cowlicks for that lunkhead, no wobbles in the part for that pretty fellow. I was five, six years old, and every morning my mother would give me the treatment, hoping to make me look like his twin brother. I can still hear the gloppity-gluggity sound as the goo came out of the bottle. It was a whitish, translucent liquid, sticky to the touch. A kind of watered-down sperm, I suppose, but who know about such things then? They probably manufactured it by hiring teenage boys to jerk off into vats. Thus are fortunes made in our great land. A penny to produce, a dollar to buy, and you figure out the rest. So my Polish mother would rub the O'Dell's Hair Trainer into my scalp, comb my disobedient locks, and then send me off to school looking like that ass-wipe kid on the bottle. I was going to be an American, by gum, and this hair meant that I belonged, that my parents knew what was fucking what.

'Before you break down and weep, my friend, let me add that O'Dell's was a sham concoction, a fraud. It didn't train hair so much as glue it into submission. For the first hour, it would seem to do its job,

but then, as the morning wore on, the glue would harden, and little by
little my hair would be turned into a mass of rigid, epoxified wires – as
if a springy metallic bonnet had been clamped over my head. It felt so
strange to the touch, I couldn't leave it alone. Even as my right hand
gripped the pencil, making with the two plus threes and six minus fives,
my left hand would be wandering around up north, poking and picking
at the alien surfaces of my head. By mid-afternoon, the O'Dell's would
be so dried out, so thoroughly drained of moisture, that each strand of
coated hair would be turned into a brittle thread. That was the moment
I was waiting for, the signal that the last act of the farce was about to
begin. One by one, I'd reach down to the base of each strand of hair
rooted in my scalp, pinch it between my thumb and middle finger, and
pull. Slowly. Very slowly, sliding my nails along the entire length of the
hair. Ah. The satisfactions were immense, incalculable. All that powder
flying off of me! The storms, the blizzards, the whirlwinds of whiteness!
It was no easy job, let me tell you, but little by little every trace of the
O'Dell's would disappear. The do would be undone, and by the time
the last bell rang and the teacher sent us home, my scalp would be tingling with happiness. It was as good as sex, *mon vieux*, as good as all the
drugs and drink I ever poured into my system. Five years old, and every
day another orgy of self-repair. No wonder I didn't pay attention at
school. I was too busy feeling myself up, too busy doing the O'Dell's
diddle.

'But enough. Enough of this tedium. Enough of this Te Deum. Hair
trainer is just the tip of the iceberg, and once I start in with this childhood drek, we'll be here for the next sixteen hours. We don't have time
for that, do we? Not for castor oil, not for pot cheese, not for lumpy porridge, not for Blackjack gum. We all grew up with that junk, but now it's
gone, isn't it, and who the hell cares anyway? Wallpaper, that's what it
was. Background music. Zeitgeist dust on the furniture of the mind. I
can bring back fifty-one thousand details, but so what? It won't do you
or me an ounce of good. Understanding. That's what I'm after, chum.
The key to the puzzle, the secret formula after four-plus decades of
groping in the dark. And still, all this stuff keeps getting in my way.
Even as I breathe my last, I'm choking on it. Useless bits of knowledge,
unwanted memories, dandelion fluff. It's all flit and fume, my boy, a
bellyful of wind. The life and times of R. Mutt. Eleanor Rigby.
Rumpelstiltskin. Who the fuck wants to know them? The Pep Boys, the
Ritz Brothers, Rory Calhoun. Captain Video and the Four Tops. The

Andrews Sisters, *Life* and *Look*, the Bobbsey Twins. There's no end to it, is there? Henry James and Jesse James, Frank James and William James. James Joyce. Joyce Cary. Cary Grant. Grant me swizzle sticks and dental floss, Dentyne gum and honey-dip doughnuts. Delete Dana Andrews and Dixie Dugan, then throw in Damon Runyon and demon rum for good measure. Forget Pall Malls and shopping malls, Milton Berle and Burl Ives, Ivory soap and Aunt Jemima pancake mix. I don't need them, do I? Not where I'm going I don't, and yet there they are, marching through my brain like long-lost brethren. That's American know-how for you. It keeps coming at you, and every minute there's new junk to push out the old junk. You'd think we would have caught on by now, wised up to the tricks they pull on us, but people can't get enough of it. They cheer, they wave flags, they hire marching bands. Yes, yes, wondrous things, miraculous things, machines to stagger the imagination, but let us not forget, no let us not forget that we are not alone in this world. Know-how knows no borders, and when you think of the bounty that pours in from across the seas, it knocks you down a peg or two and puts you in your place. I don't just mean obvious things like turkeys from Turkey or chili from Chile. I also mean pants from France. I mean pain from Spain and pity from Italy and checks from Czechoslovakia and fleece from Greece. Patriotism has its role, but in the long run it's a sentiment best kept under wraps. Yes, we Yanks have given the world the zipper and the Zippo, not to speak of zip-a-dee-doo-dah and Zeppo Marx, but we're also responsible for the H-bomb and the hula hoop. It all balances out in the end, doesn't it? Just when you think you're top gun, you wind up as bottom dog. And I don't mean you, Mr. Bones. Dog as metaphor, if you catch my drift, dog as emblem of the downtrodden, and you're no trope, my boy, you're as real as they come.

'But don't get me wrong. There's too much out there not to feel tempted. The lure of particulars, I mean, the seductions of the thing-in-itself. You'd have to be blind not to give in once in a while. I don't care what it is. Just pick a thing, and chances are a case can be made for it. The splendor of bicycle wheels, for example. Their lightness, their spidery elegance, their shining rims and gossamer spokes. Or the sound of a manhole cover rattling under a truck at three in the morning. To say nothing of Spandex, which has probably done more to spruce up the landscape than any invention since the underground telephone wire. I refer to the sight of Spandex pants plastered across the behind of a young chick as she strides by you on the street. Need I say more? You'd have to be dead not to warm to that. It darts and dives at you, keeps churning away in your head until it all melts down into a big buttery ooze. Vasco da Gama in his puffy pantaloons. FDR's cigarette holder. Voltaire's powdery wig. Cunégonde! Cunégonde! Think of what happens when you say it. See what you say when you think it. Cartography. Pornography. Stenography. Stentorian stammerings, Episcopalian floozies, Fudgicles and Frosted Flakes. I admit that I've succumbed to the charms of these things as readily as the next man, am in no wise superior to the riffraff I've rubbed shoulders with for lo these many years. I'm human, aren't I? If that makes me a hypocrite, then so be it.

'Sometimes, you just have to bow down in awe. A person comes up with an idea that no one has ever thought of, an idea so simple and perfect that you wonder how the world ever managed to survive without it. The suitcase with wheels, for example. How could it have taken us so long? For thirty thousand years, we've been lugging our burdens around with us, sweating and straining as we moved from one place to another, and the only thing that's ever come of it is sore muscles, bad backs, exhaustion. I mean, it's not as though we didn't have the wheel, is it? That's what gets me. Why did we have to wait until the end of the twentieth century for this gizmo to see the light of day? If nothing else, you'd think roller skates would have inspired someone to make the connection, to put two and two together. But no. Fifty years go by, seventy-five years go by, and people are still schlepping their bags through airports and train stations every time they leave home to visit Aunt Rita in Poughkeepsie. I'm telling you, friend, things aren't as simple as they look. The human spirit is a dull instrument, and often we're no better at figuring out how to take care of ourselves than the lowest worm in the ground.

'Whatever else I've been, I've never let myself be that worm. I've jumped, I've galloped, I've soared, and no matter how many times I've crashed back to earth, I've always picked myself up and tried again. Even now, as the darkness closes in on me, my mind holds fast and won't throw in the towel. The transparent toaster, comrade. It came to me in a vision two or three nights ago, and my head's been full of the idea ever since. Why not expose the works, I said to myself, be able to watch the bread turn from white to golden brown, to see the metamorphosis with your own eyes? What good does it do to lock up the bread and hide it behind that ugly stainless steel? I'm talking about clear glass, with the orange coils glowing within. It would be a thing of beauty, a work of art in every kitchen, a luminous sculpture to contemplate even as we go about the humble task of preparing breakfast and fortifying ourselves for the day ahead. Clear, heat-resistant glass. We could tint it blue, tint it green, tint it any color we like, and then, with the orange radiating from within, imagine the combinations, just think of the visual wonders that would be possible. Making toast would be turned into a religious act, an emanation of other-worldliness, a form of prayer. Jesus god. How I wish I had the strength to work on it now, to sit down and draw up some plans, to perfect the thing and see where we got with it. That's all I've ever dreamed of, Mr. Bones. To make the world a better place. To bring some beauty to the drab, humdrum corners of the soul. You can do it with a toaster, you can do it with a poem, you can do it by reaching out your hand to a stranger. It doesn't matter what form it takes. To leave the world a little better than you found it. That's the best a man can ever do.

'Okay, snicker if you like. If I gush, I gush, and that's all there is to it. It feels good to let the purple stuff come pouring out sometimes. Does that make me a fool? Perhaps it does. But better that than bitterness, I say, better to follow the lessons of Santa Claus than to spend your life in the claws of deceit. Sure, I know what you're thinking. You don't have to say it. I can hear the words in your head, *mein Herr*, and you won't get an argument from me. Wherefore this floundering? you ask yourself. Wherefore this flopping to and fro, this rolling in the dust, this lifelong grovel toward annihilation? You do well to ask these questions. I've asked them many times myself, and the only answer I've ever come up with is the one that answers nothing. Because I wanted it this way. Because I had no choice. Because there are no answers to questions like these.

'No apologies, then. I've always been a flawed creature, Mr. Bones, a man riddled with contradictions and inconsistencies, the tugs of too many impulses. On the one hand, purity of heart, goodness, Santa's loyal helper. On the other hand, a loud-mouthed crank, a nihilist, a besotted clown. And the poet? He fell somewhere in between, I suppose, in the interval between the best and the worst of me. Not the saint, and not the wise-cracking drunk. The man with the voices in his head, the one who sometimes managed to listen in on the conversations of stones and trees, who every now and then could turn the music of the clouds into words. Pity I couldn't have been him more. But I've never been to Italy, alas, the place where pity is produced, and if you can't afford the fare, then you just have to stay at home.

'Still, you've never seen me at my best, Sir Osso, and I regret that. I regret that you've known me only as a man in decline. It was a different story back in the old days, before my spunk petered out and I ran into this ... this engine trouble. I never wanted to be a bum. That wasn't what I had in mind for myself, that wasn't how I dreamed of my future. Scrounging for empty bottles in recycling bins wasn't part of the plan. Squirting water on windshields wasn't part of the plan. Falling down on my knees in front of churches and closing my eyes to look like an early Christian martyr so that some passerby would feel sorry for me and drop a dime or quarter in my palm – no, Signor Puccini, no, no, no, that wasn't what I was put on this earth to do. But man does not live by words alone. He needs bread, and not just one loaf, but two. One for the pocket and one for the mouth. Bread to buy bread, if you see what I mean, and if you don't have the first kind, you sure as hell aren't going to have the other.

'It was a tough blow when *Mom-san* left us. I'm not going to deny that, pupster, and I'm not going to deny that I made things worse by giving away all that money. I said no apologies, but now I want to take that back and apologize to you. I did a rash and stupid thing, and we've both paid the price. Ten thousand dollars ain't Shredded Wheat, after all. I let it slip through my fingers, watched the whole wad scatter to the winds, and the funny thing about it was that I didn't care. It made me happy to act like a big shot, to flaunt my haul like some cockamamie high-roller. Mr. Altruism. Mr. Al Truism, that's me, the one and only Alberto Verissimo, the man who took his mother's life-insurance policy and unloaded every nickel of it. A hundred dollars to Benny Shapiro. Eight hundred dollars to Daisy Brackett. Four thousand dollars to the Fresh Air Fund. Two thousand dollars to the Henry Street Settlement House. Fifteen hundred dollars to the Poets-in-the-Schools Program. It went fast, didn't it? A week, ten days, and by the time I looked up again, I had divested myself of my entire inheritance. Oh well. Easy come easy go, as the old saw says, and who am I to think I could have done otherwise? It's in my blood to be bold, to do the thing that no one else would do. Buck the buck, that's what I did. It was my one chance to put up or shut up, to prove to myself that I meant what I'd been saying for all those years, and so when the dough came in I didn't hesitate. I bucked the buck. I might have fucked myself in the process, but that doesn't mean I acted in vain. Pride counts for something, after all, and when push came to shove, I'm glad I didn't back down. I walked the plank. I went the whole distance. I jumped. Never mind the sea monsters below. I know who I am, as the good sailor Popeye never said, and for once in my life I knew exactly what I was doing.

'Too bad you had to suffer, of course. Too bad we had to hit bottom. Too bad we lost our winter hideout and had to fend for ourselves in ways we weren't accustomed to. It took its toll, didn't it? The bad grub, the lack of shelter, the hard knocks. It turned me into a sick man, and it's about to turn you into an orphan. Sorry, Mr. Bones. I've done my best, but sometimes a man's best isn't good enough. If I could just get back on my feet for a few more minutes, I might be able to figure something out. Settle you in somewhere, take care of business. But my oomph is on the wane. I can feel it dribbling out of me, and one by one things are falling away. Bear with me, dog. I'll rebound yet. Once the discombobulation passes, I'll give it the old college try again. If it passes. And if it doesn't, then I'm the one who will pass, n'est-ce pas? I just need a little more time. A few more minutes to catch my breath. Then we'll see. Or not see. And if we don't, then there'll be nothing but darkness. Darkness every-where, as far as the eye can't see. Even down to the sea, to the briny depths of nothingness, where no things are nor will ever be. Except me. Except not me. Except eternity.'

Willy stopped talking then, and the hand that had been rubbing the top of Mr. Bones's head for the past twenty-five minutes gradually went limp, then ceased moving altogether. For the life of him, Mr. Bones assumed that this was the end. How not to think that after the finality of the words just spoken? How not to think his master was gone when the hand that had been massaging his skull suddenly slid off him and fell lifelessly to the ground? Mr. Bones didn't dare look up. He kept his head planted on Willy's right thigh and waited, hoping against hope that he was wrong. For the fact was that the air was less still than it should have been. There were sounds coming from somewhere, and as he fought through the miasma of his mounting grief to listen more care-fully, he understood that they were coming from his master. Was it pos-sible? Not quite willing to believe his ears, the dog checked again, girding himself against disappointment even as his certainty grew. Yes, Willy was breathing. The air was still going in and out of his lungs, still going in and out of his mouth, still lumbering through the old dance of inhales and exhales, and though the breath was shallower than it had been just a day or two ago, no more than a faint fluttering now, a feathery sibilance confined to the throat and upper lungs, it was nevertheless breath, and where there was breath, there was life. His master wasn't dead. He had fallen asleep.

Not two seconds after that, as if to confirm the accuracy of Mr. Bones's observation, Willy began to snore.

The dog was a nervous wreck by then. His heart had jumped through a hundred hoops of dread and despair, and when he understood that a reprieve had been granted, that the hour of reckoning had been pushed back a little longer, he nearly collapsed with exhaustion. It was all too much for him. When he saw his master sit down on the ground and lean his back against the walls of Poland, he had vowed to stay awake, to keep watch over him until the bitter end. That was his duty, his fundamental responsibility as a dog. Now, as he listened to the familiar dirge of Willy's snoring, he couldn't resist the temptation to close his eyes. The tranquilizing effects of the sound were that powerful. Every night for seven years, Mr. Bones had drifted off to sleep on the waves of that music, and by now it was a signal that all was right with the world, that no matter how hungry or miserable you felt at that moment, the time had come to put aside your cares and float into the land of dreams. After some minor readjustments of position, that was precisely what Mr. Bones did. He laid his head on Willy's stomach, Willy's arm involuntarily lifted itself up into the air, then came down to rest across the dog's back, and the dog fell asleep.

That was when he dreamed the dream in which he saw Willy die. It began with the two of them waking up, opening their eyes and emerging from the sleep they had just fallen into – which was the sleep they were in now, the same one in which Mr. Bones was dreaming the dream. Willy's condition was no worse than it had been before the nap. If anything, it appeared to be a tad better because of it. For the first time in several moons, he didn't cough when he stirred, didn't lapse into another fit, didn't seize up in a gruesome frenzy of gasping, choking, and blood-tinged expectorations. He simply cleared his throat and started talking again, picking up almost exactly where he had left off earlier.

He went on for what seemed to be another thirty or forty minutes, charging ahead in a delirium of half-formed sentences and broken-off thoughts. He swam up from the bottom of the sea, took a deep breath, and began to talk about his mother. He made a list of *Mom-san*'s virtues, countered with a list of her faults, and then begged forgiveness for any sufferings he might have caused her. Before moving on to the next thing, he recalled her talent for bungling jokes, fondly regaling Mr. Bones with examples of her unerring knack for forgetting punch lines at the last minute. Then he reeled off another list – this one of all the women he had ever slept with (physical descriptions included) – and followed that with a long-winded diatribe against the perils of consumerism. Then, suddenly, he was delivering a treatise on the moral advantages of homelessness, which ended with a heartfelt apology to Mr. Bones for dragging him down to Baltimore on what had turned out to be a wild-goose chase. 'I forgot to add the letter *g*,' he said. 'I didn't come for Bea Swanson; I came to give my swan song,' and immediately after that he was reciting a new poem, an apostrophe to the invisible demiurge who was about to claim his soul. Apparently composed off the top of his head, its opening stanza went something like this:

> *O Lord of the ten thousand blast furnaces and dungeons,*
> *Of the pulverizing hammer and chain-mail gaze,*
> *Dark Lord of the salt mines and pyramids,*
> *Maestro of the sand dunes and flying fish,*
> *Listen to the prattle of your poor servant,*
> *Dying on the shores of Baltimore*
> *And headed for the Great Beyond . . .*

After the poem dribbled away, it was replaced by more laments and fugues, more unpredictable sputterings on any number of themes: the Symphony of Smells and why the experiment failed, Happy Felton and the Knothole Gang (who the hell was he?), and the fact that the Japanese ate more rice grown in America than in Japan. From there he drifted into the ups and downs of his literary career, wallowing for several minutes in a bog of pent-up grievances and morbid self-pity, then roused his spirits for a while to talk about his college roommate (the same one who had taken him to the hospital in 1968) – a guy named Anster, Omster, something like that – who had gone on to write a number of so-so books and had once promised Willy to find a publisher for his poems, but of course Willy had never sent him the manuscript and that was that, but it proved that he *could* have been published if he'd wanted to be – he just didn't want to, that's all, and who the fuck cared about that vainglorious bullshit anyway? The doing was what mattered, not what you did with it after it was done, and as far as he was concerned now,

44

not even the notebooks in the Greyhound locker were worth more than a fart and a used-up can of beans. Let them burn, for all he cared, let them be thrown out with the trash, let them be tossed into the men's room for weary travelers to wipe their asses with. He never should have lugged them down to Baltimore in the first place. A moment of weakness, that's what it was, a last-gasp move in the vile game of Ego – which was the one game that everyone loses, that no one can ever win. He paused for a few moments after that, marveling at the depth of his own bitterness, and then let out a long wheezy laugh, bravely mocking himself and the world he loved so much. From there he returned to Omster, launching into a story his friend had told him many years before about meeting an English setter in Italy who could write out sentences on a typewriter that had been custom-built for dogs. Inexplicably, Willy broke down in sobs after that, and then he began to berate himself for never having taught Mr. Bones how to read. How could he have neglected to take care of such an essential matter? Now that the dog was about to be cast out on his own, he would need every advantage he could get, and Willy had let him down, had done nothing to provide him with a new situation, was leaving him with no money, no food, no means to cope with the dangers that lay ahead. The bard's tongue was going a mile a minute by then, but Mr. Bones didn't miss a trick, and he could hear Willy's words as distinctly as he had ever heard them in life. That was what was so strange about the dream. There was no distortion, no wavy interference, no sudden switching of channels. It was just like life, and even though he was asleep, even though he was hearing the words in a dream, he was awake in the dream, and therefore the longer he went on sleeping, the more awake he felt.

Midway through Willy's speculations on canine reading skills, a police car pulled up in front of Poe's house, and two large men in uniforms climbed out. One was white and the other was black, and they were both sweating in the August heat, a pair of wide-hipped cops out on Sunday patrol, carrying the instruments of the law around their waists: revolvers and handcuffs, billy clubs and holsters, flashlights and bullets. There was no time to make a full inventory, for no sooner did the men get out of the car than one of them started talking to Willy ('Can't stay there, pal. You going to move on or what?'), and at that moment Willy turned, looked straight into his friend's eyes, and said, 'Beat it, Bonesy. Don't let them catch you,' and because Mr. Bones knew that this was it, that the dreaded moment was suddenly upon them, he

45

licked Willy's face, whimpered a brief farewell as his master patted his head for the last time, and then took off, charging down North Amity Street as fast as his legs could take him.

He heard the alarmed voice of one of the cops shouting behind him ('Frank, get the dog! Get the fucking dog, Frank!'), but he didn't stop until he reached the corner, a good eighty or ninety feet from the house. By then, Frank had already given up the idea of chasing after him. As Mr. Bones turned around to see what was happening to Willy, he saw the white cop waddling back toward the house. A moment later, urged on by the other one, who was kneeling over Willy and gesturing wildly with his hands, Frank broke into a slow trot and went to join his partner. No one was worried about the dog anymore. There was a dying man to attend to, and as long as Mr. Bones kept himself at a safe distance, nothing was going to happen to him.

So he stood on the corner and watched, panting heavily after his short run, the wind all but knocked out of him. He felt sorely tempted to open his mouth and howl, to let go with one of his dark, blood-curdling moon wails, but he suppressed the urge, knowing full well that this was no time to vent his sorrows. In the distance, he saw the black cop standing by the car, talking into the two-way radio. A muffled, static-charged response filled the empty street. The cop talked again, and gusts of incomprehensible words followed, another onslaught of noise and gibberish. A door opened across the street, and someone came out to see what was going on. A woman in a yellow house frock and a head full of pink curlers. Two children emerged from another house. A boy of about nine and a girl of about six, both of them wearing shorts and no shoes. Meanwhile, Willy was invisible, still lying where Mr. Bones had left him, blocked off from view by the white cop's broad, hulking body. A minute or two went by, then another minute or two, and then, faintly in the distance, Mr. Bones heard the sound of an approaching siren. By the time the white ambulance turned down North Amity Street and stopped in front of the house, a crowd of a dozen people had gathered, standing around with their hands in their pockets or their arms folded across their chests. Two paramedics jumped out of the back of the ambulance, wheeled a stretcher toward the house, and returned a moment later with Willy on board. It was hard to see much of anything, hard to know whether his master was alive or not. Mr. Bones considered rushing back for a last look, but he hesitated to take such a risk, and by the time he'd made up his mind to do it, the paramedics had already slid Willy into the ambulance and were slamming the doors shut.

Until then, the dream had been no different from reality. Word for word, gesture for gesture, every event had been an exact and faithful rendering of events as they happened in the world. Now, as the ambulance drove off and the people slowly returned to their houses, Mr. Bones felt himself divide in two. Half of him remained on the corner, a dog contemplating his bleak and uncertain future, and the other half of him turned into a fly. Given the nature of dreams, perhaps there was nothing unusual about that. We all change into other things while we sleep, and Mr. Bones was no exception. At one time or another, he had entered the skin of a horse, a cow, and a pig, not to speak of several different dogs, but until he had the dream that day, he had never been two things at once.

There was urgent business to attend to, and only the fly part of him could do it. So, while the dog part of him waited on the corner, the fly rose into the air and flew down the block, chasing after the ambulance as swiftly as his wings could carry him. Because it was a dream, and because the fly could fly faster than any flesh-and-blood fly, it didn't take him long to reach his goal. By the time the ambulance turned the corner on to the next street, he had already attached himself to the back-door handle, and it was in this way that he rode with Willy to the hospital, all six of his feet clamped on to the slightly rusty surface of the handle's leeward side, praying that the wind wouldn't blow him off. It turned out to be a wild jaunt, what with the pothole bumps and the swerves and the sudden stops and starts and the air streaming in on him from all directions, but he managed to hold on, and when the ambulance pulled up to the hospital emergency entrance eight or nine minutes later, his wits were still intact. He hopped off the handle just as one of the paramedics was about to grab hold of it, and then, as the doors were opened and Willy was wheeled out, he hovered a yard or so above the scene, an unobtrusive speck looking down at his master's face. At first, he couldn't tell if Willy was alive or dead, but once the gurney was all the way out and its wheels were on the ground, Mrs. Gurevitch's son opened his eyes. Not much, perhaps, just a crack to let some light in and see what was happening, but even that squint was enough to make the fly's heart skip a beat. 'Bea Swanson,' Willy mumbled. 'Three-sixteen Calvert. Gotta call her. Pronto. Gotta give her the key. Bea's key. Life and death. A matter of.'

47

'Don't worry,' one of the paramedics said. 'We'll take care of it. But don't talk now. Save your strength, Willy.'

Willy. That meant he'd said enough for them to know his name, and if he'd been talking in the ambulance, maybe that meant he wasn't as bad off as he seemed, which in turn meant that maybe with the right medicines and the proper care, he'd pull through after all. Or so mused the fly in Mr. Bones's dream, who was in fact Mr. Bones himself, and because he was a biased witness to the proceedings, we should not begrudge him the consolation of last-minute hopes, even if all traces of hope were gone. But what do flies know? And what do dogs know? And what, for that matter, do men know? It was in God's hands now, and the truth was that there was no turning back.

Nevertheless, in the seventeen hours that remained, a number of extraordinary things happened. The fly saw each one of them, looking down from the ceiling above Bed 34 in the indigents' ward of Our Lady of Sorrows Hospital, and if he hadn't been there on that August day in 1993 to see them with his own eyes, he might not have believed that such things were possible. First of all, Mrs. Swanson was found. Within three hours of Willy's admittance to the hospital, his old teacher came striding down the aisle of the ward, was shown to a chair by Sister Mary Theresa, the staff supervisor of the four p.m. to midnight shift, and from that moment until Willy left this world, she never once strayed from her student's side. Second of all, after several hours of intravenous feeding and nonstop megadoses of antibiotics and adrenaline, Willy's head seemed to clear somewhat, and he spent the last morning of his life in a state as lucid and serene as any Mr. Bones could remember. Third of all, he died without pain. No convulsions, no upheavals, no cataclysmic fires in his chest. He slipped away slowly, withdrawing from this world by small, imperceptible degrees, and in the end it was as if he were a drop of water evaporating in the sun, shrinking and shrinking until at last he wasn't there anymore.

The fly never actually saw the key change hands. It might have happened at a moment when his attention was briefly diverted, but then again, Willy might have forgotten to mention it. At the time, it hardly seemed important. Once Bea Swanson entered the room, there were so many other things to think about, so many words to follow and feelings to digest, that he could scarcely remember his own name, let alone Willy's half-cocked scheme for salvaging his literary archive.

Her hair had turned white, and she had put on thirty pounds, but the moment he saw her the fly knew who it was. Physically speaking, there was nothing to set her apart from a million other women her age. Dressed in blue-and-yellow madras shorts, a billowing white blouse, and a pair of leather sandals, she seemed to have stopped thinking about her appearance a long time ago. The plumpness of her arms and legs had grown even more pronounced over the years, and with the dimples in her pudgy knees and the varicose veins bulging from her calves and the flesh sagging from her upper arms, you could easily have mistaken her for a retirement-community golf lady, someone with nothing better to do than roam the back nine in an electric cart and worry about whether she was going to putt out in time for the early-bird special. But this woman's skin was white, not tanned, and instead of sunglasses she had on a pair of no-nonsense wire-rimmed specs. Furthermore, once you looked through the lenses of those drugstore glasses, you discovered eyes of the most remarkable shade of blue. Look into those eyes, and you were trapped. They held you with their warmth and vivacity, their intelligence and watchfulness, the depth of their Scandinavian silences. These were the eyes that Willy had fallen in love with as a boy, and now the fly understood what all the fuss had been about. Forget the short-cropped hair and the chubby legs and the humdrum clothes. Mrs. Swanson was no dowager schoolmarm. She was the goddess of wisdom, and once you fell in love with her, you loved her until the day you died.

Nor was she quite the pushover that Mr. Bones had expected her to be. After listening to Willy go on about Mrs. Swanson's kindness and generosity all the way down to Baltimore, he had imagined her as a softhearted sentimentalist, one of those flighty women prone to vast and sudden enthusiasms, who broke down and cried at the smallest provocation and bustled about straightening up after people the moment they stood up from their chairs. The real Mrs. Swanson was anything but. That is to say, the Mrs. Swanson in his dream was anything but. When Mrs. Swanson approached Willy's bed and looked into the face of her former student for the first time in almost thirty years, the fly was startled by the toughness and clarity of her reaction. 'Jesus Christ, William,' she said, 'You've sure made a mess of things, haven't you?'

'I'm afraid so,' Willy said. 'I'm what you call a world-class fuck-up, the king of the know-nothings.'

'At least you knew enough to get in touch with me,' Mrs. Swanson said, sitting down in the chair that Sister Mary Theresa had provided for her and taking hold of Willy's hand. 'The timing might not be so hot, but better late than never, huh?'

Tears started welling up in Willy's eyes, and for once in his life he was unable to speak.

'It was always touch and go with you, William,' Mrs. Swanson continued, 'so I can't really say I'm surprised. I'm sure you've done your best. But we're talking about highly combustible materials here, aren't we? You walk around with a load of nitroglycerin in your brain, and sooner or later you're going to bump into something. When it comes right down to it, it's a wonder you didn't blow yourself up a long time ago.'

'I walked all the way from New York,' Willy answered, apropos of nothing. 'Too many miles with too little gas in the tank. It just about did me in. But now that I'm here, I'm glad I came.'

'You must be tired.'

'I feel like an old sock. But at least I can die happy now.'

'Don't talk like that. They're going to fix you up and make you better. You'll see, William. In a couple of weeks, you'll be as good as new.'

'Sure. And next year I'm going to run for president.'

'You can't do that. You already have a job.'

'Not really, I'm sort of unemployed these days. Unemployable, really.'

'And what about the Santa Claus business?'

'Oh yeah. That.'

'You haven't quit, have you? When you wrote me that letter, it sounded like a lifelong commitment.'

'I'm still on the payroll. Been on it for more than twenty years now.'

'It must be hard work.'

'Yeah, it is. But I'm not complaining. Nobody forced me to do it. I signed up of my own free will, and I've never had any second thoughts. Long hours, though, and not one day off in all that time, but what do you expect? It's not easy doing good works. There's no profit in it. And when there's no money in a thing, people tend to get confused. They think you're up to something, even when you're not.'

'Do you still have the tattoo? You mentioned it in a letter, but I've never seen it.'

'Sure, it's still there. Take a look if you want.'

Mrs. Swanson leaned forward in her chair, lifted the right sleeve of Willy's hospital gown, and there it was. 'Very nice,' she said. 'That's what I'd call a proper Santa Claus.'

'Fifty bucks,' Willy said. 'And worth every penny.'

50

That was how the conversation began. It continued for the whole night and into the next morning, interrupted by occasional visits from the nurses, who came by to replenish Willy's I.V., take his temperature, and empty the bedpan. Sometimes, Willy's strength would flag, and he would suddenly doze off in mid-sentence, sleeping for ten or twenty minutes at a stretch, but he would always come back, rising up from the depths of unconsciousness to join Mrs. Swanson again. If she hadn't been there, the fly realized, it was doubtful that he would have held on as long as he did, but so great was his pleasure at being with her again that he continued to make the effort – for as long as effort was possible. Still, he did not struggle against what was coming, and even after he went through a list of things he had never done in life – never learned to drive a car, never flown in an airplane, never visited a foreign country, never learned to whistle – things he had never done and therefore would never do – it was not so much with regret as a kind of indifference, an attempt to prove to her that none of it mattered. 'Dying's no big deal,' he said, and by that he meant that he was ready to go, that he was grateful to her for seeing to it that his last hours had not been spent among strangers.

As one might have expected, his last words were about Mr. Bones. Willy had returned to the subject of his dog's future, which he had already mentioned several times before, and was emphasizing to Mrs. Swanson how important it was that she comb the city and find him, that she do everything she could to give him a new home. 'I've botched it,' he said. 'I've let my pooch down.' And Mrs. Swanson, who was alarmed to see how weak he had suddenly become, tried to soothe him with a few meaningless words, 'Don't worry, William, it's all right, it's not important,' and Willy, rousing himself for one last effort, managed to lift his head and say, 'Yes it is. It's very important –' and then, just like that, his life stopped.

Sister Margaret, the nurse on duty at that hour, walked over to the bed and checked for a pulse. When none could be found, she took a small mirror out of her pocket and held it up to Willy's mouth. A few moments later, she turned the mirror around and looked into it, but the only thing she saw there was herself. Then she put the mirror back in her pocket, reached out with her right hand, and closed Willy's eyes.

'It was a beautiful death,' she said.

For all response, Mrs. Swanson covered her face with her hands and wept.

Mr. Bones looked down at her through the eyes of the fly, listening to her grief-stricken sobs fill the ward, and wondered if there had ever been an odder, more perplexing dream than this one. Then he blinked, and he was no longer in the hospital, no longer the fly, but back on the corner of North Amity Street as his old dog self, watching the ambulance drive away into the distance. The dream was over, but he was still inside the dream, which meant that he had dreamed a dream within the dream, a parenthetical reverie of flies and hospitals and Mrs. Swansons, and now that his master was dead, he was back inside the first dream. That's what he imagined, in any case, but no sooner did this thought occur to him than he blinked a second time and woke up, and there he was again, camped out in Poland with the recumbent Willy, who was just waking up himself, and so befuddled was Mr. Bones for the next little while that he wasn't sure if he was really in the world again or had woken up in another dream.

But that wasn't all. Even after he had sniffed the air, rubbed his nose into Willy's leg, and confirmed that this was his true and authentic life, there were more mysteries to contend with. Willy cleared his throat, and as Mr. Bones waited for the inevitable coughing fit, he remembered that Willy hadn't coughed in the dream, that for once his friend had been spared that agony. Now, unexpectedly, it happened again. His master cleared his throat, and immediately after that he was talking again. At first, Mr. Bones dismissed it as a fortunate coincidence, but as Willy continued to talk, charging impetuously from one corner of his mind to another, the dog could not help but notice the resemblance between the words he was listening to and the words he had just heard in the dream. It wasn't that they were exactly the same – at least he didn't think they were – but they were close enough, *close enough*. One by one, Willy touched on each and every topic that had come up in the dream, and when Mr. Bones realized that it was happening in precisely the same order as before, he felt a chill go down his spine. First *Mom-san* and the bungled jokes. Then the catalogue of sexual adventures. Then the diatribes and the apologies, the poem, the literary battles, the whole bit. When he came to the roommate's story about the dog who could type, Mr. Bones wondered if he were going mad. Had he slipped back into the dream, or was the dream just an earlier version of what was happening now? He blinked his eyes, hoping he would wake up. He blinked them again, and again nothing happened. He couldn't wake up because he was already awake. This was his true and authentic life, and because you got to live that life only once, he knew that they had really come to the end this time. He knew that the words tumbling from his master's mouth were the last words he would ever hear Willy speak.

'I wasn't there myself,' the bard was saying, 'but I trust my witness. In all the years we were friends, I never knew him to make up stories. That's one of his problems, maybe – as a writer, I mean – not enough imagination – but as a friend he always gave it to you straight from the horse's mouth. A lovely phrase that, though I'll be damned if I know what it means. The only talking horse I ever saw was the one in those movies. Donald O'Connor, the army, three or four asinine flicks I sat through as a kid. Now that I think about it, though, it might have been a mule. A mule in the movies, and a horse on TV. What was the name of that show? *Mr. Ed.* Jesus, there I go again. I can't get rid of this garbage. Mr. Ed, Mr. Moto, Mr. Magoo, they're in there still, every last one of them. Mr. Go-Fuck-Yourself. But I'm talking about dogs, aren't I? Not horses, dogs. And not talking dogs either. Not those dogs in the stories about the guy who goes into the bar and bets his life savings because his dog can talk and nobody believes him, and then the dog never opens its mouth, and when the guy asks him about it afterward, the dog says he just couldn't think of anything to say. No, not the talking dog in those dumb jokes, but the typing dog my friend saw in Italy when he was seventeen years old. That's right, Italy. Nitty-gritty Italy, land of the witty ditty and the itty-bitty titty – yet one more place I've never been to.

'His aunt had moved there some years earlier, reasons unknown, and one summer he went to visit her for a couple of weeks. That's a fact, and what makes the dog business ring true is that the dog wasn't even the point of the story. I was reading a book. *The Magic Mountain* it was, written by one Thomas Mann – not to be confused with Thom McAn, renowned cobbler to the masses. I never finished the damned thing by the way, it was so boring, but said Herr Mann was a muckity-muck, a hotshot in the Writers Hall of Fame, and I figured I should take a look. So there I was reading this massive tome in the kitchen, hunched over a bowl of Cheerios, and my roommate Paul walks in, sees the title, and says, 'I never finished that one. Started it four times, and I never got past page two-seventy-four.' "Well," I said, "I'm on page two-seventy-one. I guess that means my time is almost up," and then he tells me, standing there in the doorway and blowing cigarette smoke out of his mouth, that he once met Thomas Mann's widow. Not bragging about it, just stating a fact. That was how he got into the story about going to Italy to visit his aunt, who turned out to be a friend of one of Mann's daughters. He had a lot of kids, old Tom did, and this girl had wound up marrying some well-heeled Italian chap and lived in a nice house up in the hills somewhere outside of God knows what little town. One day Paul and his aunt were invited to the house for lunch, and the hostess's mother was there – Thomas Mann's widow, an old woman with white hair sitting in a rocker and staring into space. Paul shook her hand, nothing of any importance was said, and then they all sat down to lunch. Blah, blah, blah, please pass the salt. Just when you think it's going nowhere, that this is the end of a truly nothing story, Paul learns that Mann's daughter is something called an animal psychologist. And what, you may ask, is an animal psychologist? Your guess is as good as mine, Mr. Bones. After lunch, she takes Paul upstairs and introduces him to an English setter named Ollie, a dog of no particular intelligence as far as he can see, and shows him a huge manual typewriter, which has to be the largest typewriter in the history of creation. It's fitted out with a set of specially designed keys, big concave cups to accommodate the dog's snout. Then she picks up a box of biscuits, calls Ollie over to the typewriter, and gives Paul a demonstration of what the hound can do.

'It was a slow, arduous business, not at all what you would expect. The sentence he was supposed to type was: "Ollie is a good dog." Instead of just saying the words to him – or instead of spelling out the words and waiting for him to hit the right letters – she went through each *sound* of each word, breaking the words down into their component phonemes, and pronouncing them so slowly, with such odd inflections and throaty timbres, that she sounded like a deaf person trying to speak. "Ohhhhh," she began, "ohhhhh," and when the dog pushed his nose down on the letter *O*, she rewarded him with a biscuit, some lovey-dovey talk, and many pats on the head, and then she went on to the next sound, "l–l–l–l, l–l–l–l," speaking as slowly and painstakingly as before, and when the dog got it right, she gave him another biscuit and more pats on the head, and so it went, letter by excruciating letter, until they came to the end of the sentence: "Ollie is a good dog."

'My friend told me that story twenty-five years ago, and I still don't know if it proves anything. But I do know this: I've been a dunce. I've wasted too much of our time on idle pleasures and frolics, frittered away the years on japes and follies, dreamy bagatelles, unrelenting fracas. We should have borne down and studied, sir, mastered the ABCs, done something useful with the short time allotted us. My fault. All my fault. I don't know about that Ollie character, but you would have achieved far greater things than that, Mr. Bones. You had the head for it, you had the will, you had the guts. But I didn't think your eyes were up to the task, and so I didn't bother. Laziness, that's what it was. Mental sloth. I should have given it a try, refused to take no for an answer. Only out of stubbornness are great things born. Instead, what did I do? I dragged you out to Uncle Al's novelty shop in Coney Island, that's what I did. Got you onto the F train by pretending to be a blind man, tapping my way down the stairs with that white stick, and there you were at my side, snug in your harness, as good a seeing-eye dog as there ever was, not one notch below those Labs and shepherds they send to school to learn the job. Thank you for that, amigo. Thank you for playing along so nobly, for indulging me in my whims and improvisations. But I should have done better by you. I should have given you a chance to reach the stars. It's possible, believe me it is. I just didn't have the courage of my convictions. But the truth is, friend, that dogs can read. Why else would they put those signs on the doors of post offices? NO DOGS ALLOWED EXCEPT FOR SEEING-EYE DOGS. Do you catch my meaning? The man with the dog can't see, so how can he read the sign? And if he can't read it, who else is left? That's what they do in those seeing-eye schools. They just don't tell us. They've kept it a secret, and by now it's one of the three or four best-kept secrets in America. For good reason, too. If word got out, just think of what would happen. Dogs as smart as men? A blasphemous assertion. There'd be riots in the streets, they'd burn down the White House, mayhem would rule. In three months, dogs would be pressing for their independence. Delegations would convene, negotiations would begin, and in the end they'd settle the thing by giving up Nebraska, South Dakota, and half of Kansas. They'd kick out the human population and let the dogs move in, and from then on the country would be divided in two. The United States of People and the Independent Republic of Dogs. Good Christ, how I'd love to see that. I'd move there and work for you, Mr. Bones. I'd fetch your slippers and light your pipe. I'd get you elected prime minister. Anything you want, boss, and I'd be your man.'

With that sentence, Willy's rhapsody came to an abrupt halt. A noise had distracted him, and when he turned his head to see what the disturbance was, he let out a little groan. A police car was inching its way down the street, moving in the direction of the house. Mr. Bones didn't have to look to know what it was, but he looked anyway. The car had

55

pulled up alongside the curb, and the two cops were getting out, patting their holsters and adjusting their belts, the black one and the white one, the same two jokers as before. Mr. Bones turned to Willy then, just as Willy was turning to him, and with the cop's words suddenly wafting in from the street ('Can't stay there, pal. You going to move on or what?'), Willy looked him in the eyes and said, 'Beat it, Bonesy. Don't let them catch you.' So he licked his master's face, stood stock-still for a moment as Willy patted his head, and then he sprinted off, flying down the street as if there were no tomorrow.

3

He didn't stop at the corner this time, and he didn't stand around and wait for the ambulance to show up. What would have been the point? He knew it was coming, and once it got there, he knew where his master was headed. The nuns and doctors would do what they could, Mrs. Swanson would hold his hand and make small talk into the night, and not long after dawn broke the next morning, Willy would be on his way to Timbuktu.

So Mr. Bones kept running, never questioning that the dream would make good on all of its promises, and by the time he rounded the corner and started down the next block, it had already dawned on him that the world wasn't going to end. He almost felt sorry about it now. He had left his master behind, and the ground had not caved in and swallowed him up. The city had not disappeared. The sky had not burst into flames. Everything was as it had been, as it would continue to be, and what was done was done. The houses were still standing, the wind was still blowing, and his master was going to die. The dream had told him that, and because the dream wasn't a dream but a vision of things to come, there was no room for doubt. Willy's fate was sealed. As Mr. Bones trotted along the sidewalk, listening to a siren approach the area he had just left, he understood that the last part of the story was about to begin. But it wasn't his story anymore, and whatever happened to Willy from this point on would have nothing to do with him. He was on his own, and like it or not, he would have to keep on moving, even if he had nowhere to go.

What a confusion those last hours had been, he said to himself, what a hodgepodge of memories and garbled thoughts – but Willy had hit the nail on the head about one thing, and even though he'd gotten a little carried away at the end, you couldn't argue with the basic idea. If Mr. Bones had known how to read, he wouldn't have been in the mess he was in now. Even with the skimpiest, most rudimentary knowledge of the alphabet, he would have been able to hunt down 316 Calvert Street, and once he got there, he would have waited by the door until Mrs. Swanson showed up. She was the only person he knew in Baltimore, but after spending all those hours with her in the dream, he was convinced that she would have been glad to let him in – and have done a crackerjack job of taking care of him to boot. You could tell that just by looking at her, just by listening to her talk. But how to find an address if you couldn't read the street signs? If Willy thought reading was so important, why hadn't he done something about it? Instead of moaning and groaning about his failures and ineptitudes, he could have saved his tears and given him a few quick lessons. Mr. Bones would have been more than willing to have a go at it. That didn't mean he would have succeeded, but how could you know unless you tried?

He turned down another street and stopped to drink from a puddle that had formed during the recent rain. As his tongue lapped up the warm, grayish water, a new thought suddenly occurred to him. Once he had pondered it for a little while, he became almost sick with regret. Forget reading, he said to himself. Forget the arguments about the intelligence of dogs. The whole problem could have been solved in a single, elegant stroke: by hanging a sign around his neck. *My name is Mr. Bones. Please take me to Bea Swanson's house at 316 Calvert Street.* On the back, Willy could have written a note to Mrs. Swanson, explaining what had happened to him and why she should give his dog a home. Once Mr. Bones had hit the streets, there was an excellent chance that some kindhearted stranger would have read the sign and carried out the request, and within a matter of hours Mr. Bones would have been curled up peacefully on the rug in the living room of his new owner's house. As he turned from the puddle and moved on, Mr. Bones wondered how this idea could have occurred to him, a mere dog, and never once have crossed Willy's mind, which was capable of such breathtaking somersaults and dazzling pirouettes. Because Willy had no sense of the practical, that's why, and because his brain was in a muddle, and because he was sick and dying and in no shape to know which end was up. At least he had talked to Mrs. Swanson about it – or at least he was going to, once Mrs. Swanson arrived at the hospital. 'Comb the city for him,' he was going to say, and after giving her a full decription of what Mr. Bones looked like, he was going to take hold of her hand and beg her to do the right thing. 'He needs a home. If you don't take him in, he's cooked.' But Willy wasn't going to die until tomorrow, and by the time Mrs. Swanson left the hospital and went home, Mr. Bones would have been wandering the streets all day, all night, and far into the next day. She might not feel up to looking for him until later, perhaps not even until the day after that, and this Baltimore was a big place, a city with ten thousand streets and alleyways, and who knew where he would be then? In order for them to find each other, they would need luck, immense amounts of luck, luck on the scale of a miracle. And Mr. Bones, who no longer believed in miracles, told himself not to count on it.

There were enough puddles to slake his thirst whenever his throat went dry, but food was another matter, and after not having swallowed a morsel for nearly two days, his stomach was crying out to be filled. So it was that his body gradually won out over his mind, and his peevish brooding over missed opportunities gave way to an all-out search for grub. It was late morning now, perhaps even early afternoon, and people were finally up and about, roused from their Sunday torpors and shuffling around their kitchens preparing breakfast and brunch. From nearly every house he trotted past he was assaulted by the smells of bacon cooking on the stove, eggs frying in the skillet, and warm toast popping out of the toaster. It was a foul trick, he felt, a cruel thing to be doing to him in his present state of angst and semi-starvation, but he resisted the urge to go begging for scraps at the doors and kept on moving. Willy's lessons had sunk in. A stray dog is nobody's friend, and if he made a nuisance of himself in front of the wrong person, he'd be carted off to the pound – the place from which no dog ever returned.

If he had developed the habit of hunting and foraging for himself, he wouldn't have felt so helpless now. But he had spent too many years at Willy's side, knocking around the world in his role as confidant and *chien à tout faire*, and whatever lupine instincts he had been born with had long since atrophied and disappeared. He had grown into a soft, civilized creature, a thinking dog instead of an athletic dog, and as far back as he could remember his bodily needs had been taken care of by someone else. But that was the bargain, wasn't it? The man gave you food and a place to sleep, and in return you gave him love and undying loyalty. Now that Willy was gone, he would have to unlearn everything he knew and start all over again. Were changes of that magnitude possible? Mr. Bones had run into homeless dogs in the past, but he had never felt anything but pity for them – pity, and a touch of disdain. The loneliness of their lives was too brutal to contemplate, and he had always kept himself at a safe distance, wary of the ticks and fleas hidden in their fur, reluctant to get too close to them for fear that the diseases and desperation they carried would rub off on him. Perhaps he had turned into a snob, but he could always recognize one of those abject creatures from a hundred yards away. They moved differently from other dogs, gliding along with that grim mendicant's lope of theirs, the tail cocked between their legs at quarter-mast, cantering down the avenues as if they were late for an appointment somewhere – when in fact they weren't going anywhere, just traveling around in circles, lost in the limbo between one nowhere and the next. Now, as he turned another corner and crossed the street, Mr. Bones discovered that he was moving just like that himself. He had kissed his master good-bye less than half an hour ago, and already he was one of them.

By and by, he came to the edge of a traffic circle with an island in the middle of it. A large statue rose up from the island, and as Mr. Bones studied the work from a distance, he concluded that it was supposed to be a soldier on horseback with his sword drawn, as if about to plunge into battle. More interestingly, a flock of pigeons had alighted on various parts of the soldier's body, not to speak of several places on the huge stone horse, and with several other species of birds in attendance below – wrens, sparrows, whatever you called them – Mr. Bones wondered if this might not be a good moment to test his prowess as a killer. If he couldn't depend on people for his food anymore, what choice did he have but to depend on himself?

The traffic had increased by then, and it took some nimble footwork for Mr. Bones to cross to the other side: dodging cars, pausing, rushing forward, waiting again, timing his moves so as not to get hit. At one point, a man on a motorcycle came roaring past him, a bolt of shining black metal that seemed to have materialized out of thin air, and Mr. Bones had to jump to the side to avoid him, which put him smack in front of an oncoming car, a big yellow job with a grille like a waffle iron, and if Mr. Bones hadn't hopped back to where he'd been a second before (returning to the spot the motorcycle had just vacated), that would have been the end of him. Two or three horns honked, a man stuck his head out of a car window and yelled something that sounded like 'funderflew' or 'chuck and chew,' and Mr. Bones felt the sting of the insult. He was ashamed of himself, humiliated by his sorry performance. He couldn't even get to the other side of the road without running into trouble, and if simple things like that were going to be hard for him, what would happen when he came to things that were really hard? In the end, he got to where he was going, but by the time he was out of danger and stepping on to the curb of the island, he felt so rattled and disgusted with himself, he wished he hadn't attempted the crossing in the first place.

Luckily, the traffic had forced him to take the long way around, and he landed on the north side of the island. From that angle, he found himself looking up at the back of the statue, the part that showed the horse's rump and the spokes of the soldier's spurs, and since most of the pigeons had congregated around in the front, Mr. Bones had a little time to catch his breath and plot his next move. He had never been one to chase after birds, but he had watched how other dogs did it, and he had learned enough from them to have formed a fairly good idea of what not to do. You couldn't just blunder in and hope for the best, for example, and you couldn't make a lot of noise, and you couldn't run, no matter how strong the temptation. You weren't out to scare the pigeons, after all. The object was to get one of them in your mouth, and the moment you started to run, they would take off into the air and fly away. That was another point to remember, he told himself. Pigeons could fly, and dogs couldn't. Pigeons might be stupider than dogs, but that was because God had given them wings instead of brains, and in order to overcome those wings, a dog had to reach down inside himself and call upon every trick that life had taught him.

Stealth was the answer. A sneak attack behind enemy lines. Mr. Bones walked over to the western face of the plinth and peered around the corner. A good eighteen or twenty pigeons were still there, parading back and forth in the sunlight. He went down into a crouch, zeroing in on the nearest bird as his belly touched the ground, and then he began to crawl forward, advancing as slowly and surreptitiously as he could. The instant he came into view, three or four sparrows rose up from the pavement and repositioned themselves on the soldier's head, but the pigeons seemed not to notice him. They continued to go about their business, cooing and strutting around in that featherheaded way of theirs, and as he moved toward his chosen victim, he could see what a fine, plump specimen she was, truly a first-rate catch. He would aim for her neck, pouncing on her from behind with his jaws open, and if he jumped at the right moment, she wouldn't have a chance. It was all a matter of patience, of knowing when to strike. He paused, not wanting to stir up any suspicions, trying to blend into the surroundings, to make himself as still and inanimate as the stone horse. He just needed to get a little closer, narrow the gap by another foot or two before springing into action for the final thrust. He was scarcely breathing by then, scarcely moving a muscle, and yet off to his right, at the outer edge of the flock, half-a-dozen pigeons suddenly flapped their wings and took off into the air, rising up toward the statue like a squadron of helicopters. It hardly seemed possible. He had been doing everything by the book, never once deviating from the plan he had set in motion, and yet they were on to him now, and if he didn't act fast, the whole operation was going to blow up in his face. The little prize in front of him waddled forward with a series of rapid, sure-footed steps, quickly retreating out of range. Another pigeon flew off, and then another, and then one more. All hell was breaking loose, and Mr. Bones, who until then had exercised the strictest, most admirable self-control, could think of nothing better to do than leap to his feet and rush after his victim. It was a desperate, thoughtless move, but it almost worked. He felt a wing flutter against his snout just as his jaws were opening, but that was as close as he got. His meal flew off into the air, escaping along with every other bird on the island, and lo and behold, there was Mr. Bones, suddenly alone, galloping back and forth in a frenzy of frustration, jumping into the air and barking, barking at all of them, barking out of rage and defeat, and long after the last bird had disappeared around the steeple of the church on the other side of the avenue, he went on barking – at himself, at the world, at nothing at all.

Two hours later, he discovered an ice-cream cone melting on the sidewalk near the Maritime Museum (cherry vanilla, with candy sprinkles studded in the soft, sugary blob), and then, not fifteen minutes after that, he chanced upon the remnants of a Kentucky Fried Chicken dinner that someone had left on a public bench – a red-and-white take-out box filled with three partially eaten legs, two untouched wings, a biscuit, and a clump of mashed potatoes soaked in brown, salty gravy. The food helped to restore his confidence somewhat, but far less than one might have supposed. The island debacle had shaken him deeply, and for hours afterward the memory of the botched attack kept knifing its way into his consciousness. He had disgraced himself, and even though he tried not to dwell on what had happened, he couldn't escape the feeling that he was old and washed up, a has-been.

He spent the night in a vacant lot, cowering under a profusion of weedy growths and pinprick stars, barely able to keep his eyes shut for more than five unbroken minutes. Bad as the day had been, the night was even worse, for this was the first night he had ever spent alone, and Willy's absence was so strong, so palpable in the air around him, that Mr. Bones did little else but lie there on his patch of ground and long for the closeness of his master's body. By the time he finally drifted off into something that resembled true sleep, it was almost morning, and three quarters of an hour later the first rays of the rising sun forced his eyes open again. He stood up and shook himself, and at that moment a terrible heaviness swept through him. It was as if everything had suddenly gone dark, as if an eclipse were taking place inside his soul, and while it was never clear to him exactly how he knew it, he was certain that the moment had come for Willy to leave this world. It was just as the dream had foretold. His master was about to die, and in another minute Sister Margaret would come into the room and put the mirror to his mouth, and then Mrs. Swanson would cover her face with her hands and start to weep.

When the fatal moment arrived, his legs buckled and he dropped to the ground. It was as if the very air had flattened him, and for the next few minutes he lay there among the bottle caps and empty beer cans, unable to move. He felt that his body was about to disintegrate, that his vital fluids were going to spill out of him, and once he had been sucked dry, he would be turned into a stiffening carcass, a lump of former dog rotting in the Maryland sun. Then, as unexpectedly as it had come on, the heaviness began to lift, and he felt his life stirring inside him again. But Mr. Bones longed for annihilation now, and rather than stand up and leave the spot where he had experienced Willy's death, he rolled on to his back and spread his legs wide open – exposing his throat, belly, and genitals to the sky. He was utterly vulnerable to attack in that position. Splayed out in puppylike innocence, he waited for God to strike him dead, fully prepared to offer himself up as a sacrifice now that his master was gone. A few more minutes went by. Mr. Bones closed his eyes, steeling himself for the bright, ecstatic blow from above, but God paid no attention to him – or else could not find him – and little by little, as the sun burned through the clouds overhead, Mr. Bones understood that he was not destined to die that morning. He rolled over and climbed to his feet. Then, tilting his head toward the sky, he filled his lungs with air and let out a long, mighty howl.

By ten o'clock, he had fallen in with a gang of six twelve-year-old boys. At first, it seemed like a stroke of good fortune, and for an hour or two he was given the royal treatment. The boys fed him pretzels, hot dogs, and crusts of pizza, and Mr. Bones returned their generosity by doing what he could to keep them entertained. He had never had much to do with children, but he had seen enough over the years to know that they were unpredictable. These boys struck him as a particularly rowdy

63

and boisterous lot. They were full of taunts and swagger and boastful remarks, and after he had been with them for a while, he noticed that they seemed to take an uncommon delight in punching each other and delivering surreptitious whacks to the head. They wound up in a park, and for an hour or so the boys played football, banging into each other's bodies with such vehemence that Mr. Bones began to grow alarmed that someone would get hurt. It was the end of summer vacation. School would be starting again soon, and the boys were hot and bored, itching to stir up trouble. After the game was over, they wandered to the edge of a pond and began skipping stones across the surface of the water. This rapidly degenerated into a contest over whose stone had made the most skips, which in turn led to several heated arguments. Mr. Bones, who despised conflict in any form, decided to break the increasingly rancorous atmosphere by diving into the water and fetching one of the stones. He had never been very interested in retrieving objects. Willy had always shunned that sport as something unworthy of Mr. Bones's intelligence, but Mr. Bones knew how impressed people were when dogs came romping back to their masters with sticks and balls between their teeth, and so he went against his own inclinations and took the plunge. The splash caused a great commotion in the pond, and even as he dove under the surface and deftly snatched a sinking stone in his jaws, he could hear one of the boys cursing him for making such a disturbance. The game was ruined, the boy shouted, and it would take five minutes before the water was still enough to start again. Maybe so, Mr. Bones said to himself as he paddled back to shore, but think how amazed he'll be when I drop this little sucker at his feet. It's not every dog who can pull off a coup like this. When he arrived in front of the angry boy and let go of the stone, however, he was greeted by a kick in the ribs. 'Dumb dog,' the boy said. 'What do you want to mess up our water for?' Mr. Bones let out a yelp of pain and surprise, and immediately after that another dispute flared up among the boys. Some condemned the kick, others applauded it, and before long two of the boys were rolling around on the ground in each other's arms, re-enacting the age-old struggle of might versus right. Mr. Bones withdrew to a safer distance several yards off, shook the water out of his fur, and then stood there waiting for one of the kinder boys to call him back. For all his willingness to bury the hatchet, no one even looked at him. The fighting continued, and when it was finally over, one of the boys spotted him, picked up a stone, and threw it in his direction. It missed by two or three feet, but Mr. Bones had seen enough by then to get the message. He turned and ran away, and even though one or two of the boys shouted after him to come back, he didn't stop running until he had reached the other end of the park.

He spent the next hour sulking under a clump of hawthorn bushes. It wasn't that the kick had hurt so much, but his morale had been bruised, and he was disappointed in himself for having misread the situation so badly. He would have to learn to be more cautious, he told himself, to be less trusting, to assume the worst in people until they had demonstrated their good intentions. It was a sad lesson to be absorbing so late in life, he realized, but if he meant to cope with the difficulties ahead, he would have to toughen up and get with the program. What he needed was to establish some general principles, firm rules of conduct that he could fall back on in moments of crisis. Based on his recent experience, it wasn't hard to come up with the first item on the list. No more kids. No more people under sixteen, especially boy people. They lacked compassion, and once you stripped that quality from a two-leg's soul, he was no better than a mad dog.

Just as he was about to climb out from under the shrub and move on, he spotted a white sneaker not two feet from his nose. It was so like the sneaker that had just landed in his gut that Mr. Bones nearly gagged on his saliva. Had the scoundrel come back to continue the job? The dog recoiled, retreating farther into the tangle of thorns and low-lying branches, snagging his fur in the process. What a dreary predicament to be in now, he thought, but what alternative did he have? He had to keep himself hidden, flattened down on all fours with a dozen spikes in his back, and hope that the bully would get tired of waiting and leave.

But such luck was not to be granted to Mr. Bones that day. The ruffian held his ground, refusing to give up, and instead of taking his mischief to some other area of the park, he crouched down in front of the bush and parted the branches to look in. Mr. Bones growled, ready to pounce on the thug if he had to.

'Don't be afraid,' the boy said. 'I'm not going to hurt you.'

Like hell you aren't, Mr. Bones thought, and because he was still too afraid to let his guard down, he failed to realize that the gentle voice floating through the branches wasn't a trick – but the voice of an altogether different boy.

'I saw what they did to you,' the new boy said. 'They're jerks, those guys. I know them from school. Ralph Hernandez and Pete Bondy. You hang around with creeps like them, and something bad is always going to happen to you.'

By then, the speaker had poked his head in far enough for Mr. Bones to get a clear view of his features, and at last he understood that he wasn't looking at his tormentor. The face belonged to a Chinese boy of ten or eleven, and in that first indelible instant, Mr. Bones felt that it was one of the loveliest human faces he had ever had the pleasure to gaze upon. So much for general principles and rules of conduct. This kid meant him no harm, and if Mr. Bones was wrong about that, then he would turn in his dog badge and spend the rest of his life as a porcupine.

'My name is Henry,' the boy said. 'Henry Chow. What's your name?'

Ha, thought Mr. Bones. A little wise guy. And how does he think I'm supposed to answer that one?

Still, with so much riding on the outcome of the conversation, he decided to give it his best shot. Buried among the twigs and dead leaves, he raised his head and emitted a series of three quick barks: wǒof, wǒof, wǒof. It was a perfect anapest, with each syllable of his name accorded the proper stress, balance, and duration. For a few brief seconds, it was as if the words *Mis|ter Bones* had been boiled down to their sonorous essence, to the purity of a musical phrase.

'Good dog,' young Henry said, holding out his right hand as a peace offering. 'You catch on fast, don't you?'

Mr. Bones barked once more to convey his agreement, and then he began to lick the open palm of the hand that was dangling in front of him. Little by little, Henry coaxed him out from the safety of his hiding place, and once Mr. Bones had fully emerged, the boy sat down on the ground with him and, in between numerous pats on the head and kisses on the face, carefully picked out the leaves and brambles that had collected in his fur.

Thus began an exemplary friendship between dog and boy. In age, they were only three and a half years apart, but the boy was young and the dog was old, and because of that discrepancy, each wound up giving to the other something he had never had before. For Mr. Bones, Henry proved that love was not a quantifiable substance. There was always more of it somewhere, and even after one love had been lost, it was by no means impossible to find another. For Henry, an only child whose parents worked long hours and had steadfastly refused to allow a pet in the apartment, Mr. Bones was the answer to his prayers.

Nevertheless, this budding alliance was not without its pitfalls and its dangers. Once Henry began to talk about his father, Mr. Bones understood that throwing in his lot with this boy was not quite the sure bet it had seemed at first glance. They were slowly wending their way toward the street where the Chow family lived, and as Henry continued to describe the various problems the two of them would be up against, Mr. Bones found himself advancing from anxiety to fear to outright terror. It was bad enough that Henry's father disliked dogs and that Mr. Bones would be barred from entering the house. Worse still was the fact that even after a place had been found for him, his presence would have to be kept a secret from Mr. Chow. If Henry's father caught so much as a whiff of the dog anywhere in the neighborhood, the boy would be punished so severely that he would wish he had never been born. Given that Mr. Chow both lived and worked in the same building, it seemed almost preposterous for them to think they could avoid discovery. The family apartment was upstairs on the second floor, the family business was downstairs on the first floor, and Henry's father was always around, either sleeping or working, morning, noon, and night.

'I know it doesn't look too good,' Henry said. 'But I'm willing to give it a try if you are.'

Well, at least the boy had spirit. And a pleasant voice to go along with it, Mr. Bones added, doing everything he could to look on the bright side and count his blessings. What he didn't know at that point, however, was that the worst was still to come. He had heard the bad, he had heard the worse, but it wasn't until Henry started talking about hiding places that he understood the full horror of what he was getting himself into.

There was the alley, Henry said. That was one option, and if Mr. Bones was willing to sleep in a cardboard box and promised not to make any noise, they might get away with it. Another possibility was the yard around in the back. It wasn't very big – just a patch of weeds, really – with some rusting refrigerators and corroded metal shelves lined up along the fence, but the waiters sometimes went out there to smoke, and on most evenings, especially when the weather was warm, his father liked to spend a few minutes walking around back there after he locked up the restaurant for the night. He called it 'drinking in the stars,' and according to Henry, he always slept better if he had his little dose of sky before going upstairs and climbing into bed.

Henry rattled on for a while about his father's sleeping habits, but Mr.

Bones was no longer listening. The fatal word had passed the boy's lips, and once Mr. Bones realized that the *restaurant* in question was not just any two-bit hot-dog stand but a *Chinese restaurant*, he was ready to turn tail and run. How many times had Willy warned him about those places? Just yesterday morning, he had lectured him for fifteen minutes on the subject, and was Mr. Bones going to ignore that advice now and betray the memory of his beloved master? This Henry was a fine little fellow, but if Willy's words contained even the smallest particle of the truth, then sticking with the boy would be like signing his own death sentence.

Still, he couldn't bring himself to bolt. He had been with Henry for only forty minutes, and already the attachment was too strong for him to dash off without saying good-bye. Torn between fear and affection, he chose a middle course, which was the only course available to him under the circumstances. He simply stopped – just came to a dead halt on the sidewalk, lay down on the ground, and began to whimper. Henry, who had little experience with dogs, had no idea what to make of this sudden, unexpected move. He crouched down beside Mr. Bones and began stroking his head, and the dog, trapped in an agony of indecision, could not help noticing what a gentle touch the boy had.

'You're bushed,' Henry said. 'Here I am blabbing away, and you're all worn out and hungry, and I haven't even bothered to feed you.'

A Big Mac followed, topped off by a bag of fries, and once Mr. Bones had devoured these delectable offerings, his heart was putty in the boy's hands. Run away from this, he told himself, and you'll die in the streets. Go home with him, and you'll die there too. But at least you'll be with Henry, and if death is everywhere, what difference does it make where you go?

And so it was that Mr. Bones went against his master's teachings and wound up living by the gates of hell.

His new home was a cardboard box that had once contained a jumbo-model Fedders air-conditioner. For caution's sake, Henry wedged it between the cyclone fence and one of the old refrigerators in the backyard. That was where Mr. Bones slept at night, curled up in his dark cell until the boy came to fetch him in the morning, and because Henry was a clever lad and had dug a hole under the fence, Mr. Bones could crawl through to the next yard – thus avoiding both the back and side doors of the restaurant – and meet up with his young master at the other end of the block to begin their daily rambles.

68

Don't think that the dog wasn't afraid, and don't think that he wasn't aware of the perils that surrounded him – but at the same time, know too that he never once regretted his decision to team up with Henry. The restaurant provided him with an inexhaustible source of savory delicacies, and for the first time since *Mom-san*'s death four years earlier, Mr. Bones had enough to eat. Spareribs and dumplings, sesame noodles and fried rice, tofu in brown sauce, braised duck and lighter-than-air won tons: the variety was endless, and once he had been initiated into the glories of Chinese cooking, he could scarcely contain himself at the thought of what Henry would be bringing him next. His stomach had never been happier, and while his digestion sometimes suffered as a result of a too-tangy spice or seasoning, those intermittent bowel eruptions seemed a small price to pay for the pleasure of the meals themselves. If there was any drawback to this heady regime, it was the pang of unknowing that pricked his soul whenever his tongue chanced upon an unidentifiable taste. Willy's prejudices had become his fears, and as he bit down on the obscure new concoction, he couldn't help wondering if he was eating a fellow dog. He would stop chewing then, suddenly frozen with remorse, but it was always too late. His salivary juices were already flowing, and with his taste buds aching for more of what they had only just discovered, his appetite would always get the better of him. After the brief pause, his tongue would dart out at the food again, and before he could tell himself that he was committing a sin, the platter would be licked clean. A moment of sadness would inevitably follow. Then, in an effort to assuage his guilty conscience, he would tell himself that if this was to be his fate as well, he only hoped that he would taste as good as the thing he had just eaten.

Henry bought several packets of radish seeds and planted them in the dirt near Mr. Bones's cardboard box. The garden was his cover story, and whenever his parents asked him why he was spending so much time in the backyard, he had only to mention the radishes and they would nod their heads and walk away. It was peculiar to start a garden so late in the season, his father said, but Henry had already prepared an answer to that question. Radishes germinate in eighteen days, he said, and they would be up long before the weather turned cold. Clever Henry. He could always talk his way out of tricky spots, and with his knack for pinching coins and stray singles from his mother's purse and his night-time raids on the kitchen leftovers, he built a more than tolerable life for himself and his new friend. It wasn't his fault that his father gave Mr. Bones several bad scares by coming out to the garden in the middle of the night to inspect the progress of the radishes. Each time the beam of his flashlight swept over the area in front of Mr. Bones's box, the dog would quake in the darkness of his cubicle, certain that the end was upon him. Once or twice, the stink of fear that rose up from his body was so pungent that Mr. Chow actually stopped to sniff the air, as if suspecting that something was wrong. But he never knew what he was looking for, and after a moment or two of puzzled reflection, he would rattle off a string of incomprehensible Chinese words and then return to the house.

Gruesome as those nights were, Mr. Bones would always forget them the moment he set eyes on Henry in the morning. Their days would begin at the secret corner, directly in front of the trash bin and the coin-operated newspaper dispenser, and for the next eight or ten hours, it was as if the restaurant and the cardboard box were no more than images from a bad dream. They would walk around the city together, drifting from here to there with no special purpose in mind, and the aimlessness of this routine was so like the helter-skelter days with Willy that Mr. Bones had no trouble understanding what was expected of him. Henry was a solitary child, a boy who was used to being alone and living in his thoughts, and now that he had a companion to share his days with, he talked continuously, unburdening himself of the smallest, most ephemeral musings that flitted through his eleven-year-old brain. Mr. Bones loved listening to him, loved the flow of words that accompanied their steps, and in that these monologic free-for-alls reminded him of his dead master as well, he sometimes wondered if Henry Chow were not the true and legitimate heir of Willy G. Christmas, the reincarnated spirit of the one and only himself.

That wasn't to say that Mr. Bones always understood what his new master was talking about, however. Henry's preoccupations were radically different from Willy's, and the dog usually found himself at a loss whenever the boy started in on his pet subjects. How could Mr. Bones be expected to know what an earned-run average was or how many games the Orioles were behind in the standings? In all the years he had spent with Willy, the poet had never once touched on the topic of baseball. Now, overnight, it seemed to have become a matter of life and death. The first thing Henry did every morning after meeting up with Mr. Bones at their corner was to put some coins into the newspaper dispenser and buy a copy of *The Baltimore Sun*. Then, hastening to a bench across the street, he would sit down, pull out the sports section, and read an account of the previous night's game to Mr. Bones. If the Orioles had won, his voice was full of happiness and excitement. If the Orioles had lost, his voice was sad and mournful, at times even tinged with anger. Mr. Bones learned to hope for wins and to dread the prospect of losses, but he never quite understood what Henry meant when he talked about the *team*. An oriole was a bird, not a group of men, and if the orange creature on Henry's black cap was indeed a bird, how could it be involved in something as strenuous and complex as base-ball? Such were the mysteries of the new world he had entered. Orioles fought with tigers, blue jays battled against angels, bear cubs warred with giants, and none of it made any sense. A baseball player was a man, and yet once he joined a team he was turned into an animal, a mutant being, or a spirit who lived in heaven next to God.

According to Henry, there was one bird in the Baltimore flock who stood out from the rest. His name was Cal, and although he was no more than a ball-playing oriole, he seemed to embody the attributes of several other creatures as well: the endurance of a workhorse, the courage of a lion, and the strength of a bull. All that was perplexing enough, but when Henry decided that Mr. Bones's new name should also be Cal – short for Cal Ripken Junior the Second – the dog was thrown into a state of genuine confusion. It's not that he objected to the principle of the thing. He was in no position to tell Henry what his real name was, after all, and since the boy had to call him something, *Cal* seemed as good a name as any other. The only problem was that it rhymed with *Al*, and the first few times he heard Henry say it, he automatically thought of Willy's old friend, dapper Al Saperstein, the man who owned that nov-elty shop they used to visit on Surf Avenue in Coney Island. He would suddenly see Uncle Al in his mind again, decked out in his lemon-yellow bow tie and hound's-tooth sport jacket, and then he would be back in the shop, watching Willy as he wandered up and down the aisles, perusing the handshake buzzers and whoopee cushions and exploding cigars. He found it painful to encounter Willy like that, to have his old master jump out from the shadows and strut about as if he were still alive, and when you combined these involuntary recollections with Henry's incessant talk about Cal the oriole, and then added in the fact that half the time Henry used the name *Cal* he was actually referring to Mr. Bones, it was hardly strange that the dog wasn't always certain about who he was anymore or what he was supposed to be.

But no matter. He had only just arrived on Planet Henry, and he knew that it would take some time before he felt completely at home there. After one week with the boy, he was already beginning to get the hang of it, and if not for a nasty trick of the calendar, there's no telling what kind of progress they would have made. But summer was not the only season of the year, and with the time approaching for Henry to return to school, the tranquil days of walking and talking and flying kites in the park were suddenly no more. The night before he was to begin the sixth grade, Henry forced himself to stay awake, lying in bed with his eyes open until he was sure his parents were asleep. Just past midnight, when the coast was finally clear, he crept down the back staircase, went into the yard, and climbed into the cardboard box with Mr. Bones. Holding the dog in his arms, he tearfully explained that things were going to be different now. 'When the sun comes up in the morning,' Henry said, 'the fun times will officially be over. I'm such an idiot, Cal. I was going to find another place for you, something better than this rotten box in this rotten backyard, and I didn't do it. I tried, but nobody would help me, and now we've run out of time. You never should have trusted me, Cal. I'm a loser. I'm a retarded piece of shit, and I mess up everything. I always have and I always will. That's what happens when you're a coward. I'm too scared to talk to my dad about you, and if I go behind his back and talk to my mom, she'll just tell him anyway, and that would only make things worse. You're the best friend I've ever had, and all I've done is let you down.'

Mr. Bones had only the dimmest idea of what Henry was talking about. The boy was sobbing too hard for his words to be understood, but as the rush of chopped-off syllables and stuttered phrases continued, it became increasingly clear that this outburst was more than just a passing mood. Something was wrong, and while Mr. Bones could scarcely imagine what that thing was, Henry's sadness was beginning to have an effect on him, and within a matter of minutes he had taken on the boy's sadness as his own. Such is the way with dogs. They might not always understand the nuances of their masters' thoughts, but they feel what they feel, and in this case there was no doubt that young Henry Chow was in bad shape. Ten minutes went by, then twenty minutes, then thirty, and there they sat, the boy and the dog, wedged together in the darkness of the cardboard box, the boy with his arms wrapped tightly around the dog, crying his eyes out, and the dog whimpering along in sympathy, raising his head every so often to lick the tears from the boy's face.

Eventually, they both fell asleep. First Henry, then Mr. Bones, and in spite of the somber occasion, in spite of the cramped quarters and the paucity of air that made breathing difficult inside the box, Mr. Bones took courage from the warmth of the body next to him, relishing the fact that he didn't have to spend another terror-filled night alone in the darkness. For the first time since Willy was taken from him, he slept soundly and deeply, untroubled by the dangers that surrounded him.

Dawn broke. Pinkish light filtered through a seam in the cardboard box, and Mr. Bones stirred, struggling to disengage himself from Henry's arms and stretch his body. A few moments of jostling ensued, but even as the dog thrashed about, knocking against the inner walls of the enclosure, the boy slept on, oblivious to all the commotion. It was remarkable how children could sleep, Mr. Bones thought, finally getting himself into a spot where he could flex his knotted muscles, but the hour was still early – just past six o'clock – and given how exhausted he had been after his late-night crying fit, it probably made sense that Henry should still be dead to the world. The dog studied the boy's face in the flickering penumbra – so smooth and round in comparison to Willy's ancient, bearded mug – and watched as little bubbles of saliva dripped down from his tongue and gathered in the corners of his half-open mouth. Tenderness welled up in Mr. Bones's heart. As long as Henry was with him, he realized, he would have been glad to stay in this box forever.

Ten seconds later, Mr. Bones was jolted from his reverie by a loud thud. The sound came crashing down on him like an explosion, and before he could identify it as a human foot kicking the outside of the box, Henry had opened his eyes and was beginning to scream. Then the box itself was rising off the ground. A rush of early-morning light engulfed Mr. Bones, and for a moment or two it was as if he had gone blind. He heard a man shouting in Chinese, and then, an instant later, the box was flying through the air in the direction of Henry's radish patch. Mr. Chow stood before them, dressed in a sleeveless undershirt and a pair of blue shorts, the veins of his thin neck bulging as the tirade of incomprehensible words continued. He jabbed the air with his finger, again and again pointing it at Mr. Bones, and Mr. Bones barked back at him, confused by the intensity of the man's anger, by the noise of Henry's wailing, by the sudden chaos of the whole hysterical scene. The man lunged at Mr. Bones, but the dog danced back, keeping himself at a safe distance. Then the man went for the boy, who was already trying to escape by crawling through the hole under the fence, and because the boy wasn't fast enough, or because he had started too late, it wasn't long before his father had yanked him to his feet and slapped him across the back of the head. By then, Mrs. Chow had come into the yard as well, charging out the back door in her flannel nightgown, and as Mr. Chow continued to shout at Henry, and as Henry continued to belt out his shrill, soprano screams, Mrs. Chow soon added her own voice to the din, venting her displeasure on both her husband and her son. Mr. Bones retreated to the opposite corner of the yard. By now, he knew that all was lost. Nothing good could come of this battle, at least not as far as he was concerned, and sorry as he felt for Henry, he felt even sorrier for himself. The only solution was to get out of there, to pull up stakes and run.

He waited until the man and the woman started dragging the boy toward the house. When they were within range of the back door, Mr. Bones scampered across the yard and crawled through the hole under the fence. He paused for a moment, waiting for Henry to disappear through the door. Just as the boy was about to go in, however, he broke free of his parents, turned in Mr. Bones's direction, and called out in that anguished, piercing voice of his: 'Cal, don't leave me! Don't leave me, Cal!' As if in response to his son's desperation, Mr. Chow picked up a stone from the ground and threw it at Mr. Bones. The dog instinctively jumped back, but the moment he did so, he felt ashamed of himself for not holding his ground. He watched the stone as it clattered harmlessly against the links of the metal fence. Then he barked three times in farewell, hoping the boy would understand that he was trying to speak to him. Mr. Chow opened the door, Mrs. Chow pushed Henry inside, and Mr. Bones began to run.

He had no idea where he was going, but he knew that he couldn't stop, that he had to keep on running until his legs gave out on him or his heart exploded in his chest. If there was any hope for him, any sliver of a chance that he would live beyond the next few days, let alone the next few hours, then he would have to get out of Baltimore. All bad things lived in this city. It was a place of death and despair, of dog-haters and Chinese restaurants, and it was only by the skin of his teeth that he hadn't wound up as a bogus appetizer in a little white take-out box. Too bad about the boy, of course, but given how quickly Mr. Bones had attached himself to his young master, it was remarkable how few regrets he had about leaving. The cardboard box no doubt had something to do with it. The nights he'd spent in there had been almost unendurable, and what good was a home if you didn't feel safe in it, if you were treated as an outcast in the very spot that was supposed to be your refuge? Shutting up a soul in a dark box wasn't right. That's what they did to you after you were dead, but as long as you were alive, as long as you had some kick left in you, you owed it to yourself and everything holy in this world not to submit to such indignities. To be alive meant to breathe; to breathe meant the open air; and the open air meant any place that was not Baltimore, Maryland.

4

He kept on running for three days, and in all that time he barely paused to sleep or look for food. When Mr. Bones finally stopped, he was somewhere in northern Virginia, sprawled out in a meadow ninety miles west of the Chows' backyard. Two hundred yards in front of him, the sun was going down behind a stand of oaks. Half-a-dozen swallows darted back and forth in the middle distance, skimming the field as they combed the air for mosquitoes, and in the darkness of the branches behind him, songbirds chirped out a few last refrains before turning in for the night. As he lay there in the tall grass, his chest heaving and his tongue dangling from his mouth, Mr. Bones wondered what would happen if he closed his eyes – and, if he did, whether he would be able to open them again in the morning. He was that tired and hungry, that muddled by the rigors of his marathon trek. If he fell asleep, it seemed perfectly possible to him that he would never wake up again.

He watched the sun as it continued to sink behind the trees, his eyes struggling to stay open as the darkness gathered around him. He didn't hold out for more than a minute or two, but even before weariness got the better of him, Mr. Bones's head had already begun to fill up with thoughts of Willy, fleeting pictures from the bygone days of smoke rings and Lucky Strikes, the goofball antics of their life together in the world of long ago. It was the first time since his master's death that he had been able to think about such things without feeling crushed by sorrow, the first time he had understood that memory was a place, a real place that one could visit, and that to spend a few moments among the dead was not necessarily bad for you, that it could in fact be a source of great comfort and happiness. Then he fell asleep, and Willy was still there with him, alive again in all his fractured glory, pretending to be a blind man as Mr. Bones led him down the steps of the subway. It was that windy day in March four and a half years ago, he realized, that funny afternoon of high hopes and dashed expectations when they rode out to Coney Island together to unveil the Symphony of Smells to Uncle Al. Willy had donned a Santa Claus hat to mark the occasion, and with the materials for the Symphony crammed inside a huge plastic garbage bag, which he had slung over his shoulder and which made him walk with a stoop, he looked for all the world like some drunk-tank version of Father Christmas himself. It's true that things didn't work out so well once they got there, but that was only because Uncle Al was in a bad mood. He wasn't a real uncle, of course, just a family friend who had lent a helping hand to Willy's parents after they arrived from Poland, and it was only out of some ancient loyalty to *Mom-san* and her husband that he allowed Willy and Mr. Bones to hang around his store. In point of fact, Al had little use for the novelty business, and with fewer and fewer customers showing up to buy his goods, there were certain items that had been languishing on the shelves for ten, twelve, and even twenty years. By now it was no more than a front for his other activities, most of them illegal, some of them not, and if the shady, fast-talking Al hadn't been turning a profit on fireworks, bookmaking, and the sale of stolen cigarettes, he wouldn't have thought twice about closing the door of that dusty emporium for ever. Who knows what scam had backfired on him that windy day in March, but when Willy traipsed in with his Symphony of Smells and started yammering to Uncle Al about how his invention was going to turn them both into millionaires, the proprietor of Whoopee-Land USA turned a deaf ear on his faux nephew's sales pitch. 'You're out of your skull, Willy,' Uncle Al said, 'you're fucking bonkers, you know that?' and promptly shooed him outside with his garbage bag of stinks and smells and collapsible cardboard labyrinths. Not to be dissuaded by a little skepticism, Willy enthusiastically set about to construct the symphony on the sidewalk, determined to prove to Uncle Al that he had indeed come up with one of the genuine marvels of all time. But the air was exceedingly gusty that day, and no sooner did Willy reach into the garbage bag and start pulling out the various elements of *Symphony No. 7* (towels, sponges, sweaters, galoshes, Tupperware boxes, gloves) than the wind caught hold of them and blew them down the street, scattering them in several different directions. Willy ran off to retrieve them, but once he let go of the bag, that too was blown away, and for all his supposed kindness to the Gurevitch family, Uncle Al just stood in the doorway and laughed.

That's what had happened four and a half years ago, but in the dream Mr. Bones had that night in the meadow, he and Willy never got off the subway. There was no question that they were on their way to Coney Island (witness the red-and-white Santa hat, the bulging garbage bag, the seeing-eye dog harness strapped around Mr. Bones's shoulders), but whereas the car of the F train had been quite crowded on the afternoon of the real journey, this time he and Willy were alone, the only two passengers riding out to the end of the line. The moment he became aware of this difference, Willy turned to him and said, 'Don't worry, Mr. Bones. It's not then. It's now.'

'And what's that supposed to mean?' the dog replied, and so naturally did these words come to him, so clearly were they the product of a long-standing, thoroughly proven ability to speak whenever he had something to say, that Mr. Bones was not the least bit astonished by the miracle that had just occurred.

'It means you're going about it all wrong,' Willy said. 'Running away from Baltimore, moping around in dumb-ass meadows, starving yourself for no good reason. It just won't do, my friend. You find yourself another master, or your fur is toast.'

'I found Henry, didn't I?' Mr. Bones said.

'A plum of a boy, that one, true blue through and through. But not good enough. That's the trouble with young ones. They might mean well, but they don't have any power. You have to go straight to the top, Mr. Bones. Find out who's boss. Find out who makes the decisions, and then attach yourself to that person. There's no other way. You need a new set-up, but it's never going to happen unless you start using your head.'

'I was desperate. How could I know his father would turn out to be such a louse?'

'Because I warned you about those places, didn't I? The moment you saw what you were getting yourself into, you should have cashed in your chips and run.'

'I did run. And when I wake up tomorrow morning, I'm going to start running again. That's my life now, Willy. I run, and I'm going to keep on running until I drop.'

'Don't give up on men, Bonesy. You've had some hard knocks, but you've got to tough it out and give it another try.'

'Men can't be trusted. I know that now.'

'You trust me, don't you?'

'You're the only one, Willy. But you're not like other men, and now that you're gone, there isn't a place on earth where I'm not in danger. Just yesterday, I nearly got myself shot. I was taking a shortcut through a field somewhere, and a guy came after me in a red pickup truck. Laughing, too, I might add, and then he pulled out a rifle and fired.

Lucky for me he missed. But who knows what's going to happen next time?'

'He's just one man. For every person like him, there's another one like Henry.'

'Your numbers are off, master. There might be a few stray fools with a soft spot for dogs, but most of them wouldn't think twice about loading up their shotguns the moment a four-leg sets foot on their land. I'm scared, Willy. Scared to go east, scared to go west. The way things stand now, I think I'd rather starve out here in the wilderness than run into one of those bullets. They'll kill you just for breathing, and when you're up against that kind of hatred, what's the use of trying?'

'All right, give up if you want to. It's no skin off my nose. I could sit here and tell you everything's going to work out, but what's the point of lying to you? Maybe it will, and maybe it won't. I'm no fortune-teller, and the truth is that not all stories have happy endings.'

'That's what I've been trying to tell you.'

'I know that. And I'm not saying you're wrong.'

Until that moment, the train had been speeding through the tunnel at a steady clip, rushing past the empty stations without stopping. Now, suddenly, Mr. Bones heard the screech of brakes, and the train began to slow down. 'What's happening?' he said. 'Why aren't we going fast anymore?'

'I have to get out,' Willy said.

'So soon?'

Willy nodded. 'I'm going now,' he said, 'but before I leave, I just want to remind you of something you might have forgotten.' He was already standing up by then, waiting for the doors to open. 'Do you remember *Mom-san*, Mr. Bones?'

'Of course I remember her. What do you take me for?'

'Well, they tried to kill her, too. They hunted her down like a dog, and she had to run for her life. People get treated like dogs, too, my friend, and sometimes they have to sleep in barns and meadows because there's nowhere else for them to go. Before you start feeling too sorry for yourself, just remember that you're not the first dog who's ever been lost.'

Sixteen hours later, Mr. Bones was ten miles south of the meadow in which he had dreamed the dream, emerging from a small patch of woods at the edge of a newly built subdivision of two-story houses. He no longer felt afraid. He was hungry, perhaps, and more than a little tired, but the terror that had been growing inside him for the past several days was largely gone. He had no idea why this should be so, but the fact was that he had woken up feeling much better than at any time since Willy's death. He knew that Willy hadn't really been there with him on the subway, and he knew that he couldn't really talk, but in the afterglow of this dream about impossible and beautiful things, he sensed that Willy was still with him, and even if he couldn't be with him, it was as if he were watching him, and even if the eyes that looked down on him were actually inside him, it made no difference in the larger scheme of things, because those eyes were the exact difference between feeling alone in the world and not feeling alone. Mr. Bones was ill-equipped to parse the subtleties of dreams, visions, and other mental phenomena, but he did know for certain that Willy was in Timbuktu, and if he himself had just been with Willy, perhaps that meant the dream had taken him to Timbuktu as well. That would explain, perhaps, why he had suddenly found himself able to speak – after so many years of struggle and failure. And if he had been to Timbuktu once, was it too much to think that he might not be able to go there again – simply by closing his eyes and chancing upon the right dream? It was impossible to say. But there was comfort in that thought, just as there had been comfort in spending that time with his old friend, even if none of it had really happened, even if none of it would ever happen again.

It was three o'clock in the afternoon, and the air was filled with the sounds of lawn mowers, sprinklers, and birds. Far away, on an invisible highway to the north, a dull bee-swarm of traffic pulsed under the suburban landscape. A radio was turned on, and a woman's voice began to sing. Closer by, someone burst out laughing. It sounded like the laugh of a small child, and as Mr. Bones finally came to the end of the woods he had been wandering in for the past half hour, he poked his snout through the twigs and saw that this was indeed the case. A towheaded boy of two or three was sitting on the ground about twelve feet in front of him, pulling up clumps of grass and flinging them into the air. Each time another shower of grass landed on his head, he broke out with a fresh round of giggles, clapping his hands and bouncing up and down as if he had discovered the most brilliant trick in the world. Ten or twelve yards beyond the boy, a girl with glasses was walking back and forth with a doll in her arms, singing softly to the imaginary infant as if she were trying to lull it to sleep. It was difficult to guess how old she was. Somewhere between seven and nine, Mr. Bones thought, but she also could have been a large six or a small ten, not to speak of an even larger five or even smaller eleven. To the left of the girl, a woman in white shorts and a white halter top was crouched over a bed of red and yellow flowers, carefully digging up weeds with a trowel. Her back was turned to Mr. Bones, and because she was wearing a straw hat with an exceedingly broad brim, her entire face was hidden from view. He was reduced to observing the curve of her spine, the freckles on her slender arms, a splash of white knee, but even with just those few elements to go on, he could tell that she wasn't old, no more than twenty-seven or twenty-eight, which probably meant that she was the mother of the two children. Wary of advancing any farther, Mr. Bones remained where he was, watching the scene from his little hideout at the verge of the woods. He had no way of knowing if this family was pro-dog or anti-dog, no way of knowing if they would treat him with kindness or chase him from their property. One thing was certain, however. He had stumbled upon a very handsome lawn. As he stood there looking at the swath of neatly tended green velvet spread out before him, he realized that it didn't take much imagination to know how good it would feel to roll around on that grass and smell the smells that came from it.

Before he could make up his mind about what to do next, the decision was taken out of his hands. The boy tossed two more fistfuls of grass into the air, and this time, instead of falling straight down on top of him as they had done before, a small breeze stirred at just that moment and carried them off in the direction of the woods. The boy turned his head to watch the flight of the green particles, and as his eyes scanned the space between them, Mr. Bones could see his expression change from one of cold, scientific detachment to one of absolute surprise. The dog had been discovered. The boy shot to his feet and began charging toward him, squealing with happiness as he waddled forth in his bloated plastic diaper, and right then and there, with his whole future suddenly on the line, Mr. Bones decided that this was the moment he had been waiting for. Not only did he not back off into the woods, and not only did he not run away, but in his calmest, most self-assured manner, he gingerly stepped out onto the grass and let the boy throw his arms around him. 'Doggy!' the little man cried, squeezing for all he was worth. 'Good doggy. Big old funny doggy.'

The girl came next, running across the lawn with the doll in her arms and calling out to the woman behind her. 'Look, Mama,' she said. 'Look what Tiger found.' Even as the boy went on hugging him, a wave of alarm passed through Mr. Bones's body. Where was this tiger she was talking about – and how could a tiger be prowling around out here where people lived? Willy had taken him to a zoo once, and he knew all about those big striped jungle cats. They were even bigger than lions, and if you ever met up with one of those sharp-fanged babies, you could kiss your future good-bye. A tiger would rip you to shreds in about twelve seconds, and whatever bits of you he didn't feel like eating would be fine stuff for the vultures and worms.

Still, Mr. Bones didn't run away. He continued to let his new friend cling to him, patiently bearing the brunt of the tyke's phenomenal strength, and hoped that his ears had been playing tricks on him, that he'd simply misheard what the girl had said. The sagging diaper was loaded with urine, and mingled in with the sharp ammonia scent he could detect traces of carrots, bananas, and milk. Then the girl was crouching down beside them, peering into Mr. Bones's face with her blue, magnified eyes, and the mystery was suddenly cleared up. 'Tiger,' she said to the boy, 'let go of him. You'll choke him to death.'

'My buddy,' Tiger said, tightening his grip even more, and although Mr. Bones was gratified to discover that he wasn't about to be devoured by a wild beast, the pressure on his throat was becoming severe enough to make him squirm now. The boy might not have been a real tiger, but that didn't mean he wasn't dangerous. In his own little way, he was more of an animal than Mr. Bones was.

Fortunately, the woman arrived just then and grabbed hold of the boy's arm, pulling him off Mr. Bones before more damage could be done. 'Careful, Tiger,' she said. 'We don't know if he's nice dog or not.'

'Oh, he's nice,' the girl said, gently patting Mr. Bones on his crown. 'All you have to do is look into his eyes. He's real nice, Mama. I'd say he's about the nicest dog I've ever seen.'

Mr. Bones was stunned by the girl's extraordinary statement, and just to show what a good sport he was, that he was indeed a dog who didn't bear grudges, he began licking Tiger's face in a great burst of slobbering affection. The little fellow howled with laughter, and even though the thrust of Mr. Bones's tongue eventually made him lose his balance, the rough-and-tumble Tiger thought it was the funniest thing that had ever happened to him, and he went on laughing under the barrage of the dog's kisses even as he thudded to the ground on his wet bottom.

'Well, at least he's friendly,' the woman said to her daughter, as if conceding an important point. 'But what an unholy mess. I don't think

I've ever seen a dirtier, scruffier, more dilapidated creature than this one.'

'There's nothing wrong with him that a little soap and water can't fix,' the girl said. 'Just look at him, Mama. He's not just nice, he's smart, too.'

The woman laughed. 'How can you know that, Alice? He hasn't done a thing but lick your brother's face.'

Alice squatted down in front of Mr. Bones and cupped his jowls in her hands. 'Show us how smart you are, old boy,' she said. 'Do a trick or something, okay? You know, like rolling over or standing up on your hind legs. Show Mama that I'm right.'

These were hardly difficult tasks for a dog of his mettle, and Mr. Bones promptly set about to demonstrate what he could do. First, he rolled over on the grass – not once but three times – and then he arched his back, lifted his front paws up to his face, and slowly rose up on his hind legs. It had been years since he had tried this last stunt, but even though his joints ached and he tottered more than he would have liked, he managed to hold the position for three or four seconds.

'See, Mama? What did I tell you?' Alice said. 'He's the smartest dog that ever was.'

The woman crouched down to Mr. Bones's level for the first time and looked into his eyes, and even though she was wearing sunglasses and still had the straw hat on her head, he could see that she was ever so pretty, with wisps of blonde hair curling down the back of her neck and a full, expressive mouth. Something shuddered inside him when she spoke to him in her slow, drawling Southern voice, and when she began patting his head with her right hand, Mr. Bones felt that surely his heart would break into a thousand pieces.

'You understand what we're saying to you, don't you, old dog?' she said. 'You're a special one, aren't you? And you're tired and beat-up, and you need something to put in your belly. That's it, old-timer, isn't it? You're lost and alone, and every inch of you is tuckered out.'

Had a poor mutt ever been luckier than Mr. Bones was that afternoon? Without any further discussion, and without any further need to charm them or prove what a good soul he was, the weary dog was led from the yard into the sanctum of the family house. There, in a radiant white kitchen, surrounded by freshly painted cabinets and shining metal utensils and an air of opulence he had never even imagined could exist on earth, Mr. Bones ate his fill, gorging himself on leftover slices of roast beef, a bowl of macaroni and cheese, two cans of tuna fish, and three uncooked hot dogs, not to mention lapping up two and a half bowls of water in between courses as well. He had wanted to hold back, to show them that he was a dog of modest appetites, really no trouble to take care of, but once the food was set down in front of him his hunger was simply too overpowering, and he forgot the vow he had made.

None of this seemed to bother his hosts. They were good-hearted people, and they knew a hungry dog when they saw one, and if Mr. Bones was that famished, then they were perfectly happy to provide for him until he wasn't. He ate in a trance of contentment, oblivious to everything but the food going into his mouth and sliding down his throat. When the meal was finally over and he looked up to check on what the others were doing, he saw that the woman had removed her hat and sunglasses. As she bent down near him to lift the bowls from the floor, he caught a glimpse of her gray-blue eyes and understood that she was in fact a great beauty, one of those women who made men stop breathing the moment they walked into a room.

'Well, old dog,' she said, running her palm over the top of his head, 'feeling better?'

Mr. Bones let out a small belch of appreciation, and then he started licking her hand. Tiger, whom he had all but forgotten by then, suddenly came rushing toward him. Drawn by the sound of the belch, which had greatly amused him, the boy leaned forward into Mr. Bones's face and let out a pretend belch of his own, which amused him even more. It was shaping up into another wild barroom scene, but before the situation could get out of hand, his mother swept him into her arms and stood up. She looked over at Alice, who was leaning against a counter and scrutinizing Mr. Bones with her serious, watchful eyes. 'What are we going to do with him, baby?' the woman said.

'I think we should keep him,' Alice answered.

'We can't do that. He probably belongs to somebody. If we kept him, it would be just like stealing.'

'I don't think he has a friend in the world. Just look at him. He's probably walked a thousand miles. If we don't take him in, he's going to die. Do you want that on your conscience, Mama?'

This girl certainly had the gift, all right. She knew just what to say and when to say it, and as Mr. Bones stood there listening to her talk to her mother, he wondered if Willy hadn't underestimated the power of some children. Alice might not have been the boss, and she might not have made the decisions, but her words cut straight to the truth, and that was bound to have an effect, to steer things in one direction rather than another.

'Check his collar, sweetheart,' the woman said. 'Maybe there's a name or an address on it or something.'

Mr. Bones knew full well that there wasn't, since Willy had never bothered with such things as licenses or registrations or fancy metal name tags. Alice knelt down beside him and began turning the collar around his neck, searching for signs of his identity or ownership, and because he already knew what the answer would be, he took advantage of the moment to enjoy the warmth of her breath as it fluttered against the back of his right ear.

'No, Mama,' she said at last. 'It's just a plain old ratty collar.'

For the first time in the short while he had known her, the dog saw the woman hesitate, and a certain confusion and sadness crept into her eyes. 'It's okay by me, Alice,' she said. 'But I can't give the thumbs-up until we've talked to your father. You know how he hates surprises. We'll wait until he comes home this evening, and then we'll all decide together. Okay?'

'Okay,' Alice said, somewhat deflated by this inconclusive response. 'But it's three against one, even if he says no. And fair is fair, right? We've just got to keep him, Mama. I'll get down on my knees and pray to Jesus for the rest of the day if it'll make Daddy say yes.'

'You don't have to do that,' the woman said. 'If you really want to help, you'll open the door and let the dog outside so he can do his business. And then we'll see if we can't clean him up a bit. That's the only way this thing is ever going to work. He's got to make a good first impression.'

The door opened for Mr. Bones not a moment too soon. After three days of privation, of eating no more than thimblefuls of scraps and garbage, of rooting around for whatever noxious edibles he could find, the richness of the meal he had just consumed hit his stomach with the force of a trauma, and with his digestive juices in full operation again, working double and even triple overtime to accommodate the recent onslaught, it was all he could do not to foul the kitchen floor and be banished into permanent exile. He trotted off behind a clump of bushes, trying to keep himself out of sight, but Alice followed him over, and to his never-ending shame and embarrassment, she was there to witness the dreadful explosion of brackish liquid that roared out of his bunghole and splattered onto the foliage beneath him. She let out a brief gasp of disgust when it happened, and he felt so mortified at offending her that for a moment or two he wished that he could shrivel up and die. But Alice was no ordinary person, and even though he thoroughly understood that by now, he never would have thought it possible for her to say what she said next. 'Poor dog,' she muttered, in a doleful, pitying voice. 'You're awfully sick, aren't you?' That was the entire statement – just two short sentences – but when Mr. Bones heard Alice say those words, he realized that Willy G. Christmas was not the only two-leg in the world who could be trusted. It turned out that there were others, and some of them were very small.

The rest of the afternoon rolled by in a blur of pleasures. They washed him down with the garden hose, lathering his fur into a mountainous pile of white suds, and as the six hands of his new companions rubbed away at his back and chest and head, he couldn't help remembering how the day had begun – and what an odd and mysterious thing it was that it should end like this. Then they rinsed him off, and after he shook himself dry and ran around the yard for a few minutes, peeing on various bushes and trees along the perimeter of the property, the woman sat with him for what seemed like the longest time, searching his body for ticks. She explained to Alice that her father had taught her how to do this in North Carolina when she was a girl and that the only foolproof method was to use your fingernails and pinch out the critters by the tops of their heads. Once you had them, you couldn't just flick them to the side, and you couldn't just crush them underfoot. You had to burn them, and while she was in no way encouraging Alice to play with matches, would she be so kind as to run into the kitchen and fetch the box of Ohio Blue Tips in the top drawer to the right of the stove? Alice did as she was asked, and for the next little while she and her mother combed through Mr. Bones's fur together, plucking out a succession of blood-swollen ticks and incinerating the culprits in little blazes of bright, phosphorescent heat. How not to be grateful for that? How not to rejoice at having this scourge of agonizing itches and sores removed from his person? Mr. Bones was so relieved by what they were doing for him that he even let Alice's next remark pass by without protest. He knew the insult was unintentional, but that didn't mean he wasn't hurt by it.

'I don't want to get your hopes up too high,' the woman said to her, 'but it might not be such a bad idea to give this dog a name before your daddy gets home. It'll make him seem more like part of the family, and that might give us a psychological edge. You understand what I'm saying, honey?'

'I already know his name,' Alice said. 'I knew it the moment I saw him.' The girl paused for a moment to collect her thoughts. 'Remember that book you used to read to me when I was little? The red one with the pictures in it and all those stories about animals? There was a dog in there that looked just like this one. He rescued a baby from a burning building and could count up to ten. Remember, Mama? I used to love that dog. When I saw Tiger hugging this one by the bushes a little while ago, it was like a dream come true.'

'What was his name?'

'Sparky. His name was Sparky the Dog.'

'All right, then. We'll call this one Sparky, too.'

When Mr. Bones heard the woman go along with this absurd choice, he felt stung. It had been bad enough trying to get used to *Cal*, but this was pushing things a little too far. He had suffered too much to be burdened with this cutesy, infantile nickname, this simpering diminutive inspired by a picture book for toddlers, and even if he lived as long again as he had lived so far, he knew that a dog of his melancholic temperament would never adjust to it, that he would cringe every time he heard it for the rest of his days.

Before Mr. Bones could work himself into a real snit, however, trouble broke out in another area of the yard. For the past ten minutes, as Alice and her mother picked away at the vermin embedded in his coat, Mr. Bones had been watching Tiger entertain himself by kicking a beach ball across the lawn. Each time it squirted away from him, he would run after it at top speed, looking like a demented soccer player in pursuit of a ball twice his size. The kid was tireless, but that didn't mean he couldn't trip and stub his toe, and when the inevitable accident finally occurred, he let out a shriek of pain that was loud enough to drive the sun from the sky and bring the clouds crashing down to the earth. The woman left off from her delicate ministrations to take care of the boy, and as she picked him up and carried him off into the house, Alice turned to Mr. Bones and said, 'That's Tiger. Nine tenths of the time, he's either laughing or crying, and when he isn't, you can be pretty sure that something weird is about to happen. You'll get used to it, Sparky. He's only two and a half, and you can't expect too much from little boys. His real name is Terry, but we all call him Tiger because he's such a roughhouser. My name is Alice. Alice Elizabeth Jones. I'm eight and three-quarters, and I just started the fourth grade. I was born with little holes in my heart, and I almost died a couple of times when I was small, even smaller than Tiger is now. I don't remember any of that, but Mama said I lived because I have an angel breathing inside me, and that angel is going to keep on protecting me forever. Mama's name is Polly Jones. She used to be Polly Danforth, but then she married Daddy and changed her name to Jones. My daddy is Richard Jones. Everyone calls him Dick, and most people say I look more like him than I look like Mama. He's an airline pilot. He flies to California and Texas and New York, all kinds of places. Once, before Tiger was born, Mama and I got to go to Chicago with him. Now we're living in this big house. We just moved in a few months ago, so it's a lucky thing you came when you did, Sparky. We've got plenty of room, and we're all settled in now, and if Daddy says we can keep you, then everything will be just about perfect around here.'

She was trying to make him feel welcome, but the net effect of Alice's rambling introduction to the family was to throw Mr. Bones into a panic and turn his stomach inside out. His future was in the hands of a person he had never seen, and after listening to the various comments that had been made about this person so far, it seemed unlikely that the decision would come down in the dog's favor. The force of these anxieties sent Mr. Bones running into the bushes again, and for the second time in an hour his intestines betrayed him. Trembling uncontrollably as the crap gushed onto the ground, he begged the god of dogdom to take care of his poor, sick body. He had entered the promised land, had fallen into a world of green lawns and gentle women and abundant food, but if it came to pass that he should be expelled from this place, then he asked only that his miseries not be prolonged beyond what he could endure.

By the time Dick's Volvo pulled into the driveway, Polly had already fed the children their dinner – hamburgers, baked potatoes, and frozen peas, some of which found its way into Mr. Bones's mouth – and the four of them were out in the yard again, watering the garden as the late afternoon turned into early evening and the sky filled with the first mottled touches of darkness. Mr. Bones had overheard Polly tell Alice that the flight from New Orleans was due in at Dulles at four forty-five, and if the plane wasn't delayed and the traffic wasn't too heavy, her father should be home by seven o'clock. Give or take a few minutes, that's just when Dick Jones arrived. He had been gone for three days, and when the children heard the sound of his approaching car, they both ran screaming from the yard and vanished around the side of the house. Polly made no move to run after them. She calmly went on watering her plants and flowers, and Mr. Bones stuck by her, unwilling to let her out of his sight. He knew that all hope was gone now, but if anybody could save him from the thing that was about to happen, she was the one.

A few moments later, the man of the house walked into the yard with Tiger in one arm and Alice tugging on the other, and because he was wearing his pilot's uniform (dark-blue pants; light-blue shirt garnished with epaulets and insignias), Mr. Bones mistook him for a cop. It was an automatic association, and with a lifetime of dread built into that response, he couldn't help recoiling as Dick approached, even though he could see with his own eyes that the man was laughing and seemed genuinely happy to be with his children again. Before Mr. Bones could sort through this jumble of doubts and conflicting impressions, he was swept up into the drama of the moment, and from then on everything seemed to happen at once. Alice had started talking to her father about the dog the instant he stepped out of the car, and she was still at it when he entered the yard and greeted his wife (a perfunctory kiss on the cheek), and the more she badgered him and raved on about the wonderful creature they had found, the more excited her little brother became. Yelling 'Sparky' at the top of his lungs, Tiger slithered out of his father's grasp, ran over to Mr. Bones, and threw his arms around his neck. Not to be outdone by her pipsqueak brother, Alice came over and got into the act as well, making a great, histrionic show of affection for the dog as she attacked him with repeated hugs and melodramatic kisses, and with the two kids suddenly mauling him like that and covering his ears with their hands and chests and faces, he missed three-quarters of what the adults were saying. About the only thing he heard with any clarity was Dick's initial statement. 'So this is the famous dog, huh? Looks like one sorry mutt to me.'

After that, it was anyone's guess as to what really happened. He saw Polly twist the nozzle of the hose, which cut off the flow of water, and then she said something to Dick. Most of it was inaudible, but from the few words and phrases that Mr. Bones managed to catch, he understood that she was pleading his case: 'wandered into the yard this afternoon,' 'intelligent,' 'the kids think . . .', and then, after Dick said something back to her, 'I don't have the foggiest idea. Maybe he ran away from the circus.' It sounded fairly encouraging, but just as he succeeded in getting his left ear free of Tiger's grip to take in a little more, Polly tossed the hose on to the ground and wandered off with Dick in the direction of the house. They stopped a few feet in front of the back door and went on talking there. Mr. Bones was certain that momentous things were being decided now, but even though their lips were moving, he could no longer hear a word they said.

He could see that Dick was watching him, however, gesturing toward him every now and then with a vague sweep of the hand as he continued his discussion with Polly, and Mr. Bones, who was growing a little bored with the raucous love-in that Tiger and Alice had started, wondered if it might not be such a bad idea to take the initiative and do something to help himself. Instead of standing around while his future hung in the balance, why not try to impress Dick with some canine derring-do, some spiffy dog thing that would turn the tide in his favor? It was true that Mr. Bones was exhausted, and it was true that his stomach still hurt and his legs felt diabolically weak, but he didn't let those things stop him from bounding off and racing to the other end of the yard. Shrieking with surprise, Tiger and Alice went running after him, and just as they were about to catch him, he bounded away from them again, abruptly charging back in the direction he had come from. Again they went after him, and again he waited until they almost had him in their hands before jumping away. He hadn't sprinted like that in aeons, but even though he knew that he was pushing himself too hard and would eventually have to pay for his exertions, he kept on going, proud to be torturing himself on behalf of such a noble cause. After three or four dashes across the lawn, he stopped in the middle of the yard and played duck-and-feint with them – the dog version of tag – and even though he could barely breathe anymore, he refused to quit before the children gave up and flopped to the ground in front of him.

Meanwhile, the sun was beginning to go down. The sky was streaked with bands of pinkish clouds, and the air had turned cooler. Now that the romp-a-thon had ended, it appeared that Dick and Polly were ready to announce their verdict. As Mr. Bones lay panting on the grass with the two children, he saw the grown-ups turn from the house and begin walking back to the yard, and while it was never clear to him whether his manic burst of high spirits had any effect on the outcome, he took heart from the satisfied little smile that was creasing the edges of Polly's mouth. 'Daddy says that Sparky can stay,' she said, and as Alice jumped up from the ground and hugged her father and Polly bent down and gathered the half-sleeping Tiger into her arms, a new chapter in Mr. Bones's life began.

Before they could break out the champagne, however, Dick butted in with a few additional points – the fine print, so to speak. It's not that he didn't want everyone to be happy, he said, but for the time being it had to be understood that they were only keeping the dog on a 'trial basis,' and unless certain conditions were met – and here he gave Alice a long, hard look – the deal was off. First: under no circumstances was the dog to be allowed in the house. Second: he would have to be taken to the vet for a full checkup. If he wasn't found to be in reasonably good health, he would have to go. Third: at the earliest possible convenience, an appointment would have to be made with a professional groomer. The dog needed a haircut, a shampoo, and a manicure, as well as a thorough going-over for ticks, lice, and fleas. Fourth: he would have to be fixed. And fifth: Alice would be responsible for feeding him and changing his water bowl – with no increase in her allowance for services rendered.

Mr. Bones had no idea what the word *fixed* meant, but he understood everything else, and all in all it didn't sound too bad, except maybe for the first point about not being allowed in the house, since he failed to grasp how a dog could become part of a family's household if he didn't have the right to enter that family's house. Alice must have been wondering the same thing, for as soon as her father came to the last item on his list, she chimed in with a question. 'What happens when winter comes?' she asked. 'We're not going to leave him out here in the cold, are we, Daddy?'

'Of course not,' Dick said. 'We'll put him in the garage, and if it's still too cold in there, we'll let him stay in the cellar. I just don't want him getting his hair all over the furniture, that's all. But we'll make it real nice for him out here, don't worry. We'll give him a first-class doghouse, and I'll set up a run for him by stringing a wire between those two trees over there. He'll have plenty of space to frisk about in, and once he gets used to it, he'll be happy as a clam. Don't feel sorry for him, Alice. He's not a person, he's a dog, and dogs don't ask questions. They make do with what they get.' With that decisive remark, Dick put his hand on Mr. Bones's head and gave it a firm, manly squeeze, as if to prove he wasn't such an ornery customer after all. 'Ain't that right, sport?' he said. 'You're not going to complain, are you? You know what you've lucked into here, and the last thing you want is to rock the boat.'

He was a can-do guy, this Dick, and even though the next day was

Sunday – which meant that both the groomer and the vet were closed –
he got up early, drove off to the lumberyard in Polly's van, and then
spent the entire morning and afternoon putting together a pre-fab doghouse (deluxe model, assembly instructions included) and rigging up a
run in the backyard. He clearly belonged to that class of men who felt
happier lugging around ladders and hammering nails into boards than
making small talk with his wife and children. Dick was a man of action,
a soldier in the war against idleness, and as Mr. Bones watched him
working away in his khaki shorts and saw the sweat glistening on his
forehead, he couldn't help but read this activity as a good sign. It meant
that all that 'trial basis' talk from yesterday had been no more than a
bluff. Dick had shelled out over two hundred dollars for this new equipment and hardware. He had toiled in the heat for the better part of a
day, and he wasn't about to let his work or money go to waste. His toes
were in the water now, and as far as Mr. Bones could tell, it was either
sink or swim from this point on.

The next morning, they all flew off in different directions. A bus
stopped in front of the house at quarter to eight and took Alice to school.
Forty minutes after that, Dick left for the airport in his pilot's uniform,
and then, shortly before nine, Polly strapped Tiger into his child-
restraint seat in the van and drove him to his morning play group. Mr.
Bones could scarcely believe what was happening. Was this what life
was going to be like around here?, he wondered. Were they simply
going to abandon him in the morning and expect him to fend for himself all day? It felt like an obscene joke. He was a dog built for companionship, for the give-and-take of life with others, and he needed to be
touched and spoken to, to be part of a world that included more than
just himself. Had he walked to the ends of the earth and found this
blessed haven only to be spat on by the people who had taken him in?
They had turned him into a prisoner. They had chained him to this
infernal bouncing wire, this metallic torture device with its incessant
squeaks and echoing hums, and every time he moved, the noises moved
with him – as if to remind him that he was no longer free, that he had
sold his birthright for a mess of porridge and an ugly, ready-made
house.

Just when it looked as if he might go ahead and do some rash, vindic-
tive thing – like digging up the flowers in the garden, for instance, or
gnawing off the bark of the young cherry tree – Polly came back, unexpectedly pulling into the driveway with her van, and the world changed

color again. Not only did she come out to the yard and release him from his bondage, and not only did she let him follow her into the house and go upstairs to her bedroom, but as she changed her clothes and brushed her hair and put on her makeup, she informed him that there were going to be two sets of rules for him to remember: Dick's rules and her rules. When Dick was around, Mr. Bones would be confined to the outdoors, but when Dick was gone, she was in charge, and that meant that dogs were allowed in the house. 'It's not that he doesn't mean well,' Polly said, 'but that man can be a squarehead sometimes, and once he's got his brain fixed on something, you're just wasting your breath if you try to talk him out of it. That's life with the Joneses, Sparky, and there's not a damn thing I can do about it. All I ask is that you keep this little arrangement under your hat. It's our secret, and not even the kids can know what we're up to. You hear me, old dog? This is strictly between you and me.'

But that wasn't all. As if this declaration of solidarity and affection hadn't been enough, later that same morning Mr. Bones got to ride in a car for the first time in nearly two years. Not scrunched up in the floor in back, where he had usually been put in the past, but right up front in the copilot's seat, riding shotgun with the window open and the sweet Virginia air rushing in on his face. It was a sublime vindication to be tooling down the road like that, with the magnificent Polly at the wheel of the Plymouth Voyager and the motion of the van rumbling inside his muscles and his nose twitching crazily at each passing smell. When it finally hit him that this van was going to be a part of his new routine, he was awed by the prospect that loomed before him. Life with Willy had been good, but maybe this was even better. For the sad truth was that poets didn't drive, and even when they traveled on foot, they didn't always know where they were going.

The visit to the groomer's was something of an ordeal, but he bore up to the multiple assaults of soaps and shears as best he could, not wanting to complain after all the kindness that had been bestowed on him. When they finished with him an hour and a half later, he emerged as an altogether different dog. Gone were the shaggy clumps of fur dangling from his hocks, the messy protrusions jutting from his withers, the hair hanging in his eyes. He was no longer a bum, no longer an embarrassment. He had been dandified, turned into a bourgeois dog-about-town, and if the novelty of the transformation made him want to gloat and preen a little bit, who could blame him for exulting in his good fortune?

'Wow,' Polly said when they finally took him out to her. 'They sure gave you the once-over, didn't they? Next thing you know, Spark Plug, you'll be winning prizes at the dog shows.'

Twenty-four hours later, they went to see the vet. Mr. Bones was glad for the chance to ride in the car again, but he'd crossed paths with those men in the white coats before, and he knew enough about their needles and thermometers and rubber gloves to dread what was coming. Mrs. Gurevitch had always been the one to schedule his appointments in the past, but after she died, Mr. Bones had been spared the agony of further dealings with the medical profession. Willy had been either too broke or too forgetful to bother anymore, and since the dog was still alive after four years of not going to the doctor, he failed to see what good a checkup was going to do him now. If you were sick enough to die, a doctor wasn't going to save you. And if you weren't sick, why let them torture you with their pricking and poking only to be told that your health was okay?

It would have been a horror if Polly hadn't stayed with him during the examination, holding him in her arms and soothing him with her soft, lovely voice. Even with her help, he trembled and shook throughout the entire visit, and three times he jumped off the table and ran for the door. The doctor's name was Burnside, Walter A. Burnside, and it made no difference that the quack seemed to like him. Mr. Bones had seen him looking at Polly, and he had smelled the arousal on the young doctor's skin. She was the one he was after, and liking her dog was only a ruse, a way to get on her good side and impress her with his understanding and skill. It didn't matter that he called Mr. Bones a wise dog and patted him on the head and laughed at his attempts to escape. He did it so he could get closer to Polly, maybe even brush up against her body, and Polly, who was so absorbed in taking care of the dog, didn't even notice what the scoundrel was up to.

'Not bad,' the doctor said at last. 'Considering what he's been through.'

'He's a tough old trouper,' Polly said, giving Mr. Bones a kiss between the eyes. 'But his stomach is shot. I hate to think about some of the things that must have gone in there.'

'He'll be all right once you get him on a regular diet. And don't forget to give him the worm pills. In a week or two, you'll probably start to see a big improvement.'

Polly thanked the doctor, and when she and Burnside shook hands on her way out, Mr. Bones couldn't help noticing that Señor Smooth held on longer than he should have. When he answered Polly's polite good-bye by saying 'The pleasure's been all mine,' the dog had a sudden urge to jump up and bite him on the leg. Polly turned to leave. Just as she was opening the door, the doctor added: 'Talk to June at the front desk. She'll schedule you in for the other matter.'

'It wasn't my idea,' Polly said. 'But that's the way my husband wants it.'

'He's right,' Burnside said. 'It simplifies things, and in the long run it'll make Sparky a whole lot happier.'

Dick returned home on Thursday night, which meant that Friday morning was much duller than the previous mornings had been. No more stealthy, luxurious hours spent in the house. No more sitting in the bathroom and watching Polly take her bath. No more scrambled eggs. No more sugary milk from the children's cereal bowls. Ordinarily, losses of that magnitude would have pained him, but on that particular Friday morning they produced no more than a stab of wistful regret. Mr. Bones had hope now, and he knew that once Dick left on Sunday afternoon, the door would open for him again. There was solace in this thought, and even though it was drizzling that day and the air had turned cool with the first traces of autumn, he settled into his doghouse with the rubber bone that Polly had bought for him at the groomer's and nibbled away at it as the family ate breakfast inside. He heard the bus come and go, he heard the van drive off, and then, in the interval before Polly returned, Dick sauntered out into the yard to say hello. Not even that could ruffle his contentment. The pilot seemed to be in a chip-per mood that morning, and when he complimented Mr. Bones on his fine haircut and asked him how he was getting along, the dog's generos-ity won out over his suspicions, and he responded with a discreet, gen-tlemanly lick of the hand. It wasn't that he was against Dick, he decided. It was just that he pitied him for not knowing how to enjoy life. The world was filled with such wonders, and it was a sad state of affairs when a man spent his time worrying about the wrong things.

Mr. Bones was anticipating a long, slow time of it, and he had pre-pared himself to while away the hours before the children came home by doing as little as possible: dozing, chewing on the bone, strolling around the yard if the rain let up. Indolence was the only chore on the agenda, but Dick kept mentioning what a big day it was, kept harping on how 'the moment of truth had finally come,' and after a while Mr. Bones began to wonder if he hadn't missed something. He had no idea what Dick was talking about, but after all these mysterious pronouncements, it didn't surprise him that once Polly returned from dropping off Tiger, he was asked to jump into the van and take another ride. It was different, of course, now that Dick was there, but who was he to object to a slight change of protocol? Dick was in the driver's seat, Polly sat next to him, and Mr. Bones rode in back, lying on a beach towel that Dick had put down to protect the car from errant dog hairs. The window couldn't be lowered in back, which reduced the pleasure of the ride considerably, but still, he enjoyed the motion for its own sake, and all in all he much preferred being where he was to where he had been.

He could sense that all was not calm between the Joneses, however. As the ride continued, it became clear that Polly was unusually subdued, gazing out the window to her right instead of looking at Dick, and after a while her silence seemed to dampen Dick's spirits as well.

'Look, Polly,' he said, 'I'm sorry. But it's really for his own good.'

'I don't want to talk about it,' she said. 'Your mind's made up, and that's the end of it. You know my opinion, so what's the point of arguing anymore?'

'It's not like I'm the only one who ever thought of it,' Dick said. 'It's common practice.'

'Oh yeah? And how would you like it if someone did it to you?'

Dick made a sound that fell halfway between a grunt and a laugh. 'Come on, honey, cut it out. He's a dog. He won't even know what happened to him.'

'Please, Dick. I don't want to talk about it.'

'Why not? If you're so upset –'

'No. Not in front of him. It's not fair.'

Dick laughed again, but this time it came out as a kind of uproarious stupefaction, a great guffaw of disbelief. 'You've got to be joking!' he said. 'I mean, Jesus Christ, Polly, we're talking about a dog!'

'Think what you like. But I'm not going to say another word about it in this car.'

And she didn't. But enough had been said for Mr. Bones to start worrying, and when the car finally came to a stop and he saw that they had pulled up in front of the same building he and Polly had visited on Tuesday morning, the same building that housed the offices of one Walter A. Burnside, doctor of veterinary medicine, he knew that something terrible was about to happen to him.

And it did. And the odd thing about it was that Dick had been right.

Mr. Bones never knew what hit him. They put him under with a needle to the rump, and after the excision had been performed and he was led back to the van, he was still too wobbly to know where he was – let alone who he was, or if he was. It was only later, when the anesthetic had worn off, that he began to feel the pain that had been inflicted on him, but even then he remained in the dark as to what had caused it. He knew where it was coming from, but that wasn't the same thing as knowing why it was there, and although he had every intention of examining the spot, he put it off for the time being, realizing that he lacked the strength to contort his body into the proper position. He was already in his dog-house then, stretched out dreamily on his left side, and Polly was on her knees in front of the open door, stroking his head and feeding him from her hand – chopped-up bits of medium-rare steak. The meat had an extraordinary flavor, but the truth was that he didn't have much of an appetite at that moment, and if he accepted what he was given, it was only to please her. The rain had stopped by then. Dick was off with Tiger somewhere, and Alice was still away at school, but being with Polly was comfort enough, and as she continued to stroke his head and assure him that everything was going to be all right, he wondered what the hell had happened to him and why he hurt so much.

In due time, he explored the damage and discovered what was missing, but because he was a dog and not a biologist or a professor of anatomy, he still had no idea what had happened to him. Yes, it was true that the sac was empty now and his old familiars were gone, but what exactly did that mean? He had always enjoyed licking that part of himself, had in fact made a regular habit of it for as long as he could remember, but aside from the tender globes themselves, everything else in the area seemed to be intact. How was he to know that those missing parts had been responsible for turning him into a father many times over? Except for his ten-day affair with Greta, the malamute from Iowa City, his romances had always been brief – impetuous couplings, impromptu flings, frantic rolls in the hay – and he had never seen any of the pups he had sired. And even if he had, how would he have been able to make the connection? Dick Jones had turned him into a eunuch, but in his own eyes he was still the prince of love, the lord of the canine Romeos, and he would go on courting the ladies until his last, dying breath. For once, the tragic dimension of his own life eluded him. The only thing that mattered was the physical pain, and once that disappeared, he never gave the operation another thought.

More days passed. He settled into the rhythms of the household, grew accustomed to the various comings and goings around him, came to understand the difference between the weekdays and the weekends, the sound of the school bus as opposed to the sound of the UPS truck, the smells of the animals who lived in the woods that bordered the yard: squirrels, raccoons, chipmunks, rabbits, all manner of birds. He knew by now that birds weren't worth the trouble, but whenever a wingless creature wandered onto the lawn, he took it upon himself to chase the varmint from the property, rushing toward him in a frenzied outburst of barks and growls. Sooner or later, they would catch on to the fact that he was hooked up to that damned wire, but for now most of them were sufficiently intimidated by his presence to keep the game interesting. Except for the cat, of course, but that was always the case with cats, and the black one from next door had already figured out the exact length of the leash that held him to the wire, which meant that he knew the limits of Mr. Bones's mobility at every point in the yard. The feline intruder would always position himself in a spot designed to cause the maximum frustration: a few inches out of the dog's range. There was nothing Mr. Bones could do about it. He could either stand there and bark his head off as the cat hissed at him and shot his claws toward his face, or he could retreat into his doghouse and pretend to ignore the cat, even though the son-of-a-bitch would then hop onto the roof and start digging his claws into the dense cedar shingles just above his head. Those were the alternatives: be scratched or be mocked, and either way it was a losing proposition. On the other hand, there were certain small miracles to be seen from that same doghouse, especially at night. A silver fox, for example, who scampered across the lawn at three a.m. and disappeared before Mr. Bones could stir a muscle, imprinting an afterimage on his mind that was so sharp, so crystalline in its perfection, that it kept coming back to him for days afterward: an apparition of weightlessness and speed, the grace of the wholly wild. And then, on a night in late September, there was the deer who stepped out of the woods, tiptoed around the grass for twenty or thirty seconds, and then, startled by the noise of a distant car, bounded off into the darkness again, leaving great divots in the lawn that were still there the following week.

Mr. Bones grew exceedingly fond of that lawn – the tufted, padded feel of it, the grasshoppers bouncing back and forth among its green stalks, the smell of earth rising up at you everywhere you turned, and as time went on, he understood that if he and Dick had anything in common, it was this deep, irrational love of lawn. It was their bond, but it was also the source of their greatest philosophical differences. For Mr. Bones, the lawn's beauty was a gift from God, and he felt it should be treated as holy ground. Dick believed in that beauty as well, but he knew that it had been born out of human effort, and if that beauty was to last, then unending care and diligence were required. The term was *lawn maintenance*, and until the middle of November not a week went by when Dick did not devote at least one full day to trimming and mowing his quarter-acre patch of sward. He had his own machine – an orange-and-white vehicle that looked like a cross between a golf cart and a midget tractor – and every time he started up the engine, Mr. Bones felt certain that he would die. He hated the noise of that contraption, hated the ear-splitting fury of its spurts and stutters, hated the gasoline smells it deposited in every corner of the air. He would hide in his doghouse whenever Dick roared out into the yard on that thing, burying his head under his blankets in a futile effort to block up his ears, but there was really no escape, no solution short of being let out of the yard altogether. But Dick had his rules, and since Mr. Bones was supposed to be in the yard, the pilot pretended not to notice the dog's suffering. The weeks rolled by, and as the assaults on Mr. Bones's ears continued, he couldn't help building up a certain resentment against Dick for refusing to take him into account.

There was no question that things were better when Dick was gone. That was a fact of life, and he learned to accept it in the same way he had once learned to accept his harsh treatment from Mrs. Gurevitch. She had been downright hostile to him in the beginning, and his first year in Brooklyn had been filled with stinging nose-slaps and grumpy tongue-lashings from the old sourpuss, a buildup of bad blood on both sides. But all that had changed, hadn't it? He had won her over in the end, and who knew if the same thing wouldn't happen with Dick as well? In the meantime, he tried not to think about it too much. He had three people to love now, and after spending his whole life as a one-man dog, that was more than enough. Even Tiger was beginning to show some promise, and once you learned how to stay clear of his pinching little fingers, he could actually be fun to be with – in small doses. With Alice, however, no dose was too large. He wished that she were able to spend more time with him, but she was off at that blasted school all day, and what with the after-school ballet lessons on Tuesday and the piano lessons on Thursday, not to speak of the homework she had to do every evening, their weekday visits were usually confined to a short early-morning conversation – as she straightened his blankets and replenished his food and water bowls – and then, after she returned home, to the period just before dinner, when she would report on what had happened to her since the morning and ask him how his day had gone. That was one of the things he liked best about her: the way she talked to him, calmly moving from point to point without leaving anything out, as if there was never any question that he couldn't understand what she was saying. Alice spent most of her time living in a world of imaginary beings, and she brought Mr. Bones into that world and made him her partner, her fellow protagonist, her male lead. Saturdays and Sundays were full of these screwball improvisations. There was the tea party they attended at the castle of the Baroness de Dunwitty, a beautiful but dangerous Machiavel plotting to take over the kingdom of Floriania. There was the earthquake in Mexico. There was the hurricane on the Rock of Gibraltar, and there was the shipwreck that left them stranded on the shores of Nemo Island, where the only food consisted of twig nubs and acorn shells, but if you managed to find the magic night crawler who lived just under the surface of the ground and ate him up in a single bite, you would be endowed with the ability to fly. (Mr. Bones swallowed the worm she gave him, and then, with Alice clinging to his back, he took off into the air and they escaped the island.)

Tiger was running and jumping. Alice was words and the meeting of minds. She was the old soul in the young body who had talked her parents into letting him stay, but now that he was there and had spent some time among them, he knew that Polly was the one who needed him most. After several dozen mornings of following her around, of listening to what she told him and watching what she did, Mr. Bones understood that she was a prisoner of circumstances just as much as he was. She had been only eighteen when she met Dick. It was just after she graduated from high school, and to earn some money before starting N.C.–Charlotte in the fall, she had taken a summer waitressing job at a seafood restaurant in Alexandria, Virginia. The first time Dick came in, he wound up asking her for a date. He was nine years older than she was, and she found him so handsome and sure of himself that she let herself go farther than she had intended. The romance continued for three or four weeks, and then she went back to North Carolina to start college. She was planning to get a degree in education and become a schoolteacher, but one month into her first term, she discovered that she

was pregnant. When she broke the news to her parents, they were outraged. They told her that she was a slut, that she had disgraced them
with her promiscuity, and then they refused to offer any help – which
caused a rift in the family that was never fully repaired, not even after
nine years of apologies and contrition on both sides. It wasn't that she
wanted to marry Dick, but after her own father turned his back on her,
where else was she going to go? Dick said he loved her. He kept telling
her that she was the prettiest, most remarkable girl on the face of the
earth, and after a couple of months of wavering back and forth, of sinking into the most desperate kinds of speculation (an abortion, giving up
the baby for adoption, keeping the baby and trying to make it on her
own), she buckled under the pressure and quit school to marry Dick.
Once the baby was old enough, she figured she would be able to go back
to college, but Alice was born with all sorts of medical problems, and for
the next four years Polly's life was taken up with doctors, hospitals, and
experimental surgeries, an endless round of cures and consultations to
keep her little girl alive. It was her proudest accomplishment as a human
being, she told Mr. Bones one morning – the way she'd looked after
Alice and pulled her through – but even though she'd been no more
than a young girl herself at the time, she wondered if it hadn't drained
her strength forever. Once Alice was well enough to go to school, Polly
began to think about going back to school herself, but then she got pregnant with Tiger, and she had to put it off again. Now it was probably too
late. Dick was starting to earn good money, and when you combined his
salary with some of the investments he'd made, they were pretty well off
now. He didn't want her to work, and whenever she said that maybe it
would be nice to work anyway, he always gave her the same answer.
She already had a career, he said. Wife and mother was a tough enough
job for any woman, and as long as he could take care of her, why change
things just for the sake of changing them? And then, to prove how much
he loved her, he went out and bought her this big, beautiful house.

Polly loved the house, but she didn't love Dick. This had become
manifestly clear to Mr. Bones, and although Polly herself didn't know it
yet, it wouldn't be long before the truth finally came crashing down on
top of her. That was why she needed Mr. Bones, and because he loved
her more than any other living person in the world, he was glad to serve
as her confidant and sounding board. There was no one else to fill this
role for her, and even though he was a mere dog who could neither
counsel her nor answer her questions, his simple presence as an ally was

enough to give her the courage to take certain steps she might not have taken otherwise. Establishing her own rules about letting him into the house was hardly a serious matter, but in its own small way it was an act of defiance against Dick, a microscopic instance of betrayal that could, in time, lead to bigger, more significant betrayals. Mr. Bones and Polly both knew that Dick didn't want him in the house, and this injunction only added to the pleasure of his visits, giving them a dangerous, clandestine quality, as if he and Polly were accomplices in a palace revolt against the king. Mr. Bones had been drafted into a war of nerves and smoldering antagonisms, and the longer he was there, the more crucial his role became. Instead of arguing about themselves, Dick and Polly now argued about him, using the dog as an excuse to advance their separate causes, and while Mr. Bones was rarely privy to the conversations, he learned enough from hearing Polly talk to her sister on the phone to know that some fierce battles had been fought on his account. The hair-on-the-carpet skirmish was just one example. Polly always took care to eliminate Mr. Bones's traces from the house when Dick was about to return, assiduously vacuuming every spot where the dog had been, even getting down on her hands and knees when necessary and using strips of scotch tape to remove any vagrant hairs that the machine had missed. Once, however, when Polly had done a less than thorough job, Dick discovered a few strands of Mr. Bones's fur lying on the living-room carpet. As Polly reported the incident to her sister Peg in Durham, those bits of fluff had led to a prolonged and churlish confrontation. 'Dick asks me what those hairs are doing there,' she said, sitting on a kitchen stool and smoking one of her infrequent morning cigarettes, 'and I tell him I don't know, maybe they fell off one of the kids. Then he goes upstairs into the bedroom and finds another one on the floor by the night table. He comes out holding the thing between his fingers and says, I suppose you don't know about this either, and I say no, why should I? Maybe it came from Sparky's brush. His brush? Dick says, what are you doing with his brush in the bedroom? Cleaning it, I say, just as calm as I can be, what difference does it make? But Dick won't let it end there. He's got to get to the bottom of the mystery, and so he keeps on pushing. Why didn't you clean it out in the yard, he says, where you're supposed to? Because it was raining, I say, telling about my fourteenth fib of the conversation. Then why didn't you do it in the garage? he asks. Because I didn't want to, I say. It's too dark in there. And so, he says, really starting to get pissed-off now, you drag in the dog's brush and clean it on the bed. That's right, I say, I cleaned it on the bed because that's where I felt like cleaning it, and he says, don't you think that's disgusting, Polly? Don't you know how much I hate that? I'm telling you, Peg, it went on like that for ten more minutes. All this petty bullshit, it drives me crazy sometimes. I can't stand lying to him, but what else am I supposed to do when we start in on these stupid disagreements? He's such a stickler, that man. His heart's in the right place, but half the time he forgets where it is. Jesus. If I told him I was letting the dog into the house, he'd probably divorce me. He'd just pack up his bags and walk out.'

Such was the marital turmoil that Mr. Bones had stumbled into. Sooner or later, something was bound to give, but until Polly woke up to herself and finally pushed that piker out the door, the atmosphere would continue to be charged with intrigues and buried animosities, the plots and counterplots of dying love. Mr. Bones did his best to adjust to all this. So much was still new to him, however, so many things still had to be studied and made sense of, that the ups and downs of Polly's marriage occupied no more than a small fraction of his energies. The Joneses had introduced him to a different world from the one he had known with Willy, and not a day went by when he didn't experience some sudden revelation or feel some pang about what had been missing from his former life. It wasn't just the daily rides in the van, and it wasn't just the regular meals or the absence of ticks and fleas from his coat. It was the barbecues on the back patio, the Porterhouse steak bones he was given to gnaw on, the weekend outings to Wanacheebee Pond and the swims with Alice in the cool water, the overall feeling of splendor and well-being that had engulfed him. He had landed in the America of two-car garages, home-improvement loans, and neo-Renaissance shopping malls, and the fact was that he had no objections. Willy had always attacked these things, railing against them in that lopsided, comic way of his, but Willy had been on the outside looking in, and he had refused to give any of it a chance. Now that Mr. Bones was on the inside, he wondered where his old master had gone wrong and why he had worked so hard to spurn the trappings of the good life. It might not have been perfect in this place, but it had a lot to recommend it, and once you got used to the mechanics of the system, it no longer seemed so important that you were tethered to a wire all day. By the time you had been there for two and a half months, you even stopped caring that your name was Sparky.

5

The concept of the family vacation was entirely unknown to him. Back in Brooklyn as a pup, he had sometimes heard Mrs. Gurevitch use the word *vacation*, but never in any way that could be connected to the word *family*. Suddenly breaking off from her housework, *Mom-san* would plop down on the sofa, throw her feet up on the coffee table, and let out a long, passionate sigh. 'That's it,' she would say. 'I'm on vacation.' According to this usage, the word seemed to be a synonym for *sofa*, or perhaps it was simply a more elegant way to describe the act of sitting down. In either case, it had nothing to do with families – and nothing to do with the idea of travel. Travel was what he did with Willy, and in all the years they had spent on the road together, he couldn't remember a single instance in which the word *vacation* had crossed his master's lips. It might have been different if Willy had been gainfully employed somewhere, but except for a few odd jobs picked up along the way (sweeping floors in a Chicago bar, messenger-service trainee for an outfit in Philadelphia), he had always been his own boss. Time had flowed without interruption for them, and with no need to break down the calendar into work periods and rest periods, no particular call to observe national holidays, anniversaries, or religious feast days, they had lived in a world apart, free of the clock-watching and hour-counting that took up so much of everyone's else's time. The only day of the year that had stood out from the others was Christmas, but Christmas wasn't a vacation, it was a work-day. Come December twenty-fifth, no matter how exhausted or hungover Willy might have been, he had always climbed straight into his Santa Claus costume and spent the day walking around the streets, spreading hope and good cheer. It was his way of honoring his spiritual father, he said, of remembering the vows of purity and self-sacrifice he had taken. Mr. Bones had always found his master's talk about peace and brotherhood a bit too sappy for his taste, but painful as it sometimes was to see their dinner money wind up in the hands of a person who was better off than they were, he knew there was a method to Willy's madness. Good begets good; evil begets evil; and even if the good you give is met by evil, you have no choice but to go on giving better than you get. Otherwise – and these were Willy's exact words – why bother to go on living?

Alice was the one who first spoke the words *family vacation* to him. It was the Saturday after Thanksgiving, and she had just come out to the yard with a clear plastic bag filled with turkey leftovers and stuffing – more miracles from Polly's white kitchen. Before Alice emptied the food into his bowl, she squatted down beside him and said, 'It's all set, Sparky. We're going on a family vacation. Next month when I'm off from school, Daddy's taking us to Disney World.' She sounded so happy and excited about it that Mr. Bones assumed it was good news, and since it never occurred to him that he wasn't included in Alice's *we* and *us*, he found himself more interested in the food he was about to eat than in the possible consequences of this new term. It took him about thirty seconds to polish off the turkey, and then, after lapping up half a bowl of water, he stretched out on the grass and listened to Alice as she filled him in on the details. Tiger was going to love seeing Mickey Mouse and Donald Duck, she said, and even though she'd outgrown those childish things herself, she could remember how much she'd loved them when she was small, too. Mr. Bones knew who this Mickey Mouse character was, and based on the things he'd been told, he wasn't too impressed. Who ever heard of a mouse with a pet dog? It was laughable, really, an insult to good taste and common sense, a perversion of the natural order of things. Any half-wit could have told you that it should be the other way around. Big creatures lorded it over small creatures, and if there was one thing he was certain about in this world, it was that dogs were bigger than mice. How puzzling it was for him, then, as he lay on the grass that Saturday afternoon in late November, to hear Alice talk so enthusiastically about their impending trip. He simply couldn't understand why people would want to travel hundreds of miles just to see a pretend mouse. There might not have been many advantages to living with Willy, but no one could accuse Mr. Bones of not having traveled. He had been everywhere, and in his time he had seen just about everything. It wasn't for him to say, of course, but if the Joneses were looking for an interesting place to visit, all they had to do was ask, and he happily would have led them to any one of a dozen lovely spots.

Nothing more was said about the subject for the remainder of the weekend. On Monday morning, however, when the dog overheard Polly talking to her sister on the phone, he realized how badly he had misunderstood what Alice had told him. It wasn't just a matter of driving down to see the mouse and then turning around and heading home, it was two weeks of discombobulation and movement. It was airplanes and hotels, rental cars and snorkeling equipment, restaurant bookings and family discount rates. Not only was there Florida, there was North Carolina as well, and as Mr. Bones listened to Polly discuss the arrangements for spending Christmas in Durham with Peg, it finally dawned on him that wherever this family vacation was going to take them, he wasn't going along. 'We need a break,' Polly was saying, 'and maybe this will do us some good. Who the hell knows, Peg, but I'm willing to give it a shot. My period's ten days late, and if that means what I think it does, then I have some pretty fast thinking to do.' Then, after a short silence: 'No. I haven't told him yet. But this trip was his idea, and I'm trying to read that as a good sign.' Another silence followed, and then, at last, he heard the words that told him what *family vacation* really meant: 'We'll put him in a kennel. There's supposed to be a nice one about ten miles from here. Thanks for reminding me, Peg. I'd better get started on it right away. Those places can get awfully crowded around Christmastime.'

He stood there and waited for her to finish, watching her with one of those dreary, stoical looks that dogs have been giving to people for forty thousand years. 'Don't worry, Spark Plug,' she said, hanging up the phone. 'It's only two weeks. By the time you start to miss us, we'll already be back.' Then, bending down to give him a hug, she added: 'Anyway, I'm going to miss you a lot more than you miss me. You've gotten under my skin, old doggy, and I can't live without you.'

All right, they were coming back. He was fairly confident of that now, but that didn't mean he wouldn't have preferred to go with them. Not that he had any great longing to be cooped up in a Florida hotel room or to ride in the baggage compartments of airplanes, but it was the principle of the thing that bothered him. Willy had never left him behind. Not once, not under any circumstances, and he wasn't used to this kind of handling. Perhaps he had been spoiled, but in his book there was more to canine happiness than just feeling wanted. You also had to feel necessary.

It was a setback, but at the same time he knew it wasn't the end of the world. He had learned that now, and all things being equal, Mr. Bones probably would have recovered from his disappointment and served out his prison term with docile good grace. He had been through worse hardships than this one, after all, but three days after receiving the bad news, he felt the first of several painful twinges in his abdomen, and over the next two and a half weeks the pains spread into his haunches, his limbs, and even into his throat. Evil spirits were lurking inside him, and he knew that Burnside was the one who had put them there. The quack had been too busy looking at Polly's legs to examine him properly, and he must have missed something, must have forgotten to run a test or look at his blood under the right microscope. The symptoms were still too vague to produce any outward manifestations (no vomiting, no diarrhea, no seizures as of yet), but as the days wore on, Mr. Bones felt less and less like himself, and instead of taking this family vacation business in his stride, he began to sulk and brood about it, to worry it into a thousand component parts, and what at first had seemed to be no more than a small bump in the road was turned into a full-scale misfortune.

It wasn't that the kennel was such a bad place. Even he could see that, and when Alice and her father deposited him there on the afternoon of December seventeenth, Mr. Bones had to admit that Polly had done her homework. Dog Haven was no Sing Sing or Devil's Island, no internment camp for abused and neglected animals. Situated on a twenty-acre property that had once been part of a large tobacco plantation, it was a four-star rural retreat, a canine hotel designed to accommodate the needs and whims of the most indulged and demanding pets. The sleeping cages lined the east and west walls of a cavernous red barn. There were sixty of them, with ample space provided for each of the boarders (more ample, in fact, than Mr. Bones's doghouse at home), and not only were they cleaned every day, but each one came with a soft, freshly laundered quilt and a chewable rawhide toy – in the shape of a bone, a cat, or a mouse, depending on the owner's preference. Just beyond the back door of the barn, there was an enclosed two-acre meadow that served as an exercise field. Special diets were available, and weekly baths were given at no extra charge.

But none of that mattered, at least not to Mr. Bones. These new surroundings failed to impress him, to arouse even the slightest show of interest, and even after he was introduced to the owner, the owner's wife, and various members of the staff (all of them solid, pleasant prodoggers), he still had no desire to stay. That didn't prevent Dick and Alice from leaving, of course, and while Mr. Bones wanted to howl out his objections to the rotten thing they'd done to him, he certainly couldn't find fault with Alice's tearful and loving farewell. In his own terse way, even Dick seemed a little sorry about having to say good-bye. Then they climbed into the van and took off, and as Mr. Bones watched them chug down the dirt road and disappear behind the main house, he had his first inkling of the kind of trouble he was in. It wasn't just a case of the blues, he realized, and it wasn't just because he was scared. Something was seriously wrong with him, and whatever mayhem had been brewing in him lately was about to come to a full boil. His head hurt, and his belly was on fire, and a weakness had invaded his knees that suddenly made standing difficult. They gave him food, but the thought of food made him sick. They offered him a bone to chew on, but he turned his head away. Only water was acceptable, but when they pushed the water in front of him, he stopped drinking after two sips.

He was put in a cage between a wheezing ten-year-old bulldog and a luscious golden Lab. Ordinarily, a female of that caliber would have sent him into spasms of lustful sniffing, but that night he barely had the strength to acknowledge her presence before dropping onto his quilt and passing out. Within moments of losing consciousness, he was dreaming about Willy again, but this dream was nothing like the ones that had come before it, and instead of gentle encouragements and soothing rationalities, he was given a full taste of his master's wrath. Perhaps it was the fever burning inside him, or perhaps something had happened to Willy in Timbuktu, but the man who came to Mr. Bones that night was not the Willy he had known in life and death for the past seven and three quarters years. This was a vengeful and sarcastic Willy, a devil Willy, a Willy bereft of all compassion and kindness, and poor Mr. Bones was so terrified of this person that he lost control of his bladder and peed on himself for the first time since he was a pup.

To confuse matters even more, the false Willy was identical in appearance to the true Willy, and when he turned up in the dream that night he was wearing the same tattered Santa Claus gear that the dog had seen him in the past seven Christmases. Even worse, the dream wasn't set in some familiar place from the past – like the one in the subway car, for instance – but in the present, in the very cage where Mr. Bones was spending the night. He closed his eyes, and when he opened them again in the dream, there was Willy, sitting in the corner just two feet away from him, leaning his back against the bars. 'I'm only going to say this once,' he began, 'so listen up and keep your trap shut. You've turned yourself into a joke, a tired and disgusting joke, and I forbid you to let me into your thoughts anymore. Don't forget that, mutt. Emblazon it upon the doorposts of your palace, and never use my name again – not in vain, not in love, not in any way at all. I'm dead, and I want to be left in peace. All this complaining, all this bitching about what's happened to you – do you think I don't hear it? I'm sick of listening to you, dog, and this is the last time you'll ever see me in your dreams. Do you understand that? Let go of me, birdbrain. Give me some room. I have friends now, and I don't need you anymore. You got it? Butt out of my business and stay out. I'm finished with you.'

By morning, the fever had shot up so high that he was seeing double. His stomach had been turned into a battleground of warring microbes, and every time he moved, stirred even an inch or two from where he was lying, another attack would begin. It felt as if depth charges were being detonated inside his bowels, as if poison gases were eating away at his inner organs. He had woken up several times during the night, retching uncontrollably until the pains had been appeased, but none of these lulls had lasted very long, and when day finally broke and light came pouring down through the rafters of the barn, he saw that he was surrounded by half-a-dozen puddles of vomit: little clumps of dried-out mucus, half-digested meat fragments, specks of congealed blood, yellowish broths that had no name.

A great racket was swirling around him by then, but Mr. Bones was too ill to take notice. The other dogs were up and about, barking in anticipation of the day ahead, but the best he could do was lie there in his torpor, contemplating the bollix his body had made of things. He knew that he was sick, but exactly how sick, and exactly where this sickness was taking him, he had no idea. A dog could die from a thing like this, he told himself, but a dog could also recover and be good as new in a couple of days. Given the choice, he would have preferred not to die. In spite of what had happened in the dream last night, he still wanted to live. Willy's unprecedented cruelty had stunned him, had made him feel miserable and unspeakably alone, but that didn't mean that Mr. Bones wasn't ready to forgive his master for what he had done. You didn't turn your back on a person for letting you down just once – not after a lifetime of friendship, you didn't, and especially not if there were extenuating circumstances. Willy was dead, and who knew if dead people didn't grow bitter and nasty after they had been dead for a while? Then again, maybe it hadn't been Willy at all. The man in the dream could have been an impostor, a demon dressed in Willy's form who had been sent from Timbuktu to trick Mr. Bones and turn him against his master. But even if it had been Willy, and even if his remarks had been stated in an excessively hurtful and mean-spirited way, Mr. Bones was honest enough to admit that they contained a germ of truth. He had spent too much time feeling sorry for himself lately, had frittered away too many precious hours pouting over infinitesimal slights and injustices, and that kind of behavior was unseemly in a dog of his stature. There was much to be thankful for, and much life still to be lived. He knew that Willy had told him never to think about him again, but Mr. Bones couldn't help it. He was in that churning, semi-delirious state that high fevers bring, and he could no more control the thoughts that flitted in and out of his head than he could stand up and unlock the door of his cage. If Willy happened to be in his thoughts now, there wasn't much he could do about it. His master would just have to cover his ears and wait until the thought went away. But at least Mr. Bones wasn't complaining anymore. At least he was trying to be good.

Less than a minute after thinking about the door of his cage, a young woman came and undid the latch. Her name was Beth, and she was wearing a puffy blue nylon parka. Chubby thighs, an inordinately round face, Little Lulu haircut. Mr. Bones remembered her from the day before. She was the one who had tried to feed him and give him water, the one who had patted him on the head and told him he would feel better in the morning. A nice girl, but not much of a diagnostician. The piles of vomit seemed to alarm her, and she crouched down and entered the cage to take a closer look. 'Not such a good night, was it, Sparky?' she said. 'I think maybe we should show you to Dad.' Dad was the man from yesterday, he remembered, the one who had given them the tour of the grounds. A burly guy with black bushy eyebrows and no hair on his head. His name was Pat – Pat Spaulding or Pat Sprowleen, he couldn't recall which. There was a wife in the picture as well, and she had accompanied them on the first part of the walk. Yes, now it was coming back to him, the odd thing about the wife. Her name was Pat, too, and Mr. Bones remembered that Alice had found that funny, had even laughed a little when she heard the two names together, and Dick had pulled her aside and told her to remember her manners. Patrick and Patricia. Pat and Pat for short. It was all so confusing, so terribly inane and confusing.

Eventually, Beth coaxed him to stand up and walk over to the house with her. He threw up once along the way, but the cold air felt good against his hot body, and once the gunk had been expelled from his system, his pains seemed to lighten considerably. Encouraged, he followed her into the house, then gratefully accepted her offer to lie down on the living-room rug. Beth went off to look for her father, and Mr. Bones, already curled up in front of the fireplace, turned his attention to the sounds coming from the grandfather clock in the hall. He heard ten ticks, twenty ticks, and then he closed his eyes. Just before he went under, there was a small disturbance of approaching footsteps, and then a man's voice said, 'Leave him be for now. We'll see how he is when he wakes up.'

He slept through the morning and deep into the afternoon, and when he woke up he sensed that the worst of it was behind him. It wasn't that he was in top form, but at least he was half alive now, and with his temperature down by a couple of degrees, he could move his muscles without feeling that his body was made of bricks. He was well enough to accept a little water, in any case, and when Beth called her father in to judge the dog's condition for himself, Mr. Bones's thirst got the better of him, and he kept drinking until the water was gone. That was a bad miscalculation. He was in no shape to handle such a prodigious amount, and the instant Pat One entered the room, Mr. Bones promptly barfed the contents of his stomach onto the living-room rug.

'I wish to hell people wouldn't dump their sick dogs on us,' the man said. 'All we need is for this one to croak. We'll have one pretty lawsuit on our hands then, won't we?'

'Do you want me to call Dr. Burnside?' Beth asked.

'Yeah. Tell him I'm on my way over.' He started to leave the room, but halfway to the door he stopped and turned to Beth again. 'On second thought, maybe your mother should do it. Things are awfully busy around here today.'

That was a lucky break for Mr. Bones. In the time it took for them to track down Pat Two and organize the trip, he was able to work out a plan. And without a plan, he never would have been able to do what he did. It made no difference to him whether he was sick or well, whether he was going to live or going to die. They had presented him with the last straw, and over his dead body would he ever allow them to take him to that moron of a vet. That was why he needed a plan. He would have only a few seconds to pull it off, and the whole thing had to be shining in his head before it happened – so he would know exactly what to do and exactly when to do it.

Pat Two was an older version of Beth. A bit broader in the beam, perhaps, with a red parka instead of a blue one, but she gave off the same air of mannish competence and stolid good humor. Mr. Bones liked both of them better than Pat One, and he felt a little sorry about abusing their trust, especially after they had treated him with such kindness, but this was an all-or-nothing proposition, and there was no time to waste on sentimentality. The woman walked him out to the car on a leash, and just as he knew she would, she opened the passenger door to let him in first, not letting go of the leash until the last possible second. The moment the door slammed shut, Mr. Bones scrambled to the other side of the car and settled into the driver's seat. That was the essence of the strategy, and the trick was to make sure that the leash didn't get tangled up on the gearshift or the steering wheel or any other protrusion (which it didn't) and to be securely in his position by the time she had walked around the front of the car and opened the door on the other side (which he was). That was how he had seen it in his mind, and that was how it happened in the world. Pat Two opened the door on the driver's side, and Mr. Bones jumped out. He hit the ground running, and before she could grab hold of his tail or step on his leash, he was gone.

He headed for the woods on the north side of the main house, trying to keep as far away from the road as possible. He heard Pat Two calling out for him to come back, and a moment later her voice was joined by those of Beth and Pat One. A little after that, he heard the engine of the car turn over and the sound of wheels skidding on dirt, but he was far into the woods by then, and he knew they would never find him. Darkness came early at that time of year, and in another hour they wouldn't be able to see.

He kept going north, trotting along through the frozen underbrush as the dim winter light faded around him. Birds scattered as he approached, soaring up into the high branches of the pines, and squirrels ran off in all directions when they heard him coming. Mr. Bones knew where he was going, and even if he didn't know exactly how to get there, he was counting on his nose to point him in the right direction. The Joneses' backyard was only ten miles away, and he figured he would arrive by tomorrow, the day after that at the latest. Never mind that the Joneses were gone and wouldn't be returning for another two weeks. Never mind that his food was locked up in the garage and he had no way of getting at it. He was only a dog, and he wasn't capable of thinking that far ahead. For now, the only thing that mattered was to get where he was going. Once he did, the rest would take care of itself.

Or so he thought. But the sad truth was that Mr. Bones thought wrong. If he had been at full strength, there's no doubt that he would have reached his destination, but his body wasn't up to the demands he was making on it, and all this jumping and running soon took its toll. Ten miles was not a long journey, not when compared to the monumental treks he had undertaken as recently as three and a half months ago, but he was traveling on an empty tank now, and a dog could go only just so far on pure willpower. Remarkably, he managed to cover almost two miles in that weakened state. He went as far as his legs could carry him, and then, between one step and the next, without the slightest premonition of what was about to happen, he sank to the ground and fell asleep.

For the second time in two nights, he dreamed about Willy, and once again the dream was unlike any of the others that had come before it. This time they were sitting on the beach in La Jolla, California, a place they had visited on their first trip together, before he was fully grown. That meant it was years and years ago, and he was back in the days when everything was new and unfamiliar to him, when everything that happened was happening for the first time. The dream started in the middle of the afternoon. The sun was shining brightly, a small breeze was stirring, and Mr. Bones was lying with his head on Willy's lap, savoring the feel of his master's fingertips as they moved back and forth across his skull. Had any of this really happened? He couldn't remember anymore, but it felt vivid enough to be real, and that was all that concerned him now. Pretty girls in bathing suits, ice-cream wrappers and tubes of suntan lotion, red Frisbees wobbling through the air. That's what he saw when he opened his eyes in the dream, and he could smell the strangeness and the beauty of it, as if a part of him already knew that he was beyond the boundaries of hard fact. It seemed to begin in silence, silence in the sense of no words, with the sound of the waves washing in and out on the shore and the wind flapping the flags and beach umbrellas. Then a pop tune started playing on a radio somewhere, and a woman's voice was singing *be my baby, be my baby, be my baby now*. It was a lovely song, a lovely and stupid song, and Mr. Bones got so caught up in listening to it that he failed to realize that Willy was talking to him. By the time he turned his attention to his master, he had already missed several sentences, perhaps whole paragraphs of vital information, and it took a few moments before he managed to piece together the gist of what Willy was saying.

'Make amends' was the first thing he heard, followed by 'sorry, old boy' and 'test.' When those words were succeeded by 'ugly business' and 'charade,' Mr. Bones was well on his way to catching on. The devil Willy had been a trick, a ruse to tempt him into hardening his heart against his master's memory. Wrenching as the ordeal had been, it was the only way to test the permanence of the dog's affections. The prankster had tried to break his spirit, and even though Mr. Bones had been scared half to death, he hadn't hesitated to forgive Willy when he woke up in the morning, to shrug off his slanders and false accusations and let bygones be bygones. In this way, without even knowing that he was being judged, he had passed the test. The reward was this dream, this visit to a world of languorous, unending summer and the chance to bask in the warmth of the sun on a cold winter's night, and yet pleasurable and well crafted as this dream was, it was no more than a prelude to something far more important.

'What thing is that?' Mr. Bones heard himself say, and suddenly he was aware of his ability to speak again, to form words as clearly and smoothly as any two-leg yapping in his mother tongue.

'That, for one thing,' Willy said.

'What *that*?' Mr. Bones said, not understanding at all. 'What thing?'

'What you're doing now.'

'I'm not doing anything. I'm just lying here with you on the sand.'

'You're talking to me, aren't you?'

'It feels like talking. It sounds like talking. But that doesn't mean I'm really doing it.'

'And what if I told you that you were?'

'I don't know. I think I'd get up and do a little dance.'

'Well, start dancing, Mr. Bones. When the time comes, you don't have to worry.'

'What time, Willy? What are you talking about?'

'When the time comes for you to go to Timbuktu.'

'You mean dogs are allowed?'

'Not all dogs. Just some. Each case is handled separately.'

'And I'm in?'

'You're in.'

'Don't kid me, master. If you're joking now, I don't think I could stand it.'

'Believe me, pooch, you're in. The decision's been made.'

'And when do I get to go?'

'When the time comes. You have to be patient.'

'I have to kick the bucket first, don't I?'

'That's the deal. In the meantime, I want you to be a good boy. Go back to Dog Haven and let them take care of you. When the Joneses come to pick you up, remember how lucky you've been. You can't ask for more than Polly and Alice. Those two are as good as it gets, take my word for it. And another thing: don't fret about that name they gave you. You'll always be Mr. Bones to me. But if it ever starts getting you down, just put it in its Latin form, and you'll feel much better. Sparkatus. It has a nice ring to it, doesn't it? Sparkatus the Dog. Behold yon Sparkatus, the noblest tail-wagger in all of Rome.'

Yes, it did have a nice ring to it, a very nice ring to it, and when Mr. Bones woke up just after dawn, the sound of it was still rattling around in his head. So much had changed while he had been asleep, so many things had happened to him between the closing and opening of his eyes, that at first he didn't notice the snow that had fallen during the night, nor did he recognize that the tinkling noises caused by the word *Sparkatus* were in fact the ice-coated branches overhead, slowly creaking in the wind. Reluctant to leave the world of the dream, Mr. Bones only gradually became aware of the intense cold around him, and then, once he began to feel the cold, he became aware of an equally intense heat. Something was burning inside him. The cold was outside, and the heat was inside; his body was covered with snow, and inside his body the fever was back, as fierce and paralyzing as it had been the day before. He took a stab at trying to stand up to shake the snow off his fur, but his legs felt like sponges, and he had to abandon the effort. Maybe later, he told himself, maybe later when the sun came out and the air warmed up a little. Meanwhile, he lay there on the ground and studied the snow. No more than an inch had fallen, but even that was enough to make the world feel like a different place. There was something eerie about the whiteness of snow, he found, something both eerie and beautiful, and as he watched two pairs of sparrows and chickadees pecking away at the ground in search of something to eat, he felt a small ache of sympathy flutter inside him. Yes, even for those useless featherbrains. He couldn't help it. The snow seemed to have brought them all together, and for once he was able to look at them not as nuisances but as fellow creatures, members of the secret brotherhood. Watching the birds, he remembered what Willy had told him about going back to Dog Haven. That was good advice, and if his body had been up to the task, he would have followed it. But it wasn't. He was too weak to go that far, and if he couldn't count on his legs to get him there, then he would have to stay where he was. For want of anything else to do, he ate some snow and tried to remember the dream.

By and by, he began to hear the sounds of cars and trucks, the rumble of early-morning traffic. The sun was just coming up then, and as the snow melted off the trees and dropped to the ground in front of him, Mr. Bones wondered if the highway was as close as it seemed to be. Sounds could be tricky sometimes, and more than once the air had fooled him into thinking a far-off thing was closer than it was. He didn't want to waste his energies on futile efforts, but if the road was where he thought it might be, then maybe he had a chance. The traffic was increasing now, and he could detect all manner of vehicles rushing down the wet highway, an unbroken parade of big cars and small cars, trucks and vans, long-distance buses. A person was at the wheel of each one of them, and if just one of those drivers was willing to stop and help him, then perhaps he would be saved. It would mean climbing up the hill in front of him, of course, and then working his way down the other side, but hard as all that was going to be, it had to be done. The road was somewhere, and he had to find it. The only drawback was that it had to be found on the first try. If he took the wrong path, he wouldn't have the strength to go back up the hill and start again.

But the road was there, and when Mr. Bones finally saw it after forty minutes of struggling past the thorns and outcrops and bulging roots that had blocked his way, after losing his footing and slipping down a dirt embankment, after drenching his fur in the muddy residues of the snow, the sick and feverish dog understood that salvation was at hand. The road was immense, and the road was dazzling: a six-lane super-highway with cars and trucks speeding past in both directions. With the moisture from the melted snow still clinging to the black surface of the road, the metal guardrails, and the branches of the trees that lined the east and west shoulders, and with the winter sun blazing in the sky and beating down on these millions of drops of water, the highway presented itself to Mr. Bones as a spectacle of pure radiance, a field of over-powering light. It was exactly what he had been hoping for, and he knew now that the idea that had come to him during those forty minutes of punishing effort up and down the hill was the only correct solution to the problem. Trucks and cars could carry him away from this place, but they could also crush his bones and make him stop breathing forever. It was all so clear once you took the long view. He didn't have to wait for the time to come; the time was upon him now. All he had to do was step into the road, and he would be in Timbuktu. He would be in the land of words and transparent toasters, in the country of bicycle wheels and burning deserts where dogs talked as equals with men. Willy would disapprove at first, but that was only because he would think that Mr. Bones had gotten there by taking his own life. But Mr. Bones wasn't proposing anything as vulgar as suicide. He was merely going to play a game, the kind of game that any sick and crazy old dog would play. And that's what he was now, wasn't it? A sick and crazy old dog.

It was called dodge-the-car, and it was a venerable, time-honored sport that allowed every old-timer to recapture the glories of his youth. It was fun, it was invigorating, it was a challenge to every dog's athletic skills. Just run across the road and see if you could avoid being hit. The more times you were able to do it, the greater the champion you were. Sooner or later, of course, the odds were bound to catch up with you, and few dogs had ever played dodge-the-car without losing on their last turn. But that was the beauty of this particular game. The moment you lost, you won.

And so it happened, on that resplendent winter morning in Virginia, that Mr. Bones, a.k.a. Sparkatus, sidekick of the late poet Willy G. Christmas, set out to prove that he was a champion among dogs. Stepping off the grass onto the east-bound shoulder of the highway, he waited for a break in the traffic, and then he began to run. Weak as he was, there was still some spring left in his legs, and once he hit his stride, he felt stronger and happier than he had felt in months. He ran toward the noise, toward the light, toward the glare and the roar that were rushing in on him from all directions.

With any luck, he would be with Willy before the day was out.

1997–1998

THE BOOK OF ILLUSIONS

Man has not one and the same life. He has many lives,
placed end to end, and that is the cause of his misery.

Chateaubriand

1

Everyone thought he was dead. When my book about his films was published in 1988, Hector Mann had not been heard from in almost sixty years. Except for a handful of historians and old-time movie buffs, few people seemed to know that he had ever existed. *Double or Nothing,* the last of the twelve two-reel comedies he made at the end of the silent era, was released on November 23, 1928. Two months later, without saying good-bye to any of his friends or associates, without leaving behind a letter or informing anyone of his plans, he walked out of his rented house on North Orange Drive and was never seen again. His blue DeSoto was parked in the garage; the lease on the property was good for another three months; the rent had been paid in full. There was food in the kitchen, whiskey in the liquor cabinet, and not a single article of Hector's clothing was missing from the bedroom drawers. According to the *Los Angeles Herald Express* of January 18, 1929, *it looked as though he had stepped out for a short walk and would be returning at any moment.* But he didn't return, and from that point on it was as if Hector Mann had vanished from the face of the earth.

For several years following his disappearance, various stories and rumors circulated about what had happened to him, but none of these conjectures ever amounted to anything. The most plausible ones – that he had committed suicide or fallen victim to foul play – could neither be proved nor disproved, since no body was ever recovered. Other accounts of Hector's fate were more imaginative, more hopeful, more in keeping with the romantic implications of such a case. In one, he had returned to his native Argentina and was now the owner of a small provincial circus. In another, he had joined the Communist Party and was working under an assumed name as an organizer among the dairy workers in Utica, New York. In still another, he was riding the rails as a Depression hobo. If Hector had been a bigger star, the stories no doubt would have persisted. He would have lived on in the things that were said about him, gradually turning into one of those symbolic figures who inhabit the nether zones of collective memory, a representative of youth and hope and the devilish twists of fortune. But none of that happened, for the fact was that Hector was only just beginning to make his mark in Hollywood when his career ended. He had come too late to exploit his talents fully, and he hadn't stayed long enough to leave a lasting impression of who he was or what he could do. A few more years went by, and little by little people stopped thinking about him. By 1932 or 1933, Hector belonged to an extinct universe, and if there were any traces of him left, it was only as a footnote in some obscure book that no one bothered to read anymore. The movies talked now, and the flickering dumb shows of the past were forgotten. No more clowns, no more pantomimists, no more pretty flapper girls dancing to the beat of unheard orchestras. They had been dead for just a few years, but already they felt prehistoric, like creatures who had roamed the earth when men still lived in caves.

I didn't give much information about Hector's life in my book. *The Silent World of Hector Mann* was a study of his films, not a biography, and whatever small facts I threw in about his offscreen activities came directly from the standard sources: film encyclopedias, memoirs, histories of early Hollywood. I wrote the book because I wanted to share my enthusiasm for Hector's work. The story of his life was secondary to me, and rather than speculate on what might or might not have happened to him, I stuck to a close reading of the films themselves. Given that he was born in 1900, and given that he had not been seen since 1929, it never would have occurred to me to suggest that Hector Mann was still alive. Dead men don't crawl out from their graves, and as far as I was concerned, only a dead man could have kept himself hidden for that long.

The book was published by the University of Pennsylvania Press eleven years ago this past March. Three months later, just after the first reviews had started to appear in the film quarterlies and academic journals, a letter turned up in my mailbox. The envelope was larger and squarer than the ones commonly sold in stores, and because it was made of thick, expensive paper, my initial response was to think there might be a wedding invitation or a birth announcement inside. My name and address were written out across the front in an elegant, curling script. If the writing wasn't that of a professional calligrapher, it no doubt came from someone who believed in the virtues of graceful penmanship, a person who had been schooled in the old academies of etiquette and social decorum. The stamp was postmarked Albuquerque, New Mexico, but the return address on the back flap showed that the letter had been written somewhere else – assuming that there was such a place, and assuming that the name of the town was real. Top and bottom, the two lines read: Blue Stone Ranch; Tierra del Sueño, New Mexico. I might have smiled when I saw those words, but I can't remember now. No name was given, and as I opened the envelope to read the message on the card inside, I caught a faint smell of perfume, the subtlest hint of lavender essence.

Dear Professor Zimmer, the note said. *Hector has read your book and would like to meet you. Are you interested in paying us a visit? Yours sincerely, Frieda Spelling (Mrs. Hector Mann).*

I read it six or seven times. Then I put it down, walked to the other end of the room, and came back. When I picked up the letter again, I wasn't sure if the words would still be there. Or, if they were there, if they would still be the same words. I read it six or seven more times, and then, still not sure of anything, dismissed it as a prank. A moment later, I was filled with doubts, and the next moment after that I began to doubt those doubts. To think one thought meant thinking the opposite thought, and no sooner did that second thought destroy the first thought than a third thought rose up to destroy the second. Not knowing what else to do, I got into my car and drove to the post office. Every address in America was listed in the zip code directory, and if Tierra del Sueño wasn't there, I could throw away the card and forget all about it. But it was there. I found it in volume one on page 1933, sitting on the line between Tierra Amarilla and Tijeras, a proper town with a post office and its own five-digit number. That didn't make the letter genuine, of course, but at least it gave it an air of credibility, and by the time I returned home, I knew that I would have to answer it. A letter like that can't be ignored. Once you've read it, you know that if you don't take the trouble to sit down and write back, you'll go on thinking about it for the rest of your life.

I haven't kept a copy of my answer, but I remember that I wrote it by hand and tried to make it as short as possible, limiting what I said to just a few sentences. Without giving it much thought, I found myself adopting the flat, cryptic style of the letter I had received. I felt less exposed that way, less likely to be taken as a fool by the person who had masterminded the prank – if indeed it was a prank. Give or take a word or two, my response went something like this: *Dear Frieda Spelling. Of course I would like to meet Hector Mann. But how can I be sure he's alive? To the best of my knowledge, he hasn't been seen in more than half a century. Please provide details. Respectfully yours, David Zimmer.*

*

We all want to believe in impossible things, I suppose, to persuade ourselves that miracles can happen. Considering that I was the author of
the only book ever written on Hector Mann, it probably made sense that
someone would think I'd jump at the chance to believe he was still alive.
But I wasn't in the mood to jump. Or at least I didn't think I was. My
book had been born out of a great sorrow, and now that the book was
behind me, the sorrow was still there. Writing about comedy had been
no more than a pretext, an odd form of medicine that I had swallowed
every day for over a year on the off chance that it would dull the pain
inside me. To some extent, it did. But Frieda Spelling (or whoever was
posing as Frieda Spelling) couldn't have known that. She couldn't have
known that on June 7, 1985, just one week short of my tenth wedding
anniversary, my wife and two sons had been killed in a plane crash. She
might have seen that the book was dedicated to them (*For Helen, Todd,
and Marco – In Memory*), but those names couldn't have meant anything
to her, and even if she had guessed their importance to the author, she
couldn't have known that for him those names stood for everything that
had any meaning in life – and that when the thirty-six-year-old Helen
and the seven-year-old Todd and the four-year-old Marco had died,
most of him had died along with them.

They had been on their way to Milwaukee to visit Helen's parents. I
had stayed behind in Vermont to correct papers and hand in the final
grades for the semester that had just ended. That was my work – professor of comparative literature at Hampton College in Hampton, Vermont
– and I had to do it. Normally, we all would have gone together on the
twenty-fourth or twenty-fifth, but Helen's father had just been operated
on for a tumor in his leg, and the family consensus was that she and the
boys should leave as quickly as possible. This entailed some elaborate,
last-minute negotiations with Todd's school so that he would be
allowed to miss the last two weeks of the second grade. The principal
was reluctant but understanding, and in the end she gave in. That was
one of the things I kept thinking about after the crash. If only she had
turned us down, then Todd would have been forced to stay at home
with me, and he wouldn't have been dead. At least one of them would
have been spared that way. At least one of them wouldn't have fallen
seven miles through the sky, and I wouldn't have been left alone in a
house that was supposed to have four people in it. There were other
things, of course, other contingencies to brood about and torture myself
with, and I never seemed to tire of walking down those same dead-end

roads. Everything was part of it, every link in the chain of cause and effect was an essential piece of the horror – from the cancer in my father-in-law's leg to the weather in the Midwest that week to the telephone number of the travel agent who had booked the airline tickets. Worst of all, there was my own insistence on driving them down to Boston so they could be on a direct flight. I hadn't wanted them to leave from Burlington. That would have meant going to New York on an eighteen-seat prop plane to catch a connecting flight to Milwaukee, and I told Helen that I didn't like those small planes. They were too dangerous, I said, and I couldn't stand the idea of letting her and the boys go on one of them without me. So they didn't – in order to appease my worries. They went on a bigger one, and the terrible thing about it was that I rushed to get them there. The traffic was heavy that morning, and when we finally got to Springfield and hit the Mass Pike, I had to drive well over the speed limit to make it to Logan in time.

I remember very little of what happened to me that summer. For several months, I lived in a blur of alcoholic grief and self-pity, rarely stirring from the house, rarely bothering to eat or shave or change my clothes. Most of my colleagues were gone until the middle of August, and therefore I didn't have to put up with many visits, to sit through the agonizing protocols of communal mourning. They meant well, of course, and whenever any of my friends came around, I always invited them in, but their tearful embraces and long, embarrassed silences didn't help. It was better to be left alone, I found, better to gut out the days in the darkness of my own head. When I wasn't drunk or sprawled out on the living room sofa watching television, I spent my time wandering around the house. I would visit the boys' rooms and sit down on the floor, surrounding myself with their things. I wasn't able to think about them directly or summon them up in any conscious way, but as I put together their puzzles and played with their Lego pieces, building ever more complex and baroque structures, I felt that I was temporarily inhabiting them again – carrying on their little phantom lives for them by repeating the gestures they had made when they still had bodies. I read through Todd's fairy-tale books and organized his baseball cards. I classified Marco's stuffed animals according to species, color, and size, changing the system every time I entered the room. Hours vanished in this way, whole days melted into oblivion, and when I couldn't stomach it anymore, I would go back into the living room and pour myself another drink. On those rare nights when I didn't pass out on the sofa, I usually slept in Todd's bed. In my own bed, I always dreamed that Helen was with me, and every time I reached out to take hold of her, I would wake up with a sudden, violent lurch, my hands trembling and my lungs gasping for air, feeling as if I'd been about to drown. I couldn't go into our bedroom after dark, but I spent a lot of time there during the day, standing inside Helen's closet and touching her clothes, rearranging her jackets and sweaters, lifting her dresses off their hangers and spreading them out on the floor. Once, I put one of them on, and another time I got into her underwear and made up my face with her makeup. It was a deeply satisfying experience, but after some additional experimentation, I discovered that perfume was even more effective than lipstick and mascara. It seemed to bring her back more vividly, to evoke her presence for longer periods of time. As luck would have it, I had given her a fresh supply of Chanel No. 5 for her birthday in March. By limiting myself to small doses twice a day, I was able to make the bottle last until the end of the summer.

I took a leave of absence for the fall semester, but rather than go away or look for psychological help, I stayed on in the house and continued to sink. By late September or early October, I was knocking off more than half a bottle of whiskey every night. It kept me from feeling too much, but at the same time it deprived me of any sense of the future, and when a man has nothing to look forward to, he might as well be dead. More than once, I caught myself in the middle of lengthy daydreams about sleeping pills and carbon monoxide gas. I never went far enough to take any action, but whenever I look back on those days now, I understand how close I came to it. The pills were in the medicine cabinet, and I had already taken the bottle off the shelf three or four times; I had already held the loose pills in my hand. If the situation had gone on much longer, I doubt that I would have had the strength to resist.

That was how things stood for me when Hector Mann unexpectedly walked into my life. I had no idea who he was, had never even stumbled across a reference to his name, but one night just before the start of winter, when the trees had finally gone bare and the first snow was threatening to fall, I happened to see a clip from one of his old films on television, and it made me laugh. That might not sound important, but it was the first time I had laughed at anything since June, and when I felt that unexpected spasm rise up through my chest and begin to rattle around in my lungs, I understood that I hadn't hit bottom yet, that there was still some piece of me that wanted to go on living. From start to finish, it couldn't have lasted more than a few seconds. As laughs go, it wasn't especially loud or sustained, but it took me by surprise, and in that I didn't struggle against it, and in that I didn't feel ashamed of myself for having forgotten my unhappiness during those few moments when Hector Mann was on-screen, I was forced to conclude that there was something inside me I had not previously imagined, something other than just pure death. I'm not talking about some vague intuition or sentimental yearning for what might have been. I had made an empirical discovery, and it carried all the weight of a mathematical proof. If I had it in me to laugh, then that meant I wasn't entirely numb. It meant that I hadn't walled myself off from the world so thoroughly that nothing could get in anymore.

It must have been a little past ten o'clock. I was anchored to my usual spot on the sofa, holding a glass of whiskey in one hand and the remote-control gadget in the other, mindlessly surfing channels. I came upon the program a few minutes after it started, but it didn't take me long to figure out that it was a documentary about silent-film comedians. All the familiar faces were there – Chaplin, Keaton, Lloyd – but they also included some rare footage of comics I had never heard of before, lesser-known figures such as John Bunny, Larry Semon, Lupino Lane, and Raymond Griffith. I followed the gags with a kind of measured detachment, not really paying attention to them, but absorbed enough not to switch to something else. Hector Mann didn't come on until late in the program, and when he did, they showed only one clip: a two-minute sequence from *The Teller's Tale*, which was set in a bank and featured Hector in the role of a hardworking assistant clerk. I can't explain why it grabbed me, but there he was in his white tropical suit and his thin black mustache, standing at a table and counting out piles of money, and he worked with such furious efficiency, such lightning speed and manic concentration, that I couldn't turn my eyes away from him. Upstairs, repairmen were installing new planks in the floor of the bank manager's office. Across the room, a pretty secretary sat at her desk, buffing her nails behind a large typewriter. At first, it looked as though nothing could distract Hector from completing his task in record time. Then, ever so gradually, little streams of sawdust began to fall on his jacket, and not many seconds after that, he finally caught sight of the girl. One element had suddenly become three elements, and from that point on the action bounced among them in a triangular rhythm of work, vanity, and lust: the struggle to go on counting the money, the effort to protect his beloved suit, and the urge to make eye contact with the girl. Every now and then, Hector's mustache would twitch in consternation, as if to punctuate the proceedings with a faint groan or mumbled aside. It wasn't slapstick and anarchy so much as character and pace, a smoothly orchestrated mixture of objects, bodies, and minds. Each time Hector lost track of the count, he would have to start over again, and that only inspired him to work twice as fast as before. Each time he turned his head up to the ceiling to see where the dust was coming from, he would do it a split second after the workers had filled in the hole with a new plank. Each time he glanced over at the girl, she would be looking in the wrong direction. And yet, through it all, Hector somehow managed to keep his composure, refusing to allow these petty frustrations to thwart his purpose or puncture his good opinion of himself. It might not have been the most extraordinary bit of comedy I had ever seen, but it pulled me in until I was completely caught up in it, and by the second or third twitch of Hector's mustache, I was laughing, actually laughing out loud.

A narrator spoke over the action, but I was too immersed in the scene to catch everything he said. Something about Hector's mysterious exit from the film business, I think, and the fact that he was considered to have been the last of the significant two-reel comedians. By the 1920s, the most successful and innovative clowns had already moved into full-length features, and the quality of short comic films had suffered a drastic decline. Hector Mann did not add anything new to the genre, the narrator said, but he was acknowledged as a talented gagman with exceptional body control, a notable latecomer who might have gone on to achieve important work if his career hadn't ended so abruptly. At that point the scene ended, and I started listening more closely to the narrator's comments. A succession of still photographs of several dozen comic actors rolled across the screen, and the voice lamented the loss of so many films from the silent era. Once sound entered the movies, silent films had been left to rot in vaults, had been destroyed by fires, had been carted away as trash, and hundreds of performances had disappeared forever. But all hope was not dead, the voice added. Old films occasionally turned up, and a number of remarkable discoveries had been made in recent years. Consider the case of Hector Mann, it said. Until 1981, only three of his films had been available anywhere in the world. Vestiges of the other nine were buried in an assortment of secondary materials – press reports, contemporary reviews, production stills, synopses – but the films themselves were presumed to be lost. Then, in December of that year, an anonymous package was delivered to the offices of the Cinémathèque Française in Paris. Apparently mailed from somewhere in central Los Angeles, it contained a nearly pristine copy of *Jumping Jacks*, the seventh of Hector Mann's twelve films. At irregular intervals over the next three years, eight similar packages were sent to major film archives around the world: the Museum of Modern Art in New York, the British Film Institute in London, Eastman House in Rochester, the American Film Institute in Washington, the Pacific Film Archive in Berkeley, and again to the Cinémathèque in Paris. By 1984, Hector Mann's entire output had been dispersed among these six organizations. Each package had emanated from a different city, traveling from places as remote from one another as Cleveland and San Diego, Philadelphia and Austin, New Orleans and Seattle, and because there was never any letter or message included with the films, it was impossible to identify the donor or even to form a hypothesis about who he was or where he might have lived. Another mystery had been added to the life and career of the enigmatic Hector Mann, the narrator said, but a great service had been done, and the film community was grateful.

I wasn't attracted to mysteries or enigmas, but as I sat there watching the final credits of the program, it occurred to me that I might want to see those films. There were twelve of them scattered among six different cities in Europe and the United States, and in order to see them all, a person would have to give up a significant chunk of his time. No less than several weeks, I imagined, but perhaps as long as a month or a month and a half. At that point, the last thing I would have predicted was that I would wind up writing a book about Hector Mann. I was just looking for something to do, something to keep me occupied in a harmless sort of way until I was ready to return to work. I had spent close to half a year watching myself go to the dogs, and I knew that if I let it go on any longer, I was going to die. It didn't matter what the project was or what I hoped to get out of it. Any choice would have been arbitrary by then, but that night an idea had presented itself to me, and on the strength of two minutes of film and one short laugh, I chose to wander around the world looking at silent comedies.

I wasn't a film person. I had started teaching literature as a graduate student in my mid-twenties, and since then all my work had been connected to books, language, the written word. I had translated a number of European poets (Lorca, Éluard, Leopardi, Michaux), had written reviews for magazines and newspapers, and had published two books of criticism. The first one, *Voices in the War Zone*, was a study of politics and literature that examined the work of Hamsun, Céline, and Pound in relation to their pro-Fascist activities during World War II. The second one, *The Road to Abyssinia*, was a book about writers who had given up writing, a meditation on silence. Rimbaud, Dashiell Hammett, Laura Riding, J. D. Salinger, and others – poets and novelists of uncommon brilliance who, for one reason or another, had stopped. When Helen and the boys were killed, I had been planning to write a new book about Stendhal. It wasn't that I had anything against the movies, but they had never been very important to me, and not once in more than fifteen years of teaching and writing had I felt the urge to talk about them. I liked them in the way that everyone else did – as diversions, as animated wallpaper, as fluff. No matter how beautiful or hypnotic the images sometimes were, they never satisfied me as powerfully as words did. Too much was given, I felt, not enough was left to the viewer's imagination, and the paradox was that the closer movies came to simulating reality, the worse they failed at representing the world – which is in us as much as it is around us. That was why I had always instinctively preferred black-and-white pictures to color pictures, silent films to talkies. Cinema was a visual language, a way of telling stories by projecting images onto a two-dimensional screen. The addition of sound and color had created the illusion of a third dimension, but at the same time it had robbed the images of their purity. They no longer had to do all the work, and instead of turning film into the perfect hybrid medium, the best of all possible worlds, sound and color had weakened the language they were supposed to enhance. That night, as I watched Hector and the other comedians go through their paces in my Vermont living room, it struck me that I was witnessing a dead art, a wholly defunct genre that would never be practiced again. And yet, for all the changes that had occurred since then, their work was as fresh and invigorating as it had been when it was first shown. That was because they had understood the language they were speaking. They had invented a syntax of the eye, a grammar of pure kinesis, and except for the costumes and the cars and the quaint furniture in the background, none of it could possibly grow old. It was thought translated into action, human will expressing itself through the human body, and therefore it was for all time. Most silent comedies hardly even bothered to tell stories. They were like poems, like the renderings of dreams, like some intricate choreography of the spirit, and because they were dead, they probably spoke more deeply to us now than they had to the audiences of their time. We watched them across a great chasm of forgetfulness, and the very things that separated them from us were in fact what made them so arresting: their muteness, their absence of color, their fitful, speeded-up rhythms. These were obstacles, and they made viewing difficult for us, but they also relieved the images of the burden of representation. They stood between us and the film, and therefore we no longer had to pretend that we were looking at the real world. The flat screen was the world, and it existed in two dimensions. The third dimension was in our head.

There was nothing to stop me from packing my bags and leaving the next day. I was off for the semester, and the next term wouldn't begin until the middle of January. I was free to do what I wanted, free to go wherever my legs wanted to take me, and the fact was that if I needed more time I could keep on going until I was past January, past September, past all the Septembers and Januarys for as long as I wished. Such were the ironies of my absurd and miserable life. The moment Helen and the boys were killed, I had been turned into a rich man. The first bit came from a life insurance policy that Helen and I had been talked into buying not long after I started teaching at Hampton – *for peace of mind*, the man said – and because it was attached to the college health plan and didn't cost much, we had been paying in a small amount every month without bothering to think about it. I hadn't even remembered that we owned this insurance when the plane went down, but less than a month later, a man showed up at my house and handed me a check for several hundred thousand dollars. A short time after that, the airline company made a settlement with the families of the victims, and as someone who had lost three people in the crash, I wound up winning the compensation jackpot, the giant booby prize for random death and unforeseen acts of God. Helen and I had always struggled to get by on my academic salary and the occasional fees she earned from freelance writing. At any point along the way, an extra thousand dollars would have made an enormous difference to us. Now I had that thousand many times over, and it didn't mean a thing. When the checks came in, I sent half the money to Helen's parents, but they sent it back by return mail, thanking me for the gesture but assuring me that they didn't want it. I bought new playground equipment for Todd's elementary school, donated two thousand dollars' worth of books and a state-of-the-art sandbox to Marco's day-care center, and prevailed upon my sister and her music-teacher husband in Baltimore to accept a large cash contribution from the Zimmer Death Fund. If there had been more people in my family to give money to, I would have done it, but my parents were no longer alive, and Deborah was the only sibling I had. Instead, I unloaded another sackful by establishing a fellowship at Hampton College in Helen's name: the Helen Markham Traveling Fellowship. The idea was very simple. Every year, a cash award would be given for excellence in the humanities to one graduating senior. The money had to be spent on travel, but other than that there were no rules, no conditions, no requirements to be fulfilled. The winner would be selected by a rotating committee of professors from several different departments (history, philosophy, English, and foreign languages), and as long as the grant was used to finance a trip abroad, the Markham Fellow could do anything with the money that he or she saw fit, no questions asked. A huge outlay was required to set this up, but large as that sum was (the equivalent of four years' salary), it put no more than a small dent in my assets, and even after I had disbursed those various amounts in the various ways that made sense to me, I still had more money than I knew what to do with. It was a grotesque situation, a sickening excess of wealth, and every penny of it had been procured with blood. If not for a sudden change of plans, I probably would have gone on giving away the money until there was nothing left. But one cold night in early November, I got it into my head to do some traveling of my own, and without the resources to pay for it, I never could have followed through on such an impulsive scheme. Until then, the money had been nothing but a torment to me. Now I saw it as a cure, a balm to ward off a terminal collapse of the spirit. Living in hotels and eating in restaurants was going to be an expensive proposition, but for once I didn't have to worry about whether I could afford to do what I wanted. Desperate and unhappy as I was, I was also a free man, and because I had gold in my pockets, I could dictate the conditions of that freedom on my own terms.

Half of the films were within driving distance of my house. Rochester was about six hours to the west, and New York and Washington were directly to the south – roughly five hours to cover the first leg of the journey, then another five to do the second. I decided to begin with Rochester. Winter was already approaching, and the longer I put off going there, the greater the chances would be of running into storms and icy roads, of bogging down in some northern inclemency. The next morning, I called Eastman House to inquire about seeing the films in their collection. I had no idea how one went about setting up such a thing, and because I didn't want to sound too ignorant when I introduced myself over the phone, I added that I was a professor at Hampton College. I was hoping that would impress them enough to take me for a serious person – and not some crank calling out of the blue, which was what I was. Oh, said the woman on the other end of the line, are you writing something about Hector Mann? She made it sound as if there was only one possible answer to the question, and after a slight pause, I mumbled the words she was expecting to hear. Yes, I said, that's it, that's it exactly. I'm writing a book about him, and I need to see the films for my research.

That was how the project began. It was a good thing it happened so early, because once I had seen the films in Rochester (*The Jockey Club* and *The Snoop*), I understood that I wasn't just wasting my time. Hector was every bit as talented and accomplished as I had hoped he would be, and if the other ten films were up to the standards of those two, then he deserved to have a book written about him, he deserved the chance to be rediscovered. Right from the start, therefore, I didn't only watch Hector's movies, I studied them. If not for my conversation with that woman in Rochester, it never would have occurred to me to take this approach. My original plan had been far simpler, and I doubt that it would have kept me busy much beyond Christmas or the first of the year. As it was, I didn't finish viewing all of Hector's films until the middle of February. The old idea had been to see each film once. Now I saw them many times, and instead of visiting an archive for just a few hours, I stuck around for days, running the films on flatbeds and Moviolas, watching Hector for entire mornings and afternoons at a stretch, winding and rewinding the prints until my eyes wouldn't stay open anymore. I took notes, consulted books, and wrote down exhaustive commentaries, detailing the cuts and camera angles and lighting positions, analyzing all aspects of every scene down to its most peripheral elements, and I never left a place until I was ready, until I had lived with the footage long enough to know every inch of it by heart.

I didn't question whether any of this was worth doing. I had my job, and the only thing that mattered to me was to stick with it and make sure that it got done. I knew that Hector was no more than a minor figure, an addendum to the list of also-rans and luckless contenders, but that didn't stop me from admiring his work and taking pleasure in his company. His films had been knocked off at the rate of one a month for a year, and they were made on budgets so small, so far below the amounts required to stage the spectacular stunts and breathless sequences normally associated with silent comedy, that it was a wonder he had managed to produce anything at all, let alone twelve perfectly watchable films. According to what I read, Hector had started out in Hollywood as a prop man, scenic painter, and sometime extra, had graduated to bit roles in a number of comedies, and had been given his chance to direct and star in his own films by a man named Seymour Hunt. Hunt, a banker from Cincinnati who wanted to break into the movie business, had gone out to California in early 1927 to set up his own production company, Kaleidoscope Pictures. By all accounts a blustering, duplicitous character, Hunt knew nothing about making movies and even less about running a business. (Kaleidoscope shut down after just a year and a half. Hunt, charged with stock fraud and embezzlement, hanged himself before his case ever came to trial.) Underfinanced, understaffed, and plagued by Hunt's constant interference, Hector nevertheless seized his opportunity and tried to make the most of it. There were no scripts, of course, and no prearranged setups. Just Hector and a pair of gagmen named Andrew Murphy and Jules Blaustein improvising as they went along, often shooting at night on borrowed sets with exhausted crews and secondhand equipment. They couldn't afford to wreck a dozen cars or to mount a cattle stampede. Houses couldn't collapse, and buildings couldn't explode. No floods, no hurricanes, and no exotic locations. Extras were at a premium, and if an idea didn't work, they didn't have the luxury of reshooting after the film was over. Everything had to be cranked out on schedule, and there was no time for second thoughts. Gags on command: three laughs a minute, and then put another coin in the meter. For all the drawbacks to the arrangement, Hector seemed to thrive on the limitations that had been imposed on him. The scale of his work was modest, but there was an intimacy to it that held your attention and forced you to respond to him. I understood why film scholars respected his work – and also why no one was terribly excited by it. He hadn't broken any new ground, and now that all his films were available again, it was clear that the history of the period would not have to be rewritten. Hector's films were small contributions to the art, but they weren't negligible, and the more I saw of them, the more I liked them for their grace and subtle wit, for the droll and affecting manner of their star. As I soon discovered, no one had seen all of Hector's films yet. The last ones had turned up too recently, and not one person had taken it upon himself to travel the whole circuit of archives and museums around the world. If I managed to carry out my plan, I would be the first one.

Before leaving Rochester, I called Smits, the dean of faculty at Hampton, and told him that I wanted to extend my leave for another semester. He was a bit put out at first, claiming that my courses had already been announced in the catalogue, but then I lied to him and said that I was undergoing psychiatric treatment, and he apologized. It was a nasty trick, I suppose, but I was fighting for my life at that point, and I didn't have the strength to explain why looking at silent movies had suddenly become so important to me. We wound up having a cordial chat, and in the end he wished me luck, but even though we both pretended that I would be returning in the fall, I think he sensed that I was already slipping away, that my heart was no longer in it.

I saw *Scandal* and *Country Weekend* in New York, then moved on to Washington for *The Teller's Tale* and *Double or Nothing*. I booked reservations for the rest of the trip with a travel agent on Dupont Circle (Amtrak to California, the *QE 2* to Europe), but the next morning, in a sudden burst of blind heroism, I canceled the tickets and opted to go by plane. It was pure folly, but now that I was off to such a promising start, I didn't want to lose my momentum. Never mind that I would have to talk myself into doing the one thing I had resolved never to do again. I couldn't slacken my pace, and if that meant seeking out a pharmacological solution to the problem, then I was prepared to ingest as many knockout pills as necessary. A woman from the American Film Institute gave me the name of a doctor. I figured the appointment would take no more than five or ten minutes. I would tell him why I wanted the pills, he would write out a prescription, and that would be that. Fear of flying was a common complaint, after all, and there would be no need to talk about Helen and the boys, no need to bare my soul to him. All I wanted was to shut down my central nervous system for a few hours, and since you couldn't buy that stuff over the counter, his sole function would be to hand me a slip of paper with his signature on it. But Dr. Singh turned out to be a thorough man, and as he went about the business of taking my blood pressure and listening to my heart, he asked me enough questions to keep me in his office for three-quarters of an hour. He was too intelligent not to want to probe, and little by little the truth came out.

We're all going to die, Mr. Zimmer, he said. What makes you think you're going to die on a plane? If you believe what the statistics tell us, you have a greater chance of dying just by sitting at home.

I didn't say I was afraid of dying, I answered, I said that I was afraid to get on a plane. There's a difference.

But if the plane isn't going to crash, why should you be worried?

Because I don't trust myself anymore. I'm afraid I'll lose control, and I don't want to make a spectacle of myself.

I'm not sure I follow you.

I imagine myself boarding the plane, and before I even get to my seat, I snap.

Snap? In what sense snap? You mean snap mentally?

Yes, I break down in front of four hundred strangers and lose my mind. I go berserk.

And what do you imagine yourself doing?

It depends. Sometimes I scream. Sometimes I punch people in the face. Sometimes I rush into the cockpit and try to strangle the pilot.

Does anyone stop you?

Of course they do. They swarm all over me and wrestle me to the ground. They beat the shit out of me.

When was the last time you were in a fight, Mr. Zimmer?

I can't remember. Back when I was a boy, I suppose. Eleven, twelve years old. School-yard stuff. Defending myself against the class bully.

And what makes you think you'll start fighting now?

Nothing. I just feel it in my bones, that's all. If something rubs me the wrong way, I don't think I'll be able to stop myself. Anything is liable to happen.

But why planes? Why aren't you afraid of losing control of yourself on the ground?

Because planes are safe. Everyone knows that. Planes are safe, fast, and efficient, and once you're up in the air, nothing can happen to you. That's why I'm afraid. Not because I think I'm going to be killed – but because I know I won't.

Have you ever attempted suicide, Mr. Zimmer?

No.

Have you ever thought about it?

Of course I have. I wouldn't be human if I hadn't.

Is that why you're here now? So you can walk off with a prescription for some nice, powerful drug and do away with yourself?

I'm looking for oblivion, Doctor, not death. The drugs will put me to sleep, and as long as I'm unconscious, I won't have to think about what I'm doing. I'll be there, but I won't be there, and to the degree that I'm not there, I'll be protected.

Protected against what?

Against myself. Against the horror of knowing that nothing is going to happen to me.

You expect to have a smooth, uneventful flight. I still don't see why that should make you afraid.

Because the odds are with me. I'm going to take off and land safely, and once I get to where I'm going, I'll step off the plane alive. Good for me, you say, but once I do that, I spit on everything I believe in. I insult the dead, Doctor. I turn a tragedy into a simple matter of bad luck. Do you understand me now? I tell the dead that they died for nothing.

He understood. I hadn't said it in so many words, but this doctor had a delicate, sophisticated mind, and he was able to figure out the rest for himself. J. M. Singh, graduate of the Royal College of Physicians, resident internist at Georgetown University Hospital, with his precise British accent and prematurely thinning hair, suddenly grasped what I had been trying to tell him in that small cubicle with the fluorescent lights and the shining metal surfaces. I was still on the examining table, buttoning my shirt and looking down at the floor (not wanting to look at him, not wanting to risk the embarrassment of tears), and just then, after what felt like a long and awkward silence, he put his hand on my shoulder. I'm sorry, he said. I'm truly sorry.

It was the first time anyone had touched me in months, and I found it disturbing, almost repulsive to be turned into an object of such compassion. I don't want your sympathy, Doctor, I said. I just want your pills.

He backed off with a slight grimace, then sat down on a stool in the corner. As I finished tucking in my shirt, I saw him pull out a prescription pad from the pocket of his white coat. I'm willing to do it, he said, but before you get up and leave, I want to ask you to reconsider your decision. I think I have an idea of what you've been through, Mr. Zimmer, and I hesitate to put you in a position that could cause you such torment. There are other methods of travel, you know. Perhaps it would be best if you avoided planes for now.

I've already been down that road, I said, and I've decided against it. The distances are just too big. My next stop is Berkeley, California, and after that I have to go to London and Paris. A train to the West Coast takes three days. Multiply that by two for the return trip, then add on another ten days to cross the Atlantic and come back, and we're talking about a minimum of sixteen lost days. What am I supposed to do with all that time? Stare out the window and soak up the scenery?

Slowing down might not be such a bad thing. It would help to take off some of the pressure.

But pressure is what I need. If I loosened my grip now, I'd fall apart. I'd fly off in a hundred different directions, and I'd never be able to put myself together again.

There was something so intense about the way I delivered those words, something so earnest and crazy in the timbre of my voice, that the doctor almost smiled – or at least appeared to be suppressing a smile. Well, we don't want that to happen, do we? he said. If you're so intent on flying, then go ahead and fly. But let's make sure you do it in only one direction. And with that whimsical comment, he removed a pen from his pocket and scratched out a series of undecipherable marks on the pad. Here it is, he said, tearing off the top sheet and putting it in my hand. Your ticket for Air Xanax.

Never heard of it.

Xanax. A potent, highly dangerous drug. Just use as directed, Mr. Zimmer, and you'll be turned into a zombie, a being without a self, a blotted-out lump of flesh. You can fly across entire continents and oceans on this stuff, and I guarantee that you'll never even know you've left the ground.

By midafternoon the following day, I was in California. Less than twenty-four hours after that, I was walking into a private screening room at the Pacific Film Archive to watch two more Hector Mann comedies. *Tango Tangle* turned out to be one of his wildest, most effervescent productions; *Hearth and Home* was one of the most careful. I spent more than two weeks with these films, returning to the building every morning at ten sharp, and even when the place was closed (on Christmas and New Year's Day), I went on working in my hotel, reading books and consolidating my notes in preparation for the next stage of my travels. On January 7, 1986, I swallowed some more of Dr. Singh's magic pills and flew directly from San Francisco to London – six thousand nonstop miles on the Catatonia Express. A larger dose was required this time, but I was worried that it wouldn't be enough, and just before I boarded the plane, I took an extra pill. I should have known better than to go against the doctor's instructions, but the thought of waking up in the middle of the flight was so terrifying to me, I nearly put myself to sleep forever. There's a stamp in my old passport that proves I entered Great Britain on January eighth, but I have no memory of landing, no memory of going through customs, and no memory of how I got to my hotel. I woke up in an unfamiliar bed on the morning of January ninth, and that was when my life started again. I had never lost track of myself so thoroughly.

There were four films left – *Cowpokes* and *Mr. Nobody* in London; *Jumping Jacks* and *The Prop Man* in Paris – and I realized that this would be my only chance to see them. I could always revisit the American archives if I had to, but a return trip to the BFI and the Cinémathèque was out of the question. I had managed to get myself to Europe, but I didn't have it in me to attempt the impossible more than once. For that reason, I wound up staying in London and Paris much longer than was necessary – almost seven weeks in all, burrowed in for half the winter like some mad, subterranean beast. I had been thorough and conscientious up to that point, but now the project was taken to a new level of intensity, a single-mindedness that verged on obsession. My outward purpose was to study and master the films of Hector Mann, but the truth was that I was teaching myself how to concentrate, training myself how to think about one thing and one thing only. It was the life of a monomaniac, but it was the only way I could live now without crumbling to pieces. When I finally returned to Washington in February, I slept off the effects of the Xanax in an airport hotel, and then, first thing the next morning, collected my car from the long-term parking lot and drove to New York. I wasn't ready to return to Vermont. If I meant to write the book, I would need a place to hole up in, and of all the cities in the world, New York struck me as the one least likely to wear on my nerves. I spent five days looking for an apartment in Manhattan, but nothing turned up. It was the height of the Wall Street boom then, a good twenty months before the '87 crash, and rentals and sublets were in short supply. Eventually, I drove across the bridge to Brooklyn Heights and took the first place I was shown – a one-bedroom apartment on Pierrepont Street that had just come on the market that morning. It was expensive, dingy, and awkwardly designed, but I felt lucky to have it. I bought a mattress for one room, a desk and a chair for the other, and then I moved in. The lease was good for a year. It began on March first, and that was the day I began writing the book.

2

Before the body, there is the face, and before the face there is the thin black line between Hector's nose and upper lip. A twitching filament of anxieties, a metaphysical jump rope, a dancing thread of discombobulation, the mustache is a seismograph of Hector's inner states, and not only does it make you laugh, it tells you what Hector is thinking, actually allows you into the machinery of his thoughts. Other elements are involved – the eyes, the mouth, the finely calibrated lurches and stumbles – but the mustache is the instrument of communication, and even though it speaks a language without words, its wriggles and flutters are as clear and comprehensible as a message tapped out in Morse code.

None of this would be possible without the intervention of the camera. The intimacy of the talking mustache is a creation of the lens. At various moments in each of Hector's films, the angle suddenly changes, and a wide or medium shot is replaced by a close-up. Hector's face fills the screen, and with all references to the environment eliminated, the mustache becomes the center of the world. It begins to move, and because Hector's skill is such that he can control the muscles in the rest of his face, the mustache appears to be moving on its own, like a small animal with an independent consciousness and will. The mouth curls a bit at the corners, the nostrils flare ever so slightly, but as the mustache goes through its antic gyrations, the face is essentially still, and in that stillness one sees oneself as if in a mirror, for it is during those moments that Hector is most fully and convincingly human, a reflection of what we all are when we're alone inside ourselves. These close-up sequences are reserved for the critical passages of a story, the junctures of greatest tension or surprise, and they never last longer than four or five seconds. When they occur, everything else stops. The mustache launches into its soliloquy, and for those few precious moments, action gives way to thought. We can read the content of Hector's mind as though it were spelled out in letters across the screen, and before those letters vanish, they are no less visible than a building, a piano, or a pie in the face.

In motion, the mustache is a tool for expressing the thoughts of all men. In repose, it is little more than an ornament. It marks Hector's place in the world, establishes the type of character he is supposed to represent, and defines who he is in the eyes of others – but it belongs to only one man, and in that it is an absurdly thin and greasy little mustache, there can never be any doubt as to who that man is. He is the South American dandy, the Latin lover, the swarthy rogue with hot blood coursing through his veins. Add in the slicked-back hair and the ever-present white suit, and the result is an unmistakable blend of dash and decorum. Such is the code of images. The meanings are understood at a single glance, and because one thing inevitably follows from another in this booby-trapped universe of missing manhole covers and exploding cigars, the moment you see a man walking down the street in a white suit, you know that suit is going to get him into trouble.

After the mustache, the suit is the most important element in Hector's repertoire. The mustache is the link to his inner self, a metonym of urges, cogitations, and mental storms. The suit embodies his relation to the social world, and with its cueball brilliance shining against the grays and blacks that surround it, it serves as a magnet for the eyes. Hector wears the suit in every film, and in every film there is at least one long gag that revolves around the perils of trying to keep it clean. Mud and crankcase oil, spaghetti sauce and molasses, chimney soot and splashing puddles – at one time or another, every dark liquid and every dark substance threaten to smudge the pristine dignity of Hector's suit. That suit is his proudest possession, and he wears it with the dapper, cosmopolitan air of a man out to impress the world. He climbs into it every morning the way a knight climbs into his armor, girding himself for whatever battles society has in store for him that day, and not once does he stop to consider that he is achieving the opposite of what he has intended. He isn't protecting himself against potential blows, he is turning himself into a target, the focal point of every mishap that can possibly occur within a hundred yards of his person. The white suit is a sign of Hector's vulnerability, and it lends a certain pathos to the jokes the world plays on him. Obstinate in his elegance, clinging to the conviction that the suit transforms him into the most attractive and desirable of men, Hector elevates his own vanity into a cause that audiences can sympathize with. Watch him flicking specks of imaginary dust from his jacket as he rings the doorbell of his girlfriend's house in *Double or Nothing*, and you're no longer watching a demonstration of self-love: you're witnessing the torments of self-consciousness. The white suit turns Hector into an underdog. It wins the audience over to his side, and once an actor has achieved that, he can get away with anything.

He was too tall to play an out-and-out clown, too handsome to act the part of innocent bungler as other comics did. With his dark, expressive eyes and elegant nose, Hector looked like a second-rate leading man, an overachieving romantic hero who had wandered onto the set of the wrong film. He was a grown-up, and the very presence of such a person seemed to run counter to the established rules of comedy. Funny men were supposed to be small, misshapen, or fat. They were imps and buffoons, dunces and outcasts, children masquerading as adults or adults with the minds of children. Think of Arbuckle's juvenile rotundity, his simpering shyness and painted, feminized lips. Remember the forefinger that flies into his mouth every time a girl looks at him. Then go down the list of props and accoutrements that shaped the careers of the acknowledged masters: Chaplin's tramp with the floppy shoes and ragged clothes; Lloyd's plucky Milquetoast with the horn-rimmed specs; Keaton's saphead with the pancake hat and frozen face; Langdon's moron with the chalk-white skin. They are all misfits, and because these characters can neither threaten us nor make us envy them, we root for them to triumph over their enemies and win the girl's heart. The only problem is that we aren't quite sure they'll know what to do with the girl once they're alone with her. With Hector, such doubts never enter our mind. When he winks at a girl, there's a better than even chance that she'll wink back. And when she does, it's clear that neither one of them is thinking about marriage.

Laughter, however, is by no means guaranteed. Hector is not what you would call a lovable figure, and he is not someone you necessarily feel sorry for. If he manages to win the viewer's sympathy, it is because he never knows when to quit. Hardworking and convivial, the perfect incarnation of *l'homme moyen sensuel*, he is not out of step with the world so much as a victim of circumstances, a man with an inexhaustible talent for running into bad luck. Hector always has a plan in mind, a purpose for doing what he does, and yet something always seems to come up to thwart him from realizing his goal. His films are fraught with bizarre physical occurrences, outlandish mechanical breakdowns, objects that refuse to behave as they should. A man with less confidence in himself would be defeated by these setbacks, but other than an occasional burst of exasperation (confined to the mustache monologues), Hector never complains. Doors slam on his fingers, bees sting him on the neck, statues fall on his toes, but again and again he shrugs off his misfortunes and continues on his way. You begin to admire him for his steadfastness, for the spiritual calm that comes over him in the face of adversity, but what holds your attention is the way he moves. Hector can charm you with any one of a thousand different gestures. Light-footed and nimble, nonchalant to the point of indifference, he threads himself through the obstacle course of life without the slightest trace of clumsiness or fear, dazzling you with his backpedals and dodges, his sudden torques and lunging pavanes, his double takes and hop-steps and rhumba swivels. Observe the thrums and fidgets of his fingers, his deftly timed exhales, the slight cock of the head when something unexpected catches his eye. These miniature acrobatics are a function of character, but they also give pleasure in and of themselves. Even when flypaper is sticking to the bottom of his shoe and the little boy of the house has just lassoed him with a rope (pinning his arms to his sides), Hector moves with uncommon grace and composure, never doubting that he'll soon be able to extricate himself from his predicament – even if another one is waiting in the next room. Too bad for Hector, of course, but those are the breaks. What matters is not how well you can avoid trouble, but how you cope with trouble when it comes.

More often than not, Hector finds himself at the bottom of the social ladder. He is married in only two of his films (*Hearth and Home* and *Mr. Nobody*), and except for the private detective he plays in *The Snoop* and his role as traveling magician in *Cowpokes*, he is a working stiff toiling for others in humble, low-salaried jobs. A waiter in *The Jockey Club*, a chauffeur in *Country Weekend*, a door-to-door salesman in *Jumping Jacks*, a dance instructor in *Tango Tangle*, a bank employee in *The Teller's Tale*, Hector is usually presented as a young man just starting out in life. His prospects are far from encouraging, but he never gives the impression of being a loser. He carries himself with too much pride for that, and to watch him go about his business with the sure-handed competence of one who trusts in his own abilities, you understand that he's a person destined for success. Accordingly, most of Hector's films end in one of two ways: either he gets the girl or he performs an act of heroism that captures the attention of his boss. And if the boss is too thick-headed to notice (the wealthy and powerful are mostly portrayed as fools), the girl will see what has happened, and that will be reward enough. Whenever there is a choice between love and money, love always has the last word. Working as a waiter in *The Jockey Club*, for example, Hector manages to nab a jewel thief while serving several tables of drunken guests at a banquet in honor of champion aviatrix Wanda McNoon. With his left hand, he knocks out the thief with a champagne bottle; with his right, he simultaneously serves up dessert to the table, and because the cork flies out of the bottle and the headwaiter is sprayed with a liter's worth of Veuve Clicquot, Hector loses his job. But no matter. The spirited Wanda is an eyewitness to Hector's exploit. She slips him her telephone number, and in the last scene they climb into her plane together and take off for the clouds.

Unpredictable in his behavior, full of contradictory impulses and desires, Hector's character is too complexly delineated for us to feel altogether comfortable in his presence. He is not a type or familiar stock figure, and for every one of his actions that makes sense to us there is another one that confounds us and throws us off balance. He displays all the striving ambitiousness of a hardworking immigrant, a man bent on overcoming the odds and winning a place for himself in the American jungle, and yet one glimpse of a beautiful woman is enough to knock him off course, to scatter his carefully laid plans to the winds. Hector has the same personality in every film, but there is no fixed hierarchy to his preferences, no way of knowing what fancy will strike him next. He is both a populist and an aristocrat, a sensualist and a closet romantic, a man of precise, even punctilious manners who never hesitates to make the grand gesture. He will give his last dime to a beggar on the street, but he will not be motivated by pity or compassion so much as by the poetry of the act itself. No matter how hard he works, no matter how diligently he performs the menial and often absurd tasks that are assigned to him, Hector conveys a sense of detachment, as if he were somehow mocking himself and congratulating himself at the same time. He seems to live in a state of ironical bemusement, at once engaged in the world and observing it from a great distance. In what is perhaps his funniest film, *The Prop Man*, he turns these opposing points of view into a unified principle of mayhem. It was the ninth short of the series, and in it Hector plays the stage manager of a small, down-at-the-heels theater troupe. The company pulls into the town of Wishbone Falls for a three-day run of *Beggars Can't Be Choosers*, a bedroom farce by noted French dramatist Jean-Pierre Saint Jean de la Pierre. When they open the truck to unload the props and carry them into the theater, they discover that the props are missing. What to do? The play can't go on without them. There is an entire living room to furnish, not to speak of replacing several important accessories: a gun, a diamond necklace, and a roasted pig. The curtain is supposed to go up at eight o'clock the next evening, and unless the entire set can be built from scratch, the company will be out of business. The director of the troupe, a pompous blowhard with an ascot wrapped around his neck and a monocle in his left eye, peers into the back of the empty truck and faints dead away. The matter is in Hector's hands. After a few brief but incisive comments from his mustache, he calmly weighs the situation, smooths out the front of his immaculate white suit, and marches off to work. For the next nine and a half minutes, the film becomes an illustration of Proudhon's well-known anarchist dictum: *all property is theft*. In a series of short, frenetic episodes, Hector rushes around town and steals the props. We see him intercepting a furniture delivery to a department store warehouse and walking off with tables, chairs, and lamps – which he packs into his own truck and promptly drives to the theater. He pilfers silverware, drinking glasses, and a full set of china from a hotel kitchen. He bluffs his way into the back room of a butcher shop with a false order form from a local restaurant and trudges out with a pig's carcass slung over his shoulder. That evening, at a private reception for the actors which is attended by the town's most prominent citizens, he manages to remove the sheriff's pistol from its holster. A little while later, he skillfully undoes the latch of a necklace worn by a bulbous, middle-aged woman as she swoons under the seductive power of Hector's charms. He is never more unctuous than in this scene. Contemptible in his simulations, loathsome in the hypocrisy of his ardor, he also comes across as a heroic outlaw, an idealist willing to sacrifice himself for the good of his cause. We recoil from his tactics, but at the same time we pray for him to pull off the theft. The show must go on, and if Hector fails to pocket the jewels, there won't be any show. To complicate the intrigue still further, Hector has just caught sight of the town belle (who happens to be the sheriff's daughter), and even as he continues his amorous assault on the aging battle-axe, he begins making furtive eyes at the young beauty. Fortunately, Hector and his victim are standing behind a velvet curtain. It hangs halfway across an open doorway that separates the entrance hall from the drawing room, and because Hector is positioned on one side of the woman and not the other, he can look into the drawing room by leaning his head slightly to the left. But the woman remains hidden from view, and even though Hector can see the girl and the girl can see Hector, she has no idea that the woman is there. This allows

Hector to pursue both of his objectives at once – the false seduction and the true seduction – and because he plays one against the other in a clever mix of cuts and camera angles, each element makes the other one funnier than it would have been on its own. That is the essence of Hector's style. One joke is never enough for him. As soon as a situation has been established, another piece of business must be added to it, and then a third, and possibly even a fourth. Hector's gags unfold like musical compositions, a confluence of contrasting lines and voices, and the more the voices interact with one another, the more precarious and unstable the world becomes. In *The Prop Man*, Hector tickles the neck of the woman behind the curtain, plays peekaboo with the girl in the other room, and finally snags the necklace when a passing waiter slips on the hem of the woman's gown and spills a trayful of drinks down her back – which gives Hector just enough time to undo the clasp. He has achieved what he has set out to do – but only by accident, rescued once again by the mutinous unpredictability of matter.

The curtain goes up the following evening, and the performance is a rousing success. The butcher, the department store owner, the sheriff, and the fat woman are all in the audience, however, and even as the actors are taking their bows and blowing kisses to the enthusiastic crowd, a constable is clamping handcuffs on Hector's wrists and carting him off to jail. But Hector is happy, and he shows not one shred of remorse. He has saved the day, and not even the threat of losing his freedom can diminish his triumph. To anyone familiar with the difficulties Hector encountered while making his films, it is impossible not to read *The Prop Man* as a parable of his life under contract to Seymour Hunt and the struggles of working for Kaleidoscope Pictures. When every card in the deck is stacked against you, the only way to win a hand is to break the rules. You beg, borrow, and steal, as the old adage goes, and if you happen to get caught in the act, at least you've gone down fighting the good fight.

This joyful disregard of consequences takes a darker turn in Hector's eleventh film, *Mr. Nobody*. Time was running out by then, and he must have known that once the contract was fulfilled, his career would be over. Sound was coming. It was an inevitable fact of life, a certainty that would destroy everything that had come before it, and the art that Hector had worked so hard to master would no longer exist. Even if he could reconfigure his ideas to accommodate the new form, it wouldn't do him any good. Hector spoke with a heavy Spanish accent, and the moment he opened his mouth on-screen, American audiences would reject him. In *Mr. Nobody*, he allows himself to indulge in a certain bitterness. The future was grim, and the present was clouded by Hunt's growing financial problems. With each passing month, the damage had spread through every aspect of Kaleidoscope's operations. Budgets were cut, salaries went unpaid, and the high interest charges on short-term loans left Hunt in constant need of ready cash. He borrowed from his distributors against future box-office revenues, and when he reneged on several of these deals, theaters began refusing to show his films. Hector was doing his best work at this point, but the sad fact was that fewer and fewer people were able to see it.

Mr. Nobody is a response to this mounting frustration. The villain of the story is called C. Lester Chase, and once you've figured out the origins of this character's odd and artificial name, it becomes hard not to see him as a metaphorical stand-in for Hunt. Translate *hunt* into French, and the result is *chasse;* drop the second *s* from *chasse*, and you wind up with *chase*. When you further consider that *Seymour* can be read as *see more* and that *Lester* can be abbreviated as *Les*, which turns C. *Lester* into C. *Les* – or *see less* – then the evidence becomes fairly compelling. Chase is the most malevolent character in any of Hector's films. He is out to destroy Hector and rob him of his identity, and he puts his plan into action not by firing a bullet into Hector's back or by plunging a knife into his heart, but by tricking him into swallowing a magic potion that makes him invisible. In effect, this is just what Hunt did to Hector's career in the movies. He put him up on-screen, and then he made it all but impossible for anyone to see him. Hector doesn't vanish in *Mr. Nobody*, but once he drinks the drink, no one can see him anymore. He is still there before our eyes, but the other characters in the film are blind to his presence. He jumps up and down, he flaps his arms, he takes off his clothes on a crowded street corner, but no one notices. When he shouts in people's faces, his voice goes unheard. He is a specter made of flesh and blood, a man who is no longer a man. He still lives in the world, and yet the world has no room for him anymore. He has been murdered, but no one has had the courtesy or the thoughtfulness to kill him. He has simply been erased.

It is the first and only time that Hector presents himself as a rich man. In *Mr. Nobody*, he has everything a person could possibly want: a beautiful wife, two young children, and an enormous house with a full staff of servants. In the opening scene, Hector is eating breakfast with his family. There are some bright slapstick bits that revolve around the buttering of toast and a wasp that lands in a pot of jam, but the narrative purpose of the scene is to present us with a picture of happiness. We are being set up for the losses that are about to occur, and without this glimpse of Hector's private life (perfect marriage, perfect kids, domestic harmony in its most rhapsodic form), the evil business that lies ahead would not have the same impact. As it is, we are devastated by what happens to Hector. He kisses his wife good-bye, and the moment he turns away from her and leaves the house, he plunges headfirst into a nightmare.

Hector is the founder and president of a thriving soft-drink concern, the Fizzy Pop Beverage Corporation. Chase is his vice president and counselor, his supposed best friend. But Chase has accumulated heavy gambling debts and is being harassed by loan sharks to pay up what he owes or else. As Hector arrives at the office in the morning and greets his staff, Chase is in another room talking to a pair of rough-looking men. Don't worry, he says. You'll have your money by the end of the week. I'll be in control of the company by then, and the stock is worth millions. The thugs agree to give him a little more time. But this is your last chance, they tell him. Any more delays, and you'll be swimming with the fishes at the bottom of the river. The men stomp off. Chase wipes the sweat from his forehead and lets out a prolonged sigh. Then he removes a letter from the top drawer of his desk. He looks it over for a moment and appears to be immensely satisfied. With a wicked smirk, he folds it up and slips it into his inside breast pocket. Wheels are obviously turning, but we have no idea where they will take us.

Cut to Hector's office. Chase enters carrying something that resembles a large thermos bottle and asks Hector if he wants to taste the new flavor. What's it called? Hector asks. Jazzmatazz, Chase answers, and Hector nods his approval, impressed by the catchy ring to the word. Suspecting nothing, Hector allows Chase to pour him a hefty sample of the new concoction. As Hector takes hold of the glass, Chase looks on with a glint in his overwatchful eye, waiting for the poisonous brew to do its work. In a medium close-up, Hector lifts the glass to his mouth and takes a small, tentative sip. His nose wrinkles in disapproval; his eyes open wide; his mustache shimmies. The tone is entirely comic, and yet as Chase urges him on and Hector lifts the glass to his mouth for a second go at it, the sinister implications of *Jazzmatazz* become more and more apparent. Hector swallows down another portion of the drink. He smacks his lips, smiles up at Chase, and then shakes his head, as if to suggest that the flavor isn't quite right. Ignoring his boss's criticism, Chase looks down at his watch, spreads out the fingers of his right hand, and begins counting off the seconds from one to five. Hector is baffled. Before he can say anything, however, Chase arrives at the fifth and last second, and just like that, without any warning, Hector pitches forward in his chair and bangs his head against the top of his desk. We assume that the drink has knocked him out, that he is temporarily unconscious, but as Chase stands there watching him with blank and pitiless eyes, Hector begins to disappear. His arms go first, slowly fading from the screen and vanishing, and then his torso, and finally his head. One part of him follows another, and in the end his entire body has dissolved into nothingness. Chase walks out of the room and shuts the door behind him. Pausing in the hallway to savor his triumph, he leans his back against the door and smiles. A title card reads: *So long, Hector. It was nice knowing you.*

Chase walks off. Once he has left the frame, the camera holds on the door for a second or two, and then, very slowly, starts pushing in on the keyhole. It is a lovely shot, full of mystery and anticipation, and as the opening grows larger and larger, taking up more and more of the screen, we are able to look through into Hector's office. An instant later, we are inside the office itself, and because we expect to find it empty, we are not at all prepared for what the camera reveals to us. We see Hector slumped over his desk. He is still unconscious, but he is visible again, and as we try to absorb this sudden and miraculous turnaround, we can come to only one conclusion. The effects of the drink must have worn off. We have just watched Hector disappear, and if we are able to see him now, it can only mean that the drink was less powerful than we thought.

Hector begins to wake up. We feel comforted by this sign of life, back on safe ground. We assume that order has returned to the universe and that Hector will now set about to exact his revenge on Chase and expose him as a scoundrel. For the next twenty-odd seconds, he goes through one of his crispest, most pungent funny-man routines. Like someone trying to fight off a bad hangover, he stands up from his chair, all woozy and disoriented, and begins to stagger about the room. We laugh at this. We believe what our eyes are telling us, and because we are confident that Hector is back to normal, we can be amused by this spectacle of buckling knees and dizzy-headed collapse. But then Hector walks over to the mirror that is hanging on the wall, and everything turns again. He wants to look at himself. He wants to straighten his hair and readjust his tie, but when he peers into the oval of smooth, shining glass, his face isn't there. He has no reflection. He touches himself to make sure that he's real, to confirm the tangibility of his body, but when he looks into the mirror again, he still can't see himself. Hector is perplexed, but he doesn't panic. Maybe there's something wrong with the mirror.

He goes out into the hall. A secretary is walking by, carrying a bundle of papers in her arms. Hector smiles at her and gives a friendly wave, but she appears not to notice. Hector shrugs. Just then, two young clerks approach from the opposite direction. Hector makes a face at them. He growls. He sticks out his tongue. One of the clerks points to the door of Hector's office. Has the boss come in yet? he asks. I don't know, the other one answers. I haven't seen him. When he speaks these words, of course, Hector is standing directly in front of him, no more than six inches from his face.

The scene shifts to the living room of Hector's house. His wife is pacing back and forth, alternately wringing her hands and weeping into a handkerchief. There is no question that she has already heard the news about Hector's disappearance. Chase enters, the ignominious C. Lester Chase, author of the diabolical plot to rob Hector of his soft-drink empire. He pretends to console the poor woman, patting her on the shoulder and shaking his head in false despair. He extracts the mysterious letter from his inside breast pocket and hands it to her, explaining that he found it on Hector's desk that morning. Cut to an insert shot of the letter in extreme close-up. *Dearest Beloved*, it says. *Please forgive me. The doc says I'm suffering from a fatal disease and have only two months to live. To spare you the agony, I've decided to end it now. Don't worry about the business. The company is in good hands with Chase. I will always love you, Hector.* It doesn't take long for these lies and deceptions to do their work. In the next shot, we see the letter slip from the wife's fingers and flutter to the floor. It is all too much for her. The world has been turned upside down, and everything in it has been broken. Less than a second after that, she faints.

The camera follows her down to the floor, and then the image of her inert, recumbent body dissolves into a wide shot of Hector. He has left the office and is wandering the streets, trying to come to terms with the strange and terrible thing that has happened to him. To prove that all hope is really gone, he stops at a crowded intersection and strips down to his underwear. He does a little dance, he walks on his hands, he sticks out his fanny at the passing traffic, and when no one pays any attention to him, he glumly climbs back into his clothes and shuffles off. After that, Hector seems resigned to his fate. He doesn't fight against his condition so much as try to understand it, and rather than look for a way to make himself visible again (by confronting Chase, for example, or by searching for an antidote that would undo the effects of the drink), he embarks on a series of weird and impulsive experiments, an investigation of who he is and what he has become. Unexpectedly – with a sudden, lightning flick of his hand – he knocks off the hat of a passerby. So that's how things are, Hector seems to be saying to himself. A man can be invisible to everyone around him, but his body can still interact with the world. Another pedestrian approaches. Hector sticks out his foot and trips him. Yes, his hypothesis is surely correct, but that doesn't mean that more research isn't required. Warming to his task now, he picks up the hem of a woman's dress and studies her legs. He kisses another woman on the cheek, then a third woman on the mouth. He crosses out the letters on a stop sign, and an instant later a motorcycle slams into a trolley. He sneaks up behind two men, and by tapping each one on the shoulder and kicking them in the shins, he instigates a brawl. There is something cruel and childish about these pranks, but they are also satisfying to watch, and each one adds another fact to the growing body of evidence. Then, as Hector picks up an errant baseball that rolls toward him on the sidewalk, he makes his second important discovery. Once an invisible man takes hold of an object, it disappears from sight. It does not hover in the air; it is sucked into the void, into the same nothingness that encloses the man himself, and the moment it enters that haunted sphere, it is gone. The boy who lost the ball runs to the spot where he thinks it must have landed. The laws of physics dictate that the ball should be there, but it isn't. The boy is mystified. Seeing this, Hector puts the ball on the ground and walks away. The boy looks down, and lo and behold, the ball is there again, lying at his feet. What in the world has happened? The little episode ends with a close-up of the boy's startled face.

Hector rounds the corner and begins walking down the next boulevard. Almost immediately, he is confronted by a repulsive sight, a thing to make one's blood boil. A fat, well-dressed gentleman is stealing a copy of the *Morning Chronicle* from a blind newspaper boy. The man is out of coins, and because he's in a hurry, too rushed to bother breaking a bill, he just takes one of the papers and walks off. Outraged, Hector runs after him, and when the man stops at the corner to wait for a red light, Hector picks his pocket. This is both funny and disturbing. We don't feel the least bit sorry for the victim, but we're dumbfounded by how blithely Hector has taken the law into his own hands. Even when he walks back to the kiosk and turns the money over to the blind boy, we are not fully assuaged. In the first moments after the theft, we are led to believe that Hector will keep the money for himself, and in that small, dark interval we understand that he has not stolen the fat man's wallet in order to correct an injustice but simply because he knew that he could get away with it. His generosity is little more than an afterthought. Everything has become possible for him now, and he no longer has to obey the rules. He can do good if he wants to, but he can also do evil, and at this point we have no idea what decision he will make.

Back at the house, Hector's wife has taken to her bed.

In the office, Chase opens a strongbox and removes a thick pile of stock certificates. He sits down at his desk and begins to count them.

Meanwhile, Hector is about to commit his first major crime. He enters a jewelry store, and in front of half a dozen unseeing witnesses, our expunged and benighted hero empties a glass display case of its contents, calmly loading his pockets with fistfuls of watches, necklaces, and rings. He seems both amused and purposeful, and he goes about his business with a small but noticeable smile creasing the corners of his mouth. It appears to be a cold-blooded and capricious act, and from the evidence before our eyes, we have no choice but to conclude that Hector has been damned.

He leaves the store. Inexplicably, the first thing he does is head straight for a trash bin sitting on the curb. He sticks his arm deep into the rubbish and pulls out a paper bag. He has obviously put it there himself, but although the bag is filled with something, we don't know what it is. When Hector walks back to the front of the store, opens the bag, and begins sprinkling a powdery substance on the sidewalk, we are thoroughly confused. It could be dirt; it could be ashes; it could be gunpowder; but whatever the stuff is, it makes no sense that Hector should be putting it on the ground. In a matter of moments, there is a thin dark line extending from the front of the jewelry store to the edge of the street. Having covered the width of the sidewalk, Hector now advances into the street itself. Dodging cars, sidestepping trolleys, hopping in and out of trouble, he continues to empty the bag as he makes his way across, looking more and more like some mad farmer trying to plant a row of seeds. The line now stretches across the avenue. As Hector steps up onto the opposite curb and extends the line still further, we suddenly catch on. He is making a trail. We still don't know where it leads, but as he opens the door of the building in front of him and disappears through the entrance, we suspect that another trick is about to be played on us. The door closes behind him, and the angle abruptly changes. We are looking at a wide shot of the building Hector has just entered: the headquarters of the Fizzy Pop Beverage Corporation.

The action accelerates after that. In a flurry of quick expository scenes, the jewelry store manager discovers that he has been robbed, rushes out onto the sidewalk and flags down a cop, and then, with urgent, panic-stricken gestures, explains what has happened. The cop glances down, notices the dark line on the pavement, and then follows it with his eyes all the way to the Fizzy Pop building across the street. Looks like a clue, he says. Let's see where it goes, the manager says, and the two of them take off in the direction of the building.

Cut back to Hector. He is walking through a corridor now, carefully putting the finishing touches on his trail. He reaches the door of an office, and as he empties the last of the dirt onto the outer half of the sill, the camera tilts up to show us what is written on the door: C. LESTER CHASE, VICE PRESIDENT. Just then, with Hector still in a crouching position, the door swings open and out steps Chase himself. Hector manages to jump back at the last second – before Chase trips over him – and then, as the door begins to close, he slips in through the opening and waddles ducklike into the office. Even as the melodrama is building toward its climax, Hector continues to pile on the gags. Alone in the office, he sees the stock certificates spread out on Chase's desk. He scoops them up, evens out the edges with a meticulous flourish, and sticks them into his jacket. Then, in a series of rapid, stabbing gestures, he reaches into his side pockets and starts pulling out the jewels, heaping a great mountain of stolen goods onto Chase's blotter. As the last ring is added to the collection, Chase returns, rubbing his hands together and looking inordinately pleased with himself. Hector steps back. His work is finished now, and all that remains is to watch his enemy get what's coming to him.

It happens in a whirl of astonishment and misapprehension, of justice done and justice betrayed. At first, the jewels distract Chase from noticing that the stocks are gone. Time is lost, and when he finally digs under the glittering pile and sees that the certificates aren't there anymore, it is too late. The door bursts open, and in rush the cop and the store manager. The jewels are identified, the crime is solved, and the thief is put under arrest. It doesn't matter that Chase is innocent. The trail has led to his door, and they've caught him red-handed with the merchandise. He protests, of course, tries to escape through the window, begins hurling Fizzy Pop bottles at his attackers, but after some wild business involving a billy club and a bayonet, he is at last overwhelmed. Hector looks on with grim insouciance. Even as Chase is put into handcuffs and led out of the office, Hector does not rejoice in his victory. His plan has worked to perfection, but what good has it done him? The day is drawing to a close now, and he is still invisible.

He goes outside again and starts walking through the streets. The downtown boulevards are deserted, and Hector appears to be the only person left in the city. What has happened to the crowds and commotion that surrounded him before? Where are the cars and trolleys, the masses of people thronging the sidewalk? For a moment we wonder if the spell has not been reversed. Perhaps Hector is visible again, we think, and everyone else has vanished. Then, out of nowhere, a truck drives by, speeding through a puddle. Plumes of water rise up from the pavement, splashing everything in sight. Hector is drenched, but when the camera turns around to show us the damage, the front of his suit is spotless. It should be a funny moment, but it isn't, and in that Hector deliberately makes it *not* funny (a long, doleful look at his suit; the disappointment in his eyes when he sees that he is not splattered with mud), this simple trick alters the mood of the film. As night falls, we see him returning to his house. He goes in, climbs the stairs to the second floor, and enters his children's bedroom. The little girl and the little boy are asleep, each one in a separate bed. He sits down beside the girl, studies her face for a few moments, and then lifts his hand to begin stroking her hair. Just as he is about to touch her, however, he stops himself, suddenly realizing that his hand could wake her, and if she woke up in the darkness and found no one there, she would be frightened. It's an affecting sequence, and Hector plays it with restraint and simplicity. He has lost the right to touch his own daughter, and as we watch him hesitate and then finally withdraw his hand, we experience the full impact of the curse that has been put on him. In that one small gesture – the hand hovering in the air, the open palm no more than an inch from the girl's head – we understand that Hector has been reduced to nothing.

Like a ghost, he stands up and leaves the room. He walks down the hall, opens a door, and goes in. It is his bedroom, and there is his wife, his Dearest Beloved, asleep in their bed. Hector pauses. She is thrashing about, tossing back and forth and kicking off the covers, in the grip of some terrifying dream. Hector approaches the bed and cautiously re-arranges the blankets, props up the pillows, and turns off the lamp on the bedside table. Her fitful movements begin to subside, and before long she has fallen into a sound and tranquil sleep. Hector backs away, blows her a little kiss, and then sits down in a chair near the foot of the bed. It looks as if he intends to stay there for the night, watching over her like some benevolent spirit. Even if he can't touch her or talk to her, he can protect her and feed on the power of her presence. But invisible men are not immune to exhaustion. They have bodies just like everyone else, and like everyone else they have to sleep. Hector's eyelids begin to grow heavy. They flutter and sag, they close and then open again, and even though he jerks himself awake a couple of times, it is clearly a los-ing battle. A moment later, he succumbs.

The screen fades to black. When the picture returns, it is morning, and daylight is flooding through the curtains. Cut to a shot of Hector's wife, still asleep in bed. Then cut to Hector, asleep in the chair. His body is contorted into an impossible position, a comic tangle of splayed limbs and twisted joints, and because we aren't prepared for the sight of this slumbering pretzel-man, we laugh, and with that laugh the mood of the film changes again. Dearest Beloved wakes first, and as she opens her eyes and sits up in bed, her face tells us everything – moving rapidly from joy to disbelief to guarded optimism. She springs out of bed and rushes over to Hector. She touches his face (which is dangling backward over the arm of the chair), and Hector's body goes into a spasm of high-voltage shocks, jumping around in a flurry of arms and legs that ulti-mately lands him in an upright position. Then he opens his eyes. Involuntarily, without seeming to remember that he is supposed to be invisible, he smiles at her. They kiss, but just as their lips come into con-tact, he recoils in confusion. Is he really there? Has the spell been bro-ken, or is he only dreaming it? He touches his face, he runs his hands over his chest, and then he looks his wife in the eyes. Can you see me? he asks. Of course I can see you, she says, and as her eyes fill with tears, she leans forward and kisses him again. But Hector is not convinced. He stands up from his chair and walks over to a mirror hanging on the wall. The proof is in the mirror, and if he is able to see his reflection, he will

know that the nightmare is over. That he does see it is a foregone conclusion, but the beautiful thing about that moment is the slowness of his
response. For a second or two, the expression on his face remains the
same, and as he peers into the eyes of the man staring back at him from
the wall, it's as if he's looking at a stranger, encountering the face of a
man he has never seen before. Then, as the camera moves in for a closer
shot, Hector begins to smile. Coming on the heels of that chilling blankness, the smile suggests something more than a simple rediscovery of
himself. He is no longer looking at the old Hector. He is someone else
now, and however much he might resemble the person he used to be, he
has been reinvented, turned inside-out, and spat forth as a new man.
The smile grows larger, more radiant, more satisfied with the face that
has been found in the mirror. A circle begins to close around it, and soon
we can see nothing but that smiling mouth, the mouth and the mustache
above it. The mustache twitches for a few seconds, and then the circle
grows smaller, then smaller still. When it finally shuts, the film is over.

In effect, Hector's career ends with that smile. He fulfilled the terms of
his contract by producing one more film, but *Double or Nothing* cannot
be counted as a new work. Kaleidoscope was all but bankrupt then, and
there wasn't enough money left to mount another full-scale production.
Instead, Hector pulled out bits of rejected material from previous films
and cobbled them together into an anthology of gags, pratfalls, and
slapstick improvisations. It was an ingenious salvage operation, but we
learn nothing from it except for what it reveals to us about Hector's talents as an editor. To assess his work fairly, we have to look at *Mr.
Nobody* as his last film. It is a meditation on his own disappearance, and
for all its ambiguity and furtive suggestiveness, for all the moral questions it asks and then refuses to answer, it is essentially a film about the
anguish of selfhood. Hector is looking for a way to say good-bye to us,
to bid farewell to the world, and in order to do that he must eradicate
himself in his own eyes. He becomes invisible, and when the magic
finally wears off and he can be seen again, he does not recognize his
own face. We are looking at him as he looks at himself, and in this eerie
doubling of perspectives, we watch him confront the fact of his own
annihilation. Double or nothing. That was the phrase he chose as the
title for his next film. Those words are not even remotely connected to
anything presented in that eighteen-minute hodgepodge of stunts and
gambols. They refer back to the mirror scene in *Mr. Nobody*, and once
Hector breaks into that extraordinary smile, we are given a brief

glimpse of what the future has in store for him. He allows himself to be
born again with that smile, but he is no longer the same person, no
longer the Hector Mann who has amused us and entertained us for the
past year. We see him transformed into someone we no longer recognize, and before we can absorb who this new Hector might be, he is
gone. A circle closes around his face, and he is swallowed up by the
blackness. An instant later, for the first and only time in any of his films,
the words THE END are written out across the screen, and that is the last
anyone ever sees of him.

I wrote the book in less than nine months. The manuscript came to more than three hundred typed pages, and every one of those pages was a struggle for me. If I managed to finish, it was only because I did nothing else. I worked seven days a week, sitting at the desk from ten to twelve hours a day, and except for my little excursions to Montague Street to stock up on food and paper, ink and typewriter ribbons, I rarely left the apartment. I had no telephone, no radio or TV, no social life of any kind. Once in April and again in August I traveled by subway to Manhattan to consult some books at the public library, but other than that I didn't budge from Brooklyn. But I wasn't really in Brooklyn either. I was in the book, and the book was in my head, and as long as I stayed inside my head, I could go on writing the book. It was like living in a padded cell, but of all the lives I could have lived at that moment, it was the only one that made sense to me. I wasn't capable of being in the world, and I knew that if I tried to go back into it before I was ready, I would be crushed. So I holed up in that small apartment and spent my days writing about Hector Mann. It was slow work, perhaps even meaningless work, but it demanded all my attention for nine straight months, and in that I was too busy to think about anything else, it probably kept me from going insane.

In late April, I wrote to Smits and asked him to extend my leave of absence through the fall semester. I was still undecided about my long-range plans, I said, but unless things changed dramatically for me in the next few months, I was probably finished with teaching – if not for good, then at least for a long while. I hoped he would forgive me. It wasn't that I had lost interest. I just wasn't sure if my legs would hold me when I stood up and tried to talk in front of students.

I was slowly getting used to being without Helen and the boys, but that didn't mean I had made any progress. I didn't know who I was, and I didn't know what I wanted, and until I found a way to live with other people again, I would continue to be something only half human. All through the writing of the book, I intentionally put off thinking about the future. A sensible plan would have been to stay in New York, to buy some furniture for the apartment I had rented and begin a new life there, but when the moment came for me to take the next step, I decided against it and returned to Vermont. I was in the last throes of revising the manuscript then, getting ready to type up the final draft and submit the book for publication, when it suddenly occurred to me that New York was the book, and once the book was over I should leave New York and go somewhere else. Vermont was probably the worst choice I could have made, but it was familiar ground to me, and I knew that if I went back there I would be close to Helen again, that I would be able to breathe the same air we had breathed together when she was still alive. There was comfort in that thought. I couldn't go back to the old house in Hampton, but there were other houses in other towns, and as long as I remained in the general area, I could carry on with my crazed, solitary life without having to turn my back on the past. I wasn't ready to let go yet. It had been only a year and a half, and I wanted my grief to continue. All I needed was another project to work on, another ocean to drown myself in.

I wound up buying a place in the town of West T—, about twenty-five miles south of Hampton. It was a ridiculous little house, a kind of pre-fab ski chalet with wall-to-wall carpeting and an electric fireplace, but its ugliness was so extreme that it verged on the beautiful. It had no charm or character, no lovingly wrought details to delude one into thinking it could ever become a home. It was a hospital for the living dead, a way station for the mentally afflicted, and to inhabit those blank, depersonalized interiors was to understand that the world was an illusion that had to be reinvented every day. For all the flaws in its design, however, the dimensions of the house struck me as ideal. They weren't so large that you felt lost in them, and they weren't so small that you felt hemmed in. There was a kitchen with skylights in the ceiling; a sunken living room with a picture window and two empty walls high enough to accommodate shelves for my books; a loggia overlooking the living room; and three identically proportioned bedrooms: one for sleeping, one for working, and one for storing the things I no longer had the heart to look at but couldn't bring myself to throw away. It was the right size and shape for a man who meant to live alone, and it had the further advantage of complete isolation. Situated halfway up a mountain and surrounded by thick stands of birch, spruce, and maple trees, it was accessible only by dirt road. If I didn't want to see anyone, I didn't have to. More important, no one would have to see me.

I moved in just after the first of the year, 1987, and for the next six weeks I devoted myself to practical matters: building bookcases, installing a wood-burning stove, selling my car and replacing it with a four-wheel-drive pickup truck. The mountain was treacherous when it snowed, and since it snowed nearly all the time, I needed something that would get me up and down without turning every trip into an adventure. I hired a plumber and an electrician to repair pipes and wires, painted walls, laid in a winter's worth of cordwood, and bought myself a computer, a radio, and a combination telephone–fax machine. Meanwhile, *The Silent World of Hector Mann* was slowly making its way through the circuitous channels of academic-press publication. Unlike other books, scholarly books are not accepted or rejected by a single in-house editor. Copies of the manuscript are sent out to various specialists in the field, and nothing happens until those people have read the submission and mailed in their reports. The fees for such work are minimal (a couple of hundred dollars at best), and since the readers tend to be professors who are busy teaching and writing books of their own, the process often drags. In my case, I waited from the middle of November until the end of March before I had an answer. By then, I was so absorbed in something else that I nearly forgot that I had sent them the manuscript. I was glad that they wanted it, of course, glad that I had something to show for my efforts, but I can't say that it meant that much to me. It was good news for Hector Mann, perhaps, good news for antique-movie hounds and connoisseurs of black mustaches, but now that the experience was behind me, I rarely thought about it anymore. On the few occasions when I did, I felt as if the book had been written by someone else.

In mid-February, I received a letter from a former graduate school classmate, Alex Kronenberg, who now taught at Columbia. I had last seen him at the memorial service for Helen and the boys, and although we hadn't spoken to each other since, I still considered him to be a solid friend. (His condolence letter had been a model of eloquence and compassion, the best letter I received from anyone.) He started off his new letter by apologizing for not having been in touch sooner. He had been thinking about me a lot, he said, and had heard through the grapevine that I was on leave from Hampton and had spent some months living in New York. He was sorry that I hadn't called. If he had known that I was there, he would have been immensely glad to see me. Those were his precise words – *immensely glad* – a typical Alex locution. In any case, the next paragraph began, he had recently been asked by Columbia University Press to edit a new series of books, the Library of World Classics. A man with the incongruous name of Dexter Feinbaum, a 1927 graduate of the Columbia School of Engineering, had bequeathed them four and a half million dollars for the purpose of starting this collection. The idea was to bring together the acknowledged masterpieces of world literature in one uniform line of books. Everything from Meister Eckhart to Fernando Pessoa would be included, and in cases where the existing translations were deemed inadequate, new translations would be commissioned. *It's a mad enterprise,* Alex wrote, *but they've put me in charge as executive editor, and in spite of all the extra work (I don't sleep anymore), I have to admit that I'm enjoying myself. In his will, Feinbaum made a list of the first one hundred titles he wanted to see published. He got rich by manufacturing aluminum siding, but you can't fault him for his taste in literature. One of the books was Chateaubriand's* Mémoires d'outre-tombe. *I still haven't read the cursed thing, all two thousand pages of it, but I remember what you said to me one night in 1971 somewhere on the Yale campus – it might have been near that little plaza just outside the Beinecke – and I'm going to repeat it to you now. 'This,' you said (holding up the first volume of the French edition and waving it in the air), 'is the best autobiography ever written.' I don't know if you still feel that way now, but I probably don't have to tell you that there have been only two complete translations since the book was published in 1848. One in 1849 and one in 1902. It's high time someone did another, don't you think? I have no idea if you're still interested in translating books, but if you are, I would love it if you agreed to do this one for us.*

I had a telephone now. It wasn't that I was hoping anyone would call me, but I figured I should have one put in just in case something went wrong. I had no neighbors up there, and if the roof fell in or the house caught fire, I wanted to be able to ring for help. This was one of my few concessions to reality, a grudging acknowledgment that I was not in fact the only person left in the world. Normally, I would have answered Alex by letter, but I happened to be in the kitchen when I opened the mail that afternoon, and the phone was right there, sitting on the counter not two feet from my hand. Alex had recently moved, and his new address and number were written out just below his signature. It was too tempting not to take advantage of all this, so I picked up the receiver and dialed.

The phone rang four times on the other end, and then an answering machine clicked on. Unexpectedly, the message was spoken by a child. After three or four words, I recognized the voice as that of Alex's son. Jacob must have been around ten at that point, roughly a year and a half older than Todd – or a year and a half older than Todd would have been if he had still been alive. The little boy said: It's the bottom of the ninth. The bases are loaded, and two men are out. The score is four to three, my team is losing, and I'm up. If I get a hit, we win the game. Here comes the pitch. I swing. It's a ground ball. I drop the bat and start running. The second baseman scoops up the grounder, throws to first, and I'm out. Yes, that's right, folks, I'm out. Jacob is out. And so is my father, Alex; my mother, Barbara; and my sister, Julie. The whole family is out right now. Please leave a message after the beep, and we'll call you back just as soon as we round the bases and come home.

It was a cute bit of nonsense, but it rattled me. When the beep sounded after the message was over, I couldn't think of anything to say, and rather than let the tape run on in silence, I hung up. I had never liked talking into those machines. They made me nervous and uncomfortable, but listening to Jacob had spun me around and knocked me off my feet, pushed me into something close to despair. There had been too much happiness in his voice, too much laughter spilling out from the edges of the words. Todd had been a bright and clever little boy, too, but he wasn't eight and a half now, he was seven, and he would go on being seven even after Jacob was a grown man.

I gave myself a few minutes, and then I tried again. I knew what to expect now, and when the message came on for the second time, I held the phone away from my ear so that I wouldn't have to listen to it. The words seemed to go on forever, but when the beep cut them off at last, I brought the phone to my ear again and started to talk. Alex, I said. I've just read your letter, and I want you to know that I'm willing to do the translation. Considering how long the book is, you shouldn't count on seeing a finished manuscript for two or three years. But I assume you're aware of that already. I'm still settling in here, but once I learn how to use the computer I bought last week, I'll get started. Thanks for the invitation. I've been casting about for something to do, and I think I'll enjoy this. Best to Barbara and the kids. Talk to you soon, I hope.

He called back that same evening, both startled and happy that I had accepted. It was just a shot in the dark, he said, but it wouldn't have felt right if I hadn't asked you first. I can't tell you how glad I am.

I'm glad you're glad, I said.

I'll tell them to send you a contract tomorrow. Just to make everything official.

Whatever you say. The fact is, I think I've already figured out how to translate the title.

Mémoires d'outre-tombe. Memoirs from Beyond the Grave.

That feels awkward to me. Too literal, somehow, and yet at the same time difficult to understand.

What do you have in mind?

Memoirs of a Dead Man.

Interesting.

It's not bad, is it?

No, not bad at all. I like it a lot.

The important thing is that it makes sense. It took Chateaubriand thirty-five years to write the book, and he didn't want it to be published until fifty years after his death. It's literally written in the voice of a dead man.

But it didn't take fifty years. The book was published in 1848, the same year he died.

He ran into financial difficulties. After the revolution of 1830, his political career was over, and he fell into debt. Madame Récamier, his mistress of the past dozen years or so – yes, *that* Madame Récamier – talked him into giving some private readings from the *Memoirs* to small, select audiences in her drawing room. The idea was to find a publisher willing to pay Chateaubriand an advance, to give him money for a work that wouldn't be coming out for years. The plan failed, but response to the book was extraordinarily good. The *Memoirs* became the most celebrated unfinished, unpublished, unread book in history. But Chateaubriand was still broke. So Madame Récamier came up with a new scheme, and this one worked – or sort of worked. A stock company was formed, and people bought shares in the manuscript. Word futures, I guess you could call them, in the same way that people from Wall Street gamble on the price of soybeans and corn. In effect, Chateaubriand mortgaged his autobiography to finance his old age. They gave him a nice chunk of money up front, which allowed him to pay off his creditors, and a guaranteed annuity for the rest of his life. It was a brilliant arrangement. The only problem was that Chateaubriand kept on living. The company was formed when he was in his mid-sixties, and he hung on until he was eighty. By then, the shares had changed hands several times, and the friends and admirers who had invested in the beginning were long gone. Chateaubriand was owned by a bunch of strangers. The only thing they were interested in was turning a profit, and the longer he went on living, the more they wanted him to die. Those last years must have been bleak for him. A frail old man crippled with rheumatism, Madame Récamier all but blind, and every one of his friends dead and buried. But he kept on revising the manuscript right up to the end.

What a cheerful story.

Not so funny, I suppose, but let me tell you, the old viscount could write one hell of a good sentence. It's an incredible book, Alex.

So you're saying you don't mind spending the next two or three years of your life with a gloomy Frenchman?

I've just spent a year with a silent-film comedian, and I think I'm ready for a change.

Silent film? I hadn't heard anything about that.

Someone named Hector Mann. I finished writing a book about him in the fall.

You've been busy, then. That's good.

I had to do something. So I decided to do that.

Why haven't I heard of this actor? Not that I know anything about movies, but the name doesn't ring a bell.

No one's heard of him. He's my own private funny man, a court jester who performs only for me. For twelve or thirteen months, I spent every waking moment with him.

You mean you were actually with him? Or is that just a figure of speech?

No one's been with Hector Mann since 1929. He's dead. As dead as Chateaubriand and Madame Récamier. As dead as Dexter What's-His-Name.

Feinbaum.

As dead as Dexter Feinbaum.

So you spent a year watching old movies.

Not exactly. I spent three months watching old movies, and then I locked myself in a room and spent nine months writing about them. It's probably the strangest thing I've ever done. I was writing about things I couldn't see anymore, and I had to present them in purely visual terms. The whole experience was like a hallucination.

And what about the living, David? Do you spend much time with them?

As little as possible.

That's what I thought you'd say.

I had a conversation in Washington last year with a man named Singh. Dr. J. M. Singh. An excellent person, and I enjoyed the time I spent with him. He did me a great service.

Are you seeing a doctor now?

Of course not. This chat we're having now is the longest talk I've had with anyone since then.

You should have called me when you were in New York.

I couldn't.

You're not even forty, David. Life isn't over, you know.

Actually, I turn forty next month. There's going to be a big bash at Madison Square Garden on the fifteenth, and I hope you and Barbara will be able to come. I'm surprised you haven't received your invitation yet.

Everyone's worried about you, that's all. I don't want to pry, but when someone you care about behaves like this, it's hard just to stand by and watch. I wish you'd give me a chance to help.

You have helped. You've offered me a new job, and I'm grateful to you.

That's work. I'm talking about life.

Is there a difference?

You're a stubborn son-of-a-bitch, aren't you?

Tell me something about Dexter Feinbaum. The man's my benefactor, after all, and I don't even know the first thing about him.

You're not going to talk about this, are you?

As our old friend in the dead-letter office used to say: I would prefer not to.

No one can live without other people, David. It's just not possible.

Maybe not. But no one's ever been me before. Maybe I'm the first one.

From the introduction to *Memoirs of a Dead Man* (Paris, April 14, 1846; revised July 28):

As it is impossible for me to foresee the moment of my death, and as at my age the days granted to men are only days of grace, or rather of suffering, I feel compelled to offer a few words of explanation.

On September fourth, I will be seventy-eight years old. It is full time for me to leave a world which is fast leaving me, and which I shall not regret . . .

Sad necessity, which has forever held its foot against my throat, has forced me to sell my Memoirs. *No one can imagine what I have suffered in being obliged to pawn my tomb, but I owed this last sacrifice to my solemn promises and the consistency of my conduct . . . My plan was to bequeath them to Madame Chateaubriand. She would have sent them out into the world or suppressed them, as she saw fit. Now more than ever, I believe the latter solution would have been preferable . . .*

These Memoirs *have been composed at different times and in different countries. For that reason, it has been necessary for me to add prologues that describe the places which were before my eyes and the feelings which were in my heart when the thread of my narrative was resumed. The changing forms of my life are thus intermingled with one another. It has sometimes happened to me in my moments of prosperity to have to speak of my days of hardship; and in my times of tribulation to retrace the periods of my happiness. My youth entering into my old age, the gravity of my later years tingeing and saddening the years of my innocence, the rays of my sun crossing and blending together from the moment of its rising to the moment of its setting, have produced in my stories a kind of confusion – or, if you will, a kind of mysterious unity. My cradle recalls something of my tomb, my tomb something of my cradle; my sufferings become pleasures, my pleasures sufferings; and, now that I have completed the perusal of these* Memoirs, *I am no longer certain if they are the product of a youthful mind or a head gray with age.*

I cannot know if this mixture will be pleasing or displeasing to the reader. There is nothing I can do to remedy it. It is the result of my changing fortunes, the inconsistency of my lot. Its storms have often left me with no table to write on but the rock on which I have been shipwrecked.

I have been urged to allow some portions of these Memoirs *to appear in my lifetime, but I prefer to speak from the depths of my tomb. My narrative will thus be accompanied by those voices which have something sacred about them because they come from the sepulchre. If I have suffered enough in this world to be turned into a happy shadow in the next, a ray from the Elysian Fields will throw a protective light on these last pictures of mine. Life sits heavily on me; perhaps death will suit me better.*

These Memoirs *have held a special importance for me. Saint Bonaventure was granted permission to go on writing his book after he was dead. I cannot hope for such a favor, but if nothing else I should like to be resurrected at some midnight hour in order to correct the proofs of mine . . .*

If any part of my labors has been more satisfying to me than the others, it is that which relates to my youth – the most hidden corner of my life. In it I have had to reawaken a world known only to myself, and as I wandered around in

THE BOOK OF ILLUSIONS

that vanished realm, I have encountered only silence and memories. Of all the people I have known, how many are still alive today?

. . . If I should die outside of France, I request that my body not be brought back to my native country until fifty years have elapsed since its first inhumation. Let my remains be spared a sacrilegious autopsy; let no one search my lifeless brain and extinguished heart to discover the mystery of my being. Death does not reveal the secrets of life. The idea of a corpse traveling by post fills me with horror, but dry and moldering bones are easily transported. They will be less weary on that final voyage than when I dragged them around this earth, burdened down by the weight of my troubles.

I started working on those pages the morning after my conversation with Alex. I could do that because I owned a copy of the book (the two-volume Pléiade edition compiled by Levaillant and Moulinier, complete with variants, notes, and appendices) and had held it in my hands just three days before Alex's letter arrived. Earlier that week, I had finished installing my new bookcases. For several hours every day, I had been unpacking books and putting them on the shelves, and somewhere in the midst of that tedious operation, I had stumbled across the Chateaubriand. I hadn't looked at the *Memoirs* in years, but that morning, in the chaos of my Vermont living room, surrounded by empty, overturned boxes and towers of unclassified books, I had impulsively opened them again. The first thing my eyes had fallen upon was a short passage in volume one. In it, Chateaubriand tells of accompanying a Breton poet on an outing to Versailles in June of 1789. It was less than a month before the taking of the Bastille, and halfway through their visit they spotted Marie-Antoinette walking by with her two children. *Casting a smiling look in my direction, she gave me the same gracious salute that I had received from her on the day of my presentation. I shall never forget that look of hers, which was soon to be no more. When Marie-Antoinette smiled, the shape of her mouth was so clear that (horrible thought!) the memory of that smile enabled me to recognize the jaw of this daughter of kings when the head of the unfortunate woman was discovered in the exhumations of 1815.*

It was a fierce, breathtaking image, and I kept thinking about it long after I had closed the book and put it on the shelf. Marie-Antoinette's severed head, unearthed from a pit of human remains. In three short sentences, Chateaubriand travels twenty-six years. He goes from flesh to bone, from piquant life to anonymous death, and in the chasm between them lies the experience of an entire generation, the unspoken years of terror, brutality, and madness. I was stunned by the passage, moved by it in a way that no words had moved me in a year and a half. Then, just three days after my accidental encounter with those sentences, I received Alex's letter asking me to translate the book. Was it a coincidence? Of course it was, but at the time I felt as though I had willed it to happen – as though Alex's letter had somehow completed a thought I was unable to finish myself. In the past, I had never been one to believe in mystical claptrap of that sort. But when you live as I was living then, all shut up inside yourself and not bothering to look at anything around you, your perspective begins to change. For the fact was that Alex's letter was dated Monday the ninth, and I had received it on Thursday the twelfth, three days later. Which meant that when he was in New York writing to me about the book, I had been in Vermont holding the book in my hands. I don't want to insist on the importance of the connection, but I couldn't help reading it as a sign. It was as if I had asked for something without knowing it, and then suddenly my wish had been granted.

So I settled down and began working again. I forgot about Hector Mann and thought only about Chateaubriand, burying myself in the massive chronicle of a life that had nothing to do with my life. That was what appealed to me most about the job: the distance, the sheer distance between myself and what I was doing. It had been good to camp out for a year in 1920s America; it was even better to spend my days in eighteenth- and nineteenth-century France. The snow fell on my little mountain in Vermont, but I scarcely paid any attention. I was in Saint-Malo and Paris, in Ohio and Florida, in England, Rome, and Berlin. Much of the work was mechanical, and because I was the servant of the text and not its creator, it demanded a different kind of energy from the one I had put into writing *The Silent World*. Translation is a bit like shoveling coal. You scoop it up and toss it into the furnace. Each lump is a word, and each shovelful is another sentence, and if your back is strong enough and you have the stamina to keep at it for eight or ten hours at a stretch, you can keep the fire hot. With close to a million words in front of me, I was prepared to work as long and as hard as necessary, even if it meant burning down the house.

For most of that first winter, I didn't go anywhere. Once every ten days, I would drive to the Grand Union in Brattleboro to shop for food, but that was the only thing I allowed to interrupt my routine. Brattleboro was a good distance out of my way, but by driving those extra twenty miles I figured I could avoid running into anyone I knew. The Hampton crowd tended to shop at another Grand Union just north of the college, and the chances of any of them turning up in Brattleboro were slim. But that didn't mean it couldn't happen, and in spite of my cautious planning, the strategy eventually backfired on me. One afternoon in March, as I was loading up my cart with toilet paper in aisle six, I found myself cornered by Greg and Mary Tellefson. This led to an invitation to dinner, and even though I did my best to worm out of it, Mary kept juggling the dates until I had run out of imaginary excuses. Twelve nights later, I drove to their house at the edge of the Hampton campus, less than a mile from where I had lived with Helen and the boys. If it had just been the two of them, it might not have been such an ordeal for me, but Greg and Mary had taken it upon themselves to invite twenty other people, and I wasn't prepared for such a crowd. They were all friendly, of course, and most of them were probably glad to see me, but I felt awkward, out of my element, and every time I opened my mouth to say something, I found myself saying the wrong thing. I wasn't up on the Hampton gossip anymore. They all assumed that I would want to hear about the latest intrigues and embarrassments, the divorces and extramarital affairs, the promotions and departmental quarrels, but the truth was that I found it unbearably dull. I would drift away from the conversation, and a moment later I would find myself surrounded by another group of people engaged in a different but similar conversation. No one was tactless enough to mention Helen (academics are too polite for that), and therefore they stuck to supposedly neutral subjects: recent news items, politics, sports. I had no idea what they were talking about. I hadn't looked at a paper in over a year, and as far as I was concerned, they could have been referring to events that had taken place in another world.

The party began with everyone milling around on the ground floor, wandering in and out of rooms, clustering together for a few minutes and then breaking apart to form new clusters in other rooms. I went from the living room to the dining room to the kitchen to the den, and at some point Greg caught up with me and put a scotch and soda in my hand. I took it without thinking, and because I was anxious and ill at ease, I drank it down in about twenty-four seconds. It was the first drop of alcohol I had had in more than a year. I had succumbed to the temptations of various hotel minibars while doing my research on Hector Mann, but I had sworn off liquor after I'd moved to Brooklyn and

171

started writing the book. I didn't particularly crave the stuff when it wasn't around, but I knew that I was only a few weak moments away from creating a bad problem for myself. My behavior after the plane crash had convinced me of that, and if I hadn't picked myself up and left Vermont when I did, I probably wouldn't have lived long enough to be attending Greg and Mary's party – not to speak of being in a position to wonder why the hell I had come back.

After I finished the drink, I went to the bar for a refill, but this time I dispensed with the soda and added only ice to the glass. For the third one, I forgot about the ice and poured it straight.

When dinner was ready, the guests lined up around the dinner table, filled their plates with food, and then scattered into other parts of the house to look for chairs. I wound up on the sofa in the den, wedged between the armrest and Karin Müller, an assistant professor in the German department. My coordination was already a bit wobbly by then, and as I sat there with a plateful of salad and beef stew balanced precariously on my knee, I turned to retrieve my drink from the back of the sofa (where I had placed it before sitting down), and no sooner did I take hold of the glass than it slipped out of my hand. A quadruple shot of Johnnie Walker splashed against Karin's neck, and then, an instant later, the glass clunked against her spine. She jumped – how could she not jump? – and when she did, she knocked over her own plate of stew and salad, which not only sent my plate crashing to the floor, but landed upside down on my lap.

It was hardly a major catastrophe, but I had drunk too much to know that, and with my pants suddenly drenched in olive oil and my shirt splattered with gravy, I chose to take offense. I don't remember what I said, but it was something cruel and insulting, an utterly uncalled-for remark. *Clumsy cow.* I think that was it. But it also might have been *stupid cow*, or else *stupid, clumsy cow*. Whatever the words were, they expressed an anger that must never be articulated under any circumstances, least of all when they can be overheard by a roomful of edgy, high-strung college professors. There is probably no need to add that Karin was neither stupid nor clumsy; and far from resembling a cow, she was an attractive, slender woman in her late thirties who taught courses on Goethe and Hölderlin and had never shown anything but the greatest respect and kindness toward me. Just seconds before the accident, she had invited me to give a talk to one of her classes, and I was clearing my throat and getting ready to tell her that I would have to think it over when the drink spilled. It was entirely my fault, and yet I immediately turned around and put the blame on her. It was a disgusting outburst, yet one more proof that I wasn't fit to be let out of my cage. Karin had made a friendly overture to me, had in fact been giving off tentative, ever so subtle signs that she was available for more intimate conversations on any number of subjects, and I, who had not touched a woman in almost two years, found myself responding to those nearly imperceptible hints and imagining, in the crude and vulgar way of a man with too much alcohol in his blood, what she would look like without any clothes on. Was that why I snapped at her so viciously? Was my self-loathing so great that I had to punish her for awakening a glimmer of sexual arousal in me? Or did I secretly know that she was doing nothing of the kind and that the whole little drama was my own invention, a moment of lust brought on by the nearness of her warm, perfumed body?

To make matters worse, I wasn't the least bit sorry when she started to cry. We were both standing by then, and when I saw Karin's lower lip begin to tremble and the corners of her eyes fill with tears, I was glad, almost jubilant over the consternation I had caused. There were six or seven other people in the room just then, and they had all turned in our direction after Karin's first yelp of surprise. The noise of clattering plates had brought several more guests to the threshold, and when I came out with my obnoxious remark, there were at least a dozen witnesses who heard it. Everything went silent after that. It was a moment of collective shock, and for the next couple of seconds no one knew what to say or do. In that small interval of breathlessness and uncertainty, Karin's hurt turned to anger.

You have no right to talk to me like that, David, she said. Who do you think you are?

Fortunately, Mary was one of the people who had come to the doorway, and before I could do any further damage, she rushed into the room and took hold of my arm.

David didn't mean it, she said to Karin. Did you, David? It was just one of those things that come flying out on the spur of the moment.

I wanted to say something harsh and contradictory, something that would prove I'd meant every word I'd said, but I held my tongue. It took all my powers of self-control to do that, but Mary had gone out of her way to act as peacemaker, and a part of me knew that I would regret causing her any more trouble. Even so, I didn't apologize, and I didn't try to make nice. Rather than say the thing I wanted to say, I freed my arm from her grasp and left the room, walking out of the den and across the living room as my former colleagues looked on and said nothing.

I went straight upstairs to Greg and Mary's bedroom. My plan was to grab my things and leave, but my parka was buried under a massive pile of coats on the bed, and I couldn't find it. After digging around for a little while, I started tossing the coats onto the floor, eliminating possibilities in order to simplify my search. Just when I had come to the halfway point – more coats off the bed than on – Mary walked into the room. She was a short, round-faced woman with blond frizzy hair and reddish cheeks, and as she stood in the doorway with her hands on her hips, I immediately understood that she'd had it with me. I felt like a child about to be scolded by his mother.

What are you doing? she said.

Looking for my coat.

It's in the downstairs closet. Don't you remember?

I thought it was here.

It's downstairs. Greg put it in the closet when you came. You were the one who found the hanger for him.

All right, I'll look for it downstairs.

But Mary wasn't about to let me off so easily. She took a few more steps into the room, bent down for a coat, and flung it angrily onto the bed. Then she picked up another coat and threw that one onto the bed as well. She went on collecting coats, and each time she thwacked another one down on the bed, she interrupted what she was saying in mid-sentence. The coats were like punctuation marks – sudden dashes, hasty ellipses, violent exclamation points – and each one broke through her words like an axe.

When you go downstairs, she said, I want you to . . . make up with Karin . . . I don't care if you have to get down on your knees . . . and beg for her forgiveness . . . Everyone's talking about it . . . and if you don't do this for me now, David . . . I'm never going to invite you to this house again.

I didn't want to come in the first place, I answered. If you hadn't twisted my arm, I never would have been here to insult your guests. You could have had the same dull and insipid party you always have.

You need help, David . . . I'm not forgetting what you've been through . . . but patience lasts just so long . . . Go and see a doctor before you ruin your life.

I live the life that's possible for me. It doesn't include going to parties at your house.

Mary threw the last coat onto the bed, and then, for no discernible reason, she abruptly sat down and began to cry.

Listen, fuckhead, she said in a quiet voice. I loved her, too. You might have been married to her, but Helen was my best friend.

No she wasn't. She was my best friend. And I was hers. This has nothing to do with you, Mary.

That put an end to the conversation. I had been so hard on her, so absolute in my rejection of her feelings that she couldn't think of anything more to say. When I left the room, she was sitting with her back to me, shaking her head back and forth and looking down at the coats.

Two days after the party, word came from the University of Pennsylvania Press that they wanted to publish my book. I was almost a hundred pages into the Chateaubriand translation at that point, and when *The Silent World of Hector Mann* was released a year later, I had another twelve hundred pages behind me. If I kept working at that pace, I would have a completed draft in seven or eight more months. Add on some extra time for revisions and changes of heart, and in less than a year I would be delivering a finished manuscript to Alex.

As it turned out, that year lasted only three months. I pushed on for another two hundred fifty pages, reaching the chapter about the fall of Napoleon in the twenty-third book (*miseries and wonders are twins, they are born together*), and then, one damp and blustery afternoon at the beginning of summer, I found Frieda Spelling's letter in my mailbox. I admit that I was thrown by it at first, but once I had sent off my response and given the matter a little thought, I managed to persuade myself that it was a hoax. That didn't mean it had been wrong to answer her, but now that I had covered my bets, I assumed that our correspondence would end there.

Nine days later, I heard from her again. She used a full sheet of paper this time, and at the top of the page there was a block of blue embossed type that bore her name and address. I realized how simple it was to produce false personal stationery, but why would anyone go to the trouble of trying to impersonate someone I had never heard of? The name Frieda Spelling meant nothing to me. She might have been Hector Mann's wife, and she might have been a crazy person who lived alone in a desert shack, but it no longer made sense to deny that she was real.

Dear Professor, she wrote. *Your doubts are perfectly understandable, and I am not at all surprised that you are reluctant to believe me. The only way to learn the truth is to accept the invitation I made to you in my last letter. Fly to Tierra del Sueño and meet Hector. If I told you that he wrote and directed a number of feature films after leaving Hollywood in 1929 – and that he is willing to screen them for you here at the ranch – perhaps that will entice you to come. Hector is almost ninety years old and in failing health. His will instructs me to destroy the films and the negatives of those films within twenty-four hours of his death, and I don't know how much longer he will last. Please contact me soon. Looking forward to your reply, I remain very truly yours, Frieda Spelling (Mrs. Hector Mann).*

Again, I didn't allow myself to get carried away. My response was concise, formal, perhaps even a bit rude, but before I committed myself to anything, I had to know that she could be trusted. *I want to believe you,* I wrote, *but I must have proof. If you expect me to go all the way to New Mexico, I need to know that your statements are credible and that Hector Mann is indeed alive. Once my doubts have been removed, I will go to the ranch. But I must warn you that I don't travel by plane. Sincerely yours, D. Z.*

There was no question that she would be back in touch – unless I had scared her off. If I had done that, then she would be tacitly admitting that she had deceived me, and the story would be over. I didn't think that was the case, but whatever she was or wasn't up to, it wasn't going to take long for me to find out the truth. The tone of her second letter had been urgent, almost imploring, and if in fact she was who she said she was, she wasn't going to waste any time before writing to me again. Silence would mean that I had called her bluff, but if she answered – and I was fully expecting her to answer – the letter would come quickly. It had taken nine days for the last one to reach me. All things being equal (no delays, no bungles by the post office), I figured the next one would come even faster than that.

I did my best to stay calm, to stick to my routine and forge ahead with the *Memoirs,* but it was no use. I was too distracted, too keyed up to give them the proper attention, and after struggling to meet my quotas for several days in a row, I finally declared a moratorium on the project. Bright and early the next morning, I crawled into the closet in the spare bedroom and pulled out my old research files on Hector, which I had packed away in cardboard boxes after finishing the book. There were six cartons in all. Five of them held the notes, outlines, and drafts of my own manuscript, but the other one was crammed with all sorts of precious material: clippings, photos, microfilmed documents, xeroxed articles, squibs from ancient gossip columns, every scrap of print I had been able to lay my fingers on that referred to Hector Mann. I hadn't looked at those papers in a long time, and with nothing to do now but wait for Frieda Spelling to contact me again, I carried the box into my study and spent the rest of the week combing through it. I don't think I was expecting to learn anything I didn't already know, but the contents of the file had become rather dim to me by then, and I felt that it deserved another look. Most of the information I had collected was unreliable: articles from the tabloid press, junk from the fan magazines, bits of movie reportage rife with hyperbole, erroneous suppositions, and out-and-out falsehoods. Still, as long as I remembered not to believe what I read, I didn't see how the exercise could do any harm.

Hector was the subject of four profiles written between August 1927 and October 1928. The first one appeared in Kaleidoscope's monthly *Bulletin*, the publicity organ of Hunt's newly formed production company. It was essentially a press release to announce the contract they had signed with Hector, and because little was known about him at that point, they were free to invent any story that served their purposes. Those were the last days of the Hollywood Latin Lover, the period just after Valentino's death when dark, exotic foreigners were still drawing large crowds, and Kaleidoscope tried to cash in on the phenomenon by billing Hector as *Señor Slapstick, the South American heart-throb with the comic touch*. To back up this assertion, they fabricated an intriguing list of credits for him, an entire career that supposedly predated his arrival in California: music hall appearances in Buenos Aires, extended vaudeville tours through Argentina and Brazil, a series of smash-hit films produced in Mexico. By presenting Hector as an already established star, Hunt could create a reputation for himself as a man with an eye for talent. He wasn't just a newcomer to the business, he was a clever and enterprising studio boss who had outbid his competitors for the right to import a well-known foreign entertainer and turn him loose on the American public. It was an easy lie to get away with. No one was paying attention to what happened in other countries, after all, and with so many imaginative possibilities to choose from, why be hemmed in by the facts?

Six months later, an article in the February issue of *Photoplay* presented a more sober view of Hector's past. Several of his films had been released by then, and with interest in his work growing around the country, the need to distort his earlier life had no doubt diminished. The story was written by a staff reporter named Brigid O'Fallon, and from her comments in the first paragraph about Hector's *piercing gaze* and *lithe muscularity*, one immediately understands that her only intention is to say flattering things about him. Charmed by his heavy Spanish accent, and yet praising him for the fluency of his English, she asks him why he has a German name. *Ees very simple*, Hector answers. *My parents was born in Germany, and so too I. We all emigrate to Argentina when I was a leetle baby. I speak the German with them at home, the Spanish at school. English come later, after I go to America. Steel not so hot.* Miss O'Fallon then asks him how long he has been here, and Hector says three years. That, of course, contradicts the information published in the Kaleidoscope *Bulletin*, and when Hector goes on to discuss some of the jobs he held after arriving in California (busboy, vacuum cleaner salesman, ditchdigger), he makes no mention of any previous work in show business. So much for the glorious Latin American career that had turned him into a household name.

It's not hard to dismiss the exaggerations of Hunt's publicity department, but just because they ignored the truth doesn't mean that the *Photoplay* story was any more accurate or believable. In the March issue of the *Picturegoer*, a journalist named Randall Simms writes of visiting Hector on the set of *Tango Tangle* and being altogether astonished to find that *this Argentinian laugh machine speaks flawless English, with scarcely the trace of an accent. If you didn't know where he was from, you would swear that he had been raised in Sandusky, Ohio.* Simms means it as a compliment, but his observation raises disturbing questions about Hector's origins. Even if one accepts Argentina as the place where he spent his childhood, he seems to have left for America much earlier than the other articles suggest. In the next paragraph, Simms reports Hector as saying: *I was a very bad boy. My parents threw me out of the house when I was sixteen, and I never looked back. Eventually, I made my way north and landed in America. Right from the start, I had only one thought in mind: to hit it big in pictures.* The man who speaks those words bears no resemblance to the man who spoke to Brigid O'Fallon one month earlier. Had he put on the heavy accent for *Photoplay* as a gag, or was Simms intentionally mangling the truth, emphasizing Hector's proficiency in English as a way to convince producers of his potential as a sound actor in the months and years ahead? Perhaps the two of them had conspired on the article together, or perhaps a third party had paid Simms off – possibly Hunt, who by then was in deep financial trouble. Could it be that Hunt was trying to increase Hector's market value in order to sell off his services to another production company? It is impossible to know, but whatever Simms's motives were, and however badly O'Fallon might have transcribed Hector's statements, the articles cannot be reconciled, no matter how many excuses one makes for the journalists.

Hector's last published interview appeared in the October issue of *Picture Play*. On the strength of what he said to B. T. Barker – or at least what Barker would have us believe he said – it seems likely that our boy had a hand in creating this confusion himself. This time, his parents are from the city of Stanislav on the eastern edge of the Austro-Hungarian Empire, and Hector's first language is Polish, not German. They leave for Vienna when he is two, stay there for six months, and then go to America, where they spend three years in New York and one year in the Midwest before pulling up stakes again and resettling in Buenos Aires. Barker interrupts to ask where they lived in the Midwest, and Hector calmly replies: Sandusky, Ohio. Just six months earlier, Randall Simms had mentioned Sandusky in his article for the *Picturegoer* – not as a real place but as a metaphor, as a representative American town. Now Hector appropriates that town and puts it in his story, perhaps for no other reason than that he is attracted to the gruff and lilting music of the words. *San-dus-ky, O-hi-o*, has a pleasant sonority to it, and the smart, triple syncopations scan with all the power and precision of a well-turned poetical phrase. His father, he says, was a civil engineer who specialized in the building of bridges. His mother, *the most beautiful woman on earth*, was a dancer, singer, and painter. Hector adored them both, was a well-behaved religious little boy (as opposed to the bad boy of Simms's piece), and until their tragic deaths in a boating accident when he was fourteen, he was planning to follow in his father's footsteps and become an engineer. The sudden loss of his parents changed all that. From the moment he became an orphan, he says, his only dream was to return to America and begin a new life there. It took a long string of miracles before that could happen, but now that he is back, he feels certain that this is the place where he was always meant to be.

Some of these statements could have been true, but not many of them, perhaps not a single one. This is the fourth version he has given of his past, and while they all have certain elements in common (German- or Polish-speaking parents, time spent in Argentina, emigration from the old world to the new), everything else is subject to change. He's hard-nosed and practical in one account; he's cowering and sentimental in the next. He's a troublemaker for one journalist, obedient and pious for another; he grew up rich, he grew up poor; he speaks with a heavy accent, he speaks with no accent at all. Put these contradictions together, and you wind up with nothing, the portrait of a man with so many personalities and family histories that he is reduced to a pile of fragments, a jigsaw puzzle whose pieces no longer connect. Every time he is asked a question, he gives a different answer. Words pour out of him, but he is determined never to say the same thing twice. He appears to be hiding something, to be protecting a secret, and yet he goes about his obfuscations with such grace and sparkling good humor that no one seems to notice. The journalists can't resist him. He makes them laugh, he amuses them with little magic tricks, and after a while they stop pressing him about the facts and give in to the power of the performance. Hector goes on winging it, careening madly from the cobbled boulevards of Vienna to the euphonious flatlands of Ohio, and eventually you begin to ask yourself if this is a game of deception or merely a blundering attempt to fight off boredom. Maybe his lies are innocent. Maybe he isn't trying to fool anyone so much as looking for a way to entertain himself. Interviews can be a dull procedure, after all. If everyone keeps asking you the same questions, maybe you have to come up with new answers just to stay awake.

Nothing was certain, but after sifting through this jumble of fraudulent memories and spurious anecdotes, I felt that I had discovered one minor fact. In the first three interviews, Hector avoids mentioning where he was born. When asked by O'Fallon, he says Germany; when asked by Simms, he says Austria; but in neither instance does he provide any details: no town, no city, no region. It is only when he talks to Barker that he opens up a bit and fills in the blanks. Stanislav had once been part of Austro-Hungary, but after the breakup of the empire at the end of the war, it had been handed over to Poland. Poland is a remote country to Americans, far more remote than Germany, and with Hector doing everything he could to downplay his foreignness, it was an odd admission for him to have named that city as his birthplace. The only possible reason for him to have done that, it seemed to me, was because it was true. I couldn't confirm this suspicion, but it makes no sense for him to have lied about it. Poland didn't help his case, and if he was intent on manufacturing a false background for himself, why bother to mention it at all? It was a mistake, a momentary lapse of attention, and no sooner does Barker hear this slip of the tongue than Hector tries to undo the damage. If he has just made himself too foreign, now he will counteract the error by insisting on his American credentials. He puts himself in New York, the city of immigrants, and then hammers home the point by traveling to the heartland. That's where Sandusky, Ohio, comes into the picture. He plucks the name out of thin air, remembering it from the profile that was written about him six months earlier, and then springs it on the unsuspecting B. T. Barker. It serves his purpose well. The journalist is sidetracked, and instead of asking more questions about Poland, he leans back in his chair and begins reminiscing with Hector about the alfalfa fields of the Midwest.

Stanislav is located just south of the Dniestr River, halfway between Lvov and Czernowitz in the province of Galicia. If that was the terrain of Hector's childhood, then there was every reason to suppose that he was born a Jew. The fact that the area was thick with Jewish settlements was not enough to persuade me, but combine the Jewish population with the fact that his family left the area, and the argument becomes quite convincing. The Jews were the ones who left that part of the world, and beginning with the Russian pogroms in the 1880s, hundreds of thousands of Yiddish-speaking immigrants fanned out across western Europe and the United States. Many of them went to South America as well. In Argentina alone, the Jewish population increased from six thousand to more than one hundred thousand between the turn of the century and the outbreak of World War I. No doubt Hector and his family helped add to those statistics. If they hadn't, then it was scarcely possible for them to have landed in Argentina. At that moment in history, the only people who traveled from Stanislav to Buenos Aires were Jews.

I was proud of my little discovery, but that didn't mean I thought it amounted to much. If Hector was indeed hiding something, and if that something turned out to be the religion he had been born into, then all I had uncovered was the most pedestrian kind of social hypocrisy. It wasn't a crime to be a Jew in Hollywood back then. It was merely something that one chose not to talk about. Jolson had already made *The Jazz Singer* at that point, and Broadway theaters were filled with audiences who paid good money to see Eddie Cantor and Fanny Brice, to listen to Irving Berlin and the Gershwins, to applaud the Marx Brothers. Being Jewish might have been a burden to Hector. He might have suffered from it, and he might have been ashamed of it, but it was difficult for me to imagine that he had been killed for it. There's always a bigot around somewhere with enough hatred in him to murder a Jew, of course, but a person who does that wants his crime to be known, to make use of it as an example to frighten others, and whatever Hector's fate might have been, the one certain fact was that his body was never found.

From the day he signed with Kaleidoscope to the day he disappeared, Hector's run lasted only seventeen months. Short as that time might have been, he achieved a certain measure of recognition for himself, and by early 1928 his name was already beginning to crop up in the Hollywood social columns. I had managed to recover about twenty of those pieces from various microfilm archives during the course of my travels. There must have been many others that I missed, not to speak of others that had been destroyed, but scant and insufficient as those mentions were, they proved that Hector was not someone who tended to sit around at home after dark. He was seen in restaurants and nightclubs, at parties and movie premieres, and nearly every time his name appeared in print, it was accompanied by a descriptive phrase that referred to his *smoldering magnetism*, his *irresistible eyes*, or his *heart-stoppingly handsome face*. This was especially true when the writer was a woman, but there were men who succumbed to his charms as well. One of them, who worked under the name Gordon Fly (the title of his column was *Fly on the Wall*), went so far as to offer the opinion that Hector was wasting his talents in comedy and should switch to drama. *With that profile, Fly wrote, it offends one's sense of aesthetic proportion to watch the elegant Señor Mann put his nose at risk by repeatedly bumping into walls and lampposts. The public would be better served if he dropped these stunts and concentrated on kissing beautiful women. Surely there are many young actresses in town who would be willing to take on that role. Sources tell me that Irene Flowers has already had several auditions, but it appears that the dashing hidalgo now has his eye on Constance Hart, the ever-popular Vim and Vigor Girl herself. We eagerly await the results of that screen test.*

Most of the time, however, Hector received no more than a glancing nod from the journalists. He wasn't much of a story yet, nothing more than one promising newcomer among others, and in fully half the columns I had on hand he appears only as a name – usually in the company of a woman, herself only a name as well. Hector Mann was spotted at the Feathered Nest with Sylvia Noonan. Hector Mann stepped out onto the dance floor of the Gibraltar Club last night with Mildred Swain. Hector Mann shared a laugh with Alice Dwyer, ate oysters with Polly McCracken, held hands with Dolores Saint John, slipped into a gin

THE BOOK OF ILLUSIONS

joint with Fiona Maar. In all, I counted the names of eight different women, but who knows how many others he went out with that year? My information was limited to the articles I had managed to find, and those eight easily could have been twenty, perhaps even more.

When the news of Hector's disappearance broke the following January, little attention was paid to his love life. Seymour Hunt had hanged himself in his bedroom just three days earlier, and instead of trying to dig up evidence of some soured romance or secret affair, the police concentrated their efforts on Hector's troubled relations with the corrupt Cincinnati banker. It was probably too tempting not to make a connection between the two scandals. After Hunt's arrest, Hector had been quoted as saying that he was relieved to know that Americans still had a sense of justice. The anonymous source, described as one of Hector's close personal friends, reported that he had announced within earshot of half a dozen people: *The man is a scoundrel. He cheated me out of thousands of dollars and tried to ruin my career. I'm glad they're locking him up. He's getting what he deserves, and I feel no pity for him.* Rumors began circulating in the press that Hector had been the one who fingered Hunt to the authorities. Advocates of this theory claimed that now that Hunt was dead, his associates had eliminated Hector in order to prevent more revelations from leaking to the public. Some versions went so far as to suggest that Hunt's death had not been a suicide but a murder arranged to look like a suicide – the first step in an elaborate conspiracy by his underworld friends to rub out the traces of their crimes.

It was the gangland reading of events. That must have felt like a plausible approach in 1920s America, but without a body to back up the hypothesis, the police investigation began to founder. The press played along for the first couple of weeks, running stories about Hunt's business practices and the rise of the criminal element in the motion picture industry, but when no definite connection could be established between Hector's disappearance and the death of his former producer, they began looking for other motives and explanations. Everyone had been tantalized by the proximity of the two events, but it was logically unsound to assume that the one had caused the other. Contiguous facts are not necessarily related facts, even though their nearness to one another would seem to suggest they are linked. Now, as other lines of inquiry began to be pursued, it turned out that many of the trails had already gone cold. Dolores Saint John, named in several of the early articles as Hector's fiancée, quietly skipped town and returned to her parents' house in Kansas. Another month went by before the journalists could find her, and when they did, she refused to talk to them, claiming that she was still too distraught over Hector's disappearance to issue a full statement. Her only comment was *My heart is broken*, and after that she was never heard from again. A fetching young actress who had appeared in half a dozen movies (among them *The Prop Man* and *Mr. Nobody*, in which she had played the sheriff's daughter and Hector's wife), she impulsively abandoned her career and vanished from the world of show business.

Jules Blaustein, the gagman who had worked with Hector on all twelve Kaleidoscope films, told a *Variety* reporter that he and Hector had been collaborating on a series of scripts for sound comedies and that his writing partner had been in *excellent spirits*. He had seen him every day since mid-December, and unlike everyone else who was interviewed about Hector, he continued to talk about him in the present tense. *It's true that things ended rather unpleasantly with Hunt,* Blaustein admitted, *but Hector wasn't the only one who got a bad shake at Kaleidoscope. We all took our knocks there, and even if he got the worst of it, he isn't someone to bear grudges. He has his whole future to look forward to, and the moment his contract with Kaleidoscope was up, he turned his mind to other things. He's been working hard with me, as hard as I've ever seen him work, and his brain has been on fire with new ideas. When he dropped out of sight, our first script was nearly finished – a side-splitter called* Dot and Dash *– and we were about to sign a contract with Harry Cohn at Columbia. Shooting was supposed to begin in March. Hector was going to direct and play a small but hilarious silent role in it, and if that sounds like someone who was planning to kill himself, then you don't know the first thing about Hector. It's absurd to think he would take his own life. Maybe someone took it for him, but that would mean he has enemies, and in all the time I've known him, I've never seen him rub a person the wrong way. The man is a prince, and I love working with him. We can sit here all day musing about what happened, but even money says he's alive somewhere, that he got one of his nutty inspirations in the middle of the night and just took off to be alone for a little while. Everyone keeps saying he's dead, but it wouldn't surprise me if Hector walked through that door right now, tossed his hat on the chair, and said, 'Okay, Jules, let's get to work.'*

Columbia confirmed that they had been negotiating with Hector and Blaustein on a three-picture contract that included *Dot and Dash* as well as two other feature comedies. Nothing had been signed yet, their spokesman said, but once the terms had been worked out to the satisfaction of both parties, the studio had been looking forward to *welcoming Hector into the family*. Blaustein's remarks, coupled with the statement from Columbia, shot down the idea that Hector's career had come to a dead end, which some of the tabloids had been pushing as a possible motive for suicide. But the facts showed that Hector's prospects had been far from bleak. The mess at Kaleidoscope had not *shattered his spirit*, as the *Los Angeles Record* announced on February 18, 1929, and since no letter or note had turned up to support the contention that Hector had taken his own life, the suicide theory began losing ground to a host of wild speculations and crackpot conjectures: kidnappings gone awry, freakish accidents, supernatural events. Meanwhile, the police were making no progress on the Hunt connection, and although they claimed to be *following up on several promising leads* (the *Los Angeles Daily News*, March 7, 1929), no new suspects were ever brought forward. If Hector had been murdered, there wasn't enough evidence to charge anyone with the crime. If he had killed himself, it wasn't for a reason that anyone could understand. A few cynics suggested that his disappearance was no more than a publicity stunt, a cheap ploy orchestrated by Harry Cohn at Columbia to bring attention to his new star, and that we could expect a miraculous reappearance any day now. That seemed to make a certain kind of cockeyed sense, but as the days passed and Hector still didn't return, that theory proved to be just as wrong as all the others. Everyone had an opinion about what had happened to Hector, but the fact was that no one knew a thing. And if someone did know, that person wasn't talking.

The case made headlines for about a month and a half, but then interest began to drop off. There were no new revelations to report, no new possibilities to examine, and eventually the press turned its attention to other matters. Late in the spring, the *Los Angeles Examiner* ran the first of several stories that appeared intermittently over the next couple of years in which Hector was supposed to have been seen by someone in an unlikely, far-flung place – the so-called Hector sightings – but these were little more than novelty items, small fillers buried at the bottom of the horoscope page, a kind of standing joke for Hollywood insiders. Hector in Utica, New York, working as a labor organizer. Hector on the pampas with his traveling circus. Hector on skid row. In March 1933, Randall Simms, the journalist who had interviewed Hector for the *Picturegoer* five years earlier, published an article in the *Herald Express* Sunday supplement entitled *Whatever Happened to Hector Mann?* It promised new information about the case, but beyond hinting at a desperate and complicated love triangle that Hector might or might not have been involved in, it was essentially a rehash of the articles that had appeared in the Los Angeles papers in 1929. A similar piece, written by someone named Dabney Strayhorn, cropped up in a 1941 issue of *Collier's*, and a book from 1957 with the trashy title *Hollywood Scandals and Mysteries*, written by Frank C. Klebald, devoted one short chapter to Hector's disappearance, which on closer examination turned out to be an almost word-for-word crib of Strayhorn's magazine article. There might have been other articles and chapters written about Hector over the years, but I wasn't aware of them. I only had what was in the box, and what was in the box was all I had managed to find.

4

Two weeks later, I still hadn't heard from Frieda Spelling. I had anticipated calls in the middle of the night, special-delivery letters, telegrams,
faxes, desperate pleas to rush to Hector's bedside, but after fourteen
days of silence, I stopped giving her the benefit of the doubt. My skepticism returned, and little by little I worked my way back to where I had
been before. The box went into the closet again, and after moping
around for another week or ten days, I picked up the Chateaubriand
manuscript and started hacking away at it again. I had been sidetracked
for nearly a month, but other than some residual feelings of disappointment and disgust, I managed to push the thought of Tierra del Sueño
out of my mind. Hector was dead again. He had died in 1929, or else he
had died the day before yesterday. It didn't matter which death was
real. He no longer belonged to this world, and I was never going to have
a chance to meet him.

I closed in on myself again. The weather swung back and forth, alternating between good stretches and bad. A day or two of sparkling light
followed by furious storms; drenching downpours, then crystal blue
skies; wind and no wind, warm and cold, mist dissolving into clarity. It
was always five degrees cooler on my mountain than in the town below,
but there were afternoons when I was able to walk around in nothing
but shorts and a T-shirt. On other afternoons, I had to light a fire and
bundle up in three sweaters. June turned into July. I had been working
steadily for about ten days then, gradually settling into the old rhythm,
digging in for what I thought would be the final push on the job. Just
after the holiday weekend, I knocked off early one day and drove into
Brattleboro to do my shopping. I spent about forty minutes at the Grand
Union, and then, after loading the bags into the cab of the truck, decided
to stick around for a while and take in a movie. It was just an impulse, a
sudden whim that came over me as I stood in the parking lot, squinting
and sweating in the late afternoon sun. My work was finished for the
day, and there was no reason not to change my plans, no reason to rush
back home if I didn't want to. I got to the Latchis Theatre on Main Street
just as the coming attractions for the six o'clock show were about to

begin. I bought a Coke and a bag of popcorn, found a seat in the middle of the last row, and sat through one of the *Back to the Future* movies. It turned out to be both ridiculous and enjoyable. After the film was over, I decided to prolong the outing by having dinner at the Korean restaurant across the street. I had eaten there once before, and judging by Vermont standards, the food wasn't half bad.

I had spent two hours sitting in the dark, and by the time I walked out of the theater, the weather had changed again. It was another one of those abrupt shifts: clouds rolling in, the temperature dropping down into the fifties, the wind starting to blow. After a day of intense and brilliant sun, there should have been some light left in the sky at that hour, but the sun had disappeared before dusk, and the long summer day had turned into a wet, chilly evening. It was already raining when I crossed the street and went into the restaurant, and as I sat down at one of the front tables and ordered my food, I watched the storm gathering force outside. A paper bag rose up from the ground and flew into the window of Sam's Army-Navy Store; an empty soda can went clattering down the street toward the river; bullets of rain pelted the sidewalk. I started off with a platter of kimchi, washing down every other bite with a swallow of beer. It was tangy stuff that burned the tongue, and when I moved on to the main course, I kept on dipping the meat into the hot sauce, which meant that I kept on drinking beer. I must have had three bottles in all, perhaps four, and by the time I paid the check, I was a little more juiced than I should have been. Sharp enough to walk a white line, I think, sharp enough to think lucid thoughts about my translation, but probably not sharp enough to drive.

Still, I'm not going to blame the beer for what happened. My reflexes might have been a bit sluggish, but there were other elements involved as well, and I doubt that the result would have been any different if beer had been removed from the equation. The rain was still pounding down when I left the restaurant, and after running several hundred yards to the municipal parking lot, I was soaked through to the skin. It didn't help that I fumbled with the keys as I tried to get them out of my wet pants, and it helped even less that once I caught hold of them and managed to pull them out, I immediately dropped them into a puddle. That meant more lost time as I crouched down to search for them in the darkness, and when I finally stood up and climbed into my truck, I was as wet as someone who had taken a shower with his clothes on. Blame the beer, but also blame those wet clothes and the water dripping into my eyes. Again and again, I had to take one hand off the wheel to wipe my forehead, and when you add that distraction to the inconvenience of a bad defrost system (which meant that when I wasn't wiping my forehead, I was using that same hand to wipe off the fogged-up windshield) and then compound the problem by throwing in defective windshield wipers (when are they not defective?), the conditions that night were hardly ones to guarantee a safe ride home.

The irony was that I was aware of all this. Shivering in my wet clothes, eager to get back and change into something warm, I nevertheless made a conscious effort to drive as slowly as I could. That's what saved me, I suppose, but at the same time it also could have been what caused the accident. If I had been driving faster, I probably would have been more alert, more attuned to the vagaries of the road, but after a while my mind began to wander, and eventually I fell into one of those long, pointless meditations that only seem to occur when you're driving alone in a car. In this case, if I remember correctly, it had to do with quantifying the ephemeral acts of daily life. How much time had I spent in the past forty years lacing up my shoes? How many doors had I opened and closed? How often had I sneezed? How many hours had I lost looking for objects I couldn't find? How many times had I stubbed my toe or banged my head or blinked away something that had crept into my eye? I found it to be a rather pleasant exercise, and I kept adding to the list as I sloshed my way through the darkness. About twenty miles out of Brattleboro, on an open stretch of road between the towns of T— and West T—, just three miles before the turnoff that would take me up the dirt road to my house, I saw the eyes of an animal gleaming in the headlights. An instant later, I saw that it was a dog. He was twenty or thirty yards ahead, a wet and ragged creature blundering through the night, and contrary to what most dogs do when they're lost, he wasn't traveling on the side of the road but trotting down the center of it – or just to the left of center, which put him smack in the middle of my lane. I swerved to avoid hitting him, and at the same moment I put my foot on the brake. I probably shouldn't have done that, but I had already done it before I could tell myself not to, and because the surface of the road was wet and oily from the rain, the tires didn't hold. I skidded across the yellow line, and before I could swing back the other way, the truck rammed into a utility pole.

I had my seat belt on, but the jolt knocked my left arm against the wheel, and with all the groceries suddenly flying out of their bags, a can of tomato juice sprang up and struck me on the chin. My face hurt like hell, and my forearm was throbbing, but I could still flex my hand, could still open and close my mouth, and I concluded that no bones had been broken. I should have felt relieved, lucky to have escaped without any serious injuries, but I was in no mood to count my blessings and speculate on how much worse it could have been. This was bad enough, and I was furious with myself for having banged up the truck. One headlight was knocked out; the fender was crumpled; the front end was smashed in. The engine was still running, though, but when I tried to back out and drive away, I discovered that the front tires were half submerged in mud. It took me twenty minutes of shoving in the glop and rain to get the thing unstuck, and by then I was too wet and exhausted to bother cleaning up the groceries that had been tossed around the inside of the cab. I just sat down behind the wheel, backed up into the road, and took off. As I later found out, I finished the drive home with a package of frozen peas wedged into the small of my back.

It was already past eleven o'clock when I pulled up in front of my house. I was shivering in my clothes, my jaw and arm were aching, and I was in a foul temper. Expect the unexpected, they say, but once the unexpected happens, the last thing you expect is that it will happen again. My guard was down, and because I was still brooding about the dog and the utility pole, still going over the details of the accident as I climbed out of the truck, I didn't notice the car that was parked to the left of the house. My headlight hadn't swept over in that direction, and when I cut the motor and turned off the light, everything went dark around me. The rain had slackened by then, but it was still drizzling, and there were no lights on in the house. Thinking that I would be back before the sun went down, I hadn't bothered to turn on the light above the front door. The sky was black. The ground was black. I groped my way to the house by memory and feel, but I couldn't see a thing.

It was common practice in southern Vermont to leave your house unlocked, but I didn't do that. I dead-bolted the door every time I went out. It was a stubborn ritual that I refused to break, even if I was going to be gone for only five minutes. Now, as I fumbled with my keys for the second time that night, I understood how stupid these precautions were. I had effectively locked myself out of my own house. The keys were already in my hand, but there were six of them on the chain, and I had no idea which was the right one. I blindly patted the door, trying to locate the lock. Once I had found it, I chose one of the keys at random and maneuvered it into the hole. It went halfway in, and then it got stuck. I would have to try another one, but before I did that, I would have to pull the first one out. That took a good deal more wiggling than I had anticipated. At the last moment, just as I was unjamming the final notch from the hole, the key gave a little jerk, and the key chain slithered out of my hand. It clattered against the wooden steps, then bounced God knows where into the night. And so the journey ended in the same way it had begun: crawling on all fours and cursing under my breath, searching for a set of invisible keys.

I couldn't have been at it for more than two or three seconds when a light went on in the yard. I glanced up, instinctively turning my head toward the light, and before I had a chance to be afraid, before I could even register what was happening, I saw that a car was sitting there – a car that had no business being on my property – and that a woman was getting out of it. She opened a large red umbrella, slammed the door shut behind her, and the light went out. Do you need some help? she said. I scrambled to my feet, and at that instant another light went on. The woman was pointing a flashlight at my face.

Who the fuck are you? I asked.

You don't know me, she answered, but you know the person who sent me.

That's not good enough. Tell me who you are, or I'll call the cops.

My name is Alma Grund. I've been waiting here for over five hours, Mr. Zimmer, and I need to talk to you.

And who's the person who sent you?

Frieda Spelling. Hector's in bad shape. She wants you to know that, and she wanted me to tell you that there isn't much time.

We found the keys with her flashlight, and when I opened the door and stepped into the house, I flicked on the light in the living room. Alma Grund came in after me – a short woman in her mid- to late thirties, dressed in a blue silk blouse and tailored gray pants. Medium-length brown hair, high heels, crimson lipstick, and a large leather purse slung over her shoulder. When she walked into the light, I saw that there was a birthmark on the left side of her face. It was a purple stain about the size of a man's fist, long enough and broad enough to resemble the map of some imaginary country: a solid mass of discoloration that covered more than half her cheek, starting at the corner of her eye and running down to her jaw. Her hair was cut in such a way as to obscure most of it, and she held her head at an awkward tilt to prevent the hair from moving. It was an ingrained gesture, I supposed, a habit acquired after a lifetime of self-consciousness, and it gave her an air of clumsiness and vulnerability, the demeanor of a shy girl who preferred looking down at the carpet to meeting you in the eye.

On any other night, I probably would have been willing to talk to her – but not that night. I was too annoyed, too put out by what had already happened, and the only thing I wanted was to peel off my wet clothes, take a hot bath, and go to bed. I had shut the door behind me after turning on the living room lights. Now I opened it again and politely asked her to leave.

Just give me five minutes, she said. I can explain everything.

I don't like it when people trespass on my property, I said, and I don't like it when people jump out at me in the middle of the night. You don't want me to have to throw you out of here, do you?

She looked up at me then, surprised by my vehemence, frightened by the undertow of rage in my voice. I thought you wanted to see Hector, she said, and as she spoke those words she took a few more steps into the house, removing herself from the vicinity of the door in case I was planning to carry out my threat. When she turned around and faced me again, I could see only her right side. She looked different from that angle, and I saw that she had a delicate, roundish face, with very smooth skin. Not unattractive, finally; perhaps almost pretty. Her eyes were dark blue, and there was a quick, nervous intelligence in them that reminded me a little of Helen.

I'm not interested in what Frieda Spelling has to say anymore, I said. She kept me waiting for too long, and I had to work too hard to get over it. I'm not going to go there again. Too much hope. Too much disappointment. I don't have the stamina for it. As far as I'm concerned, the story is over.

Before she could answer me, I finished off my little harangue with an aggressive parting shot. I'm going to take a bath, I said. When I'm done with the bath, I expect you to be gone from here. Please be good enough to close the door on your way out.

I turned my back on her and started walking toward the stairs, determined to ignore her now and wash my hands of the whole business. Halfway up the steps, I heard her say: You wrote such a brilliant book, Mr. Zimmer. You have the right to know the real story, and I need your help. If you don't hear me out, terrible things are going to happen. Just listen to me for five minutes. That's all I ask.

She was presenting her case in the most melodramatic terms possible, but I wasn't going to let it affect me. When I reached the top of the stairs, I turned around and spoke to her from the loggia. I'm not going to give you five seconds, I said. If you want to talk to me, call me tomorrow. Better yet, write me a letter. I'm not so good on the phone. And then, not bothering to wait for her reaction, I slipped into the bathroom and locked the door behind me.

I lingered in the tub for fifteen or twenty minutes. Add on another three or four minutes to dry myself off, two more minutes to examine my chin in the mirror, and then another six or seven to put on a fresh set of clothes, and I must have stayed upstairs for close to half an hour. I wasn't in any rush. I knew that she would still be there when I went downstairs again, and I was still in an ugly humor, still seething with pent-up belligerence and animosity. I wasn't afraid of Alma Grund, but my own anger frightened me, and I had no idea what was in me any-more. There had been that outburst at the Tellefsons' party the previous spring, but I had kept myself hidden since then, and I had lost the habit of talking to strangers. The only person I knew how to be with now was myself – but I wasn't really anyone, and I wasn't really alive. I was just someone who pretended to be alive, a dead man who spent his days translating a dead man's book.

She began with a stream of apologies, looking up at me from the ground floor as I stepped out onto the loggia, asking me to forgive her for her bad manners and explaining how sorry she was to have barged in on me without warning. She wasn't someone who lurked around people's houses at night, she said, and she hadn't meant to scare me. When she knocked on my door at six o'clock, the sun had been shining. She had mistakenly assumed that I would be at home, and if she wound up waiting in the yard for all those hours, it was only because she thought I would be returning at any moment.

As I descended the stairs and made my way into the living room, I saw that she had brushed her hair and put on a new coat of lipstick. She looked more pulled together now – less dowdy, less unsure of herself – and even as I walked toward her and asked her to sit down, I sensed that she wasn't quite as weak or intimidated as I had thought she was.

I'm not going to listen to you until you've answered some questions, I said. If I'm satisfied with what you tell me, I'll give you a chance to talk. If not, I'm going to ask you to leave, and I never want to see you again. Understood?

Do you want long answers or short answers?

Short answers. As short as possible.

Just tell me where to begin, and I'll do my best.

The first thing I want to know is why Frieda Spelling didn't write back to me.

She got your second letter, but just when she sat down to answer you, something happened that prevented her from continuing.

For a whole month?

Hector fell down the stairs. In one part of the house, Frieda was sitting at her desk with a pen in her hand, and in another part of the house Hector was walking toward the stairs. It was eerie how close together those two events were. Frieda wrote three words – *Dear Professor Zimmer* – and at that moment Hector tripped and fell. His leg was broken in two places. Some ribs were cracked. There was a nasty bump on the side of his head. A helicopter came to the ranch, and he was flown to a hospital in Albuquerque. During the operation to set his leg, he suffered a heart attack. They transferred him to the cardiac unit, and then, just when it looked like he was recovering, he came down with pneumonia. It was touch and go for a couple of weeks. Three or four times, we thought we were going to lose him. It just wasn't possible to write, Mr. Zimmer. Too much was happening, and Frieda couldn't think about anything else.

Is he still in the hospital?

He came home yesterday. I took the first plane out this morning, landed in Boston at around two-thirty, and drove up here in a rented car. It's faster than writing a letter, isn't it? One day instead of three or four, maybe even five. In five days, Hector could be dead.

Why didn't you just pick up the phone and call me?

I didn't want to risk it. It would have been too easy for you to hang up on me.

And why should you care? That's my next question. Who are you, and why are you involved in this?

I've known them all my life. They're very close to me.

You're not telling me you're their daughter, are you?

I'm Charlie Grund's daughter. You might not remember the name, but I'm sure you've come across it. You've probably seen it dozens of times.

The cameraman.

194

That's right. He shot all of Hector's films at Kaleidoscope. When Hector and Frieda decided to start making movies again, he left California and went to live at the ranch. That was in 1940. He married my mother in 1946. I was born there, I grew up there. It's an important place to me, Mr. Zimmer. Everything I am comes from that place.

And you never left?

I went to boarding school at fifteen. Then to college. After that, I lived in cities. New York, London, Los Angeles. I've been married and divorced, I've worked at jobs, I've done things.

But you live at the ranch now.

I moved back about seven years ago. My mother died, and I went home for the funeral. After that, I decided to stay on. Charlie died a couple of years later, but I'm still there.

Doing what?

Writing Hector's biography. It's taken me six and a half years, but I'm close to finishing now.

Little by little, it begins to make sense.

Of course it makes sense. I wouldn't have come twenty-four hundred miles to hold things back from you, would I?

That's the next question. Why me? Of all the people in the world, why did you choose me?

Because I need a witness. I talk about things in the book that no one else has seen, and my statements won't be credible unless I have another person to back me up.

But that person doesn't have to be me. It could be anyone. In your cautious, roundabout way, you've just told me that those late films exist. If there's more work of Hector's to be seen, you should contact a film scholar and ask him to look at them. You need an authority to vouch for you, someone with a reputation in the field. I'm just an amateur.

You might not be a professional movie critic, but you're an expert on the comedies of Hector Mann. You wrote an extraordinary book, Mr. Zimmer. No one is ever going to write better about those films. It's the definitive work.

Until that moment, she had given me her complete attention. Pacing back and forth in front of her as she sat on the sofa, I had felt like a prosecuting attorney cross-examining a witness. I had held the advantage, and she had looked me straight in the eye as she answered my questions. Now, suddenly, she glanced down at her watch and began to fidget, and I sensed that the mood had been broken.

It's late, she said.

I misread her comment to mean that she was getting tired. That struck me as ridiculous, an altogether absurd thing to say under the circumstances. You're the one who started this, I said. You're not going to bag out on me now, are you? We're just warming up.

It's one-thirty. The plane takes off from Boston at seven-fifteen. If we leave within an hour, we'll probably make it.

What are you talking about?

You don't think I came to Vermont just to chat, do you? I'm taking you back to New Mexico with me. I thought you understood that.

You've got to be kidding.

It's a long trip. If you have more questions to ask, I'll be happy to answer them on the way. By the time we get there, you'll know everything I know. I promise.

You're too smart to think I'd be willing to do that. Not now. Not in the middle of the night.

You have to. Twenty-four hours after Hector dies, those films are going to be destroyed. And he could be dead now. He could have died while I was traveling out here today. Don't you get it, Mr. Zimmer? If we don't leave now, there might not be enough time.

You're forgetting what I told Frieda in my last letter. I don't do planes. They're against my religion.

Without saying a word, Alma Grund reached into her purse and pulled out a small white paper bag. It was marked with a blue and green insignia, and underneath the picture there were a few lines of writing. From where I was standing, I could make out only one word, but that was the only word I needed to know in order to guess what was inside the bag. *Pharmacy*.

I haven't forgotten, she said. I brought along some Xanax to make things easier for you. That's the one you like to use, isn't it?

How do you know about that?

You wrote a magnificent book, but that didn't mean we could trust you. I had to dig around a little and check you out. I made some calls, I wrote some letters, I read your other work. I know what you've been through, and I'm very sorry – very sorry about what happened to your wife and sons. It must have been horrible for you.

You had no right. It's disgusting to pry into someone's life like that. You crash in here asking for my help, and then you turn around and tell me this? Why should I help you? You make me want to puke.

Frieda and Hector wouldn't have allowed me to invite you unless they knew who you were. I had to do it for them.

I don't accept that. I don't accept a fucking word you're saying.

We're on the same side, Mr. Zimmer. We shouldn't be shouting at each other. We should be working together as friends.

I'm not your friend. I'm not anything to you. You're a phantom who wandered in from the night, and now I want you to go back out there and leave me alone.

I can't do that. I have to take you with me, and we have to go now. Please, don't make me threaten you. It's such a stupid way to handle it.

I had no idea what she was talking about. I was eight inches taller than she was and at least fifty pounds heavier – a good-sized man on the verge of losing his temper, an unknown quantity who could burst into violence at any moment – and there she was talking to me about threats. I stayed where I was, watching her from my position near the wood-stove. We were ten or twelve feet apart, and just as she stood up from the sofa, a fresh onslaught of rain came crashing down on the roof, rattling against the shingles like a bombardment of stones. She jumped at the sound, glancing around the room with a skittish, perplexed look in her eyes, and at that moment I knew what was going to happen next. I can't explain where this knowledge came from, but whatever premonition or extrasensory alertness took hold of me when I saw that look in her eyes, I knew that she was carrying a gun in her purse, and I knew that within the next three or four seconds she was going to stick her right hand into the purse and pull out the gun.

It was one of the most sublimely exhilarating moments of my life. I was half a step in front of the real, an inch or two beyond the confines of my own body, and when the thing happened just as I thought it would, I felt as if my skin had become transparent. I wasn't occupying space anymore so much as melting into it. What was around me was also inside me, and I had only to look into myself in order to see the world.

The gun was in her hand. It was a small silver-plated revolver with a pearl handle, no more than half the size of the cap guns I had played with as a boy. As she turned in my direction and lifted her arm, I could see that the hand at the end of her arm was shaking.

This isn't me, she said. I don't do things like this. Ask me to put it away, and I will. But we have to go now.

It was the first time a gun had ever been pointed at me, and I marveled at how comfortable I felt, at how naturally I accepted the possibilities of the moment. One wrong move, one wrong word, and I could die for no reason at all. That thought should have frightened me. It should have made me want to run, but I felt no urge to do that, no inclination to stop what was happening. An immense and horrifying beauty had opened up before me, and all I wanted was to go on looking at it, to go on looking into the eyes of this woman with the strange double face as we stood in that room, listening to the rain pound on top of us like ten thousand drums scaring up the devils of the night.

Go ahead and shoot, I said. You'll be doing me a great service.

The words came out of my mouth before I knew I was going to say them. They sounded harsh and terrible to me, the kind of thing only a deranged person would say, but once I heard them, I realized that I had no intention of taking them back. I liked them. I was pleased with their bluntness and their candor, with their decisive, no-nonsense approach to the dilemma I was facing. For all the courage those words gave me, however, I'm still not sure what they meant. Was I in fact asking her to kill me, or was I looking for a way to talk her out of it and prevent myself from being killed? Did I really want her to pull the trigger, or was I trying to force her hand and trick her into dropping the gun? I've gone over these questions many times in the past eleven years, but I've never been able to come up with a conclusive answer. All I know is that I wasn't afraid. When Alma Grund pulled out that revolver and pointed it at my chest, it didn't strike fear in me so much as fascination. I understood that the bullets in that gun contained a thought that had never occurred to me before. The world was full of holes, tiny apertures of meaninglessness, microscopic rifts that the mind could walk through, and once you were on the other side of one of those holes, you were free of yourself, free of your life, free of your death, free of everything that belonged to you. I had chanced upon one of them in my living room that night. It appeared in the form of a gun, and now that I was inside that gun, I didn't care whether I got out or not. I was perfectly calm and perfectly insane, perfectly prepared to accept what the moment had offered. Indifference of that magnitude is rare, and because it can be achieved only by someone ready to let go of who he is, it demands respect. It inspires awe in those who gaze upon it.

I can remember everything up to that point, everything up to the moment when I spoke those words and a little bit beyond, but after that the sequence becomes rather murky to me. I know that I shouted at her, pounding on my chest and daring her to pull the trigger, but whether I did that before she started to cry or after is not something I can remember. Nor can I remember anything she said. That must mean that I did most of the talking, but the words were rushing out of me so fast by then that I scarcely knew what I was saying. What matters most is that she was frightened. She hadn't expected me to turn the tables on her, and when I glanced up from the gun and looked into her eyes again, I knew that she didn't have the nerve to kill me. She was all bluff and childish desperation, and the moment I started walking toward her, she immediately dropped her arm to her side. A mysterious sound escaped from her throat – a muffled, choked-off stream of breath, an unidentifiable noise that fell somewhere between a moan and a sob – and as I continued to attack her with my taunts and badgering insults, shouting at her to hurry up and get it over with, I knew – and knew absolutely, knew beyond any shadow of a doubt – that the gun wasn't loaded. Again, I don't claim to know where this certainty came from, but the instant I saw her lower her arm, I knew that nothing was going to happen to me, and I wanted to punish her for that, to make her pay for pretending to be something she was not.

I'm talking about a matter of seconds, an entire lifetime reduced to a matter of seconds. I took a step, and then another step, and suddenly I was upon her, twisting her arm and tearing the gun out of her hand. She was no longer the angel of death, but I knew what death tasted like now, and in the madness of the seconds that followed, I did what was surely the wildest, most outlandish thing I have ever done. Just to prove a point. Just to show her that I was stronger than she was. I took the gun from her, backed off a few feet, and then pointed it at my head. There were no bullets in it, of course, but she didn't know that I knew that, and I wanted to use my knowledge to humiliate her, to present her with a picture of a man who wasn't afraid to die. She had started it, and now I was going to finish it. She was screaming by then, I remember, I can still hear how she screamed and begged me not to do it, but nothing was going to stop me now.

I was expecting to hear a click, followed perhaps by a brief percussive echo from the empty chamber. I put my finger around the trigger, gave Alma Grund what must have been a grotesque and nauseating smile, and started to pull. Oh God, she screamed. Oh God, don't do it. I pulled, but the trigger didn't go anywhere. I tried again, and again nothing happened. I assumed the trigger was stuck, but when I lowered the gun to have a proper look at it, I finally saw what the trouble was. The safety catch was on. There were bullets in the gun, and the safety catch was on. She hadn't remembered to release it. If not for that mistake, one of those bullets would have been in my head.

She sat down on the sofa and went on crying into her hands. I didn't know how long it was going to last, but once she pulled herself together, I assumed that she would get up and leave. What other choice did she have? I had nearly blown my brains out because of her, and now that she had lost our sickening contest of wills, I couldn't imagine that she would have the heart to say another word to me.

I put the gun in my pocket. As soon as I was no longer touching it, I could feel the madness start to drain out of my body. Only the horror was left – a kind of hot, tactile afterglow, the memory in my right hand of trying to pull the trigger, of pressing the hard metal against my skull. If there was no hole in that skull now, it was only because I was stupid and lucky, because for once in my life my luck had won out over my stupidity. I had come within an inch of killing myself. A series of accidents had stolen my life from me and then given it back, and in the interval, in the tiny gap between those two moments, my life had become a different life.

When Alma finally lifted her face again, the tears were still running down her cheeks. Her makeup had smudged, leaving a zigzag of black lines across the center of her birthmark, and she looked so disheveled, so undone by the catastrophe she had made for herself, that I almost felt sorry for her.

Go and wash up, I said. You look terrible.

It moved me that she didn't say anything. This was a woman who believed in words, who trusted in her ability to talk her way out of tough corners, but when I gave her that command, she stood up from the sofa in silence and did what I told her to do. Just the wan trace of a smile, the barest hint of a shrug. As she walked off and found her way to the bathroom, I sensed how badly she had been defeated, how mortified she was by what she had done. Inexplicably, the sight of her leaving the room touched something in me. It turned around my thoughts somehow, and in that first little flash of sympathy and fellow feeling, I made a sudden, altogether unexpected decision. To the extent that such things can be quantified, I believe that decision was the beginning of the story I am trying to tell now.

While she was gone, I went into the kitchen to look for a place to hide the gun. After opening and shutting the cupboards above the sink, then casting about in several drawers and aluminum containers, I opted for the freezer compartment of the refrigerator. This was my first experience with a gun, and I wasn't sure if I could unload it without causing more mischief, so I laid it in the freezer as it was, bullets and all, wedging it under a bag of chicken parts and a box of ravioli. I just wanted to get the thing out of sight. After I closed the door, however, I realized that I had no great urge to get rid of it. It wasn't that I had any plans to use the gun again, but I liked the idea of having it near me, and until I thought of a better place to put it, I would let it go on sitting in the freezer. Every time I opened the door, I would remember what had happened to me that night. It would be my secret memorial, a monument to my brush with death.

She was taking a long time in the bathroom. The rain had stopped by then, and rather than sit around waiting for her to come out, I decided to clean up the mess in my truck and bring in the groceries. That took a little under ten minutes. When I had finished putting away the food, Alma was still in the bathroom. I walked over to the door to listen in, beginning to feel some twinges of worry, wondering if she hadn't gone in there with the intention of doing something rash and idiotic. Before I left the house, the water in the sink had been running. I had heard the faucets going at full blast, and when I walked by the door on my way out, I had heard her sobbing under the noise. Now the water was off, and there was no sound at all. That could have meant that her crying fit was over and that she was calmly brushing her hair and putting on her makeup. Or it could have meant that she was out cold on the floor, crumpled up with twenty Xanax pills in her stomach.

I knocked. When she didn't answer, I knocked again and asked if she was all right. She was coming, she said, she would be out in a minute, and then, after a long pause, in a voice that seemed to be struggling for breath, she told me that she was sorry, sorry for every wretched thing that had happened. She would rather die than have to leave the house before I had forgiven her, she said, she was begging me to forgive her, but even if I couldn't do that, she was going now, either way she was going, and she wouldn't trouble me again.

I stood there waiting by the door. When she came out, her eyes had that blotchy, puffed-up look you get after a long weeping jag, but her hair was in place again, and the powder and lipstick managed to hide most of the redness. She was intending to walk on past me, but I put out my hand and stopped her.

It's after two o'clock, I said. We're both exhausted, and we need to get some sleep. You can use my bed. I'll sleep downstairs on the sofa.

She was so ashamed of herself, she couldn't find the courage to lift her head and look at me. I don't understand, she said, addressing her words to the floor, and when I didn't say anything immediately after that, she said it again: I don't understand.

No one's going anywhere tonight, I said. Not me, and not you either. We can talk about tomorrow tomorrow, but for now we both stay put.

What does that mean?

It means that it's a long way to New Mexico. Better to start off fresh in the morning. I know you're in a hurry, but a few hours aren't going to make that much of a difference.

I thought you wanted me to leave.

I did. But now I've changed my mind.

Her head came up a little then, and I could see how thoroughly confused she was. You don't have to be nice to me, she said. I'm not asking for that.

Don't worry. I'm thinking about myself, not you. We have a big day ahead of us tomorrow, and if I don't sack out now, I'm not going to be able to keep my eyes open. I have to be awake to hear what you're going to tell me, don't I?

You're not saying you want to go with me. You can't be saying that. It's not possible for you to be saying that.

I can't think of anything else I have to do tomorrow. Why shouldn't I go?

Don't lie. If you're lying to me now, I don't think I could stand it. You'd be tearing the heart right out of my body.

It took several minutes for me to persuade her that I meant to go. The reversal was simply too stunning for her to comprehend, and I had to repeat myself several times before she was willing to believe me. I didn't tell her everything, of course. I didn't bother to talk about microscopic holes in the universe or the redemptive powers of temporary insanity. That would have been too difficult, and so I confined myself to telling her that my decision was personal and had nothing to do with her. We had both behaved badly, I said, and I was just as responsible for what had happened as she was. No blame, no forgiveness, no keeping score of who did what to whom. Or words to that effect, words that eventually proved to her that I had my own reasons for wanting to meet Hector and that I wasn't going for anyone but myself.

Arduous negotiations ensued. Alma couldn't accept the offer of my bed. She had inconvenienced me enough, and on top of that I was banged up from the road accident earlier that night. I needed rest, and I wasn't going to get it tossing and turning on the sofa. I insisted that I would be all right, but she wouldn't hear of such a thing, and back and forth we went, each one trying to oblige the other in an inane comedy of manners less than an hour after I had ripped a gun out of her hand and come close to firing a bullet into my head. I was too worn out to put up much of an argument, however, and in the end I let her have her way. I fetched some bedding and a spare pillow for her, plopped them down on the sofa, and then showed her where to turn off the lights. That was all. She said she didn't mind putting on the sheets herself, and after she had thanked me for the seventh time in the past three minutes, I went upstairs to my room.

There was no question that I was tired, but once I slipped in under the covers, I had trouble falling asleep. I lay there looking at the shadows on the ceiling, and when that no longer seemed interesting, I turned onto my side and listened to the faint sounds of Alma stirring around on the floor below. Alma, the feminine form of *almus*, meaning nourishing, bountiful. Eventually, the light went out under my door, and I heard the springs in the sofa shift as she settled in for the night. After that, I must have dozed off for a while, since I can't remember anything else that happened until I opened my eyes at three-thirty. I saw the time on the electric clock beside the bed, and because I was groggy, suspended in that half state between sleeping and waking, I only dimly understood that I had opened my eyes because Alma was crawling into the bed beside me and putting her head on my shoulder. It's lonely down there, she said, I can't sleep. That made perfect sense to me. I knew all about not being able to sleep, and before I was awake enough to ask her what she was doing in my bed, I had my arms around her and was kissing her on the mouth.

We set off the next morning just before noon. Alma wanted to drive, so I rode shotgun and handled the navigation duties, telling her where to turn and which highways to take as she steered her blue rented Dodge toward Boston. There were some traces of the storm left on the ground – fallen branches, wet leaves plastered to the roofs of cars, a toppled flagpole lying on someone's lawn – but the sky was clear again, and we drove through sunlight all the way to the airport.

Neither one of us said anything about what had happened in my bedroom the night before. It sat in the car with us like a secret, like something that belonged to the domain of small rooms and nocturnal thoughts and must not be exposed to the light of day. To name it would have been to risk destroying it, and therefore we didn't go much beyond an occasional sidelong glance, a fleeting smile, a hand placed cautiously on the other's knee. How could I presume to know what Alma was thinking? I was glad that she had crawled into my bed, and I was glad that we had spent those hours together in the darkness. But that was only one night, and I had no idea what was going to happen to us next.

The last time I had driven to Logan Airport, I had been in the car with Helen, Todd, and Marco. The last morning of their lives had been spent on the same roads that Alma and I were traveling now. Turn by turn, they had made the same trip; mile by mile, they had covered the same ground. Route 30 to Interstate 91; 91 to the Mass Pike; the Mass Pike to 93; 93 to the tunnel. A part of me welcomed this grotesque reenactment. It felt like some cunningly devised form of punishment, as if the gods had decided that I wouldn't be allowed to have a future until I returned to the past. Justice therefore dictated that I should spend my first morning with Alma in the same way I had spent my last morning with Helen. I had to get into a car and drive to the airport, and I had to be rushing along at ten and twenty miles over the speed limit to avoid missing a plane.

The boys had been squabbling in the back seat, I remembered, and at one point Todd had hauled off and punched his little brother on the arm. Helen had turned around to remind him that he knew better than to pick on a four-year-old, and our firstborn son had petulantly complained that M. had started it and therefore was only getting what he deserved. If someone hits you, he said, you had the right to hit him back. To which I had answered, making what was to be the last paternal pronouncement of my life, that no one had the right to hit someone smaller than he was. But Marco will always be smaller than I am, Todd said. That means I'll never be able to hit him. Well, I said, impressed by the logic of his argument, sometimes life isn't fair. It was a cretinous thing to say, and I remembered that Helen had burst out laughing when I uttered that dreadful truism. It was her way of telling me that of the four people sitting in the car that morning, Todd was the one with the best set of brains. I agreed with her, of course. They were all smarter than I was, and not for a second did I think I could hold a candle to them.

204

Alma was a good driver. As I sat there watching her weave in and out of the left and center lanes, passing everything in sight, I told her that she looked beautiful.

That's because you're looking at my good side, she said. If you were sitting over here, you probably wouldn't say that.

Is that why you wanted to drive?

The car's rented in my name. I'm the only one who's supposed to drive it.

And vanity has nothing to do with it.

It's going to take time, David. There's no point in overdoing it when we don't have to.

It doesn't bother me, you know. I'm already getting used to it.

You can't be. Not yet, anyway. You haven't looked at me enough to know what you feel.

You said you were married. It obviously hasn't stopped men from finding you attractive.

I like men. After a while, they come to like me. I might not have been around as much as some girls, but I've had my fair share of experiences. Spend enough time with me, and you won't even see it anymore.

But I like seeing it. It makes you different, someone who doesn't look like anyone else. You're the only person I've ever met who looks only like herself.

That's what my father used to say. He told me it was a special present from God, and it made me more beautiful than all the other girls.

Did you believe him?

Sometimes. And sometimes I felt cursed. It's an ugly thing, after all, and it makes you an easy target when you're a child. I kept thinking that someday I'd be able to get rid of it, that some doctor would perform an operation and make me look normal. Whenever I dreamed about myself at night, both sides of my face were the same. Smooth and white, perfectly symmetrical. That didn't stop until I was about fourteen.

You were learning how to live with it.

Maybe, I don't know. But something happened to me around then, and my thinking started to change. It was a big experience for me, a turning point in my life.

Someone fell in love with you.

No, someone gave me a book. For Christmas that year, my mother bought me an anthology of American short stories. *Classic American Tales*, a huge hardcover book with green cloth binding, and on page forty-six there was a story by Nathaniel Hawthorne. *The Birthmark*. Do you know it?

Dimly. I don't think I've read it since high school.

I read it every day for six months. Hawthorne wrote it for me. It was my story.

A scientist and his young bride. That's the situation, isn't it? He tries to remove the birthmark from her face.

A red birthmark. From the left side of her face.

No wonder you liked it.

Like isn't a strong enough word. I was obsessed by it. That story ate me alive.

The birthmark looks like a human hand, doesn't it? I'm starting to remember now. Hawthorne says that it looks like the imprint of a hand pressed against her cheek.

But small. It's the size of a pygmy's hand, the hand of an infant.

She has that one tiny flaw, but otherwise her face is perfect. She's known as an extraordinary beauty.

Georgiana. Until she marries Aylmer, she doesn't even think of it as a flaw. He's the one who teaches her to hate it, who turns her against herself and makes her want to have it removed. For him, it's not just a defect, not just something that destroys her physical beauty. It's a sign of some inner corruption, a stain on Georgiana's soul, a mark of sin and death and decay.

The stamp of mortality.

Or just simply what we think of as human. That's what makes it so tragic. Aylmer goes into his laboratory and begins experimenting with elixirs and potions, trying to come up with a formula to erase the dreaded spot, and innocent Georgiana goes along with it. That's what's so terrible. She wants him to love her. That's all she cares about, and if eliminating the birthmark is the price she has to pay for his love, she's willing to risk her life for it.

And he winds up murdering her.

But not before the birthmark disappears. That's very important. At the last second, just as she's about to die, the mark fades from her cheek. It's gone now, entirely gone, and it's only then, at that exact moment, that poor Georgiana dies.

The birthmark is who she is. Make it vanish, and she vanishes along with it.

You have no idea what that story did to me. I kept reading it, kept thinking about it, and little by little I began to see myself as I was. Other people carried their humanity inside them, but I wore mine on my face. That was the difference between me and everyone else. I wasn't allowed to hide who I was. Every time people looked at me, they were looking right into my soul. I wasn't a bad-looking girl – I knew that – but I also knew that I would always be defined by that purple blotch on my face. There was no use in trying to get rid of it. It was the central fact of my life, and to wish it away would have been like asking to destroy myself. I was never going to have an ordinary kind of happiness, but after I read that story, I realized that I had something almost as good. I knew what people were thinking. All I had to do was look at them, study their reactions when they saw the left side of my face, and I could tell whether they could be trusted or not. The birthmark was the test of their humanity. It measured the worth of their souls, and if I worked hard at it, I could see straight into them and know who they were. By the time I was sixteen or seventeen, I had the perfect pitch of a tuning fork. That doesn't mean I haven't made mistakes about people, but most of the time I've known better. I just haven't been able to stop myself.

Like last night.

No, not like last night. That wasn't a mistake.

We nearly killed each other.

It had to be that way. When you run out of time, everything gets speeded up. We couldn't afford the luxury of formal introductions, handshakes, discreet conversation over drinks. It had to be violent. Like two planets colliding at the edge of space.

Don't tell me you weren't scared.

I was scared to death. But I didn't go into this blind, you know. I had to be ready for anything.

They told you I was crazy, didn't they?

No one ever used that word. The strongest thing anyone said was nervous breakdown.

What did your tuning fork tell you when you got there?

You already know the answer to that.

You were spooked, weren't you? I spooked the hell out of you.

It was more than that. I was afraid, but at the same time I was excited, almost trembling with happiness. I looked at you, and for a couple of moments it was almost like looking at myself. That's never happened to me before.

You liked it.

I loved it. I was so lost, I thought I was going to fall to pieces.

And now you trust me.

You're not going to let me down. And I'm not going to let you down. We both know that.

What else do we know?

Nothing. That's why we're sitting together in this car now. Because we're the same, and because we don't know a damn thing other than that.

We made the four o'clock flight to Albuquerque with twenty minutes to spare. Ideally, I should have taken the Xanax by the time we reached Holyoke or Springfield, Worcester at the latest, but I was too wrapped up in talking to Alma to interrupt the conversation, and I kept putting it off. When we drove past the signs for the 495 exit, I realized that there was no point in bothering to take them. The pills were in Alma's bag, but she hadn't read the instructions on the label. She didn't know that they had to be swallowed an hour or two in advance to be effective.

At first, I was glad that I hadn't given in. Every cripple trembles at the thought of abandoning his crutch, but if I could get through the flight without disintegrating into tears or frantic ravings, perhaps I would be better for it in the end. This thought held me for another twenty or thirty minutes. Then, as we approached the outskirts of Boston, I understood that I no longer had a choice. We had been driving for more than three hours, and we still hadn't talked about Hector. I had assumed that we would do that in the car, but we had wound up talking about other things, things that no doubt had to be talked about first, that were no less important than what was waiting for us in New Mexico, and before I knew it, the first leg of the trip was nearly over. I couldn't fall asleep on her now. I had to stay awake to listen to the story she'd promised to tell me.

We sat down in the area next to the departure gate. Alma asked me if I wanted to take a pill, and that was when I told her I wasn't going to use the Xanax. Just hold my hand, I said, and I'll be all right. I'm feeling good.

She held my hand, and for a little while we necked in front of the other passengers. It was pure, adolescent abandon – not my adolescence, perhaps, but the one I had always wished for – and it was such a novel experience to be kissing a woman in public that I didn't have time to dwell on the torture ahead. When we boarded the plane, Alma was rubbing the lipstick off my cheek, and I barely noticed when we crossed the threshold and stepped inside. Walking down the center aisle posed no problem for me, nor did sitting down in my seat. I wasn't even disturbed when I had to fasten my seat belt, and even less so when the engines roared into full throttle and I felt the machine start to vibrate along my skin. We were in first class. The menu said that they would be serving us chicken for dinner. Alma, who was sitting next to the window on my left – and therefore with her right side turned to me again – took my hand in her hand, raised it to her mouth, and kissed it.

The only mistake I made was to close my eyes. When the plane backed up from the terminal and began to taxi down the runway, I didn't want to have to watch us taking off. That was the most dangerous moment, I felt, and if I could survive the transition from earth to sky, simply ignore the fact that we had lost contact with the ground, I figured I might have a chance to survive the rest. But I was wrong to want to block it out, wrong to cut myself off from the event as it unfurled itself in the actuality of the moment. To experience it would have been painful, but much worse was to remove myself from that pain and withdraw into the shell of my thoughts. The world of the present was gone. There was nothing to see, nothing to distract me from succumbing to my fears, and the longer I kept my eyes shut, the more terribly I saw what my fears wanted me to see. I had always wished that I had died with Helen and the boys, but I had never let myself fully imagine what they had lived through in the last moments before the plane went down. Now, with my eyes closed, I heard the boys screaming, and I saw Helen holding them in her arms, telling them that she loved them, whispering through the screams of the one hundred forty-eight other people who were about to die that she would always love them, and when I saw her there with the boys in her arms, I broke down and sobbed. Exactly as I had always imagined I would, I broke down and sobbed.

I put my hands over my face, and for the longest time I went on weeping into my salty, stinking palms, unable to lift my head, unable to open my eyes and stop. Eventually, I felt Alma's hand on the back of my neck. I had no idea how long it had been there, but a moment came when I started to feel it, and after a while I realized that her other hand was going up and down my left arm, stroking it very gently, using the same soft and rhythmical motion that a mother uses to comfort a miserable child. Oddly enough, the instant I became aware of this thought, aware of the fact that I had conjured up this thought about mothers and children, I imagined that I had slipped into the body of Todd, my own son, and that it was Helen who was comforting me and not Alma. That feeling lasted for only a few seconds, but it was extremely powerful, not a thing of the imagination so much as a real thing, an actual transformation that turned me into someone else, and the moment it started to go away, the worst of what had happened to me was suddenly over.

5

Half an hour later, Alma began to talk. We were seven miles up in the air by then, sailing above some nameless county in Pennsylvania or Ohio, and she went on talking all the way to Albuquerque. There was a brief pause when we landed, and then the story continued after we climbed into her car and began the two-and-a-half-hour trip to Tierra del Sueño. We drove down a series of desert highways as the late afternoon turned to dusk and the dusk then turned to night. As I remember it, the story didn't stop until we came to the gates of the ranch – and even then it wasn't quite finished. She had talked for almost seven hours, but there hadn't been enough time to fit everything in.

She jumped around a lot in the early going, darting back and forth between the past and present, and it took me a while to get my bearings and sort out the chronology of events. It was all in her book, she said, all the names and dates, all the essential facts, and there was no need to rehash the details of Hector's life prior to his disappearance – not that afternoon on the plane, in any case, not when I would be able to read the book myself in the days and weeks ahead. What mattered were the things that bore on Hector's destiny as a hidden man, the years he had spent in the desert writing and directing films that were never shown to the public. Those films were the reason why I was traveling to New Mexico with her now, and interesting as it might have been to know that Hector was born Chaim Mandelbaum – on a Dutch steamship in the middle of the Atlantic – it wasn't terribly important. It didn't matter that his mother died when he was twelve or that his father, a cabinet-maker with no interest in politics, was nearly beaten to death by an anti-Bolshevik, anti-Semitic mob during La Semana Tragica in Buenos Aires in 1919. That led to Hector's departure for America, but his father had been urging him to emigrate for some time before that, and the crisis in Argentina merely accelerated the decision. There was no point in listing the two dozen jobs he held after arriving in New York, and even less urgency to talk about what happened to him after he reached Hollywood in 1925. I knew enough about his early work as an extra, set-builder, and sometime bit player in scores of lost and forgotten films for us to pass over those years, enough about his tangled relations with Hunt not to have to dwell on them again. The experience soured Hector on the movie business, Alma said, but he wasn't ready to give up, and until the night of January 14, 1929, the last thought in his mind was that he would ever have to leave California.

One year before he vanished, he had been interviewed by Brigid O'Fallon for *Photoplay*. She had come to his house on North Orange Drive at three o'clock one Sunday afternoon, and by five o'clock they were on the floor together, rolling around on the carpet and seeking out the holes and crevices in each other's bodies. Hector was wont to behave like that with women, Alma said, and this was hardly the first time he had used his seductive powers to make a swift and decisive conquest. O'Fallon was just twenty-three, a bright Catholic girl from Spokane who had graduated from Smith and come back west to make it in journalism. As it happened, Alma had also graduated from Smith, and she used her connections there to track down a copy of the 1926 yearbook. The head shot of O'Fallon was inconclusive. Her eyes were too close together, Alma said, her chin was too broad, and her bobbed hair was not flattering to her features. Still, there was something effervescent about her, some spark of mischief or humor lurking in her gaze, a bright inner élan. In a photograph of the Drama Society's production of *The Tempest*, O'Fallon had been captured in mid-performance, decked out as Miranda in a thin white gown and sporting a single white flower in her hair, and Alma said that she was lovely in that pose, a small slip of a thing shimmering with life and energy – open-mouthed, an arm flung forward, in the act of declaiming a line. As a journalist, O'Fallon wrote in the style of the day. Her sentences were sharp and punchy, and she had a knack for sprinkling her articles with witty asides and deftly turned puns that helped her move up quickly through the ranks of the magazine. The article about Hector was an exception, far more earnest and openly admiring of her subject than any of the other pieces of hers that Alma had read. The heavy accent, however, was only a slight exaggeration. O'Fallon juiced it up a little for comic effect, but that was essentially how Hector spoke at the time. His English improved over the years, but back in the twenties he still sounded like someone who had just stepped off the boat. He might have landed on his feet in Hollywood, but yesterday he was just another bewildered foreigner, standing on the dock with all his earthly possessions crammed into a cardboard suitcase.

In the months that followed the interview, Hector went on cavorting with any number of beautiful young actresses. He enjoyed being seen in public with them, he enjoyed going to bed with them, but none of those flings lasted. O'Fallon was cleverer than the other women he knew, and once Hector had tired of his latest plaything, he would invariably call up Brigid and ask to see her again. Between early February and late June, he visited her apartment on the average of once or twice a week, and throughout the middle of that period, for most of April and May, he was with her no less than every second or third night. There was no question that he was fond of her. As the months went by, a comfortable intimacy developed between them, but whereas the less experienced Brigid took that as a sign of eternal love, Hector never deluded himself into thinking they were anything more than close friends. He saw her as his pal, as his sexual companion, as his trusted ally, but that didn't mean he had any intention of proposing marriage to her.

She was a reporter, and she must have known what Hector was up to on the nights he didn't sleep in her bed. All she had to do was open the morning paper to follow his exploits, to breathe in the innuendos about his newest crushes and dalliances. Even if most of the stories she read about him were false, there was more than enough evidence to arouse her jealousy. But Brigid wasn't jealous – or at least she didn't appear to be jealous. Every time Hector called, she welcomed him into her arms. She never talked about the other women, and because she didn't accuse him or berate him or ask him to mend his ways, his affection for her only increased. That was Brigid's plan. She had lost her heart to him, and rather than force him to make a premature decision about their life together, she decided to be patient. Sooner or later, Hector would stop running around. The frantic womanizing would lose its appeal to him. He would grow bored; he would work it out of his system; he would see the light. And when he did, she would be there for him.

So plotted the clear-thinking and resourceful Brigid O'Fallon, and for a time it looked as though she would catch her man. Hector, embroiled in his various disputes with Hunt, struggling against fatigue and the pressures of having to crank out a new film every month, became less inclined to fritter away his nights in jazz clubs and speakeasys, to expend his strength on pointless seductions. O'Fallon's apartment became a refuge for him, and the quiet evenings they spent there together helped keep his head and groin in balance. Brigid was an incisive critic, and because she was savvier about the movie business than he was, he came to rely more and more on her judgment. It was she, in fact, who suggested that he audition Dolores Saint John for the role of the sheriff's daughter in *The Prop Man*, his upcoming two-reeler. Brigid had been studying Saint John's career for the past several months, and in her opinion the twenty-one-year-old actress had the potential to become the next big thing, another Mabel Normand or Gloria Swanson, another Norma Talmadge.

Hector followed her advice. When Saint John walked into his office three days later, he had already watched a couple of her films and was committed to offering her the job. Brigid had been right about Saint John's talent, but nothing she had said and nothing he had seen of Saint John's work on film had prepared Hector for the overwhelming effect her presence would have on him. It was one thing to watch a person act in a silent movie; it was quite another to shake that person's hand and look into her eyes. Other actresses were more impressive on celluloid, perhaps, but in the real world of sound and color, in the fleshed-out, three-dimensional world of the five senses and the four elements and the two sexes, he had never met a creature to compare with this one. It wasn't that Saint John was more beautiful than other women, and it wasn't that she said anything remarkable to him during the twenty-five minutes they spent together that afternoon. To be perfectly honest, she seemed to be a bit on the dull side, of no more than average intelligence, but there was a feral quality to her, an animal energy coursing along her skin and radiating from her gestures that made it impossible for him to stop looking at her. The eyes that looked back at him were of the palest Siberian blue. Her skin was white, and her hair was the darkest shade of red, a red verging on mahogany. Unlike the hair of most American women in June of 1928, it was long, and it hung down to her shoulders. They talked for a while about nothing in particular. Then, without any preamble, Hector told her that the part was hers if she wanted it, and she accepted. She had never worked in physical comedy before, she said, and she was looking forward to the challenge. Then she rose from her chair, shook his hand, and left the office. Ten minutes later, with the image of her face still burning in his head, Hector decided that Dolores Saint John was the woman he was going to marry. She was the woman of his life, and if it turned out that she wouldn't have him, then he would never marry anyone.

She performed ably in *The Prop Man*, doing all that Hector asked of her and even contributing some clever flourishes of her own, but when he tried to sign her up for his next film, she demurred. She had been offered the main role in an Allan Dwan feature, and the opportunity was simply too great for her to turn it down. Hector, who was supposed to have the magic touch with women, was getting nowhere with her. He couldn't find the words to express himself in English, and every time he was on the point of declaring his intentions to her, he would draw back at the last moment. If the words came out wrong, he felt that he would scare her off and ruin his chances forever. Meanwhile, he continued spending several nights a week at Brigid's apartment, and because he had made no promises to her, because he was free to love any person he wanted, he said nothing to her about Saint John. When shooting on *The Prop Man* wrapped in late June, Saint John went off on location to the Tehachapi Mountains. She worked on the Dwan film for four weeks, and during that time Hector wrote her sixty-seven letters. What he hadn't been able to say to her in person, he finally found the courage to put down on paper. He said it again and again, and even though he said it differently each time he wrote, the message was always the same. At first, Saint John was puzzled. Then she was flattered. Then she began to look forward to the letters, and by the end she realized that she couldn't live without them. When she returned to Los Angeles at the beginning of August, she told Hector that the answer was yes. Yes, she loved him. Yes, she would become his wife.

No date was set for the wedding, but they were talking about January or February – time enough for Hector to have fulfilled his contract with Hunt and to have worked out his next move. The moment had come to talk to Brigid, but he kept putting it off, could never quite get around to doing it. He was working late with Blaustein and Murphy, he said, he was in the editing room, he was on a location scout, he was under the weather. Between the beginning of August and the middle of October, he invented dozens of excuses for not seeing her, but still he couldn't bring himself to break it off entirely. Even in the throes of his infatuation with Saint John, he went on visiting Brigid once or twice a week, and every time he walked through the door of the apartment, he slipped back into the same old cozy setup. One could accuse him of being a coward, of course, but one could just as easily assert that he was a man in conflict. Perhaps he was having second thoughts about marrying Saint John. Perhaps he wasn't ready to give up O'Fallon. Perhaps he was torn between the two women and felt that he needed them both. Guilt can cause a man to act against his own best interests, but desire can do that as well, and when guilt and desire are mixed up equally in a man's heart, that man is apt to do strange things.

O'Fallon suspected nothing. In September, when Hector engaged Saint John to play the role of his wife in *Mr. Nobody*, she congratulated him on the intelligence of his choice. Even when rumors filtered back from the set that there was a special *closeness* between Hector and his leading lady, she wasn't unduly alarmed. Hector liked to flirt. He always fell for the actresses he worked with, but once the shooting was finished and everyone went home, he quickly forgot about them. In this case, however, the stories persisted. Hector had already moved on to *Double or Nothing*, his last picture at Kaleidoscope, and Gordon Fly was whispering in his column that wedding bells were about to ring for a certain long-haired siren and her mustachioed, funny-man beau. It was mid-October by then, and O'Fallon, who hadn't heard from Hector in five or six days, called the editing room and asked him to come to her apartment that night. She had never asked him to do anything like that before, and so he canceled his dinner plans with Dolores and went to Brigid's place instead. And there, confronted by the question he had put off answering for the past two months, he finally told her the truth.

Hector had been praying for something decisive, an eruption of female fury that would send him staggering out onto the street and end things once and for all, but Brigid merely looked at him when he broke the news to her, took a deep breath, and said that it wasn't possible for him to love Saint John. It wasn't possible because he loved her. Yes, Hector said, he did love her, he would always love her, but the fact was that he was going to marry Saint John. Brigid started to cry then, but still she didn't accuse him of betrayal, didn't argue for herself or shout out in anger about how terribly he had wronged her. He was wrong about himself, she said, and once he realized that no one would ever love him as she loved him, he would come back to her. Dolores Saint John was a thing, she said, not a person. She was a luminous and intoxicating thing, but underneath her skin she was coarse and shallow and stupid, and she didn't deserve to be his wife. Hector should have said something to her at that point. The occasion demanded that he deliver some brutal, piercing remark that would destroy her hope forever, but Brigid's grief was too strong for him, her devotion was too strong for him, and as he listened to her speak in those small, gasping sentences of hers, he couldn't bring himself to say the words. You're right, he answered. It probably won't last more than a year or two. But I have to go through with it. I have to have her, and once I do, everything else will take care of itself.

He wound up spending the night in Brigid's apartment. Not because he thought it would do them any good, but because she begged him to stay there one last time, and he couldn't say no to her. The next morning, he slipped out before she woke up, and from that moment on, things began to change for him. The contract with Hunt ended; he started working on *Dot and Dash* with Blaustein; his wedding plans took shape. After two and a half months, he still hadn't heard from Brigid. He found her silence a little troublesome, but the truth was that he was too preoccupied with Saint John to give the matter much thought. If Brigid had disappeared, it could only be because she was a person of her word and was too proud to stand in his way. Now that he had made his intentions clear, she had backed off to let him sink or swim on his own. If he swam, he probably wouldn't see her again. If he sank, she would probably turn up at the last minute and try to pull him out of the water.

It must have soothed Hector's conscience to think these things about O'Fallon, to turn her into a form of superior being who felt no pain when knives were stuck into her body, who didn't bleed when she was wounded. But in the absence of any verifiable facts, why not indulge in a little wishful thinking? He wanted to believe that she was doing well, that she was carrying on boldly with her life. He noticed that her articles had stopped appearing in *Photoplay*, but that could have meant that she was out of town or that she had taken another job somewhere else, and for the moment he refused to look at any of the darker possibilities. It wasn't until she finally surfaced again (by slipping a letter under his door on New Year's Eve) that he learned how miserably he had fooled himself. Two days after he had walked out on her in October, she had slit her wrists in the bathtub. If not for the water that had dripped down into the apartment below, the landlady never would have unlocked the door, and Brigid wouldn't have been found until it was too late. An ambulance took her to the hospital. She pulled through after a couple of days, but her mind had crumbled, she wrote, she was incoherent and weeping all the time, and the doctors decided to hold her for observation. That led to a two-month stay in the mental ward. She was prepared to spend the rest of her life there, but that was only because her one purpose in life now was to find a way to kill herself, and it made no difference where she was. Then, just as she was gearing up for her next

217

attempt, a miracle happened. Or rather, she discovered that a miracle had already happened and that she had been living under its spell for the past two months. Once the doctors confirmed that it was a real event and not something she had imagined, she no longer wanted to die. She had lost her faith years ago, she continued. She hadn't been to confession since high school, but when the nurse came in that morning to give her the results of the test, she felt as if God had put his mouth against her mouth and breathed life into her again. She was pregnant. It had happened in the fall, on the last night they had spent together, and now she was carrying Hector's baby inside her.

After they discharged her from the hospital, she had moved out of her apartment. She had a little money saved up, but not enough to go on paying the rent without returning to work – and she couldn't do that now, since she had already quit her job at the magazine. She had found a cheap room somewhere, the letter went on, a place with an iron bedstead and a wooden cross on the wall and a colony of mice living under the floorboards, but she wasn't going to tell him the name of the hotel or even what town it was in. It would be useless for him to go out looking for her. She was registered under a false name, and she meant to lie low until her pregnancy was a little further along, when it would no longer be possible for him to try to talk her into having an abortion. She had made up her mind to let the baby live, and whether Hector was willing to marry her or not, she was determined to become the mother of his child. Her letter concluded: *Fate has brought us together, my darling, and wherever I am now, you will always be with me.*

Then more silence. Another two weeks went by, and Brigid stuck to her promise and kept herself hidden. Hector said nothing to Saint John about O'Fallon's letter, but he knew that his chances of marrying her were probably dead. He couldn't think about their future life together without also thinking about Brigid, without tormenting himself with images of his pregnant ex-lover lying in a fleabag hotel in some derelict neighborhood, slowly pushing herself into madness as his child grew within her. He didn't want to give up Saint John. He didn't want to let go of the dream of crawling into her bed every night and feeling that smooth, electric body against his naked skin, but men were responsible for their actions, and if the child was going to be born, then there was no escape from what he had done. Hunt killed himself on January eleventh, but Hector was no longer thinking about Hunt, and when he heard the news on January twelfth, he felt nothing. The past was of no importance. Only the future mattered to him, and the future was suddenly in doubt. He was going to have to break off his engagement with Dolores, but he couldn't do that until Brigid surfaced again, and because he didn't know where to find her, he couldn't move, couldn't budge from the spot where the present had stranded him. As time went on, he began to feel like a man whose feet had been nailed to the floor.

On the night of January fourteenth, he knocked off work with Blaustein at seven o'clock. Saint John was expecting him for dinner at her house in Topanga Canyon at eight. Hector would have been there well before then, but he had car trouble along the way, and by the time he finished changing the tire on his blue DeSoto, he had lost three-quarters of an hour. If not for that flat tire, the event that altered the course of his life might never have happened, for it was precisely then, as he crouched down in the darkness just off La Cienega Boulevard and began jacking up the front end of his car, that Brigid O'Fallon knocked on the door of Dolores Saint John's house, and by the time Hector had completed his little task and was back behind the wheel of the car, Saint John had accidentally fired a thirty-two-caliber bullet into O'Fallon's left eye.

That was what she said, in any case, and from the stunned and horrified look that greeted him when he walked through the front door, Hector saw no reason to doubt her. She hadn't known the gun was loaded, she said. Her agent had given it to her when she moved into this isolated house in the canyon three months ago. It was supposed to be for protection, and after Brigid started saying all those crazy things to her, ranting on about Hector's baby and her slit wrists and the bars on the windows of madhouses and the blood from Christ's wounds, Dolores had become frightened and asked her to leave. But Brigid wouldn't go, and a few minutes later she was accusing Dolores of having stolen her man, threatening her with wild ultimatums and calling her a devil, a tramp, and a low-down lousy slut. Just six months ago, Brigid had been that sweet reporter from *Photoplay* with the pretty smile and the sharp sense of humor, but now she was out of her mind, she was dangerous, she was lurching around the room and weeping at the top of her lungs, and Dolores didn't want her there anymore. That was when she thought of the revolver. It was in the middle drawer of the rolltop desk in the living room, less than ten feet from where she was standing, and so she walked over to the desk and opened the middle drawer. She hadn't meant to pull the trigger. Her only thought was that maybe the

219

sight of the gun would be enough to scare off Brigid and get her to leave. But once she took it out of the drawer and pointed it across the room, the thing went off in her hand. There hadn't been much of a sound. Just a kind of small pop, she said, and then Brigid let out a mysterious grunt and fell to the floor.

Dolores wouldn't go into the living room with him (It's too horrible, she said, I can't look at her), and so he went in alone. Brigid was lying facedown on the rug in front of the sofa. Her body was warm, and blood was still leaking from the back of her skull. Hector turned her over, and when he looked into her destroyed face and saw the hole where her left eye had been, he suddenly stopped breathing. He couldn't look at her and breathe at the same time. In order to start breathing again, he had to look away, and once he did that, he couldn't bring himself to look at her anymore. Everything gone. Everything crushed to pieces. And the unborn baby inside her, dead and gone as well. Eventually, he stood up and went into the hall, where he found a blanket in the closet. When he returned to the living room, he looked at her one last time, felt the breath clutch inside him again, and then opened the blanket and spread it over her small, tragic body.

His first impulse was to go to the police, but Dolores was afraid. What would her story sound like when they questioned her about the gun, she said, when they forced her to walk through the improbable sequence of events for the twelfth time and made her explain why a twenty-four-year-old pregnant woman was lying dead on the living room floor? Even if they believed her, even if they were willing to accept that the gun had gone off accidentally, the scandal would ruin her. Her career would be finished, and Hector's career, too, for that matter, and why should they suffer for something that wasn't their fault? They should call Reggie, she said – meaning Reginald Dawes, her agent, the same fool who had given her the gun – and let him handle it. Reggie was smart, he knew all the angles. If they listened to Reggie, he would figure out a way to save their necks.

But Hector knew that he was already past saving. It was scandal and public humiliation if they talked; it was even worse trouble if they didn't. They could be charged with murder, and once the case was presented in court, not a soul on earth would believe that Brigid's death had been an accident. Choose your poison. Hector had to decide. He had to decide for both of them, and there was no right decision to be made. Forget about Reggie, he said to her. If Dawes got wind of what she had done, he would own her. She would be groveling before him on bloody knees for the rest of her life. There couldn't be anyone else. It was either get on the phone and talk to the cops, or it was talk to no one. And if it was no one, then they would have to take care of the body themselves.

He knew that he would burn in hell for saying that, and he also knew that he would never see Dolores again, but he said it anyway, and then they went ahead and did it. It wasn't a question of good and evil anymore. It was about doing the least harm under the circumstances, about not ruining yet another life for no purpose. They took Dolores's Chrysler sedan and drove up into the mountains about an hour north of Malibu with Brigid's body in the trunk. The corpse was still in the blanket, which in turn was wrapped in the rug, and there was a shovel in the trunk as well. Hector had found it in the garden shed behind Dolores's house, and that was what he used to dig the hole with. If nothing else, he figured he owed her that much. He had betrayed her, after all, and the remarkable thing about it was that she had gone on trusting him. Brigid's stories had had no effect on her. She had dismissed them as ravings, as lunatic lies told by a jealous, unhinged woman, and even when the evidence had been pushed up flat against her beautiful nose, she had refused to accept it. It could have been vanity, of course, a monstrous vanity that saw nothing of the world except what it wanted to see, but at the same time it could have been real love, a love so blind that Hector could scarcely even imagine what he was about to lose. Needless to say, he never learned which one it had been. After they returned from their hideous errand in the hills that night, he drove back to his house in his own car, and he never saw her again.

That was when he disappeared. Except for the clothes on his back and the cash in his wallet, he left everything behind, and by ten o'clock the next morning he was heading north on a train to Seattle. He was fully expecting to be caught. Once Brigid was reported missing, it wouldn't be long before someone made a connection between the two disappearances. The police would want to question him, and at that point they would begin looking for him in earnest. But Hector was wrong about that, just as he had been wrong about everything else. He was the one who was missing, and for the time being no one even knew that Brigid was gone. She had no job anymore, no permanent address, and when she failed to return to her room at the Fitzwilliam Arms in downtown Los Angeles for the rest of that week in early 1929, the desk clerk had her belongings carried down to the basement and rented her room to someone else. There was nothing unusual about that. People disappeared all the time, and you couldn't leave a room empty when a new tenant was willing to pay for it. Even if the desk clerk had felt concerned enough to contact the police, there was nothing they could have done about it anyway. Brigid was registered under a false name, and how could you look for someone who didn't exist?

Two months later, her father called from Spokane and talked to a Los Angeles detective named Reynolds, who continued working on the case until he retired in 1936. Twenty-four years after that, the bones of Mr. O'Fallon's daughter were finally unearthed. A bulldozer dug them up on the construction site of a new housing development at the edge of the Simi Hills. They were sent to the forensic laboratory in Los Angeles, but Reynolds's paperwork was deep in storage by then, and it was no longer possible to identify the person they had belonged to.

Alma knew about those bones because she had made it her business to know about them. Hector had told her where they were buried, and when she visited the housing development in the early eighties, she talked to enough people to confirm that they had been found in that spot.

By then, Saint John was long dead as well. After returning to her parents' house in Wichita following Hector's disappearance, she had issued her statement to the press and gone into seclusion. A year and a half later, she married a local banker named George T. Brinkerhoff. They had two children, Willa and George Junior. In 1934, when the elder child was still under three, Saint John lost control of her car while driving home one night in a hard November rain. She crashed into a telephone pole, and the impact of the collision sent her hurtling through the windshield, which severed the carotid artery in her neck. According to the police autopsy report, she bled to death without regaining consciousness.

Two years later, Brinkerhoff remarried. When Alma wrote to him in 1983 to request an interview, his widow answered that he had died of kidney failure the previous fall. The children were alive, however, and Alma spoke to both of them – one in Dallas, Texas, and the other in Orlando, Florida. Neither one had much to offer. They were so young at the time, they said. They knew their mother from photographs, but they didn't remember her at all.

*

By the time Hector walked into Central Station on the morning of January fifteenth, his mustache was already gone. He disguised himself by removing his most identifiable feature, transforming his face into another face through a simple act of subtraction. The eyes and eyebrows, the forehead and slicked-back hair would also have said something to a person familiar with his films, but not long after he bought his ticket, Hector found a solution to that problem as well. In the process, Alma said, he also found a new name.

The nine twenty-one for Seattle wouldn't be boarding for another hour. Hector decided to kill the time by going into the station restaurant for a cup of coffee, but no sooner did he sit down at the counter and start breathing in the smells of bacon and eggs frying on the griddle than he was engulfed by a wave of nausea. He wound up in the men's room, locked inside one of the stalls on his hands and knees, retching up the contents of his stomach into the toilet. It all came pouring out of him, the miserable green fluids and the clotted bits of undigested brown food, a trembling purge of shame and fear and revulsion, and when the attack was over, he sank to the floor and lay there for a long while, struggling to catch his breath. His head was pushed up against the back wall, and from that angle he was in a position to see something that otherwise would have escaped his notice. In the elbow of the curved pipe just behind the toilet, someone had left a cap. Hector slid it out from its hiding place and discovered that it was a worker's cap, a sturdy thing made of wool tweed with a short bill jutting from the front – not very different from the cap he had once worn himself, back when he was new in America. Hector turned it over to make sure there was nothing inside it, that it wasn't too dirty or too foul for him to put it on. That was when he saw the owner's name written out in ink along the back of the interior leather band: Herman Loesser. It struck Hector as a good name, perhaps even an excellent name, and in any event a name no worse than any other. He was Herr Mann, was he not? If he took to calling himself Herman, he could change his identity without altogether renouncing who he was. That was the important thing: to get rid of himself for others, but to remember who he was for himself. Not because he wanted to, but precisely because he didn't.

Herman Loesser. Some would pronounce it *Lesser*, and others would read it as *Loser*. Either way, Hector figured that he had found the name he deserved.

The cap fit remarkably well. It was neither too slack nor too snug, and there was just enough give to it for him to pull the brim down over his forehead and obscure the distinctive slant of his eyebrows, to shade the fierce clarity of his eyes. After the subtraction, then, an addition. Hector minus the mustache, and then Hector plus the cap. The two operations canceled him out, and he left the men's room that morning looking like anyone, like no one, like the spitting image of Mr. Nobody himself.

He lived in Seattle for six months, moved down to Portland for a year, and then went back north to Washington, where he stayed until the spring of 1931. At first, he was pushed along by pure terror. Hector felt that he was running for his life, and in the days that followed his disappearance, his ambitions were no different from those of any other criminal: as long as he eluded capture for another day, he considered that day well spent. Every morning and afternoon, he read about himself in the papers, keeping track of the developments in the case to see how close they were to finding him. He was perplexed by what they wrote, appalled by how little effort anyone had made to know him. Hunt was only of the scantest importance, and yet every article began and ended with him: stock manipulations, bogus investments, the business of Hollywood in all its worm-eaten glory. Brigid's name was never mentioned, and until Dolores went back to Kansas, no one even bothered to talk to her. Day by day, the pressure diminished, and after four weeks of no breakthroughs and dwindling coverage in the papers, his panic began to subside. No one suspected him of anything. He could have gone back home if he had wanted to. All he had to do was hop a train for Los Angeles, and he could have picked up his life exactly where he had left it.

But Hector didn't go anywhere. There was nothing he wanted more than to be in his house on North Orange Drive, sitting on the sun porch with Blaustein as they drank their iced teas and put the finishing touches on *Dot and Dash*. Making movies was like living in a delirium. It was the hardest, most demanding work anyone had invented, and the more difficult it became for him, the more exhilarating he found it. He was learning the ropes, slowly mastering the intricacies of the job, and with a little more time he was certain that he would have developed into one of the good ones. That was all he had ever wanted for himself: to be good at that one thing. He had wanted only that, and therefore that was the one thing he would never allow himself to do again. You don't drive an innocent girl insane, and you don't make her pregnant, and you don't bury her dead body eight feet under the ground and expect to go on with your life as before. A man who had done what he had done deserved to be punished. If the world wouldn't do it for him, then he would have to do it himself.

He rented a room in a boardinghouse near the Pike Place Market, and when the money in his wallet finally ran out, he found a job with one of the local fishmongers. Up every morning at four, unloading trucks in the predawn fog, hefting crates and bushels as the damp of Puget Sound stiffened his fingers and worked its way into his bones. Then, after a brief smoke, spreading out crabs and oysters on beds of chipped ice, followed by sundry repetitive daylight occupations: the clank of shells hitting the scale, the brown paper bags, slicing open oysters with his short, lethal scimitar. When he wasn't working, Herman Loesser read books from the public library, kept a journal, and talked to no one unless absolutely compelled to. The object, Alma said, was to squirm under the stringencies he had imposed on himself, to make himself as uncomfortable as possible. When the work became too easy, he moved on to Portland, where he found a job as a night watchman in a barrel factory. After the clamor of the roofed-in market, the silence of his thoughts. There was nothing fixed about his choices, Alma explained. His penance was a continual work in progress, and the punishments he meted out to himself changed according to what he felt were his greatest deficiencies at any given moment. He craved company, he longed to be with a woman again, he wanted bodies and voices around him, and therefore he walled himself up in that vacant factory, struggling to school himself in the finer points of self-abnegation.

The stock market crashed while he was in Portland, and when the Comstock Barrel Company went out of business in mid-1930, Hector lost his job. By then, he had worked his way through several hundred books, beginning with the standard nineteenth-century novels that everyone had always talked about but which he had never taken the trouble to read (Dickens, Flaubert, Stendhal, Tolstoy), and then, once he felt that he had got the hang of it, going back to zero and deciding to educate himself in a systematic manner. Hector knew next to nothing. He had left school at sixteen, and no one had ever bothered to tell him that Socrates and Sophocles were not the same man, that George Eliot was a woman, or that *The Divine Comedy* was a poem about the afterlife and not some boulevard farce in which all the characters wound up marrying the right person. Circumstances had always pressed in on him, and there hadn't been time for Hector to worry about such things.

Now, suddenly, there was all the time in the world. Imprisoned in his private Alcatraz, he spent the years of his captivity acquiring a new language to think about the conditions of his survival, to make sense of the constant, merciless ache in his soul. According to Alma, the rigors of this intellectual training gradually turned him into someone else. He learned how to look at himself from a distance, to see himself first of all as a man among other men, then as a collection of random particles of matter, and finally as a single speck of dust – and the farther he traveled from his point of origin, she said, the closer he came to achieving greatness. He had shown her his journals from that period, and fifty years after the fact, Alma had been able to witness the agonies of his conscience firsthand. *Never more lost than now*, she recited to me, quoting a passage from memory, *never more alone and afraid – yet never more alive.* Those words were written less than an hour before he left Portland. Then, almost as an afterthought, he sat down again and added another paragraph at the bottom of the page: *I talk only to the dead now. They are the only ones I trust, the only ones who understand me. Like them, I live without a future.*

The word was that there were jobs in Spokane. The lumber mills were supposedly looking for men, and several logging camps to the east and north were said to be hiring. Hector had no interest in those jobs, but he overheard two fellows talking about the opportunities up there one afternoon not long after the barrel factory shut down, and it gave him an idea, and once he began to think the idea through, he could no longer resist it. Brigid had grown up in Spokane. Her mother was dead, but her father was still around, and there were two younger sisters in the family as well. Of all the tortures Hector could imagine, of all the pains he could possibly inflict on himself, none was worse than the thought of going to the city where they lived. If he caught a glimpse of Mr. O'Fallon and the two girls, then he would know what they looked like, and their faces would be in his mind whenever he thought about the harm he had done to them. He deserved to suffer that much, he felt. He had an obligation to make them real, to make them as real in his memory as Brigid herself.

Still known by the color of his boyhood hair, Patrick O'Fallon had owned and operated Red's Sporting Goods in downtown Spokane for the past twenty years. On the morning of his arrival, Hector found a cheap hotel two blocks west of the train station, paid in advance for one night, and then went out to look for the store. He found it within five minutes. He hadn't thought about what he would do once he got there, but for caution's sake he figured it would be best to stand outside and try to get a look at O'Fallon through the window. Hector had no idea if Brigid had mentioned him in any of her letters home. If she had, the family would have known that he talked with a heavy Spanish accent. More important, they would have paid particular attention to his disappearance in 1929, and with Brigid herself now missing for close to two years, they might have been the only people in America who had figured out the link between the two cases. All he had to do was go into the store and open his mouth. If O'Fallon knew who Hector Mann was, the odds were that his suspicions would be aroused after three or four sentences.

But O'Fallon was nowhere to be seen. As Hector pressed his nose against the glass, pretending to examine a set of golf clubs on display in the window, he had a clear view into the store, and as far as he could make out from that angle, there was no one inside. No customers, no clerk standing behind the counter. It was early yet – just past ten o'clock – but the sign on the door said OPEN, and rather than remain on the crowded street and risk calling attention to himself, Hector scrapped his plan and decided to go in. If they found out who he was, he thought, then so be it.

The door made a tinkling sound when he pulled it open, and the bare wood planks creaked underfoot as he walked toward the counter in back. It wasn't a big place, but the shelves were crammed with merchandise, and there seemed to be everything a sportsman could possibly want: fishing rods and casting reels, rubber fins and swimming goggles, shotguns and hunting rifles, tennis racquets, baseball gloves, footballs, basketballs, shoulder pads and helmets, spiked shoes and cleated shoes, kicking tees and driving tees, duck pins, barbells, and medicine balls. Two lines of regularly spaced support columns ran the length of the store, and on each one there was a framed photograph of Red O'Fallon. He had been young when the pictures were taken, and they all showed him engaged in some form of athletic activity. Wearing a baseball uniform in one, a football uniform in another, but most often running races in the skimpy garb of a track-and-field man. In one photo, the camera had caught him in full stride, both feet off the ground, two yards ahead of his closest competitor. In another, he was shaking hands with a man dressed in top hat and tails, accepting a bronze medal at the 1904 Saint Louis Olympics.

As Hector approached the counter, a young woman emerged from a back room, wiping her hands with a towel. She was looking down, her head tilted to one side, but even though her face was largely obscured from him, there was something about her walk, something about the slope of her shoulders, something about the way she rubbed the towel over her fingers that made him feel that he was looking at Brigid. For the space of several seconds, it was as if the past nineteen months had never happened. Brigid was no longer dead. She had unburied herself, clawed her way out from the dirt he had shoveled over her body, and there she was now, intact and breathing again, with no bullet in her brain and no hole where her eye had been, working as an assistant in her father's store in Spokane, Washington.

The woman kept walking toward him, pausing only to lay the towel on top of an unopened carton, and the uncanny thing about what happened next was that even after she raised her head and looked into his eyes, the illusion persisted. She had Brigid's face, too. It was the same jaw and the same mouth, the same forehead and the same chin. When she smiled at him a moment later, he saw that it was the same smile as well. Only when she had come to within five feet of him did he begin to notice any differences. Her face was covered with freckles, which had not been true of Brigid's face, and her eyes were a deeper shade of green. They were also set more widely apart, ever so slightly farther from the bridge of her nose, and this minute alteration in her features enhanced the overall harmony of her face, making her a notch or two prettier than her sister had been. Hector returned her smile, and by the time she reached the counter and spoke to him in Brigid's voice, asking if he needed help, he no longer felt that he was about to fall to the floor in a dead swoon.

He was looking for Mr. O'Fallon, he said, and he wondered if it would be possible to talk to him. He made no effort to hide his accent, pronouncing the word *Meester* with an exaggerated roll to the final *r*, and then he leaned in closer to her, studying her face for signs of a reaction. Nothing happened, or rather the conversation continued as if nothing had happened, and at that moment Hector knew that Brigid had kept him a secret. She had been raised in a Catholic family, and she must have balked at the idea of letting her father and sisters know that she was bedding down with a man engaged to another woman and that the man, whose penis was circumcised, had no intention of breaking off his engagement to marry her. If that was the case, then they probably

228

hadn't known she was pregnant. Nor that she had slit her wrists in the bathtub; nor that she had spent two months in a hospital dreaming of better and more efficient ways to kill herself. It was even possible that she had stopped writing to them before Saint John had ever appeared on the scene, when she was still confident enough to suppose that everything was going to work out as she hoped it would.

Hector's mind was galloping by then, rushing off in several directions at once, and when the woman behind the counter said that her father was out of town for the week, away on business in California, Hector felt that he knew what that business was. Red O'Fallon had gone down to Los Angeles to talk to the police about his missing daughter. He was urging them to do something about a case that had already dragged on for too many months, and if he wasn't satisfied with their answers, he was going to hire a private detective to begin the search all over again. Damn the expense, he had probably said to his Spokane daughter before he left town. Something had to be done before it was too late.

The Spokane daughter said that she was filling in at the store while her father was gone, but if Hector cared to leave his name and number, she would give him the message when he returned on Friday. No need, Hector said, he would come back on Friday himself, and then, just to be polite, or perhaps because he wanted to make a good impression on her, he asked if she had been left to run things on her own. It looked like too big of an operation to be handled by just one person, he said.

There were supposed to be three people, she answered, but the regular assistant had called in sick that morning, and the stockboy had been fired last week for pilfering baseball gloves and selling them at half price to kids in his neighborhood. The truth was that she was feeling a little lost, she said. It had been ages since she'd helped out at the store, and she couldn't tell the difference between a putter and a wood, could barely even use the cash register without pushing nine wrong buttons and bollixing the sale.

It was all very friendly and direct. She didn't seem to think twice about sharing these confidences with him, and as the conversation continued, Hector learned that she had been away for the past four years, studying to become a teacher at something she called State, which turned out to be the State College of Washington in Pullman. She had graduated in June, and now she was back home living with her father, about to begin her career as a fourth-grade teacher at the Horace Greeley Elementary School. She couldn't believe her luck, she told him.

That was the same school she had attended as a girl, and she and her two older sisters had all had Mrs. Neergaard in the fourth grade. Mrs. N. had taught there for forty-two years, and it struck her as something of a miracle that her old teacher had retired just when she herself had started looking for a job. In less than six weeks, she would be standing in front of the same classroom where she had sat every day as a ten-year-old pupil, and wasn't it strange, she said, wasn't it funny how life worked out sometimes?

Yes, very funny, Hector said, very strange. He knew now that he was talking to Nora, the youngest of the O'Fallon girls, and not to Deirdre, the one who had married at nineteen and gone off to live in San Francisco. After three minutes in her company, Hector decided that Nora was nothing like her dead sister. She might have resembled Brigid, but she had none of her tense, smart-aleck energy, none of her ambition, none of her high-strung, darting intelligence. This one was softer, more comfortable in her own flesh, more naive. He remembered that Brigid had once described herself as the only one of the O'Fallon sisters with real blood running in her veins. Deirdre was made of vinegar, she said, and Nora was composed entirely of warm milk. She was the one who should have been named Brigid, she said, after Saint Brigid, the patron saint of Ireland, for if there was ever a person destined to devote herself to a life of self-sacrifice and good works, it was her baby sister, Nora.

Again, Hector was about to turn around and leave, and once again something held him there. A new idea had entered his head – the maddest of impulses, a thing so risky and self-destructive that it amazed him that he had even thought of it, let alone that he felt he had the nerve to carry it out.

Nothing ventured, nothing gained, he said to Nora, smiling apologetically and shrugging his shoulders, but the reason why he'd come in this morning was to ask Mr. O'Fallon for a job. He'd heard about that business with the stockboy and wondered if the position was still open. That's odd, Nora said. It happened just the other day, and they hadn't gotten around to placing a notice in the want ads yet. They weren't planning to do that until after her father returned from his trip. Well, word gets around, Hector said. Yes, that was probably true, Nora answered, but why would he want to be a stockboy anyway? That was a job for nobodies, for strong-backed men with dull minds and no ambitions; surely he could do better than that. Not necessarily, Hector said.

Times were tough, and any job that paid money these days was a good job. Why not give him a chance? She was all alone in the store, and he knew that she could use some help. If she liked his work, maybe she would put in a good word for him with her father. What did Miss O'Fallon say? Did they have a deal?

He had been in Spokane for less than an hour, and already Herman Loesser was employed again. Nora shook his hand, laughing at the audacity of his proposal, and then Hector removed his jacket (the one decent article of clothing he owned), and started to work. He had turned himself into a moth, and he spent the rest of the day fluttering around a hot, burning candle. He knew that his wings could ignite at any moment, but the closer he came to touching the fire, the more he sensed that he was fulfilling his destiny. As he put it in his journal that night: *If I mean to save my life, then I have to come within an inch of destroying it.*

Against all the odds, Hector held on for close to a year. First as stockboy in the back room, then as chief clerk and assistant manager, working directly under O'Fallon himself. Nora said her father was fifty-three, but when Hector was introduced to him the following Monday, he felt he looked older than that, perhaps as old as sixty, perhaps as old as a hundred. The ex-athlete's hair was no longer red, the once lithe torso was no longer trim, and he limped sporadically from the effects of an arthritic knee. O'Fallon showed up at the store every morning at nine sharp, but the work clearly had no interest to him, and he was generally gone again by eleven or eleven-thirty. If his leg was feeling up to it, he would drive out to the country club and shoot a round of golf with two or three of his cronies. If it wasn't, he would eat a long early lunch at the Bluebell Inn, the restaurant directly across the street, and then go home and spend the afternoon in his bedroom, reading the papers and drinking from the bottles of Jameson's Irish whiskey he had smuggled in from Canada every month.

He never criticized Hector or complained about his work. Nor did he ever compliment him. O'Fallon expressed his satisfaction by saying nothing, and every so often, when he was in one of his more expansive moods, he would greet Hector with a minuscule nod of the head. For several months, there was little more contact between them than that. Hector found it jarring at first, but as time went on he learned not to take it personally. The man lived in a domain of mute inwardness, of unending resistance against the world, and he seemed to float through his days with no other purpose than to use up the hours as painlessly as possible. He never lost his temper, he seldom cracked a smile. He was fair-minded and detached, absent even when present, and he showed no more compassion or sympathy for himself than he did for anyone else.

To the degree that O'Fallon was closed off and indifferent to him, Nora was open and involved. She was the one who had hired Hector, after all, and she continued to feel responsible for him, treating him alternately as her friend, her protégé, and her human reclamation project. After her father returned from Los Angeles and the chief clerk recovered from his bout with the shingles, Nora's services were no longer required at the store. She was busy preparing for the upcoming school year, busy visiting old classmates, busy juggling the attentions of several young men, but for the rest of the summer she always managed to find time to swing by Red's in the early afternoon to see how Hector was getting on. They had worked together for only four days, but in that time they had established a tradition of sharing cheese sandwiches in the stockroom during their half-hour lunch break. Now she continued to show up with the cheese sandwiches, and they continued to spend those half hours talking about books. For Hector, the budding autodidact, it was a chance to learn something. For Nora, fresh out of college and committed to a life of instructing others, it was a chance to impart knowledge to a bright and hungry student. Hector was plowing through Shakespeare that summer, and Nora read the plays along with him, helping him out with the words he didn't understand, explaining this or that point of history or theatrical convention, exploring the psychology and motivations of the characters. During one of their backroom sessions, as Hector stumbled over the pronunciation of the words *Thou ow'st* in the third act of *Lear*, he confessed to her how much his accent embarrassed him. He couldn't learn to speak this bloody language, he said, and he would always sound like a fool when he talked in front of people like her. Nora refused to listen to such pessimism. She had minored in speech therapy at State, she said, and there were concrete remedies, practical exercises, and techniques for improvement. If he was willing to take on the challenge, she promised to get rid of the accent for him, to remove all traces of Spanish from his tongue. Hector reminded her that he was in no position to pay for such lessons. Who said anything about money? Nora answered. If he was willing to work, she was willing to help.

After school opened in September, the new fourth-grade teacher was no longer available for lunch. She and her pupil worked in the evenings instead, getting together every Tuesday and Thursday from seven to nine in the parlor of the O'Fallon house. Hector struggled mightily with the short *i* and *e*, the lisping *th*, the toothless *r*. Silent vowels, interdental plosives, labial inflections, fricatives, palatal occlusions, phonemes. Much of the time, he had no idea what Nora was talking about, but the exercises seemed to have an effect. His tongue began to produce sounds it had never made before, and eventually, after nine months of strain and repetition, he had advanced to the point where it was becoming increasingly difficult to tell where he had been born. He didn't sound like an American, perhaps, but neither did he sound like a raw, uneducated immigrant. Coming to Spokane might have been one of the worst blunders Hector ever made, but of all the things that happened to him there, Nora's pronunciation lessons probably had the deepest and most lasting effect. Every word he spoke for the next fifty years was influenced by them, and they remained in his body for the rest of his life.

O'Fallon tended to stay upstairs in his room on Tuesdays and Thursdays, or else to be out for the evening, playing poker with friends. One night in early October, the telephone rang in the middle of a lesson, and Nora went into the front hall to answer it. She talked to the operator for a few moments, and then, in a tense and excited voice, called up to her father and told him that Stegman was on the line. He was in Los Angeles, she said, and wanted to reverse the charges. Should she accept or not? O'Fallon said that he would be right down. Nora closed the sliding doors between the parlor and the front hall to give her father privacy, but O'Fallon was slightly drunk by then, and he talked in a loud enough voice for Hector to make out some of the things he said. Not every thing, but enough of them to know that the call had not brought good news.

Ten minutes later, the sliding doors opened again, and O'Fallon shuffled into the parlor. He was wearing a pair of worn-out leather slippers, and his suspenders were off his shoulders, hanging down around his knees. Both his tie and collar were gone, and he had to grip the edge of the walnut end table to steady his balance. For the next little while, he talked directly to Nora, who was sitting beside Hector on the davenport in the middle of the room. For all the attention he paid to Hector, his daughter's student might have been invisible. It wasn't that O'Fallon ignored him, and it wasn't that he pretended he wasn't there. He simply didn't notice him. And Hector, who understood every nuance of the conversation that followed, didn't dare get up and leave.

Stegman was throwing in the towel, O'Fallon said. He'd been working on the case for months, and he hadn't turned up a single promising lead. It was getting to him, he said. He didn't want to take any more of their money.

Nora asked her father how he'd responded to that, and O'Fallon said he'd told him that if he felt so bad about taking their money, why the hell did he keep reversing the charges when he called? And then he'd told him he was lousy at his job. If Stegman didn't want the work, he'd look for someone else.

No, Dad, Nora replied, you're wrong. If Stegman couldn't find her, that meant no one could. He was the best private operative on the West Coast. Reynolds said so, and Reynolds was a man they could trust.

To hell with Reynolds, O'Fallon said. To hell with Stegman. They could say whatever they goddamn liked, but he wasn't going to give up.

Nora shook her head back and forth, her eyes filling with tears. It was time to face facts, she said. If Brigid was alive somewhere, she would have written a letter. She would have called. She would have let them know where she was.

The balls she would have, O'Fallon said. She hadn't written a letter in over four years. She'd broken with the family, and that was the fact they had to face.

Not with the family, Nora said. With him. Brigid had been writing to her all along. When she was at school in Pullman, there'd been a letter every three or four weeks.

But O'Fallon didn't want to hear about that. He didn't want to discuss it anymore, and if she wasn't going to stand behind him, then he'd push on alone and damn her and her goddamn opinions. And with those words, O'Fallon let go of the table, wobbled precariously for an instant or two as he tried to regain his footing, and then staggered out of the room.

Hector wasn't supposed to have witnessed this scene. He was just the stockboy, not an intimate friend, and he had no business listening in on private conversations between father and daughter, no right to be sitting in the room as his boss staggered around in a drunken, disheveled state. If Nora had asked him to leave at that moment, the matter would have been closed forever. He wouldn't have heard what he had heard, he wouldn't have seen what he had seen, and the subject never would have been mentioned again. All she had to do was speak one sentence, make one feeble excuse, and Hector would have risen from the davenport and said good night. But Nora had no talent for dissembling. The tears were still in her eyes when O'Fallon left the room, and now that the forbidden subject was finally out in the open, why hold anything back?

Her father hadn't always been like that, she said. When she and her sisters were young, he had been a different person, and it was hard to recognize him now, hard to remember what he'd been like back in the old days. Red O'Fallon, the Northwest Flash. Patrick O'Fallon, the husband of Mary Day. Dad O'Fallon, the emperor of little girls. But think of the past six years, Nora said, think of what he'd been through, and maybe it wasn't so strange that his best friend was a man named Jameson – that grim silent fellow who lived upstairs with him, trapped in all those bottles of amber liquid. The first blow came with the death of her mother, killed by cancer at age forty-four. That had been rough enough, she said, but then bad things kept happening, one family upheaval followed by another, a punch to the stomach and then one to the face, and little by little the stuffing had been knocked out of him. Less than a year after the funeral, Deirdre got herself pregnant, and when she refused to go through with the shotgun wedding O'Fallon had arranged for her, he kicked her out of the house. That turned Brigid against him, too, Nora said. Her oldest sister was in her last year of Smith, living all the way across the country, but when she heard about what happened, she wrote to her father and said that she would never talk to him again unless he welcomed Deirdre back into the house. O'Fallon wouldn't do that. He was paying for Brigid's education, and who did she think she was telling him what to do? She paid her own tuition for the final semester, and then, after her graduation, headed straight out to California to become a writer. She didn't even stop off in Spokane for a visit. She was as stubborn as her father, Nora said, and Deirdre was twice as stubborn as both of them together. It didn't matter that Deirdre was married now and had given birth to another baby. She still wouldn't talk to her father, and neither would Brigid. Meanwhile, Nora went off to attend college in Pullman. She kept in regular contact with both her sisters, but Brigid was the better correspondent, and it was the rare month when Nora didn't receive at least one letter from her. Then, some time at the beginning of Nora's junior year,

Brigid stopped writing. At first, it didn't seem like anything to get alarmed about, but after three or four months of continuing silence, Nora wrote to Deirdre and asked if she had had any recent news from Brigid. When Deirdre answered that she hadn't heard from her in six months, Nora began to worry. She talked to her father about it, and poor O'Fallon, desperate to make amends, crushed by guilt over what he had done to his two oldest daughters, immediately contacted the Los Angeles Police Department. A detective named Reynolds was assigned to the case. The investigation took off rapidly, and within several days many of the crucial facts had already been established: that Brigid had quit her job at the magazine, that she had attempted suicide and wound up in the hospital, that she had been pregnant, that she had moved out of her apartment without leaving a forwarding address, that she was indeed missing. Dark as this news was, shattering as it was to contemplate what these facts implied, it looked as though Reynolds was on the brink of discovering what had happened to her. Then, little by little, the trail went cold. A month went by, then three months, then eight months, and Reynolds had nothing new to report. They were talking to everyone who had known her, he said, doing everything they possibly could, but once they'd traced her to the Fitzwilliam Arms, they had run into a brick wall. Frustrated by this lack of progress, O'Fallon decided to push things along by engaging the services of a private detective. Reynolds recommended a man named Frank Stegman, and for a time O'Fallon was filled with new hope. The case was all he lived for, Nora said, and whenever Stegman reported the smallest bit of new information, the tiniest hint of a lead, her father would be on the first train to Los Angeles, traveling through the night if necessary, and then knocking on the door of Stegman's office first thing the next morning. But Stegman had run out of ideas now, and he was ready to give up. Hector had heard it himself. That's what the telephone call had been about, she said, and she couldn't really fault him for wanting to quit. Brigid was dead. She knew that, Reynolds and Stegman knew that, but her father still refused to accept it. He blamed himself for everything, and unless he had some reason to hope, unless he could delude himself into believing that Brigid was going to be found, he wouldn't be able to live with himself. It was that simple, Nora said. Her father would die. The pain would be too much for him, and he would just crumple up and die.

*

After that night, Nora went on telling him everything. It made sense that she should want to share her troubles with someone, but of all the people in the world, of all the potential candidates she could have chosen from, Hector was the one who got the job. He became Nora's confidant, the repository of information about his own crime, and every Tuesday and Thursday night, as he sat next to her on the davenport and struggled through another one of his lessons, he felt a little more of his brain disintegrate in his head. Life was a fever dream, he discovered, and reality was a groundless world of figments and hallucinations, a place where everything you imagined came true. Did he know who Hector Mann was? Nora actually asked him that question one night. Stegman had come up with a new theory, she said, and after backing out of the affair two months ago, the private eye had called O'Fallon over the weekend and asked for another chance. He'd found out that Brigid had published an article about Hector Mann. Eleven months later, Mann had disappeared, and he wondered if it was just a coincidence that Brigid had disappeared at the same time. What if there was a connection between the two unsolved cases? Stegman couldn't promise any results, but at least he had something to work on now, and with O'Fallon's permission, he wanted to pursue it. If he could establish that Brigid had gone on seeing Mann after she wrote the article, there might be some cause for optimism.

No, Hector said, he'd never heard of him. Who was this Hector Mann? Nora didn't know much about him either. An actor, she said. He'd made some silent comedies a few years ago, but she hadn't seen any of them. There hadn't been enough time to go to the movies when she was in college. No, Hector said, he didn't go very often himself. They cost money, and he'd once read somewhere that movies were bad for your eyes. Nora said that she dimly remembered hearing about the case, but she hadn't followed it too closely at the time. According to Stegman, Mann had been missing for almost two years. And why had he left? Hector wanted to know. No one was sure, Nora said. He'd just vanished one day, and he hadn't been heard from since. It didn't sound too hopeful, Hector said. A man can stay hidden for just so long. If they hadn't found him by now, that probably meant he was dead. Yes, probably, Nora agreed, and Brigid was probably dead, too. But there were rumors, she continued, and Stegman was going to look into them. What kind of rumors? Hector asked. That maybe he'd gone back to South America, Nora said. That was where he was from. Brazil, Argentina, she couldn't remember which country, but it was incredible, wasn't it? How so incredible? Hector asked. That Hector Mann should have been from the same part of the world that he was. What were the odds against that? She was forgetting that South America was a big place, Hector said. South Americans were everywhere. Yes, she knew that, Nora said, but even so, wouldn't it be incredible if Brigid had gone down there with him? It made her happy just to think about it. Two sisters, two South Americans. Brigid in one place with hers, and she in another with hers.

It wouldn't have been so terrible if he hadn't liked her so much, if a part of him hadn't fallen in love with her the first day they met. Hector knew that she was off-limits, that even to contemplate the possibility of touching her would have been an unpardonable sin, and yet he kept returning to her house every Tuesday and Thursday night, dying a little death every time she sat down beside him on the davenport and nestled her twenty-two-year-old body into the burgundy velour cushions. It would have been so simple to reach out and begin stroking her neck, to run his hand down the length of her arm, to turn toward her and begin kissing the freckles on her face. Grotesque as their conversations some-times were (Brigid and Stegman, her father's deterioration, the pursuit of Hector Mann), tamping down these urges was even harder on him, and it took every ounce of his strength not to cross the line. After two hours of torture, he often found himself heading straight from the les-son toward the river, walking across town until he reached a small neighborhood of collapsing houses and two-story hotels where women could be bought for twenty or thirty minutes of their time. It was a dis-mal solution, but there were no alternatives. Less than two years before, the most attractive women in Hollywood had been fighting to jump into bed with Hector. Now he was shelling out for it in the back alleys of Spokane, squandering half a day's wages on a few minutes of release.

It never occurred to Hector that Nora might have felt anything for him. He was a lamentable figure, a man not worthy of consideration, and if Nora was willing to give him so much of her time, it was only because she pitied him, because she was a young and passionate person who fancied herself a savior of lost souls. Saint Brigid, as her sister had called her, the martyr of the family. Hector was the naked African tribesman, and Nora was the American missionary who had thrashed her way through the jungle to improve his lot. He had never met anyone so candid, so hopeful, so ignorant of the dark forces at work in the world. At times, he wondered if she wasn't just plain stupid. At other times, she seemed to be possessed of a singular, rarefied wisdom. At still other times, when she turned to him with that intense and stubborn look in her eyes, he thought his heart would break. That was the paradox of the year he spent in Spokane. Nora made life intolerable for him, and yet Nora was the only thing he lived for, the only reason why he didn't pack his bags and leave.

Half the time, he was afraid that he would confess to her. The other half of the time, he was afraid that he would be caught. Stegman followed the Hector Mann angle for three and a half months before giving up again. Where the police had failed, so had the private detective, but that didn't mean that Hector's position was any more secure. O'Fallon had gone to Los Angeles several times in the fall and winter, and it seemed likely to assume that at some point during those visits Stegman had shown him photographs of Hector Mann. What if O'Fallon had noticed the resemblance between his hardworking stockboy and the missing actor? In early February, not long after he returned from his last trip to California, O'Fallon began looking at Hector in a new way. He seemed more alert, somehow, more curious, and Hector couldn't help wondering if Nora's father wasn't on to him. After months of silence and barely restrained contempt, the old man was suddenly paying attention to the lowly lifter of boxes who toiled in the back room of his store. The indifferent nods were replaced with smiles, and every now and then, for no particular reason, he would pat his employee on the shoulder and ask him how he was doing. Even more remarkable, O'Fallon began opening the door when Hector arrived at the house for his evening lessons. He would shake his hand as though he were a welcomed guest, and then, somewhat awkwardly, but with obvious goodwill, stand around for a moment to comment on the weather before retiring to his room upstairs. With any other man, this behavior would have been seen as normal, the bare minimum required by the rules of etiquette, but in O'Fallon's case it was altogether confounding, and Hector didn't trust it. Too much was at stake to be suckered in by a few polite smiles and friendly words, and the longer this sham amiability went on, the more frightened Hector became. By the middle of February, he sensed that his days in Spokane were numbered. A trap was being set for him, and he had to be prepared to skip town at any moment, to run off into the night and never show his face to them again.

Then the other shoe dropped. Just as Hector was planning to deliver

239

his good-bye speech to Nora, O'Fallon cornered him in the back room of the store one afternoon and asked him if he was interested in a raise. Goines had given notice, he said. The assistant manager was moving to Seattle to run his brother-in-law's print shop, and O'Fallon wanted to fill the position as quickly as possible. He knew that Hector didn't have any experience in sales, but he'd been watching him, he said, he'd been keeping an eye on how he went about his business, and he didn't think it would take him long to catch on to the new job. There would be more responsibility and longer hours, but his salary would be double what it was now. Did he want to think it over, or was he ready to accept? Hector was ready to accept. O'Fallon shook his hand, congratulated him on the promotion, and then gave him the rest of the day off. Just as Hector was about to leave the store, however, O'Fallon called him back. Open the cash register and take out a twenty-dollar bill, the boss said. Then go down the block to Pressler's Haberdashery and buy yourself a new suit, some white shirts, and a couple of bow ties. You're going to be working out front now, and you need to look your best.

In practical terms, O'Fallon had handed over the operation of his business to Hector. He had given him the title of assistant manager, but the fact was that Hector didn't assist anyone. He was in charge of running the store, and O'Fallon, who was officially the manager of his own enterprise, managed nothing. Red spent too little time on the premises to concern himself with petty details, and once he understood that this go-getting foreign upstart could handle the responsibilities of the new post, he scarcely bothered to come around anymore. He was so tired of the business by then, he never even learned the new stockboy's name.

Hector excelled as de facto manager of Red's Sporting Goods. After the year-long isolation of the Portland barrel factory and the solitary confinement of O'Fallon's stockroom, he welcomed the chance to be among people again. The store was like a small theater, and the role he had been given was essentially the same one he had played in his films: Hector as conscientious underling, as snappy, bow-tie-wearing clerk. The only difference was that his name was Herman Loesser now, and he had to play it straight. No pratfalls or stubbed toes, no slapstick contortions or bumps on the head. His job was to persuade, to oversee the accounts, and to defend the virtues of sport. But no one said that he had to go about it with a glum expression on his face. He had an audience in front of him again and numerous props to work with, and once he figured out the routine, his old actor's instincts came rushing back to him.

He charmed the customers with his loquacious spiels, enthralled them with his demonstrations of catcher's gloves and fly-fishing techniques, won their loyalty with his willingness to knock off five, ten, and even fifteen percent from the list price. Wallets were thin in 1931, but games were an inexpensive distraction, a good way not to think about what you couldn't afford, and Red's continued to do a decent business. Boys would play ball no matter what the circumstances, and men would never stop casting lines into rivers and shooting bullets into the bodies of wild animals. And then, not to be forgotten, there was the matter of uniforms. Not just for the teams from the local high schools and colleges, but for the two hundred members of the Rotary Club Bowling League, the ten squads of the Catholic Charities Basketball Association, and the line-ups of three dozen amateur softball outfits as well. O'Fallon had locked up that market a decade and a half ago, and every season the orders continued to roll in, as precise and regular as the phases of the moon.

One night in the middle of April, as Hector and Nora came to the end of their Tuesday lesson, Nora turned to him and announced that she had received a proposal of marriage. The statement came out of nowhere, with no reference to anything that had come before it, and for a couple of seconds Hector wasn't sure if he had heard her correctly. An announcement of that sort was usually accompanied by a smile, perhaps even a laugh, but Nora wasn't smiling, and she didn't sound the least bit happy to be sharing this news with him. Hector asked the name of the lucky young man. Nora shook her head, then looked down at the floor and began fidgeting with her blue cotton dress. When she looked up again, there were tears glistening in her eyes. Her lips started to move, but before she managed to say anything, she abruptly rose from her seat, put her hand over her mouth, and rushed out of the parlor.

She was gone before he knew what had happened. There wasn't even enough time for him to call out to her, and when he heard Nora run up the stairs and then bang the door of her room shut, he understood that she wouldn't be coming down again that night. The lesson was over. He should be going, he said to himself, but several minutes went by, and he didn't stir from the davenport. Eventually, O'Fallon drifted into the room. It was just past nine, and Red was in his usual nocturnal condition, but not so far gone that he couldn't keep his balance. He fixed his eyes on Hector, and for the longest time he went on staring at his assistant manager, looking him up and down as a small, crooked smile formed in the lower part of his mouth. Hector couldn't tell if it was a smile of pity or mockery. It looked like both, somehow, a kind of compassionate disdain, if such a thing were possible, and Hector found it disturbing, a sign of some festering hostility that O'Fallon hadn't revealed in months. At last Hector stood up and asked: Is Nora getting married? The boss let out a brief, sarcastic laugh. How the hell should I know? he said. Why don't you ask her yourself? And then, grunting in response to his own laugh, O'Fallon turned and left the room.

Two nights later, Nora apologized for her outburst. She was feeling better now, she said, and the crisis was over. She'd turned him down, and that was that. Case closed; nothing more to worry about. Albert Sweeney was a fine person, but he was just a boy, and she was tired of being with boys, especially rich boys who lived off their fathers' money. If she was ever going to get married, it would be to a man, to someone who knew his way around the world and could take care of himself. Hector said that she couldn't blame Sweeney for having a rich father. It wasn't his fault, and besides, what was so bad about being rich, anyway? Nothing, Nora said. She just didn't want to marry him, that's all. Marriage was forever, and she wasn't going to say yes until the right man came along.

Nora soon recovered her spirits, but Hector's relations with O'Fallon seemed to have entered a new and troubling phase. The turning point had been the showdown in the parlor, with the long stare and the short, derisive laugh, and after that night Hector sensed that he was being watched again. When O'Fallon came into the store now, he took no part in transacting business or dealing with customers. Rather than lend a hand or fill in behind the cash register when things got busy, he would install himself in a chair beside the display case for tennis racquets and golf gloves and quietly read the morning papers, glancing up every now and then with that caustic smile pulling at the lower part of his mouth. It was as though he regarded his assistant as an amusing pet or wind-up toy. Hector was earning good money for him, putting in ten and eleven hours a day so that he could live in quasi retirement, but all these efforts only seemed to make O'Fallon more skeptical of him, more condescending. Wary as Hector was, he pretended not to notice. It was all right to be considered an overzealous fool, he reasoned, and maybe it wasn't even so bad when he started calling you Muchacho and El Señor, but you didn't get close to a man like that, and whenever he entered the room, you made sure that your back was turned to the wall.

When he invited you out to his country club, however, asking you to join him for eighteen holes of golf on a bright Sunday morning in early May, you didn't say no. Nor did you turn him down when he offered to buy you lunch at the Bluebell Inn, not once but twice in the span of a single week, both times insisting that you order the most expensive dishes on the menu. As long as he didn't know your secret, as long as he didn't suspect what you were doing in Spokane, you could tolerate the pressure of his constant scrutiny. You bore up to it precisely because you found it unbearable to be with him, because you pitied him for the wreck he had become, because every time you heard that cynical desolation seeping out from his voice, you knew that you were partly responsible for putting it there.

Their second lunch at the Bluebell Inn took place on a Wednesday afternoon in late May. If Hector had been prepared for what was going to happen, he probably would have reacted differently, but after twenty-five minutes of inconsequential talk, O'Fallon's question caught him by surprise. That evening, when Hector returned to his boarding-house on the other side of town, he wrote in his journal that the universe had changed shape for him in a single instant. *I have missed everything. I have misunderstood everything. The earth is the sky, the sun is the moon, the rivers are mountains. I have been looking at the wrong world.* Then, with the events of the afternoon still fresh in his mind, he wrote down a word-for-word account of his conversation with O'Fallon:

And so, Loesser, O'Fallon suddenly asked him, tell me what your intentions are.

I do not understand this word, Hector replied. A lovely steak sits in front of me, and I have every intention of eating it up. Is that what you are inquiring about?

You're a sharp fellow, Chico. You know what I mean.

Begging your pardon, sir, but these intentions bewilder me. I do not grasp them.

Long-range intentions.

Oh, yes, now I see. You refer to the future, my thoughts about the future. I can safely say that my only intentions are to go on as I am now. To continue working for you. To do the best I can for the store.

And what else?

There is no else, Mr. O'Fallon. I speak from the heart. You have given me a great opportunity, and I mean to make the most of it.

And who do you think talked me into giving you that opportunity?

I cannot say. I always thought it was your decision, that you were the one who gave me my chance.

It was Nora.

Miss O'Fallon? She never told me. I had no idea that she was responsible. I owe her so much already, and now it seems I am even further in her debt. I am humbled by what you tell me.

Do you enjoy watching her suffer?

Miss Nora suffer? Why on earth should she suffer? She is a remarkable, spirited girl, and everyone admires her. I know that family sorrows weigh on her heart – as they do on yours, sir – but other than the tears she occasionally sheds for her absent sister, I have never seen her in anything but the most lively and buoyant moods.

She's strong. She puts up a good front.

It pains me to hear this.

Albert Sweeney proposed to her last month, and she turned him down. Why do you think she did that? The boy's father is Hiram Sweeney, the state senator, the most powerful Republican in the county. She could have lived off the fat of the land for the next fifty years, and she said no. Why do you think, Loesser?

She told me she did not love him.

That's right. Because she loves someone else. And who do you think that person is?

It is impossible for me to answer that question. I know nothing about Miss Nora's feelings, sir.

You're not a pansy, are you, Herman?

Excuse me, sir?

A pansy. A homo fruit-boy.

Of course not.

Then why don't you do something?

You talk in riddles, Mr. O'Fallon. I cannot grasp.

I'm tired, son. I have nothing to live for now except one thing, and once that thing is taken care of, all I want is to croak in peace. You help me out, and I'm willing to make a bargain with you. Just say the word, amigo, and everything is yours. The store, the business, the whole works.

Are you offering to sell me your business? I have no money. I am in no position to make such bargains.

You drift into the store last summer begging for work, and now you're running the show. You're good at it, Loesser. Nora was right about you, and I'm not going to stand in her way. I'm finished standing in anyone's way. Whatever she wants, that's what she gets.

Why do you keep referring to Miss Nora? I thought you were making a business proposition.

I am. But not unless you oblige me with this one thing. It's not as though I'm asking you for something you don't want yourself. I see the way you two look at each other. All you have to do is make your move.

What are you saying, Mr. O'Fallon?

Figure it out for yourself.

I cannot, sir. I truly cannot.

Nora, stupid. You're the one she's in love with.

But I am nothing, nothing at all. Nora could not love me.

You might think that, and I might think that, but we're both wrong. The girl's heart is breaking, and I'll be damned if I sit by and watch her suffer anymore. I've lost two kids already, and it's not going to happen again.

But I must not marry Nora. I am a Jew, and such things are not permitted.

What kind of a Jew?

A Jew. There is only one kind of Jew.

Do you believe in God?

What difference does that make? I am not like you. I come from another world.

Answer the question. Do you believe in God?

No, I do not. I believe that man is the measure of all things. Both good and bad.

Then we belong to the same religion. We're the same, Loesser. The only difference is that you understand money better than I do. That means you'll be able to take care of her. That's all I want. Take care of Nora, and then I can die a good death.

You put me in a difficult position, sir.

You don't know what difficult is, hombre. You propose to her by the end of the month, or else I'm going to fire you. Do you understand? I'm going to fire you, and then I'm going to kick your ass clear out of the goddamn state.

Hector spared him the trouble. Four hours after leaving the Bluebell Inn, he closed up the store for the last time, then returned to his room and began packing his things. At some point during the evening, he borrowed his landlady's Underwood and typed out a one-page letter to Nora, signing it at the bottom with the initials H. L. He couldn't take the risk of leaving her with a sample of his handwriting, but neither could he walk off without an explanation, without inventing some story to account for his sudden, mysterious departure.

He told her that he was married. It was the biggest lie he could think of, but in the long run it was less cruel than an out-and-out rejection would have been. His wife had fallen ill in New York, and he had to rush back there to deal with the emergency. Nora would be stunned, of course, but once she understood that there had never been any hope for them, that Hector had been unavailable to her from the beginning, she would be able to recover from her disappointment without any lasting scars. O'Fallon would probably see through the deception, but even if the old man figured out the truth for himself, it was doubtful that he would share it with Nora. He was in the business of protecting his daughter's feelings, and why should he object to the removal of this inconvenient nobody who had wormed his way into her affections? He would be glad to be rid of Hector, and little by little, as the dust finally settled, young Sweeney would start coming around again, and Nora would return to her senses. In his letter, Hector thanked her for the many kindnesses she had shown him. He would never forget her, he said. She was a shining spirit, a woman above all other women, and just knowing her for the short time he had been in Spokane had permanently changed his life. All true, and yet all false. Every sentence a lie, and yet every word written with conviction. He waited until three o'clock in the morning, and then he walked to her house and slipped the letter under the front door – just as her dead sister, Brigid, on a similar errand two and a half years ago, had once slipped a letter under the door of his house.

He tried to kill himself in Montana the next day, Alma said, and three days after that he tried again in Chicago. The first time, he stuck the revolver in his mouth; the second time, he pressed the barrel against his left eye – but in neither instance was he able to go through with it. He had checked into a hotel on South Wabash at the fringes of Chinatown, and after the second failed attempt he walked out into the sweltering June night, looking for a place to get drunk. If he could pour enough liquor into his system, he figured it would give him the courage to jump into the river and drown himself before the night was over. That was the plan, in any case, but not long after he went out in search of the bottle, he stumbled onto something better than death, better than the simple damnation he'd been looking for. Her name was Sylvia Meers, and under her guidance Hector learned that he could go on killing himself without having to finish the job. She was the one who taught him how to drink his own blood, who instructed him in the pleasures of devouring his own heart.

He ran into her in a Rush Street gin mill, standing against the bar as he was about to order his second drink. She wasn't much to look at, but the price she quoted was so negligible that Hector found himself agreeing to her terms. He would be dead before the night was out anyway, and what could be more fitting than to spend his last hours on earth with a whore?

She took him across the street to a room in the White House Hotel, and once they had finished their business on the bed, she asked him if he would care to have another go at it. Hector declined, explaining that he didn't have the money for an additional round, but when she told him that there wouldn't be any extra charge, he shrugged and said why not, then proceeded to mount her for a second time. The encore soon ended with another ejaculation, and Sylvia Meers smiled. She complimented Hector on his performance, and then she asked him if he thought he had the stuff to do it again. Not right away, Hector said, but if she gave him half an hour, it probably wouldn't be any trouble. That wasn't good enough, she said. If he could make it in twenty minutes, she would give him another treat, but he would have to get hard again within ten. She looked over at the clock on the bedside table. Ten minutes from now, she said, starting when the second hand swept past the twelve. That was the deal. Ten minutes to get going, and then another ten minutes to finish the job. If he went soft on her at any point along the way, however, he would have to reimburse her for the last time. That was the penalty. Three times for the price of one, or else he coughed up retail for the whole thing. What was it going to be? Did he want to walk away now, or did he think he could come through under pressure?

If she hadn't been smiling when she asked the question, Hector would have thought she was insane. Whores didn't give away their services for free, and they didn't issue challenges to the virility of their clients. That was for the whip specialists and the secret man-haters, the ones who trafficked in suffering and bizarre humiliations, but Meers struck him as a blowsy, lighthearted sort of girl, and she didn't seem to be taunting him so much as trying to coax him into playing a game. No, not a game exactly, but an experiment, a scientific investigation into the copulative staying power of his twice-exhausted member. Could the dead be resurrected, she seemed to be asking him, and if so, how many times? Guesswork wasn't allowed. In order to provide conclusive results, the study had to be conducted under the strictest laboratory conditions.

Hector smiled back at her. Meers was sprawled out on the bed with a cigarette in her hand – confident, relaxed, perfectly at home in her nakedness. What was in it for her? Hector wanted to know. Money, she said. Lots of money. That was a good one, Hector said. There she was offering it for nothing, and in the same breath she was talking about getting rich. How dumb was that? Not dumb, she said, clever. There was money to be made, and if he could get it up again in the next nine minutes, he stood to make it with her.

She put out her cigarette and started running her hands over her body, stroking her breasts and smoothing her palms along her stomach, trailing her fingertips along the insides of her thighs and angling them into contact with her public hair, her vulva, and her clitoris, spreading herself open for him as her mouth parted and she slid her tongue over her lips. Hector was not immune to these classic provocations. Slowly but steadily the dead man inched himself out from his grave, and when Meers saw what was happening, she made a naughty little humming sound in her throat, a single prolonged note that seemed to combine both approval and encouragement. Lazarus was breathing again. She rolled over onto her stomach, muttering a string of four-letter words and moaning in feigned arousal, and then she lifted her ass into the air and told him to go into her. Hector wasn't quite ready, but as he pressed his penis against the scarlet folds of her labia, he stiffened enough to achieve penetration. He didn't have much left by the end, but something came out of him besides sweat, enough to prove the point at any rate, and when he finally slid off her and sank onto the sheets, she turned and kissed him on the mouth. Seventeen minutes, she said. He had done it three times in less than an hour, and that was all she had been looking for. If he wanted in, she was willing to make him her partner.

Hector had no idea what she was talking about. She explained it, and when he still didn't understand what she was trying to tell him, she explained it again. There were men, she said, rich men in Chicago, rich men all over the Midwest who were willing to pay good money to watch people fuck. Oh, Hector said, you mean stag films, blue movies. No, Meers replied, none of that fake stuff. Live performances. Real fucking in front of real people.

She had been doing it for a while, she said, but last month her partner had been arrested on a botched breaking-and-entering job. Poor Al. He drank too much and was having trouble getting it up anyway. Even if he hadn't put himself out of commission, it probably would have been time to start looking for a replacement. In the past couple of weeks, three or four other candidates had survived the test, but none of those fellows could measure up to Hector. She liked his body, she said, she liked the feel of his cock, and she thought he had a terrifically handsome face.

Oh no, Hector said. He would never show his face. If she wanted him to work with her, he would have to wear a mask.

He wasn't being squeamish. His films had been popular in Chicago, and he couldn't take the risk of being recognized. Holding up his end of the bargain would be hard enough, but he didn't see how he could go through with it if he had to perform in a state of fear, if every time he walked in front of an audience he would have to worry that someone was about to call out his name. That was his only condition, he said. Let him hide his face, and she could count him in.

Meers was dubious. Why would he show his dick to the world and then not let anyone see who he was? If she were a man, she said, she'd be proud to have what he had. She'd want everyone to know that it belonged to her.

But they wouldn't be there to look at him, Hector said. She was the star, and the less the audience thought about who he was, the hotter their performances would be. Put a mask on him, and he would have no personality, no distinguishing characteristics, nothing to interfere with the fantasies of the men who were watching them. They didn't want to see him fuck her, he said, they wanted to imagine they were fucking her themselves. Make him anonymous, and he would be turned into an engine of male desire, the representative of every man in the audience. The stiff-boned Sir Stud, banging away at the body of the insatiable Lady Cunt. Every man, and therefore any man. But just one woman, he said, ever and always just one woman, and her name was Sylvia Meers.

Meers bought the argument. It was her first lesson in the tactics of show business, and even if she couldn't follow everything that Hector said to her, she liked the way it sounded, she liked it that he wanted her to be the star. By the time he called her Lady Cunt, she was laughing out loud. Where had he learned to talk like that? she asked him. She'd never known a man who could make something sound so dirty and so beautiful at the same time.

Squalor has its own rewards, Hector said, purposely talking over her head. If a man decides to crawl into his tomb, who better to keep him company than a warm-blooded woman? He dies more slowly that way, and as long as his flesh is joined to her flesh, he can live off the smell of his own corruption.

Meers laughed again, unable to grasp the meaning of Hector's words. It sounded like Bible talk to her, the stuff of preachers and roadside evangelists, but Hector's little poem on death and degeneration was delivered so calmly, with such a kind and friendly smile on his face, that she assumed he was making a joke. Not for a moment did she understand that he had just confessed his innermost secrets to her, that she was looking at a man who four hours earlier had sat down on the bed in his hotel room and pressed a loaded gun against his brain for the second time that week. Hector was glad. When he saw the lack of comprehension in her eyes, he felt lucky to have fallen in with such a dim, lusterless tart. No matter how much time he spent with her, he knew that he would always be alone when they were together.

Meers was in her early twenties, a South Dakota farm girl who had run away from home at sixteen, landed in Chicago a year later, and started working the streets the same month that Lindbergh flew across the Atlantic. There was nothing compelling about her, nothing to set her apart from a thousand other whores in a thousand other hotel rooms at that same moment. A peroxide blonde with a round face, dull gray eyes, and the remnants of acne scars dotting her cheeks, she carried herself with a certain sluttish bravura, but there was no magic in her, no charm to keep one's interest alive for very long. Her neck was too short for the proportions of her body, her small breasts drooped a little, and there was already a slight buildup of flab around her hips and buttocks. As she and Hector worked out the terms of their agreement (a sixty-forty split, which Hector found more than generous), he suddenly turned away, realizing that he wouldn't be able to go through with it if he went on looking at her. What's the matter, Herm, she asked him, ain't you feelin' well? I'm fine, Hector said, his eyes still fixed on a patch of crumbling plaster at the opposite end of the room. I've never felt better in my life. I'm so happy, I could open the window and start screaming like a madman. That's how good I feel, baby. I'm out of my mind, out of my mind with joy.

Six days later, Hector and Sylvia put on their first public performance. Between that initial engagement in early June and their final show in mid-December, Alma calculated that they appeared together some forty-seven times. Most of the work took place in and around Chicago, but some bookings came in from as far away as Minneapolis, Detroit, and Cleveland. The venues ranged from nightclubs to hotel suites, from warehouses and brothels to office buildings and private homes. Their largest audience consisted of about a hundred spectators (at a fraternity party in Normal, Illinois), and the smallest had just one (repeated on ten separate occasions for the same man). The act varied according to the wishes of the clients. Sometimes Hector and Sylvia put on little plays, complete with costumes and dialogue, and at other times they did nothing more than walk in naked and screw in silence. The skits were based on the most conventional erotic daydreams, and they tended to work best in front of small- to medium-sized crowds. The most popular one was the nurse and patient routine. People seemed to like watching Sylvia take off the starched white uniform, and they never failed to applaud when she began unwrapping the gauze bandages from Hector's body. There was also the Confession Box Scandal (which ended with the priest ravishing the nun) and, more elaborately, the tale of the two libertines who meet at a masked ball in pre-revolutionary France. In almost every instance, the spectators were exclusively male. The larger gatherings were usually quite raucous (bachelor parties, birthday celebrations), while the smaller groups rarely made any noise at all. Bankers and lawyers, businessmen and politicians, athletes, stockbrokers, and representatives of the idle rich: they all watched in spellbound fascination. More often than not, at least two or three of them would open their trousers and begin to masturbate. A married couple from Fort Wayne, Indiana, who engaged the duo's services for a private performance in their home, went so far as to undress during the act and begin making love themselves. Meers had been right, Hector discovered. There was good money to be made from daring to give people what they wanted.

He rented a small efficiency apartment on the North Side, and for every dollar he earned, he gave away seventy-five cents of it to charity.

He slipped ten- and twenty-dollar bills into the collection box at Saint Anthony's Church, sent in anonymous donations to Congregation B'nai Avraham, and dispensed untold quantities of loose change to the blind and crippled beggars he encountered on the sidewalks of his neighborhood. Forty-seven performances averaged out to just under two performances a week. That left five days free, and Hector spent most of them in seclusion, holed up in his apartment reading books. His world had split in two, Alma said, and his mind and body were no longer talking to each other. He was an exhibitionist and a hermit, a mad debauchee and a solitary monk, and if he managed to survive these contradictions in himself for as long as he did, it was only because he willed his mind to go numb. No more struggles to be good, no more pretending to believe in the virtues of self-denial. His body had taken control of him, and the less he thought about what his body was doing, the more successfully he was able to do it. Alma noted that he stopped writing in his journal during this period. The only entries were dry little jottings that recorded the times and places of his jobs with Sylvia – a page and a half in six months. She took it as a sign that he was afraid to look at himself, that he was acting like a man who had covered up all the mirrors in his house.

The only time he had any trouble was the first time, or just before the first time, when he still didn't know if he would be up to the job. Fortunately, Sylvia booked their first performance for an audience of just one man. That made it bearable somehow – to go public in a private sort of way, with just one pair of eyes on him and not twenty or fifty or a hundred. In this case, the eyes belonged to Archibald Pierson, a seventy-year-old retired judge who lived alone in a three-story Tudor house in Highland Park. Sylvia had already been there once with Al, and as she and Hector climbed into a taxi on the appointed night and headed toward their destination in the suburbs, she warned him that they would probably have to go through the act twice, perhaps even three times. The coot was stuck on her, she said. He'd been calling for weeks now, desperate to know when she'd be coming back, and little by little she'd bargained the price up to two and a half C's per shot, double what it had been the last time. I ain't no slouch when it comes to talkin' bread, she announced proudly. If we play this goon right, Hermie boy, he could become our meal ticket.

Pierson turned out to be a shy and jittery old man – thin as a shoemaker's awl, with a full head of neatly combed white hair and enormous blue eyes. He had put on a green velvet smoking jacket for the occasion, and as he led Hector and Sylvia into the living room, he kept clearing his throat and smoothing down the front of the jacket, as if he felt uncomfortable in that foppish attire. He offered them cigarettes, offered them drinks (which they both declined), and then announced that he was planning to accompany their performance by playing a phonograph record of the String Sextet Number One in B flat by Brahms. Sylvia giggled when she heard the word *sextet*, failing to realize that it referred to the number of instruments in the piece, but the judge made no comment. Pierson then complimented Hector on his mask – which Hector had slipped over his face before entering the house – and said that he found it tantalizing, a clever touch. I think I'm going to enjoy this, he said. I salute you on your choice of partner, Sylvia. This one is infinitely more dashing than Al.

The judge liked to keep things simple. He wasn't interested in provocative costumes, sultry dialogue, or artificially dramatic scenes. All he wanted was to look at their bodies, he said, and once the preliminary conversation was over, he instructed them to go into the kitchen and remove their clothes. While they were gone, he put on the music, turned off the lamps, and lit candles in half a dozen spots around the room. It was theater without theatrics, a raw enactment of life itself. Hector and Sylvia were supposed to walk into the room naked, then get down to business on the Persian rug. That was the extent of it. Hector would make love to Sylvia, and when the climactic moment was upon him, he would withdraw from her and ejaculate on her breasts. Everything came down to that, the judge said. The spurt was crucial, and the farther it traveled through the air, the happier it was going to make him.

After they had taken off their clothes in the kitchen, Sylvia walked up to Hector and started running her hands over his body. She kissed him on the neck, pulled back the mask and kissed him on the face, and then cupped his flaccid penis in her hand and stroked it until it became hard. Hector was glad he had thought of the mask. It made him feel less vulnerable, less ashamed of exposing himself to the old man, but still he was nervous, and he welcomed the warmth of Sylvia's touch, appreciated that she was trying to work the butterflies out of his system. She might have been the star, but she knew that the burden of proof rested with him. Hector couldn't fake it as she could; he couldn't just go through the motions of simulated pleasure and pretend that he was enjoying it. He had to deliver something real at the end of the performance, and unless he went about it with genuine conviction, he wouldn't have a chance of getting there.

They walked into the living room holding hands, two naked savages in a jungle of gilt-edged mirrors and Louis the Fifteenth escritoires. Pierson was already installed in his seat at the far end of the room: a vast leather wing chair that seemed to swallow him up, making him look even thinner and more desiccated than he was. To his right was the phonograph machine, with the Brahms sextet revolving on the turntable. To his left was a low mahogany stand, covered with lacquered boxes, jade statuettes, and other bits of costly chinoiserie. It was a room full of nouns and unmovable objects, an enclave of thoughts. Nothing could have been more incongruous in those surroundings than the erection Hector carried in with him – than the spectacle of verbs that suddenly began to unfold not ten feet from the judge's chair.

If the old man enjoyed what he saw, he displayed no outward signs of pleasure. He stood up twice during the performance to change the record, but other than those brief, mechanical interruptions, he remained in the same position throughout, sitting on his leather throne with one leg crossed over the other and his hands in his lap. He didn't touch himself, he didn't unbutton his trousers, he didn't smile, he didn't make a sound. It was only at the end, at the moment when Hector pulled out of Sylvia and the desired eruption occurred, that a small shuddering noise seemed to catch in the judge's throat. Almost like a sob, Hector thought – and then again, almost like nothing at all.

That was the first time, Alma said, but it was also the fifth time and the eleventh time and the eighteenth time and six other times as well. Pierson became their most devoted customer, and again and again they returned to the house in Highland Park to roll around on the rug and collect their money. Nothing made Sylvia happier than that money, Hector realized, and within a couple of months she had earned enough from the act to quit peddling her wares at the White House Hotel. Not all of it went into her own pocket, but even after she turned over fifty percent to the man she called her protector, her income was two or three times greater than it had been before. Sylvia was an uneducated hick, a semi-illiterate vulgarian who spoke in a blur of double negatives and mind-bending malapropisms, but she proved to have a decent head for business. She was the one who arranged the bookings, negotiated with the clients, and took care of all practical matters: transportation to and from jobs, costume rentals, the scaring up of new work. Hector never had to concern himself with any of these details. Sylvia would call to tell him when and where they would be appearing next, and all he had to do was wait for her to swing by in a taxi to pick him up at his apartment. Those were the unspoken rules, the boundaries of their relationship. They worked together, they fucked together, they made money together, but they never bothered to become friends, and except for the times when they had to rehearse a new skit, they saw each other only when they performed.

All along, Hector assumed that he was safe with her. She didn't ask questions or pry into his past, and in the six and a half months they worked together, he never saw her look at a paper, let alone talk about the news. Once, in an oblique sort of way, he made a passing reference to that silent comedian who had disappeared a few years back. What was his name? he asked, snapping his fingers and pretending to search for the answer, but when Sylvia responded with one of those blank, indifferent looks of hers, Hector took it to mean that she wasn't familiar with the case. Somewhere along the line, however, someone must have talked to her. Hector never knew who it was, but he suspected that it was Sylvia's boyfriend – her so-called protector, Biggie Lowe, a two-hundred-forty-pound hulk who had started out in Chicago as a dance-hall bouncer and now worked as the night manager of the White House Hotel. Maybe Biggie put her up to it, filling her head with talk of quick money and foolproof extortion schemes, or maybe Sylvia was acting on her own, trying to squeeze a few extra dollars out of Hector for herself. One way or the other, greed got the better of her, and once Hector caught on to what she was planning, the only thing he could do was run.

It happened in Cleveland, less than a week before Christmas. They had gone there by train at the invitation of a wealthy tire manufacturer, had finished doing their French libertine act in front of three dozen men and women (who had gathered at the industrialist's house to participate in a semi-annual private orgy), and were now sitting in the back seat of their host's limousine, on the way to the hotel where they would be stopping for a few hours' sleep before returning to Chicago the next afternoon. They had just been paid a record amount for their work: one thousand dollars for a single, forty-minute performance. Hector's share was supposed to be four hundred dollars, but when Sylvia counted out the tire magnate's money, she gave her partner only two hundred fifty.

That's twenty-five percent, Hector said. You still owe me the other fifteen.

I don't think so, Meers replied. That's what you're gettin', Herm, and if I was you, I'd thank my lucky cards.

Oh? And to what do I owe this sudden change in fiscal policy, dear Sylvia?

It ain't physical, boyo. It's dollars and cents. I got the goods on a certain party now, and unless you want me blabbin' my trap all over town, you'll go down to twenty-five. No more forty. Them days is dead and gone.

You screw like a princess, darling. You understand sex better than any woman I have ever known, but you lack much in the thought department, don't you? You want to work out a new arrangement, fine. Sit down and talk to me about it. But you don't change the rules without consulting me first.

Okay, Mr. Hollywood. Then stop using the mask. If you do that, maybe I'll reconsider.

I see. So this is what we're driving at.

When a guy don't want to show his face, he's got a secret, don't he? And when a girl gets wind of what that secret is, it's a whole new ballgame. I shook hands on a deal with Herm. But there ain't no Herm, is there? His name is Hector, and now we got to start all over again.

She could start all over again as many times as she liked, but it wasn't going to be with him. When the limousine pulled up in front of the Hotel Cuyahoga a few seconds later, Hector told her that they would go on talking about it in the morning. He wanted to sleep on it, he said, to think it over for a while before coming to a decision, but he was sure they could come up with a solution that would satisfy them both. Then he kissed her on the hand, just as he always did when he said good-bye to her after a performance – the half-mocking, half-chivalrous gesture that had become their standard farewell. From the triumphant smirk that spread across Sylvia's face as he lifted her hand to his mouth, Hector realized that she had no idea what she had done. She hadn't blackmailed him into giving her a greater share of the profits, she had just broken up the act.

He went to his room on the seventh floor, and for the next twenty minutes he stood in front of the mirror, pressing the barrel of the gun against his right temple. He came close to pulling the trigger, Alma said, closer than he had the other two times, but when his will failed him once again, he put the gun down on the table and left the hotel. It was four-thirty in the morning. He walked to the Greyhound depot twelve blocks to the north and bought himself a ticket on the next bus out – or the next but one. The six o'clock was headed for Youngstown and points east, and the six-oh-five was going in the opposite direction. The ninth stop on the westbound coach was Sandusky. That was the town where he had never spent his childhood, and remembering how beautiful that word had once sounded to him, Hector decided to go there now – just to see what his imaginary past looked like.

It was the morning of December 21, 1931. Sandusky was sixty miles away, and he slept through most of the ride, not waking until the bus reached the terminal two and a half hours later. He had just over three hundred dollars in his pocket: the two hundred fifty from Meers, another fifty he had slipped into his wallet before leaving Chicago on the twentieth, and change from the ten he had broken for his bus ticket. He went into the depot luncheonette and ordered the breakfast special: ham and eggs, toast, home fries, orange juice, and all the coffee you could drink. Halfway through his third cup, he asked the counterman if there was anything to see in town. He was just passing through, he said, and he doubted he would ever be back this way again. Sandusky ain't much, the counterman said. It's just a little burg, you know, but if I was you, I'd go and check out Cedar Point. That's where the amusement park is. You've got your roller coasters and fun rides, the Leapfrog Railway, the Hotel Breakers, all kinds of things. That's where Knute Rockne invented the forward pass, by the way, in case you're a football fan. It's shut down for the winter now, but it might be worth a look.

The counterman drew a little diagram for him on the paper napkin, but instead of turning right out of the depot, Hector went left. That took him to Camp Street instead of Columbus Avenue, and then, to compound the error, he turned west on West Monroe instead of east. He went all the way to King Street before it dawned on him that he was walking in the wrong direction. The peninsula was nowhere in sight, and instead of cyclones and Ferris wheels, he found himself looking at a dreary expanse of broken-down factories and empty warehouses. Cold, gray weather, a threat of snow in the air, and a mangy, three-legged dog the only living creature within a hundred yards.

Hector turned around and began to retrace his steps, and the moment he turned, Alma said, he was gripped by a feeling of nullity, an exhaustion so great, so relentless, that he had to lean against the wall of a building to prevent himself from falling down. A frigid wind was blowing in off Lake Erie, and even as he felt it rush against his face, he couldn't tell if the wind was real or something he had imagined. He didn't know what month it was, what year. He couldn't remember his name. Bricks and cobblestones, his breath gusting into the air in front of it, and the three-legged dog limping around the corner and vanishing from sight. It was a picture of his own death, he later realized, the portrait of a soul in ruins, and long after he had pulled himself together and moved on, a part of him was still there, standing on that empty street in Sandusky, Ohio, gasping for breath as his existence dribbled out of him.

By ten-thirty, he was on Columbus Avenue, threading his way among a crowd of Christmas shoppers. He passed the Warner Bros. Theater, Ester Ging's manicure salon, and Capozzi's Shoe Repair, saw people going in and out of Kresge's, Montgomery Ward, and Woolworth's, heard a lone Salvation Army Santa Claus ringing a brass bell. When he came to the Commercial Banking and Trust Company, he decided to go in and convert a couple of his fifties into a stack of fives and tens and ones. It was a meaningless transaction, but he couldn't think of anything else to do just then, and rather than go on wandering in circles, he figured it might not be such a bad idea to get in out of the cold, even if only for a few minutes.

Unexpectedly, the bank was full of customers. Men and women were lined up eight and ten deep in front of the four barred tellers' windows arrayed along the west wall. Hector went to the end of the longest line, which happened to be the second one from the door. A moment after he took his spot, a young woman joined the line immediately to his left. She appeared to be in her early twenties, and she was wearing a thick woolen coat with a fur collar. Because he had nothing better to do at that moment, Hector began studying her out of the corner of his eye. She had an admirable, interesting face, he found, with high cheekbones and a gracefully defined chin, and he liked the pensive, self-sufficient look he detected in her eyes. In the old days, he would have started talking to her immediately, but now he was content simply to watch, to muse upon the flesh that was hidden beneath the coat and to imagine the thoughts churning inside that lovely, striking head of hers. At one point, she inadvertently glanced over at him, and when she saw how avidly he was staring at her, she returned his look with a brief, enigmatic smile. Hector nodded, acknowledging her smile with a brief smile of his own, and an instant later her expression changed. She narrowed her eyes into a puzzled, searching frown, and Hector knew that she had recognized him. There was no doubt about it: the woman had seen his movies. She was familiar with his face, and although she still couldn't remember who he was, it wasn't going to take her more than thirty seconds to come up with the answer.

It had happened to him several times in the past three years, and each time he had managed to slip away before the person could start asking him questions. Just as he was about to do it again, however, all hell broke loose in the bank. The young woman was standing in the line closest to the entrance, and because she had turned slightly in Hector's direction, she failed to notice that the door had opened behind her and that a man had rushed in with a red-and-white bandana tied around his face. He was carrying an empty duffel bag in one hand and a loaded pistol in the other. It was easy to tell that the pistol was loaded, Alma said, because the first thing the bank robber did was fire a shot into the ceiling. Down on the floor, he shouted, everybody down on the floor, and as the terrified customers did what the man instructed them to do, he reached out and grabbed hold of the person directly in front of him. It was all a matter of layout, architecture, topography. The young woman to Hector's left was the person closest to the entrance, and therefore she was the one who was grabbed, who wound up having the gun pointed at her head. Nobody move, the man warned, nobody move or this bird gets her brains blown out. With a brusque and violent gesture, he yanked her off her feet and began half-pushing, half-dragging her toward the tellers' windows. His left arm was wrapped around her shoulders from behind, the duffel bag was dangling from his clenched fist, and the eyes above the bandana were crazed, out of focus, incandescent with fear. It wasn't that Hector made any conscious decision to do what he did next, but the moment his knee touched the floor, he found himself standing up again. He wasn't intending to be heroic, and he certainly wasn't intending to get himself killed, but whatever else he might have been feeling at that moment, he wasn't afraid. Angry, perhaps, and more than a little worried that he was about to put the girl at risk, but not afraid for himself. The important thing was the angle of approach. Once he made his move, there wouldn't be time to stop or change direction, but if he rushed the man at full speed, and if he came at him from the right side – the duffel-bag side – there was no way that the man wouldn't turn from the girl and point the gun at him. It was the only natural response. If a wild beast comes charging at you out of nowhere, you forget about everything but the beast.

That was as far as Hector could take the story, Alma said. He could talk about what happened up to that moment, up to the moment when he started running toward the man, but he had no memory of hearing the gun go off, no memory of the bullet that tore into his chest and knocked him to the ground, no memory of seeing Frieda break loose from the man. Frieda was in a better position to see what happened, but because she was so busy twisting herself out of the man's arms, she missed many of the subsequent events as well. She saw Hector drop to the floor, she saw the hole that opened in his overcoat and the blood that came spurting out of it, but she lost track of the man and didn't see him trying to escape. The shot was still ringing in her ears, and with so many people shrieking and howling around her, she didn't hear the three additional shots that the bank guard fired into the man's back.

They were both certain of the date, however. That was fixed in their minds, and when Alma visited the microfilm vaults of the *Sandusky Evening Herald*, the Cleveland *Plain Dealer*, and several other defunct and surviving local papers, she was able to piece together the rest of the story for herself. BLOODBATH ON COLUMBUS AVENUE, BANK ROBBER DIES IN SHOOTOUT, HERO RUSHED TO HOSPITAL read some of the headlines. The man who almost killed Hector was named Darryl Knox, a.k.a. Nutso Knox, a twenty-seven-year-old ex-auto mechanic wanted in four states for a series of bank robberies and armed holdups. The journalists all celebrated his demise, calling special attention to the nifty gunwork of the guard – who managed to deliver the conclusive shot just as Knox was slipping out the door – but what interested them most was Hector's bravery, which they extolled as the finest demonstration of courage to have been seen in those parts in many years. *The girl was a goner*, one eyewitness was quoted as saying. *If that fellow hadn't taken the bull by the horns, I'd hate to think where she'd be now.* The girl was Frieda Spelling, age twenty-two, variously described as a painter, a recent graduate of Bernard College (sic), and the daughter of the late Thaddeus P. Spelling, prominent Sandusky banker and philanthropist. In article after article, she expressed her thanks to the man who had saved her life. She had been so scared, she said, so certain that she was going to die. She prayed that he would recover from his wounds.

The Spelling family offered to cover the man's medical expenses, but for the first seventy-two hours it seemed doubtful that he would pull through. He was unconscious when he arrived at the hospital, and after so much trauma and loss of blood, he was given no more than an outside chance of warding off the dangers of shock and infection, of walking out of there alive. The doctors removed his destroyed left lung, picked out the bits of exploded metal that had lodged in the tissue around his heart, and then they sewed him up again. For better or worse, Hector had found his bullet. He hadn't meant for it to happen that way, Alma said, but what he hadn't been able to do himself someone else did for him, and the irony was that Knox bungled the job. Hector didn't die from his encounter with death. He simply went to sleep, and when he woke up after his long slumber, he forgot that he had ever wanted to kill himself. The pain was too excruciating to dwell on anything as complicated as that. His insides were on fire, and all he could think about now was how to draw his next breath, how to go on breathing without bursting into flames.

At first, they had only the sketchiest idea of who he was. They emptied his pockets and examined the contents of his wallet, but they found no driver's license, no passport, no identification papers of any kind. The only thing with a name on it was a membership card for a North Side branch of the Chicago Public Library. H. Loesser, it said, but there was no address or telephone number, nothing to pinpoint where he lived. According to the newspaper articles published after the shooting, the Sandusky police were making every effort to uncover more information about him.

But Frieda knew who he was – or at least she thought she knew. She had gone to college in New York, and as a nineteen-year-old sophomore in 1928 she had managed to see six or seven of the twelve Hector Mann comedies. It wasn't that she had any interest in slapstick, but his films had been playing along with other films, part of the program of cartoons and newsreels than ran before the featured attraction, and she had become familiar enough with his looks to know who he was when she saw him. When she spotted Hector in the bank three years later, the absence of the mustache momentarily confused her. She recognized the face, but she couldn't attach a name to it, and before she could figure out who the man was, Knox rushed in behind her and pointed the gun at her head. Twenty-four hours went by before she was able to think about it again, but once the horror of her near death had begun to recede a little, the solution came to her in a flash of sudden, overpowering certainty. It didn't matter that the man's name was supposed to be Loesser. She had followed the news of Hector's disappearance in 1929, and if he wasn't dead, as most people seemed to think he was, then he had to be living under another name. What made no sense was that he had popped up in Sandusky, Ohio, but the truth was that most things made no sense, and if the laws of physics stipulated that every person in the world occupied a certain amount of space – which meant that everyone was necessarily somewhere – then why couldn't that somewhere have been Sandusky, Ohio? Three days later, when Hector emerged from his coma and started talking to the doctors, Frieda visited the hospital to thank him for what he had done. He couldn't say much, but the little he did say bore the irrefutable marks of a foreign accent. The voice clinched it for her, and when she bent over and kissed him on the forehead just before she left the hospital, she knew beyond a shadow of a doubt that her life had been saved by Hector Mann.

6

Landing turned out to be less difficult for me than taking off. I had prepared myself to be afraid, to be thrown into another frenzy of slobbering incompetence and spiritual malfunction, but when the captain told us that we were about to go into our descent, I felt curiously stable, unperturbed. There must have been a difference between going up and going down, I decided, between losing touch with the earth and returning to solid ground. One was a farewell, the other was a salutation, and perhaps beginnings were more bearable than endings, I thought, or perhaps I had discovered (quite simply) that the dead were not allowed to scream in you more than once a day. I turned toward Alma and gripped her arm. She was just getting into the early stages of Hector's romance with Frieda, moving past the night when he broke down and confessed to her and then going on to describe Frieda's startling response to that confession (The bullet absolves you, she said; you gave my life back to me, now I'm giving your life back to you), but when I put my hand on Alma's arm, she suddenly stopped talking, breaking off in mid-sentence, in mid-thought. She smiled, then leaned forward and kissed me – first on the cheek, then on the ear, and then square on the mouth. They fell hard for each other, she said. If we don't watch out, the same thing is going to happen to us.

Hearing those words must have made a difference, too – helped me to be less afraid, less prone to inner meltdown – but how apt, finally, that the word *fall* should have been the verb in the two sentences that summed up my history of the past three years. A plane falls from the sky, and all the passengers are killed. A woman falls in love, and a man falls with her, and not for an instant as the plane goes down does either one of them think about death. In midair, with the land revolving below us as we banked into our final turn, I understood that Alma was giving me the possibility of a second life, that something was still in front of me if I had the courage to walk toward it. I listened to the music of the engines as they shifted key. The noise inside the cabin grew louder, the walls shook, and then, almost as an afterthought, the wheels of the plane touched the ground.

It took a while for us to get going again. There was the opening of the hydraulic door, the walk through the terminal, the stopping in at the men's room and the women's room, the search for a telephone to call the ranch, the buying of water for the trip to Tierra del Sueño (Drink as much as you can, Alma said; the altitudes are deceiving here, and you don't want to get dehydrated), the combing of the long-term parking lot for Alma's Subaru station wagon, and then a final pause to fill up with gas before we hit the road. It was the first time I had been to New Mexico. Under normal circumstances, I would have gawked at the landscape, pointing to rock formations and demented-looking cacti, asking the name of this mountain or that gnarled shrub, but I was too caught up in Hector's story to bother with that now. Alma and I were passing through some of the most impressive country in North America, but for all the effect it had on us we could have been sitting in a room with the lights out and the shades drawn. I would travel that road several more times in the days to come, but I remember almost nothing of what I saw on that first trip. Whenever I think about riding in Alma's banged-up yellow car, the only thing that comes back to me is the sound of our voices – her voice and my voice, my voice and her voice – and the sweetness of the air rushing in on me through a crack in the window. But the land itself is invisible. It had to have been there, but I wonder now if I ever bothered to look at it. Or, if I did, if I wasn't too distracted to register what I was seeing.

They kept him in the hospital until early February, Alma said. Frieda went to visit him every day, and when the doctors finally said that he was strong enough to go, she talked her mother into letting him recuperate at their house. He was still in bad shape. It took another six months before he could move around very well.

And Frieda's mother was okay with that? Six months is an awfully long time.

She was thrilled. Frieda was a wild thing back then, one of those liberated bohemian girls who'd grown up in the late twenties, and she had nothing but contempt for Sandusky, Ohio. The Spellings had survived the crash with eighty percent of their wealth intact – which meant that they still belonged to what Frieda liked to call *the inner circle of the midwestern haute booboisie*. It was a narrow world of Republican stick-in-the-muds and foggy-headed women, and the principal entertainments consisted of joyless country club dances and long, stultifying dinner parties. Once a year, Frieda would grit her teeth and come home for the

THE BOOK OF ILLUSIONS

Christmas holidays, enduring those gruesome events for the sake of her mother and her married brother, Frederick, who still lived in town with his wife and two children. By the second or third of January, she'd rush back to New York, vowing never to return again. That year, of course, she didn't attend any parties – and she didn't go back to New York. She fell in love with Hector instead. As far as her mother was concerned, anything that kept Frieda in Sandusky was a good thing.

You're saying she had no objections to the marriage either?

Frieda had been in open rebellion for a long time. Just one day before the shooting, she'd told her mother that she was planning to move to Paris and would probably never set foot in America again. That's why she was in the bank that morning – to withdraw money from her account to buy the ticket. The last thing Mrs. Spelling ever expected to hear from her daughter's lips was the word *marriage*. In the light of this miraculous turnaround, how not to embrace Hector and welcome him into the family? Not only did Frieda's mother not object, she organized the wedding herself.

So Hector's life begins in Sandusky, after all. He plucks the name of a town out of thin air, tells a bunch of lies about it, and then he makes those lies come true. It's pretty bizarre, don't you think? Chaim Mandelbaum becomes Hector Mann, Hector Mann becomes Herman Loesser, and then what? Who does Herman Loesser become? Did he even know who he was anymore?

He went back to being Hector. That's what Frieda called him. That's what we all called him. After they were married, Hector became Hector again.

But not Hector Mann. He wouldn't have been that reckless, would he?

Hector Spelling. He took Frieda's last name.

Wow.

Not wow. Just practical. He didn't want to be Loesser anymore. That name represented everything that had gone wrong with his life, and if he was going to start calling himself something else, why not use the name of the woman he loved? It's not as if he ever went back on that. He's been Hector Spelling for more than fifty years.

How did they wind up in New Mexico?

They drove out West on their honeymoon and decided to stay. Hector had a lot of respiratory problems, and the dry air turned out to be good for him.

There were dozens of artists out there by then. The Mabel Dodge crowd in Taos, D. H. Lawrence, Georgia O'Keeffe. Did that have anything to do with it?

Nothing at all. Hector and Frieda lived in another part of the state. They never even met those people.

They moved there in 1932. Yesterday, you said that Hector started making movies again in 1940. That's eight years. What happened in the interval?

They bought four hundred acres of land. Prices were incredibly low at the time, and I don't think they paid more than a few thousand dollars for the whole property. Frieda came from a rich family, but she didn't have much money of her own. A small inheritance from her grandmother – ten or fifteen thousand dollars, something like that. Her mother kept offering to pay her bills, but Frieda wouldn't accept her help. Too proud, too stubborn, too independent. She didn't want to think of herself as a sponge. So she and Hector weren't in a position to hire large crews of workers to build a house for them. No architect, no contractor – they couldn't afford those things. Luckily, Hector knew what he was doing. He had learned carpentry from his father, had built sets for the movies, and all that experience allowed them to keep costs to a minimum. He designed the house himself, and then he and Frieda more or less built it with their own hands. It was a very simple place. A six-room adobe cottage. Just one story, and the only help they got with it came from a team of three Mexican brothers, unemployed day laborers who lived on the outskirts of town. For the first few years, they didn't even have electricity. They had water, of course, they had to have water, but it took a couple of months before they were able to find it and start digging the well. That was the first step. After that, they chose the site for the house. Then they drew up the plans and started construction. All that took time. They didn't just move there and settle in. It was blank and savage space, and they had to build everything from the ground up.

And then what? Once the house was ready, what did they do with themselves?

Frieda was a painter, and so she went back to being a painter. Hector read books and kept up with his journal, but mostly he planted trees. That became his major occupation, his work of the next few years. He cleared several acres of land around the house, and then, bit by bit, he installed an elaborate system of underground irrigation pipes. That made gardening possible, and once the garden was under way, he got busy with the trees. I've never counted them all, but there must be two or three hundred of them. Cottonwoods and junipers, willows and aspens, pinyons and white oaks. There used to be nothing but yucca and sagebrush growing there. Hector turned it into a little forest. You'll see it for yourself in a few hours, but for me it's one of the most beautiful places on earth.

That's the last thing I would have expected from him. Hector Mann, horticulturalist.

He was happy. Probably happier than at any other time in his life, but with that happiness came a total lack of ambition. The only thing that concerned him was taking care of Frieda and tending to his patch of ground. After all he'd been through in the past years, that felt like enough, like more than enough. He was still doing penance, you understand. It's just that he was no longer trying to destroy himself. Even now, he still talks about those trees as his greatest accomplishment. Better than his films, he says, better than anything else he's ever done.

What did they do for money? If things were so tight, how did they manage to get by?

Frieda had friends in New York, and many of those friends had contacts. They found jobs for her. Illustrating children's books, drawing for magazines, freelance work of one kind or another. It didn't bring in much, but it helped keep them afloat.

She must have had some talent, then.

We're talking about Frieda, David, not some upper-crust poseur. She had enormous gifts, a real passion for making art. She once told me that she didn't think she had the stuff to be a great painter, but then she added that if she hadn't met Hector when she did, she probably would have spent her life trying to become one. She hasn't painted in years, but she still draws like a demon. Fluid, sinuous lines, a terrific sense of composition. When Hector started making movies again, she did the storyboards, designed the sets and costumes, and helped establish the look of the films. She was an integral part of the whole enterprise.

I still don't understand. They were living this bare-bones existence out in the desert. Where did they come up with the money to start making movies?

Frieda's mother died. The estate was worth over three million dollars. Frieda inherited half of it, and the other half went to her brother, Frederick.

That would account for the financing, wouldn't it?

It was a lot of money back then.

It's still a lot of money today, but there's more to the story than just money. Hector made a promise never to work in films again. You told me that a few hours ago, and now he's suddenly back directing films. What made him change his mind?

Frieda and Hector had a son. Thaddeus Spelling II, named after Frieda's father. Taddy for short, or Tad, or Tadpole – they called him all sorts of things. He was born in 1935 and died in 1938. Stung by a bee one morning in his father's garden. They found him lying on the ground, all puffed up and swollen, and by the time they drove him to the doctor thirty miles away, he was already dead. Imagine the effect it had on them.

I can imagine it. If there's one thing I can imagine, I can imagine that.

I'm sorry. It was a stupid thing for me to say.

Don't be sorry. It's just that I know what you're talking about. No mental gymnastics required to understand the situation. Tad and Todd. It can't get any closer than that, can it?

Still . . .

No still. Just go on talking . . .

Hector collapsed. Months went by, and he didn't do anything at all. He sat in the house; he looked at the sky through the bedroom window; he studied the backs of his hands. It wasn't that Frieda didn't have a hard time of it, too, but he was so much more fragile than she was, so unprotected. She was tough enough to know that the boy's death was an accident, that he'd died because he was allergic to bees, but Hector saw it as a form of divine punishment. He had been too happy. Life had been too good to him, and now the fates had taught him a lesson.

The films were Frieda's idea, weren't they? After she inherited the money, she talked Hector into going back to work.

More or less. He was headed for a nervous breakdown, and she knew that she had to step in and take action. Not just to save him, but to save her marriage, to save her own life.

And Hector went along with it.

Not at first. But then she threatened to leave him, and he finally gave in. Not with any great reluctance, I should add. He was desperate to get back into it. For ten years, he'd been dreaming about camera angles, lighting setups, story ideas. It was the one thing he wanted to do, the one thing in the world that made sense to him.

But what about his promise? How did he justify breaking his word? From all you've told me about him, I don't see how he could have done that.

He did it by splitting hairs – and then he made a pact with the devil. If a tree falls in the forest and no one hears it fall, does it make a sound or not? Hector had read a lot of books by then, he knew all the tricks and arguments of the philosophers. If someone makes a movie and no one sees it, does the movie exist or not? That's how he justified what he did. He would make movies that would never be shown to audiences, make movies for the pure pleasure of making movies. It was an act of breathtaking nihilism, and yet he's stuck to the bargain ever since. Imagine knowing that you're good at something, so good that the world would be in awe of you if they could see your work, and then keeping yourself a secret from the world. It took great concentration and rigor to do what Hector did – and also a touch of madness. Hector and Frieda are both a bit mad, I suppose, but they've achieved something remarkable. Emily Dickinson wrote in obscurity, but she tried to publish her poems. Van Gogh tried to sell his paintings. As far as I know, Hector is the first artist to make his work with the conscious, premeditated intention of destroying it. There's Kafka, of course, who told Max Brod to burn his manuscripts, but when it came to the decisive moment, Brod couldn't go through with it. But Frieda will. There's no question about that. The day after Hector dies, she'll take his films into the garden and burn them all – every print, every negative, every frame he ever shot. That's guaranteed. And you and I will be the only witnesses.

How many films are we talking about?

Fourteen. Eleven features of ninety minutes or more, and three others that run under an hour.

I don't imagine he was still into comedies, was he?

Report from the Anti-World, The Ballad of Mary White, Travels in the Scriptorium, Ambush at Standing Rock. Those are some of the titles. They don't sound very funny, do they?

No, not what you'd call your standard laugh-a-thons. But not too grim, I hope.

It depends on how you define the word. I don't find them grim. Serious, yes, and often quite strange, but not grim.

How do you define strange?

Hector's films are extremely intimate, low to the ground, unflamboyant in tone. But there's always this fantastical element running through them, a weird kind of poetry. He broke a lot of rules. He did things film directors aren't supposed to do.

Like what?

Voice-overs, for one thing. Narration is considered a weakness in movies, a sign that the images aren't working, but Hector relied on it heavily in a number of his films. One of them, *The History of Light*, doesn't have a word of dialogue. It's wall-to-wall narration from start to finish.

What else did he do wrong? Wrong on purpose, I mean.

He was out of the commercial loop, and that meant he could work without constraints. Hector used his freedom to explore things other filmmakers weren't allowed to touch, especially in the forties and fifties. Naked bodies. Down-to-earth sex. Childbirth. Urination, defecation. Those scenes are a bit shocking at first, but the shock wears off rather quickly. They're a natural part of life, after all, but we're not used to seeing them presented on film, so we sit up for a couple of seconds and take notice. Hector didn't make a big point of it. Once you come to understand what's possible in his work, these so-called taboos and moments of explicitness blend into the overall texture of the stories. In a way, those scenes were a form of protection for him – just in case someone tried to walk off with one of the prints. He had to make sure that his films would be unreleasable.

And your parents went along with this.

It was a hands-on, do-it-yourself operation. Hector wrote, directed, and edited the films. My father lit them and shot them, and after the shooting was done, he and my mother did all the lab work. They processed the footage, cut the negatives, mixed the sound, and saw everything through until the final prints were in the can.

Right there at the ranch?

Hector and Frieda turned their property into a small movie studio. They began construction in May 1939 and finished in March 1940, and what they wound up with was a self-contained universe, a private compound for making films. There was a double sound stage in one building, along with additional areas for a carpentry shop, a seamstress shop, dressing rooms, and separate storage spaces for sets and costumes. Another building was for post production. They couldn't risk sending out their films to a commercial lab, so they built their own lab. That took up one wing. In the other half was the editing facility, the projection room, and an underground storage vault for prints and negatives.

All that equipment couldn't have come cheap. It cost them over a hundred fifty thousand dollars to set the place up. But they could afford it, and most things had to be bought only once. Several cameras, but only one editing machine, one pair of projectors, and one optical printer. After they had what they needed, they worked within tightly controlled budgets. Frieda's inheritance was drawing interest, and they dipped into the principal as sparingly as they could. They worked on a small scale. They had to if they meant to stretch out the money and make it last.

And Frieda was in charge of sets and costumes.

Among other things. She was also Hector's assistant editor, and when films were in production, she handled any one of several different jobs. Script supervisor, boom operator, focus puller – whatever needed doing on that day, at that moment.

And your mother?

My Faye. My beautiful, beloved Faye. She was an actress. She came to the ranch in 1945 to do a role in a film and fell in love with my father. She was still in her early twenties then. She performed in every film they made after that, mostly as the female lead, but she helped out on other fronts as well. Sewing costumes, painting scenery, advising Hector on his scripts, working with Charlie in the lab. That was the adventure of it. No one did just one thing there. They were all involved, and they all put in incredibly long hours. Months and months of laborious prep work, months and months in post production. Making films is a slow, intricate business, and with so few of them trying to do so much, they pushed along by inches. It generally took them about two years to finish a project.

I understand why Hector and Frieda wanted to be there – or partly understand it, am struggling to understand it – but your mother and father still baffle me. Charlie Grund was a gifted cameraman. I've studied his work, I know what he did with Hector in 1928, and it makes no sense that he would have walked away from his career.

My father had just been through a divorce. He was thirty-five, going on thirty-six, and he still hadn't made it into the top echelon of Hollywood DPs. After fifteen years in the business, he was working on B pictures – when he had work at all. Westerns, Boston Blackie movies, kids' serials. He had immense talent, Charlie did, but he was a quiet person, someone who never appeared to be very comfortable with himself, and people often mistook that shyness for arrogance. He kept losing out on the good jobs, and after a while it started to get to him, to eat away at his confidence. When his first wife left him, he went to hell for a few months. Drinking too much, feeling sorry for himself, not keeping up with his work. And that's when Hector called – just when he was down in that hole.

That still doesn't explain why he agreed to do it. No one makes pictures without wanting others to see them. It just isn't done. What's the point of putting film in the camera, then?

He didn't care. I know it's hard for you to believe, but the work was all that mattered to him. The results were secondary, almost of no importance. A lot of film people are like that – especially the ones below the line, the blue-collar guys, the grunts. They enjoy figuring things out. They like putting their hands on the equipment and getting it to do things for them. It's not about art or ideas. It's about working at something and making it come out right. My father had his ups and downs in the film business, but he was good at making films, and Hector gave him the opportunity to make films without having to worry about the business. If it had been anyone else, I doubt that he would have gone. But my father loved Hector. He always said that working for him at Kaleidoscope was the happiest year of his life.

He must have been shocked when Hector called. More than ten years go by, and suddenly there's a dead man on the other end of the line.

He thought someone was playing a prank on him. The only other possibility was that he was talking to a ghost, and since my father didn't believe in ghosts, he told Hector to go fuck himself and hung up the phone. Hector had to call back three more times before he was willing to accept it.

When was this?

Late thirty-nine. November or December, just after the Germans invaded Poland. By early February, my father was living at the ranch. Hector and Frieda's new house was ready by then, and he moved into the old one, the little cottage they'd built when they first got there. That's where I lived with my parents when I was growing up, and that's where I live now – in that six-room adobe house, under the shade of Hector's trees, writing my insane and endless book.

But what about the other people who came to the ranch? Actors were brought in, you said, and your father must have had some technical help. It's not possible to make a film with just four people. Even I know that. Maybe they could handle pre production and post production on their own, but not production itself. And once you have people coming in from the outside, how do you get away with it? How do you stop them from talking?

You tell them you're working for someone else. You pretend you've been hired by an eccentric millionaire from Mexico City, a man so in love with American movies that he's built his own studio in the American wilderness and commissioned you to make movies for him – movies that will never be seen by anyone but the man himself. That's the arrangement. If you come to the Blue Stone Ranch to work on a film, you do so with the understanding that your work will be seen by an audience of just one person.

That's preposterous.

Maybe so, but a lot of people swallowed the story.

You'd have to be pretty desperate to believe a thing like that.

You haven't spent much time with actors, have you? They're the most desperate people in the world. Ninety percent of them are unemployed, and if you offer them a job with a decent salary, they're not going to ask many questions. All they want is the chance to work. Hector didn't go after big names. He wasn't interested in stars. He just wanted competent professionals, and since he wrote his screenplays for small casts – sometimes just two or three roles – it wasn't difficult to find them. By the time he finished one film and was ready to go on to the next, there was a new crop of actors to choose from. Except for my mother, he never used the same actor twice.

All right, forget about everyone else. What about you? When did you first hear the name Hector Mann? You knew him as Hector Spelling. How old were you when you realized that Hector Spelling and Hector Mann were the same person?

I always knew that. We had a complete set of the Kaleidoscope films at the ranch, and I must have seen them fifty times when I was a child. The moment I learned how to read, I noticed that Hector was Mann, not Spelling. I asked my father about it, and he said that Hector had acted under a stage name when he was young, but now that he wasn't acting anymore, he'd stopped using it. It felt like a perfectly plausible explanation to me.

I thought those films were lost.

They almost were. By all rights, they should have been. But just when Hunt was about to declare bankruptcy, a day or two before the marshals came to seize his goods and padlock the door, Hector and my father broke into the Kaleidoscope offices and stole the films. The negatives weren't there, but they marched off with prints of all twelve comedies. Hector gave them to my father for safekeeping, and two months later Hector was gone. When my father moved to the ranch in 1940, he brought the the films with him.

How did Hector feel about that?

I don't understand. How should he have felt?

That's what I'm asking you. Was he pleased or displeased?

Pleased. Of course he was pleased. He was proud of those little films, and he was glad to have them back.

Then why did he wait so long before sending them out into the world again?

What makes you think he did that?

I don't know, I assumed . . .

I thought you understood. It was me. I was the one who did it.

I suspected as much.

Then why didn't you say something?

I didn't think I had the right to. In case it was supposed to be a secret.

I don't have any secrets from you, David. Whatever I know, I want you to know, too. Don't you get it? I sent out those films blind, and you were the one who found them. You're the only person in the world who found them all. That makes us old friends, doesn't it? We might not have met until yesterday, but we've been working together for years.

It was an incredible stunt you pulled. I talked to curators everywhere I went, and not one of them had any idea who you were. When I was in California, I had lunch with Tom Luddy, the head of the Pacific Film Archive. They were the last place to receive one of the Hector Mann mystery boxes. By the time theirs came, you'd already been at it for a few years, and the word was out. Tom said that he didn't even bother to open the package. He took it straight to the FBI to have it checked for fingerprints, but they couldn't find any in the box – not a single one. You didn't leave a trace.

I wore gloves. If I was going to go to the trouble of keeping a secret, I certainly wasn't going to slip up on a detail like that.

You're a clever girl, Alma.

You bet I'm clever. I'm the cleverest girl in this car, and I dare you to prove I'm not.

But how could you justify going behind Hector's back? It was his decision to make, not yours.

I talked to him about it first. It was my idea, but I didn't go ahead with it until he gave me the green light.

What did he say?

He shrugged. And then he gave me a little smile. It doesn't matter, he said. Do whatever you want, Alma.

So he didn't stop you, but he didn't help you, either. He didn't do anything.

It was November eighty-one, almost seven years ago. I'd just come back to the ranch for my mother's funeral, and it was a bad time for all of us, the beginning of the end, somehow. I didn't take it well. I admit that. She was only fifty-nine when we put her in the ground, and I hadn't been prepared for it. Pulverizing. That's the only word I can think of: a pulverizing sorrow. As if everything inside me had turned to dust. The others were so old by then. I looked up and suddenly realized that they were finished, that the great experiment was over. My father was eighty, Hector was eighty-one, and the next time I looked up, they'd all be gone. It had a tremendous effect on me. Every morning, I went into the screening room to watch my mother in her old films, and by the time I came out again, it would be dark outside and I'd be sobbing my guts out. After two weeks of that, I decided to go home. I was living in L.A. then. I had a job with an independent production company, and they needed me back at work. I was all set to go. I'd already called the airline and booked my ticket, but at the last minute – literally, on my last night at the ranch – Hector asked me to stay.

Did he give a reason?

He said he was ready to talk, and he needed someone to help him. He couldn't do it on his own.

You mean the book was his idea?

It all came from him. I never would have thought of it myself. And even if I had, I wouldn't have talked to him about it. I wouldn't have dared.

He lost his courage. That's the only explanation. Either he lost his courage or he went senile.

That's what I thought, too. But I was wrong, and you're wrong now. Hector changed his mind because of me. He told me I had a right to know the truth, and if I was willing to stay there and listen to him, he promised to tell me the whole story.

Okay, I'll accept that. You're part of the family, and now that you're an adult, you deserve to know the family secrets. But how does a private confession turn into a book? It's one thing for him to unburden himself to you, but a book is for the world, and as soon as he tells his story to the world, his life becomes meaningless.

Only if he's still alive when it's published. But he won't be. I've promised not to show it to anyone until after he's dead. He promised me the truth, and I promised him that.

And it's never occurred to you that he might be using you? You get to write your book, yes, and if all goes well, it's acknowledged as an important book, but at the same time Hector gets to live on through you. Not because of his films – which won't even exist anymore – but because of what you've written about him.

It's possible, anything is possible. But his motives don't really concern me. He could be acting out of fear, out of vanity, out of some last-minute surge of regret, but he's told me the truth. That's the only thing that counts. Telling the truth is hard, David, and Hector and I have lived through a lot together these past seven years. He's made everything available to me – all his journals, all his letters, every document he's been able to lay his hands on. At this point, I'm not even thinking about publication. Whether it comes out or not, writing this book has been the biggest experience of my life.

Where does Frieda fit into all this? Has she been helping the two of you or not?

It's been rough on her, but she's done her best to go along with us. I don't think she agrees with Hector, but she doesn't want to stand in his way. It's complicated. Everything with Frieda is complicated.

How long did it take before you decided to send out Hector's old films?

That happened right at the beginning. I still didn't know if I could trust him, and I proposed it as a test, to see if he was being honest with me. If he'd turned me down, I don't think I would have stayed. I needed him to sacrifice something, to give me a sign of good faith. He understood that. We never talked about it in so many words, but he understood. That's why he didn't do anything to stop it.

That still doesn't prove he's been honest with you. You put his old films back in circulation. Where's the harm in that? People remember him now. A crazy professor from Vermont even wrote a book about him. But none of that changes the story.

Every time he's told me something, I've gone and checked it out. I've been to Buenos Aires, I've followed the trail of Brigid O'Fallon's bones,

I've dug up the old newspaper articles about the Sandusky bank shoot-ing, I've talked to more than a dozen actors who worked at the ranch in the forties and fifties. There aren't any discrepancies. Some people couldn't be found, of course, and others turned out to be dead. Jules Blaustein, for example. And I still don't have anything on Sylvia Meers. But I did go to Spokane and talk to Nora.

She's still alive?

Very much so. At least she was three years ago.

And?

She married a man named Faraday in 1933 and had four children. Those children produced eleven grandchildren, and right around the time of my visit, one of those grandchildren was about to make them great-grandparents.

Good. I don't know why I say that, but I'm glad to hear it.

She taught the fourth grade for fifteen years, and then they made her principal of the school. She went on doing that until she retired in 1976.

In other words, Nora went on being Nora.

She was seventy-something years old when I went out there, but she still felt like the same person Hector had described to me.

And what about Herman Loesser? Did she remember him?

She cried when I mentioned his name.

What do you mean *cried*?

I mean her eyes filled up with tears, and the tears rolled down her cheeks. She cried. In the same way you and I cry. In the same way every person cries.

Good Lord.

She was so startled and embarrassed, she had to get up and leave the room. When she came back, she took hold of my hand and said that she was sorry. She'd known him a long time ago, she said, but she'd never been able to stop thinking about him. He'd been in her thoughts every day for the past fifty-four years.

You're making this up.

I don't make things up. If I hadn't been there, I wouldn't have believed it myself. But it happened. It all happened, just as Hector said it did. Every time I think he's lied to me, it turns out that he's been telling the truth. That's what makes his story so impossible, David. Because he's told me the truth.

7

There was no moon in the sky that night. When I stepped out of the car and put my feet on the ground, I remember saying to myself: Alma is wearing red lipstick, the car is yellow, and there is no moon in the sky tonight. In the darkness behind the main house, I could dimly make out the contours of Hector's trees – great hulks of shadow stirring in the wind.

Memoirs of a Dead Man opens with a passage about trees. I found myself thinking about that as we approached the front door, trying to remember my translation of the third paragraph of Chateaubriand's two-thousand-page book, the one that begins with the words *Ce lieu me plaît; il a remplacé pour moi les champs paternels* and concludes with the following sentences: *I am attached to my trees. I have addressed elegies, sonnets, and odes to them. There is not one amongst them that I have not tended with my own hands, that I have not freed from the worm that had attacked its root or the caterpillar that had clung to its leaves. I know them all by their names, as if they were my children. They are my family. I have no other, and I hope to be near them when I die.*

I wasn't expecting to see him that night. When Alma called from the airport, Frieda had told her that Hector would probably be asleep by the time we made it to the ranch. He was still hanging on, she said, but she didn't think he'd be up to talking to me until tomorrow morning – assuming he managed to last that long.

Eleven years later, I still wonder what would have happened if I had stopped and turned around before we reached the door. What if, instead of putting my arm around Alma's shoulder and walking straight toward the house, I had stopped for a moment, looked at the other half of the sky, and discovered a large round moon shining down on us? Would it still be true to say that there was no moon in the sky that night? If I didn't take the trouble to turn around and look behind me, then yes, it would still be true. If I never saw the moon, then the moon was never there.

I'm not suggesting that I didn't take the trouble. I kept my eyes open, I tried to absorb everything that was happening around me, but no doubt there was much that I missed as well. Like it or not, I can only write about what I saw and heard – not about what I didn't. This is not an admission of failure so much as a declaration of methodology, a statement of principles. If I never saw the moon, then the moon was never there.

Less than a minute after we entered the house, Frieda was taking me up to Hector's room on the second floor. There was no time for anything but the most cursory look around, the briefest of first impressions – her close-cropped white hair, the firmness of her grip when she shook my hand, the weariness in her eyes – and before I could say any of the things I was supposed to say (thank you for having me, I hope he's feeling better), she informed me that Hector was awake. He'd like to see you now, she said, and suddenly I was looking at her back as she led me up the stairs. No time to make any observations about the house, then – except to note that it was large and simply furnished, with many drawings and paintings hanging on the walls (perhaps Frieda's, perhaps not) – nor to think about the unlikely person who had opened the door, a man so diminutive that I didn't even notice him until Alma bent down and kissed him on the cheek. Frieda entered the room an instant later, and although I remember that the two women hugged, I can't recall if Alma was beside me when I walked up the stairs. I always seem to lose track of her at that point. I look for her in my mind, but I never manage to locate her. By the time I get to the top of the stairs, Frieda is inevitably gone as well. It couldn't have happened that way, but that's how I remember it. Whenever I see myself walking into Hector's room, I always go in alone.

What astonished me most, I think, was the simple fact that he had a body. Until I saw him lying there in the bed, I'm not sure that I ever fully believed in him. Not as an authentic person, at any rate, not in the way I believed in Alma or myself, not in the way I believed in Helen or even Chateaubriand. It stunned me to acknowledge that Hector had hands and eyes, fingernails and shoulders, a neck and a left ear – that he was tangible, that he wasn't an imaginary being. He had been inside my head for so long, it seemed doubtful that he could exist anywhere else.

The bony, liver-spotted hands; the gnarled fingers and thick, protruding veins; the collapsed flesh under his chin; the half-open mouth. He was lying on his back with his arms out over the covers when I entered the room, awake but still, looking up at the ceiling in a kind of trance. When he turned in my direction, however, I saw that his eyes were

Hector's eyes. Furrowed cheeks, grooved forehead, wattled throat, tufted white hair – and yet I recognized the face as Hector's face. It had been sixty years since he'd worn the mustache and the white suit, but he hadn't altogether vanished. He'd grown old, he'd grown infinitely old, but a part of him was still there.

Zimmer, he said. Sit down beside me, Zimmer, and turn off the light.

His voice was weak and clogged with phlegm, a soft rumbling of sighs and demi-articulations, but it was loud enough for me to make out what he said. The r at the end of my name had a slight roll to it, and as I reached over and turned off the lamp on the bedside table, I wondered if it wouldn't be easier for him if we continued in Spanish. After the light was off, however, I saw that a second lamp was on in the far corner of the room – a standing lamp with a broad vellum shade – and that a woman was sitting in a chair beside the lamp. She stood up the moment I glanced over at her, and I must have jumped a little when she did that – not only because I was startled, but because she was tiny, as tiny as the man who had opened the door downstairs. Neither one of them could have been more than four feet tall. I thought I heard Hector laugh behind me (a faint wheeze, the merest whisper of a laugh), and then the woman nodded at me in silence and walked out of the room.

Who was that? I said.

Don't be alarmed, Hector said. Her name is Conchita. She is part of the family.

I didn't see her, that's all. It surprised me.

Her brother Juan lives here, too. They are little people. Strange little people who cannot talk. We depend on them.

Do you want me to turn off the other light?

No, this is good. Not so hard on the eyes. I am content.

I sat down on the chair beside the bed and leaned forward, trying to position myself as close to his mouth as possible. The light from the other side of the room was no stronger than the light of a candle, but the illumination was sufficient for me to see Hector's face, to look into his eyes. A pale glow hovered over the bed, a yellowish air mixed with shadows and dark.

It is always too soon, Hector said, but I am not afraid. A man like me has to be crushed. Thank you for being here, Zimmer. I did not expect you to come.

Alma was very convincing. You should have sent her to me a long time ago.

You shook up my bones, sir. At first, I could not accept what you did. Now I think I am glad.

I didn't do anything.

You wrote a book. Again and again, I have read that book, and again and again I have asked myself: why did you choose me? What was your purpose, Zimmer?

You made me laugh. That was all it ever was. You cracked open something inside me, and after that you became my excuse to go on living.

Your book does not say that. It does honor to my old work with the mustache, but you do not talk about yourself.

I'm not in the habit of talking about myself. It makes me uncomfortable.

Alma has mentioned great sorrows, unspeakable pain. If I have helped you to bear that pain, it is perhaps the greatest good I have done.

I wanted to be dead. After listening to what Alma told me this afternoon, I gather you've been to that place yourself.

Alma was right to tell you those things. I am a ridiculous man. God has played many jokes on me, and the more you know about them, the better you will understand my films. I look forward to hearing what you say about them, Zimmer. Your opinion is very important to me.

I know nothing about films.

But you study the works of others. I have read those books, too. Your translations, your writings on the poets. It is no accident that you have spent years on the question of Rimbaud. You understand what it means to turn your back on something. I admire a man who can think like that. It makes your opinion important to me.

You've managed without anyone's opinion until now. Why this sudden need to know what others think?

Because I am not alone. Others live here, too, and I must not think only of myself.

From what I've been told, you and your wife have always worked together.

Yes, that is true. But there is Alma to consider as well.

The biography?

Yes, the book she is writing. After her mother's death, I understood that I owed her that. Alma has so little, and it seemed worth it to abandon some of my ideas about myself in order to give her a chance at life. I have begun to act like a father. It is not the worst thing that could have happened to me.

I thought Charlie Grund was her father.

He was. But I am her father, too. Alma is the child of this place. If she can turn my life into a book, then perhaps things will begin to go well for her. If nothing else, it is an interesting story. A stupid story, perhaps, but not without its interesting moments.

You're saying that you don't care about yourself anymore, that you've given up.

I have never cared about myself. Why should it bother me to turn myself into an example for others? Perhaps it will make them laugh. That would be a good outcome – to make people laugh again. You laughed, Zimmer. Perhaps others will begin to laugh with you.

We were just warming up, just beginning to get into the swing of the conversation, but before I could think of a response to Hector's last comment, Frieda walked into the room and touched me on the shoulder.

I think we should let him rest now, she said. You can go on talking in the morning.

It was demoralizing to be cut off like that, but I wasn't in a position to object. Frieda had given me less than five minutes with him, and already he had won me over, already he had made me like him more than I would have thought possible. If a dying man could exert that power, I remarked to myself, imagine what he must have been like at full strength.

I know that he said something to me before I left the room, but I can't remember what it was. Something simple and polite, but the precise words escape me now. *To be continued*, I think it was, or else *Until tomorrow, Zimmer*, a banal phrase that signified nothing of any great importance – except, perhaps, that he still believed he had a future, however short that future might have been. As I stood up from the chair, he reached out and grabbed my arm. That I do remember. I remember the cold, clawlike feel of his hand, and I remember thinking to myself: this is happening. Hector Mann is alive, and his hand is touching me now. Then I remember telling myself to remember what that hand felt like. If he didn't live until morning, it would be the only proof that I had seen him alive.

After those first hectic minutes, there was a stretch of calm that lasted for several hours. Frieda remained on the second floor, sitting in the chair I had occupied during my visit with Hector, and Alma and I went downstairs to the kitchen, which turned out to be a large, brightly lit room with stone walls, a fireplace, and a number of old appliances that seemed to have been built in the early sixties. I liked being there, and I liked sitting down at the long wooden table next to Alma and feeling her touch my arm in the same spot where Hector had touched me only a moment before. Two different gestures, two different memories – one on top of the other. My skin had become a palimpsest of fleeting sensations, and each layer bore the imprint of who I was.

Dinner was a random collection of hot and cold dishes: lentil soup, hard sausage, cheese, salad, and a bottle of red wine. The food was served to us by Juan and Conchita, the *strange little people who couldn't talk*, and while I won't deny that I was somewhat unnerved by them, I was too preoccupied with other things to give them any real attention. They were twins, Alma said, and they had started working for Hector and Frieda when they were eighteen, more than twenty years ago. I noted their perfectly formed miniature bodies, their crude peasant faces, their effervescent smiles and apparent goodwill, but I was more interested in watching Alma talk to them with her hands than I was in watching them talk to her. It intrigued me that Alma was so fluent in sign language, that she could flick off sentences with a few rapid twirls and swoops of her fingers, and because they were Alma's fingers, those were the fingers I wanted to watch. It was getting late, after all, and before long we would be going to bed. In spite of everything else that was happening just then, that was the subject I preferred to think about.

Remember the three Mexican brothers? Alma said.

The ones who helped build the original house.

The Lopez brothers. There were four girls in the family as well, and Juan and Conchita are the youngest children of the third sister. The Lopez brothers built most of the sets for Hector's films. They had eleven sons among them, and my father trained six or seven of the boys as film technicians. They were the crew. The fathers constructed the sets, and the sons worked as camera loaders and dolly operators, sound recorders and prop men, grips and gaffers. This went on for years. I used to play with Juan and Conchita when we were kids. They were the first friends I had in the world.

Eventually, Frieda came downstairs and joined us at the kitchen table. Conchita was washing a plate at the sink (standing on a footstool, working with grown-up efficiency in her seven-year-old's body), and the moment she caught sight of Frieda, she gave her a long, searching look, as if waiting for instructions. Frieda nodded, and Conchita put down the plate, dried off her hands with a dish towel, and left the room. Nothing had been said, but it was clear that she was going upstairs to sit with Hector, that they were watching over him in shifts.

By my reckoning, Frieda Spelling was seventy-nine years old. After listening to Alma's descriptions of her, I was prepared for someone ferocious – a blunt, intimidating woman, a larger-than-life character – but the person who sat down with us that evening was subdued, soft-spoken, almost reserved in her manner. No lipstick or makeup, no effort to do anything with her hair, but still feminine, still beautiful in some pared-down, incorporeal way. As I continued to look at her, I began to sense that she was one of those rare people in whom mind ultimately wins out over matter. Age doesn't diminish these people. It makes them old, but it doesn't alter who they are, and the longer they go on living, the more fully and implacably they incarnate themselves.

Forgive the confusion, Professor Zimmer, she said. You've come at a difficult time. Hector had a bad morning, but when I told him that you and Alma were on your way, he insisted on staying up. I hope it wasn't too much for him.

We had a good talk, I said. I think he's happy I came.

Happy might not be the word for it, but he's something, something very intense. You've created quite a stir in this house, Professor. I'm sure you're aware of that.

Before I could answer her, Alma broke in and changed the subject. Have you been in touch with Huyler? she asked. His breathing doesn't sound good, you know. It's much worse than it was yesterday.

Frieda sighed, then rubbed her hands over her face – exhausted from too little sleep, from too much agitation and worry. I'm not going to call Huyler, she said (talking more to herself than to Alma, as if repeating an argument she had gone through a dozen times before), because the only thing Huyler will say is *Bring him to the hospital*, and Hector won't go to the hospital. He's sick of hospitals. He made me promise, and I gave him my word. No more hospitals, Alma. So what's the point in calling Huyler?

Hector has pneumonia, Alma said. He has one lung, and he can barely breathe anymore. That's why you have to call Huyler.

He wants to die in the house, Frieda said. He's been telling me that every hour for the past two days, and I'm not going to go against him. I gave him my word.

I'll drive him to Saint Joseph's myself if you're too tired, Alma said.

Not without his permission, Frieda said. And we can't talk to him now because he's asleep. We'll try in the morning, if you like, but I'm not going to do it without his permission.

As the two women went on talking, I looked up and saw that Juan was perched on a footstool in front of the stove, scrambling eggs in a frying pan. When the food was ready, he transferred it onto a plate and carried it over to where Frieda was sitting. The eggs were hot and yellow, steaming up from the blue china in a swirl of vapor – as if the smell of those eggs had become visible. Frieda looked at them for a moment, but she didn't seem to understand what they were. They could have been a pile of rocks, or an ectoplasm that had dropped down from outer space, but they weren't food, and even if she did recognize them as food, she had no intention of putting them in her mouth. She poured herself a glass of wine instead, but after one small sip, she put the glass down again. Very delicately, she pushed the glass away from her, and then, using her other hand, she pushed away the eggs.

Bad timing, she said to me. I was hoping to be able to talk to you, to get to know you a little bit, but it doesn't look like that's going to be possible.

There's always tomorrow, I said.

Maybe, she said. Right now, I'm only thinking about now.

You should lie down, Frieda, Alma said. When was the last time you slept?

I can't remember. The day before yesterday, I think. The night before you left.

Well, I'm back now, Alma said, and David's here, too. You don't have to take on everything yourself.

I don't, Frieda said, I haven't. The little people have been an enormous help, but I have to be there to talk to him. He's too weak to sign anymore.

Get some rest, Alma said. I'll stay with him myself. David and I can do it together.

I hope you don't mind, Frieda said, but I'd feel much better if you stayed here in the house tonight. Professor Zimmer can sleep in the cottage, but I'd rather have you upstairs with me. Just in case something happens. Is that all right? I've already had Conchita make up the bed in the big guest room.

That's fine, Alma said, but David doesn't have to sleep in the cottage. He can stay with me.

Oh? Frieda said, utterly caught off guard. And what does Professor Zimmer say about that?

Professor Zimmer approves of the plan, I said.

Oh? she said again, and for the first time since she'd entered the kitchen, Frieda smiled. It was a terrific smile, I felt, full of amazement and stupefaction, and as she looked back and forth from Alma's face to my face, the smile continued to grow. My God, she said, you two work fast, don't you? Who would have expected *that*?

No one, I was about to say, but before I could get the words out of my mouth, the telephone rang. It was a bizarre interruption, and because it came so quickly after Frieda said the word *that*, there seemed to be a connection between the two events, as if the telephone had sounded in direct response to the word. It broke the mood entirely, extinguished the gleam of mirth that had been spreading across her face. Frieda stood up, and as I watched her walk to the phone (which was hanging on the wall beside the open doorway, five or six steps to her right), it occurred to me that the purpose of the call was to tell her that she wasn't allowed to smile, that smiling wasn't permitted in a house of death. It was a crazy thought, but that didn't mean my intuition was wrong. I had been on the point of saying *No one*, and when Frieda picked up the phone and asked who it was, it turned out that no one was there. Hello, she said, who is this? and when no one answered her question, she asked it again and then hung up. She turned to us with an anguished look on her face. No one, she said. Goddamn bloody no one.

Hector died a few hours later, sometime between three and four in the morning. Alma and I were asleep when it happened, naked under the covers in the guest room bed. We had made love, talked, made love again, and I can't be sure when our bodies finally gave out on us. Alma had traveled across the country twice in two days, had driven hundreds of miles to and from airports, and still she was able to rouse herself from the depths of sleep when Juan knocked on our door. I wasn't. I slept through all the noise and commotion and wound up missing everything. After years of insomnia and restless nights, I had finally slept soundly, and it happened on the one night when I should have been awake.

I didn't open my eyes until ten o'clock. Alma was sitting on the edge of the bed, stroking my cheek with her hand, whispering my name in a calm but urgent voice, and even after I had brushed out the cobwebs and lifted myself onto my elbow, she didn't tell me the news for another ten or fifteen minutes. There were kisses first, followed by some very intimate talk about the state of our feelings, and then she handed me a mug of coffee, which she allowed me to drink all the way to the bottom before starting in. I have always admired her for having the strength and the discipline to do that. By not talking about Hector right away, she was telling me that she wasn't going to let us drown in the rest of the story. We had begun our own story now, and it was just as important to her as the other – which was her life, her whole life up to the moment she had met me.

She was glad that I'd slept through it, she said. It had given her a chance to be alone for a while and to shed some tears, to get the worst of it behind her before the day started. It was going to be a rough day, she continued, a rough and eventful day for both of us. Frieda was on the warpath – charging forward on all fronts, getting ready to burn everything as quickly as she could.

I thought we had twenty-four hours, I said.

That's what I thought, too. But Frieda says it has to be *within* twenty-four hours. We had a big fight about that before she left.

Left? You mean she's not at the ranch?

It was an incredible scene. Ten minutes after Hector died, Frieda was on the phone, talking to someone at the Vista Verde Mortuary in Albuquerque. She asked them to send out a car as soon as possible. They got here at around seven, seven-thirty, which means they should almost be there by now. She plans to have Hector cremated today.

Can she do that? Don't you have to go through a lot of formalities first?

All she needs is a death certificate. Once the doctor examines the body and says that Hector died of natural causes, she'll be free to do what she wants.

She must have had this in mind all along. She just didn't tell you.

It's grotesque. We'll be out in the screening room watching Hector's films, and Hector's body will be in an oven, turning into a mound of ashes.

And then she'll come back, and the films will turn into ashes, too.

We have only a few hours. There isn't going to be enough time to watch them all, but we might be able to get through two or three if we start now.

It's not much, is it?

She was ready to burn them all this morning. At least I managed to talk her out of that.

You make it sound as if she's lost her mind.

Her husband is dead, and the first thing she has to do is destroy his work, destroy everything they made together. If she stopped to think, she wouldn't be able to go ahead with it. Of course she's out of her mind. She made this promise almost fifty years ago, and today's the day she has to carry it out. If I were in her shoes, I'd want to get it over with as fast as I could. Get it over with – and then collapse. That's why Hector gave her only twenty-four hours. He didn't want there to be any time for second thoughts.

Alma stood up then, and as she walked around the room opening the venetian blinds, I slid out of bed and put on my clothes. There were a hundred more things to say, but we would have to put them off until after we had watched the films. Sunlight rushed through the windows as Alma yanked up the blinds, filling the room with a dazzle of mid-morning brightness. She was wearing blue jeans, I remember, and a white cotton sweater. No shoes or socks, and the tips of her splendid little toes were painted red. It wasn't supposed to have worked out like this. I had been counting on Hector to keep himself alive for me, to give me a string of slow, contemplative days at the ranch with nothing to do but watch his films and sit with him in the darkness of his old man's room. It was hard to choose between disappointments, to decide which frustration was worse: never to be able to talk to him again – or to know that those films would be burned before I'd had a chance to see them all.

We passed Hector's room on the way downstairs, and when I looked inside I saw the little people stripping the sheets off the bed. The room was entirely bare now. The objects that had cluttered the surfaces of the bureau and the bedside table were gone (pill bottles, drinking glasses, books, thermometers, towels), and except for the blankets and pillows strewn about the floor, there was nothing to suggest that a man had died in there only seven hours ago. I caught them just as they were about to remove the bottom sheet. They were standing on opposite sides of the bed, hands poised in midair, getting ready to pull down from the two top corners in unison. The effort had to be coordinated because they were so small (their heads barely came above the mattress), and as the sheet momentarily billowed up from the bed, I saw that it was smudged with various stains and discolorations, the last intimate signs of Hector's presence in the world. We all die leaking out piss and blood, shitting ourselves like newborn children, suffocating in our own mucus. A second later, the sheet flattened out again, and the deaf-and-dumb servants began walking the length of the bed, moving from top to bottom as the sheet doubled over itself and then silently fell to the floor.

Alma had prepared sandwiches and drinks for us to carry over to the screening room. As she went into the kitchen to load up the picnic basket, I wandered around downstairs, looking at the art on the walls. There must have been three dozen paintings and drawings in the living room alone, another dozen in the hall: bright, undulating abstractions, landscapes, portraits, sketches in pen and ink. Nothing was signed, but they all seemed to be the work of one person, which meant that Frieda must have been the artist. I stopped in front of a small drawing that was hanging above the record cabinet. There wasn't going to be enough time to look at everything, so I decided to concentrate on that one and ignore the rest. It was an overhead view of a young child: a two-year-old sprawled out on his back with his eyes closed, evidently asleep in his crib. The paper had turned yellow and was crumbling a bit around the edges, and when I saw how old it was, I felt certain that the child in the picture was Tad, Hector and Frieda's dead son. Naked, loose-jointed arms and legs; naked torso; a bunched-up cotton diaper held together with a safety pin; a suggestion of the crib bars just beyond the crown of the head. The lines had a swift, spur-of-the-moment feel to them – a whirl of pulsing, confident strokes that had probably been executed in under five minutes. I tried to imagine the scene, to work my way back into the moment when the point of the pencil had first touched the paper. A mother is sitting next to her child as he takes his afternoon nap. She is reading a book, but when she glances up and sees him in that unguarded pose – head flung back and lolling to one side – she digs a pencil out of her pocket and begins to draw him. Since she has no paper, she uses the last page of the book, which happens to be blank. When the drawing is finished, she tears the page out of the book and puts it away – or else she leaves it there and forgets all about it. And if she forgets, years will go by before she opens the book again and rediscovers the lost drawing. Only then will she clip the brittle sheet from the binding, frame it, and hang it on the wall. There was no way for me to know when this might have happened. It could have been forty years ago, and it could have been last month, but whenever she had stumbled across that drawing of her son, the boy was already dead – perhaps long dead, perhaps dead for more years than I had been alive.

After Alma returned from the kitchen, she took my hand and led me out of the living room into an adjoining corridor with whitewashed stucco walls and a red slate floor. There's something I want you to see, she said. I know we're pressed for time, but it won't take more than a minute.

We walked to the end of the hall, passing two or three doors along the way, and then stopped in front of the last door. Alma put down the lunch basket and pulled out a fistful of keys from her pocket. There must have been fifteen or twenty keys on that ring, but she went straight to the one she wanted and slipped it into the lock. Hector's study, she said. He spent more time in here than anywhere else. The ranch was his world, but this was the center of that world.

It was filled with books. That was the first thing I noticed when I went in – how many books there were. Three of the four walls were lined with shelves from the floor to the ceiling, and every inch of those shelves was crammed with books. There were further clusters and piles of them on chairs and tables, on the rug, on the desk. Hardcovers and paperbacks, new books and old books, books in English, Spanish, French, and Italian. The desk was a long wooden table in the middle of the room – a twin to the table that stood in the kitchen – and among the titles I remember seeing there was *My Last Sigh*, by Luis Buñuel. Because the book was lying facedown and open just in front of the chair, I wondered if Hector hadn't been reading it on the day he fell and broke his leg – which was the last day he had spent any time in his study. I was about to pick it up to see where he had left off, but Alma took my hand again and led me over to the shelves in the back corner of the room. I think you'll find this interesting, she said. She pointed to a row of books several inches above her head (but exactly at my eye level), and I saw that all of them had been written by French authors: Baudelaire, Balzac, Proust, La Fontaine. A little to the left, Alma said, and as I moved my eyes to the left, scanning the spines for whatever it was she wanted to show me, I suddenly spotted the familiar green and gold of the two-volume Pléiade edition of Chateaubriand's *Mémoires d'outre-tombe*.

It shouldn't have made any difference to me, but it did. Chateaubriand wasn't an obscure writer, but it moved me to know that Hector had read the book, that he had entered the same labyrinth of memories that I had been wandering in for the past eighteen months. It was another point of contact, somehow, another link in the chain of accidental encounters and curious sympathies that had drawn me to him from the beginning. I pulled the first volume from the shelf and opened the book. I knew that Alma and I had to be on our way, but I couldn't resist the urge to run my hands over a couple of pages, to touch some of the words that Hector had read in the quiet of this room. The book fell open somewhere in the middle, and I saw that one of the sentences had been underlined faintly in pencil. *Les moments de crise produisent un redoublement de vie chez les hommes.* Moments of crisis produce a redoubled vitality in men. Or, more succinctly perhaps: Men don't begin to live fully until their backs are against the wall.

We hurried out into the hot summer morning with our sandwiches and cold drinks. One day earlier, we had been driving through the wreckage of a New England rainstorm. Now we were in the desert, walking under a sky without clouds, breathing in the thin, juniper-scented air. I saw Hector's trees off to the right, and as we maneuvered our way around the edge of the garden, cicadas clanged in the tall grass. Splashes of yarrow, fleabane, and bedstraw. I felt hyper-alert, filled with a kind of mad resolve, a jumbled-up state of fear, expectation, and happiness – as if I had three minds, and they were all working at once. A giant wall of mountains stood in the remote distance; a hawk circled overhead; a blue butterfly landed on a stone. Less than a hundred yards after setting out from the house, I could already feel sweat gathering on my forehead. Alma pointed to a long, one-story adobe building with cracked cement steps and weeds growing in front of it. The actors and technicians had slept there while films were in production, she said, but the windows were boarded up now and the water and electricity had been turned off. The post-production complex was another fifty yards ahead, but it was the building beyond that one that caught my attention. The sound stage was an enormous structure, a sprawling cube of whiteness glinting in the sun, and it looked odd to me in those surroundings, more like an airplane hangar or a truck depot than a place for shooting films. On an impulse, I squeezed Alma's hand, then shoved my fingers in with hers and laced them together. What are we going to watch first? I asked.

The Inner Life of Martin Frost.

Why that one and not another?

Because it's the shortest. We'll be able to see it through to the end, and if Frieda still isn't back when we've finished, we'll go on to the next shortest one. I couldn't think of any other way to go about it.

It's my fault. I should have come out here a month ago. You can't believe how stupid I feel.

Frieda's letters weren't very forthcoming. If I'd been in your position, I would have hesitated, too.

I couldn't accept that Hector was alive. And then, once I did accept it, I couldn't accept that he was dying. Those films have been sitting around for years. If I'd acted right away, I could have seen them all. I could have watched them two or three times, learned them by heart, digested them. Now we're scrambling to watch just one. It's absurd.

Don't beat yourself up, David. It took me months to convince them that you should come to the ranch. If it's anyone's fault, it's mine. I'm the one who was slow. I'm the one who feels stupid.

Alma opened the door with another one of her keys, and the moment we stepped across the threshold and entered the building, the temperature dropped by ten degrees. The air-conditioning was on, and unless they kept it running all the time (which I doubted), that meant Alma had already come out here earlier in the morning. It seemed like an insignificant fact, but once I'd thought about it for a couple of moments, I felt an immense surge of pity for her. She had watched Frieda drive away with Hector's body at seven or seven-thirty, and then, instead of going upstairs and waking me, she had gone over to the post-production building and turned on the air conditioner. For the next two and a half hours, she had sat in here alone, mourning Hector as the building gradually cooled off, unable to face me again until she had cried herself out. We could have spent those hours watching a movie, but she hadn't been ready to begin, and so a part of the day had slipped through our fingers. Alma wasn't tough. She was braver than I'd thought she was, but she wasn't tough, and as I followed her down the chilly hallway toward the screening room, I finally understood how terrible this day was going to be for her, how terrible it had already been.

Doors to the left, doors to the right, but no time to open any of them, no time to go in and browse around the editing suite or the sound-mixing studio, no time even to ask if the equipment was still there. At the end of the corridor, we turned left, walked down another corridor with bare cinderblock walls (pale blue, I remember), and then went through a set of double doors into the little theater. There were three rows of cushioned chairs with fold-up seats – approximately eight to ten per row – and a slight downward incline to the floor. The screen was bolted to the wall, with no stage or curtain in front of it, a rectangle of opaque white plastic with tiny perforations and a glossy oxide sheen. Behind us was the projection booth, jutting out from the back wall. The lights were on in there, and when I turned around and looked up, the first thing I noticed was that there were two projectors – and that each one was loaded with a reel of film.

Except for a few dates and numbers, Alma didn't tell me much about the movie. *The Inner Life of Martin Frost* was the fourth film Hector had made at the ranch, she said, and after completion of photography in March 1946, he had worked on it for another five months before unveiling the final version at a private screening on August twelfth. The running time was forty-one minutes. As with all of Hector's films, it had been shot in black-and-white, but *Martin Frost* was somewhat different from the others in that it could be described as a comedy (or a film with comic elements in it) and therefore was the only one of his late works with any connection to the slapstick two-reelers of the twenties. She had chosen it because of its length, she said, but that didn't mean it wasn't a good place to begin. Her mother had played her first role for Hector in this film, and if it wasn't the most ambitious work they did together, it was probably the most charming. Alma looked away for a moment. Then, after drawing in a deep breath, she turned back to me and added: Faye was so alive then, so vivid. I never get tired of watching her.

I waited for her to go on, but that was the only comment she made, the only remark that came close to offering a subjective opinion. After another short silence, she opened the picnic basket and pulled out a notebook and a ballpoint pen – which was equipped with a flashlight for writing in the dark. Just in case you want to jot something down, she said. As I took the objects from her, she leaned forward and kissed me on the cheek – a little peck, a schoolgirl's kiss – and then turned and headed for the door. Twenty seconds later, I heard a tapping sound. I looked up, and there she was again, waving at me from the glassed-in projection booth. I waved back – perhaps I even blew her a kiss – and then, just as I was installing myself in the middle seat of the front row, Alma dimmed the lights. She didn't come down again until the film was over.

It took me a while to settle into it, to figure out what was going on. The action was filmed with such deadpan realism, such scrupulous attention to the particulars of everyday life, that I failed to perceive the magic embedded in the heart of the story. The movie began like any other love comedy, and for the first twelve or fifteen minutes Hector stuck to the

293

time-worn conventions of the genre: the accidental meeting between the man and the woman, the misunderstanding that pushes them apart, the sudden turnaround and explosion of desire, the plunge into delirium, the emergence of difficulties, the grappling with doubt and the over-coming of doubt – all of which would lead (or so I thought) to a tri-umphant resolution. But then, about a third of the way into the narrative, I understood that I had it wrong. In spite of appearances, the setting of the film was not Tierra del Sueño or the grounds of the Blue Stone Ranch. It was the inside of a man's head – and the woman who had walked into that head was not a real woman. She was a spirit, a fig-ure born of the man's imagination, an ephemeral being sent to become his muse.

If the film had been shot anywhere else, I might not have been so slow to catch on. The immediacy of the landscape disconcerted me, and for the first couple of minutes I had to struggle against the impression that I was watching some kind of elaborate, highly skilled home movie. The house in the film was Hector and Frieda's house; the garden was their garden; the road was their road. Even Hector's trees were there – look-ing younger and scrawnier than they were now, perhaps, but still, they were the same trees I had passed on my way to the post-production building not ten minutes earlier. There was the bedroom I had slept in the night before, the rock on which I had seen the butterfly land, the kitchen table that Frieda had stood up from to answer the phone. Until the film began to play out on the screen in front of me, all those things had been real. Now, in the black-and-white images of Charlie Grund's camera, they had been turned into the elements of a fictional world. I was supposed to read them as shadows, but my mind was slow to make the adjustment. Again and again, I saw them as they were, not as they were meant to be.

The credits came on in silence, with no music playing in the back-ground, no auditory signals to prepare the viewer for what was to come. A progression of white-on-black cards announced the salient facts. The Inner Life of Martin Frost. Story and Direction: Hector Spelling. Cast: Norbert Steinhaus and Faye Morrison. Camera: C. P. Grund. Sets and Costumes: Frieda Spelling. The name Steinhaus meant nothing to me, and when the actor appeared on-screen a few moments later, I felt cer-tain that I had never seen him before. He was a tall, lanky fellow in his mid-thirties with sharp, observant eyes and slightly thinning hair. Not especially handsome or heroic, but sympathetic, human, with enough

294

going on in his face to suggest a certain activity of mind. I felt comfortable watching him and didn't resist believing in his performance, but it was harder for me to do that with Alma's mother. Not because she wasn't a good actress, and not because I felt let down (she was lovely to look at, excellent in her role), but simply because she was Alma's mother. No doubt that added to the dislocation and confusion I experienced at the start of the film. There was Alma's mother – but Alma's mother young, fifteen years younger than Alma was now – and I couldn't help looking for signs of her daughter in her, for traces of resemblance between them. Faye Morrison was darker and taller than Alma, undeniably more beautiful than Alma, but their bodies had a similar shape, and the look in their eyes, the tilt of their heads, and the tone in their voices bore similarities as well. I don't mean to imply that they were the same, but there were enough parallels, enough genetic echoes for me to imagine that I was watching Alma without the birthmark, Alma before I had met her, Alma as a girl of twenty-two or twenty-three – living through her mother in some alternate version of her own life.

The film begins with a slow, methodical tracking shot through the interior of the house. The camera skims along the walls, floats above the furniture in the living room, and eventually comes to a stop in front of the door. *The house was empty*, an offscreen voice tells us, and a moment later the door opens and in steps Martin Frost, carrying a suitcase in one hand and a bag of groceries in the other. As he kicks the door shut behind him, the voice-over narration continues. *I had just spent three years writing a novel, and I was feeling tired, in need of a rest. When the Spellings decided to go to Mexico for the winter, they offered me the use of their place. Hector and Frieda were close friends, and they both knew how much the book had taken out of me. I figured that a couple of weeks in the desert might do me some good, and so one morning I climbed into my car and drove from San Francisco to Tierra del Sueño. I had no plans. All I wanted was to be there and do nothing, to live the life of a stone.*

As we listen to Martin's narration, we see him wandering around in various parts of the house. He carries the groceries into the kitchen, but the moment the bag touches the counter, the scene cuts to the living room, where we find him inspecting the books on the shelves. As his hand reaches for one of the books, we jump upstairs to the bedroom, where Martin is opening and closing the drawers of the bureau, putting away his things. A drawer bangs shut, and an instant later he is sitting on the bed, testing the bounce of the mattress. It is a jagged, efficiently orchestrated montage, combining close and medium shots in a succession of slightly off-kilter angles, varied tempos, and small visual surprises. Normally, one would expect music to be playing under such a sequence, but Hector dispenses with instruments in favor of natural sound: the creaking bed-springs, Martin's footsteps on the tile floor, the rustling of the paper bag. The camera fixes on the hands of a clock, and as we listen to the last words of the opening monologue (*All I wanted was to be there and do nothing, to live the life of a stone*), the image begins to blur. Silence follows. For a beat or two, it is as if everything has stopped – the voice, the sounds, the images – and then, very abruptly, the scene shifts to the outdoors. Martin is walking in the garden. A long shot is followed by a close shot; Martin's face, and then a languid perusal of the things around him: trees and scrub, sky, a crow settling onto the branch of a cottonwood. When the camera finds him again, Martin is crouching down to observe a procession of ants. We hear the wind rush through the trees – a prolonged sibilance, roaring like the sound of surf. Martin looks up, shielding his eyes from the sun, and again we cut away from him to another part of the landscape: a rock with a lizard crawling over it. The camera tilts up an inch or two, and at the top of the frame we see a cloud floating past the rock. *But what did I know?* Martin says. *A few hours of silence, a few gulps of desert air, and all of a sudden an idea for a story was turning around in my head. That's how it always seems to work with stories. One minute there's nothing. And the next minute it's there, already sitting inside you.*

The camera pans from a close-up of Martin's face to a wide shot of the trees. The wind is blowing again, and as the leaves and branches tremble under the assault, the sound amplifies into a pulsing, breathlike wave of percussiveness, an airborne clamor of sighs. The shot lasts three or four seconds longer than we think it will. It has a strangely ethereal effect, but just when we are about to ask ourselves what this curious emphasis could signify, we are thrown back into the house. It is a harsh, sudden transition. Martin is sitting at a desk in one of the upstairs rooms, pounding away at a typewriter. We listen to the clatter of the keys, watch him work on his story from a variety of angles and distances. *It wasn't going to be long,* he says. *Twenty-five or thirty pages, forty at the most. I didn't know how much time I would need to write it, but I decided to stay in the house until it was finished. That was the new plan. I would write the story, and I wouldn't leave until it was finished.*

THE BOOK OF ILLUSIONS

The picture fades to black. When the action resumes, it is morning. A tight shot of Martin's face shows him to be asleep, his head resting on a pillow. Sunlight pours through the slatted shutters, and as we watch him open his eyes and struggle to wake up, the camera pulls back to reveal something that cannot be true, that defies the laws of common sense. Martin has not spent the night alone. There is a woman in bed with him, and as the camera continues dollying back into the room, we see that she is asleep under the covers, curled up on her side and turned toward Martin – her left arm flung casually across his chest, her long dark hair spilling out over the adjacent pillow. As Martin gradually emerges from his torpor, he notices the bare arm lying across his chest, then realizes that the arm is attached to a body, and then sits up straight in bed, looking like someone who's just been given an electric shock.

Jostled by these sudden movements, the young woman groans, buries her head in the pillow, and then open her eyes. At first, she doesn't seem to notice that Martin is there. Still groggy, still fighting her way into consciousness, she rolls onto her back and yawns. As her arms stretch out, her right hand brushes against Martin's body. Nothing happens for a second or two, and then, very slowly, she sits up, looks into Martin's confused and horrified face, and shrieks. An instant later, she flings back the covers and bounds from the bed, rushing across the room in a frenzy of fear and embarrassment. She has nothing on. Not a stitch, not a shred, not even the hint of an obscuring shadow. Stunning in her nakedness, with her bare breasts and bare belly in full view of the camera, she charges toward the lens, snatches her bathrobe from the back of a chair, and hastily thrusts her arms into the sleeves.

It takes a while to clear up the misunderstanding. Martin, no less vexed and agitated than his mysterious bed partner, slides out of bed and puts on his pants, then asks her who she is and what she's doing there. The question seems to offend her. No, she says, who is *he*, and what is *he* doing there? Martin is incredulous. What are you talking about? he says. I'm Martin Frost – not that it's any of your business – and unless you tell me who you are right now, I'm going to call the police. Inexplicably, his statement astonishes her. You're Martin Frost? she says. The real Martin Frost? That's what I just said, Martin says, growing more peevish by the second, do I have to say it again? It's just that I know you, the young woman replies. Not that I really know you, but I know who you are. You're Hector and Frieda's friend.

297

How is she connected to Hector and Frieda? Martin wants to know, and when she informs him that she's Frieda's niece, he asks her for the third time what her name is. Claire, she finally says. Claire what? She hesitates for a moment and then says, Claire . . . Claire Martin. Martin snorts with disgust. What is this, he says, some kind of joke? I can't help it, Claire says. That's my name.

And what are you doing here, Claire *Martin*?

Frieda invited me.

When Martin responds with a disbelieving look, she picks up her purse from the chair. After fumbling through its contents for several seconds, she pulls out a key and holds it up to Martin. You see? she says. Frieda sent it to me. It's the key to the front door.

With growing irritation. Martin digs into his pocket and pulls out an identical key, which he angrily holds up to Claire – jabbing it right under her nose. Then why would Hector send me this one? he says.

Because . . . Claire answers, backing away from him, because . . . he's Hector. And Frieda sent me this one because she's Frieda. They're always doing things like that.

There is an irrefutable logic to Claire's statement. Martin knows his friends well enough to understand that they're perfectly capable of getting their signals crossed. Inviting two people to the house at the same time is just the sort of thing the Spellings are apt to do.

With a defeated look, Martin begins to pace around the room. I don't like it, he says. I came here to be alone. I have work to do, and having you around is . . . well, it's not being alone, is it?

Don't worry, Claire says. I won't get in your way. I'm here to work, too.

It turns out that Claire is a student. She's preparing for a philosophy exam, she says, and has many books to read, a semester's worth of assignments to cram into a couple of weeks. Martin is skeptical. What do pretty girls have to do with philosophy? his look seems to say, and then he grills her about her studies, asking her what college she attends, the name of the professor who is giving the course, the titles of the books she has to read, and so on. Claire pretends not to notice the insult buried in these questions. She goes to Cal Berkeley, she says. Her professor's name is Norbert Steinhaus, and the course is called From Descartes to Kant: The Foundations of Modern Philosophical Inquiry.

I promise to be very quiet, Claire says. I'll move my things into another bedroom, and you won't even know I'm here.

Martin has run out of arguments. All right, he says, reluctantly giving in to her, I'll stay out of your way, and you'll stay out of mine. Do we have a deal?

They do. They even shake hands on it, and as Martin clomps out of the room to begin working on his story, the camera swings around and slowly pushes in on Claire's face. It is a simple but compelling shot, our first serious look at her in repose, and because it is accomplished with such patience and fluidity, we sense that the camera isn't trying to reveal Claire to us so much as to get inside her and read her thoughts, to caress her. She follows Martin with her eyes, watching him as he leaves the room, and an instant after the camera comes to rest in front of her, we hear the latch of the door click shut. The expression on Claire's face doesn't change. Good-bye, Martin, she says. Her voice is low, barely more than a whisper.

For the rest of the day, Martin and Claire work in their separate rooms. Martin sits at the desk in the study, typing, looking out the window, typing again, muttering to himself as he reads back the words he has written. Claire, looking like a college student in her blue jeans and sweatshirt, is sprawled out on the bed with *The Principles of Human Knowledge*, by George Berkeley. At some point, we notice that the philosopher's name is written out in block letters across the front of the sweatshirt: BERKELEY – which also happens to be the name of her school. Is this supposed to mean something, or is it simply a kind of visual pun? As the camera cuts back and forth from one room to the other, we hear Claire reading out loud to herself: *And it seems no less evident that the various sensations or ideas imprinted on the sense, however blended or combined together, cannot exist otherwise than in a mind perceiving them.* And again: *Secondly, it will be objected that there is a great difference betwixt real fire and the idea of fire, between dreaming or imagining oneself burnt, and actually being so.*

Late in the afternoon, a knock is heard at the door. Claire goes on reading, but when a second, louder knock follows the first, she puts down her book and tells Martin to come in. The door opens a few inches, and Martin pokes his head into the room. I'm sorry, he says. I wasn't very nice to you this morning. I shouldn't have acted that way. It is a stiff and bumbling apology, but delivered with such awkwardness and hesitation that Claire can't help smiling with amusement, perhaps even a trace of pity. She has one more chapter to go, she says. Why don't they meet in the living room in half an hour and have a drink? Good idea, Martin says. As long as they're stuck with each other, they might as well act like civilized people.

The action cuts to the living room. Martin and Claire have opened a bottle of wine, but Martin still seems nervous, not quite sure what to make of this strange and attractive reader of philosophy. In a clumsy stab at humor, he points to her sweatshirt and says, Does it say Berkeley because you're reading Berkeley? When you start reading Hume, will you wear one that says Hume?

Claire laughs. No, no, she says, the words are pronounced differently. *Berk*-ley and *Bark*-ley. The first one is a college, the other is a man. You know that. Everyone knows that.

It's the same spelling, Martin says. Therefore, it's the same word.

It's the same spelling, Claire says, but it's two different words.

Claire is about to go on, but then she stops, suddenly realizing that Martin is pulling her leg. She breaks into a broad smile. Holding out her glass, she asks Martin to pour her another drink. You wrote a short story about two characters with the same name, she says, and here I am lecturing you on the principles of nominalism. It must be the wine. I'm not thinking clearly anymore.

So you read that story, Martin says. You must be one of six people in the universe who knows about it.

I've read all your work, Claire answers. Both novels and the collection of stories.

But I've published only one novel.

You've just finished your second, haven't you? You gave a copy of the manuscript to Hector and Frieda. Frieda lent it to me, and I read it last week. *Travels in the Scriptorium.* I think it's the best thing you've done.

By now, whatever reservations Martin might have felt toward her have all but crumbled away. Not only is Claire a spirited and intelligent person, not only is she pleasant to look at, but she knows and understands his work. He pours himself another glass of wine. Claire discourses on the structure of his latest novel, and as Martin listens to her incisive but flattering comments, he leans back in his chair and smiles. It is the first time since the opening of the film that the brooding, everserious Martin Frost has let down his guard. In other words, he says, Miss Martin approves. Oh yes, Claire says, most definitely. Miss Martin approves of Martin. This play on their names leads them back to the Berk-ley/Bark-ley conundrum, and once again Martin asks Claire to explain the word on the sweatshirt. Which one is it? he says. The man or the college? It's both, Claire answers. It says whatever you want it to say.

At that moment, a small glint of mischief flashes in her eyes. Something has occurred to her – a thought, an impulse, a sudden inspiration. Or, Claire says, putting her glass on the table and standing up from the couch, it doesn't mean anything at all.

By way of demonstration, she peels off the sweatshirt and calmly tosses it onto the floor. She has nothing on underneath but a lacy black bra – hardly the kind of garment one would expect to discover on such an earnest student of ideas. But this is an idea, too, of course, and now that she has put it into action with such a bold and decisive gesture, Martin can only gape. Not in his wildest dreams could he have imagined that things would happen so fast.

Well, he finally says, that's one way of eliminating the confusion.

Simple logic, Claire replies. A philosophical proof.

And yet, Martin continues, speaking after another long pause, by eliminating one kind of confusion, you only create another.

Oh Martin, Claire says. Don't be confused. I'm trying to be as clear as I can.

There is a fine line between charm and aggression, between throwing yourself at someone and letting nature take its course. In this scene, which ends with the words just spoken (*I'm trying to be as clear as I can*), Claire manages to straddle both sides of the argument at once. She seduces Martin, but she goes about it in such a clever, lighthearted way that it never occurs to us to question her motives. She wants him because she wants him. That is the tautology of desire, and rather than go on discussing the endless nuances of such a proposition, she cuts directly to the chase. Removing the sweatshirt is not a vulgar announcement of her intentions. It is a moment of sublimely achieved wit, and from that moment on, Martin knows that he has met his match.

They wind up in bed. It is the same bed where they encountered each other that morning, but this time they are in no rush to separate, to fly apart on contact and scramble into their clothes. They come crashing through the door, walking and embracing at the same time, and as they fall to the bed in an awkward tangle of arms and legs and mouths, we have no doubt where all this groping and heavy breathing is going to take them. In 1946, the conventions of moviemaking would have required the scene to end there. Once the man and the woman started to kiss, the director was supposed to cut away from the bedroom to a shot of sparrows taking flight, to surf pounding against the shore, to a train speeding through a tunnel – any of several stock images to stand in for carnal passion, the fulfillment of lust – but New Mexico wasn't Hollywood, and Hector could let the camera go on rolling for as long as he liked. Clothes come off, bare flesh is seen, and Martin and Claire begin to make love. Alma had been right to warn me about the erotic moments in Hector's films, but she had been wrong to think that I would be shocked by them. I found the scene to be rather subdued, almost poignant in the banality of its intentions. The lighting is dim, the bodies are flecked with shadows, and the whole thing lasts no more than ninety or a hundred seconds. Hector doesn't want to arouse or titillate so much as to make us forget that we are watching a film, and by the time Martin starts running his mouth down Claire's body (over her breasts and along the curve of her right hip, across her pubic hair and into the soft inner part of her leg), we want to believe that we have. Again, not a note of music is played. The only sounds we hear are the sounds of breath, of rustling sheets and blankets, of bedsprings, of wind gusting through the branches of the trees in the unseen darkness outside.

The next morning, Martin begins talking to us again. Over a montage that denotes the passage of five or six days, he tells us about the progress of his story and his growing love for Claire. We see him alone at his typewriter, see Claire alone with her books, see them together in a number of different places around the house. They cook dinner in the kitchen, kiss on the living room sofa, walk in the garden. At one point, Martin is crouching on the floor beside his desk, dipping a brush into a bucket of paint and slowly writing out the letters H-U-M-E on a white T-shirt. Later on, Claire is dressed in that T-shirt, sitting Indian-style on the bed and reading a book by the next philosopher on her list, David Hume. These small vignettes are interspersed with random close-ups of objects, abstract details that have no apparent connection to what Martin is saying: a pot of boiling water, a puff of cigarette smoke, a pair of white curtains fluttering in the embrasure of a half-open window. Steam, smoke, and wind – a catalogue of formless, insubstantial things. Martin is describing an idyll, a moment of sustained and perfect happiness, and yet as this procession of dreamlike images continues to march across the screen, the camera is telling us not to trust in the surfaces of things, to doubt the evidence of our own eyes.

One afternoon, Martin and Claire are eating lunch in the kitchen.

Martin is in the middle of telling her a story (*And then I said to him, If you don't believe me, I'll show you. And then I reached into my pocket and –*) when the telephone rings. Martin gets up to answer it, and as soon as he exits the frame, the camera reverses angle and dollies in on Claire. We see her expression change from one of joyful camaraderie to concern, perhaps even alarm. It is Hector, calling long-distance from Cuernavaca, and although we can't hear his end of the conversation, Martin's comments are clear enough for us to understand what Hector is saying. It seems that a cold front is headed toward the desert. The furnace has been on the blink, and if the temperatures drop as low as they are expected to, then Martin will need to have it checked out. If anything goes wrong, the man to call is Jim, Jim Fortunato of Fortunato Plumbing and Heat.

It's no more than a mundane point of business, but Claire grows increasingly upset as she listens to the exchange. When Martin finally mentions her name to Hector (*I was just telling Claire about that bet we made the last time I was here*), Claire stands up and rushes out of the room. Martin is surprised by her sudden departure, but that surprise is nothing compared to the one that follows an instant later. *What do you mean, Who's Claire?* he says to Hector. *Claire Martin, Frieda's niece.* We don't have to listen to Hector's answer to know what he says. One look at Martin's face and we understand that Hector has just told him that he's never heard of her, that he has no idea who Claire is.

By then, Claire is already outside, running away from the house. In a series of rapid, pinpoint cuts, we see Martin burst through the door and chase after her. He calls out to Claire, but Claire keeps on running, and another ten seconds go by before he manages to catch up with her. Reaching out and grabbing her elbow from behind, he spins her around and forces her to stop. They are both out of breath. Chests heaving, lungs gasping for air, neither one of them able to talk.

At last Martin says: What's going on, Claire? Tell me, what's going on? When Claire doesn't answer him, he leans forward and shouts in her face: You have to tell me!

I can hear you, Claire says, speaking in a calm voice. You don't have to shout, Martin.

I've just been told that Frieda has one brother, Martin says. He has two children, and both of them happen to be boys. That makes two nephews, Claire, but no niece.

I didn't know what else to do, Claire says. I had to find a way to make you trust me. After a day or two, I thought you'd figure it out on your own – and then it wouldn't matter anymore.

Figure out what?

Until now, Claire has looked embarrassed, more or less contrite, not so much ashamed of her deception as disappointed that she's been found out. Once Martin confesses to his ignorance, however, the look changes. She seems genuinely astonished. Don't you get it, Martin? she says. We've been together for a week, and you're telling me you still don't get it?

It goes without saying that he doesn't – and neither do we. The bright and beautiful Claire has turned into an enigma, and the more she says, the less we are able to follow her.

Who are you? Martin asks. What the hell are you doing here?

Oh Martin, Claire says, suddenly on the verge of tears. It doesn't matter who I am.

Of course it does. It matters very much.

No, my darling, it doesn't.

How can you say that?

It doesn't matter because you love me. Because you want me. *That's* what matters. All the rest is nothing.

The picture fades out on a close-up of Claire, and before another image succeeds it, we hear the faint sounds of Martin's typewriter clicking away in the distance. A slow fade-in begins, and as the screen gradually brightens, the sounds of the typewriter seem to draw closer to us, as if we were moving from the outside to the inside of the house, walking up the stairs, and approaching the door of Martin's room. When the new image settles into focus, the entire screen is filled with an immense, tightly framed shot of Martin's eyes. The camera holds in that position for a couple of beats, and then, as the voice-over narration continues, it starts to pull back, revealing Martin's face, Martin's shoulders, Martin's hands on the keys of the typewriter, and finally Martin sitting at his desk. With no halt in its backward progress, the camera leaves the room and begins traveling down the corridor. *Unfortunately*, Martin says, *Claire was right. I did love her, and I did want her. But how can you love someone you don't trust?* The camera stops in front of Claire's door. As if by telepathic command, the door swings open – and then we are inside, moving in on Claire as she sits in front of a dressing-table mirror applying makeup to her face. Her body is sheathed in a black satin slip, her hair is swept up in a loosely knotted chignon, the back of her neck is exposed. *Claire was like no other woman,* Martin says. *She was stronger than everyone else, wilder than everyone else, smarter than everyone else. I had been waiting to meet her all my life, and yet now that we were together, I was scared. What was she hiding from me? What terrible secret was she refusing to tell? A part of me thought I should get out of there – just pack up my things and leave before it was too late. And another part of me thought: she's testing me. If I fail the test, I'll lose her.*

Eyebrow pencil, mascara, cheek rouge, powder, lipstick. As Martin delivers his confused, soul-searching monologue, Claire goes on working in front of the mirror, transforming herself from one kind of woman into another. The impulsive tomboy disappears, and in her place emerges a glamorous, sophisticated, movie-star temptress. Claire stands up from the table and wriggles into a narrow black cocktail dress, slips her feet into a pair of three-inch heels, and we scarcely recognize her anymore. She cuts a ravishing figure: self-possessed, confident, the very picture of feminine power. With a faint smile on her lips, she checks herself in the mirror one last time and then walks out of the room.

Cut to the hallway. Claire knocks on Martin's door and says: Dinner's ready, Martin. I'll be waiting for you downstairs.

Cut to the dining room. Claire is sitting at the table, waiting for Martin. She has already set out the appetizers; the wine has been uncorked; the candles have been lit. Martin enters the room in silence. Claire greets him with a warm, friendly smile, but Martin pays no attention to it. He seems wary, out of sorts, not at all sure of how he should act.

Eyeing Claire with suspicion, he walks over to the place that has been set for him, pulls out the chair, and begins to sit down. The chair appears to be solid, but no sooner does he lower his weight onto it than it splinters into a dozen pieces. Martin goes tumbling to the floor.

It is a hilarious, wholly unexpected turn of events. Claire bursts out laughing, but Martin is not at all amused. Sprawled out on his rear end, he smolders in a funk of injured pride and resentment, and the longer Claire goes on laughing at him (she can't help herself; it's simply too funny), the more ridiculous he is made to look. Without saying a word, Martin slowly climbs to his feet, kicks aside the bits of broken chair, and puts another chair in its place. He sits down cautiously this time, and when he is at last assured that the seat is strong enough to hold him, he turns his attention to the food. Looks good, he says. It is a desperate attempt to maintain his dignity, to swallow his embarrassment.

Claire seems inordinately pleased by his comment. With another smile brightening her face, she leans toward him and asks: How's your story going, Martin?

By now, Martin is holding a lemon wedge in his left hand, about to squeeze it onto his asparagus. Instead of answering Claire's question right away, he presses the lemon between his thumb and middle finger – and the juice squirts into his eye. Martin yelps in pain. Once again, Claire bursts out laughing, and once again our grumpy hero is not the least bit amused. He dips his napkin into his water glass and begins patting his eye, trying to get rid of the sting. He looks defeated, utterly humiliated by this fresh display of clumsiness. When he finally puts down the napkin, Claire repeats the question.

And so, Martin, she says, how's your story going?

Martin can barely stand it anymore. Refusing to answer Claire's question, he looks her straight in the eye and says: Who are you, Claire? What are you doing here?

Unruffled, Claire smiles back at him. No, she says, you answer my question first. How's your story going?

Martin looks as if he's about to snap. Maddened by her evasions, he just stares at her and says nothing.

Please, Martin, Claire says. It's very important.

Struggling to control his temper, Martin mumbles a sarcastic aside – not addressing Claire so much as thinking out loud, talking to himself: You really want to know?

Yes, I really want to know.

All right . . . All right, I'll tell you how it's going. It's . . . (he reflects for a moment) . . . it's (continuing to think) . . . Actually, it's going quite well.

Quite well . . . or very well?

Um . . . (thinking) . . . very well. I'd say it's going very well.

You see?

See what?

Oh, Martin. Of course you do.

No, Claire, I don't. I don't see anything. If you want to know the truth, I'm completely lost.

Poor Martin. You shouldn't be so hard on yourself.

Martin gives her a lame smile. They have reached a kind of standoff, and for the moment there is nothing more to be said. Claire digs into her food. She eats with obvious enjoyment, savoring the taste of her concoction with small tentative bites. Mmm, she says. Not bad. What do you think, Martin?

Martin lifts his fork to take a bite, but just as he is about to put the food in his mouth, he glances over at Claire, distracted by the soft moans of pleasure emanating from her throat, and with his attention briefly diverted from the matter at hand, his wrist turns downward by a few degrees. As the fork continues its journey toward his mouth, a thin trail of salad dressing comes dripping off the utensil and slides down the front of his shirt. At first, Martin doesn't notice, but as his mouth opens and his eyes return to the looming morsel of asparagus, he suddenly sees what is happening. He jumps back and lets go of the fork. Christ! he says. I've done it again!

The camera cuts to Claire (who bursts out laughing for the third time) and then dollies in on her for a close-up. The shot is similar to the one that ended the scene in the bedroom at the beginning of the film, but whereas Claire's face was motionless as she watched Martin make his exit, now it is animated, brimming with delight, expressing what seems to be an almost transcendent joy. *She was so alive then,* Alma had said, *so vivid.* No moment in the story captures that sense of fullness and life better than this one. For a few seconds, Claire is turned into something indestructible, an embodiment of pure human radiance. Then the picture begins to dissolve, breaking apart against a background of solid blackness, and although Claire's laughter goes on for several more beats, it begins to break apart as well – fading into a series of echoes, of disjointed breaths, of ever more distant reverberations.

A long stillness follows, and for the next twenty seconds the screen is dominated by a single nocturnal image: the moon in the sky. Clouds drift past, the wind rustles through the trees below, but essentially there is nothing before us but that moon. It is a stark and purposeful transition, and within moments we have forgotten the comic high jinks of the previous scene. *That night,* Martin says, *I made one of the most important decisions of my life. I decided that I wasn't going to ask any more questions. Claire was asking me to make a leap of faith, and rather than go on pressing her, I decided to close my eyes and jump. I had no idea what was waiting for me at the bottom, but that didn't mean it wasn't worth the risk. And so I kept on falling . . . and a week later, just when I was beginning to think that nothing could ever go wrong, Claire went out for a walk.*

Martin is sitting at the desk in his second-floor study. He turns from the typewriter to look out the window, and as the angle reverses to record his point of view, we see a long overhead shot of Claire walking alone in the garden. The cold front has apparently arrived. She is wearing a scarf and overcoat, her hands are in her pockets, and a light snowfall has dusted the ground. When the camera cuts back to Martin, he is still looking through the window, unable to tear his eyes away from her. Another reverse, and then another shot of Claire, alone in the garden. She takes a few more steps, and then, without warning, she collapses to the ground. It is a terrifyingly effective fall. No tottering or dizziness, no gradual buckling of the knees. Between one step and the next, Claire plunges into total unconsciousness, and from the sudden, merciless way her strength gives out on her, it looks as if she's dead.

The camera zooms in from the window, bringing Claire's inert body into the foreground. Martin enters the frame: running, out of breath, frantic. He falls to his knees and cradles her head in his hands, looking for a sign of life. We no longer know what to expect. The story has shifted into another register, and one minute after laughing our heads off, we find ourselves in the middle of a tense, melodramatic scene. Claire eventually opens her eyes, but enough time passes for us to know that it isn't a recovery so much as a stay of execution, an augur of things to come. She looks up at Martin and smiles. It is a spiritual smile, somehow, an inward smile, the smile of someone who no longer believes in the future. Martin kisses her, and then he bends down, gathers Claire into his arms, and begins carrying her toward the house. *She seemed to be all right*, he says. *Just a little fainting spell, we thought. But the next morning, Claire woke up with a high fever.*

We cut to a shot of Claire in bed. Hovering around her like a nurse, Martin takes her temperature, plies her with aspirins, dabs her forehead with a wet towel, feeds her broth with a spoon. *She didn't complain*, he continues. *Her skin was hot to the touch, but she seemed to be in good spirits. After a while, she pushed me out of the room. Go back to your story, she said. I'd rather sit here with you, I told her, but then Claire laughed, and with a funny, pouting expression on her face, she said that if I didn't go back to work this instant, she was going to jump out of bed, rip off her clothes, and run outside with nothing on. And that wasn't going to make her well, was it?*

A moment later, Martin is sitting at his desk, typing another page of his story. The sound is particularly intense here – keys clattering at a furious rhythm, great staccato bursts of activity – but then the volume diminishes, falls off into near silence, and Martin's voice returns. We go back to the bedroom. One by one, we see a succession of highly detailed close-ups, still-life renderings of the tiny world around Claire's sickbed: a glass of water, the edge of a closed book, a thermometer, the knob on the night-table drawer. *But the next morning,* Martin says, *the fever was worse. I told her that I was taking the day off, whether she liked it or not. I sat beside her for several hours, and by the middle of the afternoon, she seemed to take a turn for the better.*

The camera jumps back to a wide shot of the room, and there she is, sitting up in bed, looking like the old vivacious Claire. In a mock-serious voice, she is reading a passage from Kant out loud to Martin: . . . *things which we see are not by themselves what we see . . . so that, if we drop our subject or the subjective form of our senses, all qualities, all relations of objects in space and time, nay space and time themselves, would vanish.*

Things seem to be returning to normal. With Claire on the mend, Martin goes back to his story the next day. He works steadily for two or three hours, and then he breaks off to check in on Claire. When he enters the bedroom, she is fast asleep, bundled up under a pile of quilts and blankets. It is cold in the room – cold enough for Martin to see his own breath in front of him when he exhales. Hector warned him about the furnace, but Martin has clearly forgotten to attend to it. Too many crazy things happened after that phone call, and Fortunato's name must have slipped his mind.

There is a fireplace in the room, however, and a small stack of wood on the hearth. Martin begins preparing a fire, working as quietly as he can so as not to disturb Claire. Once the flames catch hold, he adjusts the logs with a poker, and one of them inadvertently slips out from under the others. The noise breaks in on Claire's sleep. She stirs, groaning softly as she thrashes about under the covers, and then she opens her eyes. Martin swivels around from his spot in front of the fire. I didn't mean to wake you, he says. I'm sorry.

Claire smiles. She looks weak, drained of physical resources, barely conscious. Hello, Martin, she whispers. How's my beautiful man?

Martin walks over to the bed, sits down, and puts his hand on Claire's forehead. You're burning up, he says.

I'm all right, she answers. I feel fine.

This is the third day, Claire. I think we should call a doctor.

No need for that. Just give me some more of those aspirins. In half an hour I'll be good as new.

Martin shakes out three aspirins from the bottle and hands them to her with a glass of water. As Claire swallows the pills, Martin says: This isn't good. I really think a doctor should take a look at you.

Claire gives Martin the empty glass, and he puts it back on the table. Tell me what's happening in the story, she says. That will make me feel better.

You should rest.

Please, Martin. Just a little bit.

Not wanting to disappoint her, and yet not wanting to tax her strength, Martin confines his summary to just a few sentences. It's dark now, he says. Nordstrum has left the house. Anna is on her way, but he doesn't know that. If she doesn't get there soon, he's going to walk into the trap.

Will she make it?

It doesn't matter. The important thing is that she's going to him.

She's fallen in love with him, hasn't she?

In her own way, yes. She's putting her life in danger for him. That's a form of love, isn't it?

Claire doesn't answer. Martin's question has overwhelmed her, and she is too moved to give a response. Her eyes fill up with tears; her mouth trembles; a look of rapturous intensity shines forth from her face. It's as if she has reached some new understanding of herself, as if her whole body were suddenly giving off light. How much more to go? she asks.

Two or three pages, Martin says. I'm almost at the end.

Write them now.

They can wait. I'll do them tomorrow.

No, Martin, do them now. You must do them now.

The camera lingers on Claire's face for a moment or two – and then, as if propelled by the force of her command, Martin is at his desk again, typing. This initiates a sequence of crosscuts between the two characters. We go from Martin back to Claire, from Claire back to Martin, and in the space of ten simple shots, we finally get it, we finally understand what's been happening. Then Martin returns to the bedroom, and in ten more shots he finally understands as well.

1. Claire is writhing around on the bed, in acute pain, struggling not to call out for help.

2. Martin comes to the bottom of a page, pulls it out of the machine, and rolls in another. He begins typing again.

3. We see the fireplace. The fire has nearly gone out.

4. A close-up of Martin's fingers, typing.

5. A close-up of Claire's face. She is weaker than before, no longer struggling.

6. A close-up of Martin's face. At his desk, typing.

7. A close-up of the fireplace. Just a few glowing embers.

8. A medium shot of Martin. He types the last word of his story. A brief pause. Then he pulls the page out of the machine.

9. A medium shot of Claire. She shudders slightly – and then appears to die.

10. Martin is standing beside his desk, gathering up the pages of the manuscript. He walks out of the study, holding the finished story in his hand.

11. Martin enters the room, smiling. He glances at the bed, and an instant later the smile is gone.

12. A medium shot of Claire. Martin sits down beside her, puts his hand on her forehead, and gets no response. He presses his ear against her chest – still no response. In a mounting panic, he tosses aside the manuscript and begins rubbing her body with both hands, desperately trying to warm her up. She is limp; her skin is cold; she has stopped breathing.

13. A shot of the fireplace. We see the dying embers. There are no more logs on the hearth.

14. Martin jumps off the bed. Snatching the manuscript as he goes, he wheels around and rushes toward the fireplace. He looks possessed, out of his mind with fear. There is only one thing left to be done – and it must be done now. Without hesitation, Martin crumples up the first page of his story and throws it into the fire.

15. A close-up of the fire. The ball of paper lands in the ashes and bursts into flame. We hear Martin crumpling up another page. A moment later, the second ball lands in the ashes and ignites.

16. Cut to a close-up of Claire's face. Her eyelids begin to flutter.

17. A medium shot of Martin, crouched in front of the fire. He grabs hold of the next sheet, crumples it up, and throws it in as well. Another sudden burst of flame.

18. Claire opens her eyes.

19. Working as fast as he can now, Martin goes on bunching up pages and throwing them into the fire. One by one, they all begin to burn, each one lighting the other as the flames intensify.

20. Claire sits up. Blinking in confusion; yawning; stretching out her

arms; showing no traces of illness. She has been brought back from the dead.

Gradually coming to her senses, Claire begins to glance around the room, and when she sees Martin in front of the fireplace, madly crumpling up his manuscript and throwing it into the fire, she looks stricken. What are you doing? she says. My God, Martin, what are you doing?

I'm buying you back, he says. Thirty-seven pages for your life, Claire. It's the best bargain I've ever made.

But you can't do that. It's not allowed.

Maybe not. But I'm doing it, aren't I? I've changed the rules.

Claire is overwrought, about to break down in tears. Oh Martin, she says. You don't know what you've done.

Undaunted by Claire's objections, Martin goes on feeding his story to the flames. When he comes to the last page, he turns to her with a triumphant look in his eyes. You see, Claire? he says. It's only words. Thirty-seven pages – and nothing but words.

He sits down on the bed, and Claire throws her arms around him. It is a surprisingly fierce and passionate gesture, and for the first time since the beginning of the film, Claire looks afraid. She wants him, and she doesn't want him. She is ecstatic; she is horrified. She has always been the strong one, the one with all the courage and confidence, but now that Martin has solved the riddle of his enchantment, she seems lost. What are we going to do? she says. Tell me, Martin, what on earth are we going to do?

Before Martin can answer her, the scene shifts to the outside. We see the house from a distance of about fifty feet, sitting in the middle of nowhere. The camera tilts upward, pans to the right, and comes to rest on the boughs of a large cottonwood. Everything is still. No wind is blowing; no air is rushing through the branches; not a single leaf moves. Ten seconds go by, fifteen seconds go by, and then, very abruptly, the screen goes black and the film is over.

8

Later that same day, the print of *Martin Frost* was destroyed. I should probably consider myself lucky to have seen it, to have been there for the last showing of a film at the Blue Stone Ranch, but a part of me wishes that Alma had never turned on the projector that morning, that I had never been exposed to a frame of that elegant and haunting little movie. It wouldn't have mattered if I hadn't liked it, if I had been able to dismiss it as a bad or incompetent piece of storytelling, but this was manifestly not bad, manifestly not incompetent, and now that I knew what was about to be lost, I realized that I had traveled over two thousand miles to participate in a crime. When *The Inner Life* went up in flames with the rest of Hector's work that July afternoon, it felt like a tragedy to me, like the end of the goddamn bloody world.

That was the only movie I saw. There wasn't enough time to watch another, and given that I sat through *Martin Frost* only once, it was a good thing Alma thought to provide me with the notebook and the pen. There is no contradiction in that statement. I might wish that I had never seen the film, but the fact was that I did see it, and now that the words and images had insinuated themselves inside me, I was thankful that there was a way to hold on to them. The notes I took that morning have helped me to remember details that otherwise would have slipped away from me, to keep the film alive in my head after so many years. I scarcely looked down at the page as I wrote – scribbling in the mad telegraphic shorthand I developed as a student – and if much of my writing bordered on the illegible, I eventually managed to decipher about ninety or ninety-five percent of it. It took weeks of painstaking effort to make the transcription, but once I had a fair copy of the dialogue and had broken down the story into numbered scenes, it became possible to reestablish contact with the film. I have to go into a kind of trance in order to do that (which means that it doesn't always work), but if I concentrate hard enough and get myself into the right mood, the words can actually conjure up the images for me, and it's as if I'm watching *The Inner Life of Martin Frost* again – or little flashes of it, in any case, locked in the projection room of my skull. Last year, when I began toying with the idea of writing this book, I went in for several consultations with a hypnotist. Nothing much happened the first time, but the next three visits produced astonishing results. By listening to the tape recordings of those sessions, I have been able to fill in certain blanks, to bring back a number of things that were beginning to vanish. For better or worse, it seems that the philosophers were right. Nothing that happens to us is ever lost.

The screening ended a few minutes past noon. Alma and I were both hungry by then, both in need of a short break, and so instead of plunging directly into another film, we went out into the hall with our basket lunch. It was a strange spot for a picnic – camped out on the dusty linoleum floor, digging into our cheese sandwiches under a row of blinking fluorescent lights – but we didn't want to lose any time by looking for a better place outdoors. We talked about Alma's mother, about Hector's other work, about the oddly satisfying mixture of whimsy and seriousness in the film that had just ended. Movies could trick us into believing any kind of nonsense, I said, but this time I had fallen for it. When Claire came back to life in the final scene, I had shuddered, had felt that I was watching an authentic miracle. Martin burned his story in order to rescue Claire from the dead, but it was also Hector rescuing Brigid O'Fallon, also Hector burning his own movies, and the more things had doubled back on themselves like that, the more deeply I had entered the film. Too bad we couldn't watch it again, I said. I wasn't sure if I had watched the wind closely enough, if I had paid enough attention to the trees.

I must have rattled on longer than I should have, for no sooner did Alma announce the title of the next movie we were going to see (*Report from the Anti-World*) than a door slammed somewhere in the building. We were just climbing to our feet at that point – brushing the crumbs off our clothes, taking a last swig of iced tea from the thermos, getting ready to go back inside. We heard the sound of tennis shoes flapping against the linoleum. A couple of moments later, Juan appeared at the end of the hall, and when he started coming toward us at a half trot – more running than walking – we both knew that Frieda had returned.

For the next little while, it was as if I wasn't there anymore. Juan and Alma talked to each other in silence, communicating in a flurry of hand signals, sweeping arm movements, and emphatic shakes and nods of the head. I didn't understand what they were saying, but as the remarks flew back and forth between them, I could see that Alma was becoming more and more upset. Her gestures turned harsh, truculent, almost aggressive in their denial of what Juan was telling her. Juan threw up his hands in a pose of surrender (Don't blame me, he seemed to be saying, I'm only the messenger), but Alma lashed out at him again, and his eyes clouded over with hostility. He pounded his fist in his palm, then turned and pointed a finger at my face. It wasn't a conversation anymore. It was an argument, and the argument was suddenly about me.

I kept on watching, kept on trying to understand what they were talking about, but I couldn't penetrate the code, couldn't make sense of what I was seeing. Then Juan left, and as he marched down the hall on his stocky, diminutive legs, Alma explained what had happened. Frieda got back ten minutes ago, she said. She wants to start in right away.

That was awfully fast, I said.

Hector won't be cremated until five this afternoon. She didn't want to hang around Albuquerque that long, so she decided to come home. She plans to pick up the ashes tomorrow morning.

What were you and Juan arguing about, then? I had no idea what was going on, but he pointed his finger at me. I don't like it when people point their finger at me.

We were talking about you.

So I gathered. But what do I have to do with Frieda's plans? I'm just a visitor.

I thought you understood.

I don't understand sign language, Alma.

But you saw that I was angry.

Of course I did. But I still don't know why.

Frieda doesn't want you around. It's all too private, she says, and it isn't a good time for strangers.

You mean she's booting me off the ranch?

Not in so many words. But that's the gist of it. She wants you to leave tomorrow. The plan is to drop you off at the airport on our way to Albuquerque in the morning.

But she's the one who invited me. Doesn't she remember that?

Hector was alive then. Now he's not. Circumstances have changed.

Well, maybe she has a point. I came here to watch movies, didn't I? If there aren't any movies to watch, there's probably no reason for me to stay. I got to see one of them. Now I can watch the others burn up in the fire, and then I'll be on my way.

That's just it. She doesn't want you to see that either. According to what Juan just told me, it's none of your business.

Oh. Now I see why you lost your temper.

It has nothing to do with you, David. It's about me. She knows I want you there. We talked about it this morning, and now she's broken her promise. I'm so pissed off, I could punch her in the face.

And where am I supposed to hide myself while everyone's at the barbecue?

In my house. She said you could stay in my house. But I'm going to talk to her. I'll make her change her mind.

Don't bother. If she doesn't want me there, I can't stand on my rights and make a fuss, can I? I don't have any rights. It's Frieda's land, and I have to do what she says.

Then I won't go either. She can burn the damn films with Juan and Conchita.

Of course you'll go. It's the last chapter of your book, Alma, and you have to be there to see it happen. You have to stick it out to the end.

I wanted you to be there, too. It won't be the same if you're not with me.

Fourteen prints and negatives are going to make a hell of a fire. Lots of smoke, lots of flame. With any luck, I'll be able to see it from the window of your house.

As it turned out, I did see the fire, but I saw more smoke than flame, and because the windows were open in Alma's little house, I smelled more than I saw. The burning celluloid had an acrid, stinging odor, and the airborne chemicals hovered in the atmosphere long after the smoke had drifted away. According to what Alma told me that evening, it took the four of them over an hour to haul the films out of the underground storage room. Then they strapped the cans onto hand trucks and wheeled them over the rocky ground to an area just behind the sound stage. With the help of newspapers and kerosene, they lit fires in two oil drums – one for the prints and the other for the negatives. The old nitrate stock burned easily, but the films from after 1951, which had been printed on tougher, less flammable triacetate-based stocks, had trouble igniting. They had to unspool the films from their reels and feed them into the fire one by one, Alma said, and that took time, much longer than anyone had anticipated. They had guessed that they would be finished at around three o'clock, but in point of fact they kept on working until six.

I spent those hours alone in her house, trying not to resent my exile. I had put a good face on it in front of Alma, but the truth was that I was just as angry as she was. Frieda's behavior had been unforgivable. You don't ask someone to your house and then disinvite him once he's there. And if you do, at least you offer an explanation, and not through the intermediary of a deaf-and-dumb servant, who delivers the message to someone else while pointing a finger at your face. I knew that Frieda was distraught, that she was living through a day of storms and cataclysmic sorrows, but much as I wanted to make excuses for her, I couldn't help feeling hurt. What was I doing there? Why had Alma been sent to Vermont to drag me back at gunpoint if they didn't want to see me? Frieda was the one who had written the letters, after all. She was the one who had asked me to come to New Mexico and watch Hector's films. According to Alma, it had taken her months to persuade them to invite me. I had assumed that Hector had resisted the idea and that Alma and Frieda had eventually talked him into it. Now, after eighteen hours at the ranch, I was beginning to suspect that I had been wrong.

If not for the insulting way I was treated, I probably wouldn't have given these matters a second thought. After Alma and I finished our conversation in the post-production building, we packed up the remains of our lunch and walked over to her adobe cottage, which was set on a small rise of land about three hundred yards from the main house. Alma opened the door, and sitting at our feet, just beyond the edge of the sill, was my travel bag. I had left it in the guest room of the other house that morning, and now someone (probably Conchita) had carried it over on Frieda's orders and deposited it on the floor of Alma's place. It struck me as an arrogant, imperious gesture. Again, I pretended to laugh it off (Well, I said, at least that spares me the trouble of having to do it myself), but underneath my flippant remark, I was boiling with rage. Alma left to join the others, and for the next fifteen or twenty minutes I wandered around the house, going in and out of rooms, trying to control my temper. Presently, I heard the sound of the hand trucks clattering in the distance, the clang of metal scraping against stone, the intermittent noise of stacked-up film cans clicking and vibrating against one another. The auto-da-fé was about to begin. I went into the bathroom, stripped off my clothes, and turned on the faucets of the tub at full blast.

Soaking in the warm water, I let my mind drift for a while, slowly rehearsing the facts as I understood them. Then, turning them around and looking at them from a different angle, I tried to accommodate those facts to the events that had taken place in the past hour: Juan's belligerent dialogue with Alma, Alma's vituperative response to Frieda's message (*she's broken her promise . . . I could punch her in the face*), my expulsion from the ranch. It was a purely speculative line of reasoning, but when I thought back to what had happened the night before (the graciousness of Hector's welcome, his eagerness to show me his films) and then compared it to what had happened since, I began to wonder if Frieda had not been opposed to my visit all along. I wasn't forgetting that she was the one who had invited me to Tierra del Sueño, but perhaps she had written those letters against her better judgment, buckling in to Hector's demands after months of quarrels and disagreements. If that was so, then ordering me off her land did not represent a sudden change of heart. It was merely something she could get away with now that Hector was dead.

Until then, I had thought of them as equal partners. Alma had talked about their marriage at some length, and not once had it occurred to me that their motives might have been different, that their thinking had not been in perfect harmony. They had made a pact in 1939 to produce films that would never be shown to the public, and they had both embraced the idea that the work they did together should ultimately be destroyed. Those were the conditions of Hector's return to filmmaking. It was a brutal interdiction, and yet only by sacrificing the one thing that would have given his work meaning – the pleasure of sharing it with others – could he justify his decision to do that work in the first place. The films, then, were a form of penance, an acknowledgment that his role in the accidental murder of Brigid O'Fallon was a sin that could never be pardoned. *I am a ridiculous man. God has played many jokes on me.* One form of punishment had given way to another, and in the tangled, self-torturing logic of his decision, Hector had continued to pay off his debts to a God he refused to believe in. The bullet that tore apart his chest in the Sandusky bank had made it possible for him to marry Frieda. The death of his son had made it possible for him to return to filmmaking. In neither instance, however, had he been absolved of his responsibility for what had happened on the night of January 14, 1929. Neither the physical suffering caused by Knox's gun nor the mental suffering caused by Taddy's death had been terrible enough to set him free. Make films, yes. Pour every ounce of your talents and energies into making them. Make them as though your life depended on it, and then, once your life is over, see to it that they are destroyed. You are forbidden to leave any traces behind you.

Frieda had gone along with all this, but it couldn't have been the same for her. She hadn't committed a crime; she wasn't dragged down by the weight of a guilty conscience; she wasn't pursued by the memory of putting a dead girl into the trunk of a car and burying her body in the California mountains. Frieda was innocent, and yet she accepted Hector's terms, putting aside her own ambitions to devote herself to the creation of work whose central aim was nothingness. It would have been understandable to me if she had watched him from a distance – indulging Hector in his obsessions, perhaps, pitying him for his mania, yet refusing to get involved in the mechanics of the enterprise itself. But Frieda was his accomplice, his staunchest defender, and she was up to her elbows in it from the start. Not only did she talk Hector into making films again (threatening to leave him if he didn't), but it was her money that financed the operation. She sewed costumes, drew storyboards, cut film, designed sets. You don't work that hard at something unless you enjoy it, unless you feel that your efforts have some value – but what possible joy could she have found from spending all those years in the service of nothing? At least Hector, trapped in his psycho-religious battle between desire and self-abnegation, could comfort himself with the thought that there was a purpose to what he was doing. He didn't make films in order to destroy them – but in spite of it. They were two separate actions, and the best part of it was that he wouldn't have to be around to see the second one happen. He would already be dead by the time his films went into the fire, and it would no longer make any difference to him. For Frieda, however, the actions must have been one and the same, two steps in a single, unified process of creation and destruction. All along, she was the one who had been destined to light the match and bring their work to an end, and that thought must have grown in her as the years went by until it overpowered everything else. Little by little, it had become an aesthetic principle in its own right. Even as she continued working on the films with Hector, she must have felt that the work was no longer about making films. It was about making something in order to destroy it. That was the work, and until all evidence of the work had been destroyed, the work would not exist. It would come into being only at the moment of its annihilation – and then, as the smoke rose up into the hot New Mexican day, it would be gone.

There was something chilling and beautiful about this idea. I understood how seductive it must have been for her, and yet once I allowed myself to look at it through Frieda's eyes, to experience the full power of that ecstatic negation, I also understood why she wanted to get rid of me. My presence tainted the purity of the moment. The films were supposed to die a virgin death, unseen by anyone from the outside world. It was bad enough that I had been allowed to see one of them, but now that the articles of Hector's will were about to go into effect, she could insist that the ceremony be conducted in the way she had always imagined it. The films had been born in secrecy, and they were supposed to vanish in secrecy as well. Strangers weren't permitted to watch, and although Alma and Hector had mounted a last-minute effort to bring me into the inner circle, Frieda had never viewed me as anything but a stranger. Alma was part of the family, and therefore she had been anointed as the official witness. She was the court historian, so to speak, and after the last member of her parents' generation was dead, the only memories to survive of them would be the ones recorded in her book. I was supposed to have been the witness of the witness, the independent observer brought in to confirm the accuracy of the witness's statements. It was a small role to play in such a large drama, and Frieda had cut me out of the script. As far as she was concerned, I had been unnecessary from the start.

I sat in the tub until the water grew cold, then wrapped myself in a couple of towels and lingered for another twenty or thirty minutes – shaving, dressing, combing my hair. I found it pleasant to be in Alma's bathroom, standing among the tubes and jars that lined the shelves of the medicine cabinet, that crowded the top of the small wooden chest by the window. The red toothbrush in its slot above the sink, the lipsticks in their gold and plastic containers, the mascara brush and eyeliner pencil, the box of tampons, the aspirins, the dental floss, the Chanel No. 5 eau de cologne, the prescription bottle of antimicrobial cleanser. Each one was a sign of intimacy, a mark of solitude and self-reflection. She put the pills into her mouth, rubbed the creams into her skin, ran the combs and brushes through her hair, and every morning she came into this room and stood in front of the same mirror I was looking into now. What did I know about her? Almost nothing, and yet I was certain that I didn't want to lose her, that I was ready to put up a fight in order to see her again after I left the ranch in the morning. My problem was ignorance. I had no doubt that there was trouble in the household, but I didn't know Alma well enough to be able to measure the true extent of her anger against Frieda, and because I couldn't do that, I didn't know to what degree I should be worried about what was happening. The night before, I had watched them together at the kitchen table, and there had been no trace of conflict then. I remembered the solicitude in Alma's voice, the delicate request from Frieda for Alma to spend the night in the main house, the sense of a familial bond. It wasn't unusual for people that close to lash out at each other, to say things in the heat of the moment they would later come to regret – but Alma's outburst had been particularly intense, simmering with threats of violence that were rare (in my experience) among women. *I'm so pissed off, I could punch her in the face.* How often had she said that kind of thing? Was she prone to delivering such rash, hyperbolic statements, or did this represent a new turn in her relations with Frieda, a sudden break after years of silent animosity? Had I known more, I wouldn't have had to ask the question. I would have understood that Alma's words were meant to be taken seriously, that their very extravagance proved that things were already beginning to fly out of control.

I finished up in the bathroom, then continued my aimless travels around the house. It was a small, compact place, sturdily built, somewhat clumsy in design, but in spite of the narrow dimensions, Alma seemed to live in only part of it. One room in the back was given over entirely to storage. Cardboard boxes were stacked up along one wall and half of another, and a dozen or so discarded objects were strewn about the floor: a chair with a missing leg, a rusted tricycle, a fifty-year-old manual typewriter, a black-and-white portable TV with snapped-off rabbit ears, a pile of stuffed animals, a Dictaphone, and several partially used cans of paint. Another room had nothing in it at all. No furniture, no mattress, not even a lightbulb. A large, intricate cobweb dangled from a corner of the ceiling. Three or four dead flies were trapped inside, but their bodies were so desiccated, so nearly reduced to weightless flecks of dust, that I figured the spider had abandoned her web and set up shop somewhere else.

That left the kitchen, the living room, the bedroom, and the study. I wanted to sit down and read Alma's book, but I didn't feel I had the right to do that without her permission. She had written more than six hundred pages by then, but those pages were still in rough-draft form, and unless a writer specifically asks you to comment on a work in progress, you aren't allowed to peek. Alma had pointed to the manuscript earlier (*There's the monster*, she had said), but she hadn't mentioned anything about reading it, and I didn't want to begin my life with her by betraying a trust. Instead, I killed time by looking at everything else in the four rooms she inhabited, examining the food in the refrigerator, the clothes in the bedroom closet, and the collections of books, records, and videos in the living room. I learned that she drank skim milk and buttered her bread with unsalted butter, favored the color blue (mostly in dark shades), and had wide-ranging tastes in literature and music – a girl after my own heart. Dashiell Hammett and André Breton; Pergolesi and Mingus; Verdi, Wittgenstein, and Villon. In one corner, I found all the books I had published while Helen was still alive – the two volumes of criticism, the four books of translated poems – and I realized that I had never seen all six of them together outside of my own house. On another shelf, there were books by Hawthorne, Melville, Emerson, and Thoreau. I pulled out a paperback selection of Hawthorne's stories and found "The Birthmark," which I read in front of the bookcase on the cold tile floor, trying to imagine what Alma must have felt when she'd read it as a young girl. Just as I was coming to the end (*The momentary circumstance was too strong for him; he failed to look beyond the shadowy scope of time . . .*), I caught my first whiff of kerosene wafting in through a window at the back of the house.

The smell drove me a little crazy, and I immediately climbed to my feet and started walking again. I went into the kitchen, drank a glass of water, and then continued on into Alma's study, where I paced around in circles for ten or fifteen minutes, fighting off the urge to read her manuscript. If I couldn't do anything to prevent Hector's films from being destroyed, at least I could try to understand why it was happening. None of the answers given to me so far had come close to explaining it. I had done my best to follow the argument, to penetrate the thinking that had led them to such a grim and merciless position, but now that the fires had been lit, it suddenly struck me as absurd, pointless, horrible. The answers were in the book, the reasons were in the book, the origins of the idea that had led to this moment were in the book. I sat down at Alma's desk. The manuscript was just to the left of the computer – an immense pile of pages with a stone resting on top to keep the pages from blowing away. I removed the stone, and the words underneath it read: *The Afterlife of Hector Mann*, by Alma Grund. I turned the page, and the next thing I came upon was an epigraph written by Luis Buñuel. The passage was from *My Last Sigh*, the same book I had stumbled across in Hector's study that morning. *A while later*, the quotation began, *I suggested that we burn the negative on the place du Tertre*

*in Montmartre, something I would have done without hesitation had the group
agreed. In fact, I'd still do it today; I can imagine a huge pyre in my own little
garden where all my negatives and all the copies of my films go up in flames. It
wouldn't make the slightest difference. (Curiously, however, the surrealists
vetoed my suggestion.)*

That broke the spell somewhat. I had seen some of Buñuel's films in
the sixties and seventies, but I wasn't familiar with his autobiography,
and it took me a few moments to ponder what I had just read. I glanced
up, and by turning my attention away from Alma's manuscript – however briefly – I was given time to regroup, to stop myself before I went
any further. I put the first page back where it had been, then covered up
the title with the stone. As I did so, I edged forward in my chair, changing my position enough to be able to see something I hadn't noticed
before: a small green notebook lying on the desk, midway between the
manuscript and the wall. It was the size of a school composition book,
and from the battered state of the cover and the nicks and tears along
the cloth spine, I gathered that it was quite old. Old enough to be one of
Hector's journals, I said to myself – which was exactly what it turned
out to be.

I spent the next four hours in the living room, sitting in an ancient
club chair with the notebook on my lap, reading through it twice from
beginning to end. There were ninety-six pages in all, and they covered
approximately a year and a half – from the autumn of 1930 to the spring
of 1932 – starting with an entry that described one of Hector's English
lessons with Nora and concluding with a passage about a nighttime
walk in Sandusky several days after he confessed his guilt to Frieda. If I
had been harboring any doubts about the story Alma had told me, they
were dispelled by what I read in that journal. Hector in his own words
was the same Hector she had talked about on the plane, the same tortured soul who had run from the Northwest, had come close to killing
himself in Montana, Chicago, and Cleveland, had succumbed to the
degradations of a six-month alliance with Sylvia Meers, had been shot
in a Sandusky bank and had lived. He wrote in a small, spidery hand,
often crossing out phrases and writing over them in pencil, misspelling
words, smearing ink, and because he wrote on both sides of the page, it
wasn't always easy to make out what he had written. But I managed.
Little by little, I think I got most of it, and each time I deciphered another
paragraph, the facts tallied with the ones in Alma's account, the details
matched. Using the notebook she had given me, I copied out a few of

the significant entries, transcribing them in full so as to have a record of Hector's exact words. Among them were his last conversation with Red O'Fallon at the Bluebell Inn, the dismal showdown with Meers in the back seat of the chauffeured car, and this one from the time he spent in Sandusky (living in the Spellings' house after his release from the hospital), which brought the notebook to a close:

3/31/32. Walked F.'s dog tonight. A wiggly black thing named Arp, after the artist. Dada man. The street was deserted. Mist everywhere, almost impossible to see where I was. Perhaps rain as well, but drops so fine they felt like vapor. A sense of no longer being on the ground, of walking through clouds. We approached a streetlamp, and suddenly everything began to shimmer, to gleam in the murk. A world of dots, a hundred million dots of refracted light. Very strange, very beautiful: statues of illuminated fog. Arp was pulling on the leash, sniffing. We walked on, came to the end of the block, rounded the corner. Another streetlamp, and then, stopping for a moment as Arp lifted his leg, something caught my eye. A glow on the sidewalk, a burst of brightness blinking out from the shadows. It had a bluish tint to it – rich blue, the blue of F.'s eyes. I crouched down to have a better look and saw that it was a stone, perhaps a jewel of some kind. A moonstone, I thought, or a sapphire, or maybe just a piece of cut glass. Small enough for a ring, or else a pendant that had fallen off a necklace or bracelet, a lost earring. My first thought was to give it to F.'s niece, Dorothea, Fred's four-year-old daughter. Little Dotty. She comes to the house often. Loves her grandma, loves to play with Arp, loves F. A charming sprite, crazy for baubles and ornaments, always dressing up in wild costumes. I said to myself: I'll give the stone to Dotty. So I started to pick it up, but the moment my fingers came into contact with the stone, I discovered that it wasn't what I'd thought it was. It was soft, and it broke apart when I touched it, disintegrating into a wet, slithery ooze. The thing I had taken for a stone was a gob of human spit. Someone had walked by, had emptied his mouth onto the sidewalk, and the saliva had gathered into a ball, a smooth, multifaceted sphere of bubbles. With the light shining through it, and with the reflections of the light turning it that lustrous shade of blue, it had looked like a hard and solid object. The moment I realized my mistake, my hand shot back as if I'd been burned. I felt sickened, overwhelmed by disgust. My fingers were covered in saliva. Not so bad when it's your own, perhaps, but revolting when it comes from the mouth of a stranger. I took out my handkerchief and wiped off my fingers as best I could. When I was finished, I couldn't bring myself to put the handkerchief back in my pocket. Carrying it at arm's length, I walked to the end of the street and dropped it into the first garbage can I saw.

Three months after those words were written, Hector and Frieda were married in the living room of Mrs. Spelling's house. They drove out to New Mexico on their honeymoon, bought some land, and decided to settle there. Now I understood why they had chosen to call their place the Blue Stone Ranch. Hector had already seen that stone, and he knew that it didn't exist, that the life they were about to build for themselves was founded on an illusion.

The burning ended at around six o'clock, but Alma didn't get back to the cottage until almost seven. It was still light out, but the sun was starting to go down, and I remember how the house filled up with brightness just before she came through the door: huge shafts of light plunging through the windows, an inundation of glowing golds and purples that spread into every corner of the room. It was only my second desert sunset, and I wasn't prepared for an attack of such radiance. I moved to the sofa, turning in the opposite direction to get the dazzle out of my eyes, but a few minutes after I settled into that new spot, I heard the latch turn in the door behind me. More light poured into the room: streams of red, liquefied sun, a tidal wave of luminosity. I wheeled around, shielding my eyes for protection, and there was Alma in the open doorway, almost invisible, a spectral outline with light shooting through the tips of her hair, a being on fire.

Then she closed the door, and I was able to see her face, to look into her eyes as she crossed the living room and came toward the sofa. I don't know what I was expecting from her just then. Tears, perhaps, or anger, or some excessive display of emotion, but Alma looked remarkably calm, not in turmoil anymore so much as exhausted, drained of energy. She walked around the sofa from the right, apparently unconcerned that she was showing me the birthmark on the left side of her face, and I realized that this was the first time she had done that. I wasn't sure if I should consider it a breakthrough, however, or credit it to a lapse of attention, a symptom of fatigue. She sat down next to me without saying a word, then leaned her head against my shoulder. Her hands were dirty; her T-shirt was smudged with soot. I put both arms around her and held her for a while, not wanting to press her with questions, to force her into talking when she didn't want to. Eventually, I asked her if she was all right, and when she answered yes, I'm all right, I understood that she had no desire to go into it. She was sorry it had taken so long, she said, but other than offering some explanations for the delay (which was how I heard about the oil drums, the hand trucks, and so on), we barely touched on the subject for the rest of the night. After it was over, she said, she had walked Frieda back to the main house. They had discussed tomorrow's arrangements, and then she had put Frieda to bed with a sleeping pill. She would have come straight back at that point, but the phone in the cottage was on the blink (sometimes it worked, sometimes it didn't), and rather than take a chance with it, she had called from the phone in the main house to book a ticket for me on the morning flight to Boston. The plane would be leaving Albuquerque at eight forty-seven. It was a two-and-a-half-hour drive to the airport, and because it wasn't going to be possible for Frieda to wake up early enough to get us there in time, the only solution had been to order a van to come for me instead. She had wanted to take me there herself, to see me off in person, but she and Frieda were due at the funeral home at eleven, and how could she make two runs to Albuquerque before eleven o'clock? The math didn't compute. Even if she left with me as early as five, she wouldn't be able to go back and forth and back again in under seven and a half hours. How can I do what I can't do? she said. It wasn't a rhetorical question. It was a statement about herself, a declaration of misery. How the hell can I do what I can't do? And then, turning her face in to my chest, she suddenly broke down and cried.

I got her into the bath, and for the next half hour I sat beside her on the floor, washing her back, her arms and legs, her breasts and face and hands, her hair. It took a while before she stopped crying, but little by little the treatment seemed to produce the desired effect. Close your eyes, I said to her, don't move, don't say a word, just melt into the water and let yourself drift away. I was impressed by how willingly she gave in to my commands, by how unembarrassed she was by her own nakedness. It was the first time I had seen her body in the light, but Alma acted as though it already belonged to me, as though we had already passed beyond the stage where such things needed to be questioned anymore. She went limp in my arms, surrendered to the warmth of the water, surrendered unconditionally to the idea that I was the one who was taking care of her. There was no one else. She had been living alone in this cottage for the past seven years, and we both knew that it was time for her to move on. You'll come to Vermont, I said. You'll live there with me until you finish your book, and every day I'll give you another bath. I'll work on my Chateaubriand, you'll work on your biography, and when we aren't working, we'll fuck. We'll fuck in every corner of the house.

We'll hold three-day fuckfests in the backyard and the woods. We'll fuck until we can't stand up anymore, and then we'll go back to work, and when our work is finished, we'll leave Vermont and go somewhere else. Anywhere you say, Alma. I'm willing to entertain all possibilities. Nothing is out of the question.

It was a rash thing to say under the circumstances, a supremely vulgar and outrageous proposition, but time was short, and I didn't want to leave New Mexico without knowing where we stood. So I took a risk and decided to force the issue, presenting my case in the crudest, most graphic terms I could think of. To Alma's credit, she didn't flinch. Her eyes were closed when I began, and she kept them closed until the end of the speech, but at a certain point I noticed that a smile was tugging at the corners of her mouth (I believe it started when I used the word *fuck* for the first time), and the longer I went on talking to her, the bigger that smile seemed to become. When I was finished, however, she didn't say anything, and her eyes remained closed. Well? I said. What do you think? What I think, she answered slowly, is that if I opened my eyes now, you might not be there.

Yes, I said, I see what you mean. On the other hand, if you don't open them, you'll never know if I am or not, will you?

I don't think I'm brave enough.

Of course you are. And besides, you're forgetting that my hands are in the tub. I'm touching your spine and the small of your back. If I wasn't there, I wouldn't be able to do that, would I?

Anything is possible. You could be someone else, someone who's only pretending to be David. An impostor.

And what would an impostor be doing with you here in this bathroom?

Filling my head with wicked fantasies, making me believe I can have what I want. It isn't often that someone says exactly what you want them to say. Maybe I said those words myself.

Maybe. Or maybe someone said them because the thing he wants is the same thing you want.

But not exactly. It's never *exactly*, is it? How could he say the *exact* words that were in my mind?

With his mouth. That's where words come from. From someone's mouth.

Where is that mouth, then? Let me feel it. Press that mouth against mine, mister. If it feels the way it's supposed to feel, then I'll know it's your mouth and not my mouth. Then maybe I'll start to believe you.

With her eyes still closed, Alma lifted her arms into the air, reaching up in the way small children do – asking to be hugged, asking to be carried – and I leaned over and kissed her, crushing my mouth against her mouth and parting her lips with my tongue. I was on my knees – arms in the water, hands resting on her back, elbows pinned against the side of the tub – and as Alma grabbed the back of my neck and pulled me toward her, I lost my balance and splashed down on top of her. Our heads went under the water for a moment, and when we came up again, Alma's eyes were open. Water was sloshing over the rim of the tub, we were both gasping, and yet without pausing to take in more than a gulp of air, we repositioned ourselves and started kissing in earnest. That was the first of several kisses, the first of many kisses. I can't account for the manipulations that followed, the complex maneuvers that enabled me to pull Alma out of the bath while keeping my lips planted on her lips, while managing not to lose contact with her tongue, but a moment came when she was out of the water and I was rubbing down her body with a towel. I remember that. I also remember that after she was dry, she peeled off my wet shirt and unbuckled the belt that was holding up my pants. I can see her doing that, and I can also see myself kissing her again, can see the two of us lowering ourselves onto a pile of towels and making love on the floor.

It was dark in the house when we left the bathroom. A few glimmers of light in the front windows, a thin burnished cloud stretching along the horizon, residues of dusk. We put on our clothes, drank a couple of shots of tequila in the living room, and then went into the kitchen to rustle up some dinner. Frozen tacos, frozen peas, mashed potatoes – another ad hoc assemblage, making do with what there was. It didn't matter. The food disappeared in nine minutes, and then we returned to the living room and poured ourselves another round of drinks. From that point on, Alma and I talked only about the future, and when we crawled into bed at ten o'clock, we were still making plans, still discussing what life would be like for us when she joined me on my little hill in Vermont. We didn't know when she would be able to get there, but we figured it wouldn't take longer than a week or two to wrap things up at the ranch, three at the outside limit. In the meantime, we would talk on the phone, and whenever it was too late or too early to call, we would send each other faxes. Come hell or high water, we said, we would be in touch every day.

*

328

I left New Mexico without seeing Frieda again. Alma had been hoping she would walk down to the cottage to say good-bye to me, but I wasn't expecting it. She had already crossed me off her list, and given the early hour of my departure (the van was scheduled to come at five-thirty), it seemed unlikely that she would go to the trouble of losing any sleep on my account. When she failed to show up, Alma blamed it on the pill she had taken before going to bed. That felt rather optimistic to me. According to my reading of the situation, Frieda wouldn't have been there under any circumstances – not even if the van had left at noon.

At the time, none of this seemed terribly important. The alarm went off at five, and with only half an hour to get myself ready and out the door, I wouldn't have given Frieda a single thought if her name hadn't been mentioned. What mattered to me that morning was waking up with Alma, drinking coffee with her on the front steps of the house, being able to touch her again. All groggy and tousled, all stupid with happiness, all bleary with sex and skin and thoughts about my new life. If I had been more alert, I would have understood what I was walking away from, but I was too tired and too rushed for anything but the sim-plest gestures: a last hug, a last kiss, and then the van pulled up in front of the cottage, and it was time for me to go. We went back into the house to retrieve my bag, and as we were walking out again, Alma plucked a book from the table near the door and handed it to me (To look at on the plane, she said), and then there was a last last hug, a last last kiss, and I was off to the airport. It wasn't until I was halfway there that I realized that Alma had forgotten to give me the Xanax.

On any other day, I would have told the driver to turn around and go back to the ranch. I almost did it then, but after thinking through the humiliations that would follow from that decision – missing the plane, exposing myself as a coward, reaffirming my status as neurotic weakling – I managed to curb my panic. I had already made one drugless flight with Alma. Now the trick was to see if I could do it alone. To the extent that distractions were necessary, the book she had given me proved to be an enormous help. It was over six hundred pages long, weighed almost three pounds, and kept me company the whole time I was in the air. A compendium of wildflowers with the blunt, no-nonsense title *Weeds of the West*, it had been put together by a team of seven authors (six of whom were described as Extension Weed Specialists; the seventh was a Wyoming-based Herbarium Manager) and published, aptly enough, by something called the Western Society of Weed Science, in association

with the Western United States Land Grant Universities Cooperative
Extension Services. In general, I didn't take much interest in botany. I
couldn't have named more than a few dozen plants and trees, but this
reference book, with its nine hundred color photographs and precise
prose descriptions of the habitats and characteristics of over four hundred species, held my attention for several hours. I don't know why I
found it so absorbing, but perhaps it was because I had just come from
that land of prickly, water-starved vegetation and wanted to see more of
it, had not quite had my fill. Most of the photographs had been shot in
extreme close-up, with nothing in the background but blank sky.
Occasionally, the picture would include some surrounding grass, a
patch of dirt, or, even more rarely, a distant rock or mountain.
Noticeably absent were people, the smallest reference to human activity. New Mexico had been inhabited for thousands of years, but to look
at the photos in that book was to feel that nothing had ever happened
there, that its entire history had been erased. No more ancient cliff
dwellers, no more archaeological ruins, no more Spanish conquerors,
no more Jesuit priests, no more Pat Garrett and Billy the Kid, no more
Indian pueblos, no more builders of the atomic bomb. There was only
the land and what covered the land, the meager growths of stems and
stalks and spiny little flowers that sprang up from the parched soil: a
civilization reduced to a smattering of weeds. In themselves, the plants
weren't much to look at, but their names had an impressive music, and
after I had studied the pictures and read the words that accompanied
them (*Leaf blade ovate to lanceolate in outline . . . Achenes are flattened, ribbed
and rugose, with pappus of capillary bristles*), I took a brief pause to write
down some of those names in my notebook. I started on a fresh verso,
immediately after the pages I had used to record the extracts from
Hector's journal, which in turn had followed the description of *The Inner
Life of Martin Frost*. The words had a chewy Saxon thickness to them,
and I took pleasure in sounding them out to myself, in feeling their
stolid, clanging resonances on my tongue. As I look at the list now, it
strikes me as near gibberish, a random collection of syllables from a
dead language – perhaps from the language once spoken on Mars.

Bur chervil. Spreading dogbane. Labriform milkweed. Skeletonleaf
bursage. Common sagewort. Nodding beggar-sticks. Plumeless thistle.
Squarerrose knapweed. Hairy fleabane. Bristly hawksbeard. Curlycup
gunweed. Spotted catsear. Tansy ragwort. Riddell groundsel. Blessed
milkthistle. Poverty sumpweed. Spineless horsebrush. Spiny cocklebur.

Western sticktight. Smallseed falseflax. Flixwood tansymustard. Dyer's woad. Clasping pepperweed. Bladder campion. Nettleleaf goosefoot. Dodder. Prostrate spurge. Twogrooved milkvetch. Everlasting peavine. Silky crazyweed. Toad rush. Henbit. Purple deadnettle. Spurred anoda. Panicle willowweed. Velvety gaura. Ripgut brome. Mexican sprangle-top. Fall panicum. Rattail fescue. Sharppoint fluvellin. Dalmatian toad-flax. Bilobed speedwell. Sacred datura.

Vermont looked different to me after I returned. I had been gone for only three days and two nights, but everything had become smaller in my absence: closed in on itself, dark, clammy. The greenness of the woods around my house felt unnatural, impossibly lush in comparison to the tans and browns of the desert. The air was thick with moisture, the ground was soft underfoot, and everywhere I turned I saw wild pro-liferations of plant life, startling instances of decay: the over-saturated twigs and bark fragments moldering on the trails, the ladders of fungus on the trees, the mildew stains on the walls of the house. After a while, I understood that I was looking at these things through Alma's eyes, trying to see them with a new clarity in order to prepare myself for the day when she moved in with me. The flight to Boston had gone well, much better than I had dared to hope it would, and I had walked off the plane feeling that I had accomplished something important. In the big scheme of things, it probably wasn't much, but in the small scheme of things, in the microscopic place where private battles are won and lost, it counted as a singular victory. I felt stronger than I had felt at any time in the past three years. Almost whole, I said to myself, almost ready to become real again.

    For the next several days, I kept as busy as I could, tackling chores on several fronts at once. I worked on the Chateaubriand translation, took my banged-up truck to the body shop for repairs, and cleaned the house to within an inch of its life – scrubbing floors, waxing furniture, dusting books. I knew that nothing could hide the essential ugliness of the archi-tecture, but at least I could make the rooms presentable, give them a sheen they hadn't had before. The only difficulty was deciding what to do with the boxes in the spare bedroom – which I intended to convert into a study for Alma. She would need to have a place to finish her book, a place to go to when she needed to be alone, and that room was the only one available. Storage space in the rest of the house was limited, however, and with no attic and no garage at my disposal, the only area

I could think of was the cellar. The problem with that solution was the dirt floor. Every time it rained, the cellar would fill up with water, and any cardboard box left down there was certain to be drenched. To avoid that calamity, I bought ninety-six cinder blocks and eight large rectangles of plywood. By stacking the cinder blocks three high, I managed to construct a platform that was well above the waterline of the worst flood that had visited me. For extra security against the effects of dampness, I wrapped each box in a thick plastic garbage bag and sealed up the opening with tape. That should have been satisfactory, but it took another two days for me to build up the courage to carry them downstairs. Everything that remained of my family was in those boxes. Helen's dresses and skirts. Her hairbrush and stockings. Her big winter coat with the fur hood. Todd's baseball glove and comic books. Marco's jigsaw puzzles and plastic men. The gold compact with the cracked mirror. Hooty Tooty the stuffed bear. The Walter Mondale campaign button. I had no use for these things anymore, but I had never been able to throw them away, had never even considered giving them to charity. I didn't want Helen's clothes to be worn by another woman, and I didn't want the boys' Red Sox caps to sit on the heads of other boys. Taking those things down to the cellar was like burying them in the ground. It wasn't the end, perhaps, but it was the beginning of the end, the first milestone on the road to forgetfulness. Hard to do, but not half as hard as getting on that plane to Boston had been. After I finished emptying the room, I went to Brattleboro and picked out furniture for Alma. I bought her a mahogany desk, a leather chair that rocked back and forth when you pushed a button under the seat, an oak filing cabinet, and a nifty, multicolored throw rug. It was the best stuff in the store, top-of-the-line office equipment. The bill came to more than three thousand dollars, and I paid in cash.

I missed her. However impetuous our plan might have been, I never had any doubts or second thoughts about it. I pushed on in a state of blind happiness, waiting for the moment when she would finally be able to come east, and whenever I started to miss her too much, I would open the freezer door and look at the gun. The gun proved that Alma had already been there – and if she had been there once, there was no reason to believe she wouldn't return. At first, I didn't dwell on the fact that the gun was still loaded, but after two or three days it started to bother me. I hadn't touched it in all that time, but one afternoon, just to be safe, I lifted it out of the refrigerator and carried it into the woods, where I fired all six bullets into the ground. They made a noise like a string of Chinese firecrackers, like bursting paper bags. When I returned to the house, I put the gun in the top drawer of the bedside table. It couldn't kill anymore, but that didn't mean it was any less potent, any less dangerous. It embodied the power of a thought, and every time I looked at it, I remembered how close that thought had come to destroying me.

The phone in Alma's cottage was temperamental, and I couldn't always get through to her when I called. Faulty wiring, she said, a loose connection somewhere in the system, which meant that even after I dialed her number and heard the rapid little clicks and beeps that suggested the call was going through, the bell on her end didn't ring. More often than not, however, that phone could be counted on for outgoing calls. On the day I returned to Vermont, I made several unsuccessful attempts to reach her, and when Alma finally called at eleven (nine o'clock mountain time), we decided to stick to that arrangement in the future. She would call me rather than the other way around. Every time we talked after that, we ended the conversation by fixing the time of the next call, and for three nights running the routine worked as smoothly as a trick in a magic show. We would say seven o'clock, for example, and at ten minutes to seven I would install myself in the kitchen, pour myself a straight shot of tequila (we went on drinking tequila together, even long-distance), and at seven sharp, just as the second hand on the wall clock was sweeping up to mark the hour, the telephone would ring. I came to depend on the precision of those calls. Alma's punctuality was a sign of faith, a commitment to the principle that two people in two different parts of the world could nevertheless be of one mind about nearly everything.

Then, on the fourth night (the fifth night after I had left Tierra del Sueño), Alma didn't call. I suspected that she was having trouble with her phone, and therefore I didn't act right away. I went on sitting in my spot, patiently waiting for the phone to ring, but when the silence stretched on for another twenty minutes, then thirty minutes, I began to worry. If the phone was out of order, she would have sent a fax to explain why I hadn't heard from her. Alma's fax machine was hooked up to another line, and there had never been any glitches with that number. I knew it was useless, but I picked up my own phone and called her anyway – with the expected negative result. Then, thinking that she might have been caught up in some business with Frieda, I called the number at the main house, but the result was the same. I called again, just to make sure I had dialed correctly, but again there was no answer. As a last resort, I sent a brief note by fax. *Where are you, Alma? Is everything all right? Puzzled. Please write (fax) if phone is out of order. I love you, David.*

There was only one phone in my house, and it was in the kitchen. If I went upstairs to the bedroom, I was afraid I wouldn't hear it ringing if Alma called later in the night – or, if I did, that I wouldn't be able to get downstairs in time to answer it. I had no idea what to do with myself. I waited around in the kitchen for several hours, hoping that something would happen, and then, when it finally got to be past one in the morning, I went into the living room and stretched out on the sofa. It was the same lumpy ensemble of springs and cushions that I had turned into a makeshift bed for Alma the first night we were together – a good place for thinking morbid thoughts. I kept at it until dawn, torturing myself with imagined car crashes, fires, medical emergencies, deadly stumbles down flights of stairs. At some point, the birds woke up and started singing in the branches outside. Not long after that, I unexpectedly fell asleep.

I had never thought that Frieda would do to Alma what she had done to me. Hector had wanted me to stay at the ranch and watch his films; then he died, and Frieda had prevented it from happening. Hector had wanted Alma to write his biography. Now that he was dead, why hadn't it occurred to me that Frieda would take it upon herself to prevent the book from being published? The situations were almost identical, and yet I hadn't seen the resemblance, had utterly failed to notice the similarities between them. Perhaps it was because the numbers were so far apart. Watching the films would have taken me no more than four or five days; Alma had been working on her book for close to seven years. It never crossed my mind that anyone could be cruel enough to take seven years of a person's work and rip it to shreds. I simply lacked the courage to think that thought.

If I had seen what was coming, I wouldn't have left Alma alone at the ranch. I would have forced her to pack her manuscript, pushed her into the van, and taken her with me to the airport on that last morning. Even if I hadn't acted then, it still might have been possible to do something before it was too late. We had had four telephone conversations since my return to Vermont, and Frieda's name had come up in every one of them. But I hadn't wanted to talk about Frieda. That part of the story was over for me now, and I was only interested in talking about the future. I rattled on to Alma about the house, about the room I was preparing for her, about the furniture I had ordered. I should have been asking her questions, pressing her for details about Frieda's state of mind, but Alma seemed to enjoy hearing me talk about these domestic matters. She was in the early stages of moving – filling up cardboard boxes with her clothes, deciding what to take and what to leave behind, asking me which books in my library duplicated hers – and the last thing she was expecting was trouble.

Three hours after I left for the airport, Alma and Frieda had driven to the funeral parlor in Albuquerque to collect the urn. Later that day, in a windless corner of the garden, they had scattered Hector's ashes among the rosebushes and tulip beds. It was the same spot where Taddy had been stung by the bee, and Frieda had been quite shaky throughout the ceremony, holding her own for a minute or two and then giving in to prolonged fits of silent crying. When Alma and I talked on the phone that night, she told me that Frieda had never looked so vulnerable to her, so dangerously close to collapse. Early the next morning, however, she walked over to the main house and discovered that Frieda was already awake – sitting on the floor in Hector's study, combing through mountains of papers, photographs, and drawings that were spread out in a circle around her. The screenplays were next, she told Alma, and after that she was going to make a systematic search for every other document linked to the production of the films: storyboard folios, costume sketches, set-design blueprints, lighting diagrams, notes for the actors. It would all have to be burned, she said, not a single scrap of material could be spared.

Already, then, just one day after I left the ranch, the limits of the destruction had been changed, pushed back to accommodate a broader interpretation of Hector's will. It wasn't just the movies anymore. It was every piece of evidence that could prove those movies had ever existed.

There were fires on each of the next two days, but Alma took no part in them, letting Juan and Conchita serve as helpers as she went about her own business. On the third day, scenery was dragged out from the back rooms of the sound stage and burned. Props were burned, costumes were burned, Hector's journals were burned. Even the notebook I had read in Alma's house was burned, and still we were unable to grasp where things were headed. That notebook had been written in the early thirties, long before Hector went back to making films. Its only

335

value was as a source of information for Alma's biography. Destroy that source, and even if the book was eventually published, the story it told would no longer be credible. We should have understood that, but when we talked on the phone that night, Alma mentioned it only in passing. The big news of the day had to do with Hector's silent films. Copies of those films were already in circulation, of course, but Frieda was worried that if they were discovered on the ranch, someone would make the connection between Hector Spelling and Hector Mann, and so she had decided to burn them as well. It was a gruesome job, Alma reported her as saying, but it had to be done thoroughly. If one part of the job was left unfinished, then all the other parts would become meaningless.

We arranged to talk again at nine o'clock the next evening (seven her time). Alma was going to be in Sorocco for most of the afternoon – shopping at the supermarket, taking care of personal errands – but even though it was an hour-and-a-half drive back to Tierra del Sueño, we figured that she would return to the cottage by six. When her call didn't come, my imagination immediately started filling in the blanks, and by the time I stretched out on the sofa at one o'clock, I was convinced that Alma had never made it home, that something monstrous had happened to her.

It turned out that I was both right and wrong. Wrong that she hadn't made it home, but right about everything else – although not in any of the ways I had imagined. Alma pulled up in front of her house a few minutes after six. She never locked the door, so she wasn't unduly alarmed to discover that the door of the cottage was open, but smoke was rising from the chimney, and that struck her as bizarre, altogether incomprehensible. It was a hot day in the middle of July, and even if Juan and Conchita had come to deliver fresh laundry or were taking out the trash, why on earth had they lit a fire? Alma left her groceries in the back of her car and went straight into the house. Crouched in front of the hearth in the living room, Frieda was crumpling up sheets of paper and throwing them into the fire. Gesture for gesture, it was a precise reenactment of the final scene of *Martin Frost:* Norbert Steinhaus burning the manuscript of his story in a desperate attempt to bring Alma's mother back to life. Bits of paper ash floated out into the room, hovering around Frieda like injured black butterflies. The edges of the wings glowed orange for an instant, then turned whitish gray. Hector's widow was so absorbed in her work, so intent on finishing the job she had started, that she never even looked up when Alma walked through the door. The unburned pages were spread out across her knees, a small pile of eight-and-a-half-by-eleven sheets, perhaps twenty or thirty of them, perhaps forty. If that was all there was left, then the other six hundred pages were already gone.

In her own words, Alma *went into a frenzy, a vicious tirade, an insane burst of shouting and screaming*. She charged across the living room, and when Frieda stood up to defend herself, Alma shoved her aside. That was all she could remember, she said. One violent shove, and then she was already past Frieda, running toward her study and the computer at the back of the house. The burned manuscript was only a printout. The book was in the computer, and if Frieda hadn't tampered with the hard drive or found any of the backup disks, then nothing would be lost.

Hope for an instant, a brief surge of optimism as she crossed the threshold of the room, and then no hope. Alma entered the study, and the first thing she saw was a blank space where the computer had been. The desk was bare: no more monitor, no more keyboard, no more printer, no more blue plastic box with the twenty-one labeled floppy disks and the fifty-three different research files. Frieda had carted away the whole lot. No doubt Juan had been in on it with her, and if Alma understood the situation correctly, then it was already too late to do anything about it. The computer would be smashed; the disks would be cut into little pieces. And even if that hadn't happened yet, where was she going to start looking for them? The ranch spread out over four hundred acres. All you had to do was pick a spot somewhere, dig a hole, and the book would disappear forever.

She wasn't sure how long she remained in the study. Several minutes, she thought, but it could have been longer than that, perhaps as long as a quarter of an hour. She remembered sitting down at the desk and putting her hands over her face. She wanted to cry, she said, to let loose in a jag of uninterrupted screaming and sobbing, but she was still too stunned to cry, and so she didn't do anything but sit there and listen to herself breathe through her hands. At a certain point, she began to notice how quiet it had become in the house. She assumed that meant Frieda had already left – that she had simply walked out and gone back to the other house. That was just as well, Alma thought. No amount of arguing or explaining would ever undo what had happened, and the fact was that she never wanted to talk to Frieda again. Was that true? Yes, she decided, it was true. If that was the case, then the time had

337

come to get out of there. She could pack a bag, get into her car, and drive to a motel somewhere near the airport. First thing in the morning, she could be on the plane to Boston.

That was when Alma stood up from the desk and left the study. It wasn't yet seven o'clock, but she knew me well enough to be certain that I would be in my house – hovering around the phone in the kitchen, pouring myself a tequila in anticipation of her call. She wasn't going to wait until the appointed time. Years of her life had just been stolen from her, the world was blowing up in her head, and she had to talk to me now, had to start talking to someone before the tears came and she couldn't get the words out of her mouth. The phone was in the bedroom, the next room over from the study. All she had to do was turn right when she went out the door, and ten seconds later she would have been sitting on her bed dialing my number. When she came to the threshold of the study, however, she hesitated for a moment and turned left instead. Sparks had been flying all over the living room, and before she settled in to a long conversation with me, she had to make sure that the fire was out. It was a reasonable decision, the correct thing to do under the circumstances. So she took that detour to the other side of the house, and a moment later the story of that night turned into a different story, the night became a different night. That's the horror for me: not just being unable to prevent what happened, but knowing that if Alma had called me first, it might not have happened at all. Frieda would still have been lying dead on the living room floor, but none of Alma's responses would have been the same, none of the things that happened after she discovered the body would have played out as they did. Talking to me would have made her feel a little stronger, a little less crazy, a little better prepared to absorb the shock. If she had told me about the shove, for example, had described to me how she had pushed Frieda in the chest with the flat of her hand before running past her into the study, I might have been able to warn her about the possible consequences. People lose their balance, I would have told her, they stumble backward, they fall, they hit their heads against hard objects. Go into the living room and check. Find out if Frieda is still there, and Alma would have gone into the living room without hanging up the phone. I would have been able to talk to her immediately after she discovered the body, and that would have calmed her down, given her a chance to think more clearly, made her stop and reconsider before going ahead with the terrible thing she was proposing to do. But Alma hesitated in the doorway, turned left rather than right, and when she found Frieda's body lying crumpled up on the floor, she forgot about calling me. No, I don't think she forgot, I don't mean to suggest that she forgot – but the idea was already taking shape in her head, and she couldn't bring herself to pick up the phone. Instead, she went into the kitchen, sat down with a bottle of tequila and a ballpoint pen, and spent the rest of the night writing me a letter.

I was asleep on the sofa when the fax started coming through. It was six in the morning in Vermont, but still night in New Mexico, and the machine woke me up on the third or fourth ring. I had been out for less than an hour, sunk in a coma of exhaustion, and the first rings didn't register with me except to alter the dream I was having at the moment – a nightmare about alarm clocks and deadlines and having to wake up to deliver a lecture entitled The Metaphors of Love. I don't often remember my dreams, but I remember that one, just as I remember everything else that happened to me after I opened my eyes. I sat up, understanding now that the noise wasn't coming from the alarm clock in my bedroom. The phone was ringing in the kitchen, but by the time I got to my feet and staggered across the living room, the ringing had stopped. I heard a little click in the machine, signaling that a fax transmission was about to begin, and when I finally made it to the kitchen, the first bits of the letter were curling through the slot. There were no plain-paper fax machines in 1988. The paper came in scrolls – flimsy parchment with a special electronic coating – and when you received a letter, it looked like something that had been sent from the ancient past: half of a Torah, or a message delivered from some Etruscan battlefield. Alma had spent more than eight hours composing her letter, intermittently stopping and starting, picking up the pen and putting it down again, growing steadily drunker as the night wore on, and the final accumulation ran to over twenty pages. I read it all standing on my feet, pulling on the scroll as it inched its way out of the machine. The first part recounted the things I have just summarized: the burning of Alma's book, the disappearance of the computer, the discovery of Frieda's body in the living room. The last part ended with these paragraphs:

I can't help it. I'm not strong enough to carry around a thing like this. I keep trying to get my arms around it, but it's too big for me, David, it's too heavy, and I can't even lift it off the ground.

That's why I'm not going to call you tonight. You'll tell me it was an accident, that it wasn't my fault, and I'll start to believe you. I'll want to believe you, but the truth is that I pushed her hard, much harder than you can push an eighty-year-old woman, and I killed her. It doesn't matter what she did to me. I killed her, and if I let you talk me out of it now, it would only destroy us later. There's no way around this. In order to stop myself, I would have to give up the truth, and once I did that, every good thing in me would start to die. I have to act now, you see, while I still have the courage. Thank God for alcohol. Guinness Gives You Strength, as the London billboards used to say. Tequila gives you courage.

You start from somewhere, and no matter how far you think you've traveled from that place, you always wind up there in the end. I thought you could rescue me, that I could make myself belong to you, but I've never belonged to anyone but them. Thank you for the dream, David. Ugly Alma found a man, and he made her feel beautiful. If you could do that for me, just think what you could do for a girl with only one face.

Feel lucky. It's good that it's ending before you find out who I really am. I came to your house that first night with a gun, didn't I? Don't ever forget what that means. Only a crazy person would do something like that, and crazy people can't be trusted. They snoop into other people's lives, they write books about things that don't concern them, they buy pills. Thank God for pills. Was it really an accident that you left them behind the other day? They were in my purse the whole time you were here. I kept meaning to give them to you, and I kept forgetting to do it – right up to the moment when you climbed into the van. Don't blame me. It turns out that I need them more than you do. My twenty-five little purple friends. Maximum-strength Xanax, guaranteed to provide a night of unbroken sleep.

Forgive. Forgive. Forgive. Forgive. Forgive.

I tried calling her after that, but she didn't answer the phone. I got through this time – I could hear the phone ringing on the other end – but Alma never picked up the receiver. I held on for forty or fifty rings, stubbornly hoping that the noise would break her concentration, distract her into thinking about something other than the pills. Would five more rings have made a difference? Would ten more rings have stopped her from going ahead with it? Eventually, I decided to hang up, found a piece of paper, and sent her a fax of my own. *Please talk to me,* I wrote. *Please, Alma, pick up the phone and talk to me.* I called her again a second later, but this time the line went dead after six or seven rings. I didn't understand at first, but then I realized that she must have pulled the cord out of the wall.

9

Later that week, I buried her next to her parents in a Catholic cemetery twenty-five miles north of Tierra del Sueño. Alma had never mentioned any relatives to me, and since no Grunds or Morrisons turned up to claim her body, I covered the costs of the funeral myself. There were grim decisions to be made, grotesque choices that revolved around the relative merits of embalming and cremation, the durability of various woods, the price of caskets. Then, having opted for burial, further questions about clothing, shades of lipstick, fingernail polish, hair style. I don't know how I managed to do those things, but I suspect that I went about them in the same way that everyone else does: half there and half not, half in my mind and half out. All I can remember is saying no to the idea of cremation. No more fires, I said, no more ashes. They had already cut her up to perform their autopsy, but I wasn't going to let them burn her.

On the night of Alma's suicide, I had called the sheriff's office from my house in Vermont. A deputy named Victor Guzman had been sent out to the ranch to investigate, but even though he arrived there before six a.m., Juan and Conchita had already vanished. Alma and Frieda were both dead, the letter that had been faxed to me was still in the machine, but the little people had gone missing. When I left New Mexico five days later, Guzman and the other deputies were still looking for them.

Frieda's remains were disposed of by her lawyer, according to the instructions of her will. The service was held in the arbor of the Blue Stone Ranch – just behind the main house, in Hector's little forest of willows and aspens – but I made a point of not being there. I felt too much hatred for Frieda now, and the thought of going to that ceremony turned my stomach. I never met the lawyer, but Guzman had told him about me, and when he called my motel to invite me to Frieda's funeral, I simply told him that I was busy. He rambled on for a few minutes after that, talking about poor Mrs. Spelling and poor Alma and how ghastly the whole thing had been, and then, *in strictest confidence*, barely pausing between sentences, he informed me that the estate was worth over nine million dollars. The ranch would be going up for sale once the will cleared probate, he said, and those proceeds, along with all monies acquired from the divestiture of Mrs. Spelling's stocks and bonds, would be given to a nonprofit organization in New York City. Which one? I asked. The Museum of Modern Art, he said. The entire nine million was going to be put in an anonymous fund for the preservation of old films. Pretty strange, he said, don't you think? No, I said, not strange. Cruel and sickening, maybe, but not strange. If you liked bad jokes, this one could keep you laughing for years.

I wanted to go back to the ranch one last time, but when I pulled up in front of the gate, I didn't have the heart to drive through. I had been hoping to find some photographs of Alma, to look around the cottage for some odds and ends that I could take back to Vermont with me, but the police had put up one of those crime-scene barriers with the yellow tape, and I suddenly lost my nerve. No cop was standing there to block my way, and it wouldn't have been any trouble to slip past the fence and enter the property – but I couldn't, I couldn't – and so I turned the car around and drove on. I spent my last hours in Albuquerque ordering a headstone for Alma's grave. At first, I thought I would keep the inscription to the bare minimum: ALMA GRUND 1950–1988. But then, after I had signed the contract and paid the man for the work, I went back into the office and told him that I had changed my mind. I wanted to add another word, I said. The inscription should read: ALMA GRUND 1950–1988 WRITER. Except for the twenty-page suicide note she sent me on the last night of her life, I had never read a word she had written. But Alma had died because of a book, and justice demanded that she be remembered as the author of that book.

I went home. Nothing happened on the flight back to Boston. We ran into turbulence over the Midwest, I ate some chicken and drank a glass of wine, I looked out the window – but nothing happened. White clouds, silver wing, blue sky. Nothing.

The liquor cabinet was empty when I walked into my house, and it was too late to go out and buy a new bottle. I don't know if that's what saved me, but I had forgotten that I'd finished off the tequila on my last night there, and with no hope of obliteration within thirty miles of boarded-up West T—, I had to go to bed sober. In the morning, I drank two cups of coffee and went back to work. I had been planning to fall apart, to slip into my old routine of hapless sorrow and alcoholic ruin, but in the light of that summer morning in Vermont, something in me resisted the urge to destroy myself. Chateaubriand was just coming to the end of his long meditation on the life of Napoleon, and I rejoined him in the twenty-fourth book of the memoirs, on the island of Saint Helena with the deposed emperor. *He had already been in exile for six years; he had needed less time to conquer Europe. He rarely left the house anymore and spent his days reading Ossian in Casarotti's Italian translation . . . When Bonaparte went out, he walked along rugged paths flanked by aloes and scented broom . . . or hid himself in the thick clouds that rolled along the ground. . . . At this moment in history, everything withers in a day; whoever lives too long dies alive. As we move through life, we leave behind three or four images of ourselves, each one different from the others; we see them through the fog of the past, like portraits of our different ages.*

I wasn't sure if I had tricked myself into believing that I was strong enough to go on working – or if I had simply gone numb. For the rest of the summer I felt as though I were living in a different dimension, awake to the things around me and yet removed from them at the same time, as if my body had been wrapped in transparent gauze. I put in long hours with the Chateaubriand, rising early and going to bed late, and I made steady progress as the weeks went on, gradually increasing my daily quota from three finished pages of the Pléiade edition to four. It looked like progress, it felt like progress, but that was also the period when I became prone to curious lapses of attention, fits of absentmind-edness that seemed to dog me whenever I wandered from my desk. I forgot to pay the phone bill for three months in a row, ignored every threatening notice that arrived in the mail, and didn't settle the account until a man appeared in my yard one day to disconnect the service. Two weeks later, on a shopping expedition to Brattleboro that included a visit to the post office and a visit to the bank, I managed to throw my wallet into the mailbox, thinking it was a pile of letters. These incidents confounded me, but not once did I stop to consider why they were hap-pening. To ask that question would have meant getting down on my knees and opening the trap door under the rug, and I couldn't afford to look into the darkness of that place. Most nights, after I had knocked off work and finished eating my dinner, I would sit up late in the kitchen, transcribing the notes I had taken at the screening of *The Inner Life of Martin Frost*.

I had known Alma for only eight days. For five of those days we had been apart, and when I calculated how much time we had spent together during the other three, it came to a grand total of fifty-four hours. Eighteen of those hours had been lost in sleep. Another seven had been squandered in separations of one kind or another: the six hours I spent alone in the cottage, the five or ten minutes I spent with Hector, the forty-one minutes I spent watching the film. That left a mere twenty-nine hours when I was actually able to see her and touch her, to enclose myself in the circle of her presence. We made love five times. We ate six meals together. I gave her one bath. Alma had walked in and out of my life so quickly, I sometimes felt that I had only imagined her. That was the worst part of facing her death. There weren't enough things for me to remember, and so I kept going over the same ground again and again, kept adding up the same figures and arriving at the same paltry sums. Two cars, one jet plane, six glasses of tequila. Three beds in three houses on three different nights. Four telephone conversations. I was so befuddled, I didn't know how to mourn her except by keeping myself alive. Months later, when I finished the translation and moved away from Vermont, I understood that Alma had done that for me. In eight short days, she had brought me back from the dead.

It doesn't matter what happened to me after that. This is a book of fragments, a compilation of sorrows and half-remembered dreams, and in order to tell the story, I have to confine myself to the events of the story itself. I will simply say that I live in a large city now, somewhere between Boston and Washington, D.C., and that this is the first piece of writing I have attempted since *The Silent World of Hector Mann*. I taught for a while again, found other work that was more satisfying to me, then quit teaching for good. I should also say (for those who care about such things) that I no longer live alone.

It has been eleven years since I returned from New Mexico, and in all that time I have never talked to anyone about what happened to me there. Not a word about Alma, not a word about Hector and Frieda, not a word about the Blue Stone Ranch. Who would have believed such a story if I had tried to tell it? I had no proof, no evidence to support my case. Hector's films had been destroyed, Alma's book had been destroyed, and the only thing I could have shown anyone was my pathetic little collection of notes, my trilogy of desert jottings: the breakdown of *Martin Frost*, the snippets from Hector's journal, and an inventory of extraterrestrial plants that had nothing to do with anything. Better to keep my mouth shut, I decided, and let the mystery of Hector Mann remain unsolved. Other people were writing about his work now, and when the silent comedies were put out on video in 1992 (a boxed collection of three tapes), the man in the white suit slowly began to acquire a following. It was a small comeback, of course, a minuscule event in the land of industrial entertainments and billion-dollar marketing budgets, but satisfying nevertheless, and I took pleasure in stumbling across articles that referred to Hector as a minor master of the genre or (to quote from Stanley Vaubel's piece in *Sight and Sound*) *the last great practitioner of the art of silent slapstick*. Perhaps that was enough. When a fan club was established in 1994, I was invited to become an honorary member. As the person responsible for the first and only full-length study of Hector's work, I was seen as the founding spirit of the movement, and they hoped I would give them my blessing. At last count, there were over three hundred dues-paying members of the International Brotherhood of Hector Manniacs, some of them living in such far-flung places as Sweden and Japan. Every year, the president invites me to attend their annual meeting in Chicago, and when I finally accepted in 1997, I was given a standing ovation at the end of my talk. In the question-and-answer period that followed, someone asked if I had uncovered any information relating to Hector's disappearance while conducting the research for my book. No, I said, unfortunately not. I had looked for months, but I hadn't been able to turn up a single fresh clue.

I turned fifty-one in March 1998. Six months later, on the first day of fall, just one week after I participated in a panel discussion on silent movies at the American Film Institute in Washington, I had my first heart attack. The second one came on November twenty-sixth, in the middle of Thanksgiving dinner at my sister's house in Baltimore. The first one had been fairly gentle, a so-called mild infarction, the equivalent of a short solo for unaccompanied voice. The second one ripped through my body like a choral symphony for two hundred singers and full brass orchestra, and it nearly killed me. Until then, I had refused to think of fifty-one as old. It might not have been particularly young, but neither was it the age when a man was supposed to prepare himself for the end and make his peace with the world. They kept me in the hospital for several weeks, and the news from the doctors was sufficiently discouraging for me to revise that opinion. To use a phrase I have always been fond of, I discovered that I was living on borrowed time.

I don't think I was wrong to have held on to my secrets for all those years, and I don't think I was wrong to have told them now. Circumstances changed, and once they changed, I changed my mind as well. They sent me home from the hospital in mid-December, and by early January I was writing the first pages of this book. It is late October now, and as I come to the end of my project, I note with a certain grim satisfaction that we are also closing in on the last weeks of the century – Hector's century, the century that began eighteen days before he was born and which no one in his right mind will be sorry to see end. Following Chateaubriand's model, I will make no attempt to publish what I have written now. I have left a letter of instruction for my lawyer, and he will know where to find the manuscript and what to do with it after I am gone. I have every intention of living to a hundred, but on the off chance I don't get that far, all the necessary arrangements have been made. If and when this book is published, dear reader, you can be certain that the man who wrote it is long dead.

There are thoughts that break the mind, thoughts of such power and ugliness that they corrupt you as soon as you begin to think them. I was afraid of what I knew, afraid of falling into the horror of what I knew, and therefore I didn't put the thought into words until it was too late for the words to do me any good. I have no facts to offer, no concrete evidence that would hold up in a court of law, but after playing out the events of that night again and again for the past eleven years, I am almost certain that Hector did not die a natural death. He was weak when I saw him, yes, weak and no doubt within days of dying, but his thoughts were lucid, and when he gripped my arm at the end of our conversation, he pressed his fingers into my skin. It was the grip of a man who meant to go on living. He was going to keep himself alive until we had concluded our business, and when I went downstairs after Frieda told me to leave the room, I fully expected to see him again in the morning. Think of the timing – think of how quickly the disasters accumulated after that. Alma and I went to bed, and once we fell asleep, Frieda tiptoed down the hall, went into Hector's room, and smothered him with a pillow. I'm convinced that she did it out of love. There was no anger in her, no sense of betrayal or revenge – simply a fanatic's devotion to a just and holy cause. Hector couldn't have put up much resistance. She was stronger than he was, and by cutting his life short by just a few days, she would be rescuing him from the folly of having invited me to the ranch. After years of steadfast courage, Hector had buckled in to doubts and indecision, had wound up questioning everything he had done with his life in New Mexico, and the moment I arrived in Tierra del Sueño, the beautiful thing he had made with Frieda would be smashed to bits. The craziness didn't begin until I set foot on the ranch. I was the catalyst for everything that happened while I was there, the final ingredient that triggered the fatal explosion. Frieda had to get rid of me, and the only way she could do that was by getting rid of Hector.

I often think about what happened the next day. So much of it turns on what was never said, on little gaps and silences, on the curious passivity that seemed to radiate from Alma at certain critical junctures. When I woke up in the morning, she was sitting beside me on the bed, stroking my face with her hand. It was ten o'clock – long past the time when we should have been in the screening room watching Hector's films – and yet she didn't rush me. I drank the cup of coffee she had put on the bedside table, we talked for a while, we put our arms around each other and kissed. Later on, when she returned to the cottage after the films had been destroyed, she seemed relatively unfazed by the scene she had witnessed. I'm not forgetting that she broke down and cried, but her reaction was far less intense that I had thought it would be. She didn't rant, she didn't lose her temper, she didn't curse Frieda for having lit the fires before she was compelled to do so by Hector's will. We had talked enough in the past two days for me to know that Alma was against burning the films. She was awed by the magnitude of Hector's renunciation, I think, but she also believed that it was wrong, and she'd told me that she had argued with him about it many times over the years. If that was so, then why didn't she become more upset when the films were finally destroyed? Her mother was in those films, her father had shot those films, and yet she barely said a word about them after the fires went out. I have thought about her silence for many years, and the only theory that makes sense to me, the only one that fully accounts for the indifference she displayed that evening, is that she knew the films hadn't been destroyed. Alma was a deeply clever and resourceful person. She had already made copies of Hector's early films and sent them out to half a dozen archives around the world. Why couldn't she have made copies of his late films as well? She had done a fair amount of traveling while working on her book. What would have prevented her from smuggling out a couple of negatives each time she left the ranch and taking them to a lab somewhere to strike new prints? The vault was unguarded, she had keys to all the doors, and she wouldn't have had any trouble getting the material in and out without

347

being noticed. If that was what she had done, then she would have hidden the prints somewhere and waited for Frieda to die before making them public. It would have taken years, perhaps, but Alma was patient, and how could she have known that her life would end on the same night that Frieda's did? One could argue that she would have let me in on the secret, that she wouldn't have kept such a thing to herself, but perhaps she was planning to tell me about it when she came to Vermont. She didn't refer to the films in her long, disjointed suicide letter, but Alma was in a state of anguish that night, trembling in a delirium of terror and apocalyptic self-judgments, and I don't think she was truly in this world anymore when she sat down to write me the letter. She forgot to tell me. She meant to tell me, but then she forgot. If that was the case, then Hector's films haven't been lost. They're only missing, and sooner or later a person will come along who accidentally opens the door of the room where Alma hid them, and the story will start all over again.

I live with that hope.

1999–2001

ORACLE NIGHT

for Q.B.A.S.G.
(in memory)

I had been sick for a long time. When the day came for me to leave the hospital, I barely knew how to walk anymore, could barely remember who I was supposed to be. Make an effort, the doctor said, and in three or four months you'll be back in the swing of things. I didn't believe him, but I followed his advice anyway. They had given me up for dead, and now that I had confounded their predictions and mysteriously failed to die, what choice did I have but to live as though a future life were waiting for me?

I began with small outings, no more than a block or two from my apartment and then home again. I was only thirty-four, but for all intents and purposes the illness had turned me into an old man – one of those palsied, shuffling geezers who can't put one foot in front of the other without first looking down to see which foot is which. Even at the slow pace I could manage then, walking produced an odd, airy lightness in my head, a free-for-all of mixed-up signals and crossed mental wires. The world would bounce and swim before my eyes, undulating like reflections in a wavy mirror, and whenever I tried to look at just one thing, to isolate a single object from the onrush of whirling colors – a blue scarf wrapped around a woman's head, say, or the red taillight of a passing delivery truck – it would immediately begin to break apart and dissolve, disappearing like a drop of dye in a glass of water. Everything shimmied and wobbled, kept darting off in different directions, and for the first several weeks I had trouble telling where my body stopped and the rest of the world began. I bumped into walls and trash bins, got tangled up in dog leashes and scraps of floating paper, stumbled on the smoothest sidewalks. I had lived in New York all my life, but I didn't understand the streets and crowds anymore, and every time I went out on one of my little excursions, I felt like a man who had lost his way in a foreign city.

Summer came early that year. By the end of the first week of June, the weather had turned stagnant, oppressive, rank: day after day of torpid, greenish skies; the air clogged with garbage fumes and exhaust; heat rising from every brick and concrete slab. Still, I pushed on, forcing myself down the stairs and out into the streets every morning, and as the jumble in my head began to clear and my strength slowly returned, I was able to extend my walks into some of the more far-flung crevices of the neighborhood. Ten minutes became twenty minutes; an hour became two hours; two hours became three. Lungs gasping for air, my skin perpetually awash in sweat, I drifted along like a spectator in someone else's dream, watching the world as it chugged through its paces and marveling at how I had once been like the people around me: always rushing, always on the way from here to there, always late, always scrambling to pack in nine more things before the sun went down. I wasn't equipped to play that game anymore. I was damaged goods now, a mass of malfunctioning parts and neurological conundrums, and all that frantic getting and spending left me cold. For comic relief, I took up smoking again and whiled away the afternoons in air-conditioned coffee shops, ordering lemonades and grilled cheese sandwiches as I listened in on conversations and worked my way through every article in three different newspapers. Time passed.

On the morning in question – September 18, 1982 – I left the apartment somewhere between nine-thirty and ten o'clock. My wife and I lived in the Cobble Hill section of Brooklyn, midway between Brooklyn Heights and Carroll Gardens. I usually went north on my walks, but that morning I headed south, turning right when I came to Court Street and continuing on for six or seven blocks. The sky was the color of cement: gray clouds, gray air, gray drizzle borne along by gray gusts of wind. I have always had a weakness for that kind of weather, and I felt content in the gloom, not the least bit sorry that the dog days were behind us. About ten minutes after starting out, in the middle of the block between Carroll and President, I spotted a stationery store on the other side of the street. It was wedged in between a shoe-repair shop and a twenty-four-hour bodega, the only bright façade in a row of shabby, undistinguished buildings. I gathered that it hadn't been there long, but in spite of its newness, and in spite of the clever display in the window (towers of ballpoints, pencils, and rulers arranged to suggest the New York skyline), the Paper Palace looked too small to contain much of interest. If I decided to cross the street and go in, it must have been because I secretly wanted to start working again – without knowing it, without being aware of the urge that had been gathering inside me. I hadn't written anything since coming home from the hospital in May – not a sentence, not a word – and hadn't felt the slightest inclination to do so. Now, after four months of apathy and silence, I suddenly got it into my head to stock up on a fresh set of supplies: new pens and pencils, new notebook, new ink cartridges and erasers, new pads and folders, new everything.

A Chinese man was sitting behind the cash register in front. He appeared to be a bit younger than I was, and when I glanced through the window as I entered the store, I saw that he was hunched over a pad of paper, writing down columns of figures with a black mechanical pencil. In spite of the chill in the air that day, he was dressed in a short-sleeved shirt – one of those flimsy, loose-fitting summer things with an open collar – which accentuated the thinness of his coppery arms. The door made a tinkling sound when I pulled it open, and the man lifted his head for a moment to give me a polite nod of greeting. I nodded back, but before I could say anything to him, he lowered his head again and returned to his calculations.

The traffic out on Court Street must have hit a lull just then, or else the plate glass window was exceedingly thick, but as I started down the first aisle to investigate the store, I suddenly realized how quiet it was in there. I was the first customer of the day, and the stillness was so pronounced that I could hear the scratching of the man's pencil behind me. Whenever I think about that morning now, the sound of that pencil is always the first thing that comes back to me. To the degree that the story I am about to tell makes any sense, I believe this was where it began – in the space of those few seconds, when the sound of that pencil was the only sound left in the world.

I made my way down the aisle, pausing after every second or third step to examine the material on the shelves. Most of it turned out to be standard office- and school-supply stuff, but the selection was remarkably thorough for such a cramped place, and I was impressed by the care that had gone into stocking and arranging such a plethora of goods, which seemed to include everything from six different lengths of brass fasteners to twelve different models of paper clip. As I rounded the corner and began moving down the other aisle toward the front, I noticed that one shelf had been given over to a number of high-quality imported items: leather-bound pads from Italy, address books from France, delicate rice-paper folders from Japan. There was also a stack of notebooks from Germany and another one from Portugal. The Portuguese notebooks were especially attractive to me, and with their hard covers, quadrille lines, and stitched-in signatures of sturdy, unblottable paper,

I knew I was going to buy one the moment I picked it up and held it in my hands. There was nothing fancy or ostentatious about it. It was a practical piece of equipment – stolid, homely, serviceable, not at all the kind of blank book you'd think of offering someone as a gift. But I liked the fact that it was cloth-bound, and I also liked the shape: nine and a quarter by seven and a quarter inches, which made it slightly shorter and wider than most notebooks. I can't explain why it should have been so, but I found those dimensions deeply satisfying, and when I held the notebook in my hands for the first time, I felt something akin to physical pleasure, a rush of sudden, incomprehensible well-being. There were just four notebooks left on the pile, and each one came in a different color: black, red, brown, and blue. I chose the blue, which happened to be the one lying on top.

It took about five more minutes to track down the rest of the things I'd come for, and then I carried them to the front of the shop and placed them on the counter. The man gave me another one of his polite smiles and started punching the keys on his cash register, ringing up the amounts of the various items. When he came to the blue notebook, however, he paused for a moment, held it up in the air, and ran his fingertips lightly over the cover. It was a gesture of appreciation, almost a caress.

'Lovely book,' he said, in heavily accented English. 'But no more. No more Portugal. Very sad story.'

I couldn't follow what he was saying, but rather than put him on the spot and ask him to repeat it, I mumbled something about the charm and simplicity of the notebook and then changed the subject. 'Have you been in business long?' I asked. 'It looks so new and clean in here.'

'One month,' he said. 'Grand opening on August ten.'

As he announced this fact, he seemed to stand up a little straighter, throwing out his chest with boyish, military pride, but when I asked him how business was going, he gently placed the blue notebook on the counter and shook his head. 'Very slow. Many disappointments.' As I looked into his eyes, I understood that he was several years older than I'd thought at first – at least thirty-five, perhaps even forty. I made some lame remark about hanging in there and giving things a chance to develop, but he merely shook his head again and smiled. 'Always my dream to own store,' he said. 'Store like this with pens and paper, my big American dream. Business for all people, right?'

'Right,' I said, still not exactly sure what he was talking about.

'Everybody make words,' he continued. 'Everybody write things down. Children in school do lessons in my books. Teachers put grades in my books. Love letters sent in envelopes I sell. Ledgers for accountants, pads for shopping lists, agendas for planning week. Everything in here important to life, and that make me happy, give honor to my life.'

The man delivered his little speech with such solemnity, such a grave sense of purpose and commitment, I confess that I felt moved. What kind of stationery store owner was this, I wondered, who expounded to his customers on the metaphysics of paper, who saw himself as serving an essential role in the myriad affairs of humanity? There was something comical about it, I suppose, but as I listened to him talk, it didn't once occur to me to laugh.

'Well put,' I said. 'I couldn't agree with you more.'

The compliment seemed to lift his spirits somewhat. With a small smile and a nod of the head, the man resumed punching the keys of the cash register. 'Many writers here in Brooklyn,' he said. 'Whole neighborhood full of them. Good for business maybe.'

'Maybe,' I said. 'The problem with writers is that most of them don't have much money to spend.'

'Ah,' he said, looking up from the cash register and breaking into a big smile that exposed a mouthful of crooked teeth. 'You must be writer yourself.'

'Don't tell anyone,' I answered, trying to keep the tone playful. 'It's supposed to be a secret.'

It wasn't a very funny remark, but the man seemed to think it was hilarious, and for the next little while it was all he could do not to collapse in a fit of laughter. There was a strange, staccato rhythm to his laugh – which seemed to fall somewhere between talking and singing – and it rushed out of his throat in a series of short mechanical trills: *Ha ha ha. Ha ha ha. Ha ha ha.* 'No tell nobody,' he said, once the outburst had subsided. 'Top secret. Just between you and me. Sew up my lips. *Ha ha ha.*'

He went back to his work at the cash register, and by the time he'd finished packing my things into a large white shopping bag, his face had turned serious again. 'If one day you write story in blue Portugal book,' he said, 'make me very glad. My heart fill with joy.'

I didn't know how to answer that, but before I could think of anything to say, he extracted a business card from his shirt pocket and handed it to me across the counter. The words PAPER PALACE were printed in bold letters at the top. The address and telephone number

357

followed, and then, in the lower right-hand corner, there was a last piece of information that read: *M. R. Chang, Proprietor.*

'Thank you, Mr. Chang,' I said, still looking down at the card. Then I slipped it into my own pocket and pulled out my wallet to pay the bill.

'Not mister,' Chang said, smiling his big smile again. 'M. R. Sound more important like that. More American.'

Once again, I didn't know what to say. A few ideas about what the initials stood for flashed through my mind, but I kept them to myself. Mental Resources. Multiple Readings. Mysterious Revelations. Some comments are best left unsaid, and I didn't bother to inflict my dismal wisecracks on the poor man. After a brief, awkward silence, he handed me the white shopping bag and then bowed by way of thanks.

'Good luck with your store,' I said.

'Very small palace,' he said. 'Not much stuff. But you tell me what you want, I order for you. Anything you want, I get.'

'Okay,' I said, 'it's a deal.'

I turned to leave, but Chang scuttled out from behind the counter and cut me off at the door. He seemed to be under the impression that we had just concluded a matter of highly important business, and he wanted to shake my hand. 'Deal,' he said. 'Good for you, good for me. Okay?'

'Okay,' I repeated, letting him shake my hand. I found it absurd to be making so much of so little, but it didn't cost me anything to play along. Besides, I was eager to get going, and the less I said, the sooner I would be on my way.

'You ask, I find. Whatever it is, I find for you. M. R. Chang deliver the goods.'

He pumped my arm two or three more times after that, and then he opened the door for me, nodding and smiling as I slid past him into the raw September day.[1]

I had been planning to stop in for breakfast at one of the local diners, but the twenty-dollar bill I had put in my wallet before starting out had

1. Twenty years have elapsed since that morning, and a fair amount of what we said to each other has been lost. I search my memory for the missing dialogue, but I can come up with no more than a few isolated fragments, bits and pieces shorn from their original context. One thing I'm certain of, however, is that I told him my name. It must have happened just after he found out I was a writer, since I can hear him asking me who I was – on the off chance he ran across something I had published.

>een reduced to three singles and a smattering of coins – not even
>nough for the $2.99 special when you figured in the tax and tip. If not
>or the shopping bag, I might have gone on with my walk anyway, but
:here seemed to be no point in lugging that thing around the neighbor-
1ood with me, and since the weather was in a fairly nasty state by then
(the once-fine drizzle had turned into a steady downpour), I opened my
umbrella and decided to go home.

It was a Saturday, and my wife had still been in bed when I'd left the
apartment. Grace had a regular nine-to-five job, and the weekends were
her only chance to sleep in, to indulge in the luxury of waking up without an alarm clock. Not wanting to disturb her, I had crept out as quietly
as I could, leaving a note for her on the kitchen table. Now I saw that a
few sentences had been added to the note. *Sidney: Hope you had fun on
your walk. I'm going out to do some errands. Shouldn't be long. See you back
at the ranch. Love, G.*

I went into my workroom at the end of the hall and unpacked my new
supplies. It was hardly bigger than a closet in there – just enough space
for a desk, a chair, and a miniature bookcase with four narrow shelves –
but I found it sufficient for my needs, which had never been more elaborate than to sit in the chair and put words on pieces of paper. I had
gone into the room several times since my discharge from the hospital,
but until that Saturday morning in September – what I prefer to call *the
morning in question* – I don't think I had sat down once in the chair. Now,
as I lowered my sorry, debilitated ass onto the hard wooden seat, I felt
like someone who had come home from a long and difficult journey, an
unfortunate traveler who had returned to claim his rightful place in the

---

'Orr' is what I said to him, giving my last name first, 'Sidney Orr.' Chang's English
wasn't good enough for him to understand my response. He heard Orr as *or*, and
when I shook my head and smiled, his face seemed to crumple up in embarrassed
confusion. I was about to correct the error and spell out the word for him, but before
I could say anything his eyes brightened again and he began making furious little
rowing gestures with his hands, thinking that perhaps the word I'd said to him was
oar. Again, I shook my head and smiled. Utterly defeated now, Chang emitted a
loud sigh and said: 'Terrible tongue, this English. Too tricky for my poor brain.' The
misunderstanding continued until I lifted the blue notebook from the counter and
wrote out my name in block letters on the inside front cover. That seemed to produce the desired result. After so much effort, I didn't bother to tell him that the first
Orrs in America had been Orlovskys. My grandfather had shortened the name to
make it sound more American – just as Chang had done by adding the decorative
but meaningless initials, M. R., to his.

359

world. It felt good to be there again, good to want to be there again, and in the wake of the happiness that washed over me as I settled in at my old desk, I decided to mark the occasion by writing something in the blue notebook.

I put a fresh ink cartridge in my fountain pen, opened the notebook to the first page, and looked at the top line. I had no idea how to begin. The purpose of the exercise was not to write anything specific so much as to prove to myself that I still had it in me to write – which meant that it didn't matter what I wrote, just so long as I wrote something. Anything would have served, any sentence would have been as valid as any other, but still, I didn't want to break in that notebook with something stupid, so I bided my time by looking at the little squares on the page, the rows of faint blue lines that crisscrossed the whiteness and turned it into a field of tiny identical boxes, and as I let my thoughts wander in and out of those lightly traced enclosures, I found myself remembering a conversation I'd had with my friend John Trause a couple of weeks earlier. The two of us rarely talked about books when we were together, but that day John had mentioned that he was rereading some of the novelists he had admired when he was young – curious to know if their work held up or not, curious to know if the judgments he'd made at twenty were the same ones he would make today, more than thirty years down the road. He ran through ten writers, through twenty writers, touching on everyone from Faulkner and Fitzgerald to Dostoyevsky and Flaubert, but the comment that stuck most vividly in my mind – and which came back to me now as I sat at my desk with the blue notebook open in front of me – was a small digression he'd made concerning an anecdote in one of Dashiell Hammett's books. 'There's a novel in this somewhere,' John had said. 'I'm too old to want to think about it myself, but a young punk like you could really fly with it, turn it into something good. It's a terrific premise. All you need is a story to go with it.'[2]

He was referring to the Flitcraft episode in the seventh chapter of *The Maltese Falcon*, the curious parable that Sam Spade tells Brigid

2. John was fifty-six. Not young, perhaps, but not old enough to think of himself as old, especially since he was aging well and still looked like a man in his mid- to late forties. I had known him for three years by then, and our friendship was a direct result of my marriage to Grace. Her father had been at Princeton with John in the years immediately following the Second World War, and although the two of them worked in different fields (Grace's father was a District Federal Court judge in Charlottesville, Virginia), they had remained close ever since. I therefore met him as

O'Shaughnessy about the man who walks away from his life and disappears. Flitcraft is a thoroughly conventional fellow – a husband, a father, a successful businessman, a person without a thing to complain about. One afternoon as he's walking to lunch, a beam falls from a construction site on the tenth floor of a building and nearly lands on his head. Another inch or two, and Flitcraft would have been crushed, but the beam misses him, and except for a little chip of sidewalk that flies up and hits him in the face, he walks away unhurt. Still, the close call rattles him, and he can't push the incident from his mind. As Hammett puts it: 'He felt like somebody had taken the lid off life and let him look at the works.' Flitcraft realizes that the world isn't the sane and orderly place he thought it was, that he's had it all wrong from the beginning and never understood the first thing about it. The world is governed by chance. Randomness stalks us every day of our lives, and those lives can be taken from us at any moment – for no reason at all. By the time Flitcraft finishes his lunch, he concludes that he has no choice but to submit to this destructive power, to smash his life through some meaningless, wholly arbitrary act of self-negation. He will fight fire with fire, as it were, and without bothering to return home or say good-bye to his family, without even bothering to withdraw any money from the bank, he stands up from the table, goes to another city, and starts his life all over again.

In the two weeks since John and I had discussed that passage, it hadn't once crossed my mind that I might want to take up the challenge of fleshing out the story. I agreed that it was a good premise – good because we have all imagined letting go of our lives, good because at one moment or another we have all wanted to be someone else – but that didn't mean I had any interest in pursuing it. That morning, however, as

a family friend, not as the well-known novelist I had been reading since high school – and whom I still considered to be one of the best writers we had.

He had published six works of fiction between 1952 and 1975, but nothing now for more than seven years. John had never been fast, however, and just because the break between books had been somewhat longer than usual, that didn't mean he wasn't working. I had spent several afternoons with him since my release from the hospital, and sprinkled in among our conversations regarding my health (about which he was deeply concerned, unflagging in his solicitude), his twenty-year-old son, Jacob (who had caused him much anguish of late), and the struggles of the floundering Mets (an abiding mutual obsession), he had dropped enough hints about his current activities to suggest that he was thoroughly wrapped up in something, devoting the better part of his time to a project that was well under way – and perhaps now coming to an end.

361

I sat at my desk for the first time in almost nine months, staring at my newly acquired notebook and struggling to come up with an opening sentence that wouldn't embarrass me or rob me of my courage, I decided to give the old Flitcraft episode a shot. It was no more than an excuse, a search for a possible way in. If I could jot down a couple of reasonably interesting ideas, then at least I could call it a beginning, even if I broke off after twenty minutes and never did another thing with it. So I removed the cap from my pen, pressed the point against the top line of the first page in the blue notebook, and started to write.

The words came quickly, smoothly, without seeming to demand much effort. I found that surprising, but as long as I kept my hand moving from left to right, the next word always seemed to be there, waiting to come out of the pen. I saw my Flitcraft as a man named Nick Bowen. He's in his mid-thirties, works as an editor at a large New York publishing house, and is married to a woman named Eva. Following the example of Hammett's prototype, he is necessarily good at his job, admired by his colleagues, financially secure, happy in his marriage, and so on. Or so it would appear to a casual observer, but as my version of the story begins, trouble has been stirring in Bowen for some time. He has grown bored with his work (although he is unwilling to admit it), and after five years of relative stability and contentment with Eva, his marriage has come to a standstill (another fact he hasn't had the courage to face). Rather than dwell on his burgeoning dissatisfaction, Nick spends his spare time at a garage on Desbrosses Street in Tribeca, engaged in the long-term project of rebuilding the engine of a broken-down Jaguar he bought in the third year of his marriage. He is a top young editor at a prestigious New York company, but the truth is that he prefers working with his hands.

As the story opens, the manuscript of a novel has arrived on Bowen's desk. A short work bearing the suggestive title of *Oracle Night*, it was supposedly written by Sylvia Maxwell, a popular novelist from the twenties and thirties who died nearly two decades ago. According to the agent who sent it in, this lost book was composed in 1927, the year Maxwell ran off to France with an Englishman named Jeremy Scott, a minor artist of the period who later worked as a set designer for British and American films. The affair lasted eighteen months, and when it was over Sylvia Maxwell returned to New York, leaving the novel behind with Scott. He held on to it for the rest of his life, and when he died at the age of eighty-seven, a few months before my story begins, a clause was found in his will that bequeathed the manuscript to Maxwell's granddaughter, a young American woman named Rosa Leightman. It was through her that the book was given to the agent – with explicit instructions that it be sent to Nick Bowen first, before anyone else had a chance to read it.

The package arrives at Nick's office on a Friday afternoon, just minutes after he has left for the weekend. When he returns on Monday morning, the book is sitting on his desk. Nick is an admirer of Sylvia Maxwell's other novels, and therefore he is eager to get started on this one. A moment after he turns to the first page, however, the telephone rings. His assistant informs him that Rosa Leightman is in the reception area, asking if she can see him for a few minutes. Send her in, Nick says, and before he is able to finish reading the opening sentences of the book (*The war was nearly over, but we didn't know that. We were too small to know anything, and because the war was everywhere, we didn't . . .*), Sylvia Maxwell's granddaughter enters his office. She is dressed in the simplest clothes, has almost no makeup on, wears her hair in a short, unfashionable cut, and yet her face is so lovely, Nick finds, so achingly young and unguarded, so much (he suddenly thinks) an emblem of hope and uncoiled human energy, that he momentarily stops breathing. That is precisely what happened to me the first time I saw Grace – the blow to the brain that left me paralyzed, unable to draw my next breath – so it wasn't difficult for me to transpose those feelings onto Nick Bowen and imagine them in the context of that other story. To make matters even simpler, I decided to give Grace's body to Rosa Leightman – even down to her smallest, most idiosyncratic features, including the childhood scar on her kneecap, her slightly crooked left incisor, and the beauty mark on the right side of her jaw.[3]

As for Bowen, however, I expressly made him someone I was not, an inversion of myself. I am tall, and so I made him short. I have reddish hair, and so I gave him dark brown hair. I wear size eleven shoes, and so

---

3. I happened to meet Grace in a publisher's office as well, which might explain why I chose to give Bowen the job I did. It was January 1979, not long after I had finished my second novel. My first novel and an earlier book of stories had been brought out by a small publisher in San Francisco, but now I had moved on to a larger, more commercial house in New York, Holst & McDermott. About two weeks after I signed the contract, I went to the office to see my editor, and at some point during our conversation we started discussing ideas for the cover of the book. That was when Betty Stolowitz picked up the phone on her desk and said to me, 'Why

I put him in size eight and a half. I didn't model him on anyone I knew (not consciously, at any rate), but once I had finished putting him together in my mind, he became astonishingly vivid to me – almost as if I could see him, almost as if he had entered the room and were standing next to me, looking down at the desk with his hand on my shoulder and reading the words I was writing . . . watching me bring him to life with my pen.

At last, Nick gestures for Rosa to sit down, and she settles into a chair on the opposite side of the desk. A long hesitation follows. Nick has begun breathing again, but he can't think of anything to say. Rosa breaks the ice by asking if he found time to finish the book over the weekend. No, he answers, it came in too late. I didn't get it until this morning.

---

don't we get Grace in here and see what she thinks?' It turned out that Grace worked in the art department at Holst & McDermott and had been given the job of designing the dust jacket for *Self-Portrait with Imaginary Brother* – which was what my little book of whims, reveries, and nightmare sorrows was called.

Betty and I went on talking for another three or four minutes, and then Grace Tebbetts walked into the room. She stayed for about a quarter of an hour, and by the time she walked out again and returned to her office, I was in love with her. It was that abrupt, that conclusive, that unexpected. I had read about such things in novels, but I had always assumed the authors were exaggerating the power of the first look – that endlessly talked-about moment when the man gazes into the eyes of his beloved for the first time. To a born pessimist like myself, it was an altogether shocking experience. I felt as if I had been thrust back into the world of the troubadours, reliving some passage from the opening chapter of *La Vita Nova* (. . . *when first the glorious Lady of my thoughts was made manifest to my eyes*), inhabiting the stale tropes of a thousand forgotten love sonnets. *I burned. I longed. I pined. I was rendered mute.* And all this happened to me in the dullest of precincts, under the harsh fluorescent glare of a late-twentieth-century American office – the last place on earth where one would think to stumble upon the passion of one's life.

There is no accounting for such an event, no objective reason to explain why we fall for one person and not another. Grace was a good-looking woman, but even in those first tumultuous seconds of our first encounter, as I shook her hand and watched her settle into a chair by Betty's desk, I could see that she was not inordinately beautiful, not one of those movie star goddesses who overpower you with the dazzle of their perfection. No doubt she was becoming, striking, pleasant to behold (however one chooses to define those terms), but fierce as my attraction was, I also knew that it was more than just a physical attraction, that the dream I was starting to dream was more than just a momentary surge of animal desire. Grace struck me as intelligent, but as the meeting wore on and I listened to her talk about her ideas for the cover, I understood that she wasn't a terribly articulate person (she hesitated

364

Rosa looks relieved. That's good, she says. There's been talk that the novel is a hoax, that it wasn't written by my grandmother. I couldn't be sure myself, so I hired a handwriting expert to examine the original manuscript. His report came in on Saturday, and he says it's genuine. Just so you know. *Oracle Night* was written by Sylvia Maxwell.

It sounds as if you liked the book, Nick says, and Rosa says yes, she was very moved by it. If it was written in 1927, he continues, then it came after *The Burning House* and *Redemption* but before *Landscape with Trees* – which would have made it her third novel. She was still under thirty then, wasn't she?

Twenty-eight, Rosa says. The same age I am now.

The conversation goes on for another fifteen or twenty minutes. Nick has a hundred things to do that morning, but he can't bring himself to

---

frequently between thoughts, confined her vocabulary to small, functional words, seemed to have no gift for abstraction), and nothing she said that afternoon was particularly brilliant or memorable. Other than making a few friendly remarks about my book, she gave no sign to suggest that she was even remotely interested in me. And yet there I was in a state of maximum torment – *burning* and *longing* and *pining*, a man trapped in the snares of love.

She was five feet eight inches tall and weighed a hundred and twenty-five pounds. Slender neck, long arms and long fingers, pale skin, and short dirty-blonde hair. That hair, I later realized, bore some resemblance to the hair shown in the drawings of the hero of *The Little Prince* – choppy juts of spikes and curls – and perhaps the association enhanced the somewhat androgynous aura that Grace projected. The mannish clothes she was wearing that afternoon must have played their part in creating the image as well: black jeans, white T-shirt, and a pale blue linen jacket. About five minutes into her visit, she removed the jacket and draped it over the back of her chair, and when I saw her arms, those long, smooth, infinitely feminine arms of hers, I knew there would be no rest for me until I was able to touch them, until I had earned the right to put my hands on her body and run them over her bare skin.

But I want to go deeper than Grace's body, deeper than the incidental facts of her physical self. Bodies count, of course – they count more than we're willing to admit – but we don't fall in love with bodies, we fall in love with each other, and if much of what we are is confined to flesh and bone, there is much that is not as well. We all know that, but the minute we go beyond a catalogue of surface qualities and appearances, words begin to fail us, to crumble apart in mystical confusions and cloudy, insubstantial metaphors. Some call it *the flame of being*. Others call it *the internal spark* or *the inner light of selfhood*. Still others refer to it as *the fires of quiddity*. The terms always draw on images of heat and illumination, and that force, that essence of life we sometimes refer to as soul, is always communicated to another person through the eyes. Surely the poets were correct to insist on this point. The mystery of desire ask her to leave. There is something so forthright about this girl, so lucid, so lacking in self-deception, that he wants to go on looking at her for a little while and absorb the full impact of her presence – which is beautiful, he decides, precisely because she is unaware of it, because of her absolute disregard of the effect she has on others. Nothing of consequence is said. He learns that Rosa is the daughter of Sylvia Maxwell's oldest son (who was a product of Maxwell's second marriage, to theater director Stuart Leightman) and that she was born and raised in Chicago. When Nick asks her why she was so keen on having the book sent to him first, she says she knows nothing about the publishing business, but Alice Lazarre is her favorite living novelist, and when she found out that Nick was her editor, she decided he was the man for her grandmother's book. Nick smiles. Alice will be pleased, he says, and a few minutes later, when Rosa finally stands up to make her exit, he pulls some books off a shelf in his office and gives her a stack of Alice Lazarre first editions. I hope you're not disappointed in *Oracle Night*, Rosa says. Why should I be disappointed? Nick asks. Sylvia Maxwell was a first-rate novelist. Well, Rosa says, this book is different from the others. In what way? Nick asks. I don't know, Rosa says, in every way. You'll find out for yourself when you read it.

begins by looking into the eyes of the beloved, for it is only there that one can catch a glimpse of who that person is.

Grace's eyes were blue. A dark blue flecked with traces of gray, perhaps some brown, perhaps some hints of hazelish contrast as well. They were complex eyes, eyes that changed color according to the intensity and timbre of the light that fell on them at a given moment, and the first time I saw her that day in Betty's office, it occurred to me that I had never met a woman who exuded such composure, such tranquillity of bearing, as if Grace, who was not yet twenty-seven at the time, had already moved on to some higher state of being than the rest of us. I don't mean to suggest that there was anything withheld about her, that she floated above her circumstances in some beatific haze of condescension or indifference. On the contrary, she was quite animated throughout the meeting, laughed readily, smiled, said all the appropriate things, and made all the appropriate gestures, but underneath a professional engagement in the ideas that Betty and I were proposing to her, I felt a startling absence of inner struggle, an equilibrium of mind that seemed to exempt her from the usual conflicts and aggressions of modern life: self-doubt, envy, sarcasm, the need to judge or belittle others, the scalding, unbearable ache of personal ambition. Grace was young, but she had an old and weathered soul, and as I sat with her that first day in the offices of Holst & McDermott, looking into her eyes and studying the contours of her lean, angular body, that was what I fell in love with: the sense of calm that enveloped her, the radiant silence burning within.

There were other decisions to be made, of course, a host of significant details that still had to be conjured up and worked into the scene – for purposes of fullness and authenticity, for narrative ballast. How long has Rosa been living in New York? for example. What does she do here? Does she have a job and, if so, is the job important to her or simply a means of generating enough money to cover the rent? What about the status of her love life? Is she single or married, attached or unattached, on the prowl or patiently waiting for the right person to come along? My first impulse was to make her a photographer, or perhaps an assistant film editor – work that was connected to images, not words, just as Grace's job was. Definitely unmarried, definitely never married, but perhaps involved with someone, or, even better, perhaps recently broken up after a long, tortured affair. I didn't want to dwell on any of those questions for the time being, nor on similar questions relating to Nick's wife – profession, family background, taste in music, books, and so on. I wasn't writing the story yet, I was merely sketching out the action in rough strokes, and I couldn't afford to bog myself down in the minutiae of secondary concerns. That would have forced me to stop and think, and for the moment I was only interested in forging ahead, in seeing where the pictures in my mind were going to take me. It wasn't about control; it wasn't even about making choices. My job that morning was simply to follow what was happening inside me, and in order to do that I had to keep the pen moving as fast as I could.

Nick is not a rogue or a seducer of women. He has not made a habit of cheating on his wife during the course of their marriage, and he is not aware of having any designs on Sylvia Maxwell's granddaughter now. But there is no question that he feels attracted to her, that he has been pulled in by the iridescence and simplicity of her manner, and the moment she stands up and leaves the office, it flashes through his mind – an unbidden thought, the figurative thunderclap of lust – that he would probably do anything to go to bed with this woman, even to the point of sacrificing his marriage. Men produce such thoughts twenty times a day, and just because a person experiences a momentary flicker of arousal doesn't mean he has any intention of acting on the impulse, but still, no sooner does Nick play out the thought in his head than he feels disgusted with himself, stung by a sensation of guilt. To appease his conscience, he calls his wife at her office (law firm, brokerage house, hospital – to be determined later) and announces that he is going to book a reservation at their favorite downtown restaurant and take her to dinner that night.

They meet there at eight o'clock. Things go pleasantly enough through drinks and the appetizer course, but then they begin to discuss some minor household matter (a broken chair, the imminent arrival of one of Eva's cousins in New York, a thing of no importance), and soon they have fallen into an argument. Not a vehement one, perhaps, but enough irritation enters their voices to destroy the mood. Nick apologizes and Eva accepts; Eva apologizes and Nick accepts; but the conversation has gone flat, and there is no recapturing the harmony of just a few minutes ago. By the time the main course is delivered to the table, they are both sitting there in silence. The restaurant is packed, humming with animation, and as Nick absently casts his eyes around the room, he catches sight of Rosa Leightman, sitting at a corner table with five or six other people. Eva notices him looking off in that direction and asks if he's seen someone he knows. That girl, Nick says. She was in my office this morning. He goes on to tell her something about Rosa, mentions the novel written by her grandmother, Sylvia Maxwell, and then tries to change the subject, but Eva has turned her head by then and is looking across the room at Rosa's table. She's very beautiful, Nick says, don't you think? Not bad, Eva answers. But strange hair, Nicky, and really terrible clothes. It doesn't matter, Nick says. She's alive – more alive than anyone I've met in months. She's the kind of woman who could turn a man inside out.

It's an awful thing for a man to say to his wife, especially to a wife who feels her husband has begun to drift away from her. Well, Eva says defensively, too bad you're stuck with me. Would you like me to go over there and ask her to join us? I've never seen a man turned inside out before. Maybe I'll learn something.

Realizing the thoughtless cruelty of what he's just said, Nick tries to undo the damage. I wasn't talking about myself, he replies. I just meant a man – any man. Man in the abstract.

After dinner, Nick and Eva return to their place in the West Village. It's a tidy, well-appointed duplex on Barrow Street – John Trause's apartment, in fact, which I appropriated for my Flitcraftian tale as a silent bow to the man who'd suggested the idea to me. Nick has a letter to write, some bills to pay, and as Eva prepares herself for bed, he sits down at the dining room table to attend to these small tasks. It takes him three quarters of an hour, but even though it's getting late now, he feels restless, not yet ready for sleep. He pokes his head into the bedroom, sees that Eva is still awake, and tells her he's going out to mail the letters. Just down to the box at the corner, he says. I'll be back in five minutes.

That's when it happens. Bowen picks up his briefcase (which still contains the manuscript of *Oracle Night*), tosses in the letters, and goes out on his errand. It is early spring, and a stiff wind is blowing through the city, rattling the street signs and stirring up bits of paper and debris. Still brooding about his disturbing encounter with Rosa that morning, still trying to make sense of the doubly disturbing accident of having seen her again that night, Nick walks to the corner in a fog, scarcely paying attention to where he is. He removes the letters from his briefcase and slips them into the mailbox. Something inside him has been broken, he tells himself, and for the first time since his troubles with Eva began, he's willing to admit the truth of his situation: that his marriage has failed, that his life has come to a dead end. Rather than turn around and immediately head home, he decides to go on walking for a few more minutes. He continues down the street, turns at the corner, walks down another street, and then turns again at the next corner. Eleven stories above him, the head of a small limestone gargoyle attached to the façade of an apartment building is slowly breaking loose from the rest of its body as the wind continues to attack the street. Nick takes another step, and then another step, and at the moment the gargoyle head is finally dislodged, he walks straight into the trajectory of the falling object. Thus, in slightly modified form, the Flitcraft saga begins. Hurtling down within inches of Nick's head, the gargoyle grazes his right arm, knocks the briefcase out of his hand, and then shatters into a thousand pieces on the sidewalk.

The impact throws Nick to the ground. He is stunned, disoriented, afraid. At first, he has no idea what has happened to him. A split second of alarm as the stone touched his sleeve, an instant of shock as the briefcase flew out of his hand, and then the noise of the gargoyle head exploding against the pavement. Several moments go by before he can reconstruct the sequence of events, and when he does, he picks himself up from the sidewalk understanding that he should be dead. The stone was meant to kill him. He left his apartment tonight for no other reason than to run into that stone, and if he's managed to escape with his life, it can only mean that a new life has been given to him – that his old life is finished, that every moment of his past now belongs to someone else.

A taxi rounds the corner and comes down the street in his direction. Nick raises his hand. The taxi stops, and Nick climbs in. Where to? the driver asks. Nick has no idea, and so he speaks the first word that enters his head. The airport, he says. Which one? the driver asks. Kennedy, La Guardia, or Newark? La Guardia, Nick says, and off they go to La Guardia. When they get there, Nick walks up to the ticket counter and asks when the next flight is leaving. Flight to where? the ticket salesman asks. Anywhere, Nick says. The salesman consults the schedule. Kansas City, he says. There's a flight that begins boarding in ten minutes. Fine, Nick says, handing the salesman his credit card, give me a ticket. One way or round-trip? the salesman asks. One way, Nick says, and half an hour later he's sitting on a plane, flying through the night toward Kansas City.

That was where I left him that morning – suspended in midair, winging madly toward an uncertain, implausible future. I wasn't sure how long I'd been at it, but I could feel myself beginning to run out of gas, so I put down my pen and stood up from the chair. All in all, I had covered eight pages in the blue notebook. That would suggest at least two or three hours' work, but the time had passed so quickly, I felt as if I'd been in there for only a few minutes. When I left the room, I headed down the hall and went into the kitchen. Unexpectedly, Grace was standing by the stove, preparing a pot of tea.

'I didn't know you were home,' she said.

'I got back a while ago,' I explained. 'I've been sitting in my room.'

Grace looked surprised. 'Didn't you hear me knock?'

'No, I'm sorry. I must have been pretty wrapped up in what I was doing.'

'When you didn't answer, I opened the door and peeked inside. But you weren't there.'

'Of course I was. I was sitting at my desk.'

'Well, I didn't see you. Maybe you were somewhere else. In the bathroom maybe.'

'I don't remember going to the bathroom. As far as I know, I was sitting at my desk the whole time.'

Grace shrugged. 'If you say so, Sidney,' she answered. She was clearly in no mood to pick a quarrel. Intelligent woman that she was, she gave me one of her glorious, enigmatic smiles and then turned back to the stove to finish preparing the tea.

The rain stopped at some point in the middle of the afternoon, and several hours later a battered blue Ford from one of the local car services drove us across the Brooklyn Bridge for our biweekly dinner with John

Trause. Since my return from the hospital, the three of us had made a point of getting together every other Saturday night, alternating meals at our place in Brooklyn (where we cooked for John) with elaborate culinary blowouts at Chez Pierre, an expensive new restaurant in the West Village (where John always insisted on picking up the tab). The original program for that night had been to meet at the bar of Chez Pierre at seven-thirty, but John had called earlier in the week to say that something was wrong with his leg and that he would have to cancel. It turned out to be an attack of phlebitis (an inflammation of the vein brought on by the presence of a blood clot), but then John had called back on Friday afternoon to tell us that he was feeling a little better. He wasn't supposed to walk, he said, but if we didn't mind coming to his apartment and ordering in Chinese food, maybe we could have our dinner after all. 'I'd hate to miss seeing you and Gracie,' he said. 'Since I have to eat something anyway, why don't we all do it here together? As long as I keep my leg up, it really doesn't hurt too much anymore.'[4]

I had stolen John's apartment for my story in the blue notebook, and when we got to Barrow Street and he opened the door to let us in, I had the strange, not altogether unpleasant feeling that I was entering an imaginary space, walking into a room that wasn't there. I had visited Trause's apartment countless times in the past, but now that I had spent

---

4. John was the only person in the world who still called her *Gracie*. Not even her parents did that anymore, and I myself, who had been involved with her for more than three years, had never once addressed her by that diminutive. But John had known her all her life – literally from the day she was born – and a number of special privileges had accrued to him over time, elevating him from the rank of family friend to unofficial blood relation. It was as if he had achieved the status of favorite uncle – or, if you will, godfather-without-portfolio.

John loved Grace, and Grace loved him back, and because I was the man in Grace's life, John had welcomed me into the inner circle of his affections. During the period of my collapse, he had sacrificed much of his time and energy to helping Grace through the crisis, and when I finally recovered from my brush with death, he started turning up at the hospital every afternoon to sit by my bed and keep me company – to keep me (as I later realized) in the land of the living. When Grace and I went to visit him for dinner that night (September 18, 1982), I doubt that anyone in New York was closer to John than we were. Nor was anyone closer to us than John. That would explain why he considered our Saturday nights so important and hadn't wanted to break the date, in spite of the problem with his leg. He lived alone, and since he rarely circulated in public, seeing us had become his principal form of social entertainment, his only real chance to indulge in a few hours of uninterrupted conversation.

371

several hours thinking about it in my own apartment in Brooklyn, peopling it with the invented characters of my story, it seemed to belong as much to the world of fiction as to the world of solid objects and flesh-and-blood human beings. Unexpectedly, this feeling didn't go away. If anything, it grew stronger as the night went on, and by the time the Chinese food arrived at eight-thirty, I was already beginning to settle into what I would have to call (for want of a better term) a state of double consciousness. I was both a part of what was going on around me and cut off from it, drifting freely in my mind as I imagined myself sitting at my desk in Brooklyn, writing about this place in the blue notebook, and sitting in a chair on the top floor of a Manhattan duplex, firmly anchored in my body, listening to what John and Grace were saying to each other and even adding some remarks of my own. It's not unusual for a person to be so preoccupied as to appear absent – but the point was that I wasn't absent. I was there, fully engaged in what was happening, and at the same time I wasn't there – for the there wasn't an authentic there anymore. It was an illusory place that existed in my head, and that's where I was as well. In both places at the same time. In the apartment and in the story. In the story in the apartment that I was still writing in my head.

John appeared to be in a lot more pain than he was willing to admit. He was leaning on a crutch when he opened the door, and as I watched him limp up the stairs and then hobble back to his place on the sofa – a big sagging affair festooned with a pile of pillows and blankets for propping up his leg – he was wincing noticeably, suffering with every step he took. But John wasn't about to make a big production of it. He had fought in the Pacific as an eighteen-year-old private at the end of World War II, and he belonged to that generation of men who considered it a point of honor never to feel sorry for themselves, who recoiled in disdain whenever anyone tried to fuss over them. Other than making a couple of cracks about Richard Nixon, who had given the word *phlebitis* a certain comic resonance in the days of his administration, John stubbornly refused to talk about his infirmity. No, that's not quite correct. After we entered the upstairs room, he allowed Grace to help him onto the sofa and to reposition the pillows and blankets, apologizing for what he called his 'moronic decrepitude.' Then, once he had settled into his spot, he turned to me and said, 'We're quite a pair, aren't we, Sid? You with your wobbles and nosebleeds, and now me with this leg. We're the goddamn gimps of the universe.'

Trause had never been overly attentive to his appearance, but that night he looked particularly disheveled to me, and from the rumpled condition of his blue jeans and cotton sweater – not to speak of the grayish tinge that had spread over the bottoms of his white socks – I gathered he'd been wearing that outfit for several days in a row. Not surprisingly, his hair was mussed, and the back strands had been flattened and stiffened after lying on the sofa for so many hours in the past week. The truth was that John looked haggard, considerably older than he had ever looked to me before, but when a man is in pain, and no doubt losing much sleep because of that pain, he can hardly be expected to look his best. I wasn't alarmed by what I saw, but Grace, who was normally the most unruffled person I knew, seemed flustered and upset by John's condition. Before we could get down to the business of ordering the food, she grilled him for ten solid minutes about doctors, medicines, and prognoses, and then, once he'd assured her he wasn't going to die, she moved on to a host of practical concerns: grocery shopping, cooking, trash removal, laundry, the daily routine. Madame Dumas had it all under control, John said, referring to the woman from Martinique who had been cleaning his apartment for the past two years, and when she wasn't available, her daughter came instead. 'Twenty years old,' he added, 'and very intelligent. Nice to look at, too, by the way. She doesn't walk so much as glide around the room, as if her feet weren't touching the floor. It gives me a chance to practice my French.'

The matter of John's leg aside, he seemed glad to be with us, and he talked more than he usually did on such occasions, rattling on steadily for most of the evening. I can't be certain, but I believe it was the pain that loosened his tongue and kept him going. The words must have provided a distraction from the tumult coursing through his leg, a frenzied sort of relief. That, and the vast quantities of alcohol he consumed as well. As each new bottle of wine was uncorked, John was the first to hold out his glass, and of the three bottles we drank that night, roughly half the contents wound up in his system. That makes a bottle and a half of wine, along with the two glasses of straight Scotch he drank toward the end. I had seen him drink that much a few times in the past, but no matter how well lubricated John became, he never appeared to be drunk. No slurred speech, no glassiness in the eyes. He was a big person – six-two, a shade under two hundred pounds – and he could hold it.

'About a week before this leg thing started,' he said, 'I got a call from

Tina's brother Richard.[5] I hadn't heard from him in a long time. Not since the day of the funeral, in fact, which means we're talking about eight years – more than eight years. I'd never had much to do with her family while we were married, and now that she wasn't there anymore, I hadn't bothered to stay in touch with them. Nor they with me, for that matter – not that I particularly cared. All those Ostrow brothers, with their cruddy furniture store on Springfield Avenue and their boring wives and their mediocre children. Tina had about eight or nine first cousins, but she was the only one with any spirit, the only one who'd had the gumption to break out of that little New Jersey world and try to make something of herself. So it surprised me when Richard called the other day. He lives in Florida now, he said, and had come to New York on a business trip. Would I be interested in going out to dinner with him? Somewhere nice, he said, his treat. Since I didn't have any other

---

5. Tina was John's second wife. His first marriage had lasted ten years (from 1954 to 1964) and had ended in divorce. He never talked about it in my presence, but Grace had told me that no one in her family had been particularly fond of Eleanor. The Tebbetts had seen her as a stuck-up Bryn Mawr girl from a long line of Massachusetts bluebloods, a 'cold fish' who had always looked down her nose at John's working-class Paterson, New Jersey, family. No matter that Eleanor was a respected painter whose reputation was nearly as important as John's. They weren't surprised when the marriage ended, and not one of them was sorry to see her go. The only pity, Grace said, was that John had been forced to remain in contact with her. Not through any desire on his part, but because of the ongoing antics of their troubled, wildly unstable son, Jacob.

Then he had met Tina Ostrow, a dancer-choreographer twelve years younger than he was, and when he married her in 1966, the Tebbetts clan applauded the decision. They felt confident that John had finally found the woman he deserved, and time proved them right. The small and vibrant Tina was an adorable person, Grace said, and she had loved John (in Grace's words) 'to the point of worship.' The only problem with the marriage was that Tina didn't live long enough to see her thirty-seventh birthday. Uterine cancer slowly took her from him over the course of eighteen months, and after John buried her, Grace said, he shut down for a long time, 'just froze up and sort of stopped breathing.' He moved to Paris for a year, then to Rome, then to a small village on the northern coast of Portugal. When he returned to New York in 1978 and settled into the apartment on Barrow Street, it had been three years since his last novel had been published, and the rumor was that Trause hadn't written a word since Tina's death. Four more years had passed since then, and still he hadn't produced anything – at least not anything he was willing to show anyone. But he was working. I knew he was working. He'd told me as much himself, but I didn't know what kind of work it was, for the simple reason that I hadn't found the nerve to ask.

plans, I accepted. I don't know why I did, but there wasn't any compelling reason not to, and so we arranged to meet the next night at eight o'clock.

'You have to understand about Richard. He'd always struck me as a featherweight, a person without substance. He was born a year after Tina, which would make him about forty-three now, and except for a few moments of glory as a high school basketball player, he'd stumbled around for most of his life, flunking out of two or three colleges, moving from one dismal job to the next, never marrying, never really growing up. A sweet disposition, I suppose, but shallow and uninspired, with a kind of slack-jawed dopiness that always got on my nerves. About the only thing I ever liked about him was his devotion to Tina. He loved her every bit as much as I did – that's certain, an uncontestable fact – and I'm not going to deny that he was a good brother to her, an exemplary brother. You were at the funeral, Gracie. You remember what happened. Hundreds of people showed up, and every person in the chapel was sobbing, moaning, wailing in horror. It was a flood of collective grief, suffering on a scale I'd never witnessed before. But of all the mourners in that room, Richard was the one who suffered the most. He and I together, sitting in the front pew. When the service was over, he nearly passed out when he tried to get to his feet. It took all my strength to hold him up. I literally had to throw my arms around his body to stop him from falling to the floor.

'But that was years ago. We lived through that trauma together, and then I lost track of him. When I agreed to have dinner the other night, I was expecting to have a dull time of it, to slog my way through a couple of hours of awkward conversation and then dash for the door and head home. But I was wrong. I'm happy to report that I was wrong. It always stimulates me to discover new examples of my own prejudice and stupidity, to realize that I don't know half as much as I think I do.

'It started with the pleasure of seeing his face. I'd forgotten how much he resembled his sister, how many features they had in common. The set and slant of the eyes, the rounded chin, the elegant mouth, the bridge of the nose – it was Tina in a man's body, or little flashes of her at any rate, darting out at random moments. It overwhelmed me to be with her again like that, to feel her presence again, to feel that a part of her had lived on in her brother. A couple of times Richard turned in a certain way, gestured in a certain way, did a certain something with his eyes, and I was so moved that I wanted to lean across the table and kiss him. Smack on the lips – a full-bore osculation. You'll probably laugh, but I'm actually sorry now that I didn't.

'Richard was still Richard, the selfsame Richard of yore – but better, somehow, more comfortable in his own skin. He's gotten himself married and has two little girls. Maybe that's helped. Maybe being eight years older has helped, I don't know. He's still grinding away at one of those sad-sack jobs of his – computer parts salesman, efficiency consultant, I forget what it was – and he still spends every evening in front of the television set. Football games, sitcoms, cop shows, nature specials – he loves everything about television. But he never reads, never votes, never even bothers to pretend to have an opinion about what's going on in the world. He's known me for sixteen years, and in all that time he hasn't once taken the trouble to open one of my books. I don't mind, of course, but I mention it in order to show how lazy he is, how thoroughly lacking in curiosity. And yet I enjoyed being with him the other night. I enjoyed listening to him talk about his favorite TV programs, about his wife and two daughters, about his ever-improving tennis game, about the advantages of living in Florida over New Jersey. Better climate, you understand. No more snowstorms and icy winters; summer every day of the year. So ordinary, children, so fucking complacent, and yet – how shall I put it? – utterly at peace with himself, so contented with his life that I almost envied him for it.

'So there we were, eating an unremarkable dinner in an unremarkable midtown restaurant, talking about nothing of any great importance, when Richard suddenly looked up from his plate and began to tell me a story. That's why I've been telling you all this – in order to get to Richard's story. I don't know if you'll agree with me, but it strikes me as one of the most interesting things I've heard in a long time.

'Three or four months ago, Richard was in his garage at home, looking for something in a cardboard box, when he came across an old 3-D viewer. He vaguely remembered that his parents had bought it when he was a kid, but he couldn't recall the circumstances or what they'd used it for. Unless he'd blanked out the experience, he was fairly certain he'd never looked through it, had never even held it in his hands. When he lifted it out of the box and started to examine it, he saw that it wasn't one of those cheap, flimsy things used for looking at ready-made pictures of tourist sites and pretty scenery. It was a solid, well-built optical instrument, a prize relic from the 3-D craze of the early fifties. The fad didn't last long, but the idea was to take your own 3-D pictures with a special camera, develop them as slides, and then look at them through the viewer, which served as a kind of three-dimensional photo album. The camera was missing, but Richard found a box of slides. There were just twelve of them, he said, which seemed to suggest his parents had shot only one roll of film with their novelty camera – and then had stowed it away somewhere and forgotten all about it.

'Not knowing what to expect, Richard put one of the slides in the viewer, pressed down on the background illuminator button, and had a look. In one instant, he said, thirty years of his life were erased. It was 1953, and he was in the living room of his family's house in West Orange, New Jersey, standing among the guests at Tina's sixteenth birthday party. He remembered everything now: the Sweet Sixteen bash, the caterers unpacking their food in the kitchen and lining up champagne glasses on the counter, the ringing of the doorbell, the music, the din of voices, the chignon knot in Tina's hair, the whooshing of her long yellow dress. One by one, he put each slide in the viewer and looked at all twelve of them. Everyone was there, he said. His mother and father, his cousins, his aunts and uncles, his sister, his sister's friends, and even himself, a scrawny fourteen-year-old with his protruding Adam's apple, flat-top haircut, and red clip-on bow tie. It wasn't like looking at normal photographs, he explained. It wasn't even like looking at home movies – which always disappoint you with their jerky images and washed-out colors, their sense of belonging to the remote past. The 3-D pictures were incredibly well preserved, supernaturally sharp. Everyone in them looked alive, brimming with energy, present in the moment, a part of some eternal now that had gone on perpetuating itself for close to thirty years. Intense colors, the minutest details shining in utmost clarity, and an illusion of surrounding space, of depth. The longer he looked at the slides, Richard said, the more he felt that he could see the figures breathing, and every time he stopped and went on to the next one, he had the impression that if he'd looked a little longer – just one more moment – they actually would have started to move.

'After he'd looked at each slide once, he looked at them all again, and the second time around it gradually occurred to him that most of the people in the pictures were now dead. His father, killed by a heart attack in 1969. His mother, killed by kidney failure in 1972. Tina, killed by cancer in 1974. And of his six aunts and uncles in attendance that day, four of them dead and buried as well. In one picture, he was standing on the front lawn with his parents and Tina. It was just the four of them – arms linked, leaning into one another, a row of four smiling faces, ridiculously animated, mugging for the camera – and when Richard put that one into the viewer for the second time, his eyes suddenly filled with tears. That was the one that did him in, he said, the one that was too much for him. He was standing on the lawn with three ghosts, he realized, the only survivor from that afternoon thirty years ago, and once the tears started, there was nothing he could do to stop them. He put down the viewer, lifted his hands over his face, and began to sob. That was the word he used when he told me the story: *sob*. "I sobbed my guts out," he said. "I completely lost it."

'This was Richard, remember – a man with no poetry in him, a man with the sensitivity of a doorknob – and yet once he found those pictures, he couldn't think about anything else. The viewer was a magic lantern that allowed him to travel through time and visit the dead. He would look at the pictures in the morning before he left for work, and he would look at them in the evening after he came home. Always in the garage, always by himself, always away from his wife and children – obsessively returning to that afternoon in 1953, unable to get enough of it. The spell lasted for two months, and then one morning Richard went into the garage and the viewer didn't work. The machine had jammed up, and he couldn't depress the button anymore to turn on the light. He'd probably used it too much, he said, and since he didn't know how to fix it, he assumed the adventure was over, that the marvelous thing he'd discovered had been taken away from him for good. It was a catastrophic loss, the cruelest of deprivations. He couldn't even look at the slides by holding them up to the light. Three-D pictures aren't conventional photographs, and you need the viewer to translate them into coherent images. No viewer, no image. No image, no more time travel into the past. No more time travel, no more joy. Another round of grief, another round of sorrow – as if, after bringing them back to life, he had to bury the dead all over again.

'That was the situation when I saw him two weeks ago. The machine was broken, and Richard was still trying to come to grips with what had happened to him. I can't tell you how touched I was by his story. To see this bumbling, ordinary man turned into a philosophical dreamer, an anguished soul longing for the unattainable. I told him I'd do anything I could to help. This is New York, I said, and since everything in the world can be found in New York, there has to be someone in the city who can fix it. Richard was a little embarrassed by my enthusiasm, but he thanked me for the offer, and that was where we left it. The next morning, I got busy. I called around, did some research, and within a day or two I'd tracked down the owner of a camera shop on West Thirty-first Street who thought he could do it. Richard was back in Florida by then, and when I called him that night to tell him the news, I thought he'd be excited, that we'd immediately start talking about how to pack up the viewer and ship it to New York. But there was a long pause on the other end of the line. "I don't know, John," Richard finally said. "I've thought about it a lot since I saw you, and maybe it's not such a good idea for me to be looking at those pictures all the time. Arlene was getting pretty upset, and I wasn't really paying much attention to the girls. Maybe it's better this way. You have to live in the present, right? The past is past, and no matter how much time I spend with those pictures, I'm never going to get it back."'

That was the end of the story. A disappointing end, John felt, but Grace disagreed with him. After communing with the dead for two months, Richard had put himself in danger, she said, and was perhaps running the risk of falling into a serious depression. I was about to say something then, but just as I opened my mouth to offer my opinion, I got another one of my infernal nosebleeds. They had started a month or two before I was put in the hospital, and even though most of my other symptoms had cleared up by now, the nosebleeds had persisted – always striking at the most inopportune moments, it seemed, and never failing to cause me intense embarrassment. I hated not to be in control of myself, to be sitting in a room as I was that night, for example, taking part in a conversation, and then suddenly to notice that blood was pouring out of me, splattering onto my shirt and pants, and not being able to do a damn thing to stop it. The doctors had told me not to worry – there were no medical consequences, no signs of impending trouble – but that didn't make me feel any less helpless or ashamed. Every time my nose gushed blood, I felt like a little boy who'd wet his pants.

I jumped out of the chair, pressed a handkerchief against my face, and hustled toward the nearest bathroom. Grace asked if I wanted any help, and I must have given her a somewhat peevish answer, although I can't remember what I said. 'Don't bother,' perhaps, or 'Leave me alone.' Something with enough irritation in it to amuse John, in any case, for I can distinctly remember hearing him laugh as I left the room. 'Old

Faithful strikes again,' he said. 'Orr's menstruating schnozz. Don't let it get you down, Sidney. At least you know you're not pregnant.'

There were two bathrooms in the apartment, one on each level of the duplex. Normally, we would have spent the evening downstairs in the dining room and living room, but John's phlebitic leg had pushed us up to the second floor, since that was where he was spending most of his time now. The upstairs room was a kind of supplementary parlor, a cozy little spot with large bay windows, bookshelves lining three of the walls, and built-in spaces for stereo equipment and TV – the perfect enclave for a recovering invalid. The bathroom on that floor was just off John's bedroom, and in order to reach the bedroom I had to walk through his study, the place where he wrote. I switched on the light when I entered that room, but I was too involved with my nosebleed to pay any attention to what was in it. I must have spent fifteen minutes in the bathroom squeezing my nostrils and tilting back my head, and until those old remedies began to work, so much liquid flowed out of me that I wondered if I wouldn't have to go to the hospital for an emergency transfusion. How red the blood looked against the whiteness of the porcelain sink, I thought. How vividly imagined that color was, how aesthetically shocking. The other fluids that came out of us were dull in comparison, the palest of squirts. Whitish spittle, milky semen, yellow pee, green-brown mucus. We excreted autumn and winter colors, but running invisibly through our veins, the very stuff that kept us alive, was the crimson of a mad artist – a red as brilliant as fresh paint.

After the attack was over, I lingered at the sink for a while, doing what I could to make myself presentable again. It was too late to remove the spots from my clothes (which had hardened into small rusty circles that smeared across the fabric when I tried to rub them out), but I gave my hands and face a thorough washing and wet down my hair, using John's comb to complete the job. I was feeling a bit less sorry for myself by then, a bit less battered. My shirt and pants were still adorned with ugly polka dots, but the river wasn't flowing anymore, and the stinging in my nose had mercifully abated.

As I walked through John's bedroom and entered his study, I glanced over at his desk. I wasn't really looking there, just casting my eyes around the room as I headed for the door, but lying out in full view, sur-rounded by an assortment of pens, pencils, and messy stacks of paper, there was a blue hardbound notebook – remarkably similar to the one I'd bought in Brooklyn that morning. A writer's desk is a holy place, the most private sanctuary in the world, and strangers aren't allowed to approach it without permission. I had never gone near John's desk before, but I was so startled, so curious to know if that notebook was the same as mine, that I forgot my discretion and went over to have a look. The notebook was closed, lying faceup on a small dictionary, and the moment I bent down to examine it, I saw that it was the exact double of the one lying on my desk at home. For reasons that still baffle me, I became enormously excited by this discovery. What difference did it make what kind of notebook John used? He had lived in Portugal for a couple of years, and no doubt they were a common item over there, available in any run-of-the-mill stationery store. Why shouldn't he be writing in a blue hardbound notebook that had been manufactured in Portugal? No reason, no reason at all – and yet, given the deliciously pleasant sensations I'd felt that morning when I'd bought my own blue notebook, and given that I'd spent several productive hours writing in it earlier that day (my first literary efforts in close to a year), and given that I'd been thinking about those efforts all through the evening at John's, it hit me as a startling conjunction, a little piece of black magic.

I wasn't planning to mention it when I returned to the sitting room. It was too nutty, somehow, too idiosyncratic and personal, and I didn't want to give John the impression that I was in the habit of snooping into his things. But when I walked into the room and saw him lying on the sofa with his leg up, staring at the ceiling with a grim, defeated look in his eyes, I suddenly changed my mind. Grace was downstairs in the kitchen, washing dishes and disposing of leftovers from our take-out meal, and so I sat down in the chair she had been occupying, which happened to be just to the right of the sofa, a couple of feet from John's head. He asked if I was feeling any better. Yes, I replied, much better, and then I leaned forward and said to him, 'The strangest thing happened to me today. When I was out on my morning walk, I went into a store and bought a notebook. It was such an excellent notebook, such an attractive and appealing little thing, that it made me want to write again. And so the minute I got home, I sat down at my desk and wrote in it for two straight hours.'

'That's good news, Sidney,' John said. 'You're starting to work again.'

'The Flitcraft episode.'

'Ah, even better.'

'We'll see. It's just some rough notes so far, nothing to get excited about. But the notebook seems to have charged me up, and I can't wait to write in it again tomorrow. It's dark blue, a very pleasant shade of dark blue, with a cloth strip running down the spine and a hard cover. Made in Portugal, of all places.'

'Portugal?'

'I don't know which city. But there's a little label on the inside back cover that says MADE IN PORTUGAL.'

'How on earth did you find one of those things here?'

'There's a new shop in my neighborhood. The Paper Palace, owned by a man named Chang. He had four of them in stock.'

'I used to buy those notebooks on my trips down to Lisbon. They're very good, very solid. Once you start using them, you don't feel like writing in anything else.'

'I had that same feeling today. I hope it doesn't mean I'm about to become addicted.'

'Addiction might be too strong a word, but there's no question that they're extremely seductive. Be careful, Sid. I've been writing in them for years, and I know what I'm talking about.'

'You make it sound as if they're dangerous.'

'It depends on what you write. Those notebooks are very friendly, but they can also be cruel, and you have to watch out that you don't get lost in them.'

'You don't look lost to me – and I just saw one lying on your desk when I left the bathroom.'

'I bought a big supply before I moved back to New York. Unfortunately, the one you saw is the last one I have, and I've almost filled it up. I didn't know you could get them in America. I was thinking of writing to the manufacturer and ordering some more.'

'The man in the shop told me that the company's gone out of business.'

'Just my luck. But I'm not surprised. Apparently there wasn't much of a demand for them.'

'I can pick one up for you on Monday, if you want.'

'Are there any blue ones left?'

'Black, red, and brown. I bought the last blue one.'

'Too bad. Blue is the only color I like. Now that the company's gone, I guess I'll have to start developing some new habits.'

'It's funny, but when I looked over the pile this morning, I went straight for the blue myself. I felt drawn to that one, as if I couldn't resist it. What do you think that means?'

382

'It doesn't mean anything, Sid. Except that you're a little off in the head. And I'm just as off as you are. We write books, don't we? What else can you expect from people like us?'

Saturday nights in New York are always crowded, but that night the streets were even more packed than usual, and what with one delay and another, it took us over an hour to get home. Grace managed to flag down a cab right outside John's door, but when we climbed in and told the driver we were going to Brooklyn, he made some excuse about being low on gas and wouldn't accept the fare. I wanted to make a stink about it, but Grace took hold of my arm and gently pulled me out of the cab. Nothing materialized after that, so we walked over to Seventh Avenue, threading our way past gangs of raucous, drunken kids and half a dozen demented panhandlers. The Village was percolating with energy that night, a madhouse jangle that seemed ready to erupt into violence at any moment, and I found it exhausting to be out among those crowds, trying to keep my balance as I clung to Grace's arm. We stood at the corner of Barrow and Seventh for a good ten minutes before an empty taxi approached us, and Grace must have apologized six times for having forced me out of the other one. 'I'm sorry I didn't let you put up a fight,' she said. 'It's my fault. The last thing you need is to be standing out in this chill, but I hate to argue with stupid people. It makes me too upset.'

But Grace wasn't only upset by stupid cabdrivers that night. A few moments after we got into the second taxi, she inexplicably began to cry. Not on a large scale, not with some breathless outrush of sobs, but the tears started gathering in the corners of her eyes, and when we stopped at Clarkson for a red light, the glare of the street lamps swept into the cab, and I could see the tears glistening in the brightness, welling up in her eyes like small expanding crystals. Grace never broke down like that. Grace never cried or gave way to excessive shows of feeling, and even at her most stressful moments (during my collapse, for example, and all through the desperate early weeks of my stay in the hospital), she seemed to have an inborn talent for holding herself together, for facing up to the darkest truths. I asked her what was wrong, but she only shook her head and turned away. When I put my hand on her shoulder and asked again, she shrugged me off – which was something she had never done before. It wasn't a terribly hostile gesture, but again, it was unlike Grace to act that way, and I admit that I felt a little stung by it.

Not wanting to impose myself on her or let her know I'd been hurt, I withdrew to my corner of the backseat and waited in silence as the cab inched southward along Seventh Avenue. When we came to the intersection at Varick and Canal, we were stalled in traffic for several minutes. It was a monumental jam-up: honking cars and trucks, drivers shouting obscenities at one another, New York mayhem in its purest form. In the middle of all that ruckus and confusion, Grace abruptly turned to me and apologized. 'It's just that he looked so terrible tonight,' she said, 'so done-in. All the men I love are falling apart. It's getting to be a little hard to take.'

I didn't believe her. My body was on the mend, and it seemed implausible that Grace would have been so disheartened by John's fleeting leg ailment. Something else was troubling her, some private torment she wasn't willing to share with me, but I knew that if I kept on hounding her to open up, it would only make things worse. I reached out and put my arm around her shoulder, then drew her slowly toward me. There was no resistance in her this time. I felt her muscles relax, and a moment later she was curling up beside me and leaning her head against my chest. I put my hand on her forehead and began stroking her hair with the flat of my palm. It was an old ritual of ours, the expression of some wordless intimacy that continued to define who we were together, and because I never grew tired of touching Grace, never grew tired of having my hands on some part of her body, I kept on doing it, repeating the gesture dozens of times as we made our way down West Broadway and crept toward the Brooklyn Bridge.

We didn't say anything to each other for several minutes. By the time the cab turned left on Chambers Street and started to approach the bridge, every ramp was clogged with traffic, and we could hardly advance at all. Our driver, whose name was Boris Stepanovich, muttered curses to himself in Russian, no doubt lamenting the folly of trying to cross over to Brooklyn on a Saturday night. I leaned forward and talked to him through the money slot in the scarred Plexiglas partition. Don't worry, I said, your patience will be rewarded. Oh? he said. And what means that? A big tip, I answered. As long as you get us there in one piece, you'll have your biggest tip of the night.

Grace let out a small laugh when she heard the malapropism – *What means that?* – and I took it as a sign that her funk was lifting. I settled back into the seat to resume stroking her head, and as we mounted the roadway of the bridge, crawling along at one mile an hour, suspended

over the river with a blaze of buildings behind us and the Statue of
Liberty off to our right, I started to talk to her – to talk for no other reason than to talk – in order to hold her attention and prevent her from
drifting away from me again.

'I made an intriguing discovery tonight,' I said.

'Something good, I hope.'

'I discovered that John and I have the same passion.'

'Oh?'

'It turns out that we're both in love with the color blue. In particular,
a defunct line of blue notebooks that used to be made in Portugal.'

'Well, blue is a good color. Very calm, very serene. It sits well in the
mind. I like it so much, I have to make a conscious effort not to use it on
all the covers I design at work.'

'Do colors really convey emotions?'

'Of course they do.'

'And moral qualities?'

'In what way?'

'Yellow for cowardice. White for purity. Black for evil. Green for
innocence.'

'Green for envy.'

'Yes, that too. But what does blue stand for?'

'I don't know. Hope, maybe.'

'And sadness. As in, I'm feeling blue. Or, I've got the blues.'

'Don't forget *true blue.*'

'Yes, you're right. Blue for loyalty.'

'But red for passion. Everyone agrees on that.'

'The Big Red Machine. The red flag of socialism.'

'The white flag of surrender.'

'The black flag of anarchism. The Green Party.'

'But red for love and hate. Red for war.'

'You carry the colors when you go into battle. That's the phrase, isn't
it?'

'I think so.'

'Are you familiar with the term *color war*?'

'It doesn't ring any bells.'

'It comes from my childhood. You spent your summers riding horses
in Virginia, but my mother sent me to a sleep-away camp in upstate New
York. Camp Pontiac, named after the Indian chief. At the end of the
summer, they'd divide everyone into two teams, and for the next four or

five days different groups from the two sides would compete against one another.'

'Compete at what?'

'Baseball, basketball, tennis, swimming, tug-of-war – even egg-and-spoon races and singing contests. Since the camp colors were red and white, one side was called the Red Team and the other was called the White Team.'

'And that's color war.'

'For a sports maniac like me, it was terrific fun. Some years I was on the White Team and other years on the Red. After a while, though, a third team was formed, a kind of secret society, a brotherhood of kindred souls. I haven't thought about it in years, but it was very important to me at the time. The Blue Team.'

'A secret brotherhood. It sounds like silly boys' stuff to me.'

'It was. No . . . actually it wasn't. When I think about it now, I don't find it silly at all.'

'You must have been different then. You never want to join anything.'

'I didn't join, I was chosen. As one of the charter members, in fact. I felt very honored.'

'You're already on Red and White. What's so special about Blue?'

'It started when I was fourteen. A new counselor came to the camp that year, someone a little older than the rest of the people on the staff – who were mostly nineteen- and twenty-year-old college students. Bruce . . . Bruce something . . . the last name will come to me later. Bruce had his BA and had already finished a year at Columbia Law School. A scrawny, gnomish little guy, a strict nonathlete working at a camp devoted to sports. But sharp-witted and funny, always challenging you with difficult questions. Adler. That's it. Bruce Adler. Commonly known as the Rabbi.'

'And he invented the Blue Team?'

'Sort of. To be more exact, he re-created it as an exercise in nostalgia.'

'I don't follow.'

'A few years earlier, he'd worked as a counselor at another camp. The colors of that camp were blue and gray. When color war broke out at the end of summer, Bruce was put on the Blue Team, and when he looked around and saw who was on the team with him, he realized it was everyone he liked, everyone he most respected. The Gray Team was just the opposite – filled with whining, unpleasant people, the dregs of the camp. In Bruce's mind, the words *Blue Team* came to stand for some-

thing more than just a bunch of rinky-dink relay races. They repre-
sented a human ideal, a tight-knit association of tolerant and sympa-
thetic individuals, the dream of a perfect society.'
  'This is getting pretty strange, Sid.'
  'I know. But Bruce didn't take it seriously. That was the beauty of the
Blue Team. The whole thing was kind of a joke.'
  'I didn't know rabbis were allowed to make jokes.'
  'They probably aren't. But Bruce wasn't a rabbi. He was just a law student with a summer job, looking for a little entertainment. When he
came to work at our camp, he told one of the other counselors about the
Blue Team, and together they decided to form a new branch, to reinvent
it as a secret organization.'
  'How did they choose you?'
  'In the middle of the night. I was fast asleep in my bed, and Bruce and
the other counselor shook me awake. "Come on," they said, "we have
something to tell you," and then they led me and two other boys into the
woods with flashlights. They had a little campfire going, and so we sat
around the fire and they told us what the Blue Team was, why they had
selected us as charter members, and what qualifications they were looking for – in case we wanted to recommend other candidates.'
  'What were they?'
  'Nothing specific, really. Blue Team members didn't conform to a single type, and each one was a distinct and independent person. But no
one was allowed in who didn't have a good sense of humor – however
that humor might have expressed itself. Some people crack jokes all the
time; others can lift an eyebrow at the right moment and suddenly
everyone in the room is rolling on the floor. A good sense of humor,
then, a taste for the ironies of life, and an appreciation of the absurd. But
also a certain modesty and discretion, kindness toward others, a generous heart. No blowhards or arrogant fools, no liars or thieves. A Blue
Team member had to be curious, a reader of books, and aware of the
fact that he couldn't bend the world to the shape of his will. An astute
observer, someone capable of making fine moral distinctions, a lover of
justice. A Blue Team member would give you the shirt off his back if he
saw you were in need, but he would much rather slip a ten-dollar bill
into your pocket when you weren't looking. Is it beginning to make
sense? I can't pin it down for you and say it's one thing or another. It's
all of them at once, each separate part interacting with all the others.'
  'What you're describing is a good person. Pure and simple. My

father's term for it is *honest man*. Betty Stolowitz uses the word *mensch*. John says *not an asshole*. They're all the same thing.'

'Maybe. But I like *Blue Team* better. It implies a connection among the members, a bond of solidarity. If you're on the Blue Team, you don't have to explain your principles. They're immediately understood by how you act.'

'But people don't always act the same way. They're good one minute and bad the next. They make mistakes. Good people do bad things, Sid.'

'Of course they do. I'm not talking about perfection.'

'Yes you are. You're talking about people who've decided they're better than other people, who feel morally superior to the rest of us common folk. I'll bet you and your friends had a secret handshake, didn't you? To set you apart from the riffraff and the dumbbells, right? To make you think you had some special knowledge no one else was smart enough to have.'

'Jesus, Grace. It was just a little thing from twenty years ago. You don't have to break it down and analyze it.'

'But you still believe in that junk. I can hear it in your voice.'

'I don't believe in anything. Being alive – that's what I believe in. Being alive and being with you. That's all there is for me, Grace. There's nothing else, not a single thing in the whole goddamn world.'

It was a dispiriting way for the conversation to end. My not-so-subtle attempt to tease her out of her dark mood had worked for a while, but then I'd pushed her too far, accidentally touching on the wrong subject, and she'd turned on me with that caustic denunciation. It was entirely out of character for her to talk with such belligerence. Grace seldom got herself worked up over issues of that sort, and whenever we'd had similar discussions in the past (those floating, meandering dialogues that aren't about anything, that just dance along from one random association to the next), she'd tended to be amused by the notions I'd toss out at her, rarely taking them seriously or presenting a counterargument, content to play along and let me spout my meaningless opinions. But not that night, not on the night of the day in question, and because she was suddenly fighting back tears again, engulfed by the same unhappiness that had swept over her at the beginning of the ride, I understood that she was in genuine distress, unable to stop brooding about the nameless thing that was tormenting her. There were a dozen questions I wanted to ask, but again I held back, knowing that she wouldn't confide in me until she was good and ready to talk – assuming she ever was.

We had made it over the bridge by then and were traveling down Henry Street, a narrow thoroughfare flanked by redbrick walkups that led from Brooklyn Heights to our place in Cobble Hill, just below Atlantic Avenue. It wasn't personal, I realized. Grace's little outburst hadn't been against me so much as a reaction to what I'd said – a spark produced by an accidental collision between my comments and her own train of thought. *Good people do bad things.* Had Grace done something wrong? Had someone close to her done something wrong? It was impossible to know, but someone felt guilty about something, I decided, and even though my words had triggered Grace's defensive remarks, I was fairly certain they had nothing to do with me. As if to prove that point, a moment after we crossed Atlantic Avenue and headed into the final leg of the journey, Grace reached out her hand and took hold of the back of my neck, then pulled me toward her and pressed her mouth against mine, slowly pushing in her tongue for a long, provocative kiss – *a full-bore osculation*, as Trause had put it. 'Make love to me tonight,' she whispered. 'The second we walk through the door, tear off my clothes and make love to me. Break me in two, Sid.'

We slept late the next morning, not climbing out of bed until eleven-thirty or twelve. One of Grace's cousins was in town for the day, and they were planning to meet at the Guggenheim at two, then work their way down to the Met for a few hours in the permanent collection. Looking at paintings was Grace's preferred weekend activity, and she scrambled out of the house at one in reasonably tranquil spirits.[6] I offered to walk her to the subway, but she was already running late by

---

6. Much of her graphic work was inspired by looking at art, and before my collapse at the beginning of the year, we had often spent our Saturday afternoons wandering in and out of galleries and museums together. In some sense, art had made our marriage possible, and without the intervention of art, I doubt that I would have found the courage to pursue her. It was fortunate that we had met in the neutral surroundings of Holst & McDermott, a so-called work environment. If we had been thrown together in any other way – at a dinner party, for example, or on a bus or a plane – I wouldn't have been able to contact her again without exposing my intentions, and I instinctively felt that Grace had to be approached with caution. If I tipped my hand too early, I was almost certain I would lose my chance with her forever.

Luckily, I had an excuse to call. She had been assigned to work on the cover of my book, and under the pretext of having a new idea to discuss with her, I rang up her office two days after our initial meeting and asked if I could come in and see her.

then, and since the station was a good distance from the house (all the way up on Montague Street), she didn't want me to overexert myself by having to walk so many blocks at too fast a pace. I accompanied her down the stairs and out onto the street, but at the first corner we said good-bye and walked off in opposite directions. Grace sped up Court Street toward the Heights, and I ambled down a few blocks to Landolfi's Candy Store and bought a pack of cigarettes. That was the extent of my constitutional for the day. I was eager to return to the blue notebook, and so rather than take my usual walk around the neighborhood, I immediately turned around and went home. Ten minutes later, I was in the apartment, sitting at my desk in the room at the end of the hall. I opened the notebook, turned to the page where I had left off on Saturday, and settled down to work. I didn't bother to read over what I had written so far. I just picked up the pen and started to write.

Bowen is on the plane, flying through the dark toward Kansas City. After the whirlwind of falling gargoyles and reckless dashes to the airport, a sense of growing calm, a serene blankness within. Bowen doesn't question what he is doing. He has no regrets, doesn't rethink his deci-

---

'Anytime you like,' she said. *Anytime* proved to be difficult to arrange. I had a regular job then (teaching history at John Jay High School in Brooklyn), and I couldn't make it to her office before four o'clock. As it happened, Grace's agenda was clogged with late-afternoon appointments for the rest of the week. When she suggested that we meet the following Monday or Tuesday, I told her I was going out of town to give a reading (which happened to be true, but I probably would have said it even if it wasn't), so Grace relented and offered to squeeze in some time for me after work on Friday. 'I have to be somewhere at eight,' she said, 'but if we met for an hour or so at five-thirty, it shouldn't be a problem.'

I had stolen the title of my book from a 1938 pencil drawing by Willem de Kooning. *Self-Portrait with Imaginary Brother* is a small, delicately rendered piece that depicts two boys standing side by side, one a year or two older than the other, one in long pants, the other in knickers. Much as I admired the drawing, it was the title that interested me, and I had used it not because I wanted to refer to de Kooning but because of the words themselves, which I found highly evocative and which seemed to fit the novel I had written. In Betty Stolowitz's office earlier that week, I had suggested putting de Kooning's drawing on the cover. Now I was planning to tell Grace that I thought it was a bad idea – that the pencil strokes were too faint and wouldn't be visible enough, that the effect would be too muted. But I didn't really care. If I had argued against the drawing in Betty's office, I would have been for it now. All I wanted was a chance to see Grace again – and art was my way in, the one subject that wouldn't compromise my true purpose.

Her willingness to see me after office hours gave me hope, but at the same time the news that she was going out at eight o'clock all but destroyed that hope. There was

sion to leave town and abandon his job, feels not the slightest pang of remorse about walking out on Eva. He knows how hard it will be on her, but he manages to persuade himself that she'll be better off without him in the end, that once she recovers from the shock of his disappearance, it will be possible for her to begin a new, more satisfying life. Hardly an admirable or sympathetic position, but Bowen is in the grip of an idea, and that idea is so large, so much bigger than his own paltry wants and obligations, that he feels he has no choice but to obey it – even at the cost of acting irresponsibly, of doing things that would have been morally repugnant to him just one day before. 'Men died at haphazard,' is how Hammett expressed the idea, 'and lived only while blind chance spared them . . . In sensibly ordering his affairs [Flitcraft] had got out of step, and not into step, with life. He knew before he had gone twenty feet from the fallen beam that he would never know peace again until he had adjusted himself to this new glimpse of life. By the time he had eaten his luncheon he had found his means of adjustment. Life could be ended for him at random by a falling beam: he would change his life at random by simply going away.'

---

little question that she had an appointment with a man (attractive women are always with a man on Friday night), but it was impossible to know how deeply connected she was to him. It could have been a first date, and it could have been a quiet dinner with her fiancé or live-in boyfriend. I knew she wasn't married (Betty had told me as much after Grace left her office following our first meeting), but the range of other intimacies was boundless. When I asked Betty if Grace was involved with anyone, she said she didn't know. Grace kept her private life to herself, and no one in the company had the smallest inkling of what she did outside the office. Two or three editors had asked her out since she'd started working there, but she'd turned them all down.

I quickly learned that Grace was not someone who shared confidences. In the ten months I knew her before we were married, she never once divulged a secret or hinted at any prior entanglements with other men. Nor did I ever ask her to tell me something she didn't seem willing to talk about. That was the power of Grace's silence. If you meant to love her in the way she demanded to be loved, then you had to accept the line she'd drawn between herself and words.

(Once, in an early conversation I had with her about her childhood, she reminisced about a favorite doll her parents had given her when she was seven. She named her Pearl, carried her everywhere for the next four or five years, and considered her to be her best friend. The remarkable thing about Pearl was that she was able to talk and understood everything that was said to her. But Pearl never uttered a word in Grace's presence. Not because she couldn't speak, but because she chose not to.)

There was someone in her life at the time I met her – I'm sure of that – but I never

I didn't have to approve of Bowen's actions in order to write about them. Bowen was Flitcraft, and Flitcraft had done the same thing to his own wife in Hammett's novel. That was the premise of the story, and I wasn't about to back down from the bargain I'd made with myself to stick to the premise of the story. At the same time, I understood that there was more to it than just Bowen and what happens to him after he boards the plane. There was Eva to consider as well, and no matter how wrapped up I became in following Nick's adventures in Kansas City, I wouldn't be doing the story justice unless I returned to New York and explored what was happening to her. Her fate was just as important to me as her husband's. Bowen is in search of indifference, a tranquil affirmation of things-as-they-are, whereas Eva is at war with those things, a victim of circumstances, and from the moment Nick fails to return from his errand around the corner, her mind becomes a storm field of conflicting emotions: panic and fear, sorrow and anger, despair. I relished the prospect of entering that misery, of knowing that I would be able to live those passions with her and write about them in the days ahead.

Half an hour after the plane takes off from La Guardia, Nick opens his briefcase, slides out the manuscript of Sylvia Maxwell's novel, and begins to read. That was the third element of the narrative that was taking shape in my head, and I decided that it should be introduced as early as possible – even before the plane lands in Kansas City. First, Nick's story; then, Eva's story; and finally, the book that Nick reads and

learned his name or how seriously she felt about him. Quite seriously, I would imagine, for the first six months proved to be a tempestuous time for me, and they ended badly, with Grace telling me she wanted to break it off and that I shouldn't call her anymore. Through all the disappointments of those months, however, all the ephemeral victories and tiny surges of optimism, the rebuffs and capitulations, the nights when she was too busy to see me and the nights when she allowed me to share her bed, through all the ups and downs of that desperate, failed courtship, Grace was always an enchanted being for me, a luminous point of contact between desire and the world, the implacable love. I kept my word and didn't call her, but six or seven weeks later she contacted me out of the blue and said she had changed her mind. She didn't offer any explanation, but I gathered that the man who had been my rival was now out of the picture. Not only did she want to start seeing me again, she said, but she wanted us to get married. *Marriage* was the one word I had never spoken in her presence. It had been in my head from the first moment I saw her, but I had never dared to say it, for fear it would frighten her off. Now Grace was proposing to me. I had resigned myself to living out the rest of my life with a shattered heart, and now she was telling me I could live with her instead – in one piece, my whole life in one piece with her.

continues to read as their stories unfold: the story within the story. Nick is a literary man, after all, and therefore someone susceptible to the power of books. Little by little, by force of the attention he brings to Sylvia Maxwell's words, he begins to see a connection between himself and the story in the novel, as if in some oblique, highly metaphorical way, the book were speaking intimately to him about his own present circumstances.

At that point, I had only the dimmest notion of what I wanted *Oracle Night* to be, no more than the first tentative tracings of an outline. Everything still had to be worked out concerning the plot, but I knew that it was supposed to be a brief philosophical novel about predicting the future, a fable about time. The protagonist is Lemuel Flagg, a British lieutenant blinded by a mortar explosion in the trenches of World War I. Bleeding from his wounds, disoriented and howling in pain, he wanders off from the battle and loses contact with his regiment. Thrashing forward, stumbling, with no idea where he is, he enters the Ardennes Forest and collapses to the ground. Later that same day, his unconscious body is discovered by two French children, an eleven-year-old boy and a fourteen-year-old girl, François and Geneviève. They are war orphans who live on their own in an abandoned hut in the middle of the woods – pure fairy-tale characters in a pure fairy-tale setting. They carry Flagg home and nurse him back to health, and when the war ends a few months later, he takes the children back to England with him. It is Geneviève who narrates the story, looking back from the vantage of 1927 at the strange career and eventual suicide of her adoptive father. Flagg's blindness has given him the gift of prophecy. In sudden trance-like fits, he falls to the ground and begins flailing about like an epileptic. The seizures last from eight to ten minutes, and for the length of the time they endure, his mind is overrun with images of the future. The spells come upon him without warning, and there is nothing he can do to stop them or control them. His talent is both a curse and a blessing. It brings him wealth and influence, but at the same time the attacks cause him intense physical pain – not to speak of mental pain, since many of Flagg's visions furnish him with knowledge of things he would prefer not to know. The day of his mother's death, for example, or the site of a train wreck in India where two hundred people will be killed. He struggles to lead an unobtrusive life with his children, but the astonishing accuracy of his predictions (which range from weather forecasts to the results of Parliamentary elections to the scores of cricket test matches) turns him into one of the most celebrated men in postwar Britain. Then, at the peak of his fame, things begin to go wrong for him in love, and his talent ends up destroying him. He falls for a woman named Bettina Knott, and for two years she reciprocates his love, even to the point of accepting his proposal of marriage. On the night before their wedding, however, Flagg has another one of his spells, during which he is visited by the knowledge that Bettina will betray him before the year is out. His predictions have never been wrong, and therefore he knows the marriage is doomed. The tragedy is that Bettina is innocent, utterly free of guilt, since she has not yet met the man she will betray her husband with. Unable to face the anguish that destiny has prepared for him, Flagg stabs himself in the heart and dies.

The plane lands. Bowen puts the half-read manuscript back into his briefcase, walks out of the terminal, and finds a cab. He knows nothing about Kansas City. He has never been there, has never met anyone who lives within a hundred miles of the place, and would be hard-pressed to point to it on a blank map. He asks the driver to take him to the best hotel in town, and the driver, a corpulent black man with the unlikely name of Ed Victory, bursts out laughing. I hope you're not superstitious, he says.

Superstitious? Nick replies. What's that got to do with it?

You want the best hotel. That would be the Hyatt Regency. I don't know if you read the papers, but there was a big disaster at the Hyatt about a year ago. The suspended walkways came loose from the ceiling. They crashed down into the lobby, and over a hundred people got themselves killed.

Yes, I remember that. There was a photo on the front page of the *Times.*

The place is open again now, but some folks feel pretty squeamish about staying there. If you're not squeamish, and if you're not superstitious, that's the hotel I'd recommend.

All right, Nick says. The Hyatt it is. I've already been struck by lightning once today. If it wants to hit me again, it will know where to find me.[7]

_____

7. Kansas City was an arbitrary choice for Bowen's destination – the first place that popped into my head. Possibly because it was so remote from New York, a town locked in the center of the heartland: Oz in all its glorious strangeness. Once I had Nick on his way to Kansas City, however, I remembered the Hyatt Regency catastrophe, which was a real event that had taken place fourteen months earlier (in July

Ed laughs at Nick's answer, and the two men continue talking as they drive into the city. It turns out that Ed is about to retire from the taxi business. He's been at it for thirty-four years, and tonight is his last night on the job. This is his last shift, his last airport run, and Bowen is his last fare – the final passenger who will ever travel in his cab. Nick asks what he plans on doing now to keep himself occupied, and Edward M. Victory (for that is the man's full name) reaches into his shirt pocket, pulls out a business card, and hands it to Nick. BUREAU OF HISTORICAL PRESERVATION is what the card says – with Ed's name, address, and phone number printed at the bottom. Nick is about to ask what the words mean, but before he can form the question, the car pulls up in front of the hotel, and Ed holds out his hand to receive the last fare that will ever be given to him. Bowen adds a twenty-dollar tip to the amount, wishes the now-retired taxi driver good luck, and walks through the revolving doors into the lobby of the ill-fated hotel.

Because he is low on cash and has to pay with a credit card, Nick registers under his own name. The reconstructed lobby looks as if it's just a few days old, and Nick can't help thinking that he and the hotel are more or less in the same situation: both of them trying to forget their pasts, both of them trying to begin a new life. The glittering palace with its transparent elevators and immense chandeliers and burnished metallic walls, and he with nothing but the clothes on his back, two credit cards in his wallet, and a half-read novel in his leather bag. He splurges on a suite, rides the elevator up to the tenth floor, and doesn't come down again for thirty-six hours. Naked under his hotel robe, he eats room service meals, stands by the window, studies himself in the bathroom mirror, and reads Sylvia Maxwell's book. He finishes it that first night before going to bed, and then he spends the entire next day reading it again, and then again, and then a fourth time, plowing through its two hundred and nineteen pages as if his very life depended on it. The story of Lemuel Flagg affects him deeply, but Bowen doesn't read *Oracle Night* because he is looking to be moved or entertained, and he doesn't immerse himself

1981). Close to two thousand people had been gathered in the lobby at the time – an immense open-air atrium of some seventeen thousand square feet. They were all looking up, watching a dance contest that was being held in one of the upstairs walkways (also referred to as 'floating walkways' or 'skyways'), when the wide flange beams supporting the structure broke loose from their moorings and collapsed, crashing down into the lobby four stories below. Twenty-one years later, it is still considered one of the worst hotel disasters in American history.

in the novel in order to put off making a decision about what to do next. He knows what he has to do next, and the book is the only means at hand with which to do it. He has to train himself not to think about the past. That's the key to the whole mad adventure that started for him when the gargoyle crashed to the sidewalk. If he has lost his old life, then he must act as if he has just been born, pretend that he is no more burdened by the past than an infant is. He has memories, of course, but those memories are no longer relevant, no longer a part of the life that has begun for him, and whenever he finds himself drifting into thoughts about his old life in New York – which has been erased, which is nothing more than illusion now – he does everything in his power to turn his mind from the past and concentrate on the present. That is why he reads the book. That is why he keeps reading the book. He must lure himself away from the false memories of a life that no longer belongs to him, and because the manuscript demands total surrender in order to be read, an unremitting attentiveness of both body and mind, he can forget who he was when he is lost in the pages of the novel.

On the third day, Nick finally ventures outside. He walks down the street, enters a men's clothing store, and spends the next hour browsing among the racks, shelves, and bins. Little by little, he pieces together a new wardrobe for himself, loading up on everything from pants and shirts to underwear and socks. When he hands the clerk his American Express card to pay the bill, however, the machine rejects the card. The account has been canceled, the clerk informs him. Nick is thrown by this unexpected development, but he pretends to take it in his stride. It doesn't matter, he says. I'll pay with my Visa card. But when the clerk swipes that one through the machine, it proves to be invalid as well. It's an embarrassing moment for Nick. He wants to make a joke about it, but no funny remarks spring to mind. He apologizes to the clerk for having inconvenienced him and then turns around and leaves the store.

The snafu is easily explained. Bowen has already figured it out before he returns to the hotel, and once he understands why Eva canceled the cards, he grudgingly admits that he would have done the same thing in her place. A husband goes out to mail a letter and doesn't come back. What is the wife to think? Desertion is a possibility, of course, but that thought wouldn't come until later. The first response would be alarm, and then the wife would run through a catalogue of potential accidents and dangers. Hit by a truck, knifed in the back, robbed at gunpoint and then knocked on the head. And if her husband was the victim of a robbery, then the thief would have taken his wallet and walked off with his credit cards. With no evidence to support one hypothesis or another (no reports of a crime, no dead bodies found in the street), canceling the credit cards would have been a minimum precaution.

Nick has only sixty-eight dollars in cash. He has no checks with him, and when he stops at an ATM on his way back to the Hyatt Regency, he learns that his Citibank card has been canceled as well. His situation has suddenly become quite desperate. All avenues to money have been blocked, and when the hotel finds out that the American Express card he registered with on Monday night is no longer valid, he'll be in the ugliest of predicaments, perhaps even forced to defend himself against criminal charges. He thinks about calling Eva and going home, but he can't bring himself to do it. He hasn't come all this way just to turn around and run back at the first sign of trouble, and the fact is that he doesn't want to go home; he doesn't want to go back. Instead, he takes the elevator to the tenth floor of the hotel, enters his suite, and dials Rosa Leightman's number in New York. He does it on pure impulse, without having the first idea of what he wants to say to her. Fortunately, Rosa is out, and so Nick leaves a message on her answering machine – a rambling monologue that makes little or no sense, not even to him.

I'm in Kansas City, he says. I don't know why I'm here, but I'm here now, maybe for a long time, and I need to talk to you. It would be best if we could talk in person, but it's probably too much to ask you to fly out here on such short notice. Even if you can't come, please give me a call. I'm staying at the Hyatt Regency, room Ten-forty-six. I've been through your grandmother's book several times now, and I think it's the best thing she ever wrote. Thank you for giving it to me. And thank you for coming to my office on Monday. Don't be upset when I say this, but I haven't been able to stop thinking about you. You pounded me like a hammer, and when you stood up and left the room, my brain was in little pieces. Is it possible to fall in love with someone in ten minutes? I don't know anything about you. I don't even know if you're married or live with someone, if you're free or not. But it would be so nice if I could talk to you, so nice if I could see you again. It's beautiful out here, by the way. All strange and flat. I'm standing at the window, looking out at the city. Hundreds of buildings, hundreds of roads, but everything is silent. The glass blocks out the sound. Life is on the other side of the window, but in here everything looks dead, unreal. The problem is that I can't stay at the hotel much longer. I know a man who lives at the other end

397

of town. He's the only person I've met so far, and I'm going out to look for him in a few minutes. His name is Ed Victory. I have his card in my pocket and I'll give you his number, just in case I've checked out before you call. Maybe he'll know where I am. 816-765-4321. I'll say it again: 816-765-4321. How odd. I just noticed that the numbers go down in order, one digit at a time. I've never seen a telephone number that did that before. Do you think it means something? Probably not. Unless it does, of course. I'll let you know when I find out. If I don't hear from you, I'll call again in a couple of days. Adios.

A week goes by before she listens to the message. If Nick had called twenty minutes earlier, she would have answered the telephone, but Rosa has just left her apartment, and therefore she knows nothing about his call. At the moment Nick records his words on her machine, she is sitting in a yellow cab three blocks from the entrance to the Holland Tunnel, on her way to Newark Airport, where an afternoon flight will be taking her to Chicago. It's Wednesday. Her sister is getting married on Saturday, and because the ceremony will be held at her parents' house, and because Rosa is the maid of honor, she's going out early to help with the preparations. She hasn't seen her parents in some time, so she'll take advantage of the visit to spend a few extra days with them following the wedding. Her plan is to return to New York on Tuesday morning. A man has just declared his love to her on a telephone answering machine, and a full week will go by before she knows anything about it.

In another part of New York on that same Wednesday afternoon, Nick's wife, Eva, has also turned her thoughts toward Rosa Leightman. Nick has been missing for roughly forty hours. With no word from the police concerning accidents or crimes that involve a man who matches her husband's description, with no ransom notes or telephone calls from would-be kidnappers, she begins to consider the possibility that Nick has absconded, that he walked out on her under his own steam. Until this moment, she has never suspected him of having an affair, but when she thinks back to what he said about Rosa in the restaurant on Monday night, and when she remembers how taken he was with her – even going so far as to confess his attraction out loud – she starts to wonder if he isn't off on some adulterous escapade, shacked up in the arms of the thin girl with the spiky blond hair.

She looks up Rosa's number in the phone book and calls her apartment. There's no answer, of course, since Rosa is already on the plane. Eva leaves a short message and hangs up. When Rosa fails to return the call, Eva dials again that night and leaves another message. This pattern is repeated for several days – a call in the morning and a call at night – and the longer Rosa's silence continues, the more enraged Eva becomes. Finally, she goes to Rosa's building in Chelsea, climbs three flights of stairs, and knocks on her apartment door. Nothing happens. She knocks again, pounding with her fist and rattling the door on its hinges, and still no one answers. Eva takes this as definitive proof that Rosa is with Nick – an irrational assumption, but by now Eva is beyond the pull of logic, frantically stitching together a story to explain her husband's absence that draws on her darkest anxieties, her worst fears about her marriage and herself. She scribbles a note on a scrap of paper and slips it under Rosa's door. *I need to talk to you about Nick*, it says. *Call me at once. Eva Bowen.*

By now, Nick is long gone from the hotel. He has found Ed Victory, who lives in a tiny room on the top floor of a boardinghouse in one of the worst parts of town, a fringe neighborhood of crumbling, abandoned warehouses and burned-out buildings. The few people wandering the streets are black, but this is a zone of horror and devastation, and it bears little resemblance to the enclaves of black poverty that Nick has seen in other American cities. He has not entered an urban ghetto so much as a sliver of hell, a no-man's-land strewn with empty wine bottles, spent needles, and the hulks of stripped-down, rusted cars. The boardinghouse is the one intact structure on the block, no doubt the last remnant of what the neighborhood used to be, eighty or a hundred years ago. On any other street, it would have passed for a condemned building, but in this context it looks almost inviting: a three-story house with flaking yellow paint, sagging steps and roof, and plywood planks hammered across every one of the nine front windows.

Nick raps on the door, but no one answers. He raps again, and a few moments later an old woman in a green terry-cloth robe and a cheap auburn wig is standing before him – disconcerted, mistrustful, asking what he wants. Ed, Bowen replies, Ed Victory. I talked to him on the phone about an hour ago. He's expecting me. For the longest time, the woman says nothing. She looks Nick up and down, dead eyes studying him as though he were some form of unclassifiable being, glancing down at the leather briefcase in his hand and then back up at his face, trying to figure out what a white man is doing in her house. Nick reaches into his pocket and produces Ed's business card, hoping to convince her he's there on a legitimate errand, but the woman is half blind, and as she leans forward to look at the card, Nick understands that she can't make out the words. He ain't in no trouble, is he? she asks. No trouble, Nick answers. Not that I know of, anyway. And you ain't no cop? the woman says. I'm here to get some advice, Nick tells her, and Ed is the only person who can give it to me. Another long pause follows, and finally the woman points to the staircase. Three-G, she says, the door on the left. Be sure and knock loud when you get there. Ed's usually asleep this time of the day, and he don't hear so good.

The woman knows what she's talking about, for once Nick climbs the darkened staircase and locates Ed Victory's door at the end of the hall, he has to knock ten or twelve times before the ex-cabdriver asks him to come in. Massive and round, with his suspenders hanging off his shoulders and the top of his pants unbuttoned, Nick's sole acquaintance in Kansas City is sitting on his bed and pointing a gun straight at his visitor's heart. It's the first time anyone has pointed a gun at Bowen, but before he can become sufficiently alarmed and back out of the room, Victory lowers the weapon and puts it on the bedside table.

It's you, he says. The New York lightning man.

Expecting trouble? Nick asks, belatedly feeling the terror of a potential bullet in the chest, even though the danger has passed.

These are troubled times, Ed says, and this is a troubled place. A man can never be too careful. Especially a sixty-seven-year-old man who's none too swift afoot.

No one can outrun a bullet, Nick replies.

Ed grunts by way of response, then asks Bowen to take a seat, unexpectedly referring to a passage from *Walden* as he gestures toward the one chair in the room. Thoreau said he had three chairs in his house, Ed remarks. One for solitude, two for friendship, and three for society. I've only got the one for solitude. Throw in the bed, and maybe there's two for friendship. But there's no society in here. I had my fill of that piloting my hack.

Bowen eases himself onto the straight-backed wooden chair and glances around the small, tidy room. It makes him think of a monk's cell or a hermit's refuge: a drab, spartan place with no more than the barest essentials for living. A single bed, a single chest of drawers, a hot plate, a bar-sized refrigerator, a desk, and a bookcase with several dozen books in it, among them eight or ten dictionaries and a well-worn set of *Collier's Encyclopedia* in twenty volumes. The room represents a world of restraint, inwardness, and discipline, and as Bowen turns his attention back to Victory, who is calmly watching him from the bed, he takes in one final detail, which previously escaped his notice. There are no pictures hanging on the walls, no photographs or personal artifacts on display. The only adornment is a calendar tacked to the wall just above the bureau – from 1945, open to the month of April.

I'm in a fix, Bowen says, and I thought you might be able to help me.

It all depends, Ed replies, reaching for a pack of unfiltered Pall Malls on the bedside table. He lights a cigarette with a wooden match, takes a prolonged drag, and immediately begins to cough. Years of clogged phlegm clatters inside his shrunken bronchi, and for twenty seconds the room fills with convulsive bursts of sound. When the fit subsides, Ed grins at Bowen and says: Whenever people ask me why I smoke, I tell them it's because I like to cough.

I didn't mean to bother you, Nick says. Maybe this isn't a good time.

I'm not bothered. A man gives me a twenty-dollar tip, and two days later he shows up and tells me he's got a problem. It makes me kind of curious.

I need work. Any kind of work. I'm a good auto mechanic, and it occurred to me you might have an in at the cab company you used to work for.

A man from New York with a leather briefcase and a quality suit tells me he wants to be a mechanic. He overtips a cabbie and then claims to be broke. And now you're going to tell me you don't want to answer any questions. Am I right or wrong?

No questions. I'm the man who was struck by lightning, remember? I'm dead, and whoever I used to be makes no difference anymore. The only thing that counts is now. And right now I have to earn some money.

The people who run that outfit are a pack of knaves and fools. Forget that idea, New York. If you're really desperate, though, I might have something for you at the Bureau. You need a strong back and a good head for numbers. If you meet those qualifications, I'll hire you. At a decent wage. I might look like a pauper, but I've got bags of money, more money than I know what to do with.

The Bureau of Historical Preservation. Your business.

Not a business. It's more in the nature of a museum, a private archive.

My back is strong, and I know how to add and subtract. What kind of work are you talking about?

I'm reorganizing my system. There's time, and there's space. Those are the only two possibilities. The current setup is geographic, spatial. Now I want to switch things around and make them chronological. It's a better way, and I'm sorry I didn't think of it sooner. There's some heavy lifting involved, and my body isn't up to doing it alone. I need a helper.

And if I said I'm willing to be that helper, when would I start?

Right now if you like. Just give me a chance to button up my trousers, and I'll walk you over there. Then you can decide if you're interested or not.

I broke off then for a bite to eat (some crackers and a tin of sardines) and washed down the snack with a couple of glasses of water. It was pushing five, and although Grace had said she would be back by six or six-thirty, I wanted to squeeze in a little more time with the blue notebook before she returned, to keep on going until the last possible minute. On the way back to my study at the end of the hall, I slipped into the bathroom to have a quick pee and splash some water on my face – feeling invigorated, ready to plunge on with the story. Just as I left the bathroom, however, the front door of the apartment opened, and in stepped Grace, looking wan and exhausted. Her cousin Lily was supposed to have accompanied her to Brooklyn (to have dinner with us and spend the night on the foldout sofa in the living room, then leave early in the morning for New Haven, where she was a second-year architecture student at Yale), but Grace was alone, and before I could ask her what was wrong, she gave me a weak smile, rushed down the hall in my direction, made an abrupt left, and entered the bathroom. The moment she got there, she fell to her knees and vomited into the toilet.

After the deluge ended, I helped her to her feet and guided her into the bedroom. She looked terribly pale, and with my right arm around her shoulder and my left arm around her waist, I could feel her whole body trembling – as if small currents of electricity were passing through it. Maybe it was the Chinese food from last night, she said, but I told her I didn't think so, since I'd eaten the same dishes she had and my stomach was fine. You're probably coming down with something, I said. Yes, Grace answered, you're probably right, it must be one of those bugs – using that odd little word we all fall back on to describe the invisible contagions that float through the city and worm their way into people's bloodstreams and inner organs. But I'm never sick, Grace added, even as she passively· let me take off her clothes and put her into bed. I touched her forehead, which felt neither hot nor cold, and then I fished the thermometer out of the bedside table drawer and stuck it in her mouth. Her temperature turned out to be normal. That's encouraging, I said. If you get a good night's sleep, you'll probably feel better in the morning. To which Grace replied: I have to be better. There's an important meeting at work tomorrow, and I can't miss it.

I made her a cup of weak tea and a slice of dry toast, and for the next hour or so I sat beside her on the bed, talking to her about her cousin Lily, who'd put her into a cab after the first wave of queasiness had sent her running to the women's room at the Met. After a few sips of the tea, Grace declared that the nausea was lifting – only to be overwhelmed again fifteen minutes later, which sent her on another dash to the toilet across the hall. After that second onslaught, she began to settle down, but another thirty or forty minutes went by before she was relaxed enough to fall asleep. In the meantime, we talked a little, then said nothing for a while, then talked again, and all through those minutes before she finally dropped off, I stroked her head with my open palm. It felt good to be playing nurse, I told her, even if for just a few hours. It had been the other way around for so long, I'd forgotten there could be another sick person in the house besides myself.

'You don't understand,' Grace said. 'I'm being punished for last night.'

'Punished? What are you talking about?'

'For snapping at you in the cab. I acted like a shit.'

'No you didn't. And even if you had, I doubt that God takes his revenge on people by giving them the stomach flu.'

Grace closed her eyes and smiled. 'You've always loved me, haven't you, Sidney?'

'From the first moment I saw you.'

'Do you know why I married you?'

'No. I've never been brave enough to ask.'

'Because I knew you'd never let me down.'

'You bet on the wrong horse, Grace. I've been letting you down for almost a year now. First, I drag you through hell by getting sick, and then I throw us into debt with nine hundred unpaid medical bills. Without your job, we'd be out on the street. You're carrying me on your shoulders, Ms. Tebbetts. I'm a kept man.'

'I'm not talking about money.'

'I know you're not. But you're still getting a raw deal.'

'I'm the one who owes you, Sid. More than you know – more than you'll ever know. As long as you're not disappointed in me, I can live through anything.'

'I don't understand.'

'You don't have to understand. Just keep on loving me, and everything will take care of itself.'

It was the second bewildering conversation we'd had in the past eighteen hours. Once again, Grace had been hinting at something she refused to name, some kind of inner turmoil that seemed to be dogging her conscience, and it left me at a loss, groping dumbly to figure out what was going on. And yet how tender she was that evening, how glad to accept my small ministrations, how happy to have me sit beside her on the bed. After all we'd been through together in the past year, after all her steadfastness and composure during my long illness, it seemed impossible that she could ever do anything that would disappoint me. And even if she did, I was foolish enough and loyal enough not to care. I wanted to stay married to her for the rest of my life, and if Grace had slipped at some point or done something she wasn't proud of, what difference could that make in the long run? It wasn't my job to judge her. I was her husband, not a lieutenant in the moral police, and I meant to stand by her no matter what. *Just keep on loving me.* Those were simple instructions, and unless she decided to cancel them at some future date, I intended to obey her wishes until the very end.

She fell asleep a little before six-thirty. As I tiptoed out of the room and headed toward the kitchen for another glass of water, I realized that I was glad Lily had scrapped her plan to spend the night and had caught an early train back to New Haven. It wasn't that I disliked Grace's younger cousin – in fact, I liked her very much, and enjoyed listening to her Virginia accent, which was a good deal thicker than Grace's – but having to make conversation with her all evening while Grace slept in the bedroom was a bit more than I could have coped with. I hadn't imagined I would be able to work again after they returned from Manhattan, but now that dinner was off, there was nothing to stop me from jumping back into the blue notebook. It was still early; Grace was tucked in for the night; and after my mini-meal of sardines and crackers, my hunger had been satisfied. So I walked down to the end of the hall again, took my place at my desk, and opened the notebook for the second time that day. Without once standing up from the chair, I worked steadily until three-thirty in the morning.

*

Time has passed. On the following Monday, seven days after Bowen's disappearance, his wife receives the final bill for the canceled American Express card. Scanning the list of charges, she comes to the last one at the bottom of the page – for the Delta Airlines flight to Kansas City the previous Monday – and suddenly understands that Nick is alive, that he must be alive. But why Kansas City? She struggles to imagine why her husband would have flown off to a place where he has no connections (no relatives, no authors in his stable of writers, no friends from the past) but can't think of a single possible motive. At the same time, she also begins to doubt her hypothesis concerning Rosa Leightman. The girl lives in New York, and if Nick has indeed run off with her, why on earth would he take her to the Midwest? Unless Rosa Leightman is originally from Kansas City, of course, but that strikes Eva as farfetched, the longest of long-shot solutions.

She has no theories, no guesswork narratives to rely on anymore, and the anger that has been roiling inside her for the past week gradually dissipates, then vanishes altogether. From the emptiness and confusion that follow, a new emotion emerges to fill her thoughts: hope, or something akin to hope. Nick is alive, and considering that the credit card statement records the purchase of only one ticket, there's a good chance that he is alone. Eva calls the Kansas City Police Department and asks for the Bureau of Missing Persons, but the sergeant who picks up the phone is less than helpful. Husbands disappear every day, he says, and unless there's evidence of a crime, there's nothing the police can do. Close to despair, finally giving vent to the strain and misery that have been mounting in her over past days, Eva tells the sergeant he's a cold-hearted son-of-a-bitch and hangs up. She'll catch a plane for Kansas City, she decides, and start looking for Nick herself. Too agitated to sit still anymore, she decides to leave that very night.

She calls her answering machine at work, giving elaborate instructions to her secretary about the upcoming business of that week, then explains that she has an urgent family matter to attend to. She'll be out of town for a while, she says, but will stay in touch by phone. Until now, she has told no one about Nick's disappearance except for the New York police, who have been unable to do anything for her. But she has kept her friends and co-workers in the dark, refusing even to mention it to her parents, and when Nick's office began calling on Tuesday to find out where he was, she fended them off by saying he'd come down with an intestinal virus and was stretched out flat in bed. By the next

Monday, when he should have been thoroughly recovered and back at work, she told them he was much improved, but his mother had been rushed to the hospital over the weekend after a bad fall, and he'd flown up to Boston to be with her. These lies were a form of self-protection, motivated by embarrassment, humiliation, and fear. What kind of wife was she if she couldn't account for her husband's whereabouts? The truth was a swamp of uncertainty, and the idea of confessing to anyone that Nick had deserted her did not even enter her mind.

Armed with several recent snapshots of Nick, she packs a small suit-case and heads for La Guardia, having called ahead to reserve a seat on the nine-thirty flight. When she lands in Kansas City several hours later, she finds a taxi and asks the driver to recommend a hotel, repeating almost word for word the same question her husband asked Ed Victory the previous Monday. The only difference is that she uses the word *good* instead of *best*, but for all the nuances of that distinction, the driver's response is identical. He takes her to the Hyatt, and little realizing that she's following in her husband's footsteps, Eva checks in at the front desk, asking for a single room. She isn't someone to throw away money and indulge in expensive suites, but her room is nevertheless on the tenth floor, just down the hall from where Nick stayed for the first two nights after he arrived in town. Except for the fact that her room is a mere fraction of a degree to the south of his, she has the same view of the city he had: the same expanse of buildings, the same network of roads, and the same sky of suspended clouds that he catalogued for Rosa Leightman as he stood by the window and talked into her answering machine before skipping out on the bill and leaving the place for good.

Eva sleeps badly in the unfamiliar bed, her throat dry, waking three or four times during the night to visit the bathroom, to drink another glass of water, to stare at the bright red numerals on the digital alarm clock and listen to the hum of fans whirring in the ceiling vents. She dozes off at five, sleeps uninterruptedly for about three hours, and then orders a room-service breakfast. At quarter past nine, already show-ered, dressed, and fortified with a full pot of black coffee, she rides the elevator to the ground floor to begin her search. All of Eva's hopes revolve around the photographs she's carrying in her bag. She will walk around the city and show Nick's picture to as many people as she can, beginning with hotels and restaurants, then stores and food markets, then taxi companies, office buildings, and God knows where else, praying that someone will recognize him and offer a lead. If nothing materializes after the first day, she will have copies made of one of the snapshots and plaster them all over town – on walls, lampposts, and telephone booths – and publish the picture in the *Kansas City Star*, along with any other papers that circulate in the region. Even as she stands in the elevator on her way down to the lobby, she imagines the text that will accompany the handbill. MISSING. Or: HAVE YOU SEEN THIS MAN? Followed by Nick's name, age, height, weight, and hair color. Then a contact number and the promise of a reward. She is still trying to figure out how much the amount should be when the elevator doors open. One thousand dollars? Five thousand dollars? Ten thousand dollars? If these stratagems fail, she tells herself, she will move on to the next step and engage the services of a private detective. Not just some ex-cop with an investigator's license, but an expert, a man who specializes in hunting down the vanished, the evaporated beings of the world.

Three minutes after Eva enters the lobby, something miraculous happens. She shows Nick's picture to the desk clerk on duty, and the young woman with the blonde hair and gleaming white teeth makes a positive identification. This leads to a search through the records, and even at the sluggish pace of 1982 computers, it doesn't take long to confirm that Nick Bowen was registered at the hotel, spent two nights there, and disappeared without bothering to check out. They had a credit card imprint on file, but after running the number through the American Express system, the card proved to be invalid. Eva asks to see the manager in order to settle Nick's bill, and once she's sitting in the office, handing him her own newly validated card to cover the delinquent fees, she begins to cry, breaking down in earnest for the first time since her husband went missing. Mr. Lloyd Sharkey is discomfited by this outpouring of feminine anguish, but with the smooth and unctuous manner of a veteran service professional, he offers Mrs. Bowen whatever assistance he can provide her. Several minutes later, Eva is back on the tenth floor, talking to the Mexican chambermaid responsible for cleaning room 1046. The woman informs her that the DO NOT DISTURB sign was hanging on the doorknob outside Nick's room for the entire length of his stay and she never saw him. Ten minutes after that, Eva is downstairs in the kitchen talking to Leroy Washington, the room-service waiter who served Nick some of his meals. He recognizes Eva's husband from the photo and adds that Mr. Bowen was a generous tipper, although he didn't say much and seemed 'preoccupied' by something.

Eva asks if Nick was alone or with a woman. Alone, says Washington. Unless there was a lady hiding in the bathroom or the closet, he continues, but the meals were always for one person, and as far as he could tell, only one side of the bed was ever slept in.

Now that she's paid his hotel bill, and now that she's nearly certain he hasn't run off with another woman, Eva begins to feel like a wife again, a full-fledged wife battling to find her husband and save her marriage. No more information comes from the interviews she conducts with other members of the Hyatt Regency staff. She can't begin to guess where Nick might have gone after leaving the hotel, and yet she feels encouraged, as if knowing he was here, in the same place where she is now, can be construed as a sign that he isn't far away – even if it's no more than a suggestive overlap, a spatial congruency that means nothing.

Once she steps out onto the street, however, the hopelessness of her situation comes crashing down on her again. For the fact remains that Nick left without a word – left her, left his job, left everything in New York behind him – and the only explanation she can think of now is that he's cracking up, in the throes of some violent nervous collapse. Has living with her made him that miserable? Is she the one who's driven him to take such a drastic step, who's pushed him to the point of desperation? Yes, she tells herself, she's probably done that to him. And to make matters worse, he's penniless. A miserable, half-mad soul wandering around a strange city without a penny in his pocket. And that's her fault too, she tells herself, the whole wretched business is her fault.

That same morning, as Eva begins her futile rounds of inquiry, going in and out of restaurants and shops in downtown Kansas City, Rosa Leightman flies home to New York. She unlocks the door of her apartment in Chelsea at one o'clock, and the first thing she sees is Eva's note lying on the threshold. Caught off guard, perplexed by the urgent tone of the message, she drops her bag without bothering to unpack and immediately calls the first of the two numbers listed at the bottom of the note. No one answers at the Barrow Street apartment, but she leaves a message on the machine, explaining that she's been out of town and can now be reached at her home number. Then she calls Eva's office. The secretary tells her that Mrs. Bowen is away on business, but she's due to call in later that afternoon, and when she does, the message will be passed on to her. Rosa is mystified. She has met Nick Bowen only once and knows nothing about him. The conversation in his office went extremely well, she thought, and even though she sensed that he was attracted to her (she could see it in his eyes, feel it in the way he kept looking at her), his manner was reserved and gentlemanly, even a trifle distant. A man more lost than aggressive, she remembers, with an unmistakable tinge of sadness hovering about him. Married, she now realizes, and therefore out of bounds, disqualified from consideration. But touching somehow, a sympathetic sort with kind instincts.

She unpacks her bag and looks through her mail before listening to the messages on her answering machine. It's close to two by then, and the first thing that comes on is Bowen's voice, declaring his love for her and asking her to join him in Kansas City. Rosa stands stock-still, listening in awed confusion. She is so rattled by what Nick is saying to her that she has to back up the tape to the end of the message two more times before she can be certain she's written down Ed Victory's number correctly – notwithstanding the diminuendo of evenly descending figures, which makes the number all but impossible to forget. She is tempted to stop the answering machine and call Kansas City right away, but then decides to spool through the fourteen other messages to see if Nick has called again. He has. On Friday, and again on Sunday. 'I hope you weren't scared off by what I said the other day,' the second message begins, 'but I meant every word of it. I can't get rid of you. You're in my thoughts all the time, and while you seem to be telling me you aren't interested – what else can your silence mean? – I'd appreciate it if you'd give me a call. If nothing else, we can talk about your grandmother's book. Use Ed's number, the one I gave you before: 816-765-4321. By the way, those numbers aren't random. Ed asked for them on purpose. He says they're a metaphor – of what I don't know. I think he wants me to figure it out for myself.' The last message is the shortest of the three, and by then Nick has all but given up on her. 'It's me,' he says, 'giving it one last try. Please call, even if it's only to tell me you don't want to talk.'

Rosa dials Ed Victory's number, but no one picks up on the other end, and after letting the phone ring more than a dozen times, she concludes that it's an old device, with no answering machine attached to it. Without taking the time to examine what she feels (she doesn't know what she feels), Rosa hangs up the phone convinced that she has a moral obligation to contact Bowen – and that it must be done as quickly as possible. She thinks of sending a telegram, but when she calls directory assistance in Kansas City and asks for Ed's address, the operator tells her his number is unlisted, which means she isn't allowed to give out that information. Rosa then tries Eva's office again, hoping that Nick's wife has called in by now, but the secretary tells her there's been no news. As it happens, Eva is so swept up in her Kansas City drama that she will forget to call her office for several days, and by the time she does contact the secretary, Rosa herself will be gone, on her way to Kansas City by Greyhound bus. Why does she go? Because, over the course of those several days, she has called Ed Victory close to a hundred times, and no one has answered the phone. Because, in the absence of any further communication from Nick, she has talked herself into believing that he's in trouble – perhaps serious, life-threatening trouble. Because she is young and adventurous and currently unemployed (in between jobs as a freelance illustrator) and perhaps – one can only speculate about this – because she is enamored with the idea that a man she barely knows has openly confessed that he can't stop thinking about her, that she has made a man fall in love with her at first sight.

Backing up to the previous Wednesday, to the afternoon when Bowen climbed the steps of Ed's boardinghouse and was offered the job of helper in the Bureau of Historical Preservation, I then resumed the chronicle of my latter-day Flitcraft . . .

Ed buttons up his trousers, stubs out his half-smoked Pall Mall, and leads Nick down the stairs. They walk out into the chill of the early spring afternoon and keep on going for nine or ten blocks, turning left, turning right, slowly wending their way through a network of dilapidated streets until they come to an abandoned stockyard near the river, the liquid boundary that separates the Missouri side of the city from the Kansas side. They continue walking until the water is directly in front of them, with no more buildings in sight and nothing else ahead but half a dozen sets of train tracks, which all run parallel to one another and no longer seem to be in service, given the oxidized condition of the rails and the numerous broken and splintered ties heaped about the surrounding gravel and dirt. A strong wind is blowing off the river as the two men step over the first set of rails, and Nick can't help thinking about the wind that was blowing through the streets of New York on Monday night, just before the gargoyle fell from the building and nearly crushed him to death. Wheezing from the exertion of their long walk, Ed suddenly stops as they cross the third set of rails and points to the ground. A weatherworn, unpainted square of wood is embedded in the gravel, a kind of hatch or trapdoor, and it blends in so unobtrusively with the environment that Nick doubts he would have spotted it on his own. Please be kind enough to lift that thing off the ground and put it to the side, Ed asks him. I'd do it myself, but I've grown so portly these days, I don't think I can bend down anymore without falling over.

Nick carries out his new employer's request, and a moment later the two men are climbing down an iron ladder affixed to a cement wall. They reach the bottom about twelve feet below the surface. Aided by the light shining through the open hatch above, Nick sees that they're in a narrow passageway, facing a bare plywood door. No handle or knob is visible, but there's a padlock on the right side at about chest level. Ed takes a key from his pocket and inserts it into the plug at the bottom of the casing. Once the spring mechanism is released and the padlock is in his hand, he flicks away the latch with his thumb and slides the freed end of the shackle back through the eye of the hasp. It's a smooth and practiced gesture, Nick realizes, surely the product of countless visits to this dank, subterranean hideout over the years. Ed gives the door a little push, and as it swings open on its hinges Nick peers into the darkness before him, unable to see a thing. Ed gently nudges him aside, steps across the threshold, and an instant later Nick hears the flick of a light switch, then another, then a third, and perhaps even a fourth. In a stuttering succession of flashes and buzzing oscillations, several banks of overhead fluorescent lights gradually come on, and Nick finds himself looking into a large storeroom, a windowless enclosure that measures approximately fifty by thirty feet. In precise rows running the length of the floor, gray metal bookshelves fill the entire space, each one extending all the way to the ceiling, which is somewhere between nine and ten feet high. Bowen has the impression that he's entered the stacks of some secret library, a collection of forbidden books that no one but the initiated can be trusted to read.

The Bureau of Historical Preservation, Ed says, with a small wave of the hand. Take a look. Don't touch anything, but look as long as you like.

The circumstances are so bizarre, so remote from anything Nick was expecting, he can't even begin to guess what's in store for him. He walks down the first aisle and discovers that the shelves are crammed with telephone books. Hundreds of telephone books, thousands of telephone books, arranged alphabetically by city and set out in chronological order. He happens to be in the row that contains Baltimore and Boston. Checking the dates on the spines of the directories, he sees that the earliest Baltimore book is from 1927. There are several gaps after that, but beginning with 1946 the collection is complete until the present year, 1982. The first Boston book is even older, dating from 1919, but again there are a number of missing volumes until 1946, when all years begin to be accounted for. On the strength of this scant evidence, Nick surmises that Ed started the collection in 1946, the year after the end of World War II, which also happens to be the year that Bowen himself was born. Thirty-six years devoted to a vast and apparently meaningless undertaking, which tallies exactly with the span of his own life.

Atlanta, Buffalo, Cincinnati, Chicago, Detroit, Houston, Kansas City, Los Angeles, Miami, Minneapolis, the five boroughs of New York, Philadelphia, St. Louis, San Francisco, Seattle – every American metropolis is on hand, along with dozens of smaller cities, rural counties in Alabama, suburban towns in Connecticut, and unincorporated territories in Maine. But America isn't the end of it. Four of the twenty-four double-backed rows of towering metal bookcases are given over to cities and towns in foreign countries. These archives aren't as thorough or exhaustive as their domestic counterparts, but in addition to Canada and Mexico, most nations from western and eastern Europe are represented: London, Madrid, Stockholm, Paris, Munich, Prague, Budapest. To his astonishment, Nick sees that Ed has even managed to acquire a Warsaw phone directory from 1937/38: *Spis Abonentów Warszawskiej Sieci TELEFONÓW*. As Nick fights the temptation to pull it off the shelf, it occurs to him that nearly every Jewish person listed in that book is long dead – murdered before Ed's collection was ever started.

The tour lasts for ten or fifteen minutes, and everywhere Nick goes, Ed trails after him with a little grin on his face, relishing his visitor's bafflement. When they come to the final row of shelves at the southern end of the room, Ed finally says: The man is mystified. He's asking himself, What the hell is going on?

That's one way of putting it, Nick answers.

Any thoughts – or just out and out confusion?

I'm not sure, but I have the impression it's not just a game for you. I think I understand that much. You're not someone who collects for the sake of collecting. Bottle caps, cigarette wrappers, hotel ashtrays, glass figurines of elephants. People spend their time looking for all kinds of junk. But these phone books aren't junk. They mean something to you.

This room contains the world, Ed replies. Or at least a part of it. The names of the living and the dead. The Bureau of Historical Preservation is a house of memory, but it's also a shrine to the present. By bringing those two things together in one place, I prove to myself that mankind isn't finished.

I don't think I follow.

I saw the end of all things, Lightning Man. I went down into the bowels of hell, and I saw the end. You return from a trip like that, and no matter how long you go on living, a part of you will always be dead.

When did this happen?

April 1945. My unit was in Germany, and we were the ones who liberated Dachau. Thirty thousand breathing skeletons. You've seen the pictures, but the pictures don't tell you what it was like. You have to go there and smell it for yourself; you have to be there and touch it with your own hands. Human beings did it to human beings, and they did it with a clear conscience. That was the end of mankind, Mr. Good Shoes. God turned his eyes away from us and left the world forever. And I was there to witness it.

How long were you in the camp?

Two months. I was a cook, so I worked kitchen detail. My job was to feed the survivors. I'm sure you've read the stories about how some of them couldn't stop eating. The starved ones. They'd thought about food for so long, they couldn't help it. They ate until their stomachs burst, and they died. Hundreds of them. On the second day, a woman came up to me with a baby in her arms. She'd lost her mind, this woman, I could see it, I could see it in the way her eyes kept dancing around in their sockets, and so thin, so malnourished, I couldn't understand how she managed to stay on her feet. She didn't ask for any food, but she wanted me to give the baby some milk. I was happy to oblige, but when she handed me the baby, I saw that it was dead, that it had been dead for days. Its face was shriveled up and black, blacker than my own face, a tiny thing that weighed almost nothing, just shriveled skin and dried pus and weightless bones. The woman kept begging for milk, and so I poured some onto the baby's lips. I didn't know what else to do. I poured the milk onto the dead baby's lips, and then the woman took back her child – so happy, so happy that she began to hum, almost to sing, really, to sing in this cooing, joyful sort of way. I don't know if I've ever seen anyone happier than she was at that moment, walking off with her dead baby in her arms, singing because she'd finally been able to give it some milk. I stood there watching her as she left. She staggered along for about five yards, and then her knees buckled, and before I

413

could run over there and catch her, she fell down dead in the mud. That was the thing that started it for me. When I saw that woman die, I knew I was going to have to do something. I couldn't just go home after the war and forget about it. I had to keep that place in my head, to go on thinking about it every day for the rest of my life.

Nick still doesn't follow. He can grasp the enormity of what Ed lived through, sympathize with the anguish and horror that continue to haunt him, but how those feelings found expression in the mad enterprise of collecting telephone books eludes his understanding. He can imagine a hundred other ways to translate the experience of the death camp into an enduring lifelong action, but not this strange underground archive filled with the names of people from around the world. But who is he to judge another man's passion? Bowen needs work, he enjoys Ed's company, and he has no qualms about spending the next weeks or months helping him to reorganize the storage system of the books, useless as that job might be. The two men come to terms on the matter of wages, hours, and so on, and then shake hands to seal the contract. But Nick is still in the embarrassing position of having to ask for an advance on future earnings. He needs clothes and a place to live, and the sixty-odd dollars in his billfold are not enough to cover those expenses. His new boss, however, is one step ahead of him. There's a Goodwill Mission not one mile from where we're standing, he says, and Nick can stock up on new duds for just a few dollars that afternoon. Nothing fancy, of course, but working for him will require work clothes, not expensive business suits. Besides, he already has one of those, and if he ever feels like stepping out on the town, all he has to do is climb back into it.

That problem solved, Ed immediately solves the housing problem as well. There's a one-room apartment on the premises, he informs Nick, and if Bowen isn't spooked by the thought of spending his nights underground, he's welcome to stay there free of charge. Beckoning Nick to follow him, Ed waddles down one of the center stacks, moving gingerly on his sore and swollen ankles until he reaches the gray cinderblock wall at the western limit of the room. I often stay here myself, he says, reaching into his pocket and pulling out his keys. It's a cozy place.

A metal door is fitted into the wall flush with the surface, and since it's the same shade of gray as the wall itself, Nick never even noticed it when he walked past the spot a few minutes earlier. Like the wooden entrance door at the other end of the room, this one has no knob or handle, and it opens inward with a soft push from Ed's hand. Yes, Nick says politely when he steps inside, it's a cozy place, although he finds the room rather dismal, as bare and sparsely furnished as Ed's lodgings at the boardinghouse. But all the rudiments are there – except for a window, of course, a prospect to look out on. Bed, table and chair, refrigerator, hot plate, flush toilet, a cupboard filled with canned goods. Not so terrible, really, and in the end what choice does Nick have but to accept Ed's offer? Ed seems pleased by Bowen's willingness to stay there, and as he locks the door and the two men turn around to head for the ladder that will take them aboveground again, he tells Nick that he started building the room twenty years ago. Back in the fall of 'sixty-two, he says, in the middle of the Cuban missile crisis. I thought they were going to drop the big one on us, and I figured I'd need a place to hide out in. You know, a whatchamacallit.

A fallout shelter.

Right. So I broke through the wall and added on that little room. The crisis was over before I finished, but you never know, do you? Those maniacs who run the world are capable of anything.

Nick feels a slight flush of alarm when he hears Ed talk like this. Not that he doesn't share his opinion about the rulers of the world, but he wonders now if he hasn't joined forces with an unhinged person, a destabilized and/or demented crank. It's certainly possible, he tells himself, but Ed Victory is the man fate has delivered to him, and if he means to abide by the principles of the falling gargoyle, then he must carry on and pursue the direction he's taken – for better or worse. Otherwise, his departure from New York becomes a hollow, childish gesture. If he can't accept what's happening, accept it and actively embrace it, he should admit defeat and call his wife to tell her he's coming home.

In the end, these anxieties prove groundless. The days go by, and as the two men work together in the crypt below the railroad tracks, lugging telephone books back and forth across the room in wooden apple boxes mounted on roller skates, Nick discovers that Ed is nothing less than a stalwart character, a man of his word. He never asks his helper to explain himself or tell his story, and Nick grows to admire that discretion, especially in someone as garrulous as Ed, whose very being emanates curiosity about the world. Ed's manners are so refined, in fact, that he never even asks Nick his name. At one point, Bowen mentions to his boss that he can call him Bill, but understanding that the name is an invention, Ed rarely bothers, preferring to address his employee as *Lightning Man, New York,* and *Mr. Good Shoes.* Nick is perfectly satisfied with the arrangement. Dressed in the various outfits acquired from the Goodwill Mission store (flannel shirts, jeans and khaki pants, white tube socks, and frayed basketball sneakers), he wonders about the men who originally owned the clothes he's now wearing. Castoffs can come from one of two sources, and they're given away for one of two reasons. A person loses interest in a garment and donates it to charity, or else a person dies, and his heirs dispose of his goods for a meager tax deduction. Nick warms to the idea of walking around in a dead man's clothes. Now that he has ceased to exist, it seems fitting to don the wardrobe of a man who has likewise ceased to exist – as if that double negation made the erasure of his past more thorough, more permanent.

But Bowen nevertheless has to stay on his guard. He and Ed take frequent breaks while they work, and each time they interrupt their labors Ed enjoys passing the time in conversation, often punctuating his remarks with a swig from a can of beer. Nick learns about Wilhamena, Ed's first wife, who vanished one morning in 1953 with a liquor salesman from Detroit, and about Rochelle, Wilhamena's successor, who bore him three daughters and then died of heart trouble in 1969. Bowen finds Ed an engaging raconteur, but he is careful to refrain from asking him any pointed questions – so as not to open the way to be asked any questions about himself. They have established a silent pact about not probing into each other's secrets, and much as Nick would like to know if Victory is Ed's real name, for example, or if he owns the underground space that houses the Bureau of Historical Preservation or has simply appropriated it without being caught by the authorities, he says nothing about these matters and contents himself with listening to what Ed offers of his own free will. More dangerous are the moments when Nick almost gives himself away, and each time that happens, he warns himself to keep a more careful watch over what he says. One afternoon, when Ed is talking about his experiences as a soldier in World War II, he brings up the name of a young private who joined his regiment in late 'forty-four, John Trause. Just eighteen years old, Ed says, but the quickest, brightest lad he ever ran into. He's a famous writer now, he continues, and no wonder when you think about how sharp that boy's mind was. That's when Bowen makes a near catastrophic slip. I know him, he says, and when Ed looks up and asks how John's doing these days, Nick immediately covers his tracks by clarifying the statement. Not personally, he says. I mean his books, I've read his books, and there the subject is dropped and they move on to other things. But the truth is that Nick works with John and is the editor responsible for his backlist. Not one month ago, in fact, he finished working on a set of newly commissioned covers for the paperback editions of Trause's novels. He has known him for years, and the principal reason why he applied for the job at the company he works for (or did work for until a few days ago) was that John Trause's novels were published there.

Nick starts working for Ed on Thursday morning, and the task of rearranging the telephone books is so daunting, so colossal in terms of the poundage to be dealt with – the bulk and heft of countless thousand-page volumes to be taken off the shelves, carted to other areas of the room, and lifted onto new shelves – that progress is slow, much slower than they anticipated it would be. They decide to work straight through the weekend, and by Wednesday of the following week (the same day Eva walks into a photocopy store to design the poster that will broadcast the news of her missing husband, which also happens to be the day Rosa Leightman returns to New York and listens to Bowen's lovelorn messages on her answering machine), Nick's growing concern over Ed's health finally blossoms into full-scale distress. The ex-cabbie is sixty-seven years old and at least sixty-seven pounds overweight. He smokes three packs of unfiltered cigarettes a day and has trouble walking, trouble breathing, and trouble mounting in every one of his cholesterol-packed arteries. Already the victim of two heart attacks, he is in no shape to do the work that he and Nick are trying to accomplish. Even going up and down the ladder every day requires an enormous effort of concentration and will, taxing his strength to such a point that he can barely breathe when he comes to the top or bottom of his climb. Nick has been aware of this from the beginning and has continually encouraged Ed to sit down and rest, assuring him that he's capable of handling the job himself, but Ed is a stubborn fellow, a man with a vision, and now that his dream of reorganizing his telephone-book museum is at last under way, he ignores Bowen's advice and jumps in to help at every opportunity. On Wednesday morning, things finally take a darker turn. Bowen returns from a trip to the other end of the room with his empty apple box in tow and finds Ed sitting on the floor leaning against one of the bookcases. His eyes are shut, and his right hand is pressed tightly over his heart.

Chest pains, Nick says, leaping to the obvious conclusion. How bad?

Just give me a minute, Ed says. I'll be all right.

But Nick refuses to accept that as an answer and insists on accompanying Ed to the emergency room of the nearest medical facility. After putting up a short token protest, Ed agrees to go.

More than an hour ticks by before the two of them are sitting in the backseat of a taxi on their way to Saint Anselm's Charity Hospital. First, there is the arduous business of pushing Ed's broad, voluminous body up the ladder and getting him outside; then, there is the equally desperate challenge of hunting down a cab in this grim and forsaken part of the city. Nick runs for twenty minutes before he can find a functioning pay phone, and when he finally gets hold of the Red and White Cab Company (Ed's former employer), it takes another fifteen minutes before the car shows up. Nick instructs the driver to head for the railroad tracks near the river. They retrieve the languishing Ed, who is sprawled out among the cinders in considerable pain (but still conscious, still in sufficient command of himself to crack a couple of jokes as they help him into the cab), and set off for the hospital.

This medical emergency accounts for Rosa Leightman's failure to reach Ed by telephone later that day. The man known as Victory, but whose driver's license and Medicare card show his name to be Johnson, has suffered his third heart attack. By the time Rosa calls him from her New York apartment, he is already confined to the intensive care unit at Saint Anselm's, and, based on the cardiovascular data written on the chart at the foot of his bed, he will not be returning to his boardinghouse anytime soon. From that Wednesday until she leaves for Kansas City on Saturday morning, Rosa goes on calling him at all hours of the night and day, but not once is anyone there to hear the telephone ring.

In the cab on the way to the hospital, Ed is already thinking ahead, preparing himself for what promises to be bad news, even as he pretends not to be worried. I'm a fat man, he tells Nick, and fat men never die. It's a law of nature. The world can punch us, but we don't feel a thing. That's why we have all this padding – to protect us from moments like this.

Nick tells Ed to stop talking. Save your strength, he says, and as Ed struggles to ride out the pain that's burning in his chest and down his left arm and up into his jaw, his thoughts turn to the Bureau of Historical Preservation. I'm probably going to have to spend some time in the hospital, he says, and it grieves me to think about interrupting the work we've started. Nick assures him that he's willing to carry on alone, and Ed, moved by his helper's loyalty, shuts his eyes to block the tears that are spontaneously gathering in them and calls him a good man. Then, because he's too weak to do it himself, Ed asks Bowen to stick his hand into his trouser pockets and pull out his wallet and key ring. Nick extracts the two items from Ed's pants, and a moment later Ed is telling him to open the wallet and remove the cash inside it. Just leave me twenty bucks, he says, but take the rest for yourself – an advance on services rendered. That's when Nick learns that Ed's real name is Johnson, but he quickly decides that this discovery is of little importance and makes no comment. Instead, he counts out the money, which comes to more than six hundred dollars, and puts the bundle into the right front pocket of his own pants. After that, in a near breathless litany, fighting to talk through the pain, Ed informs him of the use of each key on the ring: the front door of the boardinghouse, the door of his room upstairs, his box at the local post office, the padlock on the wooden door at the Bureau, and the door of the underground apartment. As Bowen slips his own key to the apartment onto the ring, Ed tells him that he's expecting a big shipment of European phone books this week, so Nick should remember to check in at the post office on Friday. A long silence ensues after that remark, as Ed withdraws into himself and battles to catch his breath again, but just before they reach the hospital, he opens his eyes and tells Nick that he's welcome to stay in his room at the boardinghouse while he's gone. Nick thinks about it for a moment and then turns down the offer. That's very kind of you, he says, but there's no need to change anything. I'm happy living in my hole.

He hangs around the hospital for several hours, wanting to make sure that Ed is out of danger before he leaves. Triple bypass surgery has been scheduled for the next morning, and when Nick walks out of Saint Anselm's at three o'clock, he's confident that when he returns to visit the following afternoon, Ed will be on his way to a full recovery. Or so the cardiologist has led him to believe. But nothing is certain in the realm of medical practice, least of all when it's a question of knives cutting through the flesh of diseased bodies, and when Edward M. Johnson, better known as Ed Victory, expires on the operating table Thursday morning, that same cardiologist who offered Nick such a promising diagnosis can do no more than admit he was wrong.

By then, Nick is no longer in a position to talk to the doctor and ask him why his friend didn't make it. Less than an hour after he returns to the underground archive on Wednesday, Bowen commits one of the great blunders of his life, and because he assumes Ed will live – and goes on assuming that even after his boss is dead – he has no idea how gigantic the calamity he has made for himself truly is.

Both the key ring and the cash that Ed gave him are in the right front pocket of his pants when he climbs down the ladder to the entranceway of the Bureau. After Nick undoes the padlock on the wooden door, he puts the keys into the left pocket of the aged, hand-me-down khakis bought at the Goodwill Mission store. As it happens, there's a large hole in that pocket, and the keys slide straight through it, travel down Nick's legs, and land at his feet. He bends over and picks them up, but instead of putting them back into the right pocket, he keeps them in his hand, carries them over to the place where he intends to begin working, and sets them on a shelf in front of a row of telephone books – so as not to have them bulging in his pants and digging into his leg as he goes about his chores of lifting and carting, of squatting down and standing up. The air underground is especially clammy that day. Nick works for half an hour, hoping the exercise will warm him up, but the chill settles ever more deeply into his bones, and eventually he decides to withdraw to the apartment at the back of the room, which is equipped with a portable electric heater. He remembers the keys, returns to the spot where he left the ring, and again takes hold of it in his hand. Instead of going straight to the apartment, however, he starts thinking about the Warsaw phone book from 1937/38 that caught his attention the first time he visited the Bureau with Ed. He walks to the other end of the room to look for it, wanting to take it into the apartment with him and study during his break. Again, he puts the keys down on a shelf, but this time, absorbed in his search for the book, he forgets to take them with him after the volume is located. Under normal circumstances, this wouldn't have caused a problem. He would have needed the keys to open the door of the apartment, and once he realized his mistake, he would have gone back to fetch them. But that morning, in the frenzy that followed Ed's sudden collapse, the door was left open, and as Nick walks toward that door now, already flipping through the pages of the Warsaw phone book and thinking about some of the gruesome stories Ed told him about 1945, he is distracted enough not to pay attention to what he is doing. If he thinks about the keys at all, he will take it for granted that he's put them in his right pocket, and so he walks straight into the room, turns on the overhead light, and kicks the door shut behind him – thereby locking himself in. Ed has installed a self-locking door, and once a person enters that room, he can't get out again unless he uses a key to unlock the door from the inside.

Because he imagines the key is in his pocket, Nick still isn't aware of what he has done. He switches on the electric heater, sits down on the bed, and begins reading the Warsaw phone book more carefully, giving its browned and brittle pages his full attention. An hour goes by, and when Nick feels warm enough to return to work, he finally realizes his mistake. His first response is to laugh, but as the sickening truth of what he has done to himself gradually sinks in, he stops laughing and spends the next two hours in a frantic attempt to find a way out of there.

This is a hydrogen-bomb shelter, not an ordinary room, and the double-insulated walls are four feet thick, the concrete floor extends thirty-six inches below him, and even the ceiling, which Bowen thinks will be the most vulnerable spot, is constructed of a plaster and cement combination so solid as to be impregnable. There are air vents running along the tops of all four walls, but after Bowen manages to detach one of the grates from its tight metal housing, he understands that the opening is too narrow for a man to crawl through, even a smallish man like himself.

Aboveground, in the brightness of the afternoon sun, Nick's wife is gluing pictures of his face to every wall and lamppost in downtown Kansas City, and the following day, when the residents of the greater metropolitan area climb out of bed and repair to their kitchens to down their breakfast coffee, they will stumble across that same picture on page seven of the morning paper: HAVE YOU SEEN THIS MAN?

Exhausted by his efforts, Bowen sits down on the bed and calmly tries to reassess the situation. In spite of everything, he decides there's no need to panic. The refrigerator and cupboards are stocked with food, there are abundant supplies of water and beer on hand, and if worse came to worst, he could manage to hold out for two weeks in relative comfort. But it won't be that long, he tells himself, not even half that long. Ed will be out of the hospital in just a few days, and once he's mobile enough to climb down the ladder again, he'll come to the Bureau and set him free.

With no other option available to him, Bowen settles in to wait out his solitary confinement, hoping to discover enough patience and fortitude to bear up to his absurd predicament. He passes the time reading the manuscript of *Oracle Night* and perusing the contents of the Warsaw telephone book. He thinks and dreams and does a thousand push-ups a day. He makes plans for the future. He struggles not to think about the past. Although he doesn't believe in God, he tells himself that God is testing him – and that he mustn't fail to accept his misfortune with grace and equanimity of spirit.

When Rosa Leightman's bus arrives in Kansas City on Sunday night, Nick has been in the room for five days. Deliverance is at hand, he tells himself, Ed will be coming anytime now, and ten minutes after he thinks that thought, the bulb in the overhead light burns out, and Nick finds himself sitting alone in the darkness, staring at the glowing orange coils of the electric heater.

The doctors had told me my recovery depended on keeping regular hours and getting a sufficient amount of sleep every night. Working until three-thirty in the morning was hardly an intelligent move, but I'd been too absorbed in the blue notebook to keep track of the time, and when I crawled into bed beside Grace at quarter to four, I understood that I would probably have to pay a price for departing from my regimen. Another nosebleed, perhaps, or a new attack of the wobbles, or a prolonged high-intensity headache – something that promised to rattle my system and make the next day more difficult than most. When I opened my eyes at nine-thirty, however, I felt no worse than I usually did when I woke up in the morning. Maybe rest wasn't the cure, I said to myself, but work. Maybe writing was the medicine that would make me completely well again.

After Grace's bout with the heaves on Sunday, I had assumed she would take Monday off, but when I rolled over to my left to see if she was still asleep, I discovered that her side of the bed was empty. I looked for her in the bathroom, but she wasn't there. When I went into the kitchen, I found a note lying on the table. *I'm feeling much better*, it said, *so I've gone to work. Thanks for being so nice to me last night. You're the darling of darlings, Sid, Blue Team through and through.* Then, after signing her name, she had added a P.S. at the bottom of the page. *I almost forgot. We're out of Scotch tape, and I want to wrap my father's birthday present tonight so it gets to him in time. Could you pick up a roll today when you go out on your walk?*

I knew it was just a small point, but that request seemed to symbolize everything that was good about Grace. She worked as a graphic designer for a major New York publishing house, and if there was one thing her department was well supplied with, it was Scotch tape. Nearly every white-collar worker in America steals from the office. Hordes of wage earners routinely pocket pens, pencils, envelopes, paper clips, and rubber bands, and few of them feel the vaguest twinge of conscience over these acts of petty larceny. But Grace wasn't one of those people. It had nothing to do with a fear of being caught: it simply had never crossed her mind to take something that didn't belong to her. Not out of respect for the law, not because of some priggish rectitude, not because her religious training as a child had taught her to tremble at the words of the Ten Commandments, but because the idea of theft was alien to her sense of who she was, a betrayal of all her instincts about how she wanted to live her life. She might not have supported the concept, but Grace was a permanent, dyed-in-the-wool member of the Blue Team, and it touched me that she had bothered to bring up the subject again in her note. It was another way of telling me she was sorry about her little outburst in the cab on Saturday night, a discreet and altogether characteristic form of apology. Gracie in a nutshell.

I swallowed the four pills I took every morning at breakfast, drank some coffee, ate a couple of pieces of toast, and then walked down to the end of the hall and opened the door of my workroom. I figured I would continue with the story until lunchtime. At that point, I would go out and pay another visit to Chang's store – not only to look for Grace's Scotch tape, but to buy whatever Portuguese notebooks were still in stock. It didn't matter to me that they weren't blue. Black, red, and brown would serve just as well, and I wanted to have as many of them on hand as possible. Not for the present, perhaps, but to build up a supply for future projects, and the longer I put off going back to Chang's store, the greater the chances were that they'd be gone.

Until then, writing in the blue notebook had given me nothing but pleasure, a soaring, manic sense of fulfillment. Words had rushed out of me as though I were taking dictation, transcribing sentences from a voice that spoke in the crystalline language of dreams, nightmares, and unfettered thoughts. On the morning of September 20, however, two days after the day in question, that voice suddenly went silent. I opened the notebook, and when I glanced down at the page in front of me, I realized that I was lost, that I didn't know what I was doing anymore. I had put Bowen into the room. I had locked the door and turned out the light, and now I didn't have the faintest idea of how to get him out of there. Dozens of solutions sprang to mind, but they all seemed trite, mechanical, dull. Trapping Nick in the underground bomb shelter was a compelling idea to me – both terrifying and mysterious, beyond all rational explanation – and I didn't want to let go of it. But once I'd pushed the story in that direction, I had diverged from the original premise of the exercise. My hero was no longer walking the same path that Flitcraft had followed. Hammett ends his parable with a neat comic twist, and although it has a certain air of inevitability to it, I found his conclusion a little too pat for my taste. After wandering around for a couple of years, Flitcraft winds up in Spokane and marries a woman who is nearly the double of his first wife. As Sam Spade puts it to Brigid O'Shaughnessy: 'I don't think he even knew he had settled back naturally into the same groove he had jumped out of in Tacoma. But that's the part of it I always liked. He adjusted himself to beams falling, and then no more of them fell, and he adjusted himself to them not falling.' Cute, symmetrical, and ironic – but not strong enough for the kind of story I was interested in telling. I sat at my desk for more than an hour with the pen in my hand, but I didn't write a word. Perhaps that was what John had been referring to when he spoke of the 'cruelty' of the Portuguese notebooks. You flew along in them for a while, borne away by a feeling of your own power, a mental Superman speeding through a bright blue sky with your cape flapping behind you, and then, without any warning, you came crashing down to earth. After so much excitement and wishful thinking (even, I confess, to the point of imagining I might be able to turn the story into a novel, which would have put me in a position to earn some money and begin pulling my weight in the household again), I felt disgusted, ashamed that I had allowed three dozen hastily written pages to delude me into thinking I had suddenly turned things around for myself. All I had accomplished was to back myself into a corner. Maybe there was a way out, but for the time being I couldn't see one. The only thing I could see that morning was my hapless little man – sitting in the darkness of his underground room, waiting for someone to rescue him.

The weather was warm that day, with temperatures in the low 60s, but the clouds had returned, and when I left the apartment at eleven-thirty, rain seemed imminent. I didn't bother to go back upstairs for an umbrella, however. Another trip up and down the three flights would have taken too much out of me, so I decided to risk it, banking on the chance that the rain would hold off until after I returned.

I moved down Court Street at a slow pace, starting to sag a little from the effects of my late-night work session, feeling some of the old dizziness and discombobulation. It took me over fifteen minutes to reach the block between Carroll and President. The shoe-repair shop was open, just as it had been on Saturday morning, as was the bodega two doors down, but the store in between them was empty. Just forty-eight hours earlier, Chang's business had been in full operation, with a handsomely decorated front window and an overflowing stock of stationery goods inside, but now, to my absolute astonishment, everything was gone. A padlocked gate stretched across the façade, and when I peered through the diamond-shaped openings, I saw that a small handwritten sign had been mounted on the window: STORE FOR RENT. 858-1143.

I was so puzzled, I just stood there for a while staring into the vacant room. Had business been so bad that Chang had impulsively decided to pack it in? Had he dismantled his shop in a crazy fit of sorrow and defeat, carting away his entire inventory over the course of a single weekend? It didn't seem possible. For a moment or two, I wondered if I hadn't imagined my visit to the Paper Palace on Saturday morning, or if the time sequence hadn't been scrambled in my head, meaning that I was remembering something that had happened much earlier – not two days ago, but two weeks or two months ago. I went into the bodega and talked to the man behind the counter. Mercifully, he was just as befuddled as I was. Chang's store had been there on Saturday, he said, and it was still there when he went home at seven o'clock. 'It musta happened that night,' he continued, 'or maybe yesterday. I got Sunday off. Talk to Ramón – he's the Sunday guy. When I got here this morning, the place was cleaned out. You want weird, my friend, that's weird. Just like some magician dude waves his magic wand, and poof, the Chinaman is gone.'

I bought the Scotch tape somewhere else and then walked down to Landolfi's to buy a pack of cigarettes (Pall Malls, in honor of the late Ed Victory) and some newspapers to read at lunch. Half a block from the candy store was a place called Rita's, the small, noisy coffee shop where I had whiled away most of the summer. I hadn't been there in almost a month, and I found it gratifying that the waitress and the counterman both greeted me warmly when I walked in. Out of sorts as I was that day, it felt good to know that I hadn't been forgotten. I ordered my usual grilled cheese sandwich and settled in with the papers. The *Times* first, then the *Daily News* for the sports (the Mets had lost both ends of a Sunday doubleheader to the Cardinals), and finally a look at *Newsday*. I was an old hand at wasting time by then, and with my work at a standstill and nothing urgent calling me back to the apartment, I was in no rush to leave, especially now that the rain had started and I had been too lazy to climb the stairs to fetch an umbrella before going out.

If I hadn't lingered in Rita's for so long, ordering a second sandwich and a third cup of coffee, I never would have seen the article printed at the bottom of page thirty-seven in *Newsday*. Just the night before, I had written several paragraphs about Ed Victory's experiences in Dachau. Although Ed was a fictional character, the story he told about giving milk to the dead baby was true. I borrowed it from a book I'd once read about the Second World War,[8] and with Ed's words still ringing in my ears ('That was the end of mankind'), I came across this clumsily written news item about another dead baby, another dispatch from the bowels of hell. I can quote the article verbatim because I have it in front of me now. I tore it out of the paper that afternoon twenty years ago and have been carrying it around in my wallet ever since.

BORN IN A TOILET, BABY DISCARDED

High on crack, a 22-year-old reputed prostitute gave birth over a toilet in a Bronx SRO, then dumped her dead baby in an outdoor garbage bin, police said yesterday.

The woman, police said, had been having sex with a john about 1 a.m. yesterday when she left the room they were sharing at 450 Cyrus Pl. and walked into a bathroom to smoke crack. Sitting over a toilet, the woman 'feels the water break, feels something come out,' Sgt. Michael Ryan said.

But police said the woman – wasted on crack – apparently was not aware she had given birth.

Twenty minutes later, the woman noticed the dead baby in the bowl, wrapped her in a towel, and dropped her in a garbage bin. She then returned to her customer and resumed having sex, Ryan

---

8. *The Lid Lifts* by Patrick Gordon-Walker (London, 1945). More recently, the same story was retold by Douglas Botting in *From the Ruins of the Reich: Germany 1945–1949* (New York: Crown Publishers, 1985), p. 43.

Just for the record, I should also mention that I happen to own a copy of a 1937/38 Warsaw telephone book. It was given to me by a journalist friend who went to Poland to cover the Solidarity movement in 1981. He apparently found it in a flea market somewhere, and knowing that my paternal grandparents had both been born in Warsaw, he gave it to me as a present after he returned to New York. I called it my *book of ghosts*. At the bottom of page 220, I found a married couple whose address was given as Wejnerta 19 – Janina and Stefan Orlowscy. That was the Polish spelling of my family's name, and although I wasn't sure if these people were related to me or not, I felt there was a good chance that they were.

said. A dispute over payment soon broke out, however, and police said the woman stabbed her customer in the chest about 1:15 a.m.

Police said the woman, identified as Kisha White, fled to her apartment on 188th Street. Later, White returned to the Dumpster and recovered her baby. A neighbor, however, saw her return and called the police.

When I finished reading the article for the first time, I said to myself: *This is the worst story I have ever read.* It was hard enough to absorb the information about the baby, but when I came to the stabbing incident in the fourth paragraph, I understood that I was reading a story about the end of mankind, that that room in the Bronx was the precise spot on earth where human life had lost its meaning. I paused for a few moments, trying to catch my breath, trying to stop myself from trembling, and then I read the article again. This time, my eyes filled with tears. The tears were so sudden, so unexpected, that I immediately covered my face with my hands to make sure no one saw them. If the coffee shop hadn't been

11 40 44 Orlean Ch., Karmelicka 29	11 69 91 ...
12 20 51 Orlean Josef, m., Muranowska 36	12 61 62 Orth Anna, ...
12 08 51 Orlean Josek, m., św. Jerska 9	Orthwein, Karasi...
2 37 68 Orlean Mieczysław, m., Chłodna 22	
12 07 94 Orlean Ruta, m., Gęsia 29	5 01 58 — dyrektor,
6 18 99 Orleańska Paulina, Złota 8	— „ — — (dod.) m...
2 06 98 Orleański D., m., Moniuszki 8	2 63 45 Ortman Stefa...
8 83 21 Orleński O., artystka teatr. miejsk., m., Marszałkowska 1	2 10 21 „Ortopedja",
	11 56 93 „Ortozan", f...
12 61 33 Orlewicz Stanisław, dr., płk., Pogonowskiego 42	8 75 14 Ortwein Edw...
12 69 99 Orlewicz Stefan, m., Pogonowskiego 40	2 22 30 „Orwil", Sp.
11 91 94 „Orlę", Zjedn. Polsk. Młodzieży Prac., okr. Stoł., Leszno 24	5 86 86 ,,
	9 39 69 „Oryginalna
2 14 24 Orlicki Stanisław, adwokat, Orla 6	9 55 89 Orynowski W
11 77 10 Orlik Józefa, m., Babice, parc. 165	8 14 23 Orynżyna Jan
10 06 84 Orlikowscy B-cia, handel win, wódek i tow kolonj., Ząbkowska 22	7 10 92 Orzażewski E
	10 17 29 Orzażewski K
6 24 38 Orlikowska Janina, m., Alberta 2	8 16 19 Orzażewski R
9 28 26 Orlikowski Antoni, lek. dent., pl. 3-ch Krzyży 8	11 69 79 Orzech J. B.,
10 12 19 Orlikowski Jan, skł. towarów kolonjalnych, Targowa 54	9 98 19 Orzech L., d...
	2 16 01 Orzech M.,
10 26 02 Orlikowski Jan, m., Targowa 19	
12 73 03 Orlikowski Stanisław, m., Zajączka 24	5 33 43 Orzech Maur...
4 22 70★ Orliński Bolesław, m., Racławicka 94	12 13 01 Orzech Moric...
5 85 97 Orliński Maks, dr. med., chor. nerw., Wielka 14	5 38 00 Orzech Paweł
8 11 10 Orliński Tadeusz, dziennik., Jerozolimska 31	11 84 29 Orzech Pinku...
9 96 24 Orlot Leroch Rudolf, mjr., Koszykowa 79a	6 59 39 Orzech Szym...
„Ortorog", daw. Ortowski L., Rogowicz J. i S-ka, Sp. z o. o., fabr. izol. kork.. bud. wodochr., bituminy, asfaltów	2 16 01 Orzechowa N...
	6 44 22 ,,
9 81 23 — wydz. techn., pl. 3-ch Krzyży 13	9 42 28 Orzechowska
— „ — — (dod.) gab. inż. J. Rogowicza	2 63 15 Orzechowska
— „ — — (dod.) biuro i buchalterja	9 71 24 Orzechowska
5 05 59 — fabryka, Bema 53	8 32 16 Orzechowska
8 07 66 Orłow Grzegorz, m., Mokotowska 7	10 17 31 Orzechowska
7 01 69 Orłów Ludwik, przeds. rob. budowl., Buska 9	
11 52 63 Orłow P. A., sprzed. lamp i przyb. gazowych, Zamenhofa 26	8 93 81 Orzechowska
	4 08 59★ Orzechowska
4 19 01★ Orłowscy Janina i Stefan, m., Wejnerta 19	8 84 02 Orzechowski
8 80 57 Orłowska Halina, m., Polna 72	6 50 92 Orzechowski
3 16 29 Orłowska Lilla, Kopernika 12	5 36 59 Orzechowski
4 28 36★ Orłowska Marja, kawiarnia, Rakowiecka 9	12 74 22 Orzechowski
12 52 54 Orłowska Marja, m., Cegłowska 14	
9 27 63 Orłowska-Czerwińska Sława, artystka Opery, Wspólna 37	6 35 30 Orzechowski
	5 83 80 Orzechowski
3 19 47 Orłowska Stefanja, mag. kapeluszy damsk., Chmielna 4	5 04 72 Orzechowski
9 40 41 Orłowska-Świostek Zofja, lek. dent., Wspólna 63	5 30 09 Orzechowski
8 61 75 Orłowska Zofja, m., Al. 3 Maja 5	9 66 51 Orzechowski
6 88 98 Orłowski Adam, inspektor skarb., Chłodna 52	
8 16 66 Orłowski Edward, dr. med., Hoża 15	4 35 24★ Orzechowski
2 47 59 Orłowski Feliks, szofer, Elektryczna 1	
11 06 01 Orłowski Izrael, m., Gęsia 20	12 52 55 Orzechowski
8 53 04 Orłowski Jan, m., 6-go Sierpnia 18	4 32 85★ Orzechowski
5 98 63 Orłowski Juljan, Sienna 24	5 83 22 Orzechowski
2 57 24 Orłowski M., handel win i tow. kolonj., Marjensztat 7	12 58 23 Orzechowski
	2 76 02 Orzechowski
	2 04 23 Orzechowski
5 24 65 Orłowski Maksymiljan, dr. med., rentgenolog, Graniczna 6	11 41 31 Orzelski Marj...
	6 77 66 „Orzel", zob.

crowded with customers, I probably would have collapsed in a fit of real sobbing. I didn't go that far, but it took every bit of strength in me to hold myself back.

I walked home in the rain. Once I had peeled off my wet clothes and changed into something dry, I went into my workroom, sat down at my desk, and opened the blue notebook. Not to the story I had been writing earlier, but to the last page, the final verso opposite the inside back cover. The article had churned up so much in me, I felt I had to write some kind of response to it, to tackle the misery it had provoked head on. I kept at it for about an hour, writing backward in the notebook, beginning with page ninety-six, then turning to page ninety-five, and so on. When I finished my little harangue, I closed the notebook, stood up from my desk, and walked down the hall to the kitchen. I poured myself a glass of orange juice, and as I put the carton back into the refrigerator, I happened to glance over at the telephone, which sat on a little table in the corner of the room. To my surprise, the light was flashing on the answering machine. There hadn't been any messages when I'd returned from my lunch at Rita's, and now there were two. Strange. Insignificant, perhaps, but strange. For the fact was, I hadn't heard the phone ring. Had I been so caught up in what I was doing that I hadn't noticed the sound? Possibly. But if that were so, then it was the first time it had ever happened to me. Our phone had a particularly loud bell, and the noise always carried down the hall to my workroom – even when the door was shut.

The first message was from Grace. She was rushing to meet a deadline and wouldn't be able to get out of the office until seven-thirty or eight o'clock. If I got hungry, she said, I should start dinner without her, and she would heat up the leftovers when she came home.

The second message was from my agent, Mary Sklarr. It seemed that someone had just called her from Los Angeles, asking if I was interested in writing another screenplay, and she wanted me to call her back so she could fill me in on the details.[9] I called, but it took a while before she got

9. Four years earlier, I had adapted one of the stories from my first book, *Tabula Rasa*, for a young director named Vincent Frank. It was a small, low-budget film about a musician who recovers from a long illness and slowly puts his life together again (a prophetic story, as it turned out), and when the film was released in June 1980, it did fairly well. *Tabula Rasa* played in just a few art houses around the country, but it was perceived as a critical success, and – as Mary was fond of reminding me – it helped bring my name to the attention of a so-called wider public. Sales of

down to business. Like everyone else who was close to me, Mary began the conversation by asking about my health. They'd all thought they had lost me, and even though I'd been home from the hospital for four months now, they still couldn't believe I was alive, that they hadn't buried me in some graveyard back at the beginning of the year.

'Tip-top,' I said. 'A few lulls and droops every now and then, but basically good. Better and better every week.'

'There's a rumor going around that you've started writing something. True or false?'

'Who told you that?'

'John Trause. He called this morning, and your name happened to come up.'

'It's true. But I don't know where I'm going with it yet. It could be nothing.'

'Let's hope not. I told the movie people you've started a new novel and probably wouldn't be interested.'

'But I am interested. Very interested. Especially if there's real money involved.'

'Fifty thousand dollars.'

'Good lord. With fifty thousand dollars, Grace and I would be out of the woods.'

---

my books began to improve somewhat, it's true, and when I turned in my next novel nine months later, *A Short Dictionary of Human Emotions*, she negotiated a contract with Holst & McDermott worth twice the amount I'd been given for my previous book. That advance, along with the modest sum I'd earned from the screenplay, allowed me to quit my high school teaching job, which had been my bread-and-butter work for the past seven years. Until then, I had been one of those obscure and driven writers who wrote between five and seven in the morning, who wrote at night and on weekends, who never went anywhere on his summer vacation in order to sit at home in a sweltering Brooklyn apartment and make up for lost time. Now, a year and a half after my marriage to Grace, I found myself in the luxurious position of being an independent, self-employed scribbler. We were hardly what could be called well off, but if I continued to produce work at a steady pace, our combined incomes would keep us floating along with our heads above water. Following the release of *Tabula Rasa*, a few offers came in to write more films, but the projects hadn't interested me, and I'd turned them down to push on with my novel. When Holst & McDermott brought out the book in February 1982, however, I wasn't aware that it had been published. I had already been in the hospital for five weeks by then, and I wasn't aware of anything – not even that the doctors thought I would be dead within a matter of days.

Tabula Rasa had been a union production, and in order to be given credit for my

ORACLE NIGHT

'It's a dumb project, Sid. Not your kind of thing at all. Science fiction.'
'Ah. I see what you mean. Not exactly my line of work, is it? But are we
talking about fictitious science or scientific fiction?'
'Is there a difference?'
'I don't know.'
'They're planning a remake of *The Time Machine*.'
'H. G. Wells?'
'Exactly. To be directed by Bobby Hunter.'
'The guy who makes those big-budget action movies? What does he
know about me?'
'He's a fan. Apparently, he's read all your books and loved the movie
of *Tabula Rasa*.'
'I suppose I should be flattered. But I still don't get it. Why me? I
mean, why me for this?'
'Don't worry, Sid. I'll call back and tell them no.'
'Give me a couple of days to think about it first. I'll read the book and
see what happens. You never know. Maybe I'll come up with an inter-
esting idea.'
'Okay, you're the boss. I'll tell them you're considering it. No
promises, but you want to mull it over before you decide.'
'I'm pretty sure there's a copy of the book in the apartment. An old

---

screenplay I had been obliged to join the Writers Guild. Membership entailed sending in quarterly dues and turning over a small percentage of your earnings to them,
but among the things they gave you in return was a decent health insurance policy.
If not for that insurance, my illness would have landed me in debtor's prison. Most
of the costs were covered, but as with all medical plans, there were countless other
issues to be reckoned with: deductibles, extra charges for experimental treatments,
arcane percentages and sliding-scale calculations for various medicines and dispos-
able implements, a staggering range of bills that had put me in the hole to the tune
of thirty-six thousand dollars. That was the burden Grace and I had been saddled
with, and the more my strength returned, the more I worried about how to get us
out from under this debt. Grace's father had offered to help, but the judge wasn't a
rich man, and with Grace's two younger sisters still in college, we couldn't bring
ourselves to accept. Instead, we sent in a small amount every month, trying to chip
away at the mountain slowly, but at the rate we were going, we would still be at it
when we were senior citizens. Grace worked in publishing, which meant her salary
was meager at best, and I had earned nothing now for close to a year. A few microscopic royalties and foreign advances, but that was the extent of it. That explains
why I returned Mary's call immediately after I listened to her message. I hadn't
given any thought to writing more screenplays, but if the price was right for this
one, I had no intention of turning down the job.

431

paperback I bought in junior high school. I'll start reading it now and call you back in a day or two.'

The paperback had sold for thirty-five cents in 1961, and it included two of Wells's early novels, *The Time Machine* and *War of the Worlds*. *The Time Machine* was under a hundred pages, and it didn't take me much more than an hour to finish it. I found it thoroughly disappointing – a bad, awkwardly written piece of work, social criticism disguising itself as adventure yarn and heavy-handed on both counts. It didn't seem possible that anyone would want to do a straight adaptation of the book. That version had already been done, and if this Bobby Hunter character was as familiar with my work as he claimed to be, then it must have meant that he wanted me to take the story somewhere else, to leap out of the book and find a way of doing something fresh with the material. If not, why had he asked me? There were hundreds of professional screenwriters with more experience than I had. Any one of them could have translated Wells's novel into an acceptable script – which, I imagined, would have wound up looking similar to the Rod Taylor–Yvette Mimieux film I'd seen as a boy, with more dazzling special effects.

If there was anything that grabbed me about the book, it was the underlying conceit, the notion of time travel itself. Yet Wells had some- how managed to get that wrong too, I felt. He sends his hero into the future, but the more I thought about it, the more certain I became that most of us would prefer to visit the past. Trause's story about his brother-in-law and the 3-D viewer was a good example of how power- fully the dead keep their hold on us. If given the choice of going forward or backward, I for one wouldn't have hesitated. I would much rather have found myself among the no-longer-living than the unborn. With so many historical enigmas to be solved, how not to feel curious about what the world had looked like in, say, the Athens of Socrates or the Virginia of Thomas Jefferson? Or, like Trause's brother-in-law, how to resist the urge to reencounter the people you had lost? To see your mother and father on the day they met, for example, or to talk to your grandparents when they were young children. Would anyone turn down that opportunity in exchange for a glimpse of an unknown and incomprehensible future? Lemuel Flagg had seen the future in *Oracle Night*, and it had destroyed him. We don't want to know when we will die or when the people we love will betray us. But we're hungry to know the dead before they were dead, to acquaint ourselves with the dead as living beings.

I understood that Wells needed to send his man forward in time in order to make his point about the injustices of the English class system, which could be exaggerated to cataclysmic levels if placed in the future, but even granting him the right to do that, there was another, more serious problem with the book. If a man living in London at the end of the nineteenth century could invent a time machine, then it stood to reason that other people in the future would be able to do the same thing. If not on their own, then with the time traveler's help. And if people from future generations could travel back and forth across the years and centuries, then both the past and the future would be filled with people who did not belong to the time they were visiting. In the end, all times would be tainted, thronged with interlopers and tourists from other ages, and once people from the future began to influence events in the past and people from the past began to influence events in the future, the nature of time would change. Instead of being a continuous progression of discrete moments inching forward in one direction only, it would crumble into a vast, synchronistic blur. Simply put, as soon as one person began to travel in time, time as we know it would be destroyed.

Still, fifty thousand dollars was a lot of money, and I wasn't going to let a few logical flaws stand in my way. I put down the book and started pacing around the apartment, walking in and out of rooms, scanning the titles of the books on the shelves, parting the curtains and looking through the window at the wet street below, accomplishing nothing for several hours. At seven o'clock, I went into the kitchen to prepare a meal that would be ready for Grace when she returned from Manhattan. A mushroom omelet, a green salad, boiled potatoes, and broccoli. My culinary skills were limited, but I had once worked as a short-order cook, and I had a certain talent for whipping up spare and simple dinners. The first job was to peel the potatoes, and as I started slicing away the skins over a brown paper bag, the plot of the story finally came to me. It was just a beginning, with many rough edges and a host of particulars to be added later, but I felt pleased with it. Not because I felt it was good, but because I thought it might work for Bobby Hunter – whose opinion was the only one that mattered.

There would be two time travelers, I decided, a man from the past and a woman from the future. The action would cut back and forth between them until they embark on their journeys, and then, about a third of the way into the film, they would meet up in the present. I didn't know what to call them yet, so for the time being I referred to them as Jack and Jill.

Jack is similar to the hero in Wells's book – but American, not British. It's 1895, and he lives on a ranch in Texas, the twenty-eight-year-old son of a deceased cattle baron. Independently wealthy, with no interest in running his father's business, he leaves the operation of the ranch to his mother and older sister and devotes himself to scientific research and experimentation. After two years of unrelenting work and failure, he manages to build a time machine. He takes off on his first voyage. Not thousands of years into the future as the Wellsian character does, but just sixty-eight years ahead, climbing out of his glittering contraption on a cool and sunny day in late November 1963.

Jill belongs to the world of the mid-twenty-second century. Time travel has been mastered by then, but it is practiced only rarely, and severe restrictions have been placed on its use. Understanding its potential for disruption and disaster, the government allows each person only one journey in his or her lifetime. Not for the pleasure of visiting other moments in history, but as an initiation rite into adulthood. It happens when you reach the age of twenty. A celebration is held in your honor, and that same night you're sent into the past to travel around the world for one year and observe your ancestors. You begin two hundred years before your birth, roughly seven generations back, and then gradually work your way home to the present. The purpose of the trip is to teach you humility and compassion, tolerance for your fellow men. Out of the hundreds of forebears you encounter on the voyage, the entire gamut of human possibilities will be played out before you, every number in the genetic lottery will turn up. The traveler will understand that he has come from an immense cauldron of contradictions and that among his antecedents are beggars and fools, saints and heroes, cripples and beauties, gentle souls and violent criminals, altruists and thieves. To be exposed to so many lives in such a short span of time is to gain a new understanding of yourself and your place in the world. You see yourself as part of something greater than yourself, and you see yourself as a distinct individual, an unprecedented being with your own irreplaceable future. You understand, finally, that you alone are responsible for making yourself who you are.

Certain rules are in force for the length of the journey. You must not reveal your true identity; you must not interfere with anyone's actions; you must not allow anyone to enter your machine. To break any one of these rules is to suffer banishment from your own time and live in exile for the rest of your days.

Jill's story begins on the morning of her twentieth birthday. Once the party is over, she says good-bye to her parents and friends and straps herself into her government-issued time machine. She is carrying a long list of names with her, a dossier of the ancestors she will meet on her journey. The dial on the control panel is set to November 20, 1963, exactly two hundred years before her birth. She studies the papers one last time, shoves them into her pocket, and starts up the engine of the machine. Ten seconds later, with her friends and family waving their tearful farewells, the machine vanishes into thin air, and Jill is on her way.

Jack's machine has come to a stop in a meadow on the outskirts of Dallas. It's November 27, five days after Kennedy's assassination, and Oswald is already dead, gunned down by Jack Ruby in a basement passageway of City Hall. Within six hours of his arrival, Jack has read enough newspapers and listened to enough radio and TV broadcasts to understand that he has arrived in the midst of a national tragedy. He has lived through a presidential assassination himself (Garfield, in 1881), and he has painful memories of the trauma and chaos it produced. He ponders the dilemma for a couple of days, wondering if he has a moral right to alter the facts of history, and in the end he concludes that he does. He will take action for the good of his country; he will do everything in his power to save Kennedy's life. He returns to his time machine in the meadow, sets the dial of the chronometer to November 20, and travels back nine days into the past. When he emerges from the cockpit of his vessel, he finds himself standing not ten feet from another time machine – a sleek, twenty-second-century version of his own. Jill steps out, a bit woozy and disheveled. When she sees Jack standing there, looking at her in utter stupefaction, she reaches into her pocket and pulls out her list of names. Excuse me, sir, she says, but I wonder if you happen to know where I could find a man named Lee Harvey Oswald.

I hadn't worked out many details after that. I knew Jack and Jill would have to fall in love (this was Hollywood, after all), and I knew Jack would ultimately persuade her to help him stop Oswald from murdering Kennedy – even at the risk of turning her into an outlaw, of making

435

it impossible for her to return to her own time. They would ambush Oswald on the morning of the twenty-second just as he is entering the Texas School Book Depository with his rifle, tie him up, and hold him hostage for several hours. And yet, for all their efforts, nothing would change. Kennedy would still be shot and killed, and American history would not be altered by a single comma. Oswald, the self-proclaimed patsy, had been telling the truth. Whether he had fired at the president or not, he was not the only gunman involved in the conspiracy.

Because Jill can't go home now, and because Jack loves her and can't bear the thought of leaving her behind, he chooses to stay with her in 1963. In the final scene of the movie, they destroy their time machines and bury them in the meadow. Then, with the sun rising before them, they walk off into the morning of November twenty-third, two young people who have renounced their pasts, preparing to face the future together.

It was pure rubbish, of course, fantasy drek of the lowest order, but it felt like a possible movie to me, and that was all I was hoping to accomplish: to deliver something that would fit the formula they wanted. It wasn't prostitution so much as a financial arrangement, and I didn't have any second thoughts about working for hire to scare up a pot of some much-needed cash. It had been a rocky day for me, beginning with my failure to advance the story I was working on, then the jolt of discovering Chang's store had gone out of business, and then the horrifying newspaper article I had read at lunch. If nothing else, thinking about *The Time Machine* had served as a painless distraction, and when Grace walked through the door at eight-thirty, I was in relatively good spirits. The table was set, a bottle of white wine was chilling in the refrigerator, and the omelet was ready to be poured into the pan. She was a little surprised that I had waited for her, I think, but she didn't make any comment about it. She looked worn-out, with dark circles under her eyes and a certain heaviness in her movements. After I helped her out of her coat, I immediately led her into the kitchen and sat her down at the table. 'Eat,' I said. 'You must be starved.' I put some bread and a plate of salad in front of her and then walked over to the stove to begin fixing the omelet.

She complimented me on the food, but otherwise she didn't say much during the meal. I was glad to see that her appetite had returned, but at the same time she seemed to be somewhere else, less present than usual.

When I told her about going out on my Scotch tape errand and the mysterious closing of Chang's store, she barely seemed to be listening. I was tempted to tell her about the screenplay offer, but it didn't feel like the right moment. Maybe after dinner, I thought, and then, just as I stood up and was about to start clearing the table, she looked over at me and said, 'I think I'm pregnant, Sid.'

She'd blurted out the news so unexpectedly, I didn't know what else to do but sit back down in my chair.

'It's been almost six weeks since my last period. You know how regular I am. And all that throwing up yesterday. What else can it mean?'

'You don't sound too happy about it,' I finally said.

'I don't know what I feel. We've always talked about having kids, but this seems like the worst possible moment.'

'Not necessarily. If the test comes back positive, we'll figure out something. That's what everyone else does. We're not stupid, Grace. We'll find a way.'

'The apartment's too small, we don't have any money, and I'd have to stop working for three or four months. If you were all the way back, none of that would matter. But you're still not there.'

'I got you pregnant, didn't I? Who says I'm not there? Ain't nothing wrong with my plumbing, anyway.'

Grace smiled. 'So you vote yes.'

'Of course I do.'

'That makes one yes and one no. Where do we go from there?'

'You can't be serious.'

'What do you mean?'

'An abortion. You're not thinking of getting rid of it, are you?'

'I don't know. It's a horrible idea, but it might be best to put off having kids for a while.'

'Married people don't kill their babies. Not when they love each other.'

'That's an awful thing to say, Sidney. I don't like it.'

'Last night you said, "Just go on loving me, and everything will take care of itself." That's what I'm trying to do. To love you and take care of you.'

'This isn't about love. It's about trying to figure out what's best for both of us.'

'You already know, don't you?'

'Know what?'

'That you're pregnant. You don't think you might be pregnant. You've already found out that you are. When did you have the test?'

For the first time since I'd known her, Grace turned away from me when she spoke – unable to look at me, addressing her words to the wall. I'd caught her out in a lie, and the humiliation was almost too much for her to bear. 'Saturday morning,' she said. Her voice was nearly inaudible, scarcely louder than a whisper.

'Why didn't you tell me then?'

'I couldn't.'

'Couldn't?'

'I was too shaken up. I didn't want to accept it, and I needed time to digest the news. I'm sorry, Sid. I'm really sorry.'

We went on talking for another two hours, and in the end I wore down her resistance, hammering away at her until she gave in and promised to keep the child. It was probably the worst struggle we'd ever been through together. From every practical vantage, she was right to hesitate about the pregnancy, but the very rationality of her doubts seemed to touch off some morbid, irrational fear in me, and I kept on assaulting her with wildly emotional arguments that made little sense. When it came to the money end of things, I mentioned both the screenplay and the story I'd been outlining in the blue notebook, neglecting to add that the first project was no more than a tentative query, the faintest promise of future work, and that the second project had already stalled. If neither one of them panned out, I said, I would apply for a teaching post in every creative writing department in America, and if nothing turned up there, I would go back to teaching high school history, knowing full well that I still didn't have the physical stamina to hold down a regular job. In other words, I lied to her. My only object was to talk her out of aborting the child, and I was willing to indulge in any sort of dishonesty to plead my case. The question was why. Even as I bombarded her with my endless justifications and brutally efficient rhetoric, demolishing each one of her quiet, perfectly reasonable statements, I wondered why I was battling so hard. At bottom, I wasn't at all certain that I was ready to become a father, and I knew Grace was right to contend that the timing was off, that we shouldn't start thinking about children until I was fully recovered. Months went by before I understood what I was actually up to that night. It wasn't about having a baby – it was about me. Ever since I'd met her, I had lived in mortal fear that I would lose Grace. I had lost her once before our marriage, and after falling ill and turning into a semi-invalid,

I had gradually succumbed to a kind of terminal hopelessness, a secret conviction that she would be better off without me. Having a child together would erase that anxiety and prevent her from wanting to decamp. Conversely, for her to argue against the baby was a sign that she wanted out, that she was already slipping away from me. That explains why I became so worked up that night, I think, and I defended myself as ruthlessly as any shyster lawyer, even going so low as to take that dreadful newspaper clipping out of my wallet and insist that she read it. BORN IN A TOILET, BABY DISCARDED. When she came to the end of the article, Grace looked up at me with tears in her eyes and said, 'It isn't fair, Sidney. What does this . . . this nightmare have to do with us? You talk to me about dead babies in Dachau, about couples who can't have children, and now you show me this. What's wrong with you? I'm only trying to hold our life together in the best way I can. Don't you understand that?'

The next morning, I woke up early and made breakfast for the two of us, carrying a tray into the bedroom at seven o'clock, one minute before the alarm was set to go off. I parked the tray on top of the bureau, switched off the alarm, and then sat down on the bed next to Grace. The moment she opened her eyes, I put my arms around her and began kissing her cheek, her neck, and her shoulder, pressing my head against her and apologizing for the idiotic things I'd said the night before. I told her she was free to do what she wanted, that it was up to her and I would stand behind any decision she made. Beautiful Grace, who never looked puffy or bleary in the morning, who always emerged from sleep with the alacrity of a boot-camp soldier or a young child, rising up from deepest oblivion to full alertness in a matter of seconds, wrapped her arms around me and hugged me back, not saying a word, but emitting a series of small purring sounds from the bottom of her throat that told me I was forgiven, that the disagreement was already behind us.

I served her the breakfast while she remained in bed. Orange juice first, then a cup of coffee with some milk in it, followed by a pair of two-and-a-half-minute eggs and a slice of toast. Her appetite was good, with no signs of queasiness or morning sickness, and as I drank my own coffee and ate my own piece of toast, I thought she had never looked more splendid than she did at that moment. My wife is a luminous being, I said to myself, and may lightning strike me dead if I ever forget how lucky I am to be sitting next to her now.

'I was having the strangest dream,' Grace said. 'One of those nutty, mixed-up marathons where one thing keeps changing into another. But very clear – more real than real, if you know what I mean.'

'Can you remember it?'

'Most of it, I think, but it's already starting to fade. I can't see the beginning anymore, but somewhere along the line, you and I were with my parents. We were looking for a new place to live.'

'A bigger apartment, I suppose.'

'No, not an apartment. A house. We were driving around some city. Not New York or Charlottesville, but somewhere else, a place I'd never been to before. And my father said we should check out an address on Bluebird Avenue. Where do you suppose I dug up that one? Bluebird Avenue.'

'I don't know. But it's a nice name.'

'That's just what you said in the dream. You said it was a nice name.'

'Are you sure the dream is over? Maybe we're still asleep, and we're having the dream together.'

'Don't be silly. We were riding in my parents' car. You were with me in the backseat, and you said to my mother, "That's a nice name."'

'And then?'

'We pulled up in front of an old house. It was a huge place – a mansion, really – and then the four of us went inside and started looking around. All the rooms were empty, with no furniture in them, but they were enormous, like museum galleries or basketball courts, and we could hear our steps echoing against the walls. Then my parents decided to go upstairs to have a look at the second floor, but I wanted to go down to the basement. At first, you didn't want to go, but I took your hand and sort of dragged you along with me. It turned out to be pretty much like the ground floor – one empty room after another – but right in the middle of the last room there was a trapdoor. I yanked it open and saw that there was a ladder leading to a lower level. I started climbing down, and this time you followed right after me. You were just as curious as I was by then, and it was like we were having an adventure. You know, two kids exploring a strange house, both of us a little scared, but enjoying ourselves at the same time.'

'How long was the ladder?'

'I don't know. Ten or twelve feet. Something like that.'

'Ten or twelve feet . . . And then?'

'We found ourselves in a room. Smaller than the ones upstairs, with a much lower ceiling. The whole place was filled with bookshelves. Metal

ones, painted gray, like the ones they use in libraries. We started looking at the titles of the books, and it turned out they'd all been written by
you, Sid. Hundreds and hundreds of books, and every spine had your
name on it: Sidney Orr.'

'Scary.'

'No, not at all. I felt very proud of you. After we'd looked at the books
for a while, I started walking around again, and eventually I found a
door. I opened it, and inside there was this perfect little bedroom. Very
plush, with soft Persian rugs and comfortable chairs, paintings on the
walls, incense burning on the table, and a bed with silk pillows and a
red satin comforter. I called you over, and the minute you stepped
inside, I threw my arms around you and started kissing you on the
mouth. I was completely hot. All sexed up and raring to go.'

'And me?'

'You had the biggest hard-on of your life.'

'Keep this up, Grace, and you'll give me an even bigger one now.'

'We took off our clothes and started rolling around on the bed, all
sweaty and hungry for each other. It was delicious. We both came once,
and then, without pausing for breath, we started in again, going at each
other like two animals.'

'It sounds like a porno movie.'

'It was wild. I don't know how long we kept at it, but at some point we
heard my parents' car drive away. It didn't bother us. We'll catch up
with them later, we said, and then we started screwing again. After we
were done, we both collapsed. I dozed off for a while, and when I woke
up you were standing naked by the door, pulling on the handle, looking
a little desperate. "What's wrong," I asked, and you said, "It looks like
we're locked in."'

'This is the strangest thing I've ever heard.'

'It's just a dream, Sid. All dreams are strange.'

'I haven't been talking in my sleep, have I?'

'What do you mean?'

'I know you never go into my workroom. But if you did, and if you
happened to open the blue notebook I bought on Saturday, you'd see
that the story I've been writing is similar to your dream. The ladder that
goes down to an underground room, the library bookcases, the little
bedroom at the back. My hero is locked in that room right now, and I
don't know how to get him out.'

'Weird.'

441

'It's more than weird. It's chilling.'

'The funny thing is, that's where the dream ended. You had that scared look on your face, but before I could do anything to help you, I woke up. And there you were on the bed with your arms around me, hugging me in the same way you did in the dream. It was a wonderful thing. It felt like the dream was still going on, even after I'd woken up.'

'So you don't know what happens to us after we're locked in the room.'

'I didn't get that far. But we would have found a way out. People can't die in their dreams, you know. Even if the door was locked, something would have happened to get us out. That's how it works. As long as you're dreaming, there's always a way out.'

After Grace left for Manhattan, I sat down at my typewriter and worked on the film treatment for Bobby Hunter. I tried to boil the synopsis down to four pages, but I wound up writing six. Certain matters needed more clarification, I realized, and I didn't want there to be any holes in the story. For one thing, if the initiation journey was fraught with so many dangers and the potential for such harsh punishment, why would anyone want to risk traveling into the past? I decided to make the journey optional, something one does by choice, not compulsion. For another thing, how do the people in the twenty-second century know when the traveler has broken the rules? I invented a special branch of the national police to take care of that. Time-travel agents sit in libraries poring over books, magazines, and newspapers, and when a young traveler interferes with someone's actions in the past, the words in the books change. The name Lee Harvey Oswald, for example, would suddenly disappear from every work on the Kennedy assassination. Imagining that scene, I understood that those alterations could be turned into a striking visual effect: hundreds of words scrambling around and rearranging themselves on printed pages, moving back and forth like tiny, maddened bugs.

When I finished typing, I read over the treatment once, corrected a few typos, and then walked down the hall to the kitchen and rang up the Sklarr Agency. Mary was busy on another call, but I told her assistant I would be turning up at the office in an hour or two to drop off the manuscript. 'That was fast,' she said.

'Yeah, I guess so,' I answered, 'but you know how it is, Angela. When you travel in time, you don't have a second to lose.'

Angela laughed at my feeble remark. 'All right,' she said, 'I'll tell

Mary you're on your way. But there's no big rush, you know. You could put it in the mail and save yourself the trip.'

'Don't trust the mail, ma'am,' I said, lapsing into my Oklahoma cowboy twang. 'Never did and never will.'

After we hung up, I lifted the receiver off the hook again and dialed Trause's number. Mary's office was on Fifth Avenue between 12th and 13th Streets, not far from where John lived, and it occurred to me that he might be interested in getting together for lunch. I also wanted to know how his leg was doing. We hadn't talked since Saturday night, and it was time to check up on him and get the latest report.

'Nothing new,' he said. 'It's no worse than it was, but no better. The doctor prescribed an anti-inflammatory drug, and when I took the first pill yesterday, I had a bad reaction. Upchucking, spinning head, the works. I'm still feeling a bit drained from all that.'

'I'm leaving for Manhattan in a little while to see Mary Sklarr, and I thought I'd stop by to see you afterward. Maybe have lunch or something, but it doesn't sound like a good moment.'

'Why don't you come tomorrow? I'm bound to be okay by then. At least I fucking well better be.'

I left the apartment at eleven-thirty and walked over to Bergen Street, where I caught the F train to Manhattan. There were several mysterious glitches along the way – a lengthy pause in a tunnel, a blackout in the car that lasted for four stops, an unusually slow traverse from the York Street station to the other side of the river – and by the time I made it to Mary's office, she had already gone out to lunch. I left the treatment with Angela, the chubby, chain-smoking answerer of phones and sender of packages, who surprised me by standing up from her desk and kissing me good-bye – an Italian doubleheader, one peck on each cheek. 'Too bad you're married,' she whispered. 'You and I could have made some beautiful music together, Sid.'

Angela was always horsing around like that, and after three years of diligent practice, we'd worked out a fairly polished routine. Trying to keep up my end of the game, I gave her the answer she was looking for. 'Nothing's forever,' I said. 'Just hang in there, angelic one, and sooner or later I'm bound to be free.'

There was no point in returning to Brooklyn right away, so I decided to take my afternoon walk in the Village, then round off the excursion with a bite to eat somewhere before taking the subway home. I headed west from Fifth Avenue, strolling along 12th Street with its pretty

443

brownstones and small, neatly tended trees, and by the time I'd passed the New School and was approaching Sixth Avenue, I was already lost in thought. Bowen was still trapped in the room, and with the unsettling contents of Grace's dream still echoing in my head, several new ideas had occurred to me about the story. I lost track of where I was after that, and for the next thirty or forty minutes I wandered around the streets like a blind man, more in that underground room in Kansas City than in Manhattan, taking only the scantest notice of the things around me. It wasn't until I found myself on Hudson Street, gliding past the front window of the White Horse Tavern, that my feet finally stopped moving. I had built up an appetite, I discovered, and once I became aware of that fact, the focus of my attention shifted from my head to my stomach. I was ready to sit down and eat lunch.[10]

I had been to the White Horse many times in the past, but not for several years now, and the instant I opened the door, I was happy to see that nothing had changed. It was the same woody, smoke-filled watering hole it had always been, with the same scarred tables and wobbly chairs, the same sawdust on the floor, the same big clock on the northern wall. All the tables were occupied, but there were a couple of spots open at the bar. I slid onto one of the stools and ordered a hamburger and a glass of beer. I rarely drank during the day, but being in the White Horse had put me in a nostalgic mood (remembering all the hours I'd spent there in my late teens and early twenties), and I decided to have one for old times'

10. I hadn't made any serious progress, but I understood that I could improve Bowen's condition somewhat without having to alter the central thrust of the narrative. The overhead light has burned out, but it no longer seemed necessary to keep Nick in total darkness. There could be other sources of illumination in Ed's well-equipped fallout shelter. Matches and candles, for instance, a flashlight, a table lamp – something to prevent Nick from feeling he's been buried alive. That would push any man over the edge of sanity, and the last thing I wanted was to turn Bowen's predicament into a study of terror and madness. I had left Hammett behind, but that didn't mean I intended to replace the Flitcraft story with a new version of 'The Premature Burial.' Give Nick light, then, and allow him a shred of hope. And even after the matches and candles have been used up, even after the batteries in the flashlight have lost their power, he can open the refrigerator door and cast some light into the room with the small bulb that burns inside the white enameled box.

More significant, there was the question of Grace's dream. Listening to her talk that morning, I had been too shaken by the resemblances to the story I was writing to grasp how many differences there were as well. Her room was a sanctuary to be shared by two people, a small erotic paradise. My room was a bleak cell, inhabited by one man, whose only ambition is to escape. But what if I managed to get Rosa sake. It was only after I'd settled this business with the bartender that I looked over at the man sitting to my right. I had seen him from behind when I'd entered the tavern, a thin fellow in a brown sweater hunched over a drink, and something about his posture had set off a little signal in my head. Concerning what I didn't know. Recognition, perhaps. Or perhaps something more obscure: a memory of another man in a brown sweater who'd been sitting in that same position years earlier, a lilliputian fragment from the ancient past. This man had his head down and was looking into his glass, which was half filled with Scotch or bourbon. I could only see his profile, which was partially blocked by his left wrist and hand, but there was no question that the face belonged to a person I'd thought I would never see again. M. R. Chang.

'Mr. Chang,' I said. 'How are you?'

Chang turned at the mention of his name, looking downcast and perhaps a little drunk. At first, he didn't seem to remember who I was, but then his face gradually brightened. 'Ah,' he said. 'Mr. Sidney. Mr. Sidney O. Nice fellow.'

'I went back to your store yesterday,' I said, 'but everything was gone. What happened?'

'Big trouble,' Chang replied, shaking his head and taking a sip of his drink, apparently on the verge of tears. 'Landlord raise rent on me. I tell him I have lease, but he laugh and say he seize goods with city marshal if cash not in his fist Monday morning. So I pack up my store Saturday night and leave. All Mafia men in that neighborhood. They shoot you dead if you don't play ball.'

Leightman in there with him? Nick has already fallen for her, and if they're trapped in the room together for any length of time, perhaps she would begin to reciprocate his feelings. Rosa was the physical and spiritual double of Grace, and therefore she would have the same sexual appetites as Grace – the same recklessness, the same lack of inhibition. Nick and Rosa could spend their time together reading passages out loud from *Oracle Night*, baring their souls to each other, making love. As long as there was enough food to sustain them, why would they ever want to leave?

That was the little fantasy I carried around with me through the streets of the Village. Even as I played it out in my mind, however, I knew it was deeply flawed. Grace had aroused me with her erotic dream, but in spite of the temptations it seemed to offer, it was just another dead end. If Rosa can get into the room, then Nick can get out, and once that opportunity is presented to him, he wouldn't hesitate to leave. But the point is that he can't leave. I had given him some light, but he was still locked inside that grim chamber, and without the proper tools to dig his way out, he was eventually going to die in there.

445

'You should hire a lawyer and take him to court.'

'No lawyer. Too much money. I look for new place tomorrow. Maybe Queens or Manhattan. No more Brooklyn. Paper Palace a flop. Big American dream a flop.'

I shouldn't have let myself succumb to pity, but when Chang offered to buy me a drink, I didn't have the heart to turn him down. Ingesting Scotch at one-thirty in the afternoon was not on my list of prescribed medical therapies. Even worse, now that Chang and I had become friends and were deep in conversation, I felt compelled to return the favor and order a second round. That made one glass of beer and two double Scotches in approximately an hour. Not enough to achieve full intoxication, but I was swimming pleasantly by then, and with my usual reserve growing progressively weaker as time wore on, I asked Chang a number of personal questions about his life in China and how he had come to America – something I never would have done if I hadn't been drinking. Much of what he said confused me. His ability to express himself in English slowly deteriorated as his intake of alcohol increased, but in the flow of stories I heard about his childhood in Beijing, the Cultural Revolution, and his perilous escape from the country by way of Hong Kong, one stood out in particular, no doubt because he told it early in the conversation.

'My father was math teacher,' he said, 'employed by Beijing Number Eleven Middle School. When the Cultural Revolution comes, they call him member of the Black Gang, reactionary bourgeois person. One day the Red Guard students order the Black Gang to take all books out from library not written by Chairman Mao. They hit them with belts to make them do this. These are bad books, they say. They spread capitalism and revisionist ideas, and they must be burned. My father and the other Black Gang teachers carry books out to the sports ground. The Red Guards shout at them and beat them to make them do this. They carry heavy load after heavy load, and then they have a big mountain of books. The Red Guards set them on fire, and my father begins to weep. They hit him with their belts because of this. Then the fire gets big and hot, and the Red Guards push the Black Gang right to the edge of the fire. They make them lower their heads and bend forward. They say they are being tried by the flames of the Great Cultural Revolution. It is a hot day in August, terrible sun. My father has blisters on his face and arms, cuts and bruises all over his back. At home, my mother cries when she sees him. My father cries. We all cry, Mr. Sidney. The next week, my

446

father is arrested, and we are all sent to the countryside to work as farm-ers. That is when I learn to hate my country, my China. From that day, I begin to dream of America. I get my big American dream in China, but there is no dream in America. This country is bad too. Everywhere the same. All people bad and rotten. All countries bad and rotten.'[11]

After I finished my second Cutty Sark, I shook Chang's hand and told him it was time for me to go. It was two-thirty, I said, and I had to get back to Cobble Hill to do some pre-dinner shopping. Chang looked dis-appointed. I didn't know what he was expecting from me, but perhaps he thought I was prepared to accompany him on an all-day bender.

'No problem,' he finally said. 'I drive you home.'

'You have a car?'

'Of course. Everyone have car. Not you?'

'No. You don't really need one in New York.'

'Come, Mr. Sid. You cheer me up and make me happy again. Now I drive you home.'

'No thanks. A man in your condition shouldn't drive. You're too pot-ted.'

'Potted?'

11. When Chang told this story to me twenty years ago, I was certain he was telling the truth. There was too much conviction in his voice for me to doubt his sincerity. Several months ago, however, while preparing for another project, I read a number of works on China during the period of the Cultural Revolution. In one of them, I came across an account of the same incident by Liu Yan, who was a student at the Beijing Number Eleven Middle School at the time of the book burning and wit-nessed the event. No teacher named Chang is mentioned. A female language teacher is referred to, Yu Changjiang, who broke down and wept at the sight of the burning books. 'Her tears provoked the Red Guards to give her a few extra lashes, and the belts left ugly scars on her skin.' (*China's Cultural Revolution, 1966–1969*, edited by Michael Schoenhals; Armonk, New York: M. E. Sharpe, 1996.)

I'm not saying this proves Chang was lying to me, but it does cast some suspicion over his story. Possibly, there were two teachers who wept, and Liu Yan didn't notice the other one. But it should be pointed out that the book burning was a highly publicized event in Beijing at the time and, in Liu Yan's words, 'caused a major stir all over the city.' Chang would have known about it, even if his father hadn't been there. Perhaps he told this infamous story in order to impress me. I can't say. On the other hand, his version was extremely vivid – more vivid than most secondhand accounts – which leads me to wonder if Chang wasn't present at the book burning himself. And if he was, that must have meant he'd been there as a member of the Red Guard. Otherwise, he would have told me that he'd been a student at the school – which he never did. It is even possible (this is pure speculation) that he himself was the person who lashed the weeping teacher.

'You've had too much to drink.'

'Nonsense. M. R. Chang sober as a judge.'

I smiled when I heard that old American phrase, and seeing that I was amused, Chang suddenly burst out laughing. It was the same staccato eruption I'd heard in his store on Saturday. *Ha-ha-ha. Ha-ha-ha. Ha-ha-ha.* It was a disconcerting sort of gaiety, I found, dry and soulless somehow, without the vibrant, lilting quality one usually hears when people laugh. To prove his point, Chang hopped off the bar stool and began striding back and forth across the room, demonstrating his ability to keep his balance and walk a straight line. In all fairness, I had to admit that he passed the test. His movements were steady and unforced, and he seemed to be in complete control of himself. Understanding that there was no stopping this man, that his determination to drive me home had become a passionate, single-minded cause, I reluctantly gave in and accepted his offer.

The car was parked around the corner on Perry Street, a spanking-new red Pontiac with whitewall tires and a retractable sun roof. I told Chang I thought it looked like a fresh Jersey tomato, but I didn't ask how a self-proclaimed American flop had managed to acquire such a costly machine. With evident pride, he unlocked my door first and ushered me into the passenger's seat. Then, patting the hood as he walked around the front of the car, he stepped up onto the curb and unlocked the other door. Once he'd settled in behind the wheel, he turned to me and grinned. 'Solid merchandise,' he said.

'Yes,' I replied. 'Very impressive.'

'Make yourself comfortable, Mr. Sid. Reclining seats. Go all the way back.' He leaned over and showed me where to push the button, and sure enough, the seat began propelling itself backward, coming to rest at a forty-five-degree angle. 'Like that,' Chang said. 'Always better to ride in comfort.'

I couldn't disagree with him, and in my slightly tipsy state I found it pleasant to be in something other than a vertical position. Chang started up the engine of the car, and I closed my eyes for a moment, trying to imagine what Grace would want for dinner that evening and what food I should buy when I got back to Brooklyn. That turned out to be a mistake. Instead of opening my eyes again to see where Chang was going, I promptly fell asleep – just like any other drunk on a midday binge.

I didn't wake up until the car stopped and Chang turned off the engine. Assuming I was back in Cobble Hill, I was about to thank him for the lift and open the door when I realized I was somewhere else: a crowded commercial street in an unfamiliar neighborhood, no doubt far from where I lived. When I sat up to have a better look, I saw that most of the signs were in Chinese.

'Where are we?' I asked.

'Flushing,' Chang said. 'Chinatown Number Two.'

'Why did you bring me here?'

'Driving in car, I have better idea. Nice little club on next block, good place to relax. You look tired out, Mr. Sid. I take you there, you feel better.'

'What are you talking about? It's quarter past three, and I have to get home.'

'Just half an hour. Do you a world of good, I promise. Then I drive you home. Okay?'

'I'd rather not. Just point me to the nearest subway, and I'll go home myself.'

'Please. This very important to me. Maybe a business opportunity, and I need advice from a smart man. You very smart, Mr. Sid. I can trust you.'

'I have no idea what you're talking about. First you want me to relax. Then you want me to give you advice. Which is it?'

'Both things. All things together. You see place, you relax, and then you tell me what you think. Very simple.'

'Half an hour?'

'No skin off nose. Everything on me, free of charge. Then I drive you to Cobble Hill, Brooklyn. Deal?'

The afternoon was turning stranger by the minute, but I allowed myself to be talked into going with him. I can't really explain why. Curiosity, maybe, but it also could have been just the opposite – a feeling of total indifference. Chang had begun to get on my nerves, and I couldn't take his incessant pleading anymore, especially not while cooped up in that ridiculous car of his. If another half hour of my time would satisfy him, I figured it was worth it to play along. So I climbed out of the Pontiac and followed him down the densely thronged avenue, breathing in the pungent fumes and acrid smells of the fish stores and vegetable stands that lined the block. At the first corner, we turned left, walked for about a hundred feet, and then turned left again, entering a narrow alley with a small cinder-block structure at the end of it, a tiny one-story house with no windows and a flat roof. It was a

449

classic setup for a mugging, but I didn't feel the least bit threatened. Chang was in too jolly a mood, and with his usual intensity of purpose, he seemed hell-bent on reaching our destination.

When we came to the yellow cinder-block house, Chang pressed his finger against the doorbell. A few seconds later, the door opened a crack and a Chinese man in his sixties poked out his head. He nodded in recognition when he saw Chang, they exchanged a few sentences in Mandarin, and then he let us in. The so-called club of relaxation turned out to be a small sweatshop. Twenty Chinese women sat at tables with sewing machines, stitching together brightly colored dresses made of cheap, synthetic materials. Not one of them looked up at us when we entered, and Chang rushed past them as quickly as he could, acting as if they weren't there. We kept on walking, threading our way around the tables until we came to a door at the back of the room. The old man opened it for us, and Chang and I stepped into a space that was so black, so dark in comparison to the fluorescent-lit workshop behind us, that at first I couldn't see a thing.

Once my eyes had adjusted a little, I noticed some dim low-wattage lamps glowing in various places around the room. Each one had been fitted with a bulb of a different color – red, yellow, purple, blue – and for a moment I thought about the Portuguese notebooks in Chang's bankrupt store. I wondered if the ones I'd seen on Saturday were still available and, if they were, whether he'd be willing to sell them to me. I made a mental note to ask him about it before we left.

By and by, he led me to a tall chair or stool, something made of leather or imitation leather that swiveled on its base and had a nice cushiony feel to it. I sat down, and he sat down next to me, and I realized that we were at some kind of bar – a lacquered, oval-shaped bar that occupied the center of the room. Things were becoming clearer to me now. I could make out several people sitting across from us, a couple of men in suits and ties, an Asian man in what looked like a Hawaiian shirt, and two or three women, none of whom seemed to be wearing any clothes. Ah, I said to myself, so that's what this place is. A sex club. Oddly enough, it was only then that I noticed the music playing in the background – a soft, rumbling piece that wafted in from some invisible sound system. I strained to pick out the song, but I couldn't identify it. Some Musak version of an old rock-and-roll number – maybe the Beatles, I thought, but maybe not.

'Well, Mr. Sid,' Chang said, 'what do you think?'

Before I could answer him, a bartender appeared in front of us and asked for our orders. It might have been the old man who had opened the door earlier, but I wasn't certain. It could have been his brother, or perhaps some other relative with a stake in the enterprise. Chang leaned over and whispered in my ear. 'No alcohol,' he said. 'Fake beer, 7-Up, Coke. Too risky to sell booze in place like this. No liquor license.' Now that I'd been informed of the possibilities, I opted for a Coke. Chang did the same.

'Brand-new place,' the ex-stationer continued. 'Just open on Saturday. They still iron out the kinks, but I see large potential here. They ask if I want to invest as minority partner.'

'It's a brothel,' I said. 'Are you sure you want to get mixed up in an illegal business?'

'Not brothel. Relaxation club with naked women. Help the working-man feel better.'

'I'm not going to split hairs with you. If you're so keen on it, go ahead. But I thought you were broke.'

'Money never a problem. I borrow. If profit from investment stay ahead of interest on loan, everything okay.'

'If.'

'Very little if. They find gorgeous girls to work here. Miss Universe, Marilyn Monroe, Playmate of Month. Only the hottest, most sexy women. No man can resist. Look, I show you.'

'No thanks. I'm a married man. I have everything I need at home.'

'Every man say that. But the dick always win out over duty. I prove it to you now.'

Before I could stop him, Chang wheeled around in his chair and made a beckoning gesture with his hand. I looked over in that direction myself and saw five or six cocktail booths lining the wall, something I had managed to miss when I first entered the room. Naked women sat at three of them, apparently waiting for customers, but the others had been curtained off, presumably because the women who occupied those spots were busy at work. One of the women rose from her seat and came walking toward us. 'This one the best,' Chang said, 'the most beautiful of all. They call her the African Princess.'

A tall black woman emerged from the darkness. She was wearing a pearl-and-rhinestone choker, knee-high white boots, and a white G-string. Her hair was done up in elaborate cornrow braids, ornamented with bangles at the ends that tinkled like wind chimes when she moved.

Her walk was graceful, languorous, erect – a regal sort of bearing that no doubt explained why she was called the Princess. By the time she was within six feet of the bar, I understood that Chang had not been exaggerating. She was a stunningly beautiful woman – perhaps the most beautiful woman I had ever seen. And all of twenty, perhaps twenty-two years old. Her skin looked so smooth and inviting, I found it almost impossible to resist touching it.

'Say hello to my friend,' Chang instructed her. 'I settle up with you later.'

She turned to me and smiled, exposing a set of astonishing white teeth. 'Bonjour, chéri,' she said. 'Tu parles français?'

'No, I'm sorry. I only speak English.'

'My name is Martine,' she said, with a heavy Creole accent.

'I'm Sidney,' I answered, and then, trying to make a stab at conversation, I asked her which country in Africa she came from.

She laughed. 'Pas d'Afrique! Haiti.' She pronounced the last word in three syllables, *Ha-ee-tee.* 'A bad place,' she said. 'Duvalier is very méchant. It is nicer here.'

I nodded, having no idea what to say next. I wanted to get up and leave before I got myself into trouble, but I couldn't move. The girl was too much, and I couldn't stop looking at her.

'Tu veux danser avec moi?' she said. 'You dance with me?'

'I don't know. Maybe. I'm not a very good dancer.'

'Something else?'

'I don't know. Well, maybe one thing . . . if it isn't too much to ask.'

'One thing?'

'I was wondering. . . . Would you mind terribly if I touched you?'

'Touched me? Of course. That is easy. Touch me anywhere you like.'

I reached out my hand and ran it down the length of her bare arm. 'You are very timide,' she said. 'Do you not see my breasts? Mes seins sont très jolis, n'est-ce pas?'

I was sober enough to realize that I was traveling down the road to perdition, but I didn't let that stop me. I cupped her small round breasts in my two hands and held them there for some time – long enough to feel her nipples harden.

'Ah, that is better,' she said. 'Now you let me touch you, okay?'

I didn't say yes, but neither did I say no. I assumed she had something innocent in mind – a pat on the cheek, a finger traced across my lips, a playful squeeze of the hand. Nothing to compare with what she actually did, in any case, which was to press herself against me, slide her elegant hand down into my jeans, and take hold of the erection that had been growing in there for the past two minutes. When she felt how stiff I was, she smiled. 'I think we are ready to dance,' she said. 'You come with me now, okay?'

To his credit, Chang didn't laugh at this sad little spectacle of male weakness. He had proved his point, and rather than gloat over his triumph, he merely winked at me as I walked off with Martine to her booth.

The whole transaction seemed to last no longer than the time it takes to fill a bathtub. She closed the curtain around the booth and immediately unbuckled my pants. Then she dropped to her knees and put her right hand around my penis, and after a few gentle strokes, followed by some timely licks of the tongue, she put it in her mouth. Her head began to move, and as I listened to the tinkling of her braids and looked down at her extraordinary bare back, I felt a rush of warmth rising up through my legs and into my groin. I wanted to prolong the experience and savor it for a little while, but I couldn't. Martine's mouth was a deadly instrument, and like any aroused teenage boy, I came almost at once.

Regret set in within a matter of seconds. By the time I'd pulled up my jeans and fastened my belt, regret had turned into shame and remorse. The only thing I wanted was to get out of there as quickly as I could. I asked Martine how much I owed her, but she waved me off and said my friend had already taken care of it. She kissed me when I said good-bye, an amiable little peck on the cheek, and then I parted the curtain and went back to the bar to look for Chang. He wasn't there. Perhaps he'd found a woman for himself and was already with her in another booth, testing the professional qualifications of one of his future employees. I didn't bother to stick around to find out. I walked around the bar once, just to make sure I hadn't missed him, and then I found the door that led to the dress factory and started out for home.

The next morning, Wednesday, I served Grace breakfast in bed again. There was no talk about dreams this time, and neither one of us mentioned the pregnancy or what she was planning to do about it. The issue was still up in the air, but after my disgraceful behavior in Queens the day before, I felt too embarrassed to broach the subject. In the span of thirty-six short hours, I had gone from being a self-righteous defender of moral certainties to an abject, guilt-ridden husband.

Nevertheless, I tried to keep up a good front, and even though she was unusually quiet that morning, I don't think Grace suspected anything was wrong. I insisted on walking her to the subway, holding her hand for the entire four blocks to the Bergen Street station, and for most of the way we talked about ordinary matters: a jacket she was designing for a book on nineteenth-century French photography, the film treatment I had handed in the day before and the money I hoped would come from it, what we would have for dinner that night. On the last block, however, Grace abruptly changed the tone of the conversation. She gripped my hand tightly and said: 'We trust each other, don't we, Sid?'

'Of course we do. We wouldn't be able to live together if we didn't. The whole idea of marriage is based on trust.'

'People can go through rough times, can't they? But that doesn't mean things can't work out in the end.'

'This isn't a rough time, Grace. We've been through that already, and we're beginning to pull ourselves together again.'

'I'm glad you said that.'

'I'm glad you're glad. But why?'

'Because that's what I think too. No matter what happens with the baby, everything between us is going to be fine. We're going to make it.'

'We've already made it. We're cruising down Easy Street, kid, and that's where we're going to stay.'

Grace stopped walking, put her hand on the back of my neck, and pulled my face toward her for a kiss. 'You're the best, Sidney,' she said, and then she kissed me once more for good measure. 'No matter what happens, don't ever forget that.'

I didn't understand what she was talking about, but before I could ask her what she meant, she disentangled herself from my arms and started running toward the subway. I stood where I was on the sidewalk, watching her cover the last ten yards. Then she came to the top step, grabbed hold of the railing, and disappeared down the stairs.

Back at the apartment, I kept myself busy for the next hour, killing time until the Sklarr Agency opened at nine-thirty. I washed the breakfast dishes, made the bed, tidied up the living room, and then I went back into the kitchen and called Mary. The ostensible reason was to make sure Angela had remembered to give her my pages, but knowing that she had, I was actually calling to find out what Mary thought of them. 'Good job,' she said, sounding neither greatly excited nor terribly disappointed. The fact that I had written the outline so quickly, how-ever, had enabled her to pull off a high-speed communications miracle, and that had her gushing with excitement. In those days before fax machines, e-mails, and express letters, she had sent the treatment to Cal-ifornia by private courier, which meant that my work had already trav-eled across the country on last night's red-eye. 'I had to get a contract off to another client in LA,' Mary said, 'so I hired the courier service to come by the office at three o'clock. I read your treatment right after lunch, and half an hour later the guy shows up for the contract. "This one's also going to LA," I said, "so you might as well take it too." So I handed him your manuscript, and off it went, just like that. It should be on Hunter's desk in about three hours.'

'Great,' I said. 'But what about the idea? Do you think it has a chance?'

'I only read it once. I didn't have time to study it, but it seemed fine to me, Sid. Very interesting, nicely worked out. But you never know with those Hollywood people. My guess is it's too complicated for them.'

'So I shouldn't get my hopes up.'

'I wouldn't say that. Just don't count on it, that's all.'

'I won't. But the money would be nice, wouldn't it?'

'Well, I do have some good news for you on that front. I was just going to call you, in fact, but you beat me to it. A Portuguese publisher has made an offer on your last two novels.'

'Portugal?'

'*Self-Portrait* was published in Spain while you were in the hospital. You know that, I told you. The reviews were very good. Now the Portuguese are interested.'

'That's nice. I suppose they're offering something like three hundred dollars.'

'Four hundred for each book. But I can easily get them up to five.'

'Go for it, Mary. After you deduct the agents' fees and foreign taxes, I'll wind up with about forty cents.'

'True. But at least you'll be published in Portugal. What's wrong with that?'

'Nothing. Pessoa is one of my favorite writers. They've kicked out Salazar and have a decent government now. The Lisbon earthquake inspired Voltaire to write *Candide*. And Portugal helped get thousands of Jews out of Europe during the war. It's a terrific country. I've never been there, of course, but that's where I live now, whether I like it or not.

455

Portugal is perfect. The way things have been going these past few days, it had to be Portugal.'

'What are you talking about?'

'It's a long story. I'll tell you about it some other time.'

I made it to Trause's apartment on the dot of one. As I rang the bell, it occurred to me that I should have stopped off somewhere in the neighborhood and bought take-out lunches for the two of us, but I had forgotten about Madame Dumas, the woman from Martinique who managed the household. The meal was already prepared, and it was served to us in John's den on the second floor, the same room where we had eaten our Chinese dinner on Saturday night. I should note that Madame Dumas was not on duty that day. It was her daughter, Régine, who opened the door and led me upstairs to *Monsieur John*. I remembered that Trause had called her 'nice to look at,' and now that I'd seen her myself, I was forced to admit that I, too, found her remarkably attractive – a tall, well-proportioned young woman with glowing ebony skin and keen, watchful eyes. No G-string, of course, no bare breasts or white leather boots, but this was the second twenty-year-old French-speaking black woman I had met in two days, and I found the repetition jarring, almost intolerable. Why couldn't Régine Dumas have been a short, homely girl with a bad complexion and a hump on her back? She wasn't the heart-stopping beauty that Martine of Haiti was, perhaps, but she was a fetching creature in her own right, and when she opened the door and smiled at me in her friendly, self-assured way, I felt it as a reproof, a mocking rejoinder from my own troubled conscience. I had been doing everything in my power not to think about what had happened the day before, to forget my sorry peccadillo and put it behind me, but there was no escape from what I had done. Martine had come to life again in the form of Régine Dumas. She was everywhere now, even in my friend's Barrow Street apartment, half a world away from that shabby cinder-block building in Queens.

As opposed to his unkempt appearance on Saturday night, John looked presentable this time. His hair was combed, his whiskers were gone, and he was wearing a freshly laundered shirt and clean socks. But he was still immobilized on the sofa, his left leg propped up on a mountain of pillows and blankets, and he seemed to be in considerable pain – as bad as the other night, if not worse. The clean-shaven look had thrown me. When Régine brought the lunch upstairs on a tray (turkey sandwiches, salads, sparkling water), I did everything I could not to look at her. That meant focusing my attention on John, and when I studied his features more carefully, I saw that he was exhausted, with a sunken, hollowed-out look in his eyes and a disturbing pallor to his skin. He left the sofa twice while I was there, and both times he reached for his crutch before maneuvering himself into a standing position. From the look on his face when his left foot touched the ground, the slightest pressure on the vein must have been unbearable.

I asked him when he was supposed to get better, but John didn't want to talk about it. I kept after him, however, and eventually he admitted that he hadn't told us everything on Saturday night. He hadn't wanted to alarm Grace, he said, but the truth was that there were two clots in his leg, not one. The first was in a superficial vein. It had nearly dissolved by now and posed no threat, even though it was causing most of what John referred to as his 'discomfort.' The second was lodged in a deep interior vein, and that was the one the doctor was worried about. Massive doses of blood thinner had been prescribed, and John was scheduled to have a scan at Saint Vincent's on Friday. If the results were less than satisfactory, the doctor was planning to admit him to the hospital and keep him there until the clot disappeared. Deep-vein thrombosis could be fatal, John said. If the clot broke loose, it could travel through his bloodstream and wind up in a lung, causing a pulmonary embolism and almost certain death. 'It's like walking around with a little bomb in my leg,' he said. 'If I shake it around too much, it could blow me up.' Then he added, 'Not a word to Gracie. This is strictly between you and me. Got it? Not a single goddamn word.'

Not long after that, we started talking about his son. I can't remember what led us into that pit of despair and self-recrimination, but Trause's anguish was palpable, and whatever concerns he had about his leg were nothing compared to the hopelessness he felt about Jacob. 'I've lost him,' he said. 'After the stunt he's just pulled, I'll never believe another word he says to me.'

Until the latest crisis, Jacob had been an undergraduate at SUNY Buffalo. John was acquainted with several members of the English Department there (one of them, Charles Rothstein, had published a long study of his novels), and after Jacob's disastrous, near-failing record in high school, he had pulled some strings in order to get the boy accepted. The first semester had gone reasonably well, and Jacob had managed to pass all his courses, but by the end of the second term his grades had fallen off so badly that he was put on academic probation. He needed to maintain a B average to avoid suspension, but in the fall semester of his sophomore year he cut more classes than he attended, did little or no work, and was summarily booted out for the next term. He went back to his mother in East Hampton, where she was living with her third husband (in the same house where Jacob had grown up with his much-despised stepfather, an art dealer named Ralph Singleton), and found a part-time job at a local bakery. He also formed a rock band with three of his high school friends, but there were so many tensions and squabbles among them that the group broke up after six months. He told his father he had no use for college and didn't want to go back, but John managed to talk him into it by offering certain financial incentives: a comfortable allowance, a new guitar if he kept his grades up in the first semester, a Volkswagen minibus if he finished the year with a B average. The kid went for it, and in late August he'd gone back to Buffalo to play at being a student again – with green hair, a row of safety pins dangling from his left ear, and a long black overcoat. The punk era was in full bloom then, and Jacob had joined the ever-expanding club of snarling, middle-class renegades. He was hip, he lived on the edge, and he didn't take crap from anyone.

Jacob had enrolled for the semester, John said, but a week later, without having attended a single class, he returned to the registrar's office and dropped out of school. The tuition was returned to him, and instead of sending the check to his father (who had provided him with the money in the first place), he cashed it in at the nearest bank, put the three thousand dollars in his pocket, and headed south to New York. At last word, he was living somewhere in the East Village. If the rumors circulating about him were correct, he was deep into heroin – and had been for the past four months.

'Who told you this?' I asked. 'How do you know it's true?'

'Eleanor called me yesterday morning. She'd been trying to get hold of Jacob about something, and his roommate answered the phone. Ex-roommate, I should say. He told her Jacob had left school two weeks ago.'

'And the heroin?'

'He told her about that too. There's no reason for him to lie about a thing like that. According to Eleanor, he sounded very concerned. It's not that I'm surprised, Sid. I've always suspected he was taking drugs. I just didn't know it was this bad.'

'What are you going to do about it?'

'I don't know. You're the one who used to work with kids. What would you do?'

'You're asking the wrong person. All my students were poor. Black teenagers from tumbledown neighborhoods and broken families. A lot of them took drugs, but their problems have nothing to do with Jacob's.'

'Eleanor thinks we should go out looking for him. But I can't move. I'm stuck on this couch with my leg.'

'I'll do it if you like. It's not as if I'm very busy these days.'

'No, no, I don't want you getting involved. It's not your problem. Eleanor and her husband will do it. At least that's what she said. With her, you never know if she means it or not.'

'What's her new husband like?'

'I don't know. I've never met him. The funny thing is, I can't even remember his name. I've been lying here trying to think of it, but I keep drawing blanks. Don something, I think, but I'm not sure.'

'And what's the plan once they find Jacob?'

'Get him into a drug rehab program.'

'Those things aren't cheap. Who's going to pay for it?'

'Me, of course. Eleanor's rolling in money these days, but she's so fucking tight, I wouldn't even bother to ask her. The kid chisels three thousand bucks out of me, and now I have to cough up another bundle to get him clean. If you want to know the truth, I feel like wringing his neck. You're lucky you don't have any children, Sid. They're nice when they're small, but after that they break your heart and make you miserable. Five feet, that's the maximum. They shouldn't be allowed to grow any taller than that.'

After John's last comment, I couldn't hold back from telling him my news. 'I might not be childless much longer,' I said. 'It's not clear what we're going to do about it yet, but for the moment Grace is pregnant. She had the test on Saturday.'

I didn't know what I was expecting John to say, but even after his bitter pronouncements on the agonies of fatherhood, I figured he'd manage to come out with some kind of perfunctory congratulations. Or at least wish me luck and warn me to do a better job than he'd done. Something, in any case, some little word of acknowledgment. But John didn't make a sound. For a moment he looked stricken, as if he'd just been told about the death of someone he loved, and then he turned his face away from me, abruptly swiveling his head on the pillow and looking straight into the back of the sofa.

'Poor Grace,' he muttered.

'Why do you say that?'

John slowly turned back toward me, but he stopped midway, his head aligned with the sofa, and when he talked he kept his gaze fixed on the ceiling. 'It's just that she's been through so much,' he said. 'She's not as strong as you think she is. She needs a rest.'

'She'll do exactly what she wants to do. The decision is in her hands.'

'I've known her much longer than you have. A baby is the last thing she needs right now.'

'If she goes through with it, I was thinking of asking you to be the godfather. But I don't suppose you'd be interested. Not from what you're saying now.'

'Just don't lose her, Sidney. That's all I'm asking you. If things fall apart, it would be a catastrophe for her.'

'They're not going to fall apart. And I'm not going to lose her. But even if I did, what business is it of yours?'

'Grace is my business. She's always been my business.'

'You're not her father. You might think you are sometimes, but you're not. Grace can handle herself. If she decides to have the baby, I'm not going to stop her. The truth is, I'll be glad. Having a child with her would be about the best thing that ever happened to me.'

That was the closest John and I had ever come to an out-and-out argument. It was an upsetting moment for me, and as my last words hung defiantly in the air, I wondered if the conversation wasn't about to take an even nastier turn. Fortunately, we both backed off before the flare-up developed any further, realizing that we were about to goad each other into saying things we would later regret – and which could never be expunged from memory, no matter how many apologies we made after our tempers had calmed down.

Very wisely, John picked that moment to pay a visit to the bathroom. As I watched him go through the arduous manipulations of hauling himself off the sofa and then hobble across the room, all the hostility suddenly drained out of me. He was living under extreme duress. His leg was killing him, he was grappling with the awful news about his son, and how could I not forgive him for having spoken a few harsh words? In the context of Jacob's betrayal and possible drug addiction, Grace was the adored good child, the one who had never let him down, and perhaps that was the reason why John had been so adamant in coming to her defense, butting into matters that finally didn't concern him.

He was angry at his son, yes, but that anger was also laden with a substantial dose of guilt. John knew he had more or less abdicated his responsibilities as a father. Divorced from Eleanor when Jacob was one and a half, he had allowed her to remove the child from New York when she settled in East Hampton with her second husband in 1966. After that, John had seen little of the boy: an occasional weekend together in the city, a few trips to New England and the Southwest during summer vacations. Hardly what one could call an actively involved parent, and then, after Tina's death, he had disappeared from Jacob's life for four years, seeing him only once or twice from age twelve to sixteen. Now, at twenty, his son had turned into a full-blown mess, and whether it was his fault or not, John blamed himself for the disaster.

He was gone from the room for ten or fifteen minutes. When he returned, I helped him onto the sofa again, and the first thing he said to me had nothing to do with what we'd been talking about earlier. The conflict seemed to be over – swept away during his trip down the hall and apparently forgotten.

'How's Flitcraft?' he asked. 'Making any progress?'

'Yes and no,' I said. 'I wrote up a storm for a couple of days, but then I got stuck.'

'And now you're having second thoughts about the blue notebook.'

'Maybe. I'm not sure I know what I think anymore.'

'You were so revved up the other night, you sounded like a demented alchemist. The first man to turn lead into gold.'

'Well, it was quite an experience. The first time I used the notebook, Grace tells me I wasn't there anymore.'

'What do you mean?'

'That I disappeared. I know it sounds ridiculous, but she knocked on my door while I was writing, and when I didn't answer she poked her head into the room. She swears she didn't see me.'

'You must have been somewhere else in the apartment. In the bathroom, maybe.'

'I know. That's what Grace says too. But I don't remember going to the bathroom. I don't remember anything but sitting at my desk and writing.'

'You might not remember it, but that doesn't mean it didn't happen. One tends to get a little absentminded when the words are flowing. Not true?'

'True. Of course true. But then something similar happened on

461

Monday. I was in my room writing, and I didn't hear the phone ring. When I got up from my desk and went into the kitchen, there were two messages on the machine.'

'So?'

'I didn't hear the ring. I always hear the phone when it rings.'

'You were distracted, lost in what you were doing.'

'Maybe. But I don't think so. Something strange happened, and I don't understand it.'

'Call your doctor, Sid, and set up an appointment to have your head examined.'

'I know. It's all in my head. I'm not saying it isn't, but ever since I bought that notebook, everything's gone out of whack. I can't tell if I'm the one who's using the notebook or if the notebook's been using me. Does that make any sense?'

'A little. But not much.'

'All right, let me put it another way. Have you ever heard of a writer named Sylvia Maxwell? An American novelist from the twenties.'

'I've read some books by Sylvia Monroe. She published a bunch of novels in the twenties and thirties. But not Maxwell.'

'Did she ever write a book called *Oracle Night*?'

'No, not that I know of. But I think she wrote something with the word *night* in the title. *Havana Night,* maybe. Or *London Night,* I can't remember. It shouldn't be hard to find out. Just go to the library and look her up.'

Little by little, we veered away from the blue notebook and started discussing more practical matters. Money, for one thing, and how I was hoping to solve my financial problems by writing a film script for Bobby Hunter. I told John about the treatment, giving him a quick summary of the plot I'd cooked up for my version of *The Time Machine*, but he didn't offer much of a response. *Clever,* I think he said, or some equally mild compliment, and I suddenly felt stupid, embarrassed, as though Trause looked on me as some tawdry hack trying to peddle my wares to the highest bidder. But I was wrong to interpret his muffled reaction as disapproval. He understood what a tight spot we were in, and it turned out that he was thinking, trying to come up with a plan to help me.

'I know it's idiotic,' I said, 'but if they go for the idea, we'll be solvent again. If they don't, we're still in the red. I hate to count on such flimsy prospects, but it's the only trick I have up my sleeve.'

'Maybe not,' John said. 'If this *Time Machine* thing doesn't work,

ORACLE NIGHT

maybe you could write another screenplay. You're good at it. If you got Mary to push hard enough, I'm sure you'd find someone willing to fork over a nice chunk of cash.'

'It doesn't work that way. They come to you; you don't go to them. Unless you have an original idea, of course. But I don't.'

'That's what I'm talking about. Maybe I have an idea for you.'

'A movie idea? I thought you were against writing for the movies.'

'A couple of weeks ago, I found a box with some of my old stuff in it. Early stories, a half-finished novel, two or three plays. Ancient material, written when I was still in my teens and twenties. None of it was ever published. Thankfully, I should add, but in reading over the stories, I found one that wasn't half terrible. I still wouldn't want to publish it, but if I gave it to you, you might be able to rethink it as a film. Maybe my name will help. If you tell a film producer you're adapting an unpublished story by John Trause, it might have some appeal. I don't know. But even if they don't give a shit about me, there's a strong visual component to the story. I think the images would lend themselves to film in a pretty natural way.'

'Of course your name would help. It would make a huge difference.'

'Well, read the story and let me know what you think. It's just a first draft – very rough – so don't judge the prose too harshly. And remember, I was hardly more than a kid when I wrote it. Much younger than you are now.'

'What's it about?'

'It's an odd piece, not at all like my other work, so you might be a little surprised at first. I guess I'd call it a political parable. It's set in an imaginary country in the eighteen thirties, but it's really about the early nineteen fifties. McCarthy, HUAC, the Red Scare – all the sinister things that were going on then. The idea is that governments always need enemies, even when they're not at war. If you don't have a real enemy, you make one up and spread the word. It scares the population, and when the people are scared, they tend not to step out of line.'

'What about the country? Is it a stand-in for America or something else?'

'It's part North America, part South America, but with a completely different history from either one. Way back, all the European powers had set up colonies in the New World. The colonies evolved into independent states, and then, little by little, after hundreds of years of wars and skirmishes, they gradually merge into an enormous confederation.

The question is: What happens after the empire is established? What enemy do you invent to make people scared enough to hold the confederation together?'

'And what's the answer?'

'You pretend you're about to be invaded by barbarians. The confederation has already pushed these people off their lands, but now you spread the rumor that an army of anticonfederationist soldiers has crossed into the primitive territories and is stirring up a rebellion among the people there. It isn't true. The soldiers are working for the government. They're part of the conspiracy.'

'Who tells the story?'

'A man sent to investigate the rumors. He works for a branch of the government that isn't in on the plot, and he winds up being arrested and tried for treason. To make matters more complicated, the officer in charge of the false army has run off with the narrator's wife.'

'Deceit and corruption at every turn.'

'Exactly. A man ruined by his own innocence.'

'Does it have a title?'

'"The Empire of Bones." It's not very long. Forty-five or fifty pages – but there's enough to squeeze a film out of it, I think. You decide. If you want to use it, I give you my blessing. If you don't like it, then chuck it in the garbage, and we'll forget all about it.'

I left Trause's apartment feeling overwhelmed, tongue-tied with gratitude, and not even the small torment of having to say good-bye to Régine downstairs could diminish my happiness. The manuscript was in a side pocket of my sport coat, tucked away in a manila envelope, and I kept my hand on it as I walked to the subway, itching to open it up and start reading. John had always been behind me and my work, but I knew this gift had as much to do with Grace as it did with me. I was the half-destroyed cripple responsible for taking care of her, and if there was anything he could do to help us get back on our feet, he was willing to do it – even to the extent of donating an unpublished manuscript to the cause. There was only the slimmest chance that anything would come of his idea, but whether I could turn his story into a film or not, the important thing was his readiness to go beyond the normal bounds of friendship and involve himself in our affairs. Selflessly, without any thought of profiting from what he'd done.

It was already past five o'clock when I made it to the West Fourth

Street station. Rush hour was in full swing, and as I descended the two flights of stairs to the downtown F platform, gripping the banister tightly so as not to stumble, I despaired of finding a seat on the train. There would be a crush of passengers traveling back to Brooklyn. That meant I would have to read John's story standing up, and since that would be immensely difficult, I prepared myself to fight for a little extra space if I had to. When the doors of the train opened, I ignored subway etiquette and slipped in past the jostle of disembarking passengers, entering the car before anyone else on the platform, but it didn't do me any good. A mob came pouring in behind me. I was pushed to the center of the car, and by the time the doors closed and the train left the station, I was crammed in among so many people that my arms were pinned to my sides, with no room to reach into my pocket and take out the envelope. It was all I could do not to crash into my fellow riders as we rocked and lurched our way through the tunnel. At one point, I managed to get my hand up far enough to hook my fingers onto one of the overhead bars, but that was the extent of the movement possible for me under the circumstances. Few passengers got off at the succeeding stops, and for every one who did, two others shouldered themselves in to take that person's place. Hundreds were left standing on the platforms to wait for the next train, and from the beginning of the ride to the end, I didn't have a single chance to look at the story. When we pulled into the Bergen Street station, I tried to get my hand back onto the envelope, but I was bumped from behind, squeezed from both left and right, and as I pivoted around the center pole to get ready to exit the car, the train suddenly stopped, the doors opened, and I was pushed out onto the platform before I could check to see if the envelope was still there. It wasn't. The surge of the departing crowd carried me along with it for six or seven feet, and by the time I spun around to elbow my way back into the car, the doors had already closed and the subway was moving again. I pounded my fist against a passing window, but the conductor paid no attention to me. The F glided out of the station, and a few seconds later it was gone.

I had been guilty of similar lapses of concentration since coming home from the hospital, but none was worse or more wrenching than this one. Instead of keeping the envelope in my hand, I had foolishly shoved the thing into a pocket that was too small to hold it, and now John's manuscript was lying on the floor of a subway car headed for Coney Island, no doubt trampled and smudged by half the shoes and sneakers in the borough of Brooklyn. It was an unforgivable mistake. John had entrusted me with the only copy of an unpublished story, and given the academic interest in his work, the manuscript alone was probably worth hundreds of dollars, perhaps thousands. What was I going to tell him when he asked me what I thought of it? He had said I should toss it in the garbage if I didn't like it, but that was merely a hyperbolic way of denigrating his own work, a joke. Of course he would want the manuscript back – whether I liked it or not. I had no idea how to make amends. If someone had done to me what I'd just done to Trause, I think I would have been angry enough to want to strangle him.

Demoralizing as that loss was, it was only the beginning of what turned out to be a long and difficult night. When I returned home and walked up the three flights of stairs to the apartment, I discovered that the door was open – not simply ajar, but flung back on its hinges and standing flush against the wall. My first thought was that Grace had come home early, perhaps carrying an armful of bundles and grocery bags, and had forgotten to shut the door behind her. One look at the living room, however, and I understood that Grace had nothing to do with it. Someone had broken into the apartment, most likely by climbing up the fire escape and jimmying the kitchen window. Books were strewn about the floor, our small black-and-white TV was gone, and a photograph of Grace, which had always stood on the mantel, had been torn up into little pieces and scattered onto the sofa. It was a remarkably vicious gesture, I felt, almost a personal attack. When I went over to the bookcase to inspect the damage, I saw that only the most valuable books were missing: signed copies of novels by Trause and a number of other writer friends, along with half a dozen first editions that had been given to me as presents over the years. Hawthorne, Dickens, Henry James, Fitzgerald, Wallace Stevens, Emerson. Whoever had robbed us was no ordinary thief. He knew something about literature, and he had zeroed in on the few treasures we owned.

My study appeared to be untouched, but the bedroom had been systematically and thoroughly ransacked. Every drawer had been pulled out of the bureau, the mattress had been overturned, and the Bram van Velde lithograph that Grace had bought at the Galerie Maeght in Paris in the early seventies was missing from its place on the wall above our bed. When I sifted through the contents of the bureau drawers, I discovered that Grace's jewelry box was also missing. She didn't own much, but a pair of moonstone earrings she'd inherited from her grandmother had been in that box, along with a charm bracelet from her childhood and a silver necklace I'd given to her on her last birthday. Now some stranger had walked off with these things, and it felt as cruel and pointless to me as a rape, a savage plundering of our little world.

We had no theft or home insurance, and I was disinclined to call the police to report the break-in. Burglars were never caught, and I saw no reason to pursue what struck me as a hopeless case, but before I made that decision I had to find out if anyone else in the building had been robbed. There were three other apartments in the brownstone – one above us and two below – and I began by going downstairs to the ground floor and talking to Mrs. Caramello, who shared the superintendent duties with her husband, a retired barber who spent most of his time watching television and betting on football games. Their place hadn't been touched, but Mrs. Caramello was sufficiently distressed by my news to call out to Mr. Caramello, who came shuffling to the door in his slippers and merely sighed when he was told what had happened. 'Probably one of them goddamn junkies,' he said. 'Gotta get bars on your windows, Sid. Ain't no other way to keep the trash from crawling in.'

The other two tenants had also been spared. It seemed that everyone had bars on their back windows but us, and therefore we'd been the logical target – trusting dumbbells who hadn't bothered to take the proper precautions. They all felt sorry for us, but the implicit message was that we'd deserved what we'd got.

I went back into the apartment, even more horrified now that I could survey the mess in a calmer state of mind. One by one, details I had overlooked earlier suddenly jumped out at me, further aggravating the effect of the intrusion. A standing lamp to the left of the sofa had been tipped over and broken, a flower vase lay smashed on the rug, and even our pathetic, nineteen-dollar toaster had vanished from its spot on the kitchen counter. I called Grace at her office, wanting to prepare her for the shock, but no one answered, which seemed to imply that she had already left and was on her way home. Not knowing what else to do with myself, I began straightening up the apartment. It must have been about six-thirty at that point, and even though I was expecting Grace to walk through the door at any moment, I worked steadily for over an hour, sweeping up debris, returning the books to the shelves, righting the mattress and putting it back on the bed, sliding the drawers back into the bureau. At first, I was glad to be making so much progress while Grace was still gone. The more effectively I could put the place in order, the less disconcerting it would be for her when she walked into the apartment. But then I finished what I had set out to do, and she still hadn't come home. It was seven-forty-five by then, long past the time when a subway breakdown could have accounted for her failure to reach Brooklyn. It was true that she sometimes worked late, but she always called to let me know when she would be leaving the office, and there was no message from her on the answering machine. I called her number at Holst & McDermott again, just to make sure, but again no one picked up. She wasn't at work, and she hadn't come home, and all of a sudden the break-in seemed to be of no importance, a minor irritation from the distant past. Grace was missing, and by the time eight o'clock rolled around, I had already worked myself into a feverish, all-out panic.

I made a number of calls – to friends, co-workers, even to her cousin Lily in Connecticut – but only the last person I talked to had any information to give me. Greg Fitzgerald was head of the art department at Holst & McDermott, and according to him, Grace had called the office just after nine that morning to tell him she couldn't make it to work that day. She was very sorry, but something urgent had come up that required her immediate attention. She didn't say what the something was, but when Greg asked her if she was all right, Grace had apparently hesitated before answering. 'I think so,' she'd finally said, and Greg, who had known her for years and was extremely fond of her (a gay man half in love with his prettiest female colleague), had found the response puzzling. 'Not like her' was the phrase he used, I think, but when he heard the mounting alarm in my voice, he tried to reassure me by adding that Grace had ended the conversation by telling him she would be back in the office tomorrow morning. 'Don't worry, Sidney,' Greg continued. 'When Grace says she's going to do something, she does it. I've been working with her for five years, and she hasn't let me down once.'

I sat up all night waiting for her, half out of my mind with dread and confusion. Before talking to Fitzgerald, I had convinced myself that Grace had been harmed in some violent way – mugged, molested, knocked down by a speeding truck or cab, a victim of one of the countless brutalities that can befall a woman alone on the streets of New York.

That seemed unlikely now, but if she wasn't dead or in physical danger, what had happened to her, and why hadn't she called to tell me where she was? I kept going over the conversation we'd had that morning on our walk to the subway, trying to make sense of her curiously emotional statements about trust, remembering the kisses she'd given me and how, without warning, she'd broken free of my arms and started running along the sidewalk, not even bothering to turn around and wave good-bye before disappearing down the stairs. It was the behavior of someone who had come to an abrupt and impulsive decision, whose mind had been made up about something but who was still full of doubts and uncertainties, so shaky in her resolve that she hadn't dared to pause for a single backward glance, fearing that one more look at me might destroy her determination to do whatever it was she was planning to do. I understood that much, I felt, but beyond that point I knew nothing. Grace had become a blank to me, and every thought I had about her that night quickly turned into a story, a gruesome little drama that played on my deepest anxieties about our future – which rapidly seemed to be turning into no future at all.

She came home a few minutes past seven, roughly two hours after I had resigned myself to the fact that I would never see her again. She was wearing different clothes from the ones she'd had on the previous morning, and she looked fresh and beautiful, with bright red lipstick, elegantly made-up eyes, and a hint of rouge on her cheeks. I was sitting on the sofa in the living room, and when I saw her walk in I was so taken aback that I couldn't speak, was literally unable to get any words out of my mouth. Grace smiled at me – calmly, resplendently, in full possession of herself – and then walked over to where I was sitting and kissed me on the lips.

'I know I've put you through hell,' she said, 'but it had to be this way. It won't ever happen again, Sidney. I promise.'

She sat down next to me and kissed me again, but I couldn't bring myself to put my arms around her. 'You have to tell me where you were,' I said, startled by the anger and bitterness in my voice. 'No more silence, Grace. You have to talk.'

'I can't,' she said.

'Yes you can. You have to.'

'Yesterday morning, you said you trusted me. Go on trusting me, Sid. That's all I ask.'

'When people say that, it means they're hiding something. Always.

469

It's like a mathematical law, Grace. What is it? What are you holding back from me?'

'Nothing. I just needed to be alone yesterday, that's all. I needed time to think.'

'Fine. Go ahead and think. But don't torture me by not calling to tell me where you are.'

'I wanted to, but then I couldn't. I don't know why. It was like I had to pretend I didn't know you anymore. Just for a little while. It was a rotten thing to do, but it helped me, it really did.'

'Where did you spend the night?'

'It wasn't like that, believe me. I was alone. I checked into a room at the Gramercy Park Hotel.'

'What floor? What was the number of the room?'

'Please, Sid, don't do that. It's not right.'

'I could call them and find out, couldn't I?'

'Of course you could. But that would mean you didn't believe me. And then we'd be in trouble. But we're not in trouble. That's the whole point. We're good, and the fact that I'm here now proves it.'

'I suppose you were thinking about the baby. . . .'

'Among other things, yes.'

'Any new thoughts?'

'I'm still on the fence. I'm still not sure which way to jump.'

'I spent a few hours with John yesterday, and he thinks you should have an abortion. He was very insistent about it.'

Grace looked both surprised and upset. 'John? But he doesn't know I'm pregnant.'

'I told him.'

'Oh, Sidney. You shouldn't have done that.'

'Why not? He's our friend, isn't he? Why shouldn't he know?'

She hesitated for several seconds before answering my question. 'Because it's our secret,' she finally said, 'and we haven't decided what we're going to do about it. I haven't even told my parents. If John talks to my father, things could get awfully complicated.'

'He won't. He's too worried about you to do that.'

'Worried?'

'Yes, worried. In the same way I'm worried. You haven't been yourself, Grace. Anyone who loves you is bound to be worried.'

She was becoming slightly less evasive as the conversation continued, and I meant to go on prodding her until the full story came out, until I understood what had driven her to run off on her mysterious twenty-four-hour fugue. So much was at stake, I felt, and if she didn't come clean and tell me the truth, how was I going to be able to trust her anymore? Trust was the one thing she demanded of me, and yet ever since she'd broken down in the cab on Saturday night, it had become impossible not to feel that something was wrong, that Grace was slowly crumbling under the pressure of a burden she refused to share with me. For a little while, the pregnancy had seemed to account for it, but I was no longer certain about that now. It was something else, something in addition to the baby, and before I started tormenting myself with thoughts about other men and clandestine affairs and sinister betrayals, I needed her to tell me what was going on. Unfortunately, the conversation was suddenly interrupted at that point, and I was no longer in a position to pursue my line of thought. It happened just after I told Grace how worried I was about her. I took hold of her hand, and as I pulled her toward me to kiss her on the cheek, she finally noticed that the standing lamp wasn't where it was supposed to be, that the area to the left of the sofa was vacant. I had to tell her about the burglary, and just like that the entire mood shifted, and instead of talking to her about one thing, I had no choice but to talk to her about another.

At first, Grace seemed to take the news calmly. I showed her the gap in the bookshelf where the first editions had been, pointed to the end table on which the portable TV had stood, then led her into the kitchen and informed her that we would have to buy a new toaster. Grace opened the drawers below the counter (which I had neglected to do) and discovered that our best set of silverware, which had been given to us by her parents as a first-anniversary present, was also missing. That was when anger took hold of her. She kicked the bottom drawer with her right foot and started to curse. Grace seldom used four-letter words, but for a minute or two that morning she was beside herself, and she let go with a barrage of invective that surpassed anything I'd heard from her lips before. Then we went into the bedroom, and her anger spilled over into tears. Her lower lip started to tremble when I told her about the jewelry box, but when she saw that the lithograph was gone as well, she sat down on the bed and started to cry. I did my best to comfort her, promising to look for another van Velde as soon as possible, but I knew that nothing could ever replace the one she'd bought as a twenty-year-old on her first trip to Paris: a swooping configuration of variegated, glowing blues, punctuated by a roundish blank in the center and a broken streak of red. I had

471

been living with it for several years by then, and I had never grown tired of looking at it. It was one of those works that kept giving you something, that never seemed to use itself up.[12]

It took her about fifteen or twenty minutes to pull herself together, and then she went into the bathroom to wash away the streaked mascara and reassemble her face. I waited for her in the bedroom, thinking we would be able to go on with our conversation there, but when she returned it was only to announce that she was running late and had to go to work. I tried to talk her out of it, but she wouldn't relent. She'd promised Greg she would be there this morning, she said, and after he'd been nice enough to give her yesterday off, she didn't want to take further advantage of his friendship. A promise was a promise, she said, to which I answered that we still had things to talk about. Maybe we did, she replied, but they could wait until she came home from work. As if to prove her good intentions, she sat down on the bed before leaving, threw her arms around me, and hugged me tightly for what felt like a long time. 'Don't worry about me,' she said. 'I'm really okay now. Yesterday did me a lot of good.'

I took my morning pills, returned to the bedroom, and slept until the middle of the afternoon. I didn't have any plans for the day, and the sole business on my agenda was to pass the time as quietly as possible until Grace returned home. She had promised to go on talking to me that evening, and if a promise was a promise, then I meant to hold her to it and do what I could to pull the truth from her. I wasn't terribly optimistic, but whether I failed or not, I wasn't going to get anywhere unless I buckled down and made an effort.

---

12. Grace had been a student at the Rhode Island School of Design, off on a junior-year-abroad program in Paris. Trause was the one who had written to her about van Velde, whom he had met once or twice in the fifties and who was known, he said, to be Samuel Beckett's favorite artist. (He included Beckett's dialogue with Georges Duthuit about van Velde in his letter. *My case is that van Velde is . . . the first to admit that to be an artist is to fail, as no other dare fail, that failure is his world.*) Van Velde's paintings were rare and expensive, but his graphic works from the sixties and early seventies were quite affordable at the time, and Grace had bought the piece in installments with her own money, skimping on food and other necessities in order to stay within the allowance sent each month by her father. The lithograph was an important part of her youth, an emblem of her growing passion for art as well as a sign of independence – a bridge between the last days of her girlhood and her first days as an adult – and it meant more to her than any other object she owned.

The sky was bright and clear that afternoon, but the temperature had dropped down into the 40s, and for the first time since the day in question, I could feel a touch of winter in the air, a foretaste of things to come. Once again, my normal sleep pattern had been disrupted, and I was in worse shape than usual – unsteady in my movements, at a loss for breath, tottering precariously with each step I took. It was as though I had regressed to some earlier stage of my recovery and was back in the period of swirling colors and fractured, unstable perceptions. I felt exceedingly vulnerable, as though the very air were a threat, as though an unexpected gust of wind could blow right through me and leave my body scattered in pieces on the ground.

I bought a new toaster in an appliance store on Court Street, and that simple transaction used up nearly all my physical resources. By the time I'd chosen one we could afford and had dug the money out of my wallet and handed it to the woman behind the counter, I was trembling and felt close to tears. She asked if anything was wrong. I said no, but my answer must have been unconvincing, for the next thing I knew she was asking me if I wanted to sit down and drink a glass of water. She was a fat woman in her early sixties with the faint trace of a mustache on her upper lip, and the shop she presided over was a dim and dusty hole-in-the-wall, a run-down family business with nearly half the shelves denuded of stock. Generous as her offer was, I didn't want to stay there another minute. I thanked her and moved on, staggering toward the exit and then leaning against the door to shove it open with my shoulder. I stood on the sidewalk for a few moments after that, gulping down deep drafts of the chilly air as I waited for the spell to pass. In retrospect, I realized it must have looked as if I'd been on the verge of blacking out.

I bought a slice of pizza and a large Coke at Vinny's two doors down, and by the time I stood up and left I was feeling a little better. It was about three-thirty then, and Grace wouldn't be home until six at the earliest. I didn't have it in me to trudge around the neighborhood and shop for groceries, and I knew I wasn't up to preparing dinner. Eating out was an indulgence for us then, but I figured we could order in some take-out food from the Siam Garden, a Thai restaurant that had just opened up near Atlantic Avenue. I knew that Grace would understand. Whatever difficulties we might have been having, she was concerned enough about my health not to hold that kind of thing against me.

Once I'd polished off the last of my pizza, I decided to walk over to the Clinton Street branch of the public library to see if they had any books by the novelist Trause had mentioned the day before, Sylvia Monroe. Two titles were listed in the card catalogue, *Night in Madrid* and *Autumn Ceremony*, but neither one had been checked out in over ten years. I skimmed them both, sitting at one of the long wooden tables in the reading room, and quickly discovered that Sylvia Monroe had nothing in common with Sylvia Maxwell. Monroe's books were conventional mystery stories, written in the style of Agatha Christie, and as I read through the arch, wittily contrived prose of the two novels, I felt increasingly disappointed, angry with myself for having assumed there could be a similarity between the two Sylvia M.s. At the very least, I thought maybe I'd read a book by Sylvia Monroe as a boy and had since forgotten about it, only to dredge up an unconscious memory of her in the person of Sylvia Maxwell, the pretend author of the pretend *Oracle Night*. But it seemed I'd plucked Maxwell out of thin air and *Oracle Night* was an original story, with no connection to any novel other than itself. I probably should have felt relieved, but I didn't.

When I returned to the apartment at five-thirty, there was a message from Grace on the answering machine. Bluntly and quietly, in a series of simple, forthright sentences, she dismantled the architecture of unhappiness that had been growing up around us for the past several days. She was calling from her office, she said, and had to talk in a low voice, 'but if you can hear me, Sid,' she began, 'there are four things I want you to know. First, I haven't stopped thinking about you since I left the house this morning. Second, I've decided to have the baby, and we're never going to use the word *abortion* again. Third, don't bother to make dinner. I'm leaving the office at five sharp, and from there I'm going down to Balducci's to buy some nice ready-made stuff that we can heat up in the oven. If the subway doesn't break down, I should be home by six-twenty, six-thirty. Fourth, make sure Mr. Johnson's ready for action. I'm going to attack you the minute I walk in the door, my love, so be prepared. Miss Virginia's achin' to get naked with her man.'

Miss Virginia was one of my pet names for her, but I hadn't used it since the first or second year of our marriage, and certainly not since my return from the hospital. Grace was evoking early good times with that phrase, and it moved me to know that she remembered it, since it had generally been reserved for moments of postcoital decompression: Grace rising from the bed after we had finished making love and strolling across the floor on the way to the bathroom, immodest, languid, happy in the nakedness of her body, and sometimes (it was coming back to me now), I would jokingly call her *Miss Nude Virginia*, which always made her laugh, and then, inevitably, she would stop to strike a comic cheesecake pose, which in turn would always get a laugh from me. In effect, *Miss Virginia* was shorthand for *Miss Nude Virginia*, and whenever I called her Miss Virginia in public, it was always a secret communication about our sex life, a reference to the bare skin under her clothes, an homage to her beautiful, much-adored body. Now, immediately after announcing that she wasn't going to end the pregnancy, she had reanimated the mythic personage of Miss Virginia, and by juxtaposing the one statement against the other, she was telling me that she was mine again, mine as before and yet mine in a different way as well, subtly announcing (as only Grace could) that she was prepared to enter the next phase of our marriage, that a new era of our life together was about to begin.

I called off the showdown I had been planning for that evening and didn't ask her a single question about her absence on Wednesday night. We did all the things she had warned me about on the answering machine, wrestling each other to the floor the moment she entered the apartment, then dragging our half-dressed bodies toward the bedroom, which we never quite managed to reach. Later on, after we had slipped into our bathrobes, we warmed the food in the oven and sat down to a late dinner. I showed her the new wide-slotted, bagel-compatible toaster I had bought that afternoon, and although that led to some sad talk about the robbery, it was cut short when my nose suddenly started to bleed, gushing out onto the apricot pastry that Grace had just put in front of me for dessert. She stood behind me at the sink as I tilted my head back and waited for the flow to stop, her arms wrapped around me, kissing my shoulder and my neck, all the while suggesting funny names for us to give the baby. If it was a girl, we decided, we would call her Goldie Orr. If it was a boy, we would name him after one of Kierkegaard's books, Ira Orr. We were stupidly happy that night, and I couldn't remember a time when Grace had been more giddy or effusive in her affections toward me. When the blood finally stopped flowing from my nose, she turned me around and washed my face with a damp cloth, looking steadily into my eyes as she dabbed my mouth and chin until all traces of the spill had vanished. 'We'll clean up the kitchen in the morning,' she said. Then, without adding another word, she took me by the hand and led me toward the bedroom.

*

I slept late the next morning, and when I finally rolled out of bed at ten-thirty, Grace was long gone. I went into the kitchen to take my pills and start a pot of coffee, and then slowly cleaned up the mess we had walked away from the night before. Ten minutes after I had put the last dish in the cupboard, Mary Sklarr called with bad news. Bobby Hunter's people had read my treatment, and they'd decided to pass on it.

'I'm sorry,' Mary said, 'but I'm not going to pretend I'm shocked.'

'It's all right,' I said, feeling less chagrined than I thought I would. 'The idea was a piece of shit. I'm glad they don't want it.'

'They said your plot was too cerebral.'

'I'm surprised they know what the word means.'

'I'm happy you're not upset. It wouldn't be worth it.'

'I wanted the money, that's all. A case of pure greed. I wasn't even very professional about it, was I? You're not supposed to write anything without a contract. It's the first rule of the business.'

'Well, they *were* pretty amazed. The sheer speed of it. They're not used to that kind of gung ho approach. They like to have lots of discussions with lawyers and agents first. It makes them feel as if they're doing something important.'

'I still don't understand why they thought of me.'

'Somebody there likes your work. Maybe Bobby Hunter, maybe the kid who works in the mailroom. Who knows? In any case, they're going to send you a check. As an act of goodwill. You wrote the pages without a contract, but they want to reimburse you for your time.'

'A check?'

'Just a token.'

'How much of a token?'

'A thousand dollars.'

'Well, at least that's something. It's the first money I've earned in a long time.'

'You're forgetting Portugal.'

'Ah, Portugal. How could I forget Portugal?'

'Any news on the novel you might or might not be writing?'

'Not much. There could be one piece to salvage from it, but I'm not sure. A novel within the novel. I keep thinking about it, so maybe that's a good sign.'

'Give me fifty pages, and I'll get you a contract, Sid.'

'I've never been paid for a book I haven't finished. What if I can't write page fifty-one?'

'These are desperate times, my friend. If you need money, I'll try to get you money. That's my job.'

'Let me think about it.'

'You think, and I'll wait. When you're ready to call, I'll be here.'

After we hung up, I went into the bedroom to fetch my coat from the closet. Now that the *Time Machine* business was officially dead, I had to start thinking about a new plan, and I figured a walk in the cool air might do me some good. Just as I was about to leave the apartment, however, the phone rang again. I was tempted not to answer it, but then I changed my mind and picked up on the fourth ring, hoping it would be Grace. It turned out to be Trause, probably the last person on earth I wanted to talk to just then. I still hadn't told him about losing the story, and as I prepared myself to blurt out the confession I'd been putting off for the past two days, I was so wrapped up in my own thoughts that I had trouble following him. Eleanor and her husband had found Jacob, he said. They'd already checked him into a drug clinic – a place called Smithers on the Upper East Side.

'Did you hear me?' John asked. 'They've put him in a twenty-eight-day program. That probably won't be enough, but at least it's a start.'

'Oh,' I said, in a faint voice. 'When did they find him?'

'Wednesday night, not long after you left. They had to do a lot of finagling to get him in there. Fortunately, Don knows someone who knows someone, and they managed to cut through the red tape.'

'Don?'

'Eleanor's husband.'

'Of course. Eleanor's husband.'

'Are you all right, Sid? You sound completely out of it.'

'No, no, I'm okay. Don. Eleanor's new husband.'

'The reason I called is to ask a favor. I hope you don't mind.'

'I don't mind. Whatever it is. Just ask and I'll do it.'

'Tomorrow's Saturday, and they have visiting hours at the clinic from noon to five. I was wondering if you'd go up there for me and check in on him. You don't have to stay long. Eleanor and Don can't make it. They've gone back to Long Island, and they've already done enough as it is. I just want to know if he's all right. They don't lock the doors there. It's a voluntary program, and I want to make sure he hasn't changed his mind. After all we've been through, it would be a pity if he decided to run away.'

'Don't you think you should go yourself? You're his father, after all. I barely know the kid.'

477

'He won't talk to me anymore. And whenever he forgets he's not supposed to talk to me, he feeds me nothing but lies. If I thought it would do
any good, I'd hobble up there on my crutch and see him. But it won't.'
    'And what makes you think he'll talk to me?'
    'He likes you. Don't ask me why, but he thinks you're a cool person.
That's an exact quote. "Sid's a cool person." Maybe because you look so
young, I don't know. Maybe because you once talked to him about a
rock band he's interested in.'
    'The Bean Spasms, a punk group from Chicago. One night an old
friend played a couple of their songs for me. Not very good. I think
they're gone by now.'
    'At least you knew who they were.'
    'That was the longest conversation I've ever had with Jacob. It lasted
about four minutes.'
    'Well, four minutes isn't bad. If you can get four minutes out of him
tomorrow, that would be an accomplishment.'
    'Don't you think it would be better if I took Grace along with me?
She's known him a lot longer than I have.'
    'Out of the question.'
    'What do you mean?'
    'Jacob despises her. He can't stand to be in the same room with her.'
    'No one despises Grace. You'd have to be unhinged to feel that way.'
    'Not according to my son.'
    'She's never breathed a word to me about this.'
    'It goes all the way back to when they first met. Grace was thirteen,
and Jacob was three. Eleanor and I had just gone through our divorce,
and Bill Tebbetts invited me down to his country place in Virginia to
spend a couple of weeks with his family. It was summer, and I took
Jacob with me. He seemed to get along with the other Tebbetts kids, but
every time Grace walked into the room, he'd punch her or throw things
at her. One time, he picked up a toy truck and smashed her on the knee
with it. The poor kid was bleeding all over the place. We rushed her to
a doctor, and it took ten stitches to sew up the wound.'
    'I know that scar. Grace told me about it once, but she didn't mention
Jacob. She just said it was some little boy, and that was all.'
    'He seemed to hate her right from the start, from the first moment he
laid eyes on her.'
    'He probably sensed that you liked her too much, so she became a
rival. Three-year-olds are pretty irrational creatures. They don't know

many words, and when they're angry, the only way they can talk is with their fists.'

'Maybe. But he kept it up, even after he got older. The worst time was in Portugal, about two years after Tina died. I'd just bought my little house on the northern coast, and Eleanor sent him over to stay with me for a month. He was fourteen, and he knew as many words as I did. Grace happened to be there when he showed up. She was out of college then and about to start working for Holst & McDermott in September. In July, she came to Europe to look at paintings – Amsterdam first, then Paris, and then Madrid. After that, she took the train to Portugal. I hadn't seen her in over two years, and we had a lot of catching up to do, but when Jacob got there he didn't want her around. He muttered insults at her under his breath, pretended not to hear her when she asked him questions, and once or twice even managed to spill food on her. I kept warning him to stop. One more nasty move, I said, and I'd ship him back to his mother and stepfather in America. And then he crossed the line, and I put him on a plane and sent him home.'

'What did he do?'

'He spat in her face.'

'Good God.'

'The three of us were in the kitchen, chopping vegetables for dinner. Grace made some innocuous remark about something – I can't even remember what it was – and Jacob took offense. He walked over to her waving a knife in his hand and called her a stupid bitch, and Grace finally lost her temper. That's when he spat at her. Looking back on it now, I suppose it's lucky he didn't take the knife and stab her in the chest.'

'And this is the person you want me to talk to tomorrow? What he deserves is a swift kick in the ass.'

'If I went up there myself, I'm afraid that's what would happen. It'll be a lot better for everyone if you go there for me.'

'Has anything happened since Portugal?'

'I've kept them apart. They haven't crossed paths in years, and as far as I'm concerned, the world will be a safer place if they never see each other again.'[13]

*

13. The conversation ended with my agreeing to visit Jacob – alone. I was willing to do John that small service, but I was appalled by what he'd said about the boy's animosity toward Grace. Even if there was some cause for envy on his part (the

Grace didn't have to go to work the next morning, and she was still asleep when I left the apartment. After talking to Trause on Friday, I had decided not to tell her about the promise I'd made to go to Smithers that afternoon. That would have forced me to mention Jacob, and I didn't want to run the risk of stirring up bad memories for her. We had lived through a difficult stretch of days, and I was loath to talk about anything that could cause the slightest agitation – and perhaps destroy the fragile balance we'd managed to find again in the past forty-eight hours. I left a note on the kitchen table, telling her I was going into Manhattan to visit some bookstores and would be home by six at the latest. One more lie, added to all the other little lies we had told each other in the past week. But my intention wasn't to deceive her. I simply wanted to protect her from more unpleasantness, to keep the space we shared as small and private as possible, without having to entangle ourselves in painful matters from the past.

The rehab facility was housed in a large mansion that had once belonged to the Broadway producer Billy Rose. I didn't know how or when the place had been turned into Smithers, but it was a solid example of old New York architecture, a limestone palace from an age when wealth had flaunted itself with diamonds, top hats, and white gloves.

---

neglected son cast off in favor of the beloved 'goddaughter'), I felt no sympathy for him – only disgust and contempt. I would go to the clinic for his father's sake, but I wasn't looking forward to the time I would have to spend in his company.

As far as I could remember, I had met him only twice before. Knowing nothing about his history with Grace, it had never occurred to me to question why she hadn't been with us on those occasions. The first was a Friday-night outing to Shea Stadium to see a game between the Mets and the Cincinnati Reds. Trause had been given tickets by someone who owned a season box, and because he knew I was a fan, he'd invited me to go along with him. That was in May 1979, just a few months after I'd fallen in love with Grace, and John and I had met for the first time only a couple of weeks earlier. Jacob was about to turn seventeen then, and he and one of his classmates rounded out the foursome. From the moment we entered the stadium, it was clear that neither boy had any interest in baseball. They sat through the first three innings with bored and sullen expressions on their faces, and then they stood up and left, supposedly to buy some hot dogs and 'wander around for a while,' as Jacob put it. They didn't return until the bottom of the seventh – giggling, glassy-eyed, and in far better spirits than before. It wasn't difficult to guess what they'd been up to. I was still teaching then, and I'd seen enough kids high on pot to recognize the symptoms. John was wrapped up in the game and seemed not to notice, and I didn't bother to mention it to him. I scarcely knew him at the time, and I figured that what happened between him and his son was none of my business. Beyond saying hello

How odd that it should have been inhabited now by the bottom dogs of society, an endlessly evolving population of drug addicts, alcoholics, and ex-criminals. It had become a way station for the lost, and when the door buzzed open and I went inside, I noted that a certain shabbiness had begun to set in. The bones of the building were still intact (the huge entrance hall with the black-and-white tile floor, the curving staircase with the mahogany banister), but the flesh looked sad and dirty, dilapidated after years of strain and overwork.

I asked for Jacob at the front desk, announcing myself as a family friend. The woman in charge seemed suspicious of me, and I had to empty my pockets to prove I wasn't trying to smuggle in drugs or weapons. Even though I passed the test, I felt certain that she was going to turn me away, but before I could begin arguing my case, Jacob happened to appear in the front hall, walking with three or four other residents toward the dining room for lunch. He looked taller than the last time I had seen him, but with his black clothes and green hair and excessively thin body, there was something grotesque and clownish about him, as if he were a ghostly Punchinello on his way to perform a dance for the Duke of Death. I called out his name, and when he turned and saw me, he looked shocked – not happy or unhappy, simply shocked. 'Sid,' he

and good-bye to each other, I don't think Jacob and I exchanged more than eight or ten words the whole night.

The next time I saw him was about six months later. He was in the middle of his senior year and in danger of flunking all his courses, and John had called up with a last-minute invitation to spend an evening shooting pool. He and Jacob were barely on speaking terms then, and I think he wanted me to come along to serve as a buffer, a neutral third party to prevent war from breaking out between them in a public place. That was the night Jacob and I talked about the Bean Spasms and I acquired my reputation as a cool person. He struck me as an exceedingly bright and hostile kid, determined to screw up his life in every way he could. If I detected any shadow of hope, it was in his determination to beat his father at pool. I was a lousy player and quickly fell behind in every game, but John knew what he was doing, and somewhere along the line he must have taught his son how to play. It brought out the competitiveness in both of them, and the mere fact that Jacob was concentrating on something struck me as an encouraging sign. I didn't know then that John had been an expert pool hustler in the army. If he'd wanted to, he could have run the table and wiped Jacob out, but he didn't do that. He pretended to be trying, and in the end he let the boy win. Under the circumstances, it was probably the right thing to do. Not that it did them any good in the long run, but at least Jacob cracked a smile when they finished and walked over to his father and shook his hand. For all I knew, it could have been the last time that ever happened.

muttered, 'what are you doing here?' He separated from the group and walked over to where I was standing, which prompted the woman behind the desk to ask a superfluous question: 'You know this man?' 'Yeah,' Jacob said. 'I know him. He's a friend of my father's.' That statement was enough to get me in. The woman pushed a clipboard at me, and once I'd printed my name on the sheet for visitors, I accompanied Jacob down a long hallway into the dining room.

'No one told me you were coming,' he said. 'I suppose the old man put you up to it, huh?'

'Not really. I happened to be in the neighborhood, and I thought I'd stop by and see how you were doing.'

Jacob grunted, not even bothering to comment on how thoroughly he disbelieved me. It was a transparent fib, but I'd said it in order to keep John out of the discussion, thinking I'd get more out of Jacob if I avoided talking about his family. We continued in silence for a few moments and then, unexpectedly, he put his hand on my shoulder. 'I heard you were real sick,' he said.

'I was. I seem to be getting better now.'

'They thought you were going to die, didn't they?'

'So I'm told. But I fooled them and walked out of there about four months ago.'

'That means you're immortal, Sid. You're not going to croak until you're a hundred and ten.'

The dining hall was a large sunny room with sliding glass doors that led out to a small garden, where some of the residents and their families had gone to smoke and drink coffee. The food was served cafeteria-style, and after Jacob and I loaded up our trays with meat loaf, mashed potatoes, and salad, we began looking for an empty table. There must have been fifty or sixty people in the room, and we had to circle around for a couple of minutes before we found one. The delay seemed to irritate him, as if it were a personal affront. When we finally sat down, I asked him how things were going, and he launched into a recitation of bitter grievances, nervously jiggling his left leg as he spoke.

'This place is for shit,' he said. 'All we do is go to meetings and talk about ourselves. I mean, how boring is that? As if I want to listen to these fuckups pour out their dumb stories about how rotten their childhoods were and how they stumbled off the true path and fell into the grip of Satan.'

'What happens when it's your turn? Do you get up and speak?'

'I have to. If I don't say anything, they point their fingers at me and start calling me a coward. So I make up something that sounds like what everyone else says, and then I start to cry. It always gets them. I'm a pretty good actor, you know. I tell them what a crud I am, and then I break down and can't go on anymore, and everyone's happy.'

'Why scam them? You're just wasting your time here if you do that.'

'Because I'm not an addict, that's why. I've fooled around with junk a little bit, but it's not a serious thing for me. I can take it or leave it.'

'That's what my college roommate used to say. And then one night he wound up dead from an overdose.'

'Yeah, well, he was probably stupid. I know what I'm doing, and I ain't gonna die from no overdose. I'm not hooked on the stuff. My mother thinks I am, but she doesn't know shit.'

'Then why did you agree to come here?'

'Because she said she'd cut me off if I didn't. I've already pissed off your pal, the almighty Sir John, and I don't want Lady Eleanor getting any stupid ideas about stopping my allowance.'

'You could always get a job.'

'Yeah, I could, but I don't want to. I've got other plans, and I need a little more time to work them out.'

'So you're just sitting here, waiting for the twenty-eight days to end.'

'It wouldn't be so bad if they didn't keep us busy all the time. When we're not wearing out our asses at those goddamn meetings, they make us study these terrible books. You've never read such garbage in all your life.'

'What books?'

'The AA manual, the twelve-step program, all that horseshit.'

'It might be horseshit, but it's helped a lot of people.'

'It's for cretins, Sid. All that crap about trusting in a higher power. It's like some baby-talk religion. Give yourself up to the higher power, and you'll be saved. You'd have to be a moron to swallow that stuff. There is no higher power. Take a good look at the world, and tell me where he is. I don't see him. There's just you and me and everyone else. A bunch of poor fucks doing what we can to stay alive.'

We had been together for only a few minutes, and already I felt drained, depleted by the boy's vapid, cynical talk. I wanted to get out of there as quickly as I could, but for form's sake I decided to wait until the meal was over. Trause's pale and emaciated son appeared to have little appetite for the Smithers cuisine. He picked at his mashed potatoes for a while, sampled one taste of the meat loaf, and then put down his fork. A moment later, he rose from his seat and asked me if I wanted dessert. I shook my head, and he marched off to the food line again. When he returned, he was carrying two cups of chocolate pudding, which he set before him and ate one after the other, showing considerably more interest in the sweets than he had in the main course. With no drugs around, sugar was the only substitute available, and he devoured the puddings with the relish of a small child, scooping every morsel out of each cup. Somewhere between the first and second helping, a man stopped by the table to say hello to him. He looked to be in his mid-thirties, with a rough pockmarked face and his hair pulled back in a short ponytail. Jacob introduced him as Freddy, and with the warmth and earnestness of a true rehab veteran, the older man extended his hand to me and said it was a pleasure to meet one of Jake's friends.

'Sid's a famous novelist,' Jacob announced, apropos of nothing. 'He's published about fifty books.'

'Don't listen to what he says,' I told Freddy. 'He tends to exaggerate.'

'Yeah, I know,' Freddy answered. 'This one's a real hell-raiser. Gotta keep a close eye on him. Right, kid?'

Jacob looked down at the table, and then Freddy patted him on the head and walked off. As Jacob dug into his second chocolate pudding, he informed me that Freddy was his group leader and not such a bad guy, all things considered.

'He used to steal things,' he said. 'You know, a professional shop-lifter. But he had a smart gimmick, so he never got caught. Instead of going into stores with a big overcoat on, the way most of them do it, he'd dress up as a priest. No one ever suspected him of anything. Father Freddy, the man of God. One time, though, he got himself into a weird jam. He was somewhere in midtown, about to go in and rob a drug-store, when there was this big traffic accident. A guy crossing the street was hit by one of the cars. Someone dragged him onto the sidewalk, right where Freddy was standing. There was blood all over the place, the guy was unconscious, and it looked like he was going to die. A crowd gathers around him, and suddenly a woman spots Freddy in his priest's costume and asks him to say the last rites. Father Freddy is fucked. He doesn't know the words to any of the prayers, but if he runs away, they'll know he's a fake and arrest him for impersonating a priest. So he bends down over the guy, puts his hands together to make it look like he's praying, and mumbles some solemn bullshit he once heard in a movie. Then he stands up, makes the sign of the cross, and splits. Pretty funny, huh?'

'It sounds like you're getting quite an education at those meetings.'

'That's nothing. I mean, Freddy was just a junkie trying to support his habit. A lot of the other people around here have done some pretty crazy shit. See that black guy sitting at the corner table, the big one in the blue sweatshirt? Jerome. He spent twelve years in Attica for murder. And that blonde girl at the next table with her mother? Sally. She grew up on Park Avenue and comes from one of the richest families in New York. Yesterday, she told us she's been turning tricks on Tenth Avenue over by the Lincoln Tunnel, fucking guys in cars at twenty dollars a pop. And that Hispanic guy on the other side of the room, the one in the yellow shirt? Alfonso. He went to jail for raping his ten-year-old daughter. I'm telling you, Sid, compared to most of these characters, I'm just a nice middle-class boy.'

The puddings seemed to have energized him a bit, and when we carried our dirty trays into the kitchen, he moved with a certain spring in his step, unlike the shuffling somnambulist I'd spotted in the front hall before lunch. All in all, I'd guess I was with him for thirty or thirty-five minutes – long enough to feel I'd discharged my duty to John. As we walked out of the dining hall, Jacob asked me if I'd like to go upstairs and see his room. There was going to be a big group meeting at one-thirty, he said, and family members and guests were invited to attend. I was welcome to come along if I wanted to, and in the meantime we could hang out in his room on the fourth floor. There was something pathetic about the way he'd latched on to me, about how reluctant he seemed to let me go. We were barely even acquaintances, and yet he must have been lonely enough in that place to think of me as a friend, even though he knew I'd come as a secret agent on behalf of his father. I tried to feel some pity for him, but I couldn't. He was the person who had spat in my wife's face, and even though the incident had happened six years before, I couldn't bring myself to forgive him for that. I looked at my watch and told him I was supposed to meet someone on Second Avenue in ten minutes. I saw a flash of disappointment in his eyes, and then, almost immediately, his face hardened into a mask of indifference. 'No big deal, man,' he said. 'If you gotta go, you gotta go.'

'I'll try to come back next week,' I said, knowing full well that I wouldn't.

'Whatever you like, Sid. It's your call.'

He gave me a condescending pat on the shoulder, and before I could shake his hand good-bye, he turned on his heels and started walking toward the stairs. I stood in the hall for a few moments, waiting to see if he'd look back over his shoulder for a farewell nod, but he didn't. He kept on mounting the staircase, and when he rounded the curve and disappeared from sight, I went over to the woman at the front desk and signed myself out.

It was a little past one o'clock. I rarely went to the Upper East Side, and since the weather had improved in the past hour, rapidly warming to the point where my jacket now felt like an encumbrance, I turned my daily walk into an excuse to prowl around the neighborhood. It was going to be hard to tell John how depressing the visit had been for me, and instead of calling him right away, I decided to put it off until I returned to Brooklyn. I couldn't do it from the apartment (at least not if Grace was home), but there was an ancient telephone booth in the back corner of Landolfi's, complete with a closable accordion door, and I figured I would have enough privacy to do it from there.

Twenty minutes after leaving Smithers, I was on Lexington Avenue in the low 90s, moving along among a small crowd of pedestrians and thinking about heading home. Someone knocked into me, accidentally grazing my left shoulder as he walked by, and as I turned to see who it was, something remarkable happened, something so outside the realm of probability that at first I took it for a hallucination. Directly across the avenue, at a perfect ninety-degree angle from where I was standing, I saw a small shop with a sign above the door that read PAPER PALACE. Was it possible that Chang had managed to relocate his business? It struck me as incredible, and yet given the speed with which this man conducted his affairs – closing up his store in one night, rushing around town in his red car, investing in dubious enterprises, borrowing money, spending money – why should I have doubted it? Chang seemed to live in a blur of accelerated motion, as if the clocks of the world ticked more slowly for him than they did for everyone else. A minute must have felt like an hour to him, and with so much extra time at his disposal, why couldn't he have pulled off the move to Lexington Avenue in the days since I'd last seen him?

On the other hand, it also could have been a coincidence. Paper Palace was hardly an original name for a stationery store, and there easily could have been more than one of them in the city. I crossed the street to find out, more and more certain that this Manhattan version was owned

486

by someone other than Chang. The display in the window proved to be different from the one that had caught my attention in Brooklyn the previous Saturday. There were no paper towers to suggest the New York skyline, but the replacement was even more imaginative than the old one, I felt, even more clever. A tiny doll-sized statue of a man sat at a small table with a miniature typewriter on it. His hands were on the keys, a sheet of paper had been rolled into the cylinder, and if you pressed your face against the window and looked very closely, you could read the words that had been typed on the page: *It was the best of times, it was the worst of times, it was the age of wisdom, it was the age of foolishness, it was the epoch of belief, it was the epoch of incredulity, it was the season of Light, it was the season of Darkness, it was the spring of hope, it was the winter of despair, we had everything before us, we had nothing before us . . .*

I opened the door and went in, and as I crossed the threshold I heard the same tinkling of bells I'd heard in the other Paper Palace on the eighteenth. The Brooklyn shop had been small, but this one was even smaller, with the bulk of the merchandise stacked up on wooden shelves that extended all the way to the ceiling. Once again, there were no customers in the store. At first, I didn't see anyone, but a soft, tuneless humming was wafting up from somewhere in the vicinity of the front counter, as if someone were squatting behind it – tying his shoe, perhaps, or picking up a fallen pen or pencil. I cleared my throat, and a couple of seconds later Chang rose from the floor and put his palms on the countertop, as if to steady his balance. He was wearing the brown sweater this time, and his hair was uncombed. He looked thinner than he had before, with deep creases around his mouth and slightly bloodshot eyes.

'Congratulations,' I said. 'The Paper Palace is back on its feet.'

Chang stared at me with a blank expression, either unable or unwilling to recognize me. 'Sorry,' he said. 'I don't think I know you.'

'Of course you do. I'm Sidney Orr. We spent a whole afternoon together just the other day.'

'Sidney Orr is no friend of mine. I used to think he's good guy, but no more.'

'What are you talking about?'

'You let me down, Mr. Sid. Put me in very embarrassing position. I no want to know you no more. Friendship over.'

'I don't understand. What did I do?'

'You leave me behind at dress factory. Never even say good-bye. What kind of friend is that?'

487

'I looked everywhere for you. I walked all around the bar, and when I couldn't find you I figured you were in one of the booths and didn't want to be disturbed. So I left. It was getting late, and I had to go home.'

'Home to your darling wife. Just after you get blow job from the African Princess. How funny is that, Mr. Sid? If Martine walk in here now, you do it again. Right here on floor of my shop. You fuck her like a dog and love every minute of it.'

'I was drunk. She was very beautiful, and I lost control of myself. But that doesn't mean I'd do it again.'

'You not drunk. You horny hypocrite, just like all selfish people.'

'You said no one could resist her, and you were right. You should be proud of yourself, Chang. You saw into me and found my weakness.'

'Because I knew you think bad thoughts about me, that's why. I understand what's in your mind.'

'Oh? And what was I thinking that day?'

'You think Chang in nasty business. Dirty whore-man with no heart. A man who dream only of money.'

'That's not true.'

'Yes, Mr. Sid, it's true. It's very true. Now we stop talking. You give big hurt to my soul, and now we stop. Look around if you like. I welcome you as customer to my Paper Palace, but no more friend. Friendship dead. Friendship dead and buried now. All finished.'

I don't think anyone had ever insulted me more thoroughly than Chang did that afternoon. I had caused him a great sadness, unintentionally wounding his dignity and sense of personal honor, and as he lashed out at me with those stiff, measured sentences of his, it was as if he felt I deserved to be drawn and quartered for my crimes. What made the attack even more uncomfortable was that most of his accusations were correct. I had left him at the dress factory without saying good-bye, I had allowed myself to fall into the arms of the African Princess, and I had questioned his moral integrity about wanting to invest in the club. There was little I could say to defend myself. Any denials would have been pointless, and even if my transgressions had been relatively small ones, I still felt guilty enough about my session with Martine behind the curtain not to want to bring it up again. I should have said good-bye to Chang and left the store immediately, but I didn't. The Portuguese notebooks had become too powerful a fixation by then, and I couldn't go without first checking to see if he had any in stock. I understood how unwise it was to linger in a place where I wasn't wanted, but I couldn't help myself. I simply had to know.

There was one left, sitting among a display of German and Canadian notebooks on a lower shelf at the back of the store. It was the red one, no doubt the same red one that had been in Brooklyn the previous Saturday, and the price was the same as it had been then, an even five dollars. When I carried it up to the counter and handed it to Chang, I apologized for having caused him any suffering or embarrassment. I told him he could still count on me as a friend and that I would continue to buy my stationery supplies from him, even if it meant traveling far out of my way to do so. For all the contrition I tried to express, Chang merely shook his head and patted the notebook with his right hand. 'Sorry,' he said. 'This one not for sale.'

'What do you mean? This is a store. Everything in it's for sale.' I removed a ten-dollar bill from my wallet and spread it out on the counter. 'Here's my money,' I said. 'The sticker says five dollars. Now please give me my change and the notebook.'

'Impossible. This red one the last Portuguese book in shop. Reserved for other customer.'

'If you're holding it for someone else, you should put it behind the counter where no one can see it. If it's out on the shelf, that means anyone can buy it.'

'Not you, Mr. Sid.'

'How much was the other customer going to pay for it?'

'Five dollars, just as sticker say.'

'Well, I'll give you ten for it and we'll call it a deal. How's that?'

'Not ten dollars. Ten thousand dollars.'

'*Ten thousand dollars?* Have you lost your mind?'

'This notebook not for you, Sidney Orr. You buy other notebook, and everybody happy. Okay?'

'Look,' I said, finally losing patience. 'The notebook costs five dollars, and I'm willing to give you ten. But that's all I'm going to pay.'

'You give five thousand now and five thousand on Monday. That's the deal. Otherwise, please buy other notebook.'

We had entered a domain of pure lunacy. Chang's taunts and absurd demands had finally pushed me over the edge, and rather than go on haggling with him, I snatched the notebook out from under his palm and started for the door. 'That's it,' I said. 'Take the ten and go fuck yourself. I'm leaving.'

I hadn't taken two steps when Chang jumped out from behind the counter to cut me off and block my way to the door. I tried to slip past him, using my shoulder to push him aside, but Chang held his ground, and a moment later he had his hands on the notebook and was yanking it away from me. I pulled it back and clutched it against my chest, straining to hold on to it, but the owner of the Paper Palace was a fierce little engine of wire and sinew and hard muscle, and he tore the thing from my grip in about ten seconds. I knew I would never be able to get it back from him, but I was so peeved, so wild with frustration, that I grabbed hold of his arm with my left hand and took a swing at him with my right. It was the first punch I'd thrown at anyone since grade school, and I missed. In return, Chang delivered a karate chop to my left shoulder. It crashed down on me like a knife, and the pain was so intense that I thought my arm was going to fall off. I dropped to my knees, and before I could stand up again, Chang started kicking me in the back. I yelled at him to stop, but he kept on sending the tip of his shoe into my rib cage and spine – one short brutal jab after another as I rolled toward the exit, desperately trying to get out of there. When my body was flush against the metal plate at the bottom of the door, Chang turned the handle; the latch clicked open, and I fell out onto the sidewalk.

'You stay away from here!' he shouted. 'Next time you come back, I kill you! You hear me, Sidney Orr? I cut out your heart and feed it to the pigs!'

I never told Grace about Chang or the beating or anything else that happened on the Upper East Side that afternoon. Every muscle in my body was sore, but in spite of the power of Chang's avenging foot, I had walked away from the pummeling with only the faintest bruises along the lower part of my back. The jacket and sweater I had been wearing must have protected me, and when I remembered how close I'd come to taking off the jacket as I roamed around the neighborhood, I felt lucky to have had it on when I entered the Paper Palace – although luck is perhaps an odd word to use in such a context. On warm nights, Grace and I always slept naked, but now that the weather was turning cool again, she had started going to bed in her white silk pajamas, and she didn't question me when I joined her under the covers in my T-shirt. Even when we made love (on Sunday night), it was dark enough in the bedroom for the welts to escape her notice.

I called Trause from Landolfi's when I went out for the *Times* on

Sunday morning. I told him everything I could remember about my visit with Jacob, including the fact that the safety pins were gone from his son's ear (no doubt as a protective measure), and summarized each one of the opinions he'd expressed from the moment I arrived until the moment I saw him vanish in the bend of the staircase. John wanted to know if I thought he'd stay for the whole month or skip out before the time was up, and I answered that I didn't know. He'd made some ominous remark about having plans, I said, which suggested that there were things in his life that no one in his family knew about, secrets he wasn't willing to share. John thought it might have had something to do with dealing drugs. I asked him why he suspected that, but other than making a glancing reference to the stolen tuition money, he wouldn't say. The conversation hit a lull at that point, and in the short silence that followed, I finally mustered the courage to tell him about my misadventure on the subway earlier in the week and how I'd lost 'The Empire of Bones.' I couldn't have chosen a more awkward moment to bring up the subject, and at first Trause didn't understand what I was talking about. I went through the story again. When he realized that his manuscript had probably traveled all the way to Coney Island, he laughed. 'Don't torture yourself about it,' he said. 'I still have a couple of carbons. We didn't have Xerox machines in those days, and everyone always typed at least two copies of everything. I'll put one in an envelope and have Madame Dumas mail it to you this week.'

The next morning, Monday, I went back into the blue notebook for the last time. Forty of the ninety-six pages were already filled, but there were more than enough blanks to hold another few hours' work. I started on a fresh page about halfway in, leaving the Flitcraft debacle behind me for good. Bowen would be trapped in the room forever, and I decided that the moment had finally come to abandon my efforts to rescue him. If I had learned anything from my ferocious encounter with Chang on Saturday, it was that the notebook was a place of trouble for me, and whatever I tried to write in it would end in failure. Every story would stop in the middle; every project would carry me along just so far, and then I'd look up and discover that I was lost. Still, I was furious enough with Chang to want to deny him the satisfaction of having the last word. I knew I was going to have to say good-bye to the Portuguese *caderno*, but unless I did it on my own terms, it would continue to haunt me as a moral defeat. If nothing else, I felt I had to prove to myself that I wasn't a coward.

491

PAUL AUSTER

I waded in slowly, cautiously, driven more by a sense of defiance than any compelling need to write. Before long, however, I found myself thinking about Grace, and with the notebook still open on the desk, I went into the living room to dig out one of the photo albums we kept in the bottom drawer of an all-purpose oak bureau. Mercifully, it had been left untouched by the thief during the Wednesday afternoon break-in. It was a special album, given to us as a wedding present by Grace's youngest sister, Flo, and it contained over a hundred pictures, a visual history of the first twenty-seven years of Grace's life – Grace before I had met her. I hadn't looked at this album since coming home from the hospital, and as I turned the pages in my workroom that morning, I was again reminded of the story Trause had told about his brother-in-law and the 3-D viewer, experiencing a similar kind of entrapment as the pictures pulled me into the past.

There was Grace as a newborn infant lying in her crib. There she was at two, standing naked in a field of tall grass, her arms lifted toward the sky, laughing. There she was at four and six and nine – sitting at a table drawing a picture of a house, grinning into the lens of a school photographer's camera with several teeth missing, posting in the saddle as she trotted through the Virginia countryside on a chestnut-brown mare. Grace at twelve with a ponytail, awkward, funny-looking, uncomfortable in her skin, and then Grace at fifteen, suddenly pretty, defined, the earliest incarnation of the woman she would eventually become. There were group pictures as well: Tebbetts family portraits, Grace with various unidentified friends from high school and college, Grace sitting on Trause's lap as a four-year-old with her parents on either side of them, Trause bending forward and kissing her on the cheek at her tenth or eleventh birthday party, Grace and Greg Fitzgerald making comic faces at a Holst & McDermott Christmas bash.

Grace in a prom dress at seventeen. Grace as a twenty-year-old college student in Paris with long hair and a black turtleneck sweater, sitting at an outdoor café and smoking a cigarette. Grace with Trause in Portugal at twenty-four, her hair cut short, looking like her adult self, exuding a sublime confidence, no longer uncertain of who she was. Grace in her element.

I must have looked at the pictures for more than an hour before I picked up the pen and started to write. The turmoil of the past days had happened for a reason, and with no facts to support one interpretation or another, I had nothing to guide me but my own instincts and suspi-

492

cions. There had to be a story behind Grace's dumbfounding shifts of mood, her tears and enigmatic utterances, her disappearance on Wednesday night, her struggle to make up her mind about the baby, and when I sat down to write that story, it began and ended with Trause. I could have been wrong, of course, but now that the crisis seemed to have passed, I felt strong enough to entertain the darkest, most unsettling possibilities. Imagine this, I said to myself. Imagine this, and then see what comes of it.

Two years after Tina's death, the grown-up, irresistibly attractive Grace goes to visit Trause in Portugal. He's fifty, a still vigorous and youthful fifty, and for many years now he's taken an active interest in her development – sending her books to read, recommending paintings for her to study, even helping her to acquire a lithograph that will become her most treasured possession. She's probably had a secret crush on him since girlhood, and Trause, who has known her all her life, has always been intensely fond of her. He is a lonely man now, still struggling to find his balance after his wife's death, and she is smitten, a young woman at the height of her loveliness, and ever so warm and compassionate, ever so available. Who can blame him for falling in love with her? As far as I was concerned, any man in his right mind would have fallen for her.

They have an affair. When Trause's fourteen-year-old son joins them in the house, he's revolted by their carryings-on. He has never liked Grace, and now that she's usurped his position and stolen his father from him, he sets out to sabotage their happiness. They go through a hellish time. Ultimately, Jacob makes such a nuisance of himself that he's banished from the household and sent back to his mother.

Trause loves Grace, but Grace is twenty-six years younger than he is, the daughter of his best friend, and slowly but surely guilt wins out over desire. He is bedding down with a girl he used to sing lullabies to when she was a small child. If she were any other twenty-four-year-old woman, there wouldn't be a problem. But how can he go to his oldest friend and tell him he loves his daughter? Bill Tebbetts would call him a pervert and kick him out of the house. It would cause a scandal, and if Trause held his ground and decided to marry her anyway, Grace would be the one to suffer. Her family would turn against her, and he would never be able to forgive himself for that. He tells her she belongs with someone her own age. If she sticks with him, he says, he'll turn her into a widow before she's fifty.

The romance ends, and Grace returns to New York, crushed, disbelieving, brokenhearted. A year and a half goes by, and then Trause returns to New York as well. He moves into the apartment on Barrow Street and the romance starts up again, but much as Trause loves her, the old doubts and conflicts remain. He keeps their affair a secret (to prevent the news from getting back to her father), and Grace plays along, unconcerned about the question of marriage now that she has her man again. When male co-workers at Holst & McDermott ask her out, she turns them down. Her private life is a mystery, and the tight-lipped Grace never tells anyone a thing.

At first, all goes well, but after two or three months a pattern begins to emerge, and Grace understands that she's trapped in a machine. Trause wants her and he doesn't want her. He knows he should give her up, but he can't give her up. He vanishes and reappears, withdraws and comes back, and each time he calls for her, she goes flying into his arms. He loves her for a day or a week or a month, and then his doubts return and he withdraws again. The machine goes off and on, off and on . . . and Grace isn't allowed near the control switch. There's nothing she can do to change the pattern.

Nine months after this madness begins, I enter the picture. I fall in love with Grace, and in spite of her connection to Trause, she is not wholly indifferent to me. I pursue her relentlessly, knowing there's someone else, knowing there's an unnamed rival competing for her affections, but even after she introduces me to Trause (John Trause, celebrated writer and longtime friend of the family), it never occurs to me that he's the other man in her life. For several months she goes back and forth between us, unable to make up her mind. When Trause waffles, I'm with Grace; when Trause wants her back, she's unavailable to see me. I agonize through these disappointments, continuing to hope things will turn my way, but then she breaks up with me, and I assume I've lost her forever. Perhaps she regrets her decision the moment she walks back into the machine, or perhaps Trause loves her so much that he begins to push her away, knowing that I represent a more promising future for her than the hidden, dead-end life she shares with him. It's even possible that he talks her into marrying me. That would account for her sudden, inexplicable change of heart. Not only does she want me back, but in the same breath she declares that she wants to be my wife, and the sooner we get married the better.

We live through a golden age of two years. I'm married to the woman

I love, and Trause becomes my friend. He respects my work as a writer, he takes pleasure in my company, and when the three of us are together, I detect no signs of his former involvement with Grace. He's turned himself into a doting, quasi-paternal figure, and to the degree that he looks on Grace as an imaginary daughter, he looks on me as an imaginary son. He's partly responsible for our marriage, after all, and he's not about to do anything that could put it in jeopardy.

Then catastrophe strikes. On January 12, 1982, I collapse in the 14th Street subway station and fall down a flight of stairs. There are broken bones. There are ruptured internal organs. There are two separate head injuries and neurological damage. I'm taken to Saint Vincent's Hospital and kept there for four months. For the first several weeks, the doctors are pessimistic. One morning, Dr. Justin Berg takes Grace aside and tells her they've given up hope. They doubt I'll live more than a few days, and she should prepare herself for the worst. If he were in her shoes, he says, he'd begin thinking about possible organ donations, funeral homes, and cemeteries. Grace is appalled by the bluntness and coldness of his manner, but the verdict seems final, and she has no choice but to resign herself to the prospect of my imminent death. She goes reeling out of the hospital, blasted apart by the doctor's words, and heads straight for Barrow Street, which is just a few blocks away. Who else can she turn to at such a moment but Trause? John has a bottle of Scotch in his apartment, and she begins drinking the moment she sits down. She drinks too much, and within half an hour she's crying uncontrollably. Trause reaches out to comfort her, wrapping his arms around her and stroking her head, and before she knows what she's doing, her mouth is pressing against his. They haven't touched each other in over two years, and the kiss brings it all back to them. Their bodies remember the past, and once they begin to relive what they used to be together, they can't stop themselves. The past conquers the present, and for the time being the future no longer exists. Grace lets herself go, and Trause doesn't have the strength not to go with her.

She loves me. There's no question that she loves me, but I'm a dead man now, and Grace is falling to pieces, she's half out of her mind with misery, and she needs Trause to hold her together. Impossible to blame her, impossible to blame either one of them, but as I continue to languish in Saint Vincent's over the next few weeks, not yet dead, but not yet truly alive, Grace continues to visit Trause's apartment, and little by little she falls in love with him again. She loves two men now, and even

495

after I defy the medical experts and begin my miraculous turnaround, she goes on loving both of us. When I leave the hospital in May, I'm only dimly aware of who I am anymore. I don't notice things, I stagger around in a half trance, and because a fifth pill is part of my daily regimen for the first three months, I'm in no shape to perform my duties as a husband. Grace is good to me. She's a model of kindness and patience, she's warm and affectionate, she's encouraging, but I can't give anything back to her. She continues her affair with Trause, hating herself for lying to me, hating herself for leading a double life, and the more my recovery advances, the worse her suffering becomes. In early August, two things happen that prevent our marriage from crumbling into ruin. They occur in quick succession, but neither event is related to the other. Grace finds the courage to break off with John, and I stop taking the fifth pill. My groin comes to life again, and for the first time since I left the hospital, Grace is no longer sleeping in two beds. The sky has cleared, and because I know nothing about the deceptions of the past months, I'm blissfully and ignorantly happy – an ex-cuckold who adores his wife and cherishes his friendship with the man who nearly stole her from him.

That should be the end of the story, but it isn't. A month of harmony ensues. Grace settles down with me again, and just when our troubles seem to be over, another storm breaks out. The disaster occurs on the day in question, September 18, 1982, no more than an hour or two after I find the blue notebook in Chang's store, perhaps at the very moment I sit down at my desk and write in the notebook for the first time. On the twenty-seventh, I open the notebook for the last time and record these speculations in an effort to understand the events of the past nine days. Whether they are sound or not, whether they can be verified or not, the story continues when Grace goes to the doctor and finds out she's pregnant. Glorious news, perhaps, but not if you don't know who the father is. She keeps going over the dates in her head, but she can't be sure if the baby is mine or John's. She puts off telling me about it as long as she can, but she's in torment, feeling as if her sins have come back to haunt her, feeling as if she's getting the punishment she deserves. That's why she breaks down in the cab on the night of the eighteenth and attacks me when I reminisce about the Blue Team. There's no fellowship of goodness, she says, because even the best people do bad things. That's why she begins talking about trust and weathering hard times; that's why she implores me to go on loving her.

And when she finally tells me about the baby, that's why she immediately talks about having an abortion. It has nothing to do with our lack of money – it's about not knowing. The idea of not knowing nearly destroys her. She doesn't want to start a family that way, but she can't tell me the truth, and because I'm in the dark I lash out at her and try to talk her into keeping the child. If I do anything right, it's when I back down the next morning and tell her the decision is hers. For the first time in days, she begins to feel a possibility of freedom. She runs off to be alone, scaring the life out of me when she stays out all night, but when she returns the next morning she seems calmer, more capable of thinking clearly, less afraid. It takes her just a few more hours to figure out what she wants to do, and then she leaves that extraordinary message for me on the answering machine. She decides she owes me a gesture of loyalty. She wills herself to believe the baby is mine and puts her doubts behind her. It's a leap of pure faith, and I understand now what courage it's taken her to arrive at that decision. She wants to stay married to me. The episode with Trause is finished, and as long as she continues to want to stay married to me, I will never breathe a word to her about the story I've just written in the blue notebook. I don't know if it's fact or fiction, but in the end I don't care. As long as Grace wants me, the past is of no importance.

That was where I stopped. I put the cap on my pen, stood up from the desk, and carried the photo album back into the living room. It was still early – one, maybe one-thirty in the afternoon. I rustled up some lunch for myself in the kitchen, and when I'd finished eating my sandwich, I returned to my workroom with a small plastic garbage bag. One by one, I ripped the pages out of the blue notebook and tore them into little pieces. Flitcraft and Bowen, the rant about the dead baby in the Bronx, my soap opera version of Grace's love life – everything went into the garbage bag. After a short pause, I decided to tear up the blank pages and then shoved them into the bag as well. I closed it with a tight double knot, and a few minutes later I carried the bundle downstairs when I went out for my walk. I turned south on Court Street, kept on going until I was several blocks past Chang's empty, padlocked store, and then, for no other reason than that I was far from home, I dropped the bag into a trash can on the corner, burying it under a bunch of wilted roses and the funny pages from the *Daily News*.

*

Early in our friendship, Trause told me a story about a French writer he had known in Paris in the early fifties. I can't remember his name, but John said he had published two novels and a collection of stories and was considered to be one of the shining lights of the young generation. He also wrote some poetry, and not long before John returned to America in 1958 (he lived in Paris for six years), this writer acquaintance published a book-length narrative poem that revolved around the drowning death of a young child. Two months after the book was released, the writer and his family went on a vacation to the Normandy coast, and on the last day of their trip his five-year-old daughter waded out into the choppy waters of the English Channel and drowned. The writer was a rational man, John said, a person known for his lucidity and sharpness of mind, but he blamed the poem for his daughter's death. Lost in the throes of grief, he persuaded himself that the words he'd written about an imaginary drowning had caused a real drowning, that a fictional tragedy had provoked a real tragedy in the real world. As a consequence, this immensely gifted writer, this man who had been born to write books, vowed never to write again. Words could kill, he discovered. Words could alter reality, and therefore they were too dangerous to be entrusted to a man who loved them above all else. When John told me the story, the daughter had been dead for twenty-one years, and the writer still hadn't broken his vow. In French literary circles, that silence had turned him into a legendary figure. He was held in the highest regard for the dignity of his suffering, pitied by all who knew him, looked upon with awe.

John and I talked about this story at some length, and I remember that I was quite firm in dismissing the writer's decision as an error, a misbegotten reading of the world. There was no connection between imagination and reality, I said, no cause and effect between the words in a poem and the events in our lives. It might have appeared that way to the writer, but what happened to him was no more than a horrible coincidence, a manifestation of bad luck in its cruelest, most perverse form. That didn't mean I blamed him for feeling as he did, but in spite of sympathizing with the man for his dreadful loss, I saw his silence as a refusal to accept the power of the random, purely accidental forces that mold our destinies, and I told Trause that I thought he was punishing himself for no reason.

It was a bland, commonsense argument, a defense of pragmatism and science over the darkness of primitive, magical thinking. To my surprise, John took the opposite view. I wasn't sure if he was pulling my leg or simply trying to play devil's advocate, but he said that the writer's decision made perfect sense to him and that he admired his friend for having kept his promise. 'Thoughts are real,' he said. 'Words are real. Everything human is real, and sometimes we know things before they happen, even if we aren't aware of it. We live in the present, but the future is inside us at every moment. Maybe that's what writing is all about, Sid. Not recording events from the past, but making things happen in the future.'

Roughly three years after Trause and I had that conversation, I tore up the blue notebook and threw it into a garbage can on the corner of Third Place and Court Street in Carroll Gardens, Brooklyn. At the time, it felt like the correct thing to do, and as I walked back to my apartment that Monday afternoon in September, nine days after the day in question, I was more or less convinced that the failures and disappointments of the past week were finally over. But they weren't over. The story was just beginning – the true story started only *then*, after I destroyed the blue notebook – and everything I've written so far is little more than a prelude to the horrors I'm about to relate now. Is there a connection between the *before* and the *after*? I don't know. Did the unfortunate French writer kill his child with his poem – or did his words merely predict her death? I don't know. What I do know is that I would no longer argue against his decision today. I respect the silence he imposed on himself, and I understand the revulsion he must have felt whenever he thought of writing again. More than twenty years after the fact, I now believe that Trause called it right. We sometimes know things before they happen, even if we don't know that we know. I blundered through those nine days in September 1982 like someone trapped inside a cloud. I tried to write a story and came to an impasse. I tried to sell an idea for a film and was rejected. I lost my friend's manuscript. I nearly lost my wife, and yet fervently as I loved her, I didn't hesitate to drop my pants in a darkened sex club and thrust myself into the mouth of a stranger. I was a lost man, an ill man, a man struggling to regain his footing, but underneath all the missteps and follies I committed that week, I knew something I wasn't aware of knowing. At certain moments during those days, I felt as if my body had become transparent, a porous membrane through which all the invisible forces of the world could pass – a nexus of airborne electrical charges transmitted by the thoughts and feelings of others. I suspect that condition was what led to the birth of Lemuel

Flagg, the blind hero of *Oracle Night*, a man so sensitive to the vibrations around him that he knew what was going to happen before the events themselves took place. I didn't know, but every thought that entered my head was pointing me in that direction. Stillborn babies, concentration camp atrocities, presidential assassinations, disappearing spouses, impossible journeys back and forth through time. The future was already inside me, and I was preparing myself for the disasters that were about to come.

I had seen Trause for lunch on Wednesday, but aside from our two telephone conversations later that week, I had no further contact with him before I got rid of the blue notebook on the twenty-seventh. We had talked about Jacob and the lost manuscript of his old story, but that was the extent of it, and I had no idea what he was doing with himself during those days – except lying on the sofa and taking care of his leg. It wasn't until 1994, when James Gillespie published *The Labyrinth of Dreams: A Life of John Trause*, that I finally learned the details of what John had been up to from the twenty-second to the twenty-seventh. Gillespie's massive six-hundred-page book is short on literary analysis and pays little attention to the historical context of John's work, but it is exceedingly thorough when it comes to biographical facts, and given that he spent ten years working on the project and seemed to have talked to every living person who had ever known Trause (myself included), I have no reason to doubt the precision of his chronology.

After I left John's apartment on Wednesday, he worked until dinnertime, proofreading and making minor changes on the typescript of his novel *The Strange Destiny of Gerald Fuchs*, which he had apparently finished several days before the onset of his phlebitis attack. This was the book I had suspected he was writing but had never been certain about: a manuscript of just under five hundred pages that Gillespie says Trause had started during his last months in Portugal, which meant it had taken him over four years to complete. So much for the rumor that John had stopped writing after Tina's death. So much for the rumor that a once-great novelist had given up his vocation and was living off his early accomplishments – a has-been with nothing more to say.

That evening, Eleanor called with the news that Jacob had been found, and early the next morning, Thursday, Trause telephoned his lawyer, Francis W. Byrd. Lawyers seldom make house calls, but Byrd had been representing Trause for over ten years, and when a client of

John's stature informs his attorney that he's laid up on the sofa with a bad leg and needs to see him on an urgent matter at two o'clock, the attorney will scrap his other plans and arrive at the appointed hour, equipped with all necessary papers and documents, which he will have pulled from his office files before heading downtown. When Byrd reached the Barrow Street apartment, John offered him a drink, and once the two men had finished their Scotch and sodas, they sat down to the task of rewriting Trause's will. The old one had been drawn up more than seven years earlier, and it no longer represented John's desires concerning the disposal of his estate. In the aftermath of Tina's death, he had named Jacob as his sole heir and beneficiary, appointing his brother Gilbert to serve as executor until the boy reached the age of twenty-five. Now, by the simple act of tearing up all copies of that document, Trause disinherited his son in front of his lawyer's eyes. Byrd then typed out a new will that bequeathed everything John owned to Gilbert. All cash, all stocks and bonds, all property, and all future royalties to be earned from Trause's literary works would henceforth be inherited by his younger brother. They finished at five-thirty. John shook Byrd's hand, thanking him for his help, and the lawyer left the apartment with three signed copies of the new will. Twenty minutes later, John went back to proofreading his novel. Madame Dumas served him dinner at eight, and at nine-thirty Eleanor called again, telling him that Jacob had been admitted to the program at Smithers and had been there since four o'clock that afternoon.

Friday was the day Trause was supposed to have his leg examined at Saint Vincent's Hospital, but he neglected to look at his calendar and forgot to go. In all the turmoil surrounding the business with Jacob, the appointment had slipped his mind, and at the precise moment when he should have been meeting with his doctor (a vascular surgeon named Willard Dunmore), he was on the phone with me, talking about his son's lifelong animosity toward Grace and asking me to go to Smithers for him on Saturday. According to Gillespie, the doctor called Trause's apartment at eleven-thirty to ask him why he hadn't shown up at the hospital. When Trause explained that there had been a family emergency, Dunmore delivered an angry lecture on the importance of the scan and told his patient that such a cavalier attitude toward his own health was irresponsible and could lead to dire consequences. Trause asked if it would be possible to go in that afternoon, but Dunmore said it was too late and they would have to put it off until Monday at four o'clock. He urged Trause to remember to take his medicine and to remain as still as possible over the weekend. When Madame Dumas arrived at one, she found John in his usual spot on the sofa, correcting the pages of his book.

On Saturday, while I was visiting Jacob at Smithers and tangling over the red notebook in Chang's store, Trause continued to work on his novel. His phone records indicate that he also made three long-distance calls: one to Eleanor in East Hampton, a second to his brother Gilbert in Ann Arbor (who worked as a professor of musicology at the University of Michigan), and a third to his literary agent, Alice Lazarre, at her weekend house in the Berkshires. He reported to her that he was making good progress with the book, and if he didn't run into any unforeseen problems in the days ahead, she could expect to have a finished manuscript by the end of the week.

On Sunday morning, I called from Landolfi's and gave him the rundown on my brief visit with Jacob. Then I made my confession about having lost his story, and John laughed. If I'm not mistaken, it was a laugh of relief rather than of amusement. It's difficult to know for sure, but I think Trause gave me that story for highly complex reasons – and the talk about providing me with the subject for a film was no more than an excuse, a peripheral motive at best. The story was about the cutthroat machinations of a political conspiracy, but it was also about a marital triangle (a wife running off with her husband's best friend), and if there was any truth to the speculations I put down in the notebook on the twenty-seventh, then perhaps John gave me the story in order to comment on the state of my marriage – indirectly, in the finely nuanced codes and metaphors of fiction. It didn't matter that the story had been written in 1952, the year Grace was born. 'The Empire of Bones' was a premonition of things to come. It had been put in a box and left to incubate for thirty years, and little by little it had evolved into a story about the woman we both loved – my wife, my brave and struggling wife.

I say he laughed with *relief* because I think he regretted what he had done. When we were having lunch on Wednesday, he reacted with great emotion to the news of Grace's pregnancy, and immediately after that we found ourselves on the verge of an ugly quarrel. The moment passed, but I wonder now if Trause wasn't a good deal angrier at me than he let on. He was my friend, but he also must have resented me for having won back Grace. Breaking off their affair had been her decision, and now that she was pregnant, there was no chance that he would ever be with her again. If this was true, giving me the story would have served as a veiled, cryptic form of revenge, a churlish sort of one-upmanship – as if to say, You don't know anything, Sidney. You've never known anything, but I've been around a lot longer than you have. Perhaps. There is no way to prove any of this, but if I've misunderstood his actions, how then to interpret the fact that John never sent me the story? He promised to have Madame Dumas mail me a carbon of the manuscript, but he wound up sending me something else instead, and I took that thing not only as an act of supreme generosity but as an act of contrition as well. By losing the envelope on the subway, I had spared him the embarrassment of his momentary fit of pique. He was sorry for having let his passions run away from him, and now that my clumsiness had gotten him off the hook, he was determined to make it up to me with a spectacular, altogether unnecessary gesture of kindness and goodwill.

We had talked on Sunday somewhere between ten-thirty and eleven o'clock. Madame Dumas arrived at noon, and ten minutes later Trause handed her his ATM card and instructed her to go to the neighborhood Citibank near Sheridan Square and transfer forty thousand dollars from his savings account to his checking account. Gillespie tells us that he spent the rest of the day working on his novel, and that evening, after Madame Dumas had served him dinner, he dragged himself off the sofa and limped into his study, where he sat down at his worktable and made out a check to me for thirty-six thousand dollars – the exact sum of my unpaid medical bills. Then he wrote me the following short letter:

Dear Sid:

I know I promised you a carbon of the ms., but what's the point? The whole idea was to earn you some money, so I've cut to the chase and written you the enclosed check. It's a gift, free and clear. No terms, no strings, no need to pay me back. I know you're broke, so please don't get on your high horse and tear it up. Spend it, live on it, get yourself going again. I don't want you to have to waste your time fretting about movies. Stick with books. That's where your future is, and I'm expecting great things from you.

Thanks for taking the trouble to visit the brat yesterday. It's much appreciated – nay, more than much, since I know how unpleasant it must have been for you.

Dinner this coming Saturday? Can't say where yet, since it all depends on this damn leg. Strange fact: the clot was brought on by my own cheapness. Ten days before the pain started, I made a lightning trip to Paris – back and forth in thirty-six hours – to talk at the funeral of my old friend and translator, Philippe Joubert. I flew coach, slept both ways, and the doctor says that's what did it. All cramped up in those midget seats. From now on, I only travel first class.

Kiss Gracie for me – and don't give up on Flitcraft. All you need is a different notebook, and the words will start coming again.

J.T.

He sealed up the letter and the check in an envelope and then wrote out my name and address in block letters across the front, but there were no more stamps in the house, and when Madame Dumas left Barrow Street at ten o'clock to return to her apartment in the Bronx, Trause gave her a twenty-dollar bill and asked her to swing by the post office in the morning to stock up on a new supply of first-class stamps. The ever-efficient Madame Dumas took care of the errand, and when she showed up for work on Monday at 11 a.m., John was finally able to put a stamp on the letter. She served him a light lunch at one. After the meal, he pushed on with the proofreading of his novel, and when Madame Dumas left the apartment at two-thirty to shop for groceries, Trause handed her the letter and asked her to mail it for him while she was out. She promised to return by three-thirty, at which point she would help him down the stairs and into the town car he had ordered to take him to his appointment with Dr. Dunmore at the hospital. After Madame Dumas left, Gillespie tells us we can be sure of only one thing. Eleanor called at two-forty-five and informed Trause that Jacob had gone missing. He'd walked out of Smithers sometime in the middle of the night, and no one had heard from him since. Gillespie quotes Eleanor as saying that John became 'extremely upset' and went on talking to her for fifteen or twenty minutes. 'He's on his own now,' John finally said. 'There's nothing we can do for him anymore.'

Those were Trause's last words. We have no idea what happened to him after he hung up the phone, but when Madame Dumas returned at three-thirty, she found him lying on the floor at the foot of his bed. That would seem to suggest he'd gone into the bedroom to begin changing his clothes for the appointment with Dunmore, but that is only conjecture. All we know for certain is that he died somewhere between three

504

o'clock and three-thirty on September 27, 1982 – less than two hours after I tossed the remains of the blue notebook into a garbage can on a street corner in South Brooklyn. The initial cause of death was presumed to be a heart attack, but on further investigation by the medical examiner that verdict was changed to pulmonary embolism. The blood clot that had been sitting in John's leg for the past two weeks had broken loose, traveled upward through his system, and found its target. The little bomb had finally gone off inside him, and my friend was dead at fifty-six. Too soon. Too soon by thirty years. Too soon to thank him for sending me the money and trying to save my life.

John's death was reported in a late bulletin at the end of the local six o'clock news broadcasts. Under normal circumstances, Grace and I would have turned on the television as we were setting the table and preparing our dinner, but we didn't have a television anymore, so we went through the evening without knowing that John was lying in the city morgue, without knowing that his brother Gilbert was already on a plane from Detroit to New York, without knowing that Jacob was on the loose. After dinner, we went into the living room and stretched out on the sofa together, talking about Grace's upcoming appointment with Dr. Vitale, a female obstetrician recommended by Betty Stolowitz, whose first baby had been delivered in March. The visit was scheduled for Friday afternoon, and I told Grace I wanted to be there with her and would show up at the office on West Ninth Street at four o'clock. As we were going over these arrangements, Grace suddenly remembered that Betty had given her a book about pregnancy that morning – one of those big paperback compendiums filled with charts and illustrations – and she hopped off the sofa and went into the bedroom to retrieve it from her shoulder bag. While she was gone, someone knocked on the door. I assumed it was one of our neighbors, coming to borrow a flashlight or a book of matches. It couldn't have been anyone else, since the front door of the building was always locked, and a person without a key had to push an outside buzzer and announce himself through the intercom before he could get in. I remember that I wasn't wearing any shoes, and when I climbed off the sofa and went to open the door, I picked up a small splinter in the sole of my left foot. I also remember looking at my watch and seeing that it was eight-thirty. I didn't bother to ask who it was. I simply opened the door, and once I did that, the world became a different world. I don't know how else to put it. I unlocked the door, and the thing that had been building inside me over the past days was suddenly real: the future was standing in front of me.

It was Jacob. He had dyed his hair black, and he was bundled up in a long dark overcoat that hung down to his ankles. Hands thrust into his pockets, bouncing impatiently on the balls of his feet, he looked like some futuristic undertaker who'd come to carry away a dead body. The green-headed clown I'd talked to on Saturday had been disturbing enough, but this new creature scared me, and I didn't want to let him in. 'You've got to help me,' he said. 'I'm in real trouble, Sid, and there's no one else to turn to.' Before I could tell him to go away, he pushed himself into the apartment and shut the door behind him.

'Go back to Smithers,' I said. 'There's nothing I can do for you.'

'I can't go back. They found out I was there. If I go back to that place, I'm dead.'

'Who's *they*? Who are you talking about?'

'These guys, Richie and Phil. They think I owe them money. If I don't come up with five thousand dollars, they're going to kill me.'

'I don't believe you, Jacob.'

'They're the reason I went to Smithers. It wasn't because of my mother. It was to hide from them.'

'I still don't believe you. But even if I did, I wouldn't be able to help. I don't have five thousand dollars. I don't even have five hundred dollars. Call your mother. If she turns you down, call your father. But leave Grace and me out of this.'

I heard the toilet flush down the hall, a signal that Grace would be coming back to the room at any moment. Distracted by the noise, Jacob turned his head toward that area of the apartment, and when he saw her walk into the living room with the pregnancy book in her hand, he broke into a big smile. 'Hiya, Gracie,' he said. 'Long time no see.'

Grace stopped in her tracks. 'What's he doing here?' she said, addressing her words to me. She looked stunned, and she spoke in a kind of suppressed rage, refusing to turn her eyes back in Jacob's direction.

'He wants to borrow money,' I said.

'Come on, Gracie,' Jacob said, in a half petulant, half sarcastic tone of voice. 'Won't you even say hello to me? I mean, it doesn't cost anything to be polite, does it?'

As I stood there watching the two of them, I couldn't help thinking about the torn-up photograph that had been left on the sofa after the break-in. The frame had been stolen, but only someone with a deep, long-standing grudge against the person in the portrait would have gone to the trouble of ripping it to pieces. A professional burglar would have left it intact. But Jacob wasn't a professional; he was a frantic, drug-addled kid who'd gone out of his way to hurt us – to hurt his father by going after two of his closest friends.

'That's enough,' I said to him. 'She doesn't want to talk to you, and neither do I. You're the person who robbed us last week. You crawled in through the kitchen window and smashed up the place, and then you walked off with every valuable thing you could find. Do you want me to pick up the phone and call the cops, or do you want to leave? Those are your two choices. Trust me, I'll make that call with great pleasure. I'll press charges against you, and you'll wind up going to jail.'

I was expecting him to deny the accusation, to pretend to be insulted that I would dare to think such a thing about him, but the boy was much cleverer than that. He let out a beautifully calibrated sigh of remorse, and then he sat down in a chair, slowly shaking his head back and forth, acting as if he were shocked by his own behavior. It was the same kind of self-loathing performance he'd mentioned to me on Saturday when he'd bragged about his theatrical talents. 'I'm sorry,' he said. 'But what I told you about Richie and Phil is true. They're after me, and if I don't give them their five thousand bucks, they're going to put a bullet in my head. I came here the other day thinking I'd borrow your checkbook, but I couldn't find it. So I took some other things instead. It was a dumb move. I'm really sorry. The stuff wasn't even worth that much, and I shouldn't have done it. If you want, I'll give it all back to you tomorrow. I still have it in my apartment, and I'll bring everything back first thing in the morning.'

'Bullshit,' Grace said. 'You've already sold what you could, and then you threw out the rest. Don't play that sorry-little-boy routine, Jacob. You're too big for that now. You ripped us off last week, and now you're back for more.'

'Those guys are fixing to shorten my life,' he said, 'and they need their money by tomorrow. I know you two are strapped for cash, but Christ, Gracie, your dad's a federal judge. He's not going to flinch if you ask him for a loan. I mean, what's five thousand dollars to an old southern gentleman?'

'Forget it,' I said. 'There's no way we're going to drag Bill Tebbetts into this.'

'Get him out of here, Sid,' Grace said to me, her voice tight with anger. 'I can't stand it anymore.'

'I thought we were family,' Jacob replied, staring hard at Grace, almost forcing her to look at him. He had begun to pout, but in a curiously insincere way, as though he were trying to mock her and twist her dislike for him to his own advantage. 'After all, you're sort of my unofficial stepmom, aren't you? At least you used to be. Doesn't that count for something?'

By then, Grace was already moving across the room, on her way to the kitchen. 'I'm calling the police,' she said. 'If you won't do it, Sid, I will. I want this slimeball out of here.' In order for her to reach the phone in the kitchen, however, she had to pass in front of the chair Jacob was sitting in, and before she managed to get there, he had already stood up to block her way. Until then, the confrontation had consisted entirely of words. The three of us had been talking, and no matter how distasteful that talk had been, I wasn't prepared for those words to erupt into physical violence. I was standing near the sofa, a good eight or ten feet from the chair, and when Grace tried to slip past Jacob, he grabbed hold of her arm and said, 'Not the police, stupid. Your father. The only person you're going to call is the judge – to ask for the money.' Grace tried to squirm out of his grip, bucking around like an incensed animal, but Jacob was five or six inches taller than she was, which gave him superior leverage and allowed him to bear down on her from above. I rushed toward him, slowed by my sore muscles and the splinter in my foot, but before I got there, Jacob had already locked his hands onto her shoulders and was slamming her into the wall. I jumped him from behind, trying to wrap my arms around his torso and pull him away from her, but the kid was strong, much stronger than I had expected, and without even bothering to turn around, he sent his elbow straight into my stomach. It blew the wind out of me and knocked me down, and before I could make another charge at him, he was punching Grace in the mouth and kicking her in the belly with his thick leather boots. She tried to fight back, but each time she stood up, he slugged her in the face, banged her against the wall, and threw her to the floor. Blood was pouring out of her nose when I was ready to attack again, but I knew that I was too weak to have any effect, too debilitated to stop him with my sad and frail fists. Grace was moaning and nearly unconscious by then, and I felt there was a real danger that he would beat her to death. Instead of going straight for him, I rushed into the kitchen and pulled out a large carving knife from the top drawer next to the sink. 'Stop it!' I yelled at him. 'Stop it, Jacob, or else I'm going to kill you!' I don't think he heard me at first. He was completely lost in his fury, an insane destroyer who scarcely seemed to know what he was doing anymore, but as I advanced toward him with the knife, he must have caught a glimpse of me out of the corner of his eye. He turned his head to the left, and when he saw me there with the knife raised in my hand, he suddenly stopped hitting her. His eyes had a wild, unfocused look, and sweat was sliding off his nose and falling onto his narrow, trembling chin. I felt certain he was going to come after me next. I wouldn't have hesitated to stick the knife into his body, but when he glanced down at the bleeding and immobilized Grace, he dropped his arms to his sides and said, 'Thanks a lot, Sid. Now I'm a dead man.' Then he turned around and left the apartment, vanishing into the streets of Brooklyn a few minutes before the police cars and the ambulance pulled up in front of the house.

Grace lost the baby. The blows from Jacob's boot had torn up her insides, and once the hemorrhaging began, the tiny embryo was dislodged from the wall of her uterus and came washing out in a miserable stream of blood. Spontaneous abortion, as the term goes; a miscarriage; a life that was never born. They drove her across the Gowanus Canal to Methodist Hospital in Park Slope, and as I sat beside her in the back of the ambulance, wedged in among the oxygen tanks and two paramedics, I kept looking down at her poor battered face, unable to stop myself from trembling, seizing up in continual spasms that shuddered through my chest and down the entire length of my body. Her nose was broken, the left side of her face was covered with bruises, and her right eyelid was so swollen it looked as if she would never see out of that eye again. At the hospital, they wheeled her off for X rays on the ground floor and then took her upstairs to an operating room, where they worked on her for more than two hours. I don't know how I did it, but as I waited for the surgeons to finish their job, I managed to pull myself together just long enough to call Grace's parents in Charlottesville. That was when I found out John was dead. Sally Tebbetts answered the phone, and at the end of our exhausting, interminable conversation, she told me that Gilbert had called earlier that evening with the news. She and Bill were already in shock, she said, and now I was telling her that John's son had tried to kill their daughter.

Had the world gone crazy? she asked, and then her voice choked up and she started to cry. She handed the phone to her husband, and when Bill Tebbetts came on, he got right to the point and asked me the only question worth asking. Was Grace going to live? Yes, I said, she was going to live. I didn't know that yet, but I wasn't about to tell him that Grace was in critical condition and might not pull through. I wasn't going to hex her chances by speaking the wrong words. If words could kill, then I had to keep a careful watch over my tongue and make sure never to express a single doubt or negative thought. I hadn't come back from the dead in order to watch my wife die. Losing John was terrible enough, and I wasn't going to lose anyone else. It simply wasn't going to happen. Even if I had no say in the matter, I wasn't going to allow it to happen.

For the next seventy-two hours, I sat by Grace's bed and didn't budge from my spot. I washed and shaved in the adjoining bathroom, ate meals as I watched the clear liquid in the IV line drip into her arm, and lived for those rare moments when she opened her good eye and said a few words to me. With so many painkillers circulating in her blood, she seemed to have no memory of what Jacob had done to her and only the dimmest awareness that she was in a hospital. Three or four times, she asked me where she was, but then she'd drift off again and immediately forget what I'd told her. She often whimpered in her sleep, groaning softly as she swatted at the bandages on her face, and once she woke up with tears in her eyes asking, 'Why do I hurt so much? What's wrong with me?'

People came and went during those days, but I have no more than the faintest memories of them, and I can't recall a single conversation I had with anyone. The assault occurred on a Monday night, and by Tuesday morning Grace's parents had already flown up from Virginia. Her cousin Lily drove down from Connecticut that same afternoon. Her younger sisters, Darcy and Flo, arrived the next morning. Betty Stolowitz and Greg Fitzgerald came. Mary Sklarr came. Mr. and Mrs. Caramello came. I must have talked to them and left the room every now and then, but I can't remember anything but sitting with Grace. For most of Tuesday and Wednesday, she was in a semiconscious torpor – drowsing, sleeping, waking for just a few minutes at a stretch – but by Wednesday evening she seemed to be a little more coherent and was beginning to remain conscious for longer periods of time. She slept soundly that night, and when she woke up on Thursday morning, she finally recognized me. I took hold of her hand, and as our palms touched, she muttered my name, then repeated it to herself several more times, as though that one-syllable word were an incantation that could turn her from a ghost into a living being again.

'I'm in a hospital, aren't I?' she said.

'Methodist Hospital in Park Slope,' I answered. 'And I'm sitting next to you, holding your hand. It's not a dream, Grace. We're really here, and little by little you're going to get better.'

'I'm not going to die?'

'No, you're not going to die.'

'He beat me up, didn't he? He punched me and kicked me, and I remember thinking I was going to die. Where were you, Sid? Why didn't you help me?'

'I got my arms around him, but I couldn't pull him off you. I had to threaten him with a knife. I was ready to kill him, Grace, but he ran off before anything happened. Then I called Nine-one-one, and the ambulance brought you here.'

'When was that?'

'Three nights ago.'

'And what's this stuff on my face?'

'Bandages. And a splint for your nose.'

'He broke my nose?'

'Yes. And gave you a concussion. But your head is clearing now, isn't it? You're starting to come around.'

'What about the baby? There's this big pain in my gut, Sid, and I think I know what it means. It can't be true, can it?'

'I'm afraid it is. Everything else is going to get better, but not that.'

One day later, Trause's ashes were scattered in a meadow in Central Park. There must have been thirty or forty of us in the group that morning, a gathering of friends, relatives, and fellow writers, with no official from any religion present and not one mention of the word *God* made by any of the people who spoke. Grace knew nothing about John's death, and her parents and I had decided to keep it from her as long as we could. Bill went to the ceremony with me, but Sally stayed behind at the hospital to be with Grace – who had been told I was accompanying her father to the airport for his flight back to Virginia. Grace was gradually getting better, but she still wasn't well enough to handle a blow of that magnitude. One tragedy at a time, I said to her parents, but no more. Like the single drops of liquid that fell from the plastic bag into the IV tube attached to Grace's arm, the medicine would have to be parceled out in small doses. The lost child was more than enough for now. John could wait until she was strong enough to bear a second onslaught of grief.

No one mentioned Jacob at the service, but he was present in my thoughts as I listened to John's brother and Bill and various other friends deliver their eulogies under the blazing light of that autumn morning. How rotten for a man to die before he had a chance to become old, I said to myself, how grim to contemplate the work he still had in front of him. But if John had to die now, I felt, then surely it was better that he had died on Monday, and not Tuesday or Wednesday. If he had lived another twenty-four hours, he would have found out what Jacob had done to Grace, and I was certain that knowledge would have destroyed him. As it was, he would never have to confront the fact that he had sired a monster, never have to walk around with the burden of the outrage his son had committed against the person he loved most in the world. Jacob had become the unmentionable, but I burned with hatred against him, and I was looking forward to the moment when the police finally caught up with him and I would be able to testify against him in court. To my infinite regret, I was never given that opportunity. Even as we stood in Central Park mourning his father, Jacob was already dead. None of us could have known it then, since another two months went by before his decomposing body was found – wrapped in a sheath of black plastic and buried in a Dumpster at an abandoned construction site near the Harlem River in the Bronx. He had been shot twice in the head. Richie and Phil had not been phantoms of his imagination, and when the forensic report was placed in evidence at their trial the following year, it showed that each bullet had been fired from a different gun.

That same day (October 1), the letter sent from Manhattan by Madame Dumas reached its destination in Brooklyn. I found it in my mailbox after I went home from Central Park (to change my clothes before setting out for the hospital again), and because there was no return address on the envelope, I didn't learn who it was from until I'd carried it upstairs and opened it. Trause had written the letter by hand, and the script was so jagged, so frenzied in its execution, that I had trouble deciphering it. I had to go through the text several times before I managed to crack the mysteries of its illegible curls and scratches, but once I began to translate the marks into words, I could hear John's voice talking to me – a living voice talking from the other side of death, from the other side of nowhere. Then I found the check inside the envelope, and I felt my eyes watering up with tears. I saw John's ashes streaming out of the urn in the park that morning. I saw Grace lying in her bed in the hospital. I saw myself tearing up the pages of the blue notebook, and after a while – in the words of John's brother-in-law Richard – I had my face in my hands and was sobbing my guts out. I don't know how long I carried on like that, but even as the tears poured out of me, I was happy, happier to be alive than I had ever been before. It was a happiness beyond consolation, beyond misery, beyond all the ugliness and beauty of the world. Eventually, the tears subsided, and I went into the bedroom to put on a fresh set of clothes. Ten minutes later, I was out on the street again, walking toward the hospital to see Grace.

2002–2003

THE BROOKLYN FOLLIES

for my daughter
Sophie

Overture

I was looking for a quiet place to die. Someone recommended Brooklyn, and so the next morning I traveled down there from Westchester to scope out the terrain. I hadn't been back in fifty-six years, and I remembered nothing. My parents had moved out of the city when I was three, but I instinctively found myself returning to the neighborhood where we had lived, crawling home like some wounded dog to the place of my birth. A local real estate agent ushered me around to six or seven brownstone flats, and by the end of the afternoon I had rented a two-bedroom garden apartment on First Street, just half a block away from Prospect Park. I had no idea who my neighbors were, and I didn't care. They all worked at nine-to-five jobs, none of them had any children, and therefore the building would be relatively silent. More than anything else, that was what I craved. A silent end to my sad and ridiculous life.

The house in Bronxville was already under contract, and once the closing took place at the end of the month, money wasn't going to be a problem. My ex-wife and I were planning to split the proceeds from the sale, and with four hundred thousand dollars in the bank, there would be more than enough to sustain me until I stopped breathing.

At first, I didn't know what to do with myself. I had spent thirty-one years commuting back and forth between the suburbs and the Manhattan offices of Mid-Atlantic Accident and Life, but now that I didn't have a job anymore, there were too many hours in the day. About a week after I moved into the apartment, my married daughter, Rachel, drove in from New Jersey to pay me a visit. She said that I needed to get involved in something, to invent a project for myself. Rachel is not a stupid person. She has a doctorate in bio-chemistry from the University of Chicago and works as a researcher for a large drug company outside Princeton, but much like her mother before her, it's a rare day when she speaks in anything but platitudes – all those exhausted phrases and hand-me-down ideas that cram the dump sites of contemporary wisdom.

I explained that I was probably going to be dead before the year was out, and I didn't give a flying fuck about projects. For a moment, it looked as if Rachel was about to cry, but she blinked back the tears and called me a cruel and selfish person instead. No wonder 'Mom' had finally divorced me, she added, no wonder she hadn't been able to take it anymore. Being married to a man like me must have been an unending torture, a living hell. *A living hell.* Alas, poor Rachel – she simply can't help herself. My only child has inhabited this earth for twenty-nine years, and not once has she come up with an original remark, with something absolutely and irreducibly her own.

Yes, I suppose there is something nasty about me at times. But not all the time – and not as a matter of principle. On my good days, I'm as sweet and friendly as any person I know. You can't sell life insurance as successfully as I did by alienating your customers, at least not for three long decades you can't. You have to be sympathetic. You have to be able to listen. You have to know how to charm people. I possess all those qualities and more. I won't deny that I've had my bad moments as well, but everyone knows what dangers lurk behind the closed doors of family life. It can be poison for all concerned, especially if you discover that you probably weren't cut out for marriage in the first place. I loved having sex with Edith, but after four or five years the passion seemed to run its course, and from then on I became less than a perfect husband. To hear Rachel tell it, I wasn't much in the parent department either. I wouldn't want to contradict her memories, but the truth is that I cared for them both in my own way, and if I sometimes found myself in the arms of other women, I never took any of those affairs seriously. The divorce wasn't my idea. In spite of everything, I was planning to stay with Edith until the end. She was the one who wanted out, and given the extent of my sins and transgressions over the years, I couldn't really blame her. Thirty-three years of living under the same roof, and by the time we walked off in opposite directions, what we added up to was approximately nothing.

I had told Rachel my days were numbered, but that was no more than a hotheaded retort to her meddling advice, a blast of pure hyperbole. My lung cancer was in remission, and based on what the oncologist had told me after my most recent exam, there was cause for guarded optimism. That didn't mean I trusted him, however. The shock of the cancer had been so great, I still didn't believe in the possibility of surviving it. I had given myself up for dead, and once the tumor had been cut out of me and I'd gone through the debilitating ordeals of radiation treatment and chemo, once I'd suffered the long bouts of nausea and dizziness, the loss of hair, the loss of will, the loss of job, the loss of wife, it was difficult for me to imagine how to go on. Hence Brooklyn. Hence my uncon-scious return to the place where my story began. I was almost sixty years old, and I didn't know how much time I had left. Maybe another twenty years; maybe just a few more months. Whatever the medical prognosis of my condition, the crucial thing was to take nothing for granted. As long as I was alive, I had to figure out a way to start living again, but even if I didn't live, I had to do more than just sit around and wait for the end. As usual, my scientist daughter had been right, even if I'd been too stubborn to admit it. I had to keep myself busy. I had to get off my ass and do something.

It was early spring when I moved in, and for the first few weeks I filled my time by exploring the neighborhood, taking long walks in the park, and planting flowers in my back garden – a small, junk-filled patch of ground that had been neglected for years. I had my newly resurgent hair cut at the Park Slope Barbershop on Seventh Avenue, rented videos from a place called Movie Heaven, and stopped in often at Brightman's Attic, a cluttered, badly organized used-book store owned by a flamboyant homosexual named Harry Brightman (more about him later). Most mornings, I prepared breakfast for myself in the apartment, but since I disliked cooking and lacked all talent for it, I tended to eat lunch and dinner in restaurants – always alone, always with an open book in front of me, always chewing as slowly as possible in order to drag out the meal as long as I could. After sampling a num-ber of options in the vicinity, I settled on the Cosmic Diner as my regu-lar spot for lunch. The food there was mediocre at best, but one of the waitresses was an adorable Puerto Rican girl named Marina, and I rapidly developed a crush on her. She was half my age and already mar-ried, which meant that romance was out of the question, but she was so splendid to look at, so gentle in her dealings with me, so ready to laugh at my less than funny jokes, that I literally pined for her on her days off. From a strictly anthropological point of view, I discovered that Brook-lynites are less reluctant to talk to strangers than any tribe I had previ-ously encountered. They butt into one another's business at will (old women scolding young mothers for not dressing their children warmly enough, passersby snapping at dog walkers for yanking too hard on the leash); they argue like deranged four-year-olds over disputed parking spaces; they zip out dazzling one-liners as a matter of course. One Sunday morning, I went into a crowded deli with the absurd name of La Bagel Delight. I was intending to ask for a cinnamon-raisin bagel, but the word caught in my mouth and came out as *cinnamon-reagan*. Without missing a beat, the young guy behind the counter answered, 'Sorry, we don't have any of those. How about a pumpernixon instead?' Fast. So damned fast, I nearly wet my drawers.

After that inadvertent slip of the tongue, I finally hit upon an idea that Rachel would have approved of. It wasn't much of an idea, perhaps, but at least it was something, and if I stuck to it as rigorously and faithfully as I intended to, then I would have my project, the little hobbyhorse I'd been looking for to carry me away from the indolence of my soporific routine. Humble as the project was, I decided to give it a grandiose, somewhat pompous title – in order to delude myself into thinking that I was engaged in important work. I called it *The Book of Human Folly*, and in it I was planning to set down in the simplest, clearest language possible an account of every blunder, every pratfall, every embarrassment, every idiocy, every foible, and every inane act I had committed during my long and checkered career as a man. When I couldn't think of stories to tell about myself, I would write down things that had happened to people I knew, and when that source ran dry as well, I would take on historical events, recording the follies of my fellow human beings down through the ages, beginning with the vanished civilizations of the ancient world and pushing on to the first months of the twenty-first century. If nothing else, I thought it might be good for a few laughs. I had no desire to bare my soul or indulge in gloomy introspections. The tone would be light and farcical throughout, and my only purpose was to keep myself entertained while using up as many hours of the day as I could.

I called the project a book, but in fact it wasn't a book at all. Working with yellow legal pads, loose sheets of paper, the backs of envelopes and junk-mail form letters for credit cards and home-improvement loans, I was compiling what amounted to a collection of random jottings, a hodgepodge of unrelated anecdotes that I would throw into a cardboard box each time another story was finished. There was little method to my madness. Some of the pieces came to no more than a few lines, and a number of them, in particular the spoonerisms and malapropisms I was so fond of, were just a single phrase. *Chilled greaseburger* instead of *grilled cheeseburger*, for example, which came out of my mouth sometime during my junior year of high school, or the unintentionally profound, quasi-mystical utterance I delivered to Edith while we were engaged in one of our bitter marital spats: *I'll see it when I believe it*. Every time I sat down to write, I would begin by closing my eyes and letting my thoughts wander in any direction they chose. By forcing myself to relax in this way, I managed to dredge up considerable amounts of material from the distant past, things that until then I had assumed were lost forever. A moment from the sixth grade (to cite one such memory) when a boy in our class named Dudley Franklin let out a long, trumpet-shrill fart during a silent pause in the middle of a geography lesson. We all laughed, of course (nothing is funnier to a roomful of eleven-year-olds than a gust of broken wind), but what set the incident apart from the category of minor embarrassments and elevated it to classic status, an enduring masterpiece in the annals of shame and humiliation, was the fact that Dudley was innocent enough to commit the fatal blunder of offering an apology. 'Excuse me,' he said, looking down at his desk and blushing until his cheeks resembled a freshly painted fire truck. One must never own up to a fart in public. That is the unwritten law, the single most stringent protocol of American etiquette. Farts come from no one and nowhere; they are anonymous emanations that belong to the group as a whole, and even when every person in the room can point to the culprit, the only sane course of action is denial. The witless Dudley Franklin was too honest to do that, however, and he never lived it down. From that day on, he was known as Excuse-Me Franklin, and the name stuck with him until the end of high school.

The stories seemed to fall under several different rubrics, and after I had been at the project for approximately a month, I abandoned my one-box system in favor of a multi-box arrangement that allowed me to preserve my finished works in a more coherent fashion. A box for verbal flubs, another for physical mishaps, another for failed ideas, another for social gaffes, and so on. Little by little, I grew particularly interested in recording the slapstick moments of everyday life. Not just the countless stubbed toes and knocks on the head I've been subjected to over the years, not just the frequency with which my glasses have slipped out of my shirt pocket when I've bent down to tie my shoes (followed by the further indignity of stumbling forward and crushing the glasses underfoot), but the one-in-a-million howlers that have befallen me at various times since my earliest boyhood. Opening my mouth to yawn at a Labor Day picnic in 1952 and allowing a bee to fly in, which, in my sudden panic and disgust, I accidentally swallowed instead of spitting out; or, even more unlikely, preparing to enter a plane on a business trip just seven years ago with my boarding-pass stub wedged lightly between my thumb and middle finger, being jostled from behind, losing hold of the stub, and seeing it flutter out of my hand toward the slit between the ramp and the threshold of the plane – the narrowest of narrow gaps, no more than a sixteenth of an inch, if that much – and then, to my utter astonishment, watching it slide clear through that impossible space and land on the tarmac twenty feet below.

Those are just some examples. I wrote dozens of such stories in the first two months, but even though I did my best to keep the tone frivolous and light, I discovered that it wasn't always possible. Everyone is subject to black moods, and I confess that there were times when I succumbed to bouts of loneliness and dejection. I had spent the bulk of my working life in the business of death, and I had probably heard too many grim stories to stop myself from thinking about them when my spirits were low. All the people I had visited over the years, all the policies I had sold, all the dread and desperation I'd been made privy to while talking to my clients. Eventually, I added another box to my assemblage. I labeled it 'Cruel Destinies,' and the first story I put in there was about a man named Jonas Weinberg. I had sold him a million-dollar universal life policy in 1976, an extremely large sum for the time. I remember that he had just celebrated his sixtieth birthday, was a doctor of internal medicine affiliated with Columbia-Presbyterian Hospital, and spoke English with a faint German accent. Selling life insurance is not a passionless affair, and a good agent has to be able to hold his own in what can often turn into difficult, tortuous discussions with his clients. The prospect of death inevitably turns one's thoughts to serious matters, and even if a part of the job is only about money, it also concerns the gravest metaphysical questions. What is the point of life? How much longer will I live? How can I protect the people I love after I'm gone? Because of his profession, Dr. Weinberg had a keen sense of the frailty of human existence, of how little it takes to remove our names from the book of the living. We met in his apartment on Central Park West, and once I had talked him through the pros and cons of the various policies available to him, he began to reminisce about his past. He had been born in Berlin in 1916, he told me, and after his father had been killed in the trenches of World War One, he had been raised by his actress mother, the only child of a fiercely independent and sometimes obstreperous woman who had never shown the slightest inclination to remarry. If I am not reading too much into his comments, I believe Dr. Weinberg was hinting at the fact that his mother preferred women to men, and in the chaotic years of the Weimar Republic, she must have flaunted that preference quite openly. In contrast to the headstrong Frau Weinberg, the young Jonas was a quiet, bookish boy who excelled at his studies and dreamed of becoming a scientist or a doctor. He was seventeen when Hitler took control of the government, and within months his mother was making preparations to get him out of Germany. Relatives of his father's lived in New York, and they agreed to take him in. He left in the spring of 1934, but his mother, who had already proved her alertness to the impending dangers for non-Aryans of the Third Reich, stubbornly rejected the opportunity to leave herself. Her family had been Germans for hundreds of years, she told her son, and she'd be damned if she allowed some two-bit tyrant to chase her into exile. Come hell or high water, she was determined to stick it out.

By some miracle, she did. Dr. Weinberg offered few details (it's possible he never learned the full story himself), but his mother was apparently helped by a group of Gentile friends at various critical junctures, and by 1938 or 1939 she had managed to obtain a set of false identity papers. She radically altered her appearance – not hard for an actress who specialized in eccentric character roles – and under her new Christian name she wrangled herself a job as a bookkeeper for a dry goods store in a small town outside Hamburg, disguised as a frumpy, bespectacled blonde. When the war ended in the spring of 1945, she hadn't seen her son in eleven years. Jonas Weinberg was in his late twenties by then, a full-fledged doctor completing his residency at Bellevue Hospital, and the moment he found out that his mother had survived the war, he began making arrangements for her to come visit him in America.

Everything was worked out to the smallest detail. The plane would be landing at such and such a time, would be parking at such and such a gate, and Jonas Weinberg would be there to meet his mother. Just as he was about to leave for the airport, however, he was summoned by the hospital to perform an emergency operation. What choice did he have? He was a doctor, and anxious as he was to see his mother again after so many years, his first duty was to his patients. A new plan was hastily put in motion. He telephoned the airline company and asked them to send a representative to speak to his mother when she arrived in New York, explaining that he had been called away at the last minute and that she should find a taxi to take her into Manhattan. A key would be left for her with the doorman at his building, and she should go upstairs and wait for him in the apartment. Frau Weinberg did as she was told and promptly found a cab. The driver sped off, and ten minutes into their journey toward the city, he lost control of the wheel and crashed head-on into another car. Both he and his passenger were severely injured.

By then, Dr. Weinberg was already at the hospital, about to perform his operation. The surgery lasted a little over an hour, and when he had finished his work, the young doctor washed his hands, changed back into his clothes, and hurried out of the locker room, eager to return home for his belated reunion with his mother. Just as he stepped into the hall, he saw a new patient being wheeled into the operating room.

It was Jonas Weinberg's mother. According to what the doctor told me, she died without regaining consciousness.

An Unexpected Encounter

I have rattled on for a dozen pages, but until now my sole object has been to introduce myself to the reader and set the scene for the story I am about to tell. I am not the central character of that story. The distinction of bearing the title of Hero of this book belongs to my nephew, Tom Wood, the only son of my late sister, June. Little June-Bug, as we called her, was born when I was three, and it was her arrival that precipitated our parents' departure from a crowded Brooklyn apartment to a house in Garden City, Long Island. We were always fast friends, she and I, and when she married twenty-four years later (six months after our father's death), I was the one who walked her down the aisle and gave her away to her husband, a *New York Times* business reporter named Christopher Wood. They produced two children together (my nephew, Tom, and my niece, Aurora), but the marriage fell apart after fifteen years. A couple of years later, June remarried, and again I accompanied her to the altar. Her second husband was a wealthy stockbroker from New Jersey, Philip Zorn, whose baggage included two ex-wives and a nearly grown-up daughter, Pamela. Then, at the disgustingly early age of forty-nine, June suffered a massive cerebral hemorrhage while working in her garden one scorching afternoon in the middle of August and died before the sun rose again the next day. For her big brother, it was hands down the worst blow he had ever received, and not even his own cancer and near death several years later came close to duplicating the misery he felt then.

I lost contact with the family after the funeral, and until I ran into him in Harry Brightman's bookstore on May 23, 2000, I hadn't seen Tom in almost seven years. He had always been my favorite, and even as a small tyke he had impressed me as someone who stood out from the ordinary, a person destined to achieve great things in life. Not counting the day of June's burial, our last conversation had taken place at his mother's house in South Orange, New Jersey. Tom had just graduated with high honors from Cornell and was about to go off to the University of Michigan on a four-year fellowship to study American literature. Everything I had predicted for him was coming true, and I remember that family dinner as a warm occasion, with all of us lifting our glasses and toasting Tom's success. Back when I was his age, I had hoped to follow a path similar to the one my nephew had chosen. Like him, I had majored in English at college, with secret ambitions to go on studying literature or perhaps take a stab at journalism, but I hadn't had the courage to pursue either one. Life got in the way – two years in the army, work, marriage, family responsibilities, the need to earn more and more money, all the muck that bogs us down when we don't have the balls to stand up for ourselves – but I had never lost my interest in books. Reading was my escape and my comfort, my consolation, my stimulant of choice: reading for the pure pleasure of it, for the beautiful stillness that surrounds you when you hear an author's words reverberating in your head. Tom had always shared this love with me, and starting when he was five or six, I had made a point of sending him books several times a year – not just for his birthday or Christmas, but whenever I stumbled across something I thought he would like. I had introduced him to Poe when he was eleven, and because Poe was one of the writers he had dealt with in his senior thesis, it was only natural that he should want to tell me about his paper – and only natural that I should want to listen. The meal was over by then, and all the others had gone outside to sit in the backyard, but Tom and I remained in the dining room, drinking the last of the wine.

'To your health, Uncle Nat,' Tom said, raising his glass.

'To yours, Tom,' I answered. 'And to "Imaginary Edens: The Life of the Mind in Pre-Civil War America".'

'A pretentious title, I'm sorry to say. But I couldn't think of anything better.'

'Pretentious is good. It makes the professors sit up and take notice. You got an A plus, didn't you?'

Modest as always, Tom made a sweeping gesture with his hand, as if to discount the importance of the grade. I continued, 'Partly on Poe, you say. And partly on what else?'

'Thoreau.'

'Poe and Thoreau.'

'Edgar Allan Poe and Henry David Thoreau. An unfortunate rhyme, don't you think? All those o's filling up the mouth. I keep thinking of someone shocked into a state of eternal surprise. Oh! Oh no! Oh Poe! Oh Thoreau!'

'A minor inconvenience, Tom. But woe to the man who reads Poe and forgets Thoreau. Not so?'

Tom smiled broadly, then raised his glass again. 'To your health, Uncle Nat.'

'And to yours, Dr. Thumb,' I said. We each took another sip of the Bordeaux. As I lowered my glass to the table, I asked him to outline his argument for me.

'It's about nonexistent worlds,' my nephew said. 'A study of the inner refuge, a map of the place a man goes to when life in the real world is no longer possible.'

'The mind.'

'Exactly. First Poe, and an analysis of three of his most neglected works. "The Philosophy of Furniture," "Landor's Cottage," and "The Domain of Arnheim." Taken alone, each one is merely curious, eccentric. Put them together, and what you have is a fully elaborated system of human longing.'

'I've never read those pieces. I don't think I've even heard of them.'

'What they give is a description of the ideal room, the ideal house, and the ideal landscape. After that, I jump to Thoreau and examine the room, the house, and the landscape as presented in *Walden*.'

'What we call a comparative study.'

'No one ever talks about Poe and Thoreau in the same breath. They stand at opposite ends of American thought. But that's the beauty of it. A drunk from the South – reactionary in his politics, aristocratic in his bearing, spectral in his imagination. And a teetotaler from the North – radical in his views, puritanical in his behavior, clear-sighted in his work. Poe was artifice and the gloom of midnight chambers. Thoreau was simplicity and the radiance of the outdoors. In spite of their differences, they were born just eight years apart, which made them almost exact contemporaries. And they both died young – at forty and forty-five. Together, they barely managed to live the life of a single old man, and neither one left behind any children. In all probability, Thoreau went to his grave a virgin. Poe married his teenage cousin, but whether that marriage was consummated before Virginia Clemm's death is still open to question. Call them parallels, call them coincidences, but these external facts are less important than the inner truth of each man's life. In their own wildly idiosyncratic ways, each took it upon himself to reinvent America. In his reviews and critical articles, Poe battled for a new kind of native literature, an American literature free of English and European influences. Thoreau's work represents an unending assault on the status quo, a battle to find a new way to live here. Both men believed in America, and both men believed that America had gone to hell, that it was being crushed to death by an ever-growing mountain of machines and money. How was a man to think in the midst of all that clamor? They both wanted out. Thoreau removed himself to the out-skirts of Concord, pretending to exile himself in the woods – for no other reason than to prove that it could be done. As long as a man had the courage to reject what society told him to do, he could live life on his own terms. To what end? To be free. But free to what end? To read books, to write books, to think. To be free to write a book like *Walden*. Poe, on the other hand, withdrew into a dream of perfection. Take a look at "The Philosophy of Furniture," and you'll discover that his imaginary room was designed for exactly the same purpose. As a place to read, write, and think. It's a vault of contemplation, a noiseless sanc-tuary where the soul can at last find a measure of peace. Impossibly utopian? Yes. But also a sensible alternative to the conditions of the time. For the fact was, America had indeed gone to hell. The country was split in two, and we all know what happened just a decade later. Four years of death and destruction. A human bloodbath generated by the very machines that were supposed to make us all happy and rich.'

The boy was so smart, so articulate, so well-read, that I felt honored to count myself as a member of his family. The Woods had been through their fair share of turmoil in recent years, but Tom seemed to have weathered the calamity of his parents' breakup – as well as the adoles-cent storms of his younger sister, who had rebelled against her mother's second marriage and run away from home at seventeen – with a sober, reflective, rather bemused attitude toward life, and I admired him for having kept his feet so firmly on the ground. He had little or no connec-tion with his father, who had promptly moved to California after the divorce and taken a job with the *Los Angeles Times*, and much like his sis-ter (though in far more muted form) felt no great fondness or respect for June's second husband. He and his mother were close, however, and they had lived through the drama of Aurora's disappearance as equal partners, suffering through the same despairs and hopes, the same grim expectations, the same never-ending anxieties. Rory had been one of the funniest, most fetching little girls I have ever known: a whirlwind of sass and bravura, a wise-acre, an inexhaustible engine of spontaneity and mischief. From the time she was two or three, Edith and I had always referred to her as the Laughing Girl, and she had grown up in the Wood household as the family entertainer, an ever more artful and rambunctious clown. Tom was just two years older than she was, but he had always looked out for her, and once their father left the picture, his mere presence had served as a stabilizing force in her life. But then he went off to college, and Rory went out of control – first escaping to New York, and then, after a brief reconciliation with her mother, vanishing into parts unknown. At the time of that celebratory dinner for Tom's graduation, she had already given birth to an out-of-wedlock child (a girl named Lucy), had returned home just long enough to dump the baby in my sister's lap, and had vanished again. When June died four-teen months later, Tom informed me at the funeral that Aurora had recently come back to reclaim the child – and had left again after two days. She didn't show up for her mother's burial service. Maybe she would have come, Tom said, but no one had known how or where to contact her.

In spite of these family messes, and in spite of losing his mother when he was only twenty-three, I never doubted that Tom would flourish in the world. He had too much going for him to fail, was too solid a char-acter to be thrown off course by the unpredictable winds of sorrow and bad luck. At his mother's funeral, he had walked around in a dazed stu-por, overwhelmed by grief. I probably should have talked to him more, but I was too stunned and shaken myself to offer him much of anything. A few hugs, a few shared tears, but that was the extent of it. Then he returned to Ann Arbor, and we fell out of touch. I mostly blame myself, but Tom was old enough to have taken the initiative, and he could have sent me a word whenever he'd chosen to. Or, if not me, then his first cousin, Rachel, who was also in the Midwest at the time, doing her post-graduate work in Chicago. They had known each other since infancy and had always gotten along well, but he made no move in her direction either. Every now and then, I felt a small twinge of guilt as the years passed, but I was going through a rough patch of my own (marriage problems, health problems, money problems), and I was too distracted to think about him very much. Whenever I did, I imagined him forging ahead with his studies, systematically advancing his career as he scaled the academic ladder. By the spring of 2000, I was certain he had landed a job at some prestigious place like Berkeley or Columbia – a young intellectual star already at work on his second or third book.

Imagine my surprise, then, when I walked into Brightman's Attic that Tuesday morning in May and saw my nephew sitting behind the front counter, doling out change to a customer. Luckily, I saw Tom before he saw me. God knows what regrettable words would have escaped my lips if I hadn't had those ten or twelve seconds to absorb the shock. I'm not only referring to the improbable fact that he was there, working as an underling in a secondhand bookstore, but also to his radically altered physical appearance. Tom had always been on the chunky side. He had been cursed with one of those big-boned peasant bodies constructed to bear the bulk of ample poundage – a genetic gift from his absent, semi-alcoholic father – but even so, the last time I'd seen him, he had been in relatively good shape. Burly, yes, but also muscular and strong, with an athletic bounce to his step. Now, seven years later, he had put on a good thirty or thirty-five pounds, and he looked dumpy and fat. A second chin had sprouted just below his jawline, and even his hands had acquired the pudge and thickness one normally associates with middle-aged plumbers. It was a sad sight to behold. The spark had been extinguished from my nephew's eyes, and everything about him suggested defeat.

After the customer finished paying for her book, I sidled up to the spot she had just vacated, put my hands on the counter, and leaned forward. Tom happened to be looking down at that moment, searching for a coin that had fallen to the floor. I cleared my throat and said, 'Hey there, Tom. Long time no see.'

My nephew looked up. At first, he seemed entirely befuddled, and I was afraid he hadn't recognized me. But an instant later he began to smile, and as the smile continued to spread across his face, I was heartened to see that it was the same Tom-smile of old. A touch of melancholy had been added to it, perhaps, but not enough to have changed him as profoundly as I had feared.

'Uncle Nat!' he shouted. 'What the hell are you doing in Brooklyn?'

Before I could answer him, he rushed out from behind the counter and threw his arms around me. Much to my amazement, my eyes began to water up with tears.

Farewell to the Court

Later that same day, I took him out to lunch at the Cosmic Diner. The glorious Marina served us our turkey club sandwiches and iced coffees, and I flirted with her a little more aggressively than usual, perhaps because I wanted to impress Tom, or perhaps simply because I was in such buoyant spirits. I hadn't realized how much I'd missed my old Dr. Thumb, and now it turned out that we were neighbors – living, by pure happenstance, just two blocks from each other in the ancient kingdom of Brooklyn, New York.

He had been at Brightman's Attic for the past five months, he said, and the reason why I hadn't run into him earlier was because he always worked upstairs, writing the monthly catalogues for the rare-book-and-manuscript part of Harry's business, which was far more lucrative than the secondhand-book trade downstairs. Tom wasn't a clerk, and he never operated the cash register, but the regular clerk had gone off to a doctor's appointment that morning, and Harry had asked Tom to fill in for him until he returned to the store.

The job was nothing to brag about, Tom continued, but at least it was better than driving a taxi, which was what he'd been doing ever since he'd dropped out of graduate school and come back to New York.

'When was that?' I asked, doing my best to hide my disappointment.

'Two and a half years ago,' he said. 'I finished all my course work and passed my orals, but then I got stuck with the dissertation. I bit off more than I could chew, Uncle Nat.'

'Forget this *Uncle Nat* stuff, Tom. Just call me Nathan, the way everyone else does. Now that your mother's dead, I don't feel like an uncle anymore.'

'All right, Nathan. But you're still my uncle, whether you like it or not. Aunt Edith probably isn't my aunt anymore, I suppose, but even if she's been relegated to the category of ex-aunt, Rachel's still my cousin, and you're still my uncle.'

'Just call me Nathan, Tom.'

'I will, Uncle Nat, I promise. From now on, I'll always address you as Nathan. In return, I want you to call me Tom. No more Dr. Thumb, all right? It makes me feel uncomfortable.'

'But I've always called you that. Even when you were a little boy.'

'And I've always called you Uncle Nat, haven't I?'

'Fair enough. I lay down my sword.'

'We've entered a new era, Nathan. The post-family, post-student, post-past age of Glass and Wood.'

'Post-past?'

'The *now*. And also the *later*. But no more dwelling on the *then*.'

'Water under the bridge, Tom.'

The ex-Dr. Thumb closed his eyes, tilted back his head, and shot a forefinger into the air, as if trying to remember something he'd forgotten long ago. Then, in a somber, mock-theatrical voice, he recited the opening lines of Raleigh's 'Farewell to Court':

> Like truthless dreams, so are my joys expired,
> And past return are all my dandled days,
> My love misled, and fancy quite retired:
> Of all which past, the sorrow only stays.

Purgatory

No one grows up thinking his destiny is to become a taxi driver, but in Tom's case the job had served as a particularly grueling form of penance, a way of mourning the collapse of his most cherished ambitions. It wasn't that he had ever wanted a great deal from life, but the little he had wanted turned out to have been beyond his grasp: to finish his doctorate, to find a place in some university English department, and then spend the next forty or fifty years teaching and writing about books. That was all he had ever aspired to, with a wife thrown into the bargain, maybe, and a kid or two to go along with her. It had never felt like too much to ask for, but after three years of struggling to write his dissertation, Tom finally understood that he didn't have it in him to finish. Or, if he did have it in him, he couldn't persuade himself to believe in the value of doing it anymore. So he left Ann Arbor and returned to New York, a twenty-eight-year-old has-been without a clue as to where he was headed or what turn his life was about to take.

At first, the taxi was no more than a temporary solution, a stopgap measure to pay the rent while he looked for something else. He searched for several weeks, but all the teaching jobs in private schools were filled just then, and once he settled into the grind of his twelve-hour daily shifts, he found himself less and less motivated to hunt for other work. The temporary began to feel like something permanent, and although a part of Tom knew that he was letting himself go to hell, another part of him thought that perhaps this job would do him some good, that if he paid attention to what he was doing and why he was doing it, the cab would teach him lessons that couldn't be learned anywhere else.

It wasn't always clear to him what those lessons were, but as he prowled the avenues in his rattling yellow Dodge from five in the afternoon to five in the morning six days a week, there was no question that he learned them well. The disadvantages to the work were so obvious, so omnipresent, so crushing, that unless you found a way to ignore them, you were doomed to a life of bitterness and unending complaint. The long hours, the low pay, the physical dangers, the lack of exercise –

those were the bedrock givens, and you could no more think of changing them than you could think of changing the weather. How many times had he heard his mother speak those words to him when he was a boy? 'You can't change the weather, Tom,' June would say, meaning that some things simply were what they were, and we had no choice but to accept them. Tom understood the principle, but that had never stopped him from cursing the snowstorms and cold winds that blew against his small, shivering body. Now the snow was falling again. His life had been turned into one long battle against the elements, and if there was ever a time to start grumbling about the weather, this was it. But Tom didn't grumble. And Tom didn't feel sorry for himself. He had found a method to atone for his stupidity, and if he could survive the experience without completely losing heart, then perhaps there was some hope for him after all. By sticking with the cab, he wasn't trying to make the best of a bad situation. He was looking for a way to make things happen, and until he understood what those things were, he wouldn't have the right to release himself from his bondage.

He lived in a studio apartment on the corner of Eighth Avenue and Third Street, a long-term sublet that had been passed on to him by the friend of a friend who had left New York and taken a job in another city – Pittsburgh or Plattsburgh, Tom could never remember which. It was a dingy one-closet cell with a metal shower in the bathroom, a pair of windows that looked out on a brick wall, and a pint-sized kitchenette that featured a bar refrigerator and a two-burner gas stove. One bookcase, one chair, one table, and one mattress on the floor. It was the smallest apartment he had ever lived in, but with the rent fixed at four hundred and twenty-seven dollars a month, Tom felt lucky to have it. For the first year after he moved in, he didn't spend much time there in any case. He tended to be out and about, looking up old friends from high school and college who had landed in New York, meeting new people through the old people, spending his money in bars, dating women when the opportunities arose, and generally trying to put together a life for himself – or something that resembled a life. More often than not, these attempts at sociability ended in painful silence. His old friends, who remembered him as a brilliant student and wickedly funny conversationalist, were appalled by what had happened to him. Tom had slipped from the ranks of the anointed, and his downfall seemed to shake their confidence in themselves, to open the door onto a new pessimism about their own prospects in life. It didn't help matters that Tom had gained weight, that his former plumpness now verged on an embarrassing rotundity, but even more disturbing was the fact that he didn't seem to have any plans, that he never spoke about how he was going to undo the damage he'd done to himself and get back on his feet. Whenever he mentioned his new job, he described it in odd, almost religious terms, speculating on such questions as spiritual strength and the importance of finding one's path through patience and humility, and this confused them and made them fidget in their chairs. Tom's intelligence had not been dulled by the job, but no one wanted to hear what he had to say anymore, least of all the women he talked to, who expected young men to be full of brave ideas and clever schemes about how they were going to conquer the world. Tom put them off with his doubts and soul-searchings, his obscure disquisitions on the nature of reality, his hesitant manner. It was bad enough that he drove a taxi for a living, but a philosophical taxi driver who dressed in army-navy clothes and carried a paunch around his middle was a bit too much to ask. He was a pleasant guy, of course, and no one actively disliked him, but he wasn't a legitimate candidate – not for marriage, not even for a crazy fling.

He began keeping more and more to himself. Another year went by, and so thorough was Tom's isolation by then that he wound up spending his thirtieth birthday alone. The truth was that he had forgotten all about it, and because no one called to congratulate him or wish him well, it wasn't until two o'clock the next morning that he finally remembered. He was somewhere out in Queens then, having just dropped off a pair of drunken businessmen at a strip club called the Garden of Earthly Delights, and to celebrate the beginning of the fourth decade of his existence, he drove over to the Metropolitan Diner on Northern Boulevard, sat down at the counter, and ordered himself a chocolate milk shake, two hamburgers, and a plate of French fries.

If not for Harry Brightman, there's no telling how long he would have remained in this purgatory. Harry's store was located on Seventh Avenue, just a few blocks from where Tom lived, and Tom had fallen into the habit of stopping in at Brightman's Attic as part of his daily routine. He rarely bought anything, but he liked to spend the odd hour or half hour before his shift began browsing among the used books on the ground floor. Thousands of items were crammed onto the shelves down there – everything from out-of-print dictionaries to forgotten bestsellers to leather-bound sets of Shakespeare – and Tom had always felt at home in that kind of paper mausoleum, flipping through piles of discarded books and breathing in the old dusty smells. On one of his early visits, he asked Harry a question about a certain Kafka biography, and the two of them had struck up a conversation. That was the first of many little chats, and while Harry wasn't always around when Tom came in (he spent most of his time upstairs), they talked often enough in the months that followed for Harry to have learned the name of Tom's hometown, to have been told the subject of Tom's aborted dissertation (*Clarel* – Melville's gargantuan and unreadable epic poem), and to have digested the fact that Tom had no interest in making love to men. In spite of this last disappointment, it didn't take Harry long to understand that Tom would make an ideal assistant for his rare-book-and-manuscript operation on the second floor. If he offered him the job once, he offered it a dozen times, but even though Tom continued to turn him down, Harry never gave up hope that one day he would say yes. He understood that Tom was in hibernation, wrestling blindly against a dark angel of despair, and that things would eventually change for him. That much was certain, even if Tom himself didn't know it yet. But once he did know it, all that taxi nonsense would immediately turn into yesterday's dirty laundry.

Tom enjoyed talking to Harry because Harry was such a droll and forthright person, a man of such needling patter and extravagant contradictions that you never knew what was going to come out of his mouth next. To look at him, you would have thought he was just another aging New York queen. All the surface rigmarole was calibrated to achieve that single effect – the dyed hair and eyebrows, the silk ascots and yachting club blazers, the sissified turns of speech – but once you got to know him a little, Harry turned out to be an astute and challenging fellow. There was something provocative about the way he kept coming at you, a darting, jabbing kind of intelligence that made you want to give good answers when he started reeling off those sly, overly personal questions of his. With Harry, it was never enough just to respond. There had to be some spark to what you said, some effervescent something that proved you were more than just another dullard plodding down the road of life. Since that was largely how Tom saw himself in those days, he had to work especially hard to keep up his end when talking to Harry. That work was what appealed to him most about their conversations. Tom liked having to think fast, and he found it invigorating to push his mind in unaccustomed directions for a change, to be forced to stay on his toes. Within three or four months of their first chat – at a time when they were barely even acquaintances, let alone friends or associates – Tom realized that of all the people he knew in New York, there wasn't a man or woman he talked to more openly than Harry Brightman.

And yet Tom continued to turn Harry down. For over six months he fended off the book dealer's proposals to come work for him, and in that time he invented so many different excuses, came up with so many different reasons why Harry should look for someone else, that his reluctance became a standing joke between them. In the beginning, Tom went out of his way to defend the virtues of his current profession, improvising elaborate theories about the ontological value of the cabbie's life. 'It gives you a direct path into the formlessness of being,' he would say, struggling not to smile as he mocked the jargon of his academic past, 'a unique entry point into the chaotic substructures of the universe. You drive around the city all night, and you never know where you're going next. A customer climbs into the backseat of your cab, tells you to take him to such and such a place, and that's where you go. Riverdale, Fort Greene, Murray Hill, Far Rockaway, the dark side of the moon. Every destination is arbitrary, every decision is governed by chance. You float, you weave, you get there as fast as you can, but you don't really have a say in the matter. You're a plaything of the gods, and you have no will of your own. The only reason you're there is to serve the whims of other people.'

'And what whims,' Harry would say, injecting a malicious glint into his eye, 'what naughty whims they must be. I'll bet you've caught a bundle of them in that rearview mirror of yours.'

'You name it, Harry, and I've seen it. Masturbation, fornication, intoxication in all its forms. Puke and semen, shit and piss, blood and tears. At one time or another, every human liquid has spilled onto the backseat of my cab.'

'And who wipes it up?'

'I do. It's part of the job.'

'Well, just remember, young man,' Harry would say, pressing the back of his hand against his forehead in a fake diva swoon, 'when you come to work for me, you'll discover that books don't bleed. And they certainly don't *defecate*.'

'There are good moments, too,' Tom would add, not wanting to let Harry have the last word. 'Indelible moments of grace, tiny exaltations, unexpected miracles. Gliding through Times Square at three-thirty in the morning, and all the traffic is gone, and suddenly you're alone in the center of the world, with neon raining down on you from every corner of the sky. Or pushing the speedometer up past seventy on the Belt Parkway just before dawn and smelling the ocean as it pours in on you through the open window. Or traveling across the Brooklyn Bridge at the very moment a full moon rises into the arch, and that's all you can see, the bright yellow roundness of the moon, so big that it frightens you, and you forget that you live down here on earth and imagine you're flying, that the cab has wings and you're actually flying through space. No book can duplicate those things. I'm talking about real transcendence, Harry. Leaving your body behind you and entering the fullness and thickness of the world.'

'You don't have to drive a cab to do that, my boy. Any old car will do.'

'No, there's a difference. With an ordinary car, you lose the element of drudgery, and that's fundamental to the whole experience. The exhaustion, the boredom, the mind-numbing sameness of it all. Then, out of nowhere, you suddenly feel a little burst of freedom, a moment or two of genuine, unqualified bliss. But you have to pay for it. Without the drudgery, no bliss.'

Tom had no idea why he resisted Harry in this way. He didn't believe a tenth of the things he said to him, but each time the subject of changing jobs came up again, he would dig in his heels and start spinning his ludicrous counter-arguments and self-justifications. Tom knew he would be better off working for Harry, but the thought of becoming a book dealer's assistant was hardly a thrilling prospect, hardly what he had in mind when he dreamed of overhauling his life. It was too small a step, somehow, too puny a thing to settle for after having lost so much. So the courtship continued, and the more Tom came to despise his job, the more stubbornly he defended his own inertia; and the more inert he became, the more he despised himself. The jolt of turning thirty under such bleak circumstances had an effect on him, but not enough to force him into action, and even though his meal at the counter of the Metropolitan Diner had ended with a resolution to find another job no later than one month from that night, when a month had passed he was still working for the 3-D Cab Company. Tom had always wondered what the D's stood for, and now he thought he knew. Darkness, Disintegration, and Death. He told Harry he would take his offer under consideration, and then he did nothing, just as he had always done. If not for the stuttering, juiced-up crackhead who jammed a gun into his throat at the corner of Fourth Street and Avenue B one frigid night in January, who knows how long the standoff would have continued? But Tom finally got the message, and when he went into Harry's shop the next morning and told him he had decided to accept the job, his days as a hack were suddenly over.

'I'm thirty years old,' he told his new boss, 'and forty pounds overweight. I haven't slept with a woman in over a year, and for the past twelve mornings I've dreamed about traffic jams in twelve different parts of the city. I could be wrong, but I think I'm ready for a change.'

A Wall Falls

So Tom went to work for Harry Brightman, little realizing that Harry Brightman did not exist. The name was no more than a name, and the life that belonged to it had never been lived. That didn't prevent Harry from telling stories about his past, but since that past was an invention, nearly everything Tom thought he knew about Harry was false. Forget the childhood in San Francisco with the socialite mother and the doctor father. Forget Exeter and Brown. Forget the disinheritance and the flight to Greenwich Village in the summer of 1954. Forget the vagabond years in Europe. Harry was from Buffalo, New York, and he had never been a painter in Rome, had never managed a theater in London, and had never been an auction-house consultant in Paris. The only money in the family had come from the weekly paycheck his father brought home from his job as a mail sorter at the central post office, and when Harry left Buffalo at eighteen, it wasn't to go to college but to enlist in the navy. After his discharge four years later, he did manage to earn some under-graduate credits – at De Paul University in Chicago – but he felt too old for studying by then and quit after three semesters. Chicago was where he stayed, however, and the story of how he had come to New York nine years earlier (after losing his money in a London stock fraud) was no more than another work of fiction. Nevertheless, it was true that he had been in New York for nine years, and it was also true that he hadn't known the first thing about the book business when he arrived there. But his name hadn't been Harry Brightman then; it had been Harry Dunkel. And he hadn't come to New York by way of London. He had flown in from O'Hare Airport, and for the past two and a half years his mailing address had been the federal penitentiary in Joliet, Illinois.

That would account for Harry's reluctance to tell the truth. It's no small job having to start your life again at fifty-seven, and when a man's only assets are the brain in his head and the tongue in his mouth, he has to think carefully before he decides to open that mouth and speak. Harry wasn't ashamed of what he had done (he had been caught, that was all, and since when was bad luck considered a crime?), but he certainly had no intention of talking about it. He had worked too hard and too long to fashion the little world he lived in now, and he wasn't about to let anyone know how much he had suffered. Therefore, Tom was kept in the dark about Harry's career in Chicago, which included an ex-wife, a thirty-one-year-old daughter, and an art gallery on Michigan Avenue that Harry had run for nineteen years. If Tom had known about the swindle and Harry's arrest, would he still have accepted the job Harry offered him? Possibly. But then again, perhaps not. Harry couldn't be certain, and for that reason he bit his tongue and never said a word.

Then, on a rain-soaked morning in early April, less than a month after I moved into the neighborhood, which was roughly three and a half months after Tom started working at Brightman's Attic, the great wall of secrecy came tumbling down.

It started with an unannounced visit from Harry's daughter. Tom happened to be downstairs when she walked into the store – dripping wet, with water streaming off her clothes and hair, a strange, disheveled creature with darting eyes and a foul, acrid smell hovering around her body. Tom recognized it as the smell of the permanently unwashed, the smell of the insane.

'I want to see my father,' she said, crossing her arms and clasping her elbows with trembling, nicotine-stained fingers.

Since Tom knew nothing about Harry's former life, he had no idea what she was talking about. 'You must be mistaken,' he said.

'No,' she shot back at him – suddenly agitated, bristling with anger. 'I'm Flora!'

'Well, Flora,' Tom said, 'I think you've come to the wrong place.'

'I can have you arrested, you know. What's your name?'

'Tom,' Tom said.

'Of course. Tom Wood. I know all about you. In the middle of life's journey, I lost my way in a dark wood. But you're too ignorant to know that. You're one of those little men who can't see the forest for the trees.'

'Listen,' Tom said, speaking to her in a soft, mollifying voice. 'You might know who I am, but there's nothing I can do to help you.'

'Don't get cheeky with me, mister. Just because you're made of wood, that doesn't mean you're good. *Comprendo*? I'm here to see my father, and I want to see him *right now*!'

'I don't think he's in,' Tom said, abruptly reversing his tactics.

'Like hell he isn't. The jailbird lives in the apartment upstairs. Do you think I'm stupid?'

Flora ran her fingers through her wet hair, spraying water onto a tower of newly acquired books that sat on a table near the front counter. Then, coughing deeply, she pulled out a pack of Marlboros from a pocket in her torn, loose-fitting dress. After she had lit up a cigarette, she tossed the burning match onto the floor. Tom hid his surprise and calmly snuffed it out with his foot. He didn't bother to tell her that smoking was forbidden in the shop.

'Who are we talking about?' he asked.

'Harry Dunkel. Who else?'

'Dunkel?'

'It means *dark*, in case you didn't know. My father is a dark man, and he lives in a dark wood. He pretends he's a bright man now, but that's only a trick. He's still dark. He'll always be dark – right up to the day he dies.'

Disturbing Revelations

It took Harry seventy-two hours to persuade Flora to go back on her medication – and a full week to talk her into returning to her mother in Chicago. The day after her departure, he invited Tom to join him for dinner at Mike & Tony's Steak House on Fifth Avenue, and for the first time since his release from prison nine years earlier, he spilled the beans about his past – the whole brutal, asinine story of his misspent life, alternately laughing and weeping as he unburdened himself to his incredulous assistant.

He had started out in Chicago as a salesclerk in the perfume department at Marshall Field's. After two years, he had advanced to the somewhat more exalted position of assistant window dresser, and no doubt that was where he would have stayed if not for his unlikely union with Bette (pronounced *bet*) Dombrowski, the youngest daughter of multimillionaire Karl Dombrowski, commonly referred to as the Diaper-Service King of the Midwest. The art gallery that Harry opened the following year was created entirely with Bette's money, but just because that money brought him hitherto unimaginable comforts and social status, it would be wrong to assume that he married her only because she was rich or that he walked into his new life under false pretenses. He was never anything less than frank with her on the subject of his sexual proclivities, but not even that could stop Bette from finding Harry to be the most desirable man she had ever known. She was already in her mid-thirties then, a homely, inexperienced woman who was rapidly heading toward permanent spinsterhood, and she knew that if she didn't assert herself with Harry, she was destined to live out the rest of her days in her father's house as an object of scorn, the clumsy maiden aunt of her brothers' and sisters' children, an exile stranded in the heart of her own family. Fortunately, she was less interested in sex than in companionship, and she dreamed of sharing her life with a man who would bestow on her some of the sparkle and self-confidence she lacked. If Harry wanted to indulge in an occasional dalliance or clandestine romp, she would have no objections. Just so long as they were married, she said, and just so long as he understood how much she loved him.

PAUL AUSTER

There had been women in Harry's life before. From the earliest years of his adolescence, his sexual history had been an indiscriminate catalogue of lusts and longings that fell on both sides of the fence. Harry was glad he had been built that way, glad that he was immune to the prejudice that would have forced him to spend his life spurning the charms of one half of humanity, but until Bette proposed to him in 1967, it had never occurred to him that he might enter into a fixed domestic arrangement, let alone find himself transformed into a husband. Harry had loved many times in the past, but he had rarely been loved in return, and Bette's ardor astonished him. Not only was she offering herself to him without reservation, but in the same breath she was granting him total liberty.

There were, of course, certain drawbacks to contend with as well. Bette's family, for one thing, and the bullying interference from her blowhard father, who would periodically threaten to cut his daughter out of his will unless she divorced 'that obnoxious pansy.' And then, even more unsettling perhaps, there was the matter of Bette herself. Not the person or the soul of Bette, but her body, the outer manifestations of Bette, with her small squinting eyes and the off-putting black hairs that adorned her fleshy forearms. Harry had an instinctive, highly developed taste for the beautiful, and he had never fallen for anyone who was less than attractive. If anything made him hesitate about marrying her, it was this question of her looks. But Bette was so kind, and ever so intent on pleasing him, that Harry took the plunge, knowing that his first job as a married man would be to mold his wife into a facsimile of a woman who could – in the proper light and under the proper circumstances – arouse a flicker of desire in him. Some of the improvements were simple enough to achieve. Her glasses were replaced by contact lenses; her wardrobe was revamped; her arms and legs were subjected to painful depilatory treatments at regular intervals. But there were other factors that Harry couldn't control, efforts that his new bride would have to make entirely on her own. And Bette did make them. With all the discipline and self-abnegation of a holy sister of God, she managed to diet away close to one-fifth of her body weight in the first year of their marriage, dropping from a dowdy 155 to a slender 126. Harry was moved by the struggles of his strong-willed Galatea, and as Bette blossomed under the care and scrutiny of her husband's watchful gaze, their growing admiration for each other developed into a solid, lasting friendship. Flora's birth in 1969 was not the result of some prear-

546

ranged one-night stand. Harry and Bette slept together often enough in the early years of their marriage to make a pregnancy almost inevitable, an a priori fait accompli. Who among Harry's friends would have predicted such a turnaround? He had married Bette because she had promised him his freedom, but once they settled in together, he discovered that he had little or no interest in exercising it.

The gallery opened its doors in February 1968. It was the fulfillment of a long-standing dream for the thirty-four-year-old Harry, and he did everything he could to make the operation a success. Chicago wasn't the center of the art world, but neither was it some Podunk backwater, and there was enough wealth floating around the city for a clever man to induce some of it to wind up in his pocket. After a period of deep reflection, he decided to call his gallery Dunkel Frères. Harry had no brothers, but he felt the name lent a certain Old World quality to the enterprise, hinting at a long family tradition in the business of buying and selling art. As he saw it, the marriage between the German proper noun and the French modifier would create an arresting, altogether agreeable confusion in the minds of his customers. Some would take the blending of languages to signify a background in Alsace. Others would think he was from a German-Jewish family that had emigrated to France. Still others wouldn't have the first idea what to make of him. No one would ever be certain of Harry's origins – and when a man can produce an air of mystery about himself, he always has the upper hand when dealing with the public.

He specialized in the work of young artists – paintings mostly, but also sculptures and installation pieces, along with a couple of Happenings, which were still in fashion in the late sixties. The gallery sponsored poetry readings and *soirées musicales*, and because Harry was interested in all forms of the beautiful, Dunkel Frères did not confine itself to a narrow aesthetic position. Pop and Op, minimalism and abstraction, pattern painting and photographs, video art and the New Expressionism – as the years went by, Harry and his phantom brother exhibited works that embodied every trend and inclination of the period. Most of the shows flopped. That was to be expected, but more dangerous to the future of the gallery were the defections of the half dozen or so real artists Harry discovered along the way. He would give a young kid his or her first break, promote the work with his customary flair and panache, build up a market for it, begin turning a comfortable profit, and then, after two or three shows, the artist would decamp to a gallery in New York. That was the problem with being based in Chicago, and Harry understood that for the genuinely talented ones, it was a move they had to make.

But Harry was a lucky man. In 1976, a thirty-two-year-old painter named Alec Smith walked into the gallery with a packet of slides. Harry was absent that day, but when the receptionist handed him the envelope the following afternoon, he removed a sleeve of transparencies and held it up against a window for a quick look – expecting nothing, prepared to be let down – and realized that he was looking at greatness. Smith's work had everything. Boldness, color, energy, and light. Figures swirled through fierce, slashing strokes of paint, vibrating with an incandescent roar of emotion, a human cry so deep, so true, so passionate, that it seemed to express both joy and despair at the same time. The canvases resembled nothing Harry had seen before, and so powerful was the effect they had on him that his hands began to shake. He sat down, examined all forty-seven pictures on a portable light table, and then immediately picked up the phone and called Smith to offer him a show.

Unlike the other young artists Harry had supported, Smith wanted nothing to do with New York. He had already spent six years there, and after being rejected by every gallery in town, he had returned to Chicago a bitter and angry man, seething with contempt for the art world and every blood-sucking, money-grubbing whore who was in it. Harry called him his 'surly genius,' but in spite of Smith's rude and sometimes combative nature, the roughneck was a thoroughbred at heart. He understood the meaning of loyalty, and once he was corralled into the Dunkel Frères stable, he had no intention of trying to break loose. Harry was the man who had rescued him from oblivion, and therefore Harry would remain his dealer for life.

Harry had found his first and only major artist, and for the next eight years Smith's work kept the gallery solvent. After the success of the 1976 show (all seventeen paintings and thirty-one drawings were gone by the end of the second week), Smith hightailed it out of town with his wife and young son and bought a house in Oaxaca, Mexico. From then on, the artist refused to budge, and he never set foot in America again – not even to attend the annual exhibitions of his work in Chicago, much less the museum retrospectives that were mounted in various cities around the country as his reputation began to grow. If Harry wanted to see him, he had to fly down to Mexico – which he did on average twice a year – but mostly they stayed in touch by letter and the occasional phone call. None of that posed a problem for the director of Dunkel Frères. Smith's output was prodigious, and every other month new crates of canvases and drawings would arrive at the gallery in Chicago, to be sold for ever more delicious and elevated sums. It was an ideal setup, and no doubt it would have continued for many decades if Smith hadn't filled his body with tequila three nights before his fortieth birthday and jumped off the roof of his house. His wife insisted it was a prank that had gone wrong; his mistress claimed it was suicide. One way or the other, Alec Smith was dead, and the S.S. *Harry Dunkel* was about to sink.

Enter a young artist named Gordon Dryer. Harry had given him his first show just six months before the Smith catastrophe – not because he was impressed by his work (severe, overly rational abstractions that produced not one sale nor one positive review), but because Dryer himself was an irresistible presence, a thirty-year-old who looked no older than eighteen, with a delicate, feminine face, slim, marble-white hands, and a mouth that Harry wanted to kiss from the first moment he saw it. After sixteen years of conjugal life with Bette, Tom's future employer finally succumbed. Not just to some small, fly-by-night crush, but to a delirious, full-blown intoxication, an improbable, burning love. And the ambitious Dryer, so desperate to show his work at Dunkel Frères, allowed himself to be seduced by the squat, fifty-year-old Harry. Or perhaps it was the other way around, and Dryer was the one who did the seducing. However it happened, the deed took place when the gallery owner went to the artist's studio to look at his most recent canvases. The beautiful boy-man was quick to divine Harry's intentions, and after twenty minutes of inconsequential chatter about the virtues of geometric minimalism, he casually dropped to his knees and unzipped the dealer's pants.

After the tepid response to Dryer's show, the unzippings multiplied, and before long Harry was stopping in at the painter's studio several times a week. Dryer fretted that Harry would eliminate him from the roster of his artists, and he had nothing but his body to offer as compensation. Harry was too smitten to understand that he was being used, but even if he had understood, it probably wouldn't have made a difference. Such is the madness of the human heart. He kept the affair a secret from Bette, and because the fifteen-year-old Flora was already beginning to manifest the first, incipient signs of her encroaching schizophrenia, he spent as much time at home with his family as his schedule allowed. The afternoons were for Gordon, but at night he slipped back into his role as dutiful husband and father. Then the announcement of Smith's death came crashing down on him, and Harry began to panic. There were still a number of works to be sold, but after six months or a year the stock would be exhausted. Then what? Dunkel Frères hardly broke even as it was, and Bette had already thrown too much money into the place for Harry to turn to her and ask for more help. With Smith suddenly gone, the gallery was bound to go under. If not today, then tomorrow, and if not tomorrow, then the day after that. For the truth was that Harry had failed to grasp the first thing about how to run a business. He had relied on the cantankerous Smith to support his extravagances and self-indulgent methods (the opulent parties and dinners for two hundred people, the private jets and chauffeur-driven cars, the moronic gambles on second- and third-rate talents, the monthly stipends to artists whose work didn't sell), but the goose had taken a swan dive in Mexico, and henceforth there would be no more golden eggs.

That was when Dryer came up with the plan to rescue Harry from his troubles. Sucking and fucking could go just so far, he realized, but if he could make himself truly indispensable, his career as an artist would be saved. In spite of the cold intellectualism of his work, Dryer had enormous natural gifts as a draftsman and colorist. He had suppressed them in the name of an idea, a notion of art that valued rigor and exactitude above all else. He hated Smith's gushing Romanticism, with its florid gestures and pseudo-heroic impulses, but that didn't mean he couldn't imitate the style if he chose to. Why not continue to create Smith's work after the artist was dead? The final paintings and drawings of the young master who had been cut down in his prime. A public exhibition would be too risky, of course (Smith's widow would hear about it and eventually call their bluff), but Harry could sell the pieces from the back room of the gallery to Smith's most fervent collectors, and as long as Valerie Smith knew nothing about it, the scam would yield a pure, one hundred percent profit.

Harry resisted at first. He knew that Gordon had hit on a brilliant idea, but the idea scared him – not because he was against it, but because he didn't think the boy had the stuff to pull off the job. And anything less than perfect, dead-on clones of Smith's work would probably land him in jail. Dryer shrugged, pretending it had just been a passing thought, and then started talking about something else. Five days

later, when Harry returned to the studio for another one of his afternoon visits, Dryer unveiled the first of his Alec Smith originals, and the
astonished art dealer was forced to admit that he had underestimated
the abilities of his young protégé. Dryer had reinvented himself as
Smith's double, purging every shred of his own personality in order to
slip into the mind and heart of a dead man. It was a remarkable turn of
theater, a piece of psychological witchcraft that struck both terror and
awe in poor Harry's brain. Not only had Dryer duplicated the look and
feel of one of Smith's canvases, copying the harsh palette-knife strokes,
the dense coloration, and the random, accidental drips, but he had taken
Smith ever so slightly farther than Smith had ever gone himself. It was
Smith's *next painting*, Harry realized, the one he would have started on
the morning of January twelfth if he hadn't jumped off the roof of his
house and died on the night of the eleventh.

Over the next six months, Dryer produced twenty-seven more canvases, along with several dozen ink drawings and charcoal sketches.
Then, very slowly and methodically, tamping down his enthusiasm in
an uncharacteristic display of tight-lipped control, Harry began fobbing
off the bogus works to various collectors around the world. The game
continued for more than a year, in which time twenty of the paintings
were dispensed with, netting close to two million dollars. Because
Harry was the front man – and therefore the one who stood to have his
reputation destroyed – the forgers agreed on a seventy-thirty split.
Fifteen years later, when Harry poured out his confession to Tom over
dinner in Brooklyn, he described those months as the most exhilarating
and gruesome period of his life. He was trapped in a state of constant
fear, he said, and yet notwithstanding the horror, notwithstanding the
conviction that he would ultimately be caught, he was happy, as happy
as he had ever been. Each time he managed to sell another faux-Smith to
a Japanese corporate executive or an Argentinian real estate developer,
his pounding, overtaxed heart would jump through forty-seven hoops
of joy.

In the spring of 1986, Valerie Smith sold her house in Oaxaca and
moved back to the States with her three children. In spite of her tempestuous, often violent marriage to the philandering Smith, she had always
been a staunch defender of his work, and she was familiar with every
picture he had painted from his early twenties until his death in 1984.
Following the initial show at Dunkel Frères, she and her husband had
become friendly with a plastic surgeon named Andrew Levitt, a well-

heeled collector who had bought two paintings from Harry in 1976 and had amassed a total of fourteen Smiths by the time Valerie went to dinner at his house in Highland Park ten years later. How could Harry have known that she would move back to Chicago? How could he have known that Levitt would invite her to his house – the same Levitt to whom he had sold a magnificent fake-Smith just three months earlier? Needless to say, the rich doctor proudly pointed to his new purchase on the living room wall, and needless to say, the perceptive widow instantly saw the work for what it was. She had never liked Harry, but she had always given him the benefit of the doubt for Alec's sake, knowing that the director of Dunkel Frères was the man most responsible for turning her husband's career around. But now her husband was dead, and Harry was up to no good, and the enraged Valerie Denton Smith was out to destroy him.

Harry denied everything. With seven of the sham works still locked in the storeroom of the gallery, however, it wasn't difficult for the police to mount a case against him. He continued to profess ignorance, but then Gordon skipped town, and in the aftermath of that betrayal, Harry lost all courage. In a moment of despair and self-pity, he finally broke down and told Bette the truth. Another mistake, another wrong move in a long line of stumbles and erroneous judgments. For the first time in all the years he had known her, she lashed out at him in anger – a tirade of invective that included such words as *sick, greedy, disgusting*, and *perverted*. Bette quickly apologized, but the damage had already been done, and even though she went out and hired one of the best lawyers in the city to defend him, Harry understood that his life was in ruins. The investigation dragged on for ten months, a slow gathering of evidence culled from such far-flung places as New York and Seattle, Amsterdam and Tokyo, London and Buenos Aires, and then the Cook County district attorney indicted Harry on thirty-nine counts of fraud. The press announced the news in bold front-page headlines. Harry was looking at a ten- to fifteen-year sentence if he lost his case in court. On the advice of his lawyer, he opted to plead guilty, and then, to reduce his sentence still further, implicated Gordon Dryer in the hoax, contending that the swindle had been his idea from the start and that he (Harry) had been coerced into acting as his accomplice when Dryer vowed to expose their affair. The reward for this cooperation was a maximum term of five years, with the guarantee of substantial time off for good behavior. Detectives followed Dryer's trail to New York and arrested him at a New Year's Eve party in a Christopher Street saloon, just minutes after 1988 began. He pleaded guilty as well, but with no names to give and no bargains to offer, Harry's ex-lover was sent away for seven years.

But worse was still to come. Just as Harry was preparing to go to prison, old man Dombrowski finally prevailed upon Bette to file for divorce. He employed the same intimidation tactics he had used in the past – threatening to cut her out of his will, threatening to stop her allowance – but this time he meant it. Bette was no longer in love with Harry, but neither had she been planning to desert him. In spite of the scandal, in spite of the disgrace he'd brought down on himself, it hadn't once crossed her mind to end their marriage. The problem was Flora. On the verge of nineteen now, she had already been in and out of two private mental hospitals, and her prospects for even a partial recovery were nil. Care at that level entailed staggering expenses, sums in excess of a hundred thousand dollars for each stay, and if Bette lost her father's monthly check, she would have no alternative but to send her daughter to a state institution the next time she broke down – an idea she simply refused to accept. Harry understood her dilemma, and because he had no solution to offer of his own, he reluctantly gave his blessing to the divorce, all the while swearing to kill her father the moment he was released from prison.

He had been turned into a pauper, a penniless convict without a single resource or plan, and once he had served his time in Joliet, he would be cast to the four winds like a fistful of confetti. Oddly enough, it was his much-despised father-in-law who stepped in and saved him – but at a price, at such a ruthless, exacting price that Harry never recovered from the shame and revulsion he felt when he accepted the old man's proposition. But he did it. He was too weak not to, too terrified about his future not to accept, but the moment he put his signature on the contract, he knew that he had signed away his soul and would be damned forever.

He had been in prison for almost two years at that point, and Dombrowski's terms couldn't have been simpler. Harry would move to another part of the country, and in exchange for a sufficient amount of money to set himself up in a new business, he would agree never to return to Chicago and never contact Bette or Flora again. Dombrowski considered Harry a moral degenerate, an example of some debased subspecies of organism that did not fully qualify as human, and he held him personally accountable for Flora's illness. She was crazy because Harry had impregnated Bette with his sickly, mutant sperm, and now that he had proven himself to be a fraud and a criminal as well, he would be condemned to a post-prison life of poverty and suffering unless he renounced all claims to his fatherhood. Harry renounced. He caved in to Dombrowski's ugly demands, and from that capitulation a new life became possible for him. He chose Brooklyn because it was New York and yet not New York, and the chances of running into any of his old art world colleagues were slim. There was a bookstore for sale on Seventh Avenue in Park Slope, and even though Harry knew nothing about the book business, the shop appealed to his taste for bric-a-brac and antiquarian clutter. Dombrowski bought the entire four-story building for him, and in June of 1991 Brightman's Attic was born.

Harry was crying by then, Tom said, and for the rest of the dinner he talked about Flora, remembering the last tormented day he'd spent with her before going off to prison. She was in the middle of another crack-up, spinning into the mania that would eventually land her in the hospital for the third time, but she was still lucid enough to recognize Harry as her father and talk to him in cogent sentences. Somewhere or other, she had come across a set of statistics that calculated how many people in the world were born and died each second on a given day. The numbers were stupendous, but Flora had always been good at math, and she quickly extrapolated the totals into groups of ten: ten births every forty-one seconds, ten deaths every fifty-eight seconds (or whatever the figures happened to be). This was the truth of the world, she told her father at breakfast that morning, and in order to get a grip on that truth, she had decided to spend the day sitting in the rocking chair in her room, shouting out the word *rejoice* every forty-one seconds and the word *grieve* every fifty-eight seconds to mark the passing of the ten departed souls and celebrate the arrival of the ten newly born.

Harry's heart had been broken many times, but now it was no more than a pile of ashes clogging up a hole in his chest. On the final day of his freedom, he spent twelve hours sitting on his daughter's bed watching her rock back and forth in the chair and alternately shout the words *rejoice* and *grieve* as she followed the arc of the second hand that moved steadily around the dial of the alarm clock on her bedside table. 'Rejoice!' she cried out. 'Rejoice for the ten who are born, who will be born, who have been born every forty-one seconds. Rejoice for them and do not stop. Rejoice unceasingly, for this much is certain, this much is true, and this much is beyond doubt: ten people live who did not live before. Rejoice!'

And then, gripping the arms of the chair tightly as she accelerated the pace of her rocking, she looked into her father's eyes and shouted, 'Grieve! Grieve for the ten who have vanished. Grieve for the ten whose lives are no more, who begin their journey into the vast unknown. Grieve endlessly for the dead. Grieve for the men and women who were good. Grieve for the men and women who were bad. Grieve for the old whose bodies failed them. Grieve for the young who died before their time. Grieve for a world that allows death to take us from the world. Grieve!'

On Rascals

Until I ran into Tom at Brightman's Attic, I don't think I had talked to Harry more than two or three times – and then only in passing, the shortest of short, perfunctory exchanges. After listening to Tom's tale of his boss's past, I found myself curious to learn more about this singular character, to meet the scoundrel face to face and observe him in action with my own eyes. Tom said he would be happy to introduce him to me, and so once our two-hour meal at the Cosmic Diner came to an end, I decided to accompany my nephew back to the store and fulfill my wish that very afternoon. I paid the check at the front register, then returned to our table and left a twenty-dollar tip for Marina. It was an absurdly excessive amount – nearly double the cost of the lunch itself – but I didn't care. My heart-throb beamed forth a resplendent smile of thanks, and the vision of her happiness put me in such excellent spirits that I instantly made up my mind to call Rachel that evening with the news that her long-lost cousin had been found. After her dreary, disputatious visit to my apartment in early April, I was still on my daughter's shit list, but now that I had reconnected with Tom, and now that the smiling Marina Gonzalez had just blown me a kiss as I made my way out of the restaurant, I wanted everything to be right with the world again. I had already called Rachel once to apologize for having spoken so harshly to her, but she had hung up on me after thirty seconds. Now I would call again, and this time I wouldn't stop groveling until the air had finally been cleared between us.

The bookstore was five and a half blocks from the restaurant, and as Tom and I strolled along Seventh Avenue in the softness of the May afternoon, we continued to talk about Harry, the erstwhile Dunkel of Dunkel Frères, who had fled the dark wood of his former self to emerge as a bright sun in the firmament of duplicity.

'I've always had a soft spot for rascals,' I said. 'They might not make the most reliable friends, but think how drab life would be without them.'

'I'm not sure Harry's a rascal anymore,' Tom answered. 'He's too full of regret.'·

'Once a rascal, always a rascal. People never change.'

'A matter of opinion. I say they can.'

'You never worked in the insurance business. The passion for deceit is universal, my boy, and once a man acquires a taste for it, he can never be cured. Easy money – there's no greater temptation than that. Think of all the wise guys with their staged car accidents and personal injury scams, the merchants who burn down their own stores and warehouses, the people who fake their own deaths. I watched this stuff for thirty years, and I never got tired of it. The great spectacle of human crooked-ness. It keeps coming at you from all sides, and whether you like it or not, it's the most interesting show in town.'

Tom emitted a brief noise, an outrush of air that fell midway between a snicker and a guffaw. 'I love hearing you spout your bullshit, Nathan. I hadn't realized it until now, but I've missed it. I've missed it a lot.'

'You think I'm joking,' I said, 'but I'm giving it to you straight. The pearls of my wisdom. A few pointers after a lifetime of toiling in the trenches of experience. Con men and tricksters run the world. Rascals rule. And do you know why?'

'Tell me, Master. I'm all ears.'

'Because they're hungrier than we are. Because they know what they want. Because they believe in life more than we do.'

'Speak for yourself, Socrates. If I wasn't so hungry all the time, I wouldn't be carrying around this giant gut.'

'You love life, Tom, but you don't believe in it. And neither do I.'

'You're beginning to lose me.'

'Think of Jacob and Esau. Remember them?'

'Ah. Okay. Now you're making sense.'

'It's an awful story, isn't it?'

'Yes, truly awful. It gave me no end of trouble when I was a kid. I was such a moral, upright little person back then. I never lied, never stole, never cheated, never said a cruel word to anyone. And there's Esau, a galumphing simpleton just like me. By all rights, Isaac's blessing should be his. But Jacob tricks him out of it – with his mother's help, no less.'

'Even worse, God seems to approve of the arrangement. The dishon-est, double-crossing Jacob goes on to become the leader of the Jews, and Esau is left out in the cold, a forgotten man, a worthless nobody.'

'My mother always taught me to be good. "God wants you to be good," she'd say to me, and since I was still young enough to believe in God, I believed what she said. Then I came across that story in the Bible,

557

and I didn't understand a thing. The bad guy wins, and God doesn't punish him. It didn't seem right. It still doesn't seem right.'

'Of course it does. Jacob had the spark of life in him, and Esau was a dumbbell. Good-hearted, yes, but a dumbbell. If you're going to choose one of them to lead your people, you'll want the fighter, the one with cunning and wit, the one with the energy to beat the odds and come out on top. You choose the strong and clever over the weak and kind.'

'That's pretty brutal stuff, Nathan. Take your argument one step further, and the next thing you'll be telling me is that Stalin should be revered as a great man.'

'Stalin was a thug, a psychotic murderer. I'm talking about the instinct for survival, Tom, the will to live. Give me a wily rascal over a pious sap any day of the week. He might not always play by the rules, but he's got spirit. And when you find a man with spirit, there's still some hope for the world.'

In the Flesh

When we were within a block of the store, it suddenly occurred to me that Flora's visit to Brooklyn meant that Harry was still in touch with his ex-wife and daughter – a clear violation of the contract he'd signed with Dombrowski. If so, why hadn't the old man swooped down on him and reclaimed the deed to the building on Seventh Avenue? According to my understanding of their bargain, that would have been grounds for Bette's father to have taken control of Brightman's Attic and for Harry to have been tossed out on his ear. Had I missed something, I asked Tom, or was there another wrinkle to the story he'd forgotten to tell me?

No, Tom hadn't left anything out. The contract was no longer valid for the simple reason that Dombrowski was dead.

'Did he die of natural causes,' I asked, 'or did Harry kill him?'

'Very funny,' Tom said.

'You're the one who brought it up, not me. Remember? You said Harry swore he was going to kill Dombrowski the day he got out of prison.'

'People say lots of things, but that doesn't mean they have any intention of doing them. Dombrowski kicked the bucket three years ago. He was ninety-one, and he died of a stroke.'

'According to Harry.'

Tom laughed at the remark, but at the same time I sensed that he was becoming a little annoyed by my jesting, sarcastic tone. 'Stop it, Nathan. Yes, according to Harry. Everything is according to Harry. You know that as well as I do.'

'Don't feel guilty, Tom. I'm not going to betray you.'

'Betray me? What are you talking about?'

'You're having second thoughts about letting me in on Harry's secrets. He told you his story in confidence, and now you've broken that confidence by telling the story to me. Don't worry, chum. I might act like an ass sometimes, but my lips are sealed. Got it? I don't know a god-damned thing about Harry Dunkel. The only person I'm going to shake hands with today is Harry Brightman.'

We found him in his office on the second floor, sitting behind a large

559

mahogany desk and talking to someone on the phone. He was wearing a purple velour jacket, I remember, with a multicolored silk handkerchief sprouting from the left front pocket. The hanky resembled some rare tropical flower, an efflorescence that immediately caught one's eye in the brownish, grayish environment of the book-lined room. Other sartorial particulars escape me now, but I wasn't interested in Harry's clothes so much as in examining his broad, jowly face, his exceedingly round, somewhat bulging blue eyes, and the curious configuration of his upper teeth – which fanned out in a way that suggested a jack-o'-lantern, with small gaps between them. He was a strange little pumpkin-head of a man, I decided, a popinjay with utterly hairless hands and fingers, and only his voice, a smooth and resonant baritone, undercut the overall foppishness of his manner.

As I listened to that voice talk into the phone, Harry waved a greeting to Tom, then lifted an index finger into the air, silently telling him that he'd be with us in a minute. The subject of the conversation eluded me, since Brightman did less talking than his invisible interlocutor, but I gathered that he was discussing the sale of a nineteenth-century first edition with a customer or fellow book dealer. The title of the work wasn't mentioned, however, and my thoughts soon began to wander. To keep myself occupied, I walked around the room inspecting the books on the shelves. By my rough count, there must have been seven or eight hundred volumes in that neatly organized space, with works ranging from the quite old (Dickens and Thackeray) to the relatively new (Faulkner and Gaddis). The older books were mostly leather-bound, whereas the contemporary ones all had transparent protective covers wrapped around their dust jackets. Compared to the jumble and chaos of the shop downstairs, the second floor was a paradise of tranquility and order, and the total value of the collection must have run well into the fat six figures. For a man who hadn't had a pot to piss in less than a decade earlier, the former Mr. Dunkel had done rather nicely for himself, rather nicely indeed.

The telephone conversation ended, and when Tom explained who I was, Harry Brightman stood up from his chair and shook my hand. Perfectly friendly, flashing his jack-o'-lantern teeth with a welcoming smile, the very model of decorum and good manners.

'Ah,' he said, 'the famous Uncle Nat. Tom's spoken of you often.'

'I'm just Nathan now,' I said. 'We dropped the uncle business a few hours ago.'

'*Just Nathan*,' Harry replied, furrowing his brows in mock consterna-tion, 'or *Nathan* pure and simple? I'm a little confused.'

'Nathan,' I said. 'Nathan Glass.'

Harry pressed a finger against his chin, striking the pose of a man lost in thought. 'How interesting. Tom Wood and Nathan Glass. Wood and Glass. If I changed my name to Steel, we could open an architecture firm and call ourselves Wood, Glass, and Steel. Ha ha. I like that. Wood, Glass, and Steel. *You want it, we'll build it.*'

'Or I could change my name to Dick,' I said, 'and people could call us Tom, Dick, and Harry.'

'One never uses the word *dick* in polite society,' Harry said, pretend-ing to be scandalized by my use of the term. 'One says *male organ*. In a pinch, the neutral term *penis* is acceptable. But *dick* won't do, Nathan. It's far too vulgar.'

I turned to Tom and said, 'It must be fun working for a man like this.'

'Never a dull moment,' Tom answered. 'He's the original barrel of monkeys.'

Harry grinned, then shot an affectionate glance at Tom. 'Yes, yes,' he said. 'The book business is so amusing, we get stomach-aches from laughing so hard. And you, Nathan, what line of work are you in? No, I take that back. Tom's already told me. You're a life insurance salesman.'

'Ex-life insurance salesman,' I said. 'I took early retirement.'

'Another ex,' Harry said, sighing wistfully. 'By the time a man gets to be our age, Nathan, he's little more than a series of exes. *N'est-ce pas?* In my own case, I could probably reel off a dozen or more. Ex-husband. Ex-art dealer. Ex-navy man. Ex-window dresser. Ex-perfume salesman. Ex-millionaire. Ex-Buffalonian. Ex-Chicagoan. Ex-convict. Yes, yes, you heard me right. Ex-convict. I've had my spots of trouble along the way, as most men have. I'm not afraid to admit it. Tom knows all about my past, and what Tom knows, I want you to know, too. Tom's like family to me, and since you're related to Tom, you're in my family as well. You, the ex-Uncle Nat, now known as Nathan, pure and simple. I've paid my debt to society, and my conscience is clear. X marks the spot, my friend. Now and forever, X marks the spot.'

I hadn't been prepared for Harry to come out with such a naked admission of guilt. Tom had warned me that his boss was a man filled with contradictions and surprises, but in the context of such a farcical and rambunctious conversation, I found it baffling that he suddenly should have seen fit to confide in a total stranger. Perhaps it had something to do with his earlier confession to Tom, I thought. He'd found the courage to let the cat out of the bag, so to speak, and now that he'd done it once, maybe it wasn't so difficult for him to do it a second time. I couldn't be certain, but for the moment it seemed to be the only hypothesis that made sense. I would have preferred to ponder the question a little longer, but circumstances didn't allow it. The conversation went charging ahead, full of the same silly remarks as before, the same ludicrous witticisms, the same blithering japery and pseudo-histrionic turns, and all in all I had to admit that I was favorably impressed by my pumpkin-headed rascal. He was somewhat exhausting to be with, perhaps, but he didn't disappoint. By the time I left the bookstore, I had already invited Tom and Harry to join me for dinner on Saturday night.

It was a little past four when I returned to my apartment. Rachel was still on my mind, but it was too early to call her (she didn't get home from work until six), and as I imagined myself picking up the phone and dialing her number, I realized that it was probably just as well. Relations had turned so bitter between us, I felt there was a good chance she would hang up on me again, and I dreaded the prospect of another rebuff from my daughter. Instead of calling, I decided to write her a letter. It was a safer approach, and if I kept my name and return address off the envelope, the odds were that she would open the letter and read it rather than tearing it up and throwing it in the garbage.

I thought it would be simple, but it took me six or seven shots before I felt I'd struck the right tone. Asking forgiveness from someone is a complicated affair, a delicate balancing act between stiff-necked pride and tearful remorse, and unless you can truly open up to the other person, every apology sounds hollow and false. As I worked on the successive drafts of the letter (growing more and more dejected in the process, blaming myself for everything that had gone wrong with my life, whipping my poor, rotten soul like some medieval penitent), I was reminded of a book Tom had sent me for my birthday eight or nine years back, in the golden age before June died and Tom was still the brilliant and promising Dr. Thumb. It was a biography of Ludwig Wittgenstein, a philosopher I had heard of but never read – not an unusual circumstance, since most of my reading was confined to fiction, with nary the smallest dabble in other fields. I found it to be an absorbing, well-written book, but one story stood out from all the others, and it had stayed with me ever since. According to the author, Ray Monk, after Wittgenstein wrote his *Tractatus* as a soldier during World War One, he felt that he had solved all the problems of philosophy and was finished with the subject for good. He took a job as a schoolmaster in a remote Austrian mountain village, but he proved unfit for the work. Severe, ill-tempered, even brutal, he scolded the children constantly and beat them when they failed to learn their lessons. Not just ritual spankings, but blows to the head and face, angry pummelings that wound up causing serious injuries to a number of children. Word got out about this outrageous conduct, and Wittgenstein was forced to resign his post. Years went by, at least twenty years if I'm not mistaken, and by then Wittgenstein was living in Cambridge, once again pursuing philosophy, by then a famous and respected man. For reasons I forget now, he went through a spiritual crisis and suffered a nervous breakdown. As he began to recover, he decided that the only way to restore his health was to march back into his past and humbly apologize to each person he had ever wronged or offended. He wanted to purge himself of the guilt that was festering inside him, to clear his conscience and make a fresh start. That road naturally led him back to the small mountain village in Austria. All his former pupils were adults now, men and women in their mid- and late twenties, and yet the memory of their violent schoolmaster had not dimmed with the years. One by one, Wittgenstein knocked on their doors and asked them to forgive him for his intolerable cruelty two decades earlier. With some of them, he literally fell to his knees and begged, imploring them to absolve him of the sins he had committed. One would think that a person confronted with such a sincere display of contrition would feel pity for the suffering pilgrim and relent, but of all of Wittgenstein's former pupils, not a single man or woman was willing to pardon him. The pain he had caused had gone too deep, and their hatred for him transcended all possibility of mercy.

In spite of everything, I felt reasonably certain that Rachel didn't hate me. She was pissed off at me, she resented me, she was frustrated with me, but I didn't think her animosity was strong enough to create a permanent rift between us. Still, I couldn't take any chances, and by the time I got around to composing the final draft of the letter, I was in a state of full and utter repentance. 'Forgive your stupid father for shooting his mouth off,' I began, 'and saying things he now mortally regrets. Of all the people in the world, you're the one who means the most to me. You're the heart of my heart, the blood of my blood, and it torments me to think that my idiotic remarks could have caused any bad blood between us. Without you, I am nothing. Without you, I am no one. My darling, beloved Rachel, please give your moronic old man a chance to redeem himself.'

I went on in that vein for several more paragraphs, ending the letter with the good news that her cousin Tom had magically popped up in Brooklyn and was looking forward to seeing her again and meeting Terrence (her English-born husband, who taught biology at Rutgers). Perhaps we could all have dinner together in the city one night. Sometime soon, I hoped. In the coming days or weeks – whenever she was free.

It had taken me over three hours to finish the job, and I felt exhausted, both physically and mentally drained. It wouldn't do to have the letter sitting around the apartment, however, so I immediately went out and mailed it, dropping it into one of the boxes in front of the post office on Seventh Avenue. It was dinnertime by then, but I didn't feel the least bit hungry. Instead, I walked on for several more blocks and went into Shea's, the local liquor store, and bought myself a fifth of Scotch and two bottles of red wine. I am not a heavy drinker, but there are moments in a man's life when alcohol is more nourishing than food. This happened to be one of them. Reconnecting with Tom had given a big boost to my morale, but now that I was alone again, it suddenly hit me what a pathetic, isolated person I had become – an aimless, disconnected lump of human flesh. I am not normally prone to bouts of self-pity, but for the next hour or so I pitied myself with all the abandon of a morose adolescent. Eventually, after two Scotches and half a bottle of wine, the gloom began to lift, and I sat down at my desk and added another chapter to *The Book of Human Folly*, a choice anecdote about the toilet bowl and the electric razor. It went back to the time when Rachel was in high school and still living at home, a chilly Thanksgiving Thursday, roughly three-thirty in the afternoon, with a dozen guests about to descend on the house at four. At no small expense, Edith and I had just remodeled the upstairs bathroom, and everything in it was spanking new: the tiles, the cupboards, the medicine cabinet, the sink, the bathtub and shower, the toilet, the whole works. I was in the bedroom, standing before the closet mirror and knotting my tie; Edith was down in the kitchen, basting the turkey and attending to last-minute details; and the sixteen- or seventeen-year-old Rachel, who had spent the morning and early afternoon writing up a physics lab report, was in the bathroom, scrambling to get ready before the guests arrived. She had just finished showering in the new shower, and now she was standing in front of the new toilet, her right foot perched on the rim of the bowl, shaving her leg with a battery-operated Schick razor. At some point, the machine slipped out of her hand and fell into the water. She reached in and tried to pull it out, but the razor had lodged itself tightly in the flush-hole of the toilet, and she couldn't get a purchase on it. That was when she opened the door and cried out, 'Daddy,' (she still called me *Daddy* then) 'I need some help.'

Daddy came. What tickled me most about our predicament was that the razor was still buzzing and vibrating in the water. It was a strangely insistent and irritating noise, a perverse aural accompaniment to what was already a bizarre, perhaps even unprecedented conundrum. Add in the noise, and it became both bizarre and hilarious. I laughed when I saw what had happened, and once Rachel understood that I wasn't laughing at her, she laughed along with me. If I had to choose one moment, one memory to hoard in my brain from all the moments I've spent with her over the past twenty-nine years, I believe that one would be it.

Rachel's hands were much smaller than mine. If she couldn't get the razor out, there was little hope that I could do any better, but I gave it a shot for form's sake. I removed my jacket, rolled up my sleeves, flung my tie over my left shoulder, and reached in. The buzzing instrument was locked in so firmly, I didn't have a chance.

A plumber's snake might have been useful, but we didn't have a plumber's snake, so I undid a wire hanger and stuck that in instead. Slender as the wire was, it was far too thick to help.

The doorbell rang then, I remember, and the first of Edith's many relatives arrived. Rachel was still in her terry-cloth robe, sitting on her knees as she watched my futile attempts to trick the razor out with the wire, but time was marching on, and I told her she should probably get dressed. 'I'm going to disconnect the toilet and turn it upside down,' I said. 'Maybe I can poke the little fellow out from the other end.' Rachel smiled, patted me on the shoulder as if she thought I'd gone mad, and stood up. As she was leaving the bathroom, I said, 'Tell your mother I'll be down in a few minutes. If she asks you what I'm doing, tell her it's none of her business. If she asks again, tell her I'm up here fighting for world peace.'

There was a toolbox in the linen closet next to the bedroom, and once I'd turned off the valve to the toilet, I took out a pair of pliers and detached the toilet from the floor. I don't know how much the thing weighed. I managed to lift it off the ground, but it was too heavy for me to feel confident that I could turn it over without dropping it, especially in such a cramped space. I had to get it out of the room, and because I was afraid of damaging the wood floor if I put it down in the hall, I decided to carry it downstairs and take it into the backyard.

With every step I took, the toilet seemed to become a few pounds heavier. By the time I reached the bottom of the stairs, I felt as if I were holding a small white elephant in my arms. Fortunately, one of Edith's brothers had just entered the house, and when he saw what I was doing, he came over and lent a hand.

'What's going on, Nathan?' he asked.

'I'm carrying a toilet,' I said. 'We're going to take it outside and put it in the backyard.'

All the guests had arrived by then, and everyone gawked at the weird spectacle of two men in ties and white shirts carrying a musical toilet through the rooms of a suburban house on Thanksgiving Day. The smell of turkey was everywhere. Edith was serving drinks. A Frank Sinatra song was playing in the background ('My Way,' if I remember correctly), and dear, overly self-conscious Rachel looked on with a mortified expression on her face, knowing that she was responsible for disrupting her mother's carefully planned party.

We got the elephant outside and turned it over on the brown autumn grass. I can't recall how many different tools I pulled out of the garage, but not one of them worked. Not the rake handle, not the screwdriver, not the awl and hammer – nothing. And still the razor buzzed on, singing its interminable one-note aria. A number of guests had joined us in the yard, but they were becoming hungry, cold, and bored, and one by one they all drifted back into the house. But not me, not the single-minded, see-it-to-the-end Nathan Glass. When I finally understood that all hope was lost, I took a sledgehammer to the toilet and smashed it to bits. The indomitable razor slid out onto the ground. I switched it off, put it in my pocket, and handed it to my blushing daughter when I returned to the house. For all I know, the damned thing is still working today.

After throwing the story into the box labeled 'Mishaps,' I polished off the other half of the bottle and then climbed into bed. Truth be told (how can I write this book if I don't tell the truth?), I put myself to sleep by masturbating. Doing my best to imagine what Marina Gonzalez looked like without any clothes on, I tried to trick myself into believing that she was just about to enter the room and slip under the covers with me, impatient to coil her smooth, warm flesh around mine.

The Sperm Bank Surprise

As it happened, masturbation turned out to be one of the topics Tom and I discussed over lunch the following afternoon (in a Japanese restaurant this time, since it was Marina's day off at the diner). It started when I asked him if he had managed to reestablish contact with his sister. As far as I knew, the last time anyone in the family had seen her was before June's death, when she had come home to New Jersey to reclaim the infant Lucy. That was in 1992, a good eight years ago now, and from the fact that Tom hadn't mentioned her to me the day before, I assumed my niece had somehow dropped off the face of the earth, never to be heard from again.

Not so. In late 1993, less than a year after my sister's burial, Tom and a pair of his graduate student buddies came up with a scheme to earn some quick cash. There was an artificial-insemination clinic on the outskirts of Ann Arbor, and the three of them decided to offer their services as donors to the sperm bank. It was undertaken as a lark, Tom said, and not one of them stopped to consider the consequences of what they were doing: filling up vials of ejaculated semen in order to impregnate women they would never see or hold in their arms, who in turn would give birth to children – *their children* – whose names, lives, and destinies would remain forever unknown to them.

They were each led into a small, private room, and in order to get them into the spirit of the project, the clinic had thoughtfully provided the donors with a stack of dirty magazines – picture after picture of young naked women in alluring erotic poses. Given the nature of the male beast, such images rarely fail to induce stiff and pulsing erections. Always serious about his work, Tom diligently sat down on the bed and began flipping through the magazines. After a minute or two, his pants and underwear were down around his ankles, his right hand was gripping his cock, and as his left hand continued to turn the pages of the magazines, it was only a matter of time before the job would be finished. Then, in a publication he later identified as *Midnight Blue*, he saw his sister. There was no doubt that it was Aurora – one glance, and Tom knew who it was. Nor had she even bothered to disguise her name. The six-page spread of more than a dozen photos was entitled 'Rory the Magnificent,' and it featured her in various stages of undress and provocation: decked out in a transparent nightie in one picture, a garter belt and black stockings in another, knee-high patent-leather boots in another, but by the fourth page it was pure Rory from top to bottom, fondling her small breasts, touching her genitals, sticking out her ass, opening her legs so wide as to leave nothing to the imagination, and in every picture she was grinning, at times even laughing, her eyes all lit up in an exuberant rush of happiness and abandon, with no trace of reluctance or anxiety, looking as if she were having the time of her life.

'It nearly killed me,' Tom said. 'In two seconds, my dick went soft as a marshmallow. I pulled up my pants, buckled my belt, and got out of there as fast as I could. It knocked me flat, Nathan. My little sister, vamping in a skin magazine. And to find out about it in such a terrible way – out of the blue, sitting in that goddamn clinic at the very moment I'm trying to jerk off. It made me sick, sick to my stomach. Not just because I hated seeing Rory like that, but because I hadn't heard from her in two years, and those pictures seemed to confirm my worst nightmares about what had happened to her. She was only twenty-two, and already she'd fallen into the lowest, most degrading kind of work: selling her body for money. It was all so sad, it made me want to cry for a month.'

When you've lived as long as I have, you tend to think you've heard everything, that there's nothing left that can shock you anymore. You grow a little complacent about your so-called knowledge of the world, and then, every once in a while, something comes along that jolts you out of your smug cocoon of superiority, that reminds you all over again that you don't understand the first thing about life. My poor niece. The genetic lottery had been too kind to her, and she had come up with all the winning numbers. Unlike Tom, who had inherited his shape from the Woods, Aurora was a Glass through and through, and as a family we are universally thin, angular, and tall. She had developed into a carbon copy of her mother – a long-legged, dark-haired beauty, as lithe and supple as June herself. Natasha from *War and Peace*, as opposed to her brother's big-footed, awkward Pierre. It goes without saying that everyone wants to be beautiful, but beauty in a woman can sometimes be a curse, especially if you're a young woman like Aurora: a high school dropout with no husband and a three-year-old kid to support, with a wild and rebellious streak in you, willing to thumb your nose at the world and take on any risk that comes your way. If you're hard up for money, and if your looks are your prime selling point, why would you hesitate to strip off your clothes and reveal yourself to the camera? As long as you can handle the situation, giving in to an offer like that can mean the difference between eating and not eating, between living well and barely living at all.

'Maybe she only did it that one time,' I said, doing what little I could to comfort Tom. 'You know, she's having trouble paying the bills, and a photographer comes along and proposes the job to her. One day's work for a nice bundle of cash.'

Tom shook his head, and from the sullen expression on his face, I understood that my remark was no more than a futile exercise in wishful thinking. Tom didn't know all the facts, but he was certain that the story had neither begun nor ended with that photo session for *Midnight Blue*. Aurora had been a topless dancer in Queens (at the Garden of Earthly Delights, of all places, the very club where Tom had dropped off the drunken businessmen on the night of his thirtieth birthday), had appeared in more than a dozen porn films, and had posed for nudie magazines six or seven times. Her career in the sex business had lasted a solid eighteen months, and because she was well paid for her work, she probably would have kept at it a good deal longer if not for something that occurred just nine or ten weeks after Tom spotted her picture in *Midnight Blue*.

'Nothing bad, I hope,' I said to him.

'Worse than bad,' Tom replied, suddenly on the verge of tears. 'She was gang-raped on the set of a film. By the director, the cameraman, and half the crew.'

'Jesus Christ.'

'They really worked her over, Nathan. She was bleeding so much by the end, she had to check herself into a hospital.'

'I'd like to kill the fucks who did that to her.'

'Me too. Or at least put them in jail, but she refused to press charges. All she wanted was to get away, to get the hell out of New York. That's when I heard from her. She wrote me a letter in care of the English department at the university, and when I realized what kind of spot she was in, I called her and said she should come out to Michigan with Lucy and live with me. She's a good person, Nathan. You know that. I know that. Everyone who's ever come near her knows that. There isn't a bad bone in her body. A bit out of control, maybe, a bit headstrong, but entirely innocent and trusting, the least cynical person in the world.

Good for her that she wasn't ashamed of working in porn, I suppose. She thought it was fun. Fun! Can you imagine? She didn't understand that the business is filled with creeps, the vilest cruds in the universe.'

So Aurora and the three-year-old Lucy moved to the Midwest and settled into the top two floors of a rented house with Tom. Aurora had been making decent money before her departure, but most of it had gone into rent, clothes, and a full-time nanny for Lucy, which meant that her savings were nearly exhausted. Tom had his fellowship, but he was living on a restricted graduate-student budget, with a part-time job at the university library to help make ends meet. They talked about calling their father in California to ask for a loan, but in the end they decided against it. The same with their stepfather in New Jersey, Philip Zorn. Rory's belligerent teenage antics had ravaged the household for years, and they were reluctant to turn to a man who had grown to despise his stepdaughter during the great battles of those earlier days. Tom never said a word to his sister about it, but he knew that Zorn secretly blamed Aurora for their mother's death. She had put June through a prolonged siege of turmoil and despair, and the only recompense for all that suffering had been the unexpected gift of being able to raise her infant granddaughter. Then that was snatched away from her as well, and Zorn felt it was the anguish of having to part with the child that had killed her. It was a sentimental reading of the story, perhaps, but who's to say he wasn't right? To be perfectly honest, on the day of the funeral the same thought had also occurred to me.

Instead of asking for handouts, Rory found herself a job waiting tables at the priciest French restaurant in town. She had no experience, but she charmed the owner with her smile, her long legs, and her pretty face, and because she was a clever girl, she caught on quickly and mastered the routine within days. It was a big comedown from her high-voltage life in New York, perhaps, but the last thing Aurora was looking for now was excitement. Chastened and bruised, still haunted by the vicious thing that had been done to her, she longed for nothing more than a dull and uneventful respite, a chance to recover her strength. Tom mentioned bad dreams, sudden outbursts of sobbing, long, moody silences. For all that, he also remembered the months she spent with him as a happy time, a time of great solidarity and mutual affection, and now that he had his sister back, there was the unrelenting pleasure of being able to assume the role of big brother again. He was her friend and protector, her guide and support, her rock.

As Aurora slowly regained the spunk and élan of her former self, she started talking about getting a high school equivalency diploma and applying to college. Tom encouraged her to go ahead with the plan, promising to help with the work if she found any of it too difficult. It's never too late, he kept telling her, it's never too late to start again, but in some sense it already was. Weeks passed, and as Rory continued to put off the decision, Tom understood that her heart wasn't in it. On her days off from the restaurant, she began turning up on open-mike nights at a local club, singing blues songs with three musicians she had met one evening while serving them dinner, and before long the quartet had decided to band together and form a group. They called them-selves Brave New World, and once Tom saw them perform, he knew that Rory's fleeting impulse to go on with her education had been stopped dead in its tracks. His sister could sing. She'd always had a good voice, but now that she was older, and now that her lungs had been subjected to the tars and fumes of fifty thousand cigarettes, a new and compelling quality had been added to it – something deep and throaty and sensual, an aching, hard-knocks candor that made you sit up in your chair and listen. Tom was both happy and frightened for her. Within a month, she had taken up with the bass guitarist, and he knew it was only a matter of time before she and Lucy would be leav-ing with him and the two others for some larger city – Chicago or New York, Los Angeles or San Francisco, anywhere in America that wasn't Ann Arbor, Michigan. Deluded or not, Aurora saw herself as a star, and she would never find joy or fulfillment unless the eyes of the world were looking at her. Tom understood that now, and he made no more than a weak, pro forma attempt to talk her out of going. Skin movies yesterday; blues songs today; God knows what tomorrow. He prayed that the bass guitarist, whose name also happened to be Tom, wasn't as stupid as he looked.

When the inevitable moment arrived, Brave New World and their lit-tle mascot climbed into a used Plymouth van with eighty thousand miles on it and headed for Berkeley, California. Seven months went by before Tom heard from her again: a telephone call in the middle of the night, and her voice on the other end singing 'Happy Birthday' to him, as sweet and innocent as ever.

Then nothing. Aurora vanished as thoroughly and mysteriously as she had before turning up in Michigan, and for the life of him Tom couldn't understand why. Wasn't he her friend? Wasn't he someone

571

she could count on no matter what kind of trouble she was in? He felt hurt, then angry, then miserable, and as the long months of silence stretched on for more than another year, his misery mutated into a deep and ever-growing despond, a conviction that something terrible had happened to her. In the fall of 1997, he finally gave up on his doctoral thesis. The night before he left Ann Arbor, he collected all his notes, all his diagrams and lists, all the countless rough drafts of his thirteen-part debacle, and one by one burned every page in an oil drum in the backyard. As soon as the great Melvillean bonfire was extinguished, one of his housemates drove him to the bus depot, and an hour later he was on the road to New York. Three weeks after his arrival, he began his stint as a yellow cab man, and then, just six weeks after that, Aurora unexpectedly called. Neither frantic nor upset, Tom said, neither in desperate straits nor asking for money – she just wanted to see him.

They met for lunch the next day, and for the first twenty or thirty minutes he couldn't stop looking at her. She was twenty-six now and still lovely, as lovely as any woman on earth, but her entire presentation of self had changed. She still looked like Aurora, but it was a different Aurora who sat in front of him now, and Tom couldn't decide if he preferred the new version or the old. In the past, she had worn her lavish, tumbling hair long; there had been makeup, large jewelry, rings on every finger, and a flair for decking herself out in inventive, unorthodox clothes: green leather boots and Chinese slippers, motorcycle jackets and silk skirts, lacy gloves and outrageous scarves, a demi-punk, demi-glamorous style that seemed to express her youth and brave fuck-you spirit. Now, in comparison, she looked positively prim. Her hair had been cut in a short bob; she had no makeup on except for the tiniest slash of rouge on her lips; and her clothes were conventional to a fault: blue pleated skirt, white cashmere sweater, and a pair of nondescript brown high heels. No earrings, just one ring on the fourth finger of her right hand, and nothing around her neck. Tom hesitated to ask, but he wondered if the big eagle tattoo on her left shoulder was still there – or if, in some effort to purify herself, to expunge all traces of her former life, she had gone through the painful procedure of having the ornate, multicolored bird removed.

There was no question that she was glad to see him, but at the same time he sensed how reluctant she was to talk about anything but the present. She offered no apologies for having been out of touch for so long, and when it came to her comings and goings since leaving Ann Arbor, she skimmed over the facts in just a few sentences. Brave New World broke up after less than a year; she sang with a couple of other groups in northern California; there were men, and then more men, and she began taking too many drugs. Eventually, she parked Lucy with two of her friends – a lesbian couple in their late forties who lived in Oakland – and checked herself into a rehab clinic, where she managed to get herself clean after six months. The entire saga was recounted in under two minutes, and because it had flown by him so quickly, Tom was too bewildered to press her for more details. Then she started talking about someone named David Minor, her group leader at the clinic, who had already turned himself around by the time she left detox and entered the program. He was single-handedly responsible for saving her, she said, and without him she never would have pulled through. More than that, he was the only man she had ever met who didn't think she was dumb, who didn't have sex on the brain twenty-four hours a day, who wasn't after her just for her body. Except Tom, of course, but sisters weren't allowed to marry their brothers, were they? It was against the law, and so she was going to marry David instead. They had already moved to Philadelphia and were staying with his mother while they both looked for work. Lucy was in a good school, and David was planning to adopt her after the wedding. That was why she had come to New York: to ask for Tom's blessing and find out if he would be willing to give her away at the ceremony. Yes, Tom said, of course he would, he would be honored. But what about their father, he asked, wasn't it his job to walk down the aisle with his daughter? Maybe so, Aurora said, but he didn't care about either one of them, did he? He was all wrapped up with his new wife and new kids, and besides, he was too cheap to spring for the airfare from L.A. to Philadelphia. No, she said, it had to be Tom. Tom and no one else.

He asked her to tell him something more about David Minor, but she spoke only in the vaguest generalities, which seemed to suggest that she didn't know as much about her future husband as she should have. David loved her, he respected her, he was kind to her, and so on, but there was nothing solid enough in those phrases for Tom to form a picture of who the man was. Then, her voice dropping almost to a whisper, Aurora added, 'He's very religious.'

'Religious? What sort of religion?' Tom asked, trying not to sound alarmed.

'Christianity. You know, Jesus and all that stuff.'

'What does that mean? Does he belong to a specific denomination, or are we talking about a born-again fundamentalist?'

'Born-again, I guess.'

'And what about you, Rory? Do you believe in all that?'

'I try to, but I don't think I'm very good at it. David says I need to be patient, that one day my eyes will open and I'll see the light.'

'But you're half Jewish. By Jewish law, you're all Jewish.'

'I know. Because of Mom.'

'And?'

'David says it doesn't matter. Jesus was Jewish, too, and he was the son of God.'

'David seems to say a lot of things. Is he the one who got you to cut your hair and change the way you dress?'

'He never forces me to do anything. I did it because I wanted to.'

'With David's encouragement.'

'Modesty befits a woman. David says it helps my self-esteem.'

'David says.'

'Please, Tommy, try to be nice. I know you don't approve, but I've finally found a chance for a little happiness, and I'm not going to let it slip through my fingers. If David wants me to dress this way, what difference does it make? I used to walk around looking like a slut. This is better for me. I feel safer, more pulled together. After all the screwed-up things I did, I'm lucky I'm still alive.'

Tom backed off and changed his tone, and they parted company that afternoon with fierce hugs and earnest kisses, swearing never to fall out of touch again. Tom was convinced that Aurora meant it this time, but as the date of the wedding approached, he still hadn't received an invitation from her – nor a letter, nor a telephone message, nor a word of any kind. When he called the number with the Philadelphia area code she had scribbled onto a paper napkin for him during lunch, a mechanical voice announced that the number was no longer in service. He then tried to track her down through local information, but of the three David Minors he spoke to, not one of them had heard of a woman named Aurora Wood. True to form, Tom blamed himself. His negative comments about Minor's religion had probably hurt Rory's feelings, and if she had gone ahead and told her fiancé about her atheist brother in New York, perhaps he had forbidden her to invite him to the wedding. From the little Tom had heard about Minor, he sounded like that

574

kind of man: one of those overbearing zealots who laid down the law to others, a sanctimonious prick.

'Any news from her since?' I asked.

'Nothing,' Tom said. 'It's been about three years since we had that lunch, and I have no idea where she is.'

'What about the telephone number she gave you? Do you think it was real?'

'Rory has her faults, but lying isn't one of them.'

'If they moved, then, you should have been able to contact her through the mother.'

'I tried, but nothing came of it.'

'Strange.'

'Not really. What if her name wasn't Minor? Husbands die, after all. People get divorced. Maybe she married again and was using her second husband's name.'

'I feel sorry for you, Tom.'

'Don't. It's not worth it. If Rory wanted to see me, she'd call. I'm pretty much resigned to it by now. I miss her, of course, but what the hell can I do about it?'

'And your father. When was the last time you saw him?'

'About two years ago. He had to come to New York for an article he was working on, and he invited me out to dinner.'

'And?'

'Well, you know what he's like. Not the easiest man in the world to talk to.'

'And what about the Zorns? Are you still in touch with them?'

'A little. Philip invites me out to New Jersey for Thanksgiving every year. I never liked him much when he was married to my mother, but I've gradually changed my mind about him. Her death really tore him apart, and when I understood how much he'd loved her, I couldn't bear a grudge anymore. So we have a mild, respectful sort of friendship now. The same with Pamela. She'd always struck me as a brainless snob, one of those people who cared too much about what college you went to and how much money you earned, but she seems to have improved over the years. She's thirty-five or thirty-six now and lives in Vermont with her lawyer husband and two kids. If you want to go to New Jersey with me this Thanksgiving, I'm sure they'd be happy to see you.'

'I'll have to think it over, Tom. For the time being, you and Rachel are about the only family I can stomach. One more ex-relative, and I'm liable to choke.'

'How is old cousin Rachel? I haven't even asked.'

'Ah, there's the rub, my boy. In herself, I believe she's fine. Good job, decent husband, comfortable apartment. But we had a little tiff a couple of months ago, and the fence is far from mended. In a word, there's a good chance she never wants to talk to me again.'

'I feel sorry for you, Nathan.'

'Don't. It's not worth it. I'd rather you let me feel sorry for you.'

The Queen of Brooklyn

When Tom and I met again for lunch the following afternoon, we both understood that we were in the process of creating a small ritual. We didn't articulate it in so many words, but excepting the times when other plans or obligations arose, we would make it our business to get together as often as possible to share our midday meal. No matter that I was twice his age and had once been known as Uncle Nat. As Oscar Wilde once put it, after twenty-five everyone is the same age, and the truth was that our present circumstances were almost identical. We both lived alone, neither one of us was involved with a woman, and neither one of us had many friends (in my case none at all). What better way to break the monotony of solitude than to chow down with your confrère, your *semblable*, your long-lost Tomassino, and chew the fat as you shoveled in your grub?

Marina was on duty that day, looking terrific in a pair of tight-fitting jeans and an orange blouse. It was a delectable combination, since it gave me something to study and admire when she came toward us (the front view of her ample, poignant breasts) and also when she walked away (the back view of her rounded, somewhat bulky rear end). After my recent fantasy of our late-night tryst, I felt a little more reticent with her than I normally did, but there was still the matter of the outrageous gratuity I'd left for her the last time I'd been in, and she was all smiles with us when she took our orders, knowing (I think) that she had conquered my heart forever. I can't recall a word we said to each other, but I must have wound up with a rather dopey smile on my face, for once she walked off toward the kitchen, Tom remarked on how odd I looked and asked if anything was wrong. I assured him I was in top form, and then, in the next breath, I heard myself confessing to my mad, unrequited crush. 'I'd move heaven and earth for that girl,' I said, 'but it won't do me a bit of good. She's married, and one hundred percent Catholic to boot. But at least she gives me a chance to dream.'

I braced myself for Tom to burst out laughing at me, but he did nothing of the kind. With an utterly solemn expression on his face, he reached his

577

arm across the table and patted me on the hand. 'I know just how you feel, Nathan,' he said. 'It's a terrible thing.'

Now it was Tom's turn to confess. Now I was hearing my nephew tell me that he, too, was in love with an unattainable woman. He called her the B.P.M. The initials stood for the Beautiful Perfect Mother, and not only had he never spoken a word to her, he didn't even know her name. She lived in a brownstone on a block midway between his apartment and Harry's bookstore, and every morning on his way to breakfast he would see her sitting on the front stoop of her building with her two young children, waiting for the yellow bus to arrive and take them to school. She was remarkably attractive, Tom said, with long black hair and luminous green eyes, but what stirred him most about her was the way she held and touched her children. He had never seen maternal love expressed so eloquently or simply, with more tenderness or outright joy. Most mornings, the B.P.M. would be sitting between the two children, an arm wrapped around each of their waists as they leaned into her for support, nuzzling and kissing them in turn, or else dandling them on her knees as she enclosed them in a double embrace, an enchanted circle of hugging, singing, and laughter. 'I walk by as slowly as I can,' Tom continued. 'A spectacle like that needs to be savored, and so I usually pretend I've dropped something on the ground, or pause to light a cigarette – anything to prolong the pleasure by just a few seconds. She's so beautiful, Nathan, and to see her with those kids, it almost makes me want to start believing in humanity again. I know it's ridiculous, but I probably think about her twenty times a day.'

I kept my feelings to myself, but I didn't like the sound of it. Tom was just thirty years old, in the prime of his young manhood, and yet when it came to women and the pursuit of love, he had all but given up on himself. His last steady girlfriend had been a fellow graduate student named Linda Something-or-other, but they had broken up six months before he left Ann Arbor, and since then his luck had been so bad that he'd gradually withdrawn from circulation. Two days earlier, he'd told me that he hadn't been out on a date in over a year, which meant that his silent worship of the B.P.M. now constituted the full extent of his love life. I found that pathetic. The boy needed to gather up his courage and start making an effort again. If nothing else, he needed to get laid – and stop frittering away his nights dreaming about some beatific earth mother. I was in the same boat, of course, but at least I knew my dream girl's name, and whenever I repaired to the Cosmic Diner and sat down at my regular table, I could actually talk to her. That was enough for an old has-been like myself. I had already danced my dance and had my fun, and what happened to me was of little importance. If the opportunity came along to add another notch to my belt, I wouldn't have said no, but it was hardly a matter of life and death. For Tom, everything hinged on having the guts to barrel himself back into the thick of the game. Otherwise, he would go on languishing in the darkness of his private, two-by-four hell, and as the years went by he would slowly turn bitter, slowly turn into someone he wasn't meant to be.

'I'd like to see this creature for myself,' I said. 'You make her sound like an apparition from another world.'

'Anytime, Nathan. Just come to my apartment one morning at a quarter to eight, and we can walk down her block together. You won't be disappointed, I guarantee it.'

And so it was that we met early the next morning and walked down Tom's favorite street in Brooklyn. I assumed he was exaggerating when he started talking about the 'hypnotic power' of the Beautiful Perfect Mother, but it turned out that I was wrong. The woman was indeed perfect, indeed a sublime incarnation of the angelic and the beautiful, and to watch her sitting on the front steps of her house with her arms wrapped around those two small kids was enough to bring a flutter to an old curmudgeon's heart. Tom and I were standing on the other side of the street, tactfully positioned behind the trunk of a tall locust tree, and what moved me most about my nephew's beloved was the absolute freedom of her gestures, an unselfconscious abandon that allowed her to live fully in the moment, in an ever-present, ever-expanding now. I guessed her age to be around thirty, but her bearing was as light and unpretentious as a young girl's, and I found it refreshing that such a lovely figure of a woman would show herself in public dressed in a pair of white overalls and a checkered flannel shirt. It was a sign of confidence, I felt, an indifference to the opinions of others that only the steadiest, most grounded souls possess. I wasn't about to abandon my secret infatuation with Marina Gonzalez, but by every objective standard of feminine beauty, I knew she couldn't hold a candle to the B.P.M.

'I'll bet she's an artist,' I said to Tom.

'What makes you say that?' he replied.

'The overalls. Painters always like to wear overalls. Too bad Harry's gallery went out of business. We could have organized a show for her.'

579

'It could be that she's pregnant again. I've seen her with her husband a couple of times. A tall blond guy with big shoulders and a wispy beard. She's just as affectionate with him as she is with the kids.'

'Maybe she's both.'

'Both?'

'Both pregnant and an artist. A pregnant artist in her dual-purpose overalls. On the other hand, take note of her slender form. I cast my eyes toward the region of her belly, but I detect no bulge.'

'That's why she's wearing the overalls. They're loose enough to hide it.'

As Tom and I continued to speculate on the meaning of the overalls, the school bus pulled up in front of the house across the street, and the B.P.M. and her two little ones were momentarily blocked from view. I realized that I didn't have a moment to spare. In another few seconds, the bus would drive off down the block, and the B.P.M. would turn around and go back into her house. I had no intention of spying on the woman again (there are some things you just don't do), and if this was my only chance, then I had to act immediately. For the sake of my bashful, lovesick nephew's mental health, I felt obliged to destroy the spell he was living under, to demystify the object of his longing and turn her into what she really was: a happily married Brooklyn housewife with two kids and perhaps another on the way. Not some saintly, unapproachable goddess, but a flesh-and-blood woman who ate and shat and fucked – just like everyone else.

Given the circumstances, there was only one possible choice. I had to cross the street and talk to her. Not just a few words, but a full-fledged conversation that would go on long enough for me to wave Tom over and force him to join in. At the very least, I wanted him to shake her hand, to touch her, so he would finally get it through his thick skull that she was a tangible being and not some disembodied spirit who lived in the clouds of his imagination. So off I went – rashly, impulsively, without the first idea of what I was going to say to her. The bus was just beginning to move again when I got to the other side of the street, and there she was, standing on the curb directly in front of me, blowing a last kiss to her two darlings, who had already found their seats on the bus and were now part of a mob of three dozen howling tots. Putting on my most pleasant and reassuring salesman's face, I advanced toward her and said, 'Excuse me, but I wonder if I could ask you a question.'

'A question?' she answered, a bit taken aback, I think, or else merely startled that a man was now standing in front of her where just a moment before there had been a bus.

'I've just moved into the neighborhood,' I continued, 'and I'm looking for a decent art supply store. When I saw you standing here in your overalls, I thought maybe you were an artist yourself. Ergo, it popped into my head to ask.'

The B.P.M. smiled. I couldn't tell whether it was because she didn't believe me or because she was amused by the lameness of my question, but as I studied her face and saw the crinkles forming around her eyes and mouth, I understood that she was a tad older than I had thought at first. Perhaps thirty-four or thirty-five – not that it made the least bit of difference or detracted from her youthful luster in any way. She had spoken only two words to me so far – *A question?* – but in those three short syllables I had heard the resonant tonality of a born Brooklynite, that unmistakable accent so ridiculed in other parts of the country, but which I find to be the most welcoming, most human of all American voices. On the strength of that voice, the gears started rotating in my head, and by the time she spoke to me again, I had already sketched out the story of her life. Born here, I said to myself, and raised here as well, perhaps in the very house she was standing in front of now. Working-class parents, since the Brooklyn gentrification boom didn't begin until the mid-seventies, meaning that at the time of her birth (mid- to late sixties) the neighborhood had still been a shabby, rundown area inhabited by struggling immigrants and blue-collar families (the Brooklyn of my own childhood), and the four-story brownstone that loomed behind her, which was now worth at least eight or nine hundred thousand dollars, had been bought for next to nothing. She attends the local schools, stays in the city for college, loves several men and breaks more than a few hearts, eventually marries, and when her parents die she inherits the house she lived in as a girl. If not precisely that, then something very close to it. The B.P.M. was too comfortable in her surroundings to have been a stranger, too settled in her own skin to have come from somewhere else. This was her place, and she reigned over the block as if it had been her realm from the first minute of her life.

'Do you always judge people by what they wear?' she asked.

'It wasn't a judgment,' I said, 'just a guess. Maybe a stupid guess, but if you're not a painter or a sculptor or an artist of some kind, then it's the first time I've ever guessed wrong about anyone. That's my specialty. I look at people and figure out who they are.'

She cracked another smile and laughed. Who is this silly person, she must have been wondering, and why is he talking to me like this? I decided the moment had come to introduce myself. 'I'm Nathan, by the way,' I said. 'Nathan Glass.'

'Hello, Nathan. I'm Nancy Mazzucchelli. And I'm not an artist.'

'Oh?'

'I make jewelry.'

'That's cheating. Of course you're an artist.'

'Most people would call it a craft.'

'I suppose it depends on how good your work is. Do you sell the things you make?'

'Of course. I have my own business.'

'Is your store in the neighborhood?'

'I don't have a store. But a bunch of places on Seventh Avenue carry my stuff. I also sell things out of the house.'

'Ah, I see. Have you lived here long?'

'All my life. Born and bred on this very spot.'

'A Park Sloper through and through.'

'Yeah. Right down to the marrow in my bones.'

There it was: a full confession. Sherlock Holmes had done it again, and as I marveled at my devastating powers of deduction, I wished there had been two of me so I could have patted myself on the back. I know it sounds arrogant, but how often does one achieve a mental triumph of that magnitude? After listening to her speak just two words, I had nailed the whole bloody thing. If Watson had been there, he would have been shaking his head and muttering under his breath.

Meanwhile, Tom was still standing on the other side of the street, and I figured it was long past time to bring him into the conversation. As I turned around and gestured for him to come over, I informed the B.P.M. that he was my nephew and that he ran the rare-book-and-manuscript division of Brightman's Attic.

'I know Harry,' Nancy said. 'I even worked for him one summer before I was married. A hell of a guy.'

'Yeah, a hell of a guy. They don't make them like that anymore.'

I knew that Tom was peeved at me for dragging him into a situation he wanted no part of, but he nevertheless came over and joined us – blushing, his head down, looking like a dog who was about to be whipped. I suddenly regretted what I was doing to him, but it was too late to put a stop to it, too late to offer any apologies, and so I plunged ahead and introduced him to the Queen of Brooklyn, all the while swearing on my sister's grave that I would never, never butt into the affairs of anyone else again.

'Tom,' I said, 'this is Nancy Mazzucchelli. She and I were having a discussion about local art supply stores, but then we got sidetracked onto the subject of jewelry. Believe it or not, she's lived in this house all her life.'

Without daring to lift his eyes from the ground, Tom extended his right arm and shook Nancy's hand. 'It's a pleasure to meet you,' he said.

'Nathan tells me you work for Harry Brightman,' she replied, blissfully unaware of the momentous thing that had just happened. Tom had finally touched her, had finally heard her speak, and regardless of whether that would be enough to break the spell of his enchantment, contact had been made, which meant that Tom would henceforth have to confront her on new ground. She was no longer the B.P.M. She was Nancy Mazzucchelli, and pretty as she was to look at, she was just an ordinary girl who made jewelry for a living.

'Yes,' Tom said, 'I've been there for about six months. I like it.'

'Nancy used to work in the store herself,' I said. 'Before she was married.'

Instead of answering my comment, Tom looked at his watch and announced that he had to be going. Still understanding nothing, the object of his adoration calmly waved good-bye. 'Nice to meet you, Tom,' she said. 'See you around, I hope.'

'I hope so, too,' he answered, and then, much to my surprise, he turned to me and shook my hand. 'We're still on for lunch, right?'

'Absolutely,' I said, relieved to know that he wasn't as upset as I had imagined. 'Same time, same place.'

And off he went, shambling down the block with his heavy-footed gait, gradually shrinking into the distance.

Once he was out of earshot, Nancy said, 'He's very shy, isn't he?'

'Yes, very shy. But a good and noble person. One of the best people on earth.'

The B.P.M. smiled. 'Do you still want the name of an art store?'

'Yes, I do. But I'd also be interested in looking at your jewelry. My daughter's birthday is coming up, and I still haven't bought her a present. Maybe you can help pick something out for me.'

'Maybe. Why don't we go inside and have a look?'

On the Stupidity of Men

I wound up buying a necklace that cost something in the neighborhood of a hundred and sixty dollars (thirty dollars off the original price because I paid in cash). It was a fine and delicate piece of work, with bits of topaz, garnet, and cut glass strung along a thin gold chain, and I felt certain it would look attractive sitting around Rachel's slender neck. I had lied about her birthday – which was still three months down the road – but I figured it wouldn't hurt matters to send an additional peace offering as a follow-up to the letter I'd written on Tuesday. When all else fails, bombard them with tokens of your love.

Nancy's workshop was in a back room on the bottom floor of the house, and the windows looked out on the garden, which wasn't a garden so much as a tiny playground, with a swing set in one corner, a plastic slide in another, and a host of toys and rubber balls in between. As I sifted through the various rings, necklaces, and earrings she had for sale, we chatted in a comfortable sort of way about any number of topics. She was an easy person to talk to – very open, very generous, altogether warm and friendly – but, alas, not so terribly bright as it turned out, since it wasn't long before I learned that she was a devoted believer in astrology, the power of crystals, and all kinds of other New Age hokum. Oh, well. Nobody's perfect, as the old movie line goes – not even the Beautiful Perfect Mother. Too bad for Tom, I thought. He was going to be sorely disappointed if he ever managed to get into a serious conversation with her. But then again, perhaps that was all for the best.

I had figured out some of the essential facts of her life, but I was still curious to know if my other Holmesian theories were valid or not. I therefore continued to question her – not making a big point of it, but jumping in whenever the opportunity presented itself, trying to go about it as subtly as I could. The results were somewhat mixed. I had been right about the matter of her schooling (P.S. 321, Midwood High, Brooklyn College for two years before dropping out to test her luck as an actress, which hadn't come to anything) but wrong about inheriting the house from her deceased parents. Her father was dead, but her

584

mother was very much above ground. She occupied the largest bed-room on the top floor, rode her bicycle through Prospect Park every Sunday, and at fifty-eight was still working as a secretary for a law firm in midtown Manhattan. So much for my infallible genius. So much for Glass's unerring eye.

Nancy had been married for seven years and referred to her husband as both Jim and Jimmy. When I asked if he was Mazzucchelli or if she'd kept her maiden name, she laughed and said that he was pure Irish. Well, I answered, at least Italy and Ireland both began with the letter *I*. That got another laugh out of her, and then, still laughing, she told me that her mother's first name and her husband's last name were identical.

'Oh,' I said. 'And what name is that?'

'Joyce.'

'Joyce?' I paused for a moment in a kind of addled wonder. 'Are you telling me you're married to a man named James Joyce?'

'Uh-huh. Just like the writer.'

'Incredible.'

'The funny thing is, Jim's parents don't know the first thing about lit-erature. They hadn't even heard of James Joyce. They named Jim after his mother's father, James Murphy.'

'Well, I hope your Jim isn't a writer. It wouldn't be much fun trying to publish work with that name branded on your head.'

'No, no, my Jim doesn't write. He's a Foley walker.'

'A what?'

'A Foley walker.'

'I have no idea what that is.'

'He makes sound effects for movies. It's part of postproduction. The mikes don't always pick up everything on the set. But say the director wants to have the sound of someone's feet crunching on a gravel drive-way, you know? Or turning the page of a book, or opening a box of crackers – that's what Jimmy does. It's a cool job. Very exact, very inter-esting. They really work hard at getting things right.'

When Tom and I met for lunch at one o'clock, I duly reported every scrap of information I'd managed to glean from my talk with Nancy. He was in particularly jovial spirits, and more than once he thanked me for having taken the initiative that morning and coerced him into his face-to-face encounter with the B.P.M.

'I didn't know how you'd react,' I said. 'By the time I got to the other side of the street, I was pretty sure you'd be angry with me.'

'You took me by surprise, that's all. You did a good thing, Nathan, a brave and excellent thing.'

'I hope so.'

'I'd never seen her up close before. She's absolutely stunning, isn't she?'

'Yes, very pretty. The prettiest girl in the neighborhood.'

'And kind. That most of all. You can feel the kindness radiating from every pore of her body. She's not one of those stuck-up, standoffish beauties. She likes people.'

'Down to earth, as the saying goes.'

'Yes, that's it. Down to earth. I don't feel intimidated anymore. The next time I see her, I'll be able to say hello, to talk to her. Little by little, we might even become friends.'

'I hate to disillusion you, but after talking to her this morning, I don't think you two have much in common. Yes, she's a lovely kid, but there ain't too much going on upstairs, Tom. Average intelligence at best. College dropout. No interest in books or politics. If you asked her who the secretary of state was, she wouldn't be able to tell you.'

'So what? I've probably read more books than any person in this restaurant, and what good has it done me? Intellectuals suck, Nathan. They're the most boring people in the world.'

'That could be. But the first thing she'll want to know about you is what your astrological sign is. And then you'll have to talk about horoscopes for the next twenty minutes.'

'I don't care.'

'Poor Tom. You're really stuck on her, aren't you?'

'I can't help it.'

'So what's the next step? Marriage, or just a plain old affair?'

'If I'm not mistaken, I believe she's married to someone else.'

'A minor detail. If you want him out of the picture, all you have to do is ask. I have good connections, son. But for you, I'd probably take care of the job myself. I can see the headlines now: EX-LIFE INSURANCE SALESMAN MURDERS JAMES JOYCE.'

'Ha ha.'

'I'll say one thing about your Nancy, though. She makes very nice jewelry.'

'Do you have the necklace with you?'

I reached into my inside breast pocket and pulled out the long, narrow box that contained my morning's purchase. Just as I was opening the lid, Marina arrived at the table with our sandwiches. Not wanting to exclude her from the unveiling, I slid the box in her direction so she could look as well. The necklace was mounted lengthwise on a bed of white cotton wool, and as she leaned over to examine it, she promptly announced her verdict. '*Ah, qué linda,*' she said, 'such a pretty thing.' Tom seconded her opinion with a silent nod, no doubt too moved to speak because he was thinking about his darling Nancy, whose celestial hands had wrought the small glimmering object that sat before him.

I lifted the necklace from the box and held it out toward Marina. 'Why don't you put it on?' I said. 'So we can see what it looks like.'

That was my original intention – simply to have her model it for us – but once she took the necklace in her hands and held it up against her light brown skin (that small area of exposed flesh just below the unfastened top button of her turquoise blouse), I suddenly changed my mind. I wanted to give it to her as a present. I could always buy another necklace for Rachel, but this one suited Marina so perfectly that it already seemed to belong to her. At the same time, if I gave the impression that I was coming on to her (which I was, of course, but with no hope), she might have felt that I was putting her in an awkward position and refused to accept it.

'No, no,' I said. 'Don't just hold it up. Put it on, so we can make sure it hangs right.' As she fumbled with the clasp in back, I hastily tried to think of something that would overcome her resistance. 'Someone told me it's your birthday today,' I said. 'Is that true, Marina, or was that guy just pulling my leg?'

'Not today,' she answered. 'Next week.'

'This week, next week, what difference does it make? It's coming soon, and that means you're already living inside the birthday aura. It's written all over your face.'

Marina finished putting on the necklace and smiled. 'Birthday aura? What's that?'

'I bought this necklace today for no particular reason. I wanted to give it to someone, but I didn't know who that person was. Now that I see how good it looks on you, I want you to have it. That's what the birthday aura is. It's a powerful force, and it makes people do all sorts of strange things. I didn't know it at the time, but I was buying the necklace for you.'

At first she seemed happy, and I thought there wasn't going to be a problem. From the way she looked at me with those vivid brown eyes of hers, there was no question that she wanted to keep it, that she was touched and flattered by the gesture, but then, once the initial surge of pleasure had passed, she began to think about it a little, and I saw doubt and confusion enter those same brown eyes. 'You're a terrific guy, Mr. Glass,' she said, 'and I really appreciate it. But I can't take presents from you. It ain't right. You're a customer.'

'Don't worry about that. If I want to give something to my favorite waitress, who's going to stop me? I'm an old man, and old men are free to do what they want.'

'You don't know Roberto,' she said. 'He's a very jealous guy. He won't like me taking things from other men.'

'I'm not a man,' I said. 'I'm just a friend who wants to make you happy.'

At that point, Tom finally added his two cents to the discussion. 'I'm sure he doesn't mean any harm,' he said. 'You know what Nathan's like, Marina. He's a nutty person – always doing crazy, impulsive things.'

'He's crazy, all right,' she said. 'And also very nice. It's just that I don't want any trouble. You know how it is. One thing leads to another, and then boom.'

'Boom?' Tom said.

'Yeah, boom,' she replied. 'And don't ask me to explain what that means.'

'All right,' I said, suddenly understanding that her marriage was far less tranquil than I had supposed. 'I think I have a solution. Marina keeps the necklace, but she doesn't take it home. It stays here in the restaurant at all times. She wears it at work, and then she stores it in the cash register overnight. Tom and I can come in every day and admire the necklace, and Roberto will never know a thing.'

It was such a preposterous, underhanded proposal, such a devious, rawboned bit of chicanery that Tom and Marina both cracked up laughing.

'Wow,' Marina said. 'You're one hell of a sneaky old man, Nathan.'

'Not as old as all that,' I said.

'And what happens if I forget I'm wearing the necklace?' she asked. 'What happens if I go home one night and still have it on?'

'You'd never do that,' I said. 'You're too smart.'

And so I forced the birthday present on the young and guileless Marina Luisa Sanchez Gonzalez, and for my efforts I received a kiss on the cheek, a prolonged and tender kiss that I will remember to the end of my days. Such are the perks allotted to stupid men. And I am nothing if not a stupid, stupid man. I got my kiss and my beaming smile of thanks, but I also got more than I'd bargained for. Its name was Trouble, and when I reach the point in my story when I was introduced to Mr. Trouble, I will give a full account of what happened. But it is only Friday afternoon now, and there are other, more pressing matters to attend to. The weekend is about to begin, and less than thirty hours after Tom and I left the Cosmic Diner, we were both sitting in another restaurant with Harry Brightman, eating dinner, drinking wine, and wrestling with the mysteries of the universe.

A Night of Eating and Drinking

Saturday evening. May 27, 2000. A French restaurant on Smith Street in Brooklyn. Three men are sitting at a round table in the rear left corner of the room: Harry Brightman (formerly known as Dunkel), Tom Wood, and Nathan Glass. They have just finished giving their orders to the waiter (three different appetizers, three different main courses, two bottles of wine – one red, one white) and have resumed drinking the aperitifs that were brought to the table not long after they entered the restaurant. Tom's glass is filled with bourbon (Wild Turkey), Harry is sipping a vodka martini, and as Nathan downs another mouthful of his neat, single-malt Scotch (twelve-year-old Macallan), he won- ders if he isn't in the mood for a second drink before the meal is served. So much for the setting. Once the conversation begins, further stage directions will be kept to a minimum. It is the author's opinion that only the words spoken by the above-mentioned characters are of any importance to the narrative. For that reason, there will be no descriptions of the clothes they are wearing, no com- ments on the food they eat, no pauses when one of them stands up to visit the men's room, no interruptions from the waiter, and not one word about the glass of red wine that Nathan spills on his pants.

TOM: I'm not talking about saving the world. At this point, I just want to save myself. And some of the people I care about. Like you, Nathan. And you, too, Harry.

HARRY: Why so glum, boy? You're about to eat the best dinner you've had in years, you're the youngest person sitting at this table, and as far as I know, you still haven't contracted a major disease. Look at Nathan over there. He's had lung cancer, and he never even smoked. And I've had two heart attacks. Do you see us grumbling? We're the happiest men in the world.

TOM: No you're not. You're just as miserable as I am.

NATHAN: Harry's right, Tom. It's not as bad as all that.

TOM: Yes it is. If anything, it's even worse.

HARRY: Please define 'it.' I don't even know what we're talking about anymore.

TOM: The world. The big black hole we call the world.

HARRY: Ah, the world. Well, of course. That goes without saying. The world stinks. Everyone knows that. But we do our best to avoid it, don't we?

TOM: No we don't. We're right in the thick of it, whether we like it or not. It's all around us, and every time I lift my head and take a good look at it, I'm filled with disgust. Sadness and disgust. You'd think World War Two would have settled things, at least for a couple of hundred years. But we're still hacking each other to pieces, aren't we? We still hate each other as much as we ever did.

NATHAN: So that's what we're talking about. Politics.

TOM: Among other things, yes. And economics. And greed. And the horrible place this country has turned into. The maniacs on the Christian Right. The twenty-year-old dot-com millionaires. The Golf Channel. The Fuck Channel. The Vomit Channel. Capitalism triumphant, with nothing to oppose it anymore. And all of us so smug, so pleased with ourselves, while half the world is starving to death and we don't lift a finger to help. I can't take it anymore, gentlemen. I want out.

HARRY: Out? And where are you going to go? Jupiter? Pluto? Some asteroid in the next galaxy? Poor Tom-All-Alone, like the Little Prince marooned on his rock in the middle of space.

TOM: You tell me where to go, Harry. I'm open to any and all suggestions.

NATHAN: A place to live life on your own terms. That's what we're talking about, isn't it? 'Imaginary Edens' revisited. But in order to do that, you have to be willing to reject society. That's what you told me. It was a long time ago, but I think you also used the word *courage*. Do you have the courage, Tom? Does any one of us have the courage to do that?

TOM: You still remember that old paper, huh?

NATHAN: It made a big impression on me.

591

TOM: I was just a wee undergraduate back then. I didn't know much, but I was probably smarter than I am now.

HARRY: We're referring to what?

NATHAN: The inner refuge, Harry. The place a man goes to when life in the real world is no longer possible.

HARRY: Oh. I used to have one of those. I thought everyone did.

TOM: Not necessarily. It takes a good imagination, and how many people have that?

HARRY *(closing his eyes; pressing his forefingers against his temples):* It's all coming back to me now. The Hotel Existence. I was just ten years old, but I can still remember the exact moment when the idea occurred to me, the exact moment when I found the name. It was a Sunday afternoon during the war. The radio was on, and I was sitting in the living room of our house in Buffalo with a copy of *Life* magazine, looking at pictures of the American troops in France. I had never been inside a hotel, but I had walked past enough of them on my trips downtown with my mother to know that they were special places, fortresses that protected you from the squalor and meanness of everyday life. I loved the men in the blue uniforms who stood in front of the Remington Arms. I loved the sheen of the brass fittings on the revolving doors at the Excelsior. I loved the immense chandelier that hung in the lobby of the Ritz. The sole purpose of a hotel was to make you happy and comfortable, and once you signed the register and went upstairs to your room, all you had to do was ask for something and it was yours. A hotel represented the promise of a better world, a place that was more than just a place, but an opportunity, a chance to live inside your dreams.

NATHAN: That explains the hotel part. Where did you find the word *existence*?

HARRY: I heard it on the radio that Sunday afternoon. I was only half listening to the program, but someone was talking about *human existence,* and I liked the way it sounded. *The laws of existence,* the voice said, and *the perils we must face in the course of our existence.* Existence was bigger than just life. It was everyone's life all together, and even if you lived in Buffalo, New York, and had never been more than ten miles from home, you were part of the puzzle, too. It didn't matter how small your life was. What happened to you was just as important as what happened to everyone else.

TOM: I still don't follow. You invent a place called the Hotel Existence, but where is it? What was it for?

HARRY: For? Nothing, really. It was a retreat, a world I could visit in my mind. That's what we're talking about, no? Escape.

NATHAN: And where did the ten-year-old Harry escape to?

HARRY: Ah. That's a complicated question. There were two Hotel Existences, you see. The first one, the one I made up that Sunday afternoon during the war, and then a second one, which didn't get going until I was in high school. Number one, I'm sorry to say, was pure corn and boyish sentimentality. But I was just a small fellow back then, and the war was everywhere, everyone talked about it all the time. I was too young to fight, but like most fat, dumb little boys, I dreamed of becoming a soldier. Ugh. Oh, ugh and double ugh. What empty dolts we mortals be. So I imagine this place called the Hotel Existence, and I immediately turn it into a refuge for lost children. I'm talking about European children, of course. Their fathers had been shot down in battle, their mothers were lying under the ruins of collapsed churches and buildings, and there they were, wandering through the rubble of bombed-out cities in the cold of winter, scavenging for food in forests, children alone, children in pairs, children in gangs of four and six and ten, rags tied around their feet instead of shoes, their gaunt faces splattered with mud. They lived in a world without grown-ups, and because I was such a fearless, altruistic soul, I anointed myself as their savior. That was my mission, my purpose in life, and every day for the rest of the war I would parachute into some demolished corner of Europe to rescue the lost and starving boys and girls. I would struggle down burning mountainsides, swim across exploding lakes, machine-gun my way into dank wine cellars, and each time I found another orphan, I would take the child by the hand and lead him to the Hotel Existence. It didn't matter what country I was in. Belgium or France, Poland or Italy, Holland or Denmark – the hotel was never far away, and I always managed to get the kid there before nightfall. Once I'd guided him through the formalities of registering at the front desk, I would turn around and leave. It wasn't my job to run the hotel – only to find the children and take them there. Anyway, heroes don't rest, do they? They aren't allowed to sleep in soft beds with down comforters and three pillows, and they don't have time to sit down in the hotel kitchen to eat a helping of lamb stew with all those succulent potatoes and carrots steaming in the bowl. They have to go back into the night and do their job. And my job was to save the children. Until the last bullet had been fired, until the last bomb had been dropped, I had to go on looking for them.

TOM: What happened after the war was over?

HARRY: I gave up my dreams of manly courage and noble self-sacrifice. The Hotel Existence shut down, and when it opened again a few years later, it was no longer sitting in a meadow somewhere in the Hungarian countryside, and it no longer looked like a baroque castle plucked from the boulevards of Baden-Baden. The new Hotel Existence was a much smaller and shabbier affair, and if you wanted to find it now, you had to go to one of those big cities where real life began only after dark. New York, maybe, or Havana, or some dingy side street in Paris. To enter the Hotel Existence was to think of words like *hobnob, chiaroscuro,* and *fate.* It was men and women eyeing you discreetly in the lobby. It was perfume and silk suits and warm skin, and everyone always walked around with a highball in one hand and a burning cigarette in the other. I'd seen it all in the movies, and I knew how it was supposed to look. The regulars downstairs in the piano bar sipping their dry martinis. The casino on the second floor with the roulette table and the muffled dice bouncing on the green felt, the baccarat dealer whispering in an oily foreign accent. The ballroom on the lower level with the plush leather booths and the singer in the spotlight with her smoky voice and shimmering silver dress. Those were the props that helped get things started, but no one came just for the drinks or the gambling or the songs, even if the singer that night was Rita Hayworth, flown in from Buenos Aires for one performance only by her current husband and manager, George Macready. You had to ease yourself into the flow, get a few shots into you before you could settle down to business. Not business, really, but the game, the infinitely pleasurable game of deciding which person you would go upstairs with later that night. The first move was always with the eyes – never anything but the eyes. You would let them wander around from this one to that one for a few minutes, calmly drinking your drink and smoking your cigarette, testing out the possibilities, searching for a glance that might be aimed in your direction, maybe even luring some-

594

one with a little smile or a flick of the shoulder to start looking at you. Men and women both, it didn't matter to me. I was still a virgin in those days, but I already knew enough about myself to know that I didn't care. Once, Cary Grant sat down next to me in the piano bar and began rubbing my leg. Another time, the dead Jean Harlow came back from her grave and made passionate love to me in room four-twenty-seven. But there was also my French teacher, Mademoiselle Des Forêts, the slender Québecoise with the pretty legs and the bright red lipstick and the liquid brown eyes. Not to speak of Hank Miller, the varsity quarterback and hotshot ladies' man of the senior class. Hank probably would have punched me to death if he'd known what I was doing to him in my dreams, but the fact was that he didn't know. I was only a sophomore then, and I never would have had the courage to address such an august figure as Hank Miller during the day, but at night I could meet him in the bar at the Hotel Existence, and after a few drinks and some friendly small talk, I could take him upstairs to room three-oh-one and introduce him to the secrets of the world.

TOM: Adolescent jerk-off material.

HARRY: You could say that. But I prefer to think of it as the product of a rich inner life.

TOM: This is getting us nowhere.

HARRY: Where do you want us to go, dear Tom? We're sitting here waiting for the next course, drinking a splendid bottle of Sancerre, and entertaining ourselves with meaningless stories. There's nothing wrong with that. In most parts of the world, it would be considered the height of civilized behavior.

NATHAN: The kid's in the dumps, Harry. He needs to talk.

HARRY: I'm aware of that. I have eyes in my head, don't I? If Tom doesn't approve of my Hotel Existence, then maybe he should tell us something about his. Every man has one, you know. And just as no two men are alike, each man's Hotel Existence is different from all the others.

TOM: I'm sorry. I don't mean to be a bore. This was supposed to be a fun night, and I'm spoiling it for both of you.

NATHAN: Forget about it. Just answer Harry's question.

TOM (*a long silence; then in a low voice, as if speaking to himself*): I want to live in a new way, that's all. If I can't change the world, then at least I can try to change myself. But I don't want to do it alone. I'm alone too much as it is, and whether it's my fault or not, Nathan is right. I'm in the dumps. Ever since we talked about Aurora the other day, I haven't stopped thinking about her. I miss her. I miss my mother. I miss everyone I've lost. I get so sad sometimes, I can't believe I don't just drop dead from the weight that's crushing down on me. What's my Hotel Existence, Harry? I don't know, but maybe it has something to do with living with others, with getting away from this rathole of a city and sharing a life with people I love and respect.

HARRY: A commune.

TOM: No, not a commune – a community. There's a difference.

HARRY: And where would this little utopia of yours be?

TOM: Somewhere out in the country, I suppose. A place with a lot of land and enough buildings to accommodate all the people who wanted to live there.

NATHAN: How many people are you talking about?

TOM: I don't know. It's not as if I've worked anything out yet. But both of you would be more than welcome.

HARRY: I'm flattered that I'm so high on your list. But if I move to the country, what happens to my business?

TOM: You'd move it with you. You make ninety percent of your money through the mail as it is. What difference does it make what post office you use? Yes, Harry, of course I'd want you to be a part of it. And maybe Flora, too.

HARRY: My dear, demented Flora. But if you asked her, Bette would also have to be invited. She's ailing now, you know. Trapped in a wheelchair with Parkinson's, the poor woman. I can't say how she'd react, but in the end she might welcome the idea. And then there's Rufus.

NATHAN: Who's Rufus?

HARRY: The young man who works behind the counter at the bookstore. The tall, light-skinned Jamaican with the pink boa. A few years ago, I found him crying his heart out in front of a building in the West Village and brought him home. By now, I've more or less adopted him. The bookstore job helps pay his rent, but he's also one of the best drag queens in the city. He works on the weekends under the name of Tina Hott. A fabulous performer, Nathan. You should catch his act sometime.

NATHAN: Why would he want to leave the city?

HARRY: Because he loves me, for one thing. And because he's H.I.V. positive and scared out of his wits. A change of scenery might do him some good.

NATHAN: Fine. But where are we going to come up with the money to buy a country estate? I could chip in something, but it wouldn't be nearly enough.

TOM: If Bette wants to join us, maybe she'd be willing to open the coffers and help.

HARRY: Out of the question. A man has his pride, sir, and I'd rather croak ten times over before I asked that woman for another penny.

TOM: Well, if you sold your building in Brooklyn, that might raise enough to swing it.

HARRY: A mere drop in the bucket. If I'm going to spend my waning years in the boondocks, I want to do it in grand style. No bumpkin stuff for me, Tom. I turn myself into a country squire, or the deal is off.

TOM: A little here, then, and a little there. We'll think of some other people who might want to get involved, and if we pool our resources, maybe we can pull it off.

HARRY: Don't fret, boys. Uncle Harry will take care of everything. At least he hopes he will. If all goes according to plan, we can expect a large infusion of cash in the near future. Enough to tip the balance and make our dream come true. That's what we're talking about, isn't it? A dream, a wild dream of removing ourselves from the cares and sorrows of this miserable world and creating a world of our own. A long shot, yes, but who's to say it can't happen?

TOM: And where is this 'infusion of cash' going to come from?

HARRY: Let's just say I have a business venture in the works, and we'll put the matter aside until further notice. If my ship comes in, the new Hotel Existence is a sure thing. If it doesn't – well, at least I'll have gone down fighting the good fight. A man can't do any more than that, can he? I'm sixty-six years old, and after all the ups and downs of my . . . my somewhat dubious career, this is probably my last chance to walk off with some big-time money. And when I say big, I mean very big. Bigger than either one of you can imagine.

Cigarette Break

At the time, I didn't take any of this talk seriously. Tom was in low spirits – that was all – and Harry was simply trying to cheer him up, to put some wind in his sails and lift him out of the doldrums. I must say that I liked Harry for humoring Tom and playing along with his impractical fantasy, but the idea that Harry would actually leave Brooklyn and move to some remote country settlement struck me as pure nonsense. The man was made for the city. He was a creature of crowds and commerce, of good restaurants and expensive clothes, and even if he was only half gay, his closest friend turned out to be a black transvestite who went to work sporting a pair of rhinestone clip-on earrings and a pink feather boa. Put a man like Harry Brightman in some rustic backwater, and the neighboring peasants would run him out of town with pitchforks and knives.

On the other hand, I felt reasonably certain that Harry's business venture was on the level. The old reprobate had some new deal cooking, and I was burning with curiosity to find out what it was. Even if he didn't want to talk about it in front of Tom, I hoped he would make an exception for me. My opportunity came just after we ordered dessert, when Tom excused himself and went into the bar area to smoke a cigarette (his newest tactic in the ongoing campaign to shed some pounds).

'Big money,' I remarked to Harry. 'Sounds interesting.'

'The chance of a lifetime,' he said.

'Any particular reason you don't want to talk about it?'

'I'm afraid of disappointing Tom, that's all. Some minor issues still have to be worked out, and until the business is settled, there's no point in getting overly excited.'

'I have some extra money lying around, you know. Quite a lot, in fact. If you need another investor to go in with you, I might be willing to help.'

'That's very generous of you, Nathan. Fortunately, I'm not looking for a partner. But that doesn't mean I wouldn't welcome your advice. I'm fairly confident my associates are on the up-and-up – but not one hundred percent confident. And doubt is a burdensome thing to live with, especially with so much at stake.'

'How about another dinner, then? Just the two of us. You can lay the whole thing out for me, and I'll tell you what I think.'

'Sometime next week?'

'Just pick a day, and I'll be there.'

On the Stupidity of Men (2)

At eleven o'clock the next morning, I stopped in at one of the local jewelry stores to buy a substitute necklace for Rachel. I didn't want to disturb the B.P.M. by ringing her bell on a Sunday morning, but I specifically asked the saleswoman to show me any and all pieces they carried that bore Nancy Mazzucchelli's mark. The woman smiled, said she was an old friend of Nancy's, and then promptly opened a glass cabinet from which she extracted eight or ten examples of her work, placing them on the counter for me one article at a time. As luck would have it, the last necklace turned out to be almost identical to the one that now slept at night in the cash register at the Cosmic Diner.

I was planning to head straight back to my apartment. A couple of anecdotes had occurred to me while walking to the store, and I was eager to return to my desk and add them to the ever-expanding *Book of Human Folly.* I hadn't bothered to count up the entries I'd written so far, but there must have been close to a hundred by then, and from the way they kept coming to me, surging up at all hours of the day and night (sometimes even in my dreams), I suspected there was more than enough material to go on with the project for years. Not twenty seconds after leaving the store, however, who should I run into but Nancy Mazzucchelli, the B.P.M. herself? I had been living in the neighborhood for two months, had taken long walks every morning and afternoon, had gone into countless shops and restaurants, had sat outdoors at the Circle Café watching hundreds of people stride down the avenue, but until that Sunday morning I had never once caught a glimpse of her in public. I don't mean to imply that she had escaped my notice. I look at everyone, and if I had seen this woman before (who was no less than the reigning monarch of Park Slope), I would have remembered her. Now, following our impromptu meeting in front of her house on Friday, the pattern abruptly changed. Like a word you add to your vocabulary late in life – and which you then start hearing everywhere you turn – Nancy Mazzucchelli was suddenly everywhere I turned. It began with that Sunday encounter, and from then on scarcely a day went by when I didn't run into her at the bank or the post office or on some street in the neighborhood. Eventually,

I was introduced to her children (Devon and Sam); her mother Joyce; and her Foley-walker husband, Jim, the James Joyce who was not James Joyce. From total stranger, the B.P.M. rapidly became one of the fixtures of my life. Even if she is referred to only seldom in the future pages of this book, she is always there. Watch for her between the lines.

That first Sunday, nothing of any importance was said. Hi Nathan, hi Nancy, how are you, not bad, how's Tom, beautiful weather, nice seeing you, and so on. Small-town chat in the heart of the big city. If there is any detail significant enough to report, it would be the fact that she wasn't wearing her overalls. The day was unusually warm, and Nancy was dressed in a pair of blue jeans and a white cotton T-shirt. Because the shirt was tucked into the pants, I could see that her stomach was flat. That didn't mean she wasn't pregnant, of course, but even if she was in the early days of her first trimester, she hadn't been wearing the overalls on Friday to mask any bulge. I made a mental note to tell Tom about it the next time I saw him.

First thing Monday morning, I sent the necklace to Rachel, along with a short note *(Thinking of you – Love, Dad)*, but by nine o'clock that evening I was beginning to worry. I had mailed my letter to her on Tuesday night. Assuming it had gone out early Wednesday morning, it should have reached her by Saturday – Monday at the latest. My daughter had never been much of a letter writer (she did most of her communicating by e-mail, which I didn't have), and therefore I was expecting her to contact me by phone. Saturday and Sunday had already come and gone without a word, which meant that Monday had to be the day she would call. Anytime after six, when she came home from work and read my letter. No matter how badly I had offended her, I found it inconceivable that Rachel wouldn't respond to what I had written. I sat in my apartment waiting for the phone to ring, but by nine o'clock nothing had happened. Even if she had decided to put off calling until after dinner, dinner would have been over by nine. A little desperate, a little afraid, more than a little embarrassed by how desperate and afraid I was, I finally summoned the courage to dial her number. No one there. The answering machine clicked on after four rings, but I hung up before the beep sounded.

Same result on Tuesday.

Same result on Wednesday.

Not knowing what else to do, I decided to call Edith and ask her what was going on. She and Rachel were in constant touch, and while I felt some trepidation about having to talk to my ex, there was no reason to suppose she wouldn't give me a straight answer. X marks the spot, as Harry had so eloquently put it. By now, the only contact I had with my former helpmeet was looking at her signature on the backs of my canceled alimony checks. She had filed for divorce in November 1998, and one month later, long before the decree came through, I was diagnosed with cancer. To her credit, Edith allowed me to stay on in the house for as long as necessary, which explained why we had been so slow to put it on the market. After the sale, she'd used a portion of her money to buy a condo in Bronxville – which Rachel, with her usual flair for colorful language, had told me was 'very nice.' She'd also started taking adult education classes at Columbia, had traveled at least once to Europe, and, if the gossip mill was correct, was getting it on with an old lawyer friend of ours, Jay Sussman. His wife had died two years earlier, and since he'd always had the hots for Edith (husbands are good at detecting such things), it was only natural that he should make a move on her once I exited the scene. The merry widower and the gay divorcée. Well, good for both of them. Jay was pushing seventy, of course, but who was I to object to a tango dinner or two and some twilight nooky? To be perfectly frank, I wouldn't have minded a dose of that for myself.

'Hi there, Edith,' I said when she answered the phone. 'It's the ghost of Christmas past.'

'Nathan?' She sounded surprised to hear from me – and also a little disgusted.

'I'm sorry to bother you, but I need some information, and you're the only person who can give it to me.'

'This isn't one of your bad jokes, is it?'

'I wish.'

She sighed loudly into the receiver. 'I'm busy right now. Make it fast, okay?'

'Busy entertaining, I presume.'

'Presume whatever you like. I don't have to tell you a thing, do I?' She let out a strange, piercing laugh – a laugh that was so bitter, so triumphant, so full of smoldering, contradictory impulses, that I scarcely knew what to make of it. The laugh of a liberated ex-wife, perhaps. The last laugh.

'No, of course not. You're free to do what you want. All I'm asking for is some information.'

'About what?'

'Rachel. I've been trying to get in touch with her since Monday, but no one seems to be home. I just want to make sure that she and Terrence are all right.'

'You're such an idiot, Nathan. Don't you know anything?'

'Apparently not.'

'They went to England on May twentieth and won't be back until June fifteenth. The Rutgers semester ended. Rachel was invited to give a paper at a conference in London, and now they're spending some time with Terrence's parents in Cornwall.'

'She never told me.'

'Why should she tell you anything?'

'Because she's my daughter, that's why.'

'If you acted more like a father, maybe she would. That was a crummy thing you did to her, Nathan, blowing up at her like that. Who gives you the right? She was so hurt . . . so fucking hurt.'

'I called to apologize, but she hung up on me. Now I've written her a long letter. I'm trying to repair the damage, Edith. I really do love her, you know.'

'Then get down on your knees and beg for mercy. But don't expect any help from me. My days as a mediator are over.'

'I'm not asking for your help. But if she happens to call from England, you might want to mention that there's a letter waiting for her when she gets home. And a necklace, too.'

'Forget it, bub. I ain't saying a word. Not a single goddamn word. Got it?'

So much for the myth of tolerance and goodwill among divorced couples. By the time the conversation ended, I was half in the mood to hop on the next train to Bronxville and strangle Edith with my bare hands. The other half of me wanted to spit. But give the old girl her due. Her wrath had been so violent, so blistering in its denunciations and contempt, it actually helped me come to a decision. I would never call her again. Never again for the rest of my life. Under no circumstances, not ever again. The divorce had disentangled us in the eyes of the law, dissolving the marriage that had held us together for so many years, but even so, there was one thing we still had in common, and because we would go on being Rachel's parents for as long as we lived, I had assumed that connection would prevent us from sinking into a state of permanent animosity. But no longer. That telephone call was the end, and from now on Edith would be no more than a name to me – five tiny letters that signified a person who had ceased to exist.

The next day, Thursday, I ate lunch alone. Tom was in Manhattan with Harry that afternoon, negotiating with the widow of a recently dead novelist about the books in her husband's library. According to Tom, this novelist seemed to have known every important writer of the past fifty years, and his shelves were crammed with books that had been signed and dedicated to him by his illustrious friends. 'Association copies,' as these books were called in the business, and because they were much sought after by collectors, Tom said, they invariably fetched good prices. He also said that outings of this sort were the thing he liked best about working for Harry. Not only did they allow him to quit the confines of his second-floor office in Brooklyn, but they gave him a chance to watch his boss in action. 'He puts on quite a show,' he said. 'Never stops talking. Never stops bargaining. Flatter, denigrate, cajole – an endless feint and dodge. I don't believe in reincarnation, but if I did, I'd swear he'd been a Moroccan rug merchant in another life.'

Wednesday was Marina's day off. Without Tom to keep me company, I was particularly looking forward to seeing her on Thursday, but when I walked into the Cosmic Diner at one o'clock, she wasn't there. I talked to Dimitrios, the owner of the restaurant, and he explained that she'd called in sick that morning and would probably be out for a few days. I felt deeply and absurdly dejected. After the tongue-lashing I'd been given by my ex-wife the night before, I wanted to reaffirm my faith in the female sex, and who better to help me than the gentle Marina Gonzalez? Before entering the restaurant, I had already imagined her wearing the necklace (which had been the case on Monday and Tuesday), and I knew that the mere sight of her would do me a world of good. With a heavy heart, therefore, I slid into an empty booth and placed my order with Dimitrios, who was filling in for my absent love. As usual, I was carrying a book in my jacket pocket (*Confessions of Zeno*, which I'd bought on Tom's recommendation), and given that I had no one to talk to that day, I opened Svevo's novel and began to read.

After two paragraphs, the man known as Mr. Trouble came knocking at my door. This was the encounter I alluded to some fifteen or twenty pages ago, and now that the moment has arrived for me to talk about it, I cringe at the memory of what happened between us. This person, this thing I prefer to call Trouble, this nightmare being who emerged from the depths of nowhere, masqueraded himself as a thirty-year-old U.P.S. deliveryman with a muscular, well-toned body and an angry expression in his eyes. No, *anger* doesn't do justice to what I saw in that face. *Fury* would be closer to it, I think, or perhaps *rage*, or even *homicidal madness*. Whatever it was, when he stormed into the restaurant and asked Dimitrios in a loud, bellicose voice if Nathan was there, Nathan Glass, I knew Mr. Trouble went by the code name of Roberto Gonzalez. I also knew that the necklace was no longer in the cash register. Poor Marina had forgotten to take it off when she went home on Tuesday night. A small blunder, perhaps, but I couldn't help thinking of how she had employed the word *boom* when she tried to turn down my gift, and when I coupled that word with Dimitrios's announcement that she would be out 'for a few days,' I wondered how badly the son-of-a-bitch had beaten her.

Marina's husband parked himself on the bench directly opposite me and leaned across the table. 'Are you Nathan?' he asked. 'Nathan fucking Glass?'

'That's right,' I said. 'But my middle name isn't Fucking. It's Joseph.'

'Okay, smart-ass. Tell me why you did it.'

'Did what?'

He reached into his pocket and slammed the necklace down on the table. 'This.'

'It was a birthday present.'

'To my wife.'

'Yes. To your wife. What's wrong with that? Marina serves me lunch every day. She's a terrific girl, and I wanted to show my gratitude. I tip her when I pay my bill, don't I? Well, consider the necklace a big tip.'

'It ain't right, man. You don't fuck around with married women.'

'I'm not fucking around. I just gave her a present, that's all. I'm old enough to be her father.'

'You got a dick, don't you? You still got balls, don't you?'

'The last time I looked, they were still there.'

'I'm warning you, mister. You lay off Marina. She's my bitch, and I'll kill you if you ever come near her again.'

'Don't call her a bitch. She's a woman. And you're damn lucky to have her as a wife.'

'I'll call her whatever I want, asshole. And this,' he said, as he picked up the necklace and dangled it before my eyes, 'this piece of shit you can eat for breakfast tomorrow morning.' He grabbed hold of it with his two hands, and with one sharp jerk of the wrists snapped apart the gold chain. Some of the beads slid off and bounced on the Formica table; others landed in his palm, and as he stood up to take his leave, he threw them in my face. If not for my glasses, I might have caught one in the eye. 'Next time, I kill you!' he shouted, jabbing his finger at me like some deranged marionette. 'You lay off her, you bastard, or you're dead!'

By now, everyone in the restaurant was looking at us. It wasn't every day that you sat down to lunch and were treated to such an absorbing spectacle, but now that Mr. Trouble had told me off, the action seemed to be coming to an end. Or so I thought. Gonzalez had already turned from me and was heading in the direction of the door, but the path between the booths and tables was narrow, and before he could make his exit, the towering, broad-bellied Dimitrios was standing in his way. Thus began Act Two. Hemmed in, his brains still on fire, the overwrought Gonzalez started yelling at the top of his voice. 'You keep that scum-bag out of here!' he said (referring to me). 'You keep him out, or else Marina don't work for you no more! She quits!'

'Then she quits,' said the owner of the Cosmic Diner. 'This is my restaurant, and nobody tells me what to do in *my restaurant*. Without my customers, I don't have nothing. So get your ass out of here and tell Marina she's done. I don't want to see her no more. And you – you come in my place again, I call the cops.'

There was some pushing and shoving after that, but strong and muscular as Gonzalez was, Dimitrios was too big for him, and eventually, following another wave of threats and counter-threats, Marina's husband vanished from the premises. The fool had lost his wife her job. But worse than that – far worse than that – I realized I would probably never see her again.

Once calm had been restored to the diner, Dimitrios walked over to my table and sat down. He apologized for the disturbance and offered me lunch on the house, but when I tried to talk him out of firing Marina, he wouldn't budge. He had been a willing co-conspirator in our necklace-cash register ploy, but business was business, he said, and even though he liked Marina 'a hell of a lot,' he didn't want to take any chances with that crazy husband of hers. Then he said something that burned into me like the scald of a branding iron. 'Don't worry about it,' he said. 'It's not your fault.'

But it was my fault. I was to blame for the whole mess, and I despised myself for the wrong I'd done to the innocent Marina. Her first impulse had been to refuse the necklace. She understood what kind of man her husband was, but rather than listen to what she said to me, I had forced her to take it, and that stupid move, that stupid, stupid move, had led to nothing but trouble. God damn me, I said to myself. Cast my body into hell, and let me burn there for a thousand years.

That was the last time I had lunch at the Cosmic Diner. I continue to pass it every day on my walks down Seventh Avenue, but I still haven't found the courage to go back in.

Monkey Business

That evening (Thursday) I met Harry for dinner at Mike & Tony's Steak House on the corner of Fifth Avenue and Carroll Street. This was the same restaurant where he had made his disturbing revelations to Tom a couple of months earlier, and I believe he chose it because he felt comfortable there. The front half of the establishment was a neighborhood bar where the smoking of cigarettes and cigars was actively encouraged, and sporting events could be watched on a large TV mounted on the wall near the entrance. Walk through that room, however, open the thickly paned double glass doors at the rear, and you found yourself in an altogether different environment. The restaurant at Mike & Tony's was a small, carpeted chamber with shelves of books lining one wall, a few black-and-white photographs hanging on another, and no more than eight or ten tables. In other words, a quiet, intimate beanery, blessed with the further advantage of tolerant acoustics that allowed one to be heard even while speaking in a hushed voice. To Harry's mind, the place must have felt as snug and private as a confessional box. At any rate, that's where he preferred to do his confessing – first to Tom, and now to me.

As far as Harry knew, my understanding of his pre-Brooklyn life was limited to just a few basic facts: born in Buffalo, ex-husband of Bette, father of Flora, time spent in prison. He wasn't aware that Tom had already supplied me with a host of particulars, but I wasn't about to let him know that. I therefore played dumb as Harry marched me through the familiar story of the Alec Smith bamboozle and his subsequent falling out with Gordon Dryer. At first I didn't understand why he was bothering to tell me these things. What connection did they have with his current business deal? I wondered, and then, ever more confused, I put the question directly to Harry. 'Just bear with me,' he said. 'In due time, all will come clear.'

I didn't say much through the early part of the meal. The uproar at the diner that afternoon had left me badly shaken, and as Harry rattled on with his story, my thoughts kept wandering off to Marina and her idiot husband and the whole chain of circumstances that had led me to buy that cursed bauble from the B.P.M. But Tom's boss was in good form that night, and with the aid of a predinner Scotch and the wine I drank to accompany my platter of Blue Point oysters, I gradually pulled out of my funk and started to focus on the business at hand. Harry's account of his Chicago crimes matched neatly with Tom's retelling of them, but with one notable and amusing difference. With Tom, Harry had broken down and wept. He had been overcome by remorse, berating himself for having destroyed his marriage, his livelihood, his name. With me, on the other hand, he sounded thoroughly unrepentant, even boasting of the remarkable coup he'd managed to keep going for two solid years, and he looked back at his adventure in art forgery as one of the most glorious periods of his life. How to explain this radically altered tone? Had he been putting on an act for Tom to win his sympathy and understanding? Or, coming on the heels of Flora's disastrous visit to Brooklyn, had that first confession been a true cry from the heart? Perhaps. All men contain several men inside them, and most of us bounce from one self to another without ever knowing who we are. Up one day and down the next; morose and silent in the morning, laughing and cracking jokes at night. Harry had been low when he talked to Tom, but now that his business venture was in the works, he was flying high with me.

Our T-bones were brought to the table, we switched to a bottle of red, and then, at long last, the other shoe dropped. Harry had all but told me he was building up to a surprise, but even if he'd given me a hundred chances to guess what it was, I never would have predicted the startling piece of news that calmly fell from his lips.

'Gordon's back,' he said.

'Gordon,' I repeated, too stunned to say anything else. 'You mean Gordon Dryer?'

'Gordon Dryer. My old comrade in sin and frolic.'

'How in the world did he track you down?'

'You make it sound like a bad thing, Nathan. It's not. I'm very, very happy.'

'After what you did to him, I'd think he'd want to kill you.'

'That's what I thought at first, but it's all over now. The rancor, the bitterness. The poor fellow threw himself into my arms and asked me to forgive him. Can you imagine that? He wanted me to forgive *him*.'

'But you're the one who put him in jail.'

'Yes, but the scheme was Gordon's idea in the first place. Without him to get things rolling, neither one of us would have served any time. That's what he blames himself for. He's done a lot of soul-searching over the years, and he told me he'd gotten to the point where he couldn't live with himself if I thought he still bore me a grudge. Gordon's not a child anymore. He's forty-seven now, and he's grown up a lot since the old days in Chicago.'

'How many years did he spend in prison?'

'Three and a half. Then he moved to San Francisco and started painting again. Without much success, I'm sorry to report. He kept himself together by giving private drawing lessons, an odd temp job here and there, and then he fell for a man who lives in New York. That's why he's in the city now. He left San Francisco and moved in with him early last month.'

'Someone with money, I suppose.'

'I don't know all the details. But I think he earns enough to support them both.'

'Lucky Gordon.'

'Not so lucky. Not really, when you think of all he's been through. And besides, I'm the one he loves. He's very attached to his friend, but I'm the one he loves. And I love him back.'

'I don't mean to dig into your private life, but what about Rufus?'

'Rufus is my heart, but our relations are strictly platonic. In all the years I've known him, we haven't spent a single night together.'

'But Gordon is different.'

'Very different. He's not young anymore, but he's still a beautiful man. I can't tell you how kind he is to me. We don't get to see each other often, but you know what secret affairs are like. So many lies to be told, so many arrangements to be made. But whenever it happens, the old spark is still there. I'd thought I was finished with all that, over the hill, but Gordon's rejuvenated me. Bare skin, Nathan. It's the only thing worth living for.'

'One thing anyway, I'll grant you that.'

'If you can think of a better one, let me know.'

'I thought we came here to discuss business.'

'That's precisely what we're doing. Gordon's a part of it, you see. We're in it together.'

'Again?'

'It's a tremendous plan. So brilliant, I get goose bumps every time I think about it.'

'Why do I have this crazy feeling you're about to tell me you're involved in another fraud? Is the business legal or illegal?'

'Illegal, of course. Where's the fun if there's no risk?'

'You're incorrigible, Harry. After all that's happened to you, I'd think you'd want to toe the straight and narrow for the rest of your life.'

'I've tried. For nine long years I've tried, but it's no use. There's an imp inside me, and if I don't let him out to make some mischief now and then, the world just gets too damned dull. I hate feeling grumpy and bored. I'm an enthusiast, and the more dangerous my life becomes, the happier I am. Some people gamble at cards. Other people climb mountains or jump out of airplanes. I like tricking people. I like seeing how much I can get away with. Even as a kid, one of my dreams was to publish an encyclopedia in which all the information was false. Wrong dates for every historical event, wrong locations for every river, biographies of people who never existed. What kind of person imagines doing a thing like that? A crazy person, I suppose, but Christ, how that idea used to make me laugh. When I was in the navy, I was almost court-martialed for mislabeling a set of nautical maps. I did it on purpose. I don't know why, but the urge came over me, and I couldn't stop myself. I talked my commanding officer into believing it was an honest mistake, but it wasn't. That's who I am, Nathan. I'm generous, I'm kind, I'm loyal, but I'm also a born prankster. A couple of months ago, Tom mentioned a theory someone had come up with about classical literature. It was all a hoax, he said. Aeschylus, Homer, Sophocles, Plato, the whole lot of them. Invented by some clever Italian poets during the Renaissance. Isn't that just the most wonderful thing you've ever heard? The great pillars of Western civilization, and every one of them a fake. Ha! How I would have loved to have taken part in that little gag.'

'So what is it this time? More forged paintings?'

'No, a forged manuscript. I'm in the book business now, remember?'

'Gordon's idea, no doubt.'

'Well, yes. He's extremely smart, you know, and he understands my weaknesses.'

'Are you sure you want to tell me about it? How do you know I can be trusted?'

'Because you're a man of honor and discretion.'

'How do you know that?'

'Because you're Tom's uncle. And he's a man of honor and discretion as well.'

'Then why not tell Tom?'

'Because Tom is too pure. He's too good, and he doesn't have a head for business. You've been around the block, Nathan, and I'm relying on your experience for some intelligent counsel.'

'My advice would be to drop the whole thing.'

'I can't do that. The venture is too far along for me to back out now. And besides, I don't want to.'

'All right. But when this thing blows up in your face, don't forget that I warned you.'

'*The Scarlet Letter.* You're familiar with the title, yes?'

'I read it in English class my junior year. Miss O'Flaherty, fourth period.'

'We all had to read it in high school, didn't we? An American classic. One of the most famous books ever written.'

'Are you telling me that you and Gordon are going to forge a manuscript of *The Scarlet Letter*? What about Hawthorne's original?'

'That's the beauty of it. Hawthorne's manuscript disappeared. Except for the title page – which is sitting in a vault at the Morgan Library as we speak. But no one knows what happened to the rest of the book. Some people think it was burned, either by Hawthorne himself or in a warehouse fire. Others say the printers simply threw the sheets in the garbage – or else used them to light their pipes. That's my favorite version. A ragtag crew of Boston print-shop workers lighting their corncobs with *The Scarlet Letter*. But whatever the real story is, there's enough uncertainty to the business to imagine that the manuscript was never lost. Just misplaced, so to speak. What if Hawthorne's publisher, James T. Fields, took it home with him and put it in a box somewhere with a pile of other papers? Eventually, the box is moved to the attic. Years later, the box is inherited by one of Fields's children, or else it's left in the house, and when the house is sold, the box becomes the property of the new owners. Do you see what I'm talking about? There are enough doubts and mysteries to lay the groundwork for a miraculous discovery. It happened with a stash of Melville letters and manuscripts just a few years ago in a house in upstate New York. If Melville papers can be found, why not Hawthorne?'

'Who's forging the manuscript? Gordon isn't qualified to do something like that, is he?'

'No. He's going to be the person who finds it, but the actual work is being done by a man named Ian Metropolis. Gordon heard about him from someone he met in prison, and apparently he's the best there is, an out-and-out genius. He's forged Lincoln, Poe, Washington Irving, Henry James, Gertrude Stein, and God knows who else, but in all the years he's been at it, he hasn't been caught once. No record, no suspicions hovering around him. A shadow-man lurking in the dark. It's a complex and demanding job, Nathan. First of all, there's the matter of finding the right paper – mid-nineteenth-century paper that will hold up to X-rays and ultraviolet exams. Then you have to study all of Hawthorne's extant manuscripts and learn how to imitate his handwriting – which was quite sloppy, by the way, almost illegible at times. But mastering the physical technique is only a small part of it. It's not as if you just sit down with a printed version of *The Scarlet Letter* and copy it out by hand. You have to know every one of Hawthorne's private tics, the errors he made, his idiosyncratic use of hyphens, his inability to spell certain words correctly. *Ceiling* was always *cieling*; *steadfast* was always *stedfast*; *subtle* was always *subtile*. Whenever Hawthorne wrote *Oh*, the typesetters would change it to *O*. And so on and so on. It takes a lot of preparation and hard work. But well worth it, my friend. A complete manuscript will probably go for three to four million dollars. Gordon's offered me twenty-five percent for my services, which means that we're looking at something close to a million bucks. Not too shabby, is it?'

'And what are you supposed to do for your twenty-five percent?'

'Sell the manuscript. I'm the humble but respected purveyor of rare books, autographs, and literary curios. It lends legitimacy to the project.'

'Have you come up with a buyer yet?'

'That's the part that worries me. I suggested that we sell it directly to one of the libraries in town – the Berg Collection, the Morgan, Columbia University – or else put it up for auction at Sotheby's. But Gordon has his heart set on a private collector. He says it's safer to keep the business from going public, and I suppose I see his point. Still, it makes me wonder if he has real confidence in Metropolis's work.'

'What does Metropolis say?'

'I don't know. I've never met him.'

'You're involved in a four-million-dollar swindle with a man you've never met?'

'He doesn't allow anyone to see his face. Not even Gordon. All their contacts have been by phone.'

'I don't like the sound of this, Harry.'

'Yes, I know. A little too cloak-and-daggery for my taste as well. Nevertheless, things seem to be moving forward now. We've found our buyer, and two weeks ago we let him have a sample page. Believe it or not, he's taken it around to a number of experts, and they've all confirmed that it's genuine. I just got a check from him for ten thousand dollars. As a down payment, so we won't offer the manuscript to anyone else. We're supposed to conclude the sale after he comes back from Europe next Friday.'

'Who is he?'

'A stocks-and-bonds man named Myron Trumbell. I've looked him up. A Park Avenue blueblood, positively rolling in money.'

'Where did Gordon find him?'

'He's a friend of his friend, the man he's living with now.'

'Whom you haven't met either.'

'No. Nor do I want to. Gordon and I are secret lovers. Why would I want to meet my rival?'

'I think you're walking into a trap, old man. They're setting you up.'

'Setting me up? What are you talking about?'

'How many pages of the manuscript have you seen?'

'Just the one. The page I handed over to Trumbell two weeks ago.'

'What if it's the only one, Harry? What if there is no Ian Metropolis? What if Gordon's new friend turns out to be none other than Myron Trumbell himself?'

'Impossible. Why would anyone go to such lengths . . . '

'Revenge. One bad turn deserves another. Tit for tat. All those wonderful qualities human beings are so renowned for. I'm afraid your Gordon isn't what you think he is.'

'That's too dark, Nathan. I refuse to believe it.'

'Have you deposited Trumbell's check?'

'I put it in the bank three days ago. As a matter of fact, I've already spent half of it on a pile of new clothes.'

'Send the money back.'

'I don't want to.'

'If you don't have enough in your account, you can borrow the rest from me to make up the difference.'

'Thank you, Nathan, but I don't need your charity.'

'They've got you by the balls, Harry, and you don't even know it.'

'Think what you like, but I'm not bowing out now. I'm marching ahead, come hail, sleet, or flood. If you're right about Gordon, then my life's finished anyway. So what difference does it make? And if you're wrong – which I know you are – then I'll invite you to another dinner and you can toast my success.'

A Knock on the Door

Saturdays and Sundays, Tom slept in. Harry's store was open on the weekends, but Tom didn't have to go to work, and since there was no school on those days, rising early would have been pointless. He wouldn't have found the B.P.M. on the front steps of her house waiting for the bus to pick up her children, and without that lure to pull him from the warm sheets of his bed, he didn't bother to set his alarm clock. Shades drawn, his body enveloped in the womblike dark of his tiny home, he would sleep until his eyes opened of their own accord – or, as often happened, a noise from somewhere in the building jolted him awake. On Sunday, June fourth (three days after my disastrous run-in with Roberto Gonzalez, which was also the day of my disconcerting talk with Harry Brightman), it was a noise that tore my nephew from the depths of slumber – in this case, the noise of a small hand knocking softly and tentatively on his door. It was a few minutes past nine, and once Tom managed to register the sound, once he roused himself from his bed and stumbled across the room to open the door, his life took a new and startling turn. To put it bluntly, everything changed for him, and it is only now, after much laborious preparation, after much raking and hoeing of the ground, that my chronicle of Tom's adventures begins to take flight.

It was Lucy. A silent, nine-and-a-half-year-old Lucy with short dark hair and her mother's round hazel eyes, a tall, preadolescent girl dressed in ragged red jeans, scuffed white Keds, and a Kansas City Royals T-shirt. No bag, no jacket or sweater slung over her arm, nothing but the clothes on her back. Tom hadn't seen her in six years, but he recognized her at once. Altogether different somehow, and yet exactly as she'd been – in spite of a full new set of adult teeth, in spite of the longer, thinner look to her face, in spite of the many inches she had grown. There she stood at the door, smiling up at her disheveled, sleep-worn uncle, studying him with the rapt, unblinking eyes he remembered so well from the old days in Michigan. Where was her mother? Where was her mother's husband? Why was she alone? How had she gotten there? Tom paused after each question, but not a single word came from

Lucy's mouth. For a few moments, he wondered if she hadn't gone deaf, but then he asked her if she remembered who he was, and she nodded her head. Tom opened his arms, and she walked readily into his embrace, pressing her forehead against his chest and hugging him back as tightly as she could. 'You must be starving,' Tom said at last, and then he opened the door wide and let her into the dismal coffin he called his room.

He fixed her a bowl of Cheerios, poured her a glass of orange juice, and by the time he'd finished making a pot of coffee for himself, both the glass and the bowl were empty. He asked if she wanted something more, and when she nodded yes and smiled, he set about preparing a couple of pieces of French toast for her, which she doused in a puddle of maple syrup and scarfed down in a minute and a half. At first, Tom attributed her silence to exhaustion, to anxiety, to hunger, to any one of several possible causes, but the fact was that Lucy didn't look tired, appeared to be perfectly comfortable in her surroundings, and now that she had polished off the food, hunger had been scratched from the list as well. And yet she continued to say nothing in response to his questions. A few nods and shakes of the head, but no words, no sounds, no effort to use her tongue at all.

'Have you forgotten how to talk, Lucy?' Tom asked.

A shake of the head.

'What about the T-shirt? Does it mean you came here from Kansas City?'

No response.

'What do you want me to do with you? I can't send you back to your mother if you don't tell me where she lives.'

No response.

'Would you like me to give you a pencil and a pad of paper? If you don't want to talk, then maybe you could write down your answers for me.'

A shake of the head.

'Have you stopped talking forever?'

Another shake of the head.

'Good. I'm glad to hear it. And when are you allowed to start talking again?'

Lucy thought for a moment, then held two fingers up to Tom.

'Two. But two what? Two hours? Two days? Two months? Tell me, Lucy.'

No response.

'Is your mother all right?'

A nod.

'Is she still married to David Minor?'

Another nod.

'Why did you run away, then? Don't they treat you well?'

No response.

'How did you get to New York? By bus?'

A nod.

'Do you still have your ticket receipt?'

No response.

'Let's see what's in your pockets. Maybe we'll find some answers there.'

Lucy obliged by digging her hands into all four pockets of her jeans and yanking out the contents, but nothing of significance was found. A hundred and fifty-seven dollars in cash, three sticks of chewing gum, six quarters, two dimes, four pennies, and a piece of paper with Tom's name, address, and phone number written on it – but no bus ticket, no clue to tell him where her trip had begun.

'All right, Lucy,' Tom said. 'Now that you're here, what are you planning to do? Where are you going to live?'

Lucy pointed her finger at her uncle.

Tom let out a short, incredulous laugh. 'Take a good look at where you are,' he said. 'There's barely enough room for one person here. Where do you think you're going to sleep, little girl?'

A shrug, followed by a large, ever more beautiful smile – as if to say, *We'll figure it out*.

But there was no figuring it out, at least not in Tom's mind. He knew nothing about children, and even if he'd been living in a twelve-room mansion with a full staff of servants, he still wouldn't have had the faintest interest in becoming his niece's substitute parent. A normal child would have been challenging enough, but a child who refused to talk and stubbornly resisted giving out any information about herself was a simple impossibility. And yet what was he going to do? For the time being he was stuck with her, and unless he could force her to tell him where her mother was, there would be no getting rid of her. That didn't mean he wasn't fond of Lucy or felt indifferent to her welfare, but he knew she had come to the wrong person. Of all the people even remotely connected to her, he was the worst man for the job.

I had no interest in taking care of her either, but at least there was an extra room in my apartment, and when Tom called later that morning and told me about his predicament (panic in his voice, almost screeching into the phone), I said I would be willing to put her up until we found a solution to the problem. They arrived at my place on First Street just after eleven. Lucy smiled when Tom introduced her to her great-uncle Nat, and she seemed happy to receive the welcoming kiss I planted on the crown of her head, but I soon discovered that she was no more willing to talk to me than she was to him. I had been hoping to trick a few words out of her, but all I got were the same nods and shakes of the head that Tom had been subjected to earlier. Strange, unsettling little person. I was no expert in child psychology, but it seemed clear to me that there was nothing physically or mentally wrong with her. No retardation, no signs of autism, nothing organic to impede her interaction with others. She looked you straight in the eye, understood everything you said, and smiled as often and affectionately as any two children put together. What was it, then? Had she suffered some terrible trauma that had shut down her ability to talk? Or, for reasons that were still impenetrable, had she decided to take a vow of silence, pushing herself into voluntary mutism in order to test her will and courage – a kid's game that she would eventually grow tired of? Her face and arms were free of bruises, but at some point during the day I was determined to coax her into the bath to get a look at the rest of her body. Just to satisfy myself that no one had beaten or abused her.

I put her in front of the TV in the living room and switched on the set to a twenty-four-hour cartoon channel. Her eyes lit up with pleasure when she saw the animated figures prance across the screen – so much so that it occurred to me that she wasn't in the habit of watching television, which in turn led me to start thinking about David Minor and the harshness of his religious beliefs. Had Aurora's husband banned TV from the house? Were his convictions so strong that he wanted to shield his adopted daughter from the frenzied carnival of American pop culture – that godless free-for-all of glitz and garbage that poured out endlessly from every cathode tube in the land? Perhaps. We wouldn't know anything about Minor until Lucy told us where she lived, and for now she wasn't saying a word. Tom had guessed Kansas City because of the T-shirt, but she had refused to confirm or deny it, which meant that she didn't want us to know – for the simple reason that she was afraid we would send her back. She had run away from home, after all, and happy children did not run away from home. That much was certain, whether the home had a TV in it or not.

With Lucy parked on the floor of the living room, eating pistachio nuts and watching an episode of *Inspector Gadget*, Tom and I withdrew to the kitchen, where she wouldn't be able to overhear our conversation. We talked for a good thirty or forty minutes, but nothing came of it except ever-mounting confusion and worry. So many mysteries and imponderables to be dealt with, so little evidence on which to build a plausible case. Where had Lucy found the money for the trip? How had she known Tom's address? Had her mother helped her get away, or had she absconded on her own? And if Aurora had been involved, why hadn't she contacted Tom in advance or at least sent a note with Lucy? Perhaps there had been a note, we said, and Lucy had lost it. One way or another, what did the girl's departure tell us about Aurora's marriage? Was it the disaster we both feared, or had Tom's sister finally seen the light and embraced her husband's vision of the world? And yet, if harmony reigned in the household, what was their daughter doing in Brooklyn? Round and round it went, the two of us traveling in circles, talking, talking, talking, but unable to answer a single question.

'Time will tell,' I said at last, not wanting to prolong the agony. 'But first things first. We have to find a place for her to live. You can't keep her, and neither can I. So what do we do?'

'I'm not putting her in foster care, if that's what you mean,' Tom said.

'No, of course not. But there must be someone we know who'd be willing to take her in. Temporarily, I mean. Until we manage to track down Aurora.'

'That's asking a lot, Nathan. It could go on for months. Maybe forever.'

'What about your stepsister?'

'You mean Pamela?'

'You said she's pretty well off. Big house in Vermont, two kids, lawyer husband. If you told her it's just for the summer, maybe she'd go along with it.'

'She detests Rory. All the Zorns do. Why would she want to put herself out for Rory's kid?'

'Compassion. Generosity. You said she's improved over the years, didn't you? Well, if I promise to cover Lucy's expenses, maybe she'd see it as a joint family venture. All of us pulling together for the common good.'

621

'You're a persuasive old coot, aren't you?'

'Just trying to get us out of a tight squeeze, Tom. Nothing more than that.'

'All right, I'll get in touch with Pamela. She'll turn me down, but I might as well give it a shot.'

'That's the spirit, son. Lay it on good and thick. A double grease job with syrup and molasses.'

He didn't want to make the call from my apartment, however. Not only because Lucy was there, he said, but because he would feel too self-conscious knowing I was around. Delicate, finicky Tom, the most sensitive soul in the world. No problem, I replied, but there wasn't any need for him to walk back to his place. Lucy and I would go out, and he could be alone when he talked to Pamela, with the added bonus of being able to charge the long-distance call to my bill. 'You saw what the kid is wearing,' I said. 'Those ratty jeans and worn-out sneakers. It just won't do, will it? You call Vermont, and I'll take her out to buy some new clothes.'

That settled the matter. After a hastily prepared lunch of tomato soup, scrambled eggs, and salami sandwiches, Lucy and I went on a shopping binge. Silent or not, she seemed to enjoy the expedition as much as any other young girl would have under similar circumstances: total freedom to choose whatever she wanted. At first we stuck mostly to the basics (socks, underwear, long pants, short pants, pajamas, a hooded sweatshirt, a nylon windbreaker, nailclippers, toothbrush, hairbrush, and so on), but then followed the hundred-and-fifty-dollar pair of neon-blue sneakers, the all-wool Brooklyn Dodgers replica baseball cap, and, somewhat to my surprise, a glistening duo of authentic, patent-leather Mary Janes, along with the red-and-white cotton dress we bought at the end – the old classic, with the round collar and the sash that tied in back. By the time we carried our haul to my apartment, it was well past three o'clock, and Tom was no longer there. A note was sitting on the kitchen table.

Dear Nathan

Pamela said yes. Don't ask me how I did it, but I had to work on her for over an hour before she finally gave in. One of the most grueling, punishing conversations I've ever had. For now, it's only on a 'trial basis,' but the good news is that she wants us to get Lucy up there tomorrow. Something to do with Ted's schedule and some shindig at the local country club. I assume we can use your car, yes? I'll drive if you don't feel up to it. I'm off to the bookstore now to talk to Harry about taking some time off. I'll wait for you there.

A presto.

Tom

It hadn't occurred to me that things would happen so fast. I felt relieved, of course, glad that our problem had been solved in such a quick and efficient way, but a part of me also felt disappointed, perhaps even a little bereft. I was beginning to like Lucy, and all during our shopping trip through the neighborhood, I had gradually warmed to the prospect of having her around for a while – days, I imagined, perhaps even weeks. It wasn't that I had changed my mind about the situation (she couldn't live in my apartment forever), but a short period would have been more than bearable for me. I had missed so many opportunities with Rachel when she was young, and now, suddenly, here was a little girl who needed looking after, who needed someone to buy clothes for her and put food in her stomach, who needed an adult with enough time on his hands to pay attention to her and try to draw her out of her baffling silence. I had no objections to assuming that role, but the show was apparently traveling from Brooklyn to New England, and I had been replaced by another actor. I tried to comfort myself with the thought that Lucy would be better off in the country with Pamela and her kids, but what did I know about Pamela? I hadn't seen her in years, and our few encounters in the past had left me cold.

Lucy wanted to wear her new dress and the Mary Janes to the bookstore, and I agreed on the condition that she take a bath first. I was an old hand at giving baths to children, I said, and to prove my point I pulled a photo album from the bookcase and showed her some pictures of Rachel – one of which, miraculously, showed my daughter sitting in a bubble bath at age six or seven. 'That's your cousin,' I said. 'Did you know that she and your mother were born just three months apart? They used to be great friends.' Lucy shook her head and flashed one of her biggest smiles of the day. She was beginning to trust her Uncle Nat, I felt, and a moment later we marched down the hall to the bathroom. As I filled the tub with water, Lucy compliantly stripped off her clothes and waded in. Except for a small, mostly hardened scab on her left knee, there wasn't a scratch on her. Clean, smooth back; clean, smooth legs; and no swelling or abrasions around her genitals. It was only a quick eyeball exam, but whatever the cause of her silence, I saw nothing to suggest that she had been roughed up or molested. To celebrate my discovery, I sang her the full version of 'Polly Wolly Doodle' as I washed and rinsed her hair.

Fifteen minutes after I pulled her out of the tub, the telephone rang. It was Tom, calling from the bookstore, wondering what had happened to us. He had finished talking to Harry (who had granted his request for a few days off) and was eager to get out of there.

'I'm sorry,' I said. 'Shopping took longer than expected, and then I decided Lucy could use a bath. Say good-bye to the little ragamuffin, Tom. Our girl looks like she's about to go to a birthday party at Windsor Castle.'

A short discussion followed about what to do for dinner. Since Tom wanted to get an early start in the morning, he thought it would be best if we planned something for around six o'clock. Besides, he added, Lucy's appetite was so big, she'd probably be ravenous by then anyway.

I turned to Lucy and asked her what she thought of pizza. When she replied by licking her lips and patting her stomach, I told Tom to meet us at Rocco's Trattoria – which served the best pizza in the neighborhood. 'Six o'clock,' I said. 'Meanwhile, Lucy and I will go to the video store and look for a movie we can all watch after dinner.'

The movie turned out to be *Modern Times*, which struck me as a weirdly inspired choice. Not only had Lucy never seen or heard of Chaplin (further evidence of the collapse of American education), but this was the film in which the tramp talks for the first time. The words might be gibberish, but sounds nevertheless came flying from his mouth, and I wondered if that moment wouldn't stir up something in Lucy, perhaps give her pause to reflect on the meaning of her intractable silence. In the best of all possible worlds, I thought maybe it would even snap her out of it for good.

Until the dinner at Rocco's, she had been on her best behavior. Everything I had asked of her she had done willingly and obediently, and not once had a frown creased her forehead. But Tom, in a rare burst of thoughtlessness, abruptly dropped the news of our impending trip to Vermont just minutes after we sat down at the table. There was no buildup, no propaganda extolling the wonders of Burlington, no argument about why she would be better off with Pamela than with her two uncles in Brooklyn. That was when I saw her frown for the first time, then cry for the first time, then sulk through the better part of the meal.

Hungry as she must have been, she didn't touch her pizza when it was set down before her, and it was only my nonstop talking that delivered us from what might have escalated into a full-blown war of nerves. I began by doing the groundwork Tom had neglected to take care of: the hymns and panegyrics, the Chamber of Commerce tap dance, the lengthy encomium on Pamela's legendary kindness. When those speeches failed to produce the desired result, I switched tactics and promised her that Tom and I would stay around until she was comfortably settled in, and then, going even further, took the supreme risk of assuring her that the decision was entirely in her hands. If she didn't like it there, we would gather up her things and drive back to New York. But she had to give it a real chance, I said, no less than three or four days. Agreed? She nodded her head. And then, for the first time in half an hour, she smiled. I called for the waiter and asked him if it wouldn't be too much trouble to reheat her pizza in the kitchen. Ten minutes later, he carried it back to the table, and Lucy dug in.

The Chaplin experiment yielded only mixed results. Lucy laughed, emitting the first sounds we had heard from her all day (even her tears at dinner had rolled down her cheeks in silence), but several minutes before we came to the restaurant scene, the spot in the film where Charlie breaks into his memorable nonsense song, her eyes had already closed and she had drifted off to sleep. Who could blame her? She had arrived in New York only that morning, having traveled God knows how many hundreds of miles, which meant that for much if not all of the previous night she had been sitting on the bus. I carried her into the spare bedroom as Tom opened the already made-up sofa bed and pulled down the top sheet and blanket. No one sleeps more soundly than the young, especially the exhausted young. Even as I lowered her body onto the mattress and tucked her in, she didn't open her eyes once.

The next day began with a curious and troubling event. At seven o'clock, I walked in on the sleeping Lucy with a glass of orange juice, a plate of scrambled eggs, and two pieces of buttered toast. I put the food down on the floor and then reached out and gently shook her arm. 'Wake up, Lucy,' I said. 'It's time for breakfast.' After three or four seconds, she opened her eyes, and then, following a short spell of absolute bewilderment *(Where am I? Who is this strange man looking down at me?)*, she remembered who I was and smiled. 'How did you sleep?' I asked.

'Real good, Uncle Nat,' she answered, pronouncing the words with what sounded like a southern accent. 'Like a big old stone at the bottom of a well.'

Bang. There it was. Lucy had talked. Without prompting or encouragement, without pausing to consider what she was about to do, she had calmly opened her mouth and talked. Was the reign of silence officially over, I wondered, or had she simply forgotten about it in the stupor of emerging wakefulness?

'I'm glad,' I said, not wanting to jinx things by mentioning what had just happened.

'Are we still going to stinky Vermont today?' she asked.

Each new word, each new sentence added to my cautious feeling of hope.

'In about an hour,' I said. 'Look, Lucy, juice and toast and eggs.'

As I bent down and lifted the food off the floor, she broke into another one of her big smiles. 'Breakfast in bed,' she announced. 'Just like Queen Nefertiti.'

I thought we were out of the woods by then, but what did I know – what did I know about anything? I had the glass of juice in my right hand, and just as she was reaching out to take it from me, the sky fell on top of her. I have rarely witnessed a face change expression more rapidly than hers did at that moment. In a single flash, the bright smile turned into a look of piercing, devastating horror. She clamped her hand over her mouth, and within seconds her eyes were brimming with tears.

'Don't worry, sweetheart,' I said. 'You haven't done anything wrong.'

But she had. According to her lights she had, and from the look on that tormented little face of hers, it was as if she had committed an unpardonable sin. In a sudden blast of anger at herself, she started banging the side of her head with the heel of her left hand, a wild pantomime display that seemed to express how stupid she thought she was. She did it three times, four times, five times, but just as I was about to grab her arm and make her stop, she thrust out her left hand and held up one finger, emphatically jabbing it toward my face. She was in a fury. Eyes burning with disgust and self-loathing, she began slapping her left hand with her right, as if rebuking the hand for having had the gall to hold up that one finger. Then the slapping stopped, and she thrust out her left hand again. This time she was holding up two fingers. As before, she jabbed the air with bitter emphasis. First one finger, then two fingers. What was she trying to tell me? I couldn't be sure, but I suspected it had something to do with time, with the number of days that were left before she would allow herself to speak again. She had been down to one day when she woke up that morning, but now that some words had accidentally slipped out of her, she had to punish herself by adding another day to her silence. One, therefore, had become two.

'Is that it?' I asked. 'Are you telling me you'll start talking again in two days?'

No response. I asked again, but Lucy wasn't about to divulge her secret. No nod of the head, no shake of the head, no nothing. I sat down beside her and started stroking her hair.

'Here, Lucy,' I said, handing her the glass of orange juice. 'Time to eat your breakfast.'

Riding North

The car was a relic from my old life. I had no use for the thing in New York, but I had been too lazy to bother selling it, and so it sat in a parking garage on Union Street between Sixth and Seventh Avenues, never once driven or looked at since my move to Brooklyn. A 1994 lime-green Oldsmobile Cutlass, a shockingly ugly piece of hardware. But the car did what it was supposed to do, and after two long months of idleness, the engine kicked over with the first turn of the key.

Tom was the pilot; I rode shotgun; Lucy sat in back. In spite of the promises I'd made to her the night before, she still wanted nothing to do with Pamela and Vermont, and she resented the fact that we were taking her there against her will. Logically speaking, she had a point. If the ultimate decision was in her hands, what was the purpose of driving over three hundred miles to get her there when the only result would be to drive another three hundred miles to bring her back? I had told her she had to give the Pamela experiment a legitimate chance. She had pretended to agree, but I knew her mind was already made up and nothing was going to change it. So she sat in the backseat of the car, looking sullen and withdrawn, a pouting, innocent victim of our cruel machinations. She fell asleep as we were passing the outskirts of Bridgeport on I-95, but until then she did little else but stare out the window, no doubt thinking evil thoughts about her two wicked uncles. As later events would prove, I was wrong about that. Lucy was far more resourceful than I had imagined, and rather than sit there fuming with anger, she was planning and thinking, using her considerable intelligence to hatch a plot that would turn the tables on us and put her in control of her own destiny. It was a brilliant scheme, if I do say so myself, a true rascal's scheme, and one can only tip one's hat to ingenuity taken to such an exalted level. But more about that anon.

While Lucy cogitated and napped in the rear, Tom and I talked in the front. He hadn't been behind the wheel of a car since quitting his taxi job in January, and the mere fact that he was driving again seemed to work like a tonic on his system. I had been with him nearly every day for the past two weeks, and not once had I seen him lighter or happier than he was that morning in early June. After he'd negotiated us through the city traffic, we hit the first of several highways that would take us north, and it was out there on those open roads that he began to relax, to slough off the burden of his miseries and temporarily stop hating the world. A relaxed Tom was a talkative Tom. That was rule of thumb for the ex-Dr. Thumb, and from approximately eight-thirty in the morning until well past noon, he showered me with a torrent of words – a veritable flood of stories, jokes, and lectures on matters both pertinent and arcane.

It started with a comment about *The Book of Human Folly*, my diminutive, half-assed work in progress. He wanted to know how it was coming along, and when I told him I was charging ahead with no end in sight, that each story I wrote seemed to give birth to another story and then another story and then another story, he clapped me on the shoulder with his right hand and pronounced this astonishing verdict: 'You're a writer, Nathan. You're becoming a real writer.'

'No, I'm not,' I said. 'I'm just a retired life insurance salesman who has nothing better to do with himself. It helps pass the time, that's all.'

'You're wrong, Nathan. After years of wandering in the desert, you've finally found your true calling. Now that you don't have to work for money anymore, you're doing the work you were meant to do all along.'

'Ridiculous. No one becomes a writer at sixty.'

The former graduate student and literary scholar cleared his throat and begged to differ with me. There were no rules when it came to writing, he said. Take a close look at the lives of poets and novelists, and what you wound up with was unalloyed chaos, an infinite jumble of exceptions. That was because writing was a disease, Tom continued, what you might call an infection or influenza of the spirit, and therefore it could strike anyone at any time. The young and the old, the strong and the weak, the drunk and the sober, the sane and the insane. Scan the roster of the giants and semi-giants, and you would discover writers who embraced every sexual proclivity, every political bent, and every human attribute – from the loftiest idealism to the most insidious corruption. They were criminals and lawyers, spies and doctors, soldiers and spinsters, travelers and shut-ins. If no one could be excluded, what prevented an almost sixty-year-old ex-life insurance agent from joining their ranks? What law declared that Nathan Glass had not been infected by the disease?

I shrugged.

'Joyce wrote three novels,' Tom said. 'Balzac wrote ninety. Does it make a difference to us now?'

'Not to me,' I said.

'Kafka wrote his first story in one night. Stendhal wrote *The Charterhouse of Parma* in forty-nine days. Melville wrote *Moby-Dick* in sixteen months. Flaubert spent five years on *Madame Bovary*. Musil worked for eighteen years on *The Man Without Qualities* and died before he could finish. Do we care about any of that now?'

The question didn't seem to call for a response.

'Milton was blind. Cervantes had one arm. Christopher Marlowe was stabbed to death in a barroom brawl before he was thirty. Apparently, the knife went straight through his eye. What are we supposed to think of that?'

'I don't know, Tom. You tell me.'

'Nothing. A big fat nothing.'

'I tend to agree with you.'

'Thomas Wentworth Higginson "corrected" Emily Dickinson's poems. A puffed-up ignoramus who called *Leaves of Grass* an immoral book dared to touch the work of the divine Emily. And poor Poe, who died crazy and drunk in a Baltimore gutter, had the misfortune to select Rufus Griswold as his literary executor. Little knowing that Griswold despised him, that this so-called friend and supporter would spend years trying to destroy his reputation.'

'Poor Poe.'

'Eddie had no luck. Not while he lived, and not even after he died. They buried him in a Baltimore cemetery in 1849, but it took twenty-six years before a stone was erected over his grave. A relative commissioned one immediately after his death, but the job ended in one of those black-humor fuck-ups that leave you wondering who's in charge of the world. Talk about human folly, Nathan. The marble yard happened to be situated directly below a section of elevated railroad tracks. Just as the carving of the stone was about to be finished, there was a derailment. The train toppled into the yard and crushed the stone, and because the relative didn't have enough money to order another one, Poe spent the next quarter century lying in an unmarked grave.'

'How do you know all this stuff, Tom?'

'Common knowledge.'

'Not to me it isn't.'

'You never went to graduate school. While you were out there making the world safe for democracy, I was sitting in a library carrel, cramming my head full of useless information.'

'Who finally paid for the stone?'

'A bunch of local teachers formed a committee to raise the funds. It took them ten years, if you can believe it. When the monument was finished, Poe's remains were exhumed, carted across town, and reburied in a Baltimore churchyard. On the morning of the unveiling, there was a special ceremony held at something called the Western Female High School. A terrific name, don't you think? *The Western Female High School.* Every important American poet was invited, but Whittier, Longfellow, and Oliver Wendell Holmes all found excuses not to come. Only Walt Whitman bothered to make the trip. Since his work is worth more than all the others' put together, I look at it as an act of sublime poetic justice. Interestingly enough, Stéphane Mallarmé was also there that morning. Not in the flesh – but his famous sonnet, 'Le Tombeau d'Edgar Poe,' was written for the occasion, and even if he didn't manage to finish it in time for the ceremony, he was nevertheless there in spirit. I love that, Nathan. Whitman and Mallarmé, the twin fathers of modern poetry, standing together in the Western Female High School to honor their mutual forebear, the disgraced and disreputable Edgar Allan Poe, the first true writer America gave to the world.'

Yes, Tom was in excellent form that day. Somewhat manic, I suppose, but there was no question that his rambling, erudite chatter helped cut the tedium of the drive. He would jog along in one direction for a while, come to a fork in the road, and then veer off sharply in another direction, never pausing to decide if left was better than right or vice versa. All roads led to Rome, so to speak, and since Rome was nothing less than all of literature (about which he seemed to know everything), it didn't matter which decision he made. From Poe, he suddenly bounced forward to Kafka. The link was the age of the two men at the time of their deaths: Poe at forty years and nine months, Kafka forty years and eleven months. It was the kind of obscure fact that only Tom would have remembered or cared about, but having spent half my life studying actuarial tables and thinking about the death rates of men in various professions, I found it rather interesting myself.

'Too young,' I said. 'If they'd been around today, there's a good chance that drugs and antibiotics would have saved them. Look at me. If I'd had my cancer thirty or forty years ago, I probably wouldn't be sitting in this car now.'

'Yes,' Tom said. 'Forty is too young. But think of how many writers didn't even make it that far.'

'Christopher Marlowe.'

'Dead at twenty-nine. Keats at twenty-five. Georg Büchner at twenty-three. Imagine. The greatest German playwright of the nineteenth century, dead at twenty-three. Lord Byron at thirty-six. Emily Brontë at thirty. Charlotte Brontë at thirty-nine. Shelley, just one month before he would have turned thirty. Sir Philip Sidney at thirty-one. Nathanael West at thirty-seven. Wilfred Owen at twenty-five. Georg Trakl at twenty-seven. Leopardi, Garcia Lorca, and Apollinaire all at thirty-eight. Pascal at thirty-nine. Flannery O'Connor at thirty-nine. Rimbaud at thirty-seven. The two Cranes, Stephen and Hart, at twenty-eight and thirty-two. And Heinrich von Kleist – Kafka's favorite writer – dead at thirty-four in a double suicide with his lover.'

'And Kafka is your favorite writer.'

'I think so. From the twentieth century, anyway.'

'Why didn't you do your dissertation on him?'

'Because I was stupid. And because I was supposed to be an Americanist.'

'He wrote *Amerika*, didn't he?'

'Ha ha. Good point. Why didn't I think of that?'

'I remember his description of the Statue of Liberty. Instead of a torch, the old girl is holding an upraised sword in her hand. An incredible image. It makes you laugh, but at the same time it scares the shit out of you. Like something from a bad dream.'

'So you've read Kafka.'

'Some. The novels and maybe a dozen stories. A long time ago now, back when I was your age. But the thing about Kafka is that he stays with you. Once you've dipped into his work, you don't forget it.'

'Have you looked at the diaries and letters? Have you read any biographies?'

'You know me, Tom. I'm not a very serious person.'

'A pity. The more you learn about his life, the more interesting his work becomes. Kafka wasn't just a great writer, you see, he was a remarkable man as well. Did you ever hear the story about the doll?'

'Not that I can remember.'

'Ah. Then listen carefully. I offer it to you as the first piece of evidence in support of my case.'

'I'm not sure I follow.'

'It's very simple. The object is to prove that Kafka was indeed an extraordinary person. Why begin with this particular story? I don't know. But ever since Lucy turned up yesterday morning, I haven't been able to get it out of my head. There must be a connection somewhere. I still haven't figured out exactly how, but I think there's a message in it for us, some kind of warning about how we're supposed to act.'

'Too much preamble, Tom. Just get down to it and tell the story.'

'I'm blathering again, aren't I? All this sunshine, all these cars, all this rushing along at sixty and seventy miles an hour. My brain's exploding, Nathan. I feel pumped up, ready for anything.'

'Good. Now tell me the story.'

'All right. The story. The story of the doll . . . It's the last year of Kafka's life, and he's fallen in love with Dora Diamant, a young girl of nineteen or twenty who ran away from her Hasidic family in Poland and now lives in Berlin. She's half his age, but she's the one who gives him the courage to leave Prague – something he's been wanting to do for years – and she becomes the first and only woman he lives with. He gets to Berlin in the fall of 1923 and dies the following spring, but those last months are probably the happiest months of his life. In spite of his deteriorating health. In spite of the social conditions in Berlin: food shortages, political riots, the worst inflation in German history. In spite of the certain knowledge that he is not long for this world.

'Every afternoon, Kafka goes out for a walk in the park. More often than not, Dora goes with him. One day, they run into a little girl in tears, sobbing her heart out. Kafka asks her what's wrong, and she tells him that she's lost her doll. He immediately starts inventing a story to explain what happened. "Your doll has gone off on a trip," he says. "How do you know that?" the girl asks. "Because she's written me a letter," Kafka says. The girl seems suspicious. "Do you have it on you?" she asks. "No, I'm sorry,' he says, 'I left it at home by mistake, but I'll bring it with me tomorrow." He's so convincing, the girl doesn't know what to think anymore. Can it be possible that this mysterious man is telling the truth?

'Kafka goes straight home to write the letter. He sits down at his desk, and as Dora watches him write, she notices the same seriousness and tension he displays when composing his own work. He isn't about to cheat the little girl. This is a real literary labor, and he's determined to get it right. If he can come up with a beautiful and persuasive lie, it will supplant the girl's loss with a different reality – a false one, maybe,

633

but something true and believable according to the laws of fiction.

'The next day, Kafka rushes back to the park with the letter. The little girl is waiting for him, and since she hasn't learned how to read yet, he reads the letter out loud to her. The doll is very sorry, but she's grown tired of living with the same people all the time. She needs to get out and see the world, to make new friends. It's not that she doesn't love the little girl, but she longs for a change of scenery, and therefore they must separate for a while. The doll then promises to write the girl every day and keep her abreast of her activities.

'That's where the story begins to break my heart. It's astonishing enough that Kafka took the trouble to write that first letter, but now he commits himself to the project of writing a new letter every day – for no other reason than to console the little girl, who happens to be a complete stranger to him, a child he ran into by accident one afternoon in a park. What kind of man does a thing like that? He kept it up for three weeks, Nathan. *Three weeks.* One of the most brilliant writers who ever lived sacrificing his time – his ever more precious and dwindling time – to composing imaginary letters from a lost doll. Dora says that he wrote every sentence with excruciating attention to detail, that the prose was precise, funny, and absorbing. In other words, it was Kafka's prose, and every day for three weeks he went to the park and read another letter to the girl. The doll grows up, goes to school, gets to know other people. She continues to assure the girl of her love, but she hints at certain complications in her life that make it impossible for her to return home. Little by little, Kafka is preparing the girl for the moment when the doll will vanish from her life forever. He struggles to come up with a satisfactory ending, worried that if he doesn't succeed, the magic spell will be broken. After testing out several possibilities, he finally decides to marry off the doll. He describes the young man she falls in love with, the engagement party, the wedding in the country, even the house where the doll and her husband now live. And then, in the last line, the doll bids farewell to her old and beloved friend.

'By that point, of course, the girl no longer misses the doll. Kafka has given her something else instead, and by the time those three weeks are up, the letters have cured her of her unhappiness. She has the story, and when a person is lucky enough to live inside a story, to live inside an imaginary world, the pains of this world disappear. For as long as the story goes on, reality no longer exists.'

Our Girl, or *Coke Is It*

There are two ways to travel from New York City to Burlington, Vermont: the fast way and the slow way. For the first two-thirds of the trip, we chose the fast way, a trajectory that included such urban roads as Flatbush Avenue, the BQE, Grand Central Parkway, and Route 678. After we crossed the Whitestone Bridge into the Bronx, we continued north for several miles until we came to I-95, which led us out of the city, through the eastern part of Westchester County, and on through lower Connecticut. At New Haven, we turned off onto I-91. That was where we spent the bulk of the journey, traversing what remained of Connecticut and all of Massachusetts until we reached the southern border of Vermont. The quickest route to Burlington would have been to stay on I-91 until White River Junction and then turn west onto I-89, but once we found ourselves on the outskirts of Brattleboro, Tom declared that he was sick of superhighways and preferred switching over to smaller, emptier back-country roads. And so it was that we abandoned the fast way for the slow way. It would add another hour or two to the trip, he said, but at least we would have a chance to see something other than a procession of fast-moving, lifeless cars. Woods, for example, and wildflowers along the edge of the road, not to mention cows and horses, farms and meadows, village greens and an occasional human face. I had no objection to this change of plans. What did I care whether we made it to Pamela's house at three o'clock or five o'clock? Now that Lucy had opened her eyes again and was staring out the side window in back, I felt so guilty about what we were doing to her that I wanted to put off getting there as long as we could. I opened our Rand McNally road atlas and studied the map of Vermont. 'Get off at Exit Three,' I said to Tom. 'We're looking for Route Thirty, which squiggles up diagonally to the northwest. After about forty miles, we'll start bobbing and weaving until we get to Rutland, find Route Seven, and take that straight to Burlington.'

Why do I linger over these trivial details? Because the truth of the story lies in the details, and I have no choice but to tell the story exactly as it happened. If we hadn't made that decision to get off the highway at

Brattleboro and follow our noses to Route 30, many of the events in this book never would have taken place. I am thinking especially of Tom when I say that. Both Lucy and I profited from the decision as well, but for Tom, the long-suffering hero of these Brooklyn Follies, it was probably the most important decision of his life. At the time, he had no inkling of the consequences, no knowledge of the whirlwind he had set in motion. Like Kafka's doll, he thought he was simply looking for a change of scenery, but because he left one road and took another, Fortune unexpectedly reached out her arms to him and carried our boy into a different world.

The gas tank was nearly empty; our stomachs were nearly empty; our bladders were full. About fifteen or twenty miles northwest of Brattleboro, we stopped for lunch at a crummy roadside restaurant called Dot's. FOOD AND GAS, as the highway signs aptly put it, and that was the order in which we chose to fulfill our needs. Food and gas at Dot's, and then more gas at the Chevron station across the road. Here, too, our casual decision to do things one way and not another turned out to have a significant effect on the story. If we had filled up the gas tank first, Lucy never would have been able to pull off her electrifying stunt, and no doubt we would have continued all the way to Burlington as planned. But because the tank was still empty when we sat down to eat, the opportunity was suddenly there, and the little one didn't hesitate. It felt like a catastrophe at the time, but if our girl hadn't done what she did, our boy never would have fallen into the nurturing arms of Dame Fortune, and leaving or not leaving the highway would have been a moot point.

Even now, I can't quite comprehend how she did it. Certain contingencies worked in her favor, but even taking into account those stray bits of luck, there was something almost demonic about the daring and efficiency of her sabotage. Yes, the restaurant was set back from the road by about a hundred feet, which protected her from the eyes of passing motorists. Yes, all the parking places directly in front of the restaurant were full, which meant that we left our car off to the side, out of range of the two picture windows built into the façade of the sagging one-story building. And yes, there was the double bonus that Tom and I happened to sit down with our backs to those windows. But how in the world could she have thought quickly enough to translate the presence of an outdoor Coke machine (fortuitously positioned within ten feet of our parked car) into a weapon in her fight against the Burlington

636

Solution? The three of us entered the restaurant together, and the first thing we did was head straight for the toilets. Then we sat down at a table and ordered our hamburgers and tuna salads and grilled cheese sandwiches. The moment the waitress was finished with us, Lucy made it known by pointing to her lap that she had more business to attend to in the bathroom. No problem, I said, and off she went, looking like any other American girl in her paisley shorts and hundred-and-fifty-dollar neon-blue sneakers. While she was gone, Tom and I talked about how pleasant it was to be out of the city, even sitting in a dark and mangy joint like Dot's, surrounded by truckers and farmers in yellow and red baseball caps emblazoned with logos from companies that manufactured work tools and heavy machinery. Tom was still going at full verbal tilt, and I got so caught up in what he was saying that I lost track of Lucy. Little did we know at the time (the facts didn't come out until later) that our girl had left the restaurant through a rear door and was frantically feeding coins and dollar bills into the Coke machine outside. She bought at least twenty cans of that gooey, sugar-laden concoction, and one by one she poured the entire contents of each can into the gas tank of my once healthy Oldsmobile Cutlass. How could she have known that sugar was a deadly poison to internal combustion engines? How could the brat have been so damn clever? Not only did she bring our journey to an abrupt and conclusive halt, but she managed to do it in record time. Five minutes would be my guess, seven at the most. However long it was, we were still waiting for our food when she returned to the table. She was suddenly full of smiles again, but how could I have guessed the cause of her happiness? If I had bothered to think about it at all, I would have assumed it was because she had taken a good shit.

When the meal was over and we climbed back into the car, the engine coughed forth one of the most peculiar noises in automotive history. I have sat here thinking about that noise for the past twenty minutes, but I still haven't found the correct words to describe it, the one unforgettable phrase that would do it justice. *Raucous chortling? Hiccupping pizzicati? A pandemonium of guffaws?* I'm probably not up to the task – or else language is too feeble an instrument to capture what I heard, which resembled something that might have come from the mouth of a choking goose or a drunken chimpanzee. Eventually, the guffaws modulated into a single, drawn-out note, a loud, tuba-like eructation that could have passed for a human burp. Not exactly the belch of a satisfied beer drinker, but a sound that recalled the slow, agonizing rumble of indigestion, a basso discharge of air seeping from the throat of a man afflicted with terminal heartburn. Tom cut the engine and tried again, but the second turn of the key produced no more than a faint groan. The third resulted in silence. The symphony had come to an end, and my poisoned Olds was in cardiac arrest.

'I think we're out of gas,' Tom said.

It was the only sensible conclusion to be drawn, but when I leaned to my left and looked at the fuel gauge, it showed that the tank was about one-eighth full. I pointed my finger at the red needle. 'Not according to this,' I said.

Tom shrugged. 'It must be broken. Lucky for us there's a gas station across the road.'

As Tom presented his flawed diagnosis of the car's condition, I turned around to glance at said gas station through the rear window – a tumbledown, two-pump garage that looked as if it hadn't had a paint job since 1954. In doing so, my eyes came into contact with Lucy's. She was sitting directly behind Tom, and because I had no idea that she was responsible for the mess we found ourselves in, I was somewhat puzzled by the serene, almost supernatural contentment I saw on her face. The engine had just poured out its cacophonous jungle medley, and under normal circumstances you would think those laughable sounds would have gotten a rise out of her: alarm, amusement, agitation, something. But Lucy had withdrawn deep into herself – floating weightlessly on a cloud of indifference, a pure spirit detached from her own body. I understand now that she was rejoicing over the success of her mission, giving silent thanks to the all-powerful one for helping her accomplish a miracle. Sitting with her in the car that afternoon, however, I was merely perplexed.

'Are you still with us, Lucy?' I asked.

She gave me a long, impassive stare, and then she nodded her head.

'Don't be upset,' I continued. 'We'll have the car running again in no time.'

Needless to say, I was wrong. It would be tempting to give a blow-by-blow account of the comedy that ensued, but I don't want to try the reader's patience by discussing matters that are not, strictly speaking, relevant to the story. In the case of the car, the upshot is all that counts. I will therefore dispense with the jerrican of high-octane gas that Tom lugged back from the garage across the road (since it didn't help) and omit any references to the tow truck that eventually hauled the Cutlass over to that same garage (what other choice did we have?). The only fact that bears mentioning is that neither one of the fellows who ran the garage (a father-and-son team known as Al Senior and Al Junior) could figure out what was wrong with the car. Junior and Senior were roughly the same ages as Tom and myself respectively, but whereas I was thin and Tom was stout, the bodies of the young Al and the old Al resembled ours in reverse: the son was lean, the father was fat.

After examining the engine for several minutes and finding nothing, Al Junior slammed the hood shut. 'I'm going to have to take this baby apart,' he said.

'It's that bad, huh?' I replied.

'I'm not saying it's bad. But it's not too good either. No sir, not too good at all.'

'How long will it take to fix it?'

'That depends. Maybe a day, maybe a week. First thing, I got to locate the problem. If it's something simple, no sweat. If it's not, we might have to order you some new parts from the dealer, and that could drag on for a while.'

It sounded like a fair and honest assessment, and given that I was thoroughly ignorant on the subject of cars, I didn't see what else I could do but offer him the job – no matter how long it took. Tom, who was no mechanic either, seconded that course of action. All well and good, perhaps, but now that we were stranded on a back road in rural Vermont, what were we going to do with ourselves while the two Als worked on resuscitating our ailing machine? One option was to rent a car and push on to Burlington, then spend the rest of the week with Pamela and pick up the Oldsmobile on our way back to New York. Or, more simply, rent rooms at a local inn and pretend that we were on vacation until the car was ready.

'I've had enough driving for today,' Tom said. 'I vote for staying put. At least until tomorrow.'

I was inclined to agree with him. As for Lucy – the wordless, ever-watchful Lucy – one can well imagine how little she protested our decision.

Al Senior recommended a couple of spots in Newfane, a village we had driven through about ten miles back. I went into the office and called both numbers, but it turned out that neither inn had any rooms available. When I reported what had happened, the big man looked

639

miffed. 'Cruddy tourists,' he said. 'It's only the first week of June, and summer's already in full swing.'

For the next half minute or so, we all stood around with our hands in our pockets, watching father and son think. At long last, Al Junior broke the silence. 'What about Stanley, Dad?'

'Hmmm,' his father said. 'I don't know. What makes you think he's back in business?'

'I heard he's planning to open up this year,' the young man answered. 'That's what Mary Ellen told me. She bumped into Stanley at the post office last week.'

'Who's Stanley?' I asked.

'Stanley Chowder,' Al Senior said, lifting his arm and pointing west. 'He used to have an inn about three miles up that hill there.'

'Stanley Chowder,' I repeated. 'That's one hell of a funny name.'

'Yeah,' big Al said. 'But Stanley doesn't care. I think he kind of likes it.'

'I once knew a man named Elmer Doodlebaum,' I said, suddenly realizing that I enjoyed talking to the two Als. 'How'd you like to be saddled with that moniker all your life?'

Al Senior grinned. 'Not much, mister. Not much at all. But at least people would remember it. I've been Al Wilson since the day I was born, which is maybe half a step up from being called John Doe. There's nothing to sink your teeth into with a name like that. Al Wilson. There must be a thousand Al Wilsons in Vermont alone.'

'I think I'll give Stanley a try,' Al Junior said. 'You never can tell. If he isn't outside mowing that lawn of his, maybe he'll pick up . . .'

As the slender son went into the office to make the call, his plump father leaned back against my car, pulled a cigarette from his shirt pocket (which he put in his mouth but didn't light), and then told us the sad story of the Chowder Inn.

'That's what Stanley does now,' he said. 'He mows his lawn. From early in the morning until late in the afternoon, he rides around on his red John Deere and mows his lawn. It starts when the snow melts in April, and it doesn't stop until the snow starts falling again in November. Every day, rain or shine, he's out there riding around his property, mowing the lawn for hours on end. When winter comes, he stays inside and watches television. And when he can't stand watching television anymore, he gets into his car and drives down to Atlantic City. He checks into one of the casino hotels and plays blackjack for ten straight days. Sometimes he wins, sometimes he loses, but Stanley doesn't care. He has enough money to live on, and if he squanders a few bucks every now and then, so what?

'I've known him a long time – more than thirty years now, I think. He used to be a C.P.A. down in Springfield, Mass. Back around sixty-eight or sixty-nine, he and his wife Peg bought that big white house up on the hill, and after that they'd come for the weekends, for summer vacations, for the Christmas holidays, whenever they could. Their big dream was to turn the place into an inn and live there full-time after Stanley retired. So four years ago, Stanley quits his job as a C.P.A., he and Peg sell their house in Springfield, and they move up here to open the Chowder Inn. I'll never forget how hard they worked that first spring, rushing to get things ready for the Memorial Day weekend. Everything goes as planned. They pretty up the place until it sparkles like a jewel. They hire a chef and two housemaids, and then, just when they're about to book their first reservations, Peg has a stroke and dies. Right there in the kitchen in the middle of the day. One minute she's alive, talking to Stanley and the chef, and the next minute she's crumpled up on the floor, breathing her last. It happened so quick, she died before the ambulance ever left the hospital.

'That's why Stanley mows his lawn. Some people think he's gone a little crazy, but whenever I talk to him, he's the same old Stanley I met thirty years ago, the same guy he's always been. He's grieving for his Peg, that's all. Some men take to drink. Some men look for a new wife. Stanley mows his lawn. There's no harm in that, is there?

'I haven't seen him in a while, but if Mary Ellen got the story right – and I've never known her not to – then that's good news. It means that Stanley's getting better, that he wants to start living again. Al Junior's been gone for a couple of minutes now. I could be wrong, but I'll bet Stanley picked up the phone, and they're working out the arrangements for getting you three up the hill. That would be something, wouldn't it? If Stanley's open for business, you'll be the first paying customers in the history of the Chowder Inn. My oh my. That would really be something, wouldn't it?'

Dream Days at the Hotel Existence

I want to talk about happiness and well being, about those rare, unexpected moments when the voice in your head goes silent and you feel at one with the world.

I want to talk about the early June weather, about harmony and blissful repose, about robins and yellow finches and bluebirds darting past the green leaves of trees.

I want to talk about the benefits of sleep, about the pleasures of food and alcohol, about what happens to your mind when you step into the light of the two o'clock sun and feel the warm embrace of air around your body.

I want to talk about Tom and Lucy, about Stanley Chowder and the four days we spent at the Chowder Inn, about the thoughts we thought and the dreams we dreamed on that hilltop in southern Vermont.

I want to remember the cerulean dusks, the languorous, rosy dawns, the bears yelping in the woods at night.

I want to remember it all. If all is too much to ask, then some of it. No, more than some of it. Almost all. Almost all, with blanks reserved for the missing parts.

The taciturn yet convivial Stanley Chowder, practiced mower of lawns, astute poker player and Ping-Pong dervish, aficionado of old American movies, Korean War veteran, father of a thirty-two-year-old daughter with the unlikely name of Honey – a fourth-grade public school teacher who lives in Brattleboro. Stanley is sixty-seven but fit for his age, with a full head of hair and clear blue eyes. Five-eightish, stockily built, a firm grip when he shakes my hand.

He drives down the hill to pick us up. After greeting Al Junior and Al Senior, he introduces himself to us and then pitches in as we transfer our bags from the trunk of my car to the back of his Volvo station wagon. I notice that he moves quickly, almost rushing as he walks between the two vehicles. There is a nimble, nervous proficiency to his gestures. Stanley is no dawdler. Idleness breeds thought, and thoughts can be dangerous, as anyone who lives alone will readily understand.

After listening to Al Senior's account of Peg's demise, I see Stanley as a lost and tormented figure. Accommodating, generous to a fault, but uncomfortable in his own skin, a shattered man struggling to pick up the pieces.

We say good-bye to the Wilsons and thank them for their help. Al Junior promises to give me daily progress reports on the state of my car.

A steep dirt road flanked by woods on both sides; bumpy terrain; an occasional low-hanging branch sweeps across the windshield as we climb toward the top of the hill. Stanley apologizes in advance for any problems we might encounter at the inn. He's been working alone for the past two weeks trying to get it into shape, but there's still much to be done. He was planning to open for the Fourth of July, but after Al Junior called and told him about our predicament, he 'wouldn't have felt right' about not putting us up for a few days. No staff has been hired yet, but he will make the beds and see to it that we're as comfortable as circumstances allow. He has already talked to his daughter in Brattleboro, and she has agreed to come to the inn every day and cook dinner for us. He assures us that she cooks well. Tom and I thank him for his kindness. Preoccupied with these multiple concerns, Stanley fails to notice that Lucy has yet to speak.

A three-story white house with sixteen rooms and a wraparound front porch. The sign at the edge of the driveway says *The Chowder Inn*, but a part of me already understands that we have come to the Hotel Existence. For the moment, I decide not to share this thought with Tom.

Before we are shown to our rooms, Tom calls Pamela from the ground-floor parlor to explain what happened to us. Stanley is upstairs making the beds. Lucy wanders off toward the sofa, and a moment later she is down on her knees petting Stanley's dog, an aging black Lab named Spot. Without wanting to, I think of Harry and the inane words that have been stuck in my head for the past two weeks: *X marks the spot*. The spot has now been turned into a four-legged animal, and as I watch the dog lick Lucy's face, I stand close to Tom on the off chance I'll be called upon to say a few words to Pamela. I'm not, but as I listen to Tom's end of the conversation, I'm surprised by his stepsister's irritable response to the news that our arrival in Burlington will be delayed. As if the trouble with the car were our fault. As if unforeseen events didn't occur all the time. But Pamela has just spent an hour and a half at the supermarket and is now in the kitchen 'working her head off' to get dinner ready for us before we show up. As a sign of hospitality and welcome, she's planned an elaborate, multicourse meal that includes everything from gazpacho to a home-baked pecan pie, and she's put out, nay furious, when she learns that all her efforts have been in vain. Tom offers a dozen apologies, but Pamela nevertheless continues to scold him. Is this the new and improved Pamela I've heard so much about? If she can't take a small disappointment in her stride, what kind of a stand-in mother will she be for Lucy? The last thing the girl needs is a neurotic bourgeois woman bearing down on her with impatient and impossible demands.

Even before Tom hangs up the phone, I decide that the Burlington Solution is dead. I cross Pamela's name off the list and appoint myself as Lucy's temporary guardian. Am I better qualified to take care of Lucy than Pamela is? No, in most ways probably not, but my gut tells me that I'm responsible for her – whether I like it or not.

Tom hangs up the phone and shakes his head. 'That's one pissed-off lady,' he says.

'Forget Pamela,' I answer.

'What do you mean?'

'I mean we're not going to Burlington.'

'Oh? Since when?'

'Since now. We'll stay here until the car is fixed, and then we'll all go back to Brooklyn together.'

'And what are you planning to do with Lucy?'

'She'll live with me in my apartment.'

'When we talked about it yesterday, you said you weren't interested.'

'I've changed my mind.'

'So we've driven all the way up here for nothing.'

'Not really. Look around you, Tom. We've landed in paradise. A couple of days of rest and relaxation, and we'll go home feeling like new men.'

Lucy is no more than ten feet from us as we exchange these words, and she hears every syllable we say. When I turn to look at her, she's blowing kisses to me with both hands – arms extended after each smack of her lips, like a triumphant leading lady on opening night. I'm happy to see her so happy, but I'm also scared. Do I have any idea what I'm getting myself into?

Suddenly, I remember a line from a film I saw back in the late seventies. The title eludes me, both the story and characters have passed into oblivion, but the words are still ringing in my head, as if I heard them only yesterday. 'Children are a consolation for everything – except having children.'

As Stanley shows us to our rooms on the top floor, he explains that Peg, the late Mrs. Chowder ('dead for four years now'), was responsible for choosing the furniture, the bed linens, the wallpaper, the Venetian blinds, the rugs, the lamps, the curtains, and every one of the many small objects that sit on top of the various tables, nightstands, and bureaus: the lace doilies, the ashtrays, the candlestick holders, the books. 'A woman of impeccable taste,' he says. To my mind, the décor is overly precious, a nostalgic attempt to re-create the atmosphere of a bygone New England that was in fact much grimmer and sparer than the soft, girlish rooms I am looking at now. But no matter. Everything is clean and comfortable, and there is one redeeming element that undercuts the otherwise pervasive tone of kitsch and fussiness: the pictures hanging on the walls. Contrary to what one might expect, there are no needlepoint samplers, no badly executed watercolors of snowy Vermont landscapes, no Currier and Ives reproductions. The walls are covered with eight-by-ten black-and-white photographs of old Hollywood comedy stars. This is Stanley's single contribution to the look of the rooms, but it makes all the difference, injecting a dose of wit and levity into the staid surroundings. Of the three rooms he has prepared for us, one is devoted to the Marx Brothers, another to Buster Keaton, and the last to Laurel and Hardy. Tom and I give Lucy first choice, and she opts for Stan and Ollie at the end of the hall. Tom selects Buster, and I wind up between them with Groucho, Harpo, Chico, Zeppo, and Margaret Dumont.

First perusal of the grounds. Immediately after unpacking our bags, we go outside to visit Stanley's famous lawn. For several minutes, I am prey to a steady flow of shifting sensations. The feel of the soft, well-tended grass underfoot. The sound of a horsefly buzzing past my ear. The smell of the grass. The smells of the honeysuckle and lilac bushes. The bright red tulips planted around the edge of the house. The air begins to vibrate, and a moment later a small breeze is wafting over my face.

I drift along with my three companions and the dog, musing about absurd things. Stanley informs us that the property extends over a hundred acres, and I imagine how simple it would be to construct more buildings if the population of the Hotel Existence outgrows the capacity of the main house. I am dreaming Tom's dream and reveling in the possibilities. Sixty acres of woods. A pond. A neglected apple orchard, a collection of abandoned beehives, a shack in the woods for distilling maple syrup. And the grass of Stanley's lawn – the lovely, unending grass, stretching all around us and beyond.

It will never happen, I tell myself. Harry's scheme is bound to fail, and even if it doesn't, why should I presume Stanley would be willing to sell his house? On the other hand, what if Stanley stays with us and becomes a partner in the enterprise? Is he the sort of man who would grasp what Tom is hoping to achieve? I decide that I have to get to know him better, that I must spend as much time in his company as I can.

After twenty minutes or so, we circle back in the direction of the house. Stanley dashes into the garage to fetch some lawn chairs for us, and once we're installed, he excuses himself and disappears into the house. He has work to do, but the first paying guests in the history of the Chowder Inn are free to loaf in the sunlight as long as they want.

For a couple of minutes, I watch Lucy run across the lawn, throwing sticks to the dog. To my left, Tom is reading a play by Don DeLillo. I look up at the sky and study the passing clouds. A hawk wheels into view and then vanishes. When the hawk returns, I close my eyes. Within seconds, I am fast asleep.

At five o'clock, Honey Chowder makes her first appearance, pulling up in front of the house with a carload of groceries and two cases of wine. By now, Tom and I have left the lawn chairs and are sitting on the porch, talking about politics. We interrupt our denunciations of Bush II and the Republican Party, walk down the steps to the white Honda, and introduce ourselves to Stanley's daughter.

She's a large, freckle-faced woman with beefy upper arms and a bone-crunching handshake. She brims with confidence, with humor, with good will. A bit overbearing, perhaps, but what can you expect from a fourth-grade schoolteacher? Her voice is loud and somewhat hoarse, but I like it that she seems so ready to laugh, is unafraid of the bigness of her personality. She's a competent, can-do girl, I decide, and no doubt good fun in bed. Not pretty, but not not-pretty either. Radiant blue eyes, full lips, a thick mane of reddish-blonde hair. As we help her unload the grocery bags from the trunk of the car, I see her eyeing Tom with something more than detached curiosity. The lunkhead notices nothing, but I begin to wonder if this bossy, brainy young woman isn't the answer to my prayers. No more ethereal B.P.M.s, but an unmarried woman desperate to hook a man. A steamroller. A tornado. A hungry, fast-talking wench who could flatten our boy into submission.

For the second time that afternoon, I decide to keep my thoughts to myself and say nothing to Tom.

As Stanley promised, she cooks us an excellent dinner. Watercress soup, a pork loin roast, string beans with almonds, crème caramel for dessert, and generous pourings of wine. I feel a twinge of sympathy for Pamela and the aborted feast she was preparing for us, but I doubt the fare in Burlington could surpass what bedecks the table at the Chowder Inn.

The victorious Lucy, now liberated from her impending bondage, shows up at the table wearing her red-and-white checkered dress, her black patent-leather shoes, and her white anklets with the lacy fringes on top. I don't know if Stanley is impervious to the behavior of others or just overly discreet, but he still hasn't commented on Lucy's silence. Ten minutes into the meal, however, his blunt, sharp-eyed daughter begins asking questions.

'What's wrong with her?' she says. 'Doesn't she know how to talk?'

'Of course she does,' I reply. 'She just doesn't want to.'

'Doesn't want to?' Honey says. 'What does that mean?'

'It's a test,' I explain, blurting out the first lie that pops into my head. 'Lucy and I were talking the other day about hard things, and we decided that not talking is about the hardest thing a person can do. So we made a pact. Lucy agreed not to say a word for three days. If she can hold up her end of the bargain, I've promised to give her fifty dollars. Isn't that right, Lucy?'

Lucy nods.

'And how many days are left?' I continue.

Lucy holds up two fingers.

Ah, I say to myself, there we have it. The kid has finally fessed up. In two more days, the torture will come to an end.

Honey squints her eyes, at once dubious and alarmed. Children are her business, after all, and she senses that something is off. But I'm a stranger to her, and rather than press me about the queer and unhealthy game I've been playing with this little girl, she comes at the problem from another angle.

'Why isn't the child in school?' she asks. 'It's Monday, June fifth. Summer vacation doesn't begin for another three weeks.'

'Because . . .' I say, scrambling to concoct another fib, 'Lucy goes to a private school . . . and the academic year is shorter there than at public schools. She had her last class on Friday.'

Again, I'm convinced that Honey doesn't believe me. But short of crossing the line into an unacceptable rudeness, she can't very well go on interrogating me about matters that don't concern her. I like this chunky, forthright Chowder of a woman, and I also like her old man, who is sitting across the table from me, quietly chewing his food and sipping his wine, but I have no intention of letting them in on our family secrets. It's not that I'm ashamed of who we are – but my God, I tell myself, what a family it is. What a motley bunch of messed-up, floundering souls. What stunning examples of human imperfection. A father whose daughter wants nothing to do with him anymore. A brother who hasn't seen or heard from his sister in three years. And a little girl who's run away from home and refuses to speak. No, I'm not about to expose the Chowders to the truth of our fractured, good-for-nothing little clan. Not tonight I'm not. Not tonight, and no doubt not ever.

Tom must be thinking thoughts similar to mine, for he hastily jumps in and tries to steer the table talk in another direction. He begins by asking Honey about her work. How long has she been doing it, what motivated her to become a teacher in the first place, what does she think of the Brattleboro system, and so on. His questions are bland, stultifying in their banality, and as I look at his face while he talks to Honey, I can tell that he has no interest in her – not as a woman, not even as a person. But Honey is too tough to allow Tom's indifference to prevent her from giving bright and charming answers, and before long she is the one guiding the conversation, bombarding our boy with dozens of questions of her own. Her aggressiveness rocks Tom back on his heels for a few moments, but when he understands that his interlocutor is fully as clever as he is, he rises to the occasion and starts giving as good as he gets. Stanley and I scarcely say a word, but we are both amused by the verbal sparring match that has broken out before our eyes. Inevitably, the talk veers to politics and the upcoming elections in November. Tom rails against the right-wing takeover of America. He cites the near destruction of Clinton, the anti-abortion movement, the gun lobby, the fascist propaganda of talk-radio shows, the cowardice of the press, the ban on the teaching of evolution in certain states. 'We're marching backward,' he says. 'Every day, we lose another piece of our country. If Bush is elected, there won't be anything left.' To my surprise, Honey is in total agreement with him. Peace reigns for approximately thirty seconds, and then she announces that she's planning to vote for Nader.

'Don't do that,' Tom says. 'A vote for Nader is a vote for Bush.'

'No, it's not,' Honey says. 'It's a vote for Nader. Besides, Gore will win Vermont. If I wasn't sure of that, I'd vote for him. This way I can make my little protest and still keep Bush out of office.'

'I don't know about Vermont,' Tom says, 'but I do know it's going to be a close election. If enough people think like you in the swing states, Bush will win.'

Honey struggles to suppress a smile. Tom is so damned earnest, she's itching to knock him from his high horse with some loopy, off-the-wall remark. I can see the joke coming, and I cross my fingers that it's a good one.

'Do you know what happened the last time a nation listened to a bush?' Honey asks.

No one says a word.

'Its people wandered in the desert for forty years.'

In spite of himself, Tom bursts out laughing.

The jousting contest has been brought to a sudden, decisive end, and Honey is the clear winner.

I don't want to get carried away, but I suspect that Tom has met his match. Whether anything comes of it is another story, to be told by time and the mysterious inclinations of the flesh. I tell myself to stay tuned for further developments.

Early the next morning, I call Al Junior at the gas station, but he still hasn't solved the riddle of the car. 'I'm working on it now,' he says. 'As soon as I have the answer, I'll be in touch.'

I marvel at how little this news affects me. If anything, I'm glad to be stuck on our hilltop for another day, glad not to have to think about returning to New York just yet.

I have a job to do that morning, but it's impossible to get Stanley to sit down long enough to engage him in a serious conversation. He cooks and serves us breakfast, but the moment he puts the plates in front of us, he rushes out of the kitchen and goes upstairs to make the beds. After that, he's busy with various projects around the house: screwing in lightbulbs, beating carpets, repairing broken window sashes. There's nothing to be done but look for an opportunity later in the day.

The morning air is cool and misty. We're wearing sweaters as we walk out onto the front porch and scan the wet, dew-drenched lawn. Eventually, the clouds will burn away and we'll be given another sparkling afternoon, but for now the shrubs and trees are barely visible.

Lucy has found a book in her room, and she carries it with her onto the porch. It's a small paperback, and since her hand is covering the title, I ask her to show me what it is. *Riders of the Purple Sage*, by Zane Grey. I ask her if it's any good, and she gives a vigorous nod of approval. Not just good, she seems to be telling me, but a masterpiece for all time. I find it a curious choice for a nine-year-old girl, but who am I to object? The kid likes to read, I say to myself, and I consider that a positive development, proof that our little runaway is no mental sluggard.

Tom plants himself in the chair next to mine as Lucy stretches out on the glider with her Western. He lights up an after-breakfast cigarette and says, 'Do you think Al Junior will ever fix the car?'

'Probably,' I answer. 'But I'm in no rush to get out of here. Are you?'

'No, not really. I'm beginning to like this place.'

'Do you remember our dinner with Harry last week?'

'When you spilled the red wine on your pants? How could I forget it?'

'I've been thinking about some of the things you said that night.'

'As I remember it, I said a lot of things. Most of them stupid things. Monumentally stupid things.'

'You were out of sorts. But you didn't say anything stupid.'

'You must have been too drunk to notice.'

'Drunk or not, there's one thing I have to know. Did you mean it about wanting to get out of the city – or was it just talk?'

'I meant it, but it was also just talk.'

'It can't be both. It has to be one or the other.'

'I meant it, but I also know it will never happen. Therefore, it was just talk.'

'And what about Harry's deal?'

'Just talk. You should know that about Harry by now. If anyone is "just talk," it's our old friend Harry Brightman.'

'I'm not going to disagree with you. But just for the sake of argument, imagine he was telling the truth. Imagine he's about to come into big money and would be willing to dump it into a country house. What would you say then?'

'I'd say, 'Let's go ahead and do it.''

'Good. Now think carefully. If you could buy any place in the world, where would you want it to be?'

'I haven't thought that far ahead. Somewhere isolated, though. A place where other people wouldn't be right on top of us.'

'Somewhere like the Chowder Inn?'

'Yeah. Now that you mention it, this spot would work just fine.'

'Why don't we ask Stanley if he's willing to sell?'

'What for? We don't have enough money to buy.'

'You're forgetting Harry.'

'No, I'm not. Harry has his good points, but he's the last man I'd count on for something like this.'

'I admit it's a million-to-one shot, but just in case Harry's horse comes in, why not talk to Stanley? Just for the fun of it. If he says he's interested, at least we'll know what the Hotel Existence looks like.'

'Even if we never live here.'

'Exactly. Even if we never come back for the rest of our days.'

It turns out that Stanley had been thinking about selling the place for years. Only inertia and apathy have stopped him from 'taking the bull by the horns,' he says, but if the price is right, he'd chuck the whole thing in a minute. He can't stand living with Peg's ghost anymore. He can't stand the brutal winters. He can't stand the isolation. He's had it with Vermont, and all he dreams about is moving to the tropics, to some Caribbean island where the weather is warm every day of the year.

Then why work so hard at whipping the Chowder Inn into shape? I ask. No reason, he says. He has nothing better to do, and it helps ward off the boredom.

It's lunchtime. The four of us are sitting around the dining room table, eating cold cuts, fruit, and cheese. Now that the fog has lifted, sunlight blasts through the open windows, and every object in the room seems more defined, more vivid, more saturated with color. Our host is pouring out the sorrows of his life to us, but I feel remarkably happy just to be where I am, sitting in my own body, looking at the things on the table, breathing air in and out of my lungs, relishing the simple fact that I am alive. What a pity that life ends, I tell myself, what a pity that we aren't allowed to go on living forever.

Tom explains that we don't have the money to make an offer on the house now, but we might be in a position to do so in the coming weeks.

Stanley says he doesn't know what the property is worth, but he can contact a local real estate agent and find out. The more we talk, the more enthusiastic he becomes. I don't know if he believes a word we say, but just being able to imagine a new life for himself seems to have turned him into a different man.

Why have I encouraged such nonsense? Everything hinges on the sale of a forged manuscript of *The Scarlet Letter*, and not only am I morally opposed to Harry's criminal scheme, I have no faith in it to begin with. More to the point: even if I did, I don't have any interest in moving to Vermont. I have only recently begun a new life of my own, and I'm perfectly content with the decision I made to settle in Brooklyn. After all those years in the suburbs, I find that the city agrees with me, and I've already grown attached to my neighborhood, with its shifting jumble of white and brown and black, its multilayered chorus of foreign accents, its children and its trees, its striving middle-class families, its lesbian couples, its Korean grocery stores, its bearded Indian holy man in his white robes bowing to me whenever we cross paths on the street, its dwarfs and cripples, its aged pensioners inching along the sidewalk, its church bells and ten thousand dogs, its underground population of solitary, homeless scavengers, pushing their shopping carts down the avenues and digging for bottles in the trash.

If I don't want to leave all that, why have I pushed Tom into this pointless discussion about real estate with Stanley Chowder? To please Tom, I think. To show him that he can count on me to support his project, even though we both understand that the new Hotel Existence is built on a foundation of 'just talk.' I play along with Tom to prove that I'm on his side, and because Tom appreciates the gesture, he plays along with me. It's a mutual exercise in clear-eyed self-deception. Nothing will ever come of it, and therefore we can dream along together without having to worry about the consequences. Now that we've dragged Stanley into our little game, it almost begins to look real. But it isn't. It's still just hot air and hopeless fantasy, an idea as fake as Harry's Hawthorne manuscript – which probably doesn't even exist. But that doesn't mean the game isn't fun. You'd have to be dead not to enjoy talking about outlandish things, and what better place to do it than on a hilltop in the middle of a quiet New England nowhere?

After lunch, the rejuvenated Stanley challenges me to a Ping-Pong match in the barn. I tell him I'm rusty, that I haven't played in years, but he won't take no for an answer. The exercise will do me good, he says, 'get the juices flowing again,' and so I reluctantly agree to play a game or two. Lucy accompanies us to the barn to witness the action, but Tom stays put, settling into a chair on the porch to smoke and read.

I quickly learn that Stanley doesn't play the kind of Ping-Pong I'm used to. The paddles and ball are the same, but in his hands it isn't a polite parlor activity so much as a full-blown, strenuous sport, a demonic, miniaturized form of tennis. He delivers his serves with a devastating, unhittable topspin, stands ten feet back from the table, and counters every shot I make as though I'm no more skilled than a four-year-old. He beats me three straight times – 21-0, 21-0, 21-0 – and once the massacre is over, there's nothing I can do but bow humbly to the victor and drag my exhausted body out of the barn.

Covered in sweat, I return to the house for a quick shower and a change of clothes. As I climb the steps of the front porch with Lucy, Tom tells me he called Brooklyn fifteen minutes ago. Harry is out on an errand, but Tom has left word with Rufus to have him call us back. 'To see if he's still interested,' Tom says. 'There's no point in getting Stanley's hopes up if Harry's changed his mind.'

I've been in the barn for less than half an hour, but in that brief interlude I sense that Tom has been deep in thought. Something in his eyes tells me that our lunchtime talk with Stanley has altered his position concerning the new Hotel Existence. He's beginning to believe it can work. He's beginning to hope.

As it happens, the telephone rings the instant I step into the front hall. I pick up the receiver, and there's Brightman himself, chirping away on the other end of the line. I tell him about our car trouble, about the Chowder Inn, and about Stanley's eagerness to strike a bargain with us. 'This is the spot,' I continue. 'Tom's idea might have sounded a little strange when we were sitting in that restaurant in the city, but once you get up here the whole thing looks eminently reasonable. That's why he called. To find out if you're still in.'

'In?' Harry booms, sounding like some half-mad nineteenth-century actor. 'Of course I'm in. We shook hands on it, didn't we?'

'Not that I remember.'

'Well, maybe it wasn't an actual physical handshake. But we all agreed. I distinctly remember that.'

'A mental handshake.'

'That's it. A mental handshake. A true meeting of minds.'

'All contingent on the outcome of your little deal, of course.'

'Of course. That goes without saying.'

'So you're still planning to go ahead with it.'

'I know you're skeptical, but all the pieces are suddenly falling into place.'

'Oh?'

'Yes. And I'm happy to report an excellent bit of news. Don't think I didn't take your advice to heart, Nathan. I told Gordon I was having second thoughts, and if he didn't arrange a meeting for me with the elusive Mr. Metropolis, I was backing out.'

'And?'

'I met him. Gordon brought him to the store, and I met him. A most interesting man. Barely said a word, but I knew that I was in the presence of a real pro.'

'Did he bring samples of his work?'

'A love letter from Charles Dickens to his mistress. A beautiful specimen.'

'I wish you luck, Harry. If not for your sake, then at least for Tom's.'

'You'll be proud of me, Nathan. After our talk the other night, I decided I needed to take some precautions. Just in case things go wrong. Not that they will – but when you've been around as many years as I have, you'd be a fool not to consider all the possibilities.'

'I don't think I follow.'

'You don't have to. Not now, in any case. If and when the time comes, you'll understand everything. It's probably the smartest move I've made in my life. A grand gesture, Nathan. The splurge of splurges. A vast swan dive into eternal greatness.'

I have no idea what he's talking about. Harry is in full bombastic flight, blustering forth his enigmatic pronouncements for the pure, self-indulgent pleasure of listening to his own voice, and I see no point in prolonging the conversation. Tom is standing next to me by then. Without bothering to say another word, I pass the phone to him and walk upstairs to take my shower.

The next morning, Lucy finally opens her mouth and speaks.

I am expecting answers and revelations, the unwrapping of manifold mysteries, a great beam of light shining into the darkness. I should have known better than to count on language as a more efficient form of communication than nods and shakes of the head. Lucy has resisted our attempts to pry something out of her for three solid days, and once she allows herself to talk, her words are scarcely more helpful to us than her silence was.

I begin by asking her where she lives.

'Carolina,' she says, drawling out the syllables with the same backwoods southern accent I had heard on Monday morning.

'North Carolina or South Carolina?'

'Carolina Carolina.'

'There's no such place, Lucy. You know that. You're a big girl. It's either North Carolina or South Carolina.'

'Don't be mad, Uncle Nat. Mama said not to tell.'

'Was it your mother's idea for you to go to Uncle Tom in Brooklyn?'

'Mama said go, and so I went.'

'Were you sad to leave her?'

'Real sad. I love my mama, but she knows what's right.'

'And what about your father? Does he know what's right?'

'Definitely. He's about the rightest man under the sun.'

'Why didn't you talk, Lucy? What made you keep quiet for so many days?'

'I did it for Mama. So she'd know I was thinking about her. That's how we do things back home. Daddy says silence purifies the spirit, that it prepares us to receive the word of God.'

'Do you love your father as much as your mother?'

'He's not my real father. I'm adopted. But I came out of Mama's womb. She carried me inside her for nine months, so she's the one I belong to.'

'Did she tell you why she wanted you to come north?'

'She said go, and so I went.'

'Don't you think Tom and I should talk to her? He's her brother, you know, and I'm her uncle. My sister was her mother.'

'I know. Grandma June. I used to live with her, but now she's dead.'

'If you give me your phone number, it will make things a lot simpler for all of us. I won't send you back if you don't want to go. I just want to talk to your mother.'

'We don't have a phone.'

'What?'

'Daddy doesn't like phones. We used to have one, but then he gave it back to the store.'

'All right, then. What about your address? You must know that.'

'Yeah, I know it. But Mama said not to tell, and when Mama tells me something, that's what I do.'

This maddening, breakthrough conversation takes place at seven o'clock in the morning. Lucy has woken me up by knocking on my door, and she sits beside me on the bed as I rub my eyes open and begin my futile questioning. Next door, Tom is still asleep in the Buster Keaton room, but when he comes downstairs for breakfast an hour later, he is no more successful than I am in extracting information from her. Together, we go on grilling her for half the morning, but the kid is made of steel and won't budge. She won't even tell us what kind of work her father does ('He has a job') or if her mother still has the tattoo on her left shoulder ('I never see her without her clothes on'). The one fact she's willing to share with us is irrelevant to our purposes: her best friend is a girl named Audrey Fitzsimmons. Audrey wears glasses, we're told, but she's the best arm wrestler in the fourth grade. Not only does she beat all the girls, but she's stronger than all the boys as well.

Eventually, we give up in frustration, but not before Lucy reminds me that I promised to pay her fifty dollars the moment she started talking again.

'I never said that,' I tell her.

'Yes, you did,' she answers. 'The other night at dinner. When Honey asked you why I didn't speak.'

'I was trying to protect you. I didn't really mean it.'

'That makes you a liar, then. Daddy says liars are the lowest worms in the universe. Is that what you are, Uncle Nat? A no-good, lowly worm?'

Tom, who just a moment before was on the point of wringing her neck, suddenly bursts out laughing. 'You better cough up,' he says. 'You don't want her to lose respect for you, do you, Nathan?'

'Yeah,' Lucy chimes in. 'You want me to love you, don't you, Uncle Nat?'

Reluctantly, I take out my wallet and hand over the fifty dollars.

'You're some operator, Lucy,' I mumble.

'I know I am,' she says, tucking the bills into her pocket and gracing me with one of her gigantic smiles. 'Mama told me always to stick up for myself. A bargain's a bargain, right? If I let you welsh on the deal, you wouldn't like me anymore. You'd think I was a softy.'

'What makes you think I like you?' I ask.

'Because I'm so cute,' she says. 'And because you changed your mind about Pamela.'

It's all very funny, perhaps, but once she runs off to play with the dog, I turn to Tom and ask, 'How the hell are we going to get her to talk?'

'She's talking,' he says. 'She's just not saying the right words.'

'Maybe I should threaten her.'

'That's not your style, Nathan.'

'I don't know. What if I tell her I've changed my mind again? If she doesn't answer our questions, we'll drive her up to Pamela and dump her there. No ifs, ands, or buts.'

'Fat chance.'

'I'm worried about Rory, Tom. If the kid doesn't open up, we'll never know what's going on.'

'I'm worried, too. For the past three years, the only thing I've done is worry. But frightening Lucy isn't going to help anyone. She's already been through enough.'

At eleven o'clock that same morning, Al Junior calls from the garage down the hill and tells me the problem has been solved. Sugar in the gas tank and fuel lines, he says. This pronouncement is so mystifying to me, I scarcely know what he's talking about.

'Sugar,' he repeats. 'It looks like someone poured about fifty cans of Coke into the tank. You want to mess up a person's car, there's no faster or simpler way to do it.'

'Good God,' I say. 'Are you telling me someone did it on purpose?'

'That's what I'm saying. Coke cans don't have legs, do they? They don't have hands and fingers to flick themselves open with. The only explanation is that someone got it into his head to do a number on your car.'

'It had to have happened while we were eating lunch. The car was working fine until we parked in front of the restaurant. The question is: why would anyone do a shitty thing like that?'

'A hundred reasons, Mr. Glass. Some rowdy kids, maybe. You know, a bunch of bored teenagers out to play a prank. That kind of vandalism goes on around here all the time. Or else it was someone who doesn't like people from New York. He sees the license plates on your car and decides to teach you a lesson.'

'That's ridiculous.'

'You'd be surprised. There's a lot of resentment against out-of-staters in this part of Vermont. The New York and Boston folks most of all, but I've even seen some morons pick fights with people from New Hampshire. It happened just the other day at Rick's Bar on Route Thirty. A guy walks in from Keene, New Hampshire, which is about one inch from the Vermont border, and some drunken local – I won't mention any names – smashes a chair over his head. "Vermont for Vermonters!" he's yelling. "Get your New Hampshire ass out of here!" It turned into a real slugfest. From what they tell me, it probably would have gone on all night if the cops hadn't broken it up.'

'You make it sound like we're living in Yugoslavia.'

'Yeah, I know what you mean. Every idiot's got his turf to defend, and damn the poor stranger who doesn't belong to your tribe.'

Al Junior rattles on for another minute or two, lamenting the state of the world in a doleful, disbelieving voice, and I imagine him shaking his head as the words come out of his mouth. Eventually, we resume talking about my sabotaged green sedan, and I'm told that he's about to get started on flushing the engine and fuel lines clean. I'm going to have to spring for new spark plugs, a new distributor cap, and sundry other replacement parts, but all I care about is getting the old jalopy up and running again. Al Junior predicts a clean bill of health by the end of the day. If he and his father have time, they'll drive up the hill in two cars and deliver the Cutlass to me that evening. If not, I should expect them the following morning. I don't bother to ask him what the repairs will cost. My mind is temporarily stuck in Yugoslavia, and I'm thinking about the horrors of Sarajevo and Kosovo, about the thousands of slaughtered innocents who died for no other reason than that they were supposedly different from the people who killed them.

Dark thoughts dog me until lunchtime, and I walk around the property alone, leaving Tom and Lucy to their own devices. It is the only grim patch during my stay at the Chowder Inn, but nothing has gone right this morning, and suddenly I feel the world pressing down on me from all sides. Lucy's deft, tight-lipped evasions; the growing anxiety about her mother; the malicious attack on my car; the unstoppable brooding about massacres in distant places – all of these things pour into my head and remind me there is no escape from the wretchedness that stalks the earth. Not even on the remotest hilltop in southern Vermont. Not even behind the locked doors and bolted porticoes of the make-believe sanctuary known as the Hotel Existence.

I cast about for a counter-argument, for an idea that will put the scales in balance, and eventually I start thinking about Tom and Honey. Nothing is certain at this point, but at dinner the previous night I sensed a considerable softening in his attitude toward her. Honey has been begging her father to move for years, and when Stanley told her about our potential interest in buying the house, she raised her glass and offered us a toast of thanks. Then she turned to Tom and asked him why on earth would he want to trade his life in the city for a dirt road in Vermont? Instead of mocking her with a facetious answer, he gave a full and measured explanation, reiterating many of the points he had made at our dinner with Harry on Smith Street in Brooklyn, but somehow he was more eloquent than he had been that night – more urgent, more persuasive as he delved into his despair over the future of America. It was Tom at his scintillating best, and as I watched Honey looking at him across the table, I saw little tears gathering in the corners of her eyes, and I knew, knew beyond any shadow of a doubt, that Stanley's buxom, big-hearted daughter was smitten with my nephew.

But what about Tom? I could see that he had begun to take notice of her, to talk to her in a less guarded and aggressive way, but what did that mean? It could have been a sign of growing interest, and it also could have been simple good manners.

One small moment from the end of the evening. Whether it answers the question or not, I submit it as a final piece of evidence.

By the time we finished dessert, Lucy was already upstairs in bed, and the four adults were all a bit drunk. Stanley proposed a friendly game of poker, and as he shuffled the cards and talked about his new life in the tropics (sitting under a palm tree with a rum punch in one hand and a Montecristo in the other, watching the surf roll in and out on the white shore at sunset), he quietly proceeded to beat our pants off, winning three out of every four hands we played. After the drubbing he'd given me at Ping-Pong that afternoon, how could I have expected any less? It seemed there was nothing the man didn't excel at, and both Tom and Honey laughed at their ineptitude, making wilder and wilder bets as Stanley continued to outsmart us all. It was a complicitous sort of laughter, I felt, and I made a conscious effort not to join in, studying the two youngsters from behind the shield of my cards. Then, as the game was breaking up, Tom said something that took me by surprise. 'Don't go back to Brattleboro,' he said to Honey. 'It's after midnight, and you've had too much to drink.'

Simple good manners – or a devious ploy to woo her into bed?

'I can drive that road with my eyes shut,' Honey answered. 'Don't worry about me, kiddo.'

She went on to explain that she had to get up especially early the next morning (something to do with a teacher-parent conference), but I could see that Tom's solicitude had touched her, or at least I imagined it had. Then she kissed everyone good-bye. First her father, next a light peck on the jaw for me, and last of all Tom. Not only did he get his kiss on the lips, but he was the recipient of a hug as well – a big hug, which went on several seconds longer than the situation seemed to call for.

'Night, all,' Honey said, waving to us as she walked to the front door. 'See you fellows tomorrow.'

She shows up the next day at four, bearing five lobsters, three bottles of champagne, and two different desserts. Another feast is prepared for us by our extravagantly gifted chef, and now that Lucy is willing to join in on the conversation, the fourth-grade teacher and the fourth-grade student talk shop for a good part of the meal, batting back and forth the titles of their favorite books. Al Junior and Al Senior have yet to show up with my car, but I announce that the Olds has been fixed and should be in our hands by tomorrow. With so much high-spirited talk flying around the table, I neglect to mention the cause of the breakdown, since I don't want to spoil the mood by bringing up such an unpleasant subject. Tom knows all about it by now, but he too is reluctant to report on the nasty trick that was played on us. Honey and Lucy are singing nonsense songs as they crack open their lobsters, and why interrupt their fun with a disheartening account of class resentments and provincial animosities?

When I take Lucy upstairs to bed, I realize that I'm too worn out to sit up late for a second night in a row, belting back glass after glass of wine with the others. The Chowders can both hold their alcohol, and with his great bulk and prodigious appetites, Tom can match them drink for drink, but I'm a skinny ex-cancer patient with a small capacity, and I dread waking up the next morning with a hangover.

I park myself on the edge of Lucy's bed and read to her from the Zane Grey novel until she closes her eyes and falls asleep. As I walk to my own room next door, I can hear laughter seeping up from the dining room below. I catch Stanley say something about being 'tuckered out,' and then Honey adds something about 'the Charlie Chaplin room' and 'maybe it's not such a bad idea.' It's difficult to know what they're talking about, but one possibility could be this: Stanley is about to go to bed, and Honey has drunk too much to drive home and plans to spend the night at the inn. If I'm not mistaken, the Charlie Chaplin room is the one immediately next to Tom's.

I crawl into my own bed and begin reading Italo Svevo's *As a Man Grows Older*. It's my second Svevo novel in less than two weeks, but *The Confessions of Zeno* made such a strong impression on me, I've decided to read everything by the author I can put my hands on. The original title in Italian is *Senilità*, and I find it a perfect book for an aging fart like me. An older man and his young mistress. The sorrows of love. Dashed hopes. After every paragraph or two, I pause for a moment and think about Marina Gonzalez, aching at the thought that I will never see her again. I'm tempted to masturbate, but I resist the urge because the rusty bedsprings are bound to give me away. Nevertheless, I slip my hand under the covers from time to time and briefly touch my cock. Just to make sure it's still there, to verify that my ancient friend is still with me.

Half an hour later, I hear footsteps tramping up the stairs. Two pairs of legs, two whispering voices: Tom and Honey. They walk down the hall in the direction of my door, then stop. I strain to catch a few words of their conversation, but they're talking too low for me to make anything out. Eventually, I hear Tom say 'good-night,' and a moment later the door of the Charlie Chaplin room opens and shuts. Three seconds after that, the same thing happens to the door of the Buster Keaton room.

The wall between me and Tom is thin – the flimsiest of Sheetrock partitions – and every sound he makes is audible to me. I hear him take off his shoes and unbuckle his belt, I hear him brush his teeth at the sink, I hear him sigh, I hear him hum, I hear him crawl under the covers of his creaking bed. I'm about to close my book and turn out the light, but no sooner do I reach for the lamp than I hear a faint knock on Tom's door. Honey's voice says, 'Are you asleep?' Tom says no, and when Honey asks if she can come in, our boy says yes, and by saying yes the hidden purpose of our turn off the interstate highway onto Route 30 is about to be fulfilled.

The sounds are so clear to me, I have no trouble following every detail of the action that unfolds on the other side of the wall.

'Don't get any ideas,' Honey says. 'It's not that I do this sort of thing every day.'

'I know,' Tom answers.

'It's just that it's been a long time.'

'For me, too. A very long time.'

I hear her slip into bed with him, and I hear everything that happens after that. Sex is such a strange and sloppy business, why bother to recount every slurp and moan that ensued? Tom and Honey deserve their privacy, and for that reason I will end my report of the night's activities here. If some readers object, I ask them to close their eyes and use their imaginations.

The next morning, Honey is long gone before the rest of the house rolls out of bed. It's another splendid day, perhaps the most beautiful day of the spring, but it turns out to be a day of surprises as well, and in the end those jolts will overwhelm the perfection of the landscape and the weather, pushing them to the back of my mind. If I remember that day at all, it's only as an unassembled jigsaw puzzle, a mass of isolated impressions. A patch of blue sky here; a silver birch there, reflecting the light of the sun off its bark. Clouds that look like human faces, like the maps of countries, like ten-legged dream animals. The sudden glimpse of a garter snake wending its way through the grass. The four-note lament of an unseen mockingbird. The thousand leaves of an aspen tree fluttering like wounded moths as the wind slides through the branches. One by one, each element is there, but the whole is lacking, the parts don't cohere, and I can do no more than search for the remnants of a day that doesn't fully exist.

It begins with the arrival of Al Junior and Al Senior at nine o'clock. Tom is still upstairs in the Buster Keaton room, comatose after his all-night romp with Honey. Lucy and I have been up since eight, and we're just leaving the house to go for a walk when the Wilsons show up in their two-vehicle convoy: a red Mustang convertible and my lime-green Cutlass. I let go of Lucy's hand to shake hands with those stalwart gentlemen. They tell me my car is as good as new, Al Senior presents me with a bill for their services, and I write them a check on the spot. Then, just when I think the transaction is over, Al Junior drops the first bomb of the day.

'The kicker is, Mr. Glass,' he says, patting the roof of my car, 'it's a good thing that dope messed with your gas tank.'

'What do you mean?' I say, not knowing how to interpret this peculiar statement.

'After we talked yesterday morning, I thought I'd have the job finished in a couple of hours. That's why I said we'd be able to deliver the car to you last night. Remember?'

'Yes, I remember. But you also said it might not happen until today.'

'Yeah, I did say that, but the reason I gave you then isn't the reason why we couldn't get here till now.'

'No? What happened in the meantime?'

'I took your Olds out for a spin. Just to make sure everything was back to normal. It wasn't.'

'Oh?'

'I pushed the car up to sixty-five, seventy, and then I tried to slow down. Mighty hard to do when the brakes are shot. Lucky I didn't get myself killed.'

'The brakes . . .'

'Yeah, the brakes. I got the car back to the garage and had a look. The lining was worn thin, Mr. Glass, just about to go.'

'What are you saying?'

'I'm saying that if you hadn't had that other problem with the gas tank, you never would have found out about this problem with the brakes. If you'd gone on driving much longer, you would have run into some pretty bad trouble. Accident trouble. Death trouble. All kinds of trouble.'

'So the shithead who poured Coke into the gas tank actually saved our lives.'

'That's what it looks like. Pretty weird, huh?'

After the Wilsons drive off in their red convertible, Lucy begins tugging on my sleeve.

'It wasn't no S-head that did it, Uncle Nat,' she says.

'S-head?' I answer. 'What are you talking about?'

'You said a naughty word. I'm not allowed to talk like that.'

'Oh, I see. *S*. Short for you-know-what.'

'Yeah. The S-word.'

'You're right, Lucy. I shouldn't use that kind of language when you're around.'

'You shouldn't use it, period. Whether I'm around or not.'

'You're probably right. But I was angry, and when a person's angry, he can't always control what he says. A bad man tried to wreck our car. For no reason. Just to be cruel, to hurt us. I'm sorry I used that word, but you can't really blame me for being upset.'

'It wasn't a bad man. It was a bad girl.'

663

'A girl? How do you know that? Did you see it happen?'

For a brief moment, she relapses into her old silence, nodding her head in answer to my question. Already, tears have begun to well up in her eyes.

'Why didn't you tell me?' I ask. 'If you saw it happen, you should have told me, Lucy. We could have caught the girl and put her in jail. And if the men at the garage had known what the problem was, they could have fixed the car right away.'

'I was scared,' she says, bowing her head, afraid to look me in the eye. The tears are spilling out of her in earnest now, and I see them land on the dry dirt below – salty ephemera, shining globules that momentarily darken and then vanish into the dust.

'Scared? Why should you be scared?'

Instead of responding to my question, she grabs hold of me with her right arm and digs her face into my ribs. I begin stroking her hair, and as I feel her body shudder against mine, I suddenly understand what she's been trying to tell me. I register a moment of genuine shock, then feel a wave of anger pass through me, but once the wave passes, it is gone. Anger gives way to pity, and I realize that if I begin scolding her now, I might lose her trust forever.

'Why did you do it?' I ask.

'I'm sorry,' she says, tightening her grip on me and blubbering into my shirt. 'I'm real, real sorry. I just kind of went crazy, Uncle Nat, and before I knew what I was doing, it was already done. Mama told me about Pamela. She's a mean person, and I didn't want to go there.'

'I don't know if she's mean or not, but it all turned out for the best, didn't it? You did a wrong thing, Lucy. A very wrong thing, and I never want you to behave like that again. But this time – this one time – the wrong thing turned out to be the right thing, too.'

'How can a wrong thing be a right thing? That's like saying a dog's a cat, or a mouse is an elephant.'

'Don't you remember what Al Junior told us about the brakes?'

'Yeah, I remember. I saved your life, didn't I?'

'Not to speak of your own life. And Tom's life, too.'

At long last, she disengages herself from my shirt, wipes the tears from her eyes, and gives me an intense, thoughtful look. 'Don't tell Uncle Tom I did it, okay?'

'Why not?'

'He won't like me anymore.'

'Of course he will.'

'No, he won't. And I want him to like me.'

'I still like you, don't I?'

'You're different.'

'In what way?'

'I don't know. You don't take things as hard as Uncle Tom. You're not as serious.'

'That's because I'm older.'

'Just don't tell him, okay? Swear to me you won't tell him.'

'All right, Lucy. I swear.'

She smiles then, and for the first time since she turned up on Sunday morning, I catch a glimpse of her mother as a young girl. Aurora. The absent Aurora, lost somewhere in the mythical land of Carolina Carolina, a shadow-woman beyond the reach of the living. If she is anywhere now, it is only in her daughter's face, in the little girl's loyalty to her, in Lucy's unbroken promise not to tell us where she is.

Tom rises at last. I find it difficult to read his state of mind, which seems to oscillate between somber contentment and a fidgety, awkward self-consciousness. At lunch he says not a word about the previous night's events, and I refrain from asking any questions, curious though I am to learn his side of the story. Has he fallen for the ebullient Miss C., I wonder, or does he plan to brush her off as a one-night fling? Is it all sex and nothing but sex, or are feelings involved in the equation as well? After we finish our lunch, Lucy trots off with Stanley to ride on the tractor and help him mow the lawn. Tom retires to the porch for his postprandial smoke, and I settle into the chair next to his.

'How did you sleep last night, Nathan?' he asks.

'Pretty well,' I answer. 'Considering the thinness of the walls, it could have been a lot worse.'

'I was afraid of that.'

'It's not your fault. You didn't build the house.'

'I kept telling her to keep it down, but you know how it is. A person gets carried away, and there's nothing you can do about it.'

'Not to worry. To tell the truth, I was glad. I felt happy for you.'

'Me too. For one night, I was glad.'

'You'll have other nights, old man. That was only the beginning.'

'Who knows? She left early this morning, and it's not as if we did much talking while she was here. I have no idea what she wants.'

'More to the point – what do you want?'

'It's too early to tell. Everything happened so fast, I haven't had time to think about it.'

'Not that you've asked me, but in my opinion you two are a good match.'

'Yeah. Two fatsos colliding in the night. I'm surprised the bed didn't collapse.'

'Honey isn't fat. She's what they call "statuesque."'

'She's not my type, Nathan. Too tough. Too confident. Too many opinions. I've never been attracted to women like that.'

'That's why she'd be good for you. She'd keep you on your toes.'

Tom shakes his head and sighs. 'It would never work. She'd wear me out in less than a month.'

'So you're ready to give up after one night.'

'There's nothing wrong with that. One good night, and that's the end of it.'

'And what happens if she crawls into your bed again? Are you going to kick her out?'

Tom puts a match to a second cigarette, then pauses for a long moment. 'I don't know,' he says at last. 'We'll see.'

Unfortunately, neither Tom nor anyone else gets a chance to see.

A last surprise is waiting for us, and this one proves to be so large, so stinging, so colossal in its ramifications, that we have no choice but to hit the road that very afternoon. Our holiday at the Chowder Inn comes to a sudden and bewildering end.

Good-bye hilltop. Good-bye lawn. Good-bye Honey.

Good-bye to the dream of the Hotel Existence.

Tom utters the words 'We'll see' at approximately one o'clock. After Lucy's tractor ride with Stanley, I take her to the pond for a swim. When we return to the house forty minutes later, Tom delivers the news. Harry is dead. Rufus has just called from Brooklyn, weeping into the phone, barely able to get a word out of his mouth, to tell us that Harry has died, that Harry is gone. According to Tom, Rufus was too choked up to say any more. We understand nothing. Beyond the fact that we must leave Vermont at once, we understand nothing.

I pay Stanley what we owe him. As I sign the check with a trembling hand, I tell him that our partner is dead and that we're no longer in a position to buy the house. Stanley shrugs. 'I knew it wasn't serious,' he

666

says. 'But that doesn't mean I didn't enjoy talking about it.'

Tom hands him a piece of paper with his address and telephone number on it. 'Please give this to Honey,' he says. 'And tell her I'm sorry.'

We pack our bags. We climb into the car. We go.

Double-Cross

I considered it a homicide. It didn't matter that no one laid a hand on him, that no one shot him or stabbed him in the chest, that no one ran him down with a car. Even if words were his killers' only weapons, the violence they subjected him to was no less physical than a blow to the head with a hammer. Harry was not a young man. He had suffered two coronaries in the past three years, his blood pressure was high, his arteries were in a state of imminent collapse. How much torture could a body in that condition withstand? Not much, in my opinion. Not much at all.

There was only one witness to the outrage, but even though Rufus heard every word they said, he understood only the smallest part of it. That was because Harry hadn't bothered to tell him about the scheme he was hatching with Gordon Dryer, and when Dryer walked into the store early that afternoon with Myron Trumbell, Rufus took them for a pair of fellow dealers. He led them upstairs to Harry's office, and because Harry seemed exceptionally tense and excited when he opened the door, not at all himself, pumping the hands of his visitors like some windup doll, Rufus began to grow alarmed. Rather than return to his post at the cash register downstairs, he decided to stay where he was and listen in on the conversation by pressing his ear against the door.

They toyed with Harry for a few minutes before they circled in with their daggers, softening him up for the kill. Friendly greetings all around, casual remarks about the weather, unctuous compliments about Harry's taste in office furniture, admiring references to the neat array of first editions stacked along the shelves. For all the pleasant banter, Harry must have been confused. Metropolis hadn't finished his work on the manuscript, and without a completed forgery to hand over to Trumbell, he didn't understand why Gordon had chosen to drop by now.

'It's always a pleasure to see you,' he said, 'but I don't want Mr. Trumbell to be disappointed. The manuscript is locked away in a vault at the Citibank on Fifty-Third Street in Manhattan. If you'd called in advance, I would have had it for you today. But unless I'm wrong, we weren't supposed to get together until next Monday afternoon.'

'In a bank vault?' Gordon said. 'So that's where you stashed away my discovery. I didn't know.'

'I thought I'd told you,' Harry continued, improvising as he went along, still unable to comprehend what Gordon was doing there with Trumbell four days before their scheduled meeting.

'I'm having second thoughts,' Trumbell said.

'Yes,' Gordon added, jumping in before Harry had a chance to reply. 'You see, Mr. Brightman, a sale like this can't be taken lightly. Not when there's so much money involved.'

'I'm aware of that,' Harry said. 'That's why we had the first page examined by those experts. Not just one man, but two.'

'Not two,' Trumbell said. 'Three.'

'Three?'

'Three,' Gordon said. 'You can never be too careful, can you? Myron also took it to a curator at the Morgan Library. One of the top men in the field. He gave his verdict this morning, and he's convinced it's a forgery.'

'Well,' Harry stammered, 'two out of three isn't bad. Why trust this man's opinion over the two others?'

'He was very persuasive,' Trumbell said. 'If I'm going to buy this manuscript, there can't be any doubt. No doubt whatsoever.'

'I see,' Harry said, struggling to elude the trap they had set for him, but no doubt already beginning to lose heart, already demoralized beyond all imagining. 'I just want you to know that I've acted in good faith, Mr. Trumbell. Gordon found the manuscript in his grandmother's attic and brought it to me. We had it checked out and were told it was genuine. You became interested in buying it. If you've changed your mind, I can only say I'm sorry. We can cancel the deal right now.'

'You're forgetting the ten thousand dollars you took from Myron,' Gordon said.

'No, I'm not,' Harry answered. 'I'll give him back the money, and then we're quits.'

'I don't think it's going to be that simple, Mr. Brightman,' Trumbell said. 'Or should I call you Mr. *Dunkel*? Gordon's told me quite a bit about you, Harry. Chicago. Alec Smith. Twenty-odd forged paintings. Prison. A new identity. You're a champion liar, Harry, and with a record like yours, I'd just as soon you kept those ten thousand dollars. That way I'll be able to press charges. You were planning to rip me off, weren't you? I don't like it when people try to take my money. It irritates me.'

'Who is this man, Gordon?' Harry said, his voice suddenly shaking, out of control.

'Myron Trumbell,' Gordon answered. 'My benefactor. My friend. The man I love.'

'So this is the one,' Harry said. 'There never was that other person.'

'Just the one,' Gordon replied. 'Always just the one.'

'Nathan was right,' Harry moaned. 'Nathan was right all along. Goddamn it, why didn't I listen to him?'

'Who's Nathan?' Gordon asked.

'A man I know,' Harry said. 'It doesn't matter. Someone I know. A fortune-teller.'

'You never could take good advice, could you, Harry?' Gordon said. 'Too fucking greedy. Too fucking full of yourself.'

That was when Harry began to crack. The cruelty in Gordon's voice was too much for him, and he was no longer able to pretend that he was talking business, discussing the ins and the outs of a deal that had gone wrong. This was love that had gone wrong, deception on a scale he had never encountered before, and the pain of it destroyed any power he might have had to resist the onslaught.

'Why, Gordon?' he said. 'Why are you doing this to me?'

'Because I hate you,' his ex-lover said. 'Haven't you figured that out by now?'

'No, Gordon. You love me. You've always loved me.'

'Everything about you disgusts me, Harry. Your bad breath. Your varicose veins. Your dyed hair. Your awful jokes. Your fat belly. Your knobby knees. Your puny cock. Everything. Every part of you makes me sick.'

'Then why come back after all these years? Couldn't you have left well enough alone?'

'After what you did to me? Are you insane? You destroyed my life, Harry. Now it's my turn to destroy yours.'

'You ran out on me, Gordon. You betrayed me.'

'Think again, Harry. Who turned me over to the cops? Who cut a deal for himself by pointing his finger at me?'

'And so now you turn me over to the cops. Two wrongs don't make a right, Gordon. At least you're alive. At least you're young enough to have something to look forward to. You put me back in jail, and I'm finished. I'm a dead man.'

'We don't want you to die, Harry,' Trumbell said, suddenly reentering the conversation. 'We want to make a bargain with you.'

'A bargain? What kind of bargain?'

'We're not out for blood. We're only looking for justice. Gordon suffered because of you, and now we feel he deserves some compensation. Fair is fair, after all. If you cooperate with us, we won't say a word to the law.'

'But you're rich. Gordon has all the money he needs.'

'Certain members of my family are rich. Unfortunately, I'm not one of them.'

'I don't have any cash. I can scrape up the ten thousand I owe you, but that's about it.'

'You might be short on cash, but you have other assets we'd be willing to settle for.'

'Other assets? What are you talking about?'

'Look around you. What do you see?'

'No. You can't do that. You've got to be kidding.'

'I see books, Harry, don't you? I see hundreds of books. And not just any books, but first editions, even signed first editions. Not to speak of what's sitting in the drawers and cabinets below. Manuscripts. Letters. Autographs. Give us the contents of this room, and we'll consider the account square.'

'I'll be ruined. I'll be wiped out.'

'Consider the alternatives, Mr. Dunkel-Brightman. Which would you prefer: arrest on charges of fraud, or a quiet, peaceful life as the owner of a used-book store? Think about it carefully. Gordon and I will come back tomorrow with a large van and a team of moving men. It won't take more than a couple of hours, and then you'll be rid of us forever. If you try to stop us, I'll simply pick up the phone and call the police. You decide, Harry. Life or death. An empty room – or a second trip to prison. If you don't give us the books tomorrow, you're going to lose them anyway. You understand that, don't you? Be smart, Harry. Don't fight it. If you give up without a struggle, you'll be doing everyone a favor – especially yourself. Expect us between eleven and noon. I wish I could be more precise, but it's so hard to predict the traffic these days. *A demain*, Harry. Ta ta.'

The door opened then, and as Dryer and Trumbell pushed their way past him, Rufus looked into the office and saw Harry sitting at his desk with his head in his hands, sobbing like a young boy. If only Harry had stayed there for a few minutes and taken the time to reflect on what had just happened, he would have understood that Dryer and Trumbell had no case against him, that threatening to turn him in to the police was no more than an artless, heavy-handed bluff. How could they have proved that Harry knowingly tried to sell a forged manuscript without also implicating themselves? By confessing to their knowledge of the forgery, they would have been obliged to deliver the forger to the police, and what were the chances that Ian Metropolis would have admitted he was involved in the hoax? Assuming there was such a person as Ian Metropolis, of course, which struck me as less than likely. Ditto with the three so-called experts who had supposedly examined his work. My hunch was that Dryer and Trumbell had manufactured the Hawthorne page themselves, and with a gullible man like Harry as their victim, how hard would it have been to persuade him that he was looking at the penmanship of a master forger? Harry had told me he'd met Metropolis while we were in Vermont, but how could he be certain that man was who he claimed to be? The Dickens letter was of no importance. Whether genuine or fake, the letter had no bearing on the story. From start to finish, the plot to crush Harry had been a two-man operation, with a brief appearance by a third person posing as someone else. Two not-so-clever crooks and their anonymous crony. Bastards all.

But Harry wasn't thinking clearly that day. How could he think when his mind had been turned into an open wound, a suppurating mass of scrambled brain matter, exploded neurons, and short-circuited electrical impulses? Where was reason when the adored one of your life has just insulted you with a litany of monstrous denunciations, ripping apart your hapless self with the hatchet blows of his contempt? Where was mental equilibrium when that same man and his new cohort have declared their intention to rob you of everything you own and you feel powerless to stop them? Could anyone criticize Harry for lacking the wherewithal to take the long view? Could anyone fault him for being in a state of pure, animal panic?

When Rufus entered the office, Harry stood up from his desk and began to howl. He was beyond words then, incapable of forming a single coherent sentence, and the sounds that rushed out of his throat were so ghastly, Rufus said, so agonizing in their torment, that he began to shake with fear. Dryer and Trumbell were still on their way down the stairs to the ground floor, and without bothering to acknowledge Rufus's presence, Harry bolted out from behind his desk and began chasing after them. Rufus followed – but slowly, cautiously, nearly immobilized with dread. By the time he got to the bottom of the stairs,

Dryer and Trumbell had already left the shop, and Harry was yanking open the front door – still howling, still in pursuit. A yellow cab was parked at the curb with its engine and meter running, and the two men climbed into the backseat before Harry could catch up with them. He shook his fist at the departing taxi, paused for a moment to scream two words – *Murderers! Murderers!* – and then, totally out of his mind, began charging down Seventh Avenue as fast as his legs could take him, bumping into pedestrians, staggering, falling down, picking himself up, but not stopping until he reached the next corner and the cab vanished from sight. Rufus watched it all from a distance, following the blurred form of Harry's body as tears streamed down his face.

At the moment Harry stopped at the corner, Nancy Mazzucchelli rounded that same corner and approached her former boss, stunned to see him in such a gruesome state. His cheeks were bright red, he was gasping for breath, the elbow of his jacket was torn, and his eternally well-groomed hair was flopping around on all sides of his scalp.

'Harry,' she said. 'What's wrong?'

'They've killed me, Nancy,' Harry replied, clutching his chest and continuing to gasp for air. 'They stuck a knife in my heart and killed me.'

Nancy put her arms around him and gently patted his back. 'Don't worry,' she said. 'Everything is going to be all right.'

But it wasn't all right; it wasn't the least bit all right. Just after Nancy spoke those words, Harry let out a long, faint groan, and then she felt his body go limp against hers. She tried to hold him up, but he was too heavy for her, and little by little they both sank to the ground. And so it was that Harry Brightman, once known as Harry Dunkel, father of Flora and ex-husband of Bette, died on a Brooklyn sidewalk one sultry after-noon in the year 2000, cradled in the arms of the B.P.M.

Counterattack

Tom drove fast, and we made it back to Park Slope in less than five hours, pulling up in front of the store just as the sun was beginning to go down. Rufus and Nancy were waiting for us in Harry's upstairs apartment, huddled together in the darkened bedroom. It felt right to me that she should be present, but until Rufus began telling us what had happened earlier that day, I didn't understand why she was there. With so many pressing matters to attend to, it never even occurred to me to ask.

Neither one of them had met Lucy before, so introductions became the first point of business. Then Tom took our girl into the living room and planted her in front of the TV. Normally, that would have been my job, but I believe Tom was so startled to encounter the B.P.M. in such an unlikely setting that he had to withdraw for a moment to catch his breath. His queen had miraculously surfaced again, and no doubt his heart was racing, pounding madly in his lovesick chest.

Rufus was a good deal calmer than he had been on the phone that afternoon. The shock had begun to wear off a bit, and he was able to get through the story without too many interruptions. He and Nancy were sitting on the bed, and every time he broke down and cried, she would put her arms around him and hold on firmly until the tears had passed. She was somewhat weepy herself, but kindness was her specialty, and she understood that of all the people in the apartment that night, Rufus was the most desperate, the one most in need of comforting. As he went on talking to us in his slow, lilting Jamaican voice, my mind kept conjuring up images of Harry's corpse, which was laid out in a freezer at Methodist Hospital, just a few blocks from where we sat.

I hadn't known Harry well, but I had been fond of him in a peculiar sort of way (part fascination, part awe, part disbelief), and if he had died under any other circumstances, I doubt that I would have been as affected as I was. More than shock, more than sadness, I was filled with anger over the grotesque thing that had been done to him. It didn't help matters that I had predicted Dryer's double-cross, that my instincts had told me the Hawthorne scam was no more than a ruse, an elaborate hoax within a hoax, and that revenge had been the single motive from the start. What good is knowledge if you don't use it to stop your friends from being destroyed? I had tried to warn Harry, but I hadn't been emphatic enough – I hadn't put in sufficient time and effort to make him understand why he should have backed out of the deal. And now he was dead – murdered in cold blood, and murdered in such a way that his killers would never be charged for their crime.

After Rufus had finished talking, my immediate impulse was to partake in some vengeance of my own. Tom had only the fuzziest idea of what the dispute with Dryer and Trumbell had been about (he knew it was connected to Harry's deal in some way, but that was all), and Rufus and Nancy were in the dark about everything. Unlike Tom, they had never even heard of Gordon Dryer, and neither one of them was aware of Harry's less than sterling past. I didn't take the trouble to fill them in on the details. There wouldn't have been any point. The only point was to get on the phone as quickly as possible – and make sure that no van turned up at the store the next morning. Dryer and his boyfriend might have killed Harry, but I wasn't going to let them rob him as well.

I asked Tom for the key to the downstairs office, and since he was in a state of extreme discombobulation at that moment (mourning the unexpected death of his boss, trembling with joy and terror at his sudden proximity to the B.P.M., doing what he could to console the all but inconsolable Rufus), he absentmindedly reached into his pocket and gave it to me. It was only when I was walking out the door that he came to his senses long enough to ask me what I was doing. 'Nothing,' I said vaguely. 'I just need to check on something. I'll be right back.'

I installed myself at Harry's desk and opened the top center drawer, thinking it might be a logical place for him to have put Dryer's telephone number. I was prepared to call information and track down Trumbell if necessary, but I was hoping to save a little time by looking in the drawer first. For once in my life, I got lucky. Affixed to a business-size envelope at the very top of the drawer was a square green Post-it with two words scribbled on it in ink – *Gordon's cell* – followed by a ten-digit number that began with a 917 area code. When I removed the Post-it from the envelope and stuck it on the desk beside the phone, I saw that the envelope had writing on it as well: *To Be Opened In The Event Of My Death.*

There were twelve typed pages folded up inside, a Last Will and Testament prepared by the Court Street law firm of Flynn, Bernstein, and Vallero, duly signed, witnessed, and executed on June 5, 2000, just one day before I had talked to Harry on the phone at the Chowder Inn. I scanned the contents of the document, and within three minutes I understood what he'd meant by his *grand gesture*, his *splurge of splurges*, his *vast swan dive into eternal greatness*. He had been referring to the will I now held in my hands, which was indeed something great, something altogether surprising and great, and which proved that he had listened to my warnings far more closely than I had imagined. Even as he'd refused to follow my advice, he had hedged his bets by embracing the possibility that Gordon was about to turn on him, and if such a betrayal were to come to pass, he felt that his life would be over – if not literally, then at least in the sense that the inner destruction would be more than he could bear. He had said as much to me at our dinner on June first: *If you're right about Gordon, then my life's finished anyway.* To think about Gordon as a duplicitous avenger was also to think about his own death. The first thought led naturally to the second, and in the end the two thoughts were one and the same. Hence the will. It was an overly dramatic step, perhaps, a near-hysterical response to the distress roiling inside him, but who could fault him for wanting to take (in his words) *some precautions*? In light of what had happened earlier that day, it turned out to be an act of supreme wisdom.

The two beneficiaries named in the will were Tom Wood and Rufus Sprague. They were to inherit the building on Seventh Avenue along with the business known as Brightman's Attic, including all goods and moneys that appertained to said business. Other, smaller bequests were mentioned as well – various books, paintings, and articles of jewelry to be given to people whose names were unfamiliar to me – but the bulk of Harry's estate was going to Tom and Rufus, with all income from Brightman's Attic to be divided equally between them. Considering that there was no mortgage on the building, and considering the value of the books and manuscripts in the room where I was currently sitting, the inheritance would amount to a small fortune, more money than either one of them had ever dreamed of. At the last possible moment, Harry had pulled off his grand gesture, his splurge of splurges. He had taken care of his boys.

I realized then how badly I had underestimated him. The man might have grown up into an imp and a scoundrel, but a part of him had remained the ten-year-old child who had fantasized about rescuing orphans from the bombed-out cities of Europe. For all his wisecracking irreverence, for all his peccadilloes and falsehoods, he had never stopped believing in the principles of the Hotel Existence. Good old Harry Brightman. Funny old Harry Brightman. If there had been a bottle of something on the desk, I would have poured myself a glass and raised a toast to his memory. Instead, I picked up the phone and dialed Gordon's number. In the long run, that probably amounted to the same thing.

He didn't answer, but a message came on after four rings and I heard his voice for the first time – an unusually calm and guarded voice, I felt, with little affect or inflection. Fortunately, he gave a second number where he could be reached (I assumed Trumbell's), which spared me the bother of having to look it up myself. I dialed again, fully expecting no one to be in, imagining that Dryer and Trumbell were out somewhere whooping it up, celebrating their triumph in Brooklyn that afternoon. Just as I was beginning to wonder if I should leave a message on the machine, the phone stopped ringing and I heard Dryer's voice for the second time in thirty seconds. To play it safe, I asked if I could talk to Gordon Dryer, even though I knew for certain that he was the man on the other end of the line.

'Speaking,' he said. 'Who is this?'

'Nathan,' I replied. 'We've never met, but I believe you've heard of me. Harry Brightman's friend. The fortune-teller.'

'I don't know what you're talking about.'

'Of course you do. When you and your friend visited Harry today, someone was standing on the other side of the door, listening in on your conversation. At one point, Harry mentioned my name. "I should have listened to Nathan," he said, and you asked him, "Who's Nathan?" That's when Harry told you I was a fortune-teller. Remember now? We're not talking about the distant past, Mr. Dryer. You heard those words just a few hours ago.'

'Who are you?'

'I'm the messenger of bad tidings. I'm the man who issues threats and warnings, who tells people what to do.'

'Oh? And what am I supposed to do?'

'I like your sarcasm, Gordon. I hear that coldness in your voice, and it confirms my feelings about who you are. Thank you. Thank you for making my job so simple.'

'All I have to do is hang up the phone, and that's the end of the conversation.'

'But you're not going to hang up, are you? You're scared shitless, and you'll do anything to find out what I know. Am I right or wrong?'

677

'You don't know a damn thing.'

'Guess again, Gordon. Let me try out some names on you, and we'll see what I know and don't know.'

'Names?'

'Dunkel Frères. Alec Smith. Nathaniel Hawthorne. Ian Metropolis. Myron Trumbell. How's that? Do you want me to go on?'

'All right, so you know who I am. Big deal.'

'Yes, big deal. Because I know what I know, I'm in a position to get what I want from you.'

'Ah. So that's it. You want money. You want us to cut you in on the deal.'

'Wrong again, Gordon. I'm not interested in money. There's just one thing you have to do for me. A very easy thing. It won't take but a minute of your time.'

'One thing?'

'Call up the moving company you hired for tomorrow and cancel the order. Tell them you've changed your mind and won't be needing the van.'

'Why would I do that?'

'Because your scam has done gone backfired on you, Gordon. The whole thing blew up in your face about five minutes after you left Harry's store.'

'What do you mean?'

'Harry's dead.'

'What?'

'Harry's dead. He went running after you along Seventh Avenue as you were driving away in the cab. The strain was too much for him. His heart gave out, and he died there on the street.'

'I don't believe you.'

'Believe it, buster. Harry's dead, and you killed him. Poor, stupid Harry. All he ever did was love you, and you pay him back by luring him into some crummy extortion scheme. Nice work, kid. You must be very proud of yourself.'

'It's not true. Harry's alive.'

'Call the morgue at Methodist Hospital in Brooklyn, then. You don't have to take my word for it. Just ask the guys in the white coats.'

'I will. That's exactly what I'll do.'

'Good. In the meantime, don't forget to call the movers. Harry's books stay in Harry's store. If you show up at Brightman's Attic tomor-

row, I'll break your neck. And then I'll turn you over to the cops. Do you
understand me, Gordon? I'm letting you off easy. I know all about the
forged manuscript page, the ten-thousand-dollar check, everything. It's
just that I don't want to see Harry's name get dragged into it. The man's
dead, and I'll be damned if I do anything to hurt his reputation now. But
that's only if you act like a good boy. You do what I tell you to do, or else
I switch to Plan B and go after you with everything I've got. Do you hear
me? I'll have you busted and thrown into jail. I'll fuck you up so bad,
you won't want to live anymore.'

Adieu

Rufus wanted no part of the building or the store. He wanted no part of Brooklyn, no part of New York City, no part of America. The only America he believed in was the one that had Harry Brightman in it, and now that Harry had left the country, Rufus felt it was time for him to be going home.

'I'll live with my granny in Kingston,' he said. 'She's my friend, the only friend I have in the world.'

Such was his startling reaction to the news of Harry's will. As for Tom, he just sat there in silence, not knowing what to think.

I returned to the upstairs apartment a little past ten. Nancy had already gone home to be with her children; Lucy had fallen asleep in front of the television and had since been transferred to Harry's bed, where she was stretched out on top of the covers with her clothes on and her mouth open, gurgling softly in the warm New York night; Tom and Rufus were in the living room, sitting in chairs and smoking. Tom looked pensive as he dragged on his Camel Filter. Rufus, who was puffing on what appeared to be a joint, looked a little crazed.

High or not, he talked with great clarity after I read Harry's will to them. His mind was made up, and no matter what Tom said to him, he wouldn't budge from his position. The only thing he wanted was to talk about Harry, which he proceeded to do at great length, giving a long-winded, emotional account of their first meeting – Rufus in tears, having just been thrown out of the apartment he shared with his friend Tyrone, and Harry stepping out of the darkness, putting his arm around his shoulder, and asking if there was anything he could do to help – and then moving on to the thousand selfless acts Harry had bestowed on him over the past three years, in particular the offer of a job, but also paying for the costumes and jewelry he used in his Tina Hott performances, not to speak of Harry's unflagging generosity with the doctors' bills and his willingness to spring for the expensive medicines that were keeping Rufus alive. Was there ever a man as good as Harry Brightman? he asked. Not that he knew of, he said, answering his own question, and then, for the umpteenth time that night, he broke down and wept.

'You don't have any choice,' Tom said, finally emerging from his dazed silence. 'Whether you stay here or not, the money belongs to both of us. We're partners, and there's no way I'm going to steal your share. Half and half, Rufus. We split everything right down the middle.'

'Just send me the money for my meds,' Rufus whispered. 'I don't want anything else.'

'We'll sell the building and the store,' Tom said. 'We'll get rid of everything and share the profits.'

'No, Tommy,' Rufus said. 'You keep it. You're so smart, man, you'll make yourself rich if you hold on. This place isn't for me. I don't know nothing about books. I'm just a freak, man, a little colored freak who doesn't belong here. A girl in a boy's body. A dying boy who wants to go home.'

'You're not going to die,' Tom said. 'Your health is good.'

'We all die, baby,' Rufus said, lighting up another joint. 'Don't take it so hard. I'm cool with it, man. My granny will take good care of me. Just remember to call every once in a while, okay? Promise me that, Tommy. If you forget my birthday, I don't think I'll ever forgive you.'

As I listened to this exchange between the two young men, I began to feel somewhat choked up myself. It wasn't like me to succumb to strong displays of sentiment, but I was still reeling from my talk with Dryer, which had taken a lot more out of me than I had expected it would. I had assumed the role of tough guy for the confrontation, and I had borne down on him with a viciousness that made me sound like some gravel-voiced hood from an old B-movie. It wasn't that Dryer didn't deserve the full treatment, but until the words came out of my mouth, I hadn't known I was capable of such coarseness, of such brutality. Now, just minutes after that talk had ended, I was in the upstairs apartment again, listening to Rufus Sprague turn down the very things Dryer had wanted to steal from Harry. The contrast was too stark, too overwhelming not to feel moved by the differences between the two men. And yet Harry had loved them both, had stuck by each one of them with the same helpless ardor, the same unquestioning devotion. How was such a thing possible? I asked myself. How could a person so thoroughly misjudge one man and at the same time so accurately penetrate the true character of another? Rufus was just twenty-six or twenty-seven years old. Physically, he resembled an exotic creature from some alien planet, and with his small, perfect head, his honey-colored face, and his slender, elongated limbs, he was the very embodiment of the weakling, the

681

pushover, the pansy. But there was something fierce in him as well, an unusual sort of idealism that rejected the vanities and desires that make the rest of us so vulnerable to the temptations of the world. For his sake, I hoped he would change his mind about the inheritance. I hoped he would start thinking like the rest of us and accept the property that had been left to him, but as I listened to Tom argue with him for the next two hours, I realized it was never going to happen.

The following day was given over to practical chores. Phone calls to Harry's friends (handled by Rufus), calls to Bette in Chicago and fellow book dealers in New York (handled by Tom), and calls to various funeral parlors around Brooklyn (handled by me). In his will, Harry had left instructions that his body should be cremated, but he hadn't stipulated how or where the ashes should be disposed of. After a lengthy discussion, it was decided that we would scatter them in a wooded area of Prospect Park. By New York City law, you aren't supposed to dump the ashes of dead people in public places, but we figured that if we secluded ourselves in some remote, rarely traveled spot, no one would notice us. The bill for burning Harry's body and securing the remains in a metal box tallied up to just over fifteen hundred dollars. With no one else in a position to contribute, I covered the entire cost myself.

On the afternoon of the ceremony – Sunday, June eleventh – I left Lucy with a babysitter and walked to the park with Tom, who carried the box of ashes in a green shopping bag with the Brightman's Attic logo on it. The weather had been vile since the start of the weekend, a sweltering, oppressive, ninety-six-degree onslaught of humidity and pounding light, and Sunday was the worst day of all, one of those barely breathable moments when New York is turned into an equatorial jungle outpost, the hottest, foulest place on earth. Simply to move was to feel your body awash in sweat.

The weather was probably responsible for the sparse turnout. Harry's Manhattan friends had opted to stay at home in their air-conditioned apartments, and our number was therefore reduced to a smattering of neighborhood loyalists. Among them were three or four Seventh Avenue shopkeepers, the owner of Harry's regular lunch spot, and the woman who had cut and dyed his hair. Nancy Mazzucchelli was present, of course, as was her husband, the ersatz James Joyce, better known as Jim or Jimmy. It was the first time I had met him, and I'm sorry to report that I was not favorably impressed. He was as tall and handsome as Tom had advertised, but he kept grumbling about the heat and the gnats swarming in the woods, and I took those complaints as a sign of childishness and inappropriate self-regard, particularly when he had come to pay his last respects to a man who would no longer have the pleasure of complaining about anything.

But no matter. There was only one thing that counted that day, and it wasn't connected to Nancy's husband or the weather. It was all about Rufus, who turned up twenty minutes after the rest of the party had assembled, striding into the gnat-filled copse just as we were about to begin the ceremony without him. By then, the prevailing opinion was that he had chickened out, that the prospect of seeing Harry reduced to an urnful of ashes had been too much for him, and he hadn't been up to the ordeal. Nevertheless, we gave him the benefit of the doubt, standing around in the turgid, suffocating air for all those minutes as we mopped our faces and checked the time on our wristwatches, hoping we had been wrong. When he finally appeared, it took a few moments before anyone recognized him. It wasn't Rufus Sprague who had joined us – it was Tina Hott, and the transformation was so radical, so mesmerizing, that I actually heard someone behind me gasp.

He was one of the most beautiful women I had ever seen. Decked out in full widow's regalia, with a tight black dress, three-inch black heels, and a black pillbox hat with a delicate black veil, he had turned himself into an incarnation of absolute femininity, an idea of the feminine that surpassed anything that existed in the realm of natural womanhood. The auburn wig looked like real hair; the breasts looked like real breasts; the makeup had been applied with skill and precision; and Tina's legs were so long and lovely to look at, it was impossible to believe that they were attached to a man.

But there was more to the effect she created than mere surface trappings, more than just clothes or wigs or makeup. The inner light of the feminine was there as well, and Tina's dignified, sorrowful bearing was a perfect representation of grieving widowhood, a performance by an actress of immense talent. All through the ceremony, she didn't say a word, standing among us in total silence as people delivered short speeches about Harry and Tom then opened the box and spread the ashes out on the ground. It seemed as if our business had been concluded, but before we turned to go, a chubby black boy of about twelve emerged from the fringes of the small forest and approached the group. There was a portable CD player in his outstretched arms, and he carried it as if he were bearing a crown on a velvet pillow. The boy, who was later identified as Rufus's cousin, placed the boom box at Tina's feet and pushed a button. Suddenly, Tina opened her mouth, and as the first bars of orchestral music came pouring through the speakers, she began lip-synching the words of the song that followed. After a moment or two, I recognized the voice of Lena Horne, singing the old song from *Show Boat*, 'Can't Help Lovin' Dat Man.' This was how Tina Hott performed in her Saturday night cabaret appearances: not as a singer, but as a faux-singer, mouthing the words of show tunes and jazz standards as sung by legendary female vocalists. It was magnificent and absurd. It was funny and heartbreaking. It was moving and comical. It was everything it was and everything it wasn't. And there was Tina, gesturing with her arms as she pretended to belt out the words of the song. Her face was all tenderness and love. Her eyes were wet with tears, and we all stood there transfixed, not knowing whether to cry with her or to laugh. As far as I'm concerned, it was one of the strangest, most transcendent moments of my life.

> Fish gotta swim, birds gotta fly
> I gotta love one man 'til I die . . .

That evening, Rufus boarded a plane and flew home to Jamaica. To the best of my knowledge, he has not been back since.

Further Developments

Tom was confused. So much had happened in such a short period of time, he felt unprepared to deal with the wealth of possibilities that had opened before him. Did he want to take over Harry's business and spend the rest of his days trafficking in rare and used books from a Park Slope storefront? Or, as he had proposed on the night of Harry's death, should he simply sell the whole operation and split the proceeds with Rufus? The fact that Rufus didn't want the money was of little importance. The building was a valuable piece of property, and if Rufus persisted in turning down his half of the sale, Tom would see to it that his grandmother accepted for him. Selling would generate a large sum of cash, no less than several hundred thousand dollars for each of them, and with his share Tom would be able to reinvent himself from the bottom up, to take off in any direction he wanted. But what did he want? That was the fundamental question, and for the time being it was the one question that had no answer. Was Tom still interested in pursuing the idea of the Hotel Existence? Or would he prefer to return to his original post-Michigan plan and look for a job as a high school English teacher? And, if so, where? Did he want to stay in New York, or was he ready to pack it in and move to the country? We discussed these matters a hundred times in the days that followed, but other than giving up his tiny apartment and temporarily installing himself in Harry's place above the store, Tom continued to waffle, to brood, to sulk. Fortunately, he was under no immediate pressure to make a decision. Harry's will was about to commence its laborious journey through probate, and it would be months before the deed to the building was turned over to the beneficiaries. As for Harry's other assets – his meager bank account, a few stocks and bonds – those were frozen as well. Tom was sitting on a mountain of gold, but until the lawyers at Flynn, Bernstein, and Vallaro wrapped up the affairs of Harry's estate, he would actually be worse off than he had been before. He had lost his weekly salary, and unless he kept Brightman's Attic running at full tilt, he would scarcely have any income at all. I offered to lend him money, but he refused to consider it. Nor was he terribly keen on my suggestion that he shut down the

685

business for the summer and go on a long vacation with Lucy and me. He owed it to Harry to keep the Attic alive, he said. It was a moral debt, and he felt honor-bound to stick it out to the end. Fine, I said. But how are you going to run the store on your own? Rufus is gone, which means you don't have a salesclerk. And you can't afford to hire a new one, can you? Where's his salary going to come from?

For the first time in all the years I had known him, Tom lost his temper. 'Fuck it, Nathan,' he said. 'Who the hell cares? I'll figure something out. Just mind your own business, okay?'

But Tom's business was also my business, and it pained me to see him in such a difficult spot. That's when I volunteered my services to the cause – for the nominal salary of one dollar a month. I would take over for Rufus, I said, and for as long as necessary I would suspend my retirement to carry out the taxing responsibilities of salesclerk on the ground floor of Brightman's Attic. If Tom wanted me to, I would even be happy to call him Boss.

And so it was that a new era of our lives began. I enrolled Lucy in a summer arts camp at the Berkeley Carroll School on Lincoln Place, and every morning after walking her the seven and a half blocks between apartment and camp, I would stroll back down the avenue and take my place behind the counter of the store. My work on *The Book of Human Follies* suffered from this altered routine, but I kept my hand in as best I could, scribbling during the late-night hours after Lucy had gone to bed, stealing fifteen minutes here or twenty minutes there whenever business in the store was slow. Much to my regret, the daily lunches with Tom were discontinued. There simply wasn't enough time to indulge in long, sit-down meals anymore, so we turned ourselves into brown baggers instead, eating our sandwiches and drinking our iced coffees in the stuffy confines of the Attic, polishing off the food in a matter of minutes. At four o'clock, Tom would relieve me of my duties behind the counter so I could fetch Lucy at camp. I would bring her back to the shop, and until we closed up at six, she would entertain herself by reading one of the four thousand two hundred books that lined the shelves on the ground floor.

Lucy remained a puzzle to me. In many respects, she was a model child, and the better we got to know each other, the more I liked her, the more I enjoyed having her around. Forgetting the question of her mother for a moment, there were a thousand positive things to be said about our girl. A complete stranger to big-city life, she adapted quickly to her new surroundings and began to feel at home in the neighborhood almost at once. Wherever Carolina Carolina might have been, the only language spoken there was English. Now, as we took our walks up and down Seventh Avenue, passing the dry cleaner, the grocery store, the bakery, the beauty parlor, the newsstand, the coffee shop, she was assaulted by a plethora of different tongues. She heard Spanish and Korean, Russian and Chinese, Arabic and Greek, Japanese, German, and French, but rather than feel intimidated or perplexed, she exulted in this variety of human sound. 'I want to talk like that,' she said to me one morning as we walked by the open door of some establishment or other and saw a dumpy little woman screaming at an old man. *'Mira! Mira! Mira!'* Lucy said, aping the woman's voice with uncanny exactitude. *'Hombre! Gato! Sucio!'* A minute later, she was doing a similar rendition of a man calling out to someone across the street in Arabic – words I wouldn't have been able to pronounce if my life had depended on it. The kid had an ear, and eyes to see with, and a mind to think with, and a heart to feel with. She had no trouble making friends at the camp, and by the end of the first week she had already been invited over by three different girls for so-called play dates. She didn't recoil from my good-night kisses and hugs; she wasn't picky about her food; she rarely made a fuss about anything. In spite of her frequently atrocious grammar (which I decided not to correct) and in spite of her fixation with watching TV cartoons (I put my foot down and limited her to one hour a day), I never once regretted having taken her in.

Still, there was the unsettling fact of her refusal to talk about her mother. Aurora was the unseen presence who dominated our little household, and no matter how many questions I asked, no matter how often I tried to trick Lucy into divulging some scrap of pertinent information, I continued to get nowhere. I suppose there was something admirable about such willpower in one so young, but I found it infuriating, and the longer the standoff went on, the more frustrated I became.

'You miss your mother, Lucy, don't you?' I asked her one night.

'I miss her something terrible,' she said. 'I miss her so bad, my heart aches.'

'You want to see her again, don't you?'

'More than anything. Every night I pray to God she'll come back to me.'

'She will. All you have to do is tell me where we can find her.'

'I'm not supposed to, Uncle Nat. I keep telling you the same thing, but it's like you don't hear what I'm saying.'

'I hear you. It's just that I don't want you to be sad anymore.'

'I can't talk about it. I made a promise, and if I break my promise, I'll burn in hell. Hell is forever, and I'm still a little girl. I'm not ready to burn forever.'

'There is no hell, Lucy. And you're not going to burn, not for one minute. Everyone loves your mother, and all we want to do is help her.'

'No, sir. That ain't the way it is. Please, Uncle Nat. Don't ask me any more questions about Mama. She's all right, and one day she'll come back to me. That's what I know, and that's the only thing I can tell you. If you keep it up, I'll just go back to the way I was when I first came here. I'll clamp my lips shut and won't say a word to you. And where would that get us? We have such a nice time when we talk together. As long as you're not asking me about Mama, it's about the best fun I have. Talking to you, I mean. You're such a jolly old soul, Uncle Nat. We don't want to spoil a good thing, do we?'

Outwardly, she appeared to be the happiest, most contented of children, but it disturbed me to think of the torments she must have been living through in order to hold on to her secret. It was too much to ask a nine-and-a-half-year-old person to walk around with such a heavy responsibility. Damage was being done to her, and I couldn't figure out a way to stop it. I talked to Tom about sending her to a psychiatrist, but he thought it would only be a waste of time and money. If Lucy wouldn't talk to us, then she certainly wouldn't talk to a stranger. 'We have to be patient,' he said. 'Sooner or later, it will become too much for her, and then everything will come pouring out. But she won't say a word until she's good and ready.' I took Tom's advice and temporarily bagged the idea of a doctor, but that didn't mean I thought much of his opinion. The kid was never going to be ready. She was so tough, so stubborn, so damned unbreakable, I was convinced she could hold out forever.

I started working for Tom on the fourteenth, three days after Harry's ashes were scattered in Prospect Park and Rufus went home to his Jamaican granny. The day after that, my daughter returned from England. I had been thinking about the fifteenth ever since my disastrous conversation with the now unmentionable one who had mothered my child, but in the maelstrom of events that followed our abrupt departure from the Chowder Inn, I had been too preoccupied to keep track of dates. It was indeed the fifteenth of June, but I was too out of it by then to know that. After closing up the store at six, Tom, Lucy, and I had an early dinner at the Second Street Café, and then Lucy and I returned to my apartment, where we were planning to spend the evening battling each other at a game of Monopoly or Clue. That was when I heard Rachel's message on the answering machine. Her plane had landed at one; she had walked into her house at three; she had read my letter at five. From the tone of her voice when she spoke the word *letter*, I understood that all was forgiven. 'Thank you, Dad,' she said. 'You have no idea how important it is to me. So much bad stuff has been happening lately, it's exactly what I needed to hear. If I can count on you now, I think I'll be able to get through anything.'

The next night, Tom babysat for Lucy, and I had dinner with Rachel in midtown Manhattan, not far from my old office at Mid-Atlantic Accident and Life. How rapidly the world shifts around us; how rapidly one problem is replaced by another, with scarcely a moment to bask in our victories. For close to a month, I had been fretting over the note I'd sent to my angry, alienated daughter, praying that my abject words of apology would cut through years of resentment and give me a second chance with her. By some miracle, the letter had accomplished everything I had hoped it would. We were back on solid ground together, and with all the acrimonies of the past now forgotten, the dinner that night should have been a joyous reunion, a time for jokes and laughter and whimsical recollections. But no sooner had I reestablished myself as Rachel's father than I was called upon to help her through the worst predicament of her adult life. My girl was going through 'bad stuff.' She was in crisis, and who else could she turn to but her old man – incompetent fool though he might have been?

I booked a table for us at La Grenouille, the same exorbitantly priced, fussily decorated old New York-style French restaurant where (name deleted) and I had taken her to celebrate her eighteenth birthday. She showed up wearing the necklace I had sent her, the twin to the one that had caused so much grief at the Cosmic Diner, and glad as I was to see how well it suited her, how attractive it looked against the darkness of her eyes and hair, I couldn't help thinking about the other necklace at the same time, which provoked several pangs of remorse as I relived the disaster I had brought down on Marina Gonzalez. So many young women in their late twenties and early thirties, I said to myself, so many young female lives swirling around me. Marina. Honey Chowder.

Nancy Mazzucchelli. Aurora. Rachel. Of all the women in that group, my daughter struck me as the most balanced and successful, the most solid, the one least likely to be swamped with difficulties, and yet there she was sitting across the table from me with tears in her eyes, telling me that her marriage was falling apart.

'I don't understand,' I said. 'The last time I saw you, everything was going well. Terrence was terrific. You were terrific. You'd just had your second anniversary, and you told me they'd been the happiest two years of your life. When was that? Late March? Early April? Marriages don't crumble that fast. Not when people are in love.'

'I'm still in love,' Rachel answered. 'It's Terrence I'm worried about.'

'The guy chased you halfway around the world to talk you into marrying him. Remember? He was the one who went after you. At first, you weren't even sure if you liked him.'

'That was a long time ago. This is now.'

'The last time we talked about now, you said you were thinking about having babies. You said Terrence was dying to become a father. Not a father in the abstract – but the father of your child. That's what men say when they're in love with the woman they live with.'

'I know. That's what I thought, too. But then we went to England.'

'America, England. What's the difference? You're still the same people wherever you are.'

'Maybe so. But Georgina isn't in America. She's in England.'

'Ah. So that's where we're going. Why didn't you come right out and say it?'

'It's hard. Just mentioning her name turns my stomach.'

'If it's any comfort, I find it a ridiculous name. Georgina. It makes me think of some giggly Victorian girl with golden ringlets and fat red jowls.'

'She's a mousy little brunette with greasy hair and bad skin.'

'Doesn't sound like much competition to me.'

'She and Terrence went to university together. She was his first big love. Then she fell for someone else and broke up with him. That's when he came to America. He was so depressed, Dad. He told me he thought of committing suicide.'

'And now the someone else is out of the picture.'

'I'm not sure. All I know is that when we were in London, the three of us had dinner together, and Terrence couldn't take his eyes off her. It was like I wasn't even there. After that, he wouldn't stop talking about her.'

Georgina is so smart. Georgina is so funny. Georgina is such a good person. Two days later, he had lunch with her alone. Then we went to Cornwall to visit his parents, but after three or four days he took the train back to London to talk to his publisher about the book he's been writing. Or so he said. I think he went back to be with stupid Georgina Watson, the love of his life. It was so awful. He just left me out there in the country with his right-wing, anti-Semitic parents, and all I could do was pretend I was enjoying every minute of it. He slept with her. I know he did. He slept with her, and now he doesn't love me anymore.'

'Did you ask him?'

'You bet I did. The minute he came back to his parents' house. We had a terrible fight. The worst fight since I've known him.'

'And what did he say?'

'He denied it. He said I was jealous and making up stories.'

'That's a good sign, Rachel.'

'Good? What do you mean good? He was lying to me, and now I'm never going to be able to trust him again.'

'Assume the worst. Assume that he slept with her and then came back and lied to you. It's still a good sign.'

'How can you keep saying that?'

'Because it means he doesn't want to lose you. He doesn't want the marriage to end.'

'What kind of marriage is that? When you can't trust the man you're married to, it's like not being married at all.'

'Look, dumpling, far be it from me to offer you advice. When it comes to marriage, I'm the least qualified person in the world to tell anyone what to do. You lived in the same house with me for the first eighteen years of your life, and I don't have to remind you what a botch of it I made with your mother. There were moments when I felt so sick of her, I actually wished she would die. I would imagine car crashes, train wrecks, falls down enormous flights of stairs. This is a terrible confession to make, and I don't want you to think I'm proud of myself – but it's important that you understand what a bad marriage is. Your mother and I had a bad marriage. We loved each other for a while, and then it all went bad. But still, we stuck it out for a long time, and bad as we were together, we managed to make you. You're the happy ending to the whole tragic story, and because you are who you are, I don't have a single regret about anything. Do you understand me, Rachel? I don't know Terrence well enough to have an opinion about him. But I do know that you don't have a bad marriage. People slip up. They do dumb things. But Georgina is on the other side of the ocean now, and unless you've linked yourself up with an incurable skirt chaser, I suspect this little episode is over and done with. Stick it out for a while and see what happens. Don't do anything rash. He told you he was innocent, and who's to say he wasn't telling the truth? Old loves are hard to get out of your system. Maybe Terrence had his head turned for a couple of moments, but now he's back in America with you, and if you love him as much as you say you do, there's a good chance everything will work out. As long as he doesn't turn into the kind of shit husband your father was, there's hope. Lots of hope. Hope for a happy future together. Hope for babies. Hope for cats and dogs. Hope for trees and flowers. Hope for America. Hope for England. Hope for the world.'

I had no idea what I was saying. The words tumbled out of me in a mad rush, an unstoppable deluge of nonsense and overcooked emotions, and when I came to the end of my ridiculous speech, I saw that Rachel was smiling, smiling for the first time since she had walked into the restaurant. Perhaps that was all I could hope to accomplish. To let her know that I was with her, that I believed in her, and that the situation probably wasn't as dark as she thought it was. If nothing else, the smile told me that she was beginning to calm down, and as I kept on talking, I slowly steered her away from the subject at hand, knowing that the best medicine would be to make her forget Terrence for a while, to stop her from dwelling on the problem that had been obsessing her for weeks. Chapter by chapter, I filled her in on all the things that had happened to me since we'd last been together. Essentially, it was a truncated version of everything I've set down in this book so far. No, not quite everything – since I edited out the story of Marina and the other necklace (too sad, too humiliating), said nothing about my ugly telephone conversation with the unmentionable one, and spared her the painful details of the *Scarlet Letter* hoax. But nearly all the other elements were accounted for: *The Book of Human Folly*, cousin Tom, Harry Brightman, little Lucy, the trip to Vermont, Tom's fling with Honey Chowder, the contents of Harry's will, Tina Hott mouthing the words of 'Can't Help Lovin' Dat Man.' Rachel listened closely, doing her best to absorb so much startling information as she swallowed her food and drank her wine. As for me, the more I talked, the more I enjoyed myself. I had slipped into the role of ancient mariner, and I could have gone on spinning my tales until the end of the night. Rachel was especially eager to meet Lucy, and so we arranged for her to visit my apartment the following Sunday – with or without her husband, as she preferred. She was also looking forward to seeing Tom, she said, and then she asked the sixty-four-thousand-dollar question, 'What about Honey? Do you think anything is going to happen?'

'I doubt it,' I said. 'Tom left his number with her father and asked him to give it to her, but she hasn't called. And as far as I know, Tom hasn't called her. If I were a betting man, I'd say we've seen the last of Honey. Too bad, but the case appears to be closed.'

As usual, I was wrong. Exactly two weeks after my dinner with Rachel, on the last Friday of the month, Honey Chowder came striding into the bookstore wearing a white summer dress and a large straw hat with a floppy brim. It was five o'clock in the afternoon. Tom was sitting behind the front counter, reading an old softcover edition of *The Federalist Papers*. I had already picked up Lucy at camp, and she and I were in the back of the store, rearranging books in the History section. Not a single customer had been in for the past two hours, and the only sound to be heard was the muffled whir of an electric fan.

Lucy's face brightened when she saw Honey walk in. She was about to go running toward her, but I put my hand on her arm and whispered, 'Not yet, Lucy. Give them a chance to talk first.' Honey, whose eyes were fixed on Tom, hadn't noticed we were there. Like two secret agents, our girl and yours truly hid behind one of the bookcases and observed the following exchange.

'Hey there, Tom,' Honey said, plopping her purse down on the counter. Then she removed her hat and shook out her long, opulent hair. 'How's life?'

Tom glanced up from his book and said, 'Good Lord, Honey. What are you doing here?'

'We'll get to that later. First, I want to know how you are.'

'Not bad. Busy, a bit stressed out, but not bad. A lot has happened since I last saw you. My boss died, and it seems that I've inherited this store. I'm still trying to figure out what to do with it.'

'I'm not talking about business. I'm talking about you. The inner workings of your heart.'

'My heart? It's still beating. Seventy-two times a minute.'

'Which means you're still alone, doesn't it? If you'd fallen in love with someone, it would beat much faster than that.'

'Love? What are you talking about?'

'You haven't met anyone in the past month, have you?'

'No. Of course not. I've been much too busy.'

'Do you remember Vermont?'

'How could I forget it?'

'And the last night you were there. Do you remember that?'

'Yes. I remember that night.'

'And?'

'And what?'

'What do you see when you look at me, Tom?'

'I don't know, Honey. I see you. Honey Chowder. A woman with an impossible name. An impossible woman with an impossible name.'

'Do you know what I see when I look at you, Tom?'

'I'm not sure I want to know.'

'I see a great man, that's what I see. I see the finest person I've ever met.'

'Oh?'

'Yes, *oh*. And because that's what I see when I look at you, I've chucked everything and come down to Brooklyn to be part of your life.'

'Chucked everything?'

'That's right. The school year ended two days ago, and I gave them notice. I'm free as a bird.'

'But Honey, I'm not in love with you. I hardly even know you.'

'You will.'

'Will what?'

'First, you'll get to know me. And then you'll start to love me.'

'Just like that.'

'Yes. Just like that.' She paused for a moment and smiled. 'How's Lucy, by the way?'

'Lucy's fine. She's living with Nathan on First Street.'

'Poor Nathan. He's not up to all that work. The girl needs a mother. From now on, she'll live with us.'

'You're awfully damn sure of yourself, aren't you?'

'I have to be, Tom. If I wasn't sure of myself, I wouldn't be here. I wouldn't have all my bags waiting outside in the car. I wouldn't know that you were the man of my life.'

At that point, I figured they had said enough to each other, and I let Lucy come out of hiding. She rushed across the room, heading straight for Honey.

'There you are, my little munchkin,' the ex-schoolteacher said, wrapping our girl in her arms and lifting her off the ground. When she finally put her down again, she asked, 'Did you hear what Tom and I were saying?'

Lucy nodded.

'And what do you think?'

'I think it's a nice plan,' Lucy said. 'If I live with you and Uncle Tom, I won't have to eat in restaurants anymore. You'll stuff me with all that tasty food you cook. And Uncle Nat can eat with us whenever he likes. And when you and Uncle Tom go out on the town, he can be my babysitter.'

Honey grinned. 'And you're going to be a good girl, aren't you? The best girl in the world.'

'No, ma'am,' Lucy said, looking back at her with the deadest of deadpan faces. 'I'm gonna be bad. I'm gonna be the baddest, meanest, cussingest little girl in the whole of God's creation.'

Hawthorn Street or Hawthorne Street?

Months passed. By the middle of October, the lawyers had finished their work on Harry's estate, and Tom and Rufus had become the legitimate owners of Brightman's Attic and the building it was housed in. Tom and Honey were already married by then, and Lucy, silent as ever on the subject of her mother's whereabouts, was enrolled as a fifth grader at the local public school, P.S. 321. Rachel was still with Terrence. One week after the Wood-Chowder wedding, she called to tell me that she was two months pregnant.

I continued to work in the bookstore, but after Honey's dramatic appearance at the end of June, we began sharing the job, which meant that I had to be there only half the time. On my days off I continued jotting down anecdotes for *The Book of Human Folly*, and just as Lucy had suggested, I filled in as babysitter whenever Tom and Honey went out at night. In their first months together, that proved to be a common occurrence. Honey had felt starved in the provinces, and now that she had landed in New York, she wanted to take advantage of everything the city had to offer: plays, movies, concerts, dance performances, poetry readings, moonlight jaunts on the Staten Island ferry. It did me good to see how the slothful, bovine Tom flourished under the energetic influence of his newfound wife. Within days of Honey's arrival, he ceased dithering about what to do with the inheritance and decided to put the building on the market. With their half of the money from the sale, they would have more than enough to buy a two- or three-bedroom apartment in the neighborhood, along with something left over to carry them until they found regular jobs – most likely as teachers in a private school for the next academic year. Months passed, and by mid-October Tom had lost close to twenty pounds, which brought him halfway back to resembling the young Dr. Thumb of yore. Home cooking obviously agreed with him, and in spite of his predictions to the contrary, Honey didn't wear him out or beat him down or crush his spirit. Day by day, she slowly turned him into the man he was always destined to become.

With so many positive developments in the love department, the reader might be lulled into thinking that universal happiness reigned over our little patch of Brooklyn. Alas, not all marriages are destined to survive. Everyone knows that, but who among us would have guessed that the least happy person in the neighborhood during those months was Tom's former flame, the Beautiful Perfect Mother? It was true that her husband had made a bad impression on me in the woods of Prospect Park, but not in a hundred years would I have supposed he was dumb enough to take a wife like his for granted. The Nancy Mazzucchellis of this world are few and far between, and if a man should be lucky enough to win a Mazzucchelli heart, his job from that point on is to do everything in his power not to lose it. But men (as I have amply demonstrated in earlier chapters of this book) are stupid creatures, and pretty boy James Joyce turned out to be stupider than most. Because Nancy's mother and I struck up a friendship that summer (more about that later), I was a frequent dinner guest of the family, and it was within the precincts of their house on Carroll Street that I learned about Jimmy's past transgressions and saw his marriage to Nancy burst asunder. The tomfoolery had started even before there was such a person as the B.P.M. – a good six years back, when Nancy was pregnant with her first child, Devon. When she learned about her husband's affair with a Tribeca barmaid, she temporarily threw him out of the house, but once the baby was born, she didn't have the strength to resist his tearful promises that it would never happen again. But words count for little in such matters, and who knows how many secret liaisons followed? By Joyce's estimate, there were no less than seven or eight, counting one-night stands and quick fucks in the back stairwell at work. Nancy, ever generous and forgiving, tended to discount the rumors. But then Jim fell for fellow Foley walker Martha Ives, and that was that. He said he was in love, and on August 11, 2000, two months after I first saw him at Harry's funeral service, he packed up his bags and left.

Twelve days later, my oncologist told me that my lungs were still clean.

A scant four days after that, Rachel, in cahoots with Tom and Honey, hatched a devilish plot to trick me into thinking I was about to attend a ball game at Shea Stadium – when in fact it was a surprise party for my sixtieth birthday. The plan was for me to pick up Tom at his apartment, but the moment I walked through the door, a dozen people mobbed me with hugs, kisses, and slaps on the back, not to mention an outburst of wild shouting and singing. I was so unprepared for this assault of good will, I nearly threw up from the shock it gave to my system. The festivities lasted well into the night, and at one point I was prevailed upon to stand up and deliver a speech. The champagne had long since gone to my head, and I think I rambled for some time, spouting gibberish and incoherent jokes as my half-potted audience struggled to follow what I was saying. About the only thing that comes back to me from that screwy discourse is a brief aside on the linguistic acumen of Casey Stengel. If memory serves me right, I think I even ended my talk with a quotation from the master himself. 'They didn't call him the Old Professor for nothing,' I said. 'Not only was he the first manager of our beloved Mets, but, even more essential to the general good of mankind, he was the author of numerous sentences that have reshaped our understanding of the English language. Before I sit down, allow me to leave you with this priceless, unforgettable pearl, which sums up my own experience more accurately than any statement I've come across in the sixty years I've dwelled inside this flesh: "There comes a time in every man's life, and I've had plenty of them."'

The Subway Series came and went; the weather turned cool; Gore was running against Bush. To my mind, the outcome was never in doubt. Even with Nader gumming up the works, it seemed impossible that the Democrats could be defeated, and wherever I went in the neighborhood, almost everyone I talked to was of the same opinion. Only Tom, the most pessimistic of men when it came to American politics, looked worried. He believed it was too close to call, and if Bush turned out to be the winner, he said, we could forget all that claptrap about 'compassionate conservatism.' The man wasn't a conservative. He was an ideologue of the extreme right, and the instant he was sworn into office, the government would be controlled by lunatics.

Just one week before the election, Aurora finally surfaced – only to vanish again within thirty seconds. Contact came in the form of a telephone call to Tom, but no one was in the apartment that morning, and therefore we had nothing to go on but a truncated message left on the answering machine. I don't know how many times I listened to that message with Tom and Honey, but we rewound the tape often enough for me to have memorized every sentence of it. Each time I heard her voice, she sounded a little more despairing, a little more on edge, a little more afraid. She spoke softly, barely rising above a whisper from start to finish, but her words were so deadly, they carried all the impact of a scream.

Tom. It's me, Rory. I'm calling from a pay phone and I don't have much time. I know you've probably had it with me, but I've been missing Lucy so much, I just wanted to find out how she is. Don't think it was fun, Tommy. I thought and thought, but you were the only person I could count on. She couldn't stay here anymore. It's all going to pieces. It's bad news. I've been trying to get out myself, but it's too hard, I'm never alone . . . Write me a letter, okay? I don't have a phone, but you can reach me at eighty-seven Hawthorn Street in . . . Shit. Gotta go. Sorry. Gotta go.

The receiver slammed down on the hook, and the long-awaited call came to a sudden, inconclusive end. Our darkest anxieties had assumed the weight of fact, and still we had no idea where she was. Tom had been through similar moments with his sister in the past, and though he felt every bit as worried about her as I did, his alarm was tempered by exhaustion, by irritation, by years of disappointment and regret. 'She's the most irresponsible person I've ever known,' he said. 'Lucy's finally beginning to settle in with us, and now, after how many goddamn months, she calls to say she's missing her. What kind of mother is that? She wants me to write to her, and then she doesn't even tell us what town she lives in. It isn't fair, Nathan. Honey and I are doing all we can to help, and the last thing we need is more confusion, more drama. Enough is enough.'

'It might not be fair,' I said, 'but Rory's in some kind of trouble, and we have to find her. There's no other choice. Spare me your judgments until later, all right?'

The entire world changed for me after that. The 2000 election disaster was just a few days down the road, but even as Tom and Honey sat horrified in front of their television set for the next five weeks, watching the Republican Party call in their thugs to challenge the Florida returns and then manipulate the Supreme Court into staging a legal coup on their behalf, even as these offenses were committed against the American people and my nephew and his wife marched in demonstrations, sent letters to their congressman, and signed countless protests and petitions, I was preoccupied with only one thing: to hunt down Rory and bring her back to New York.

Eighty-seven Hawthorn Street. Or maybe it was Hawthorne Street, named after a man instead of a shrub – perhaps even Nathaniel Hawthorne, the long-dead novelist who had inadvertently caused the death of our sad, luckless friend. A bitter conjunction, signifying little or nothing, but spooky for all that, as if the same word appearing in two different contexts established a subterranean link between Harry and Aurora: the one gone forever, the other just beyond reach, both denizens of the invisible. Apart from that single clue, everything was blind guesswork, but because Lucy spoke with a southern accent, and because she had placed her mother in the nonexistent land of Carolina Carolina, I decided to begin my search in the real Carolinas, North and South. The pity was that Aurora and her husband didn't have a phone. If they had been listed in the book, it would have been possible to call information for every town and city in both states and find them by asking for the number of David Minor at 87 Hawthorn(e) Street. A laborious task, but one that was bound to yield a positive result. Since that option wasn't available to me, I had no choice but to proceed in reverse. One Sunday, I took the train down to Princeton Junction and spent twelve hours sitting in front of a computer screen with my pregnant daughter and her meek, chastened husband. Terrence might have lacked charm, but he was a technological superhero, and by the time I returned home the next morning, I had a printout that listed every Hawthorn Street and Hawthorne Street in both Carolinas. To my stupefaction, there were several hundred of them. Too many. In order to visit every number 87 on the list, I would have been on the road for six months.

That was when I turned to Henry Peoples, my old associate at Mid-Atlantic Accident and Life. He had been one of the company's top investigators, and over the years we had worked on a number of cases together, the most spectacular one being the so-called Dubinsky Affair, which had turned Henry into something of a minor legend in the field. Arthur Dubinsky had faked his death at fifty-one by killing a homeless man from the streets of New York and substituting that body for his own in a fiery car crash off a cliff in the Rockies. Maureen, his twenty-eight-year-old third wife, collected on the one-point-six-million-dollar policy, and then, just one month later, sold her Manhattan co-op and vanished from sight. Henry, who had been suspicious of Dubinsky from the start, had continued keeping tabs on Maureen, and when she suddenly upped and left New York, he filed a report with his department chief, who granted him permission to go after her. It took nine months of arduous legwork before he found Mrs. Dubinsky – living with her perfectly intact husband on the island of Saint Lucia. We managed to recover eighty-five percent of the policy; Arthur Dubinsky wound up in prison for murder; and Henry and I were rewarded with large bonuses.

I worked with Peoples for more than twenty years, but I'm not going to pretend I ever liked him. He was an odd, unpleasant man who adhered to a strict vegetarian diet and demonstrated all the warmth and personality of an extinguished lamppost. Rumpled polyester suits (mostly brown), thick horn-rim glasses, perpetual dandruff, and an unnerving revulsion against small talk of any kind. You could show up at the office with your arm in a sling or a patch over your eye, and Henry wouldn't say a word. He would stare at you for a while, absorb the details of your injury, and then, without asking how you'd hurt yourself or whether you were in pain, calmly put his report on your desk.

Still, he had a knack for wriggling into holes and scaring up missing people, and now that he was retired, I wondered if he wouldn't be willing to take on the job for me. Fortunately, he hadn't moved from his old apartment in Queens, which he shared with his widowed sister and four cats. When I dialed his number, he picked up on the second ring.

'Just name a price,' I said. 'I'll pay anything you ask.'

'I don't want your money, Nathan,' he answered. 'Just cover my expenses, and it's a deal.'

'It could take months. I'd hate to see you lose so much time and get nothing out of it.'

'That's all right. It's not as if I have anything better to do with myself these days. I'll climb back into the saddle, and I'll get to live the glory years all over again.'

'The glory years?'

'Sure. All those good times we had together, Nathan. Dubinsky. Williamson. O'Hara. Lupino. You remember those cases, don't you?'

'Of course I remember them. I didn't know you were such a sentimentalist, Henry.'

'I'm not. Or at least I didn't think I was. But you can count on me. For old times' sake.'

'I'm assuming North Carolina or South Carolina. But I could be wrong.'

'Don't worry. As long as Minor used to have a phone, I'll be able to find him. It's in the bag.'

Six weeks later, Henry called me in the middle of the night and muttered four syllables into my ear: 'Winston-Salem.'

The next morning I was on a plane, flying south into the heart of tobacco country.

The Laughing Girl

Eighty-seven Hawthorne Street was a shabby two-story house on a half-rural, half-suburban road about three miles from the center of town. I lost my way several times before I found it, and when I parked my rented Ford Escort in the dirt driveway, I noticed that all the blinds on the front windows had been drawn. It was a gloomy, overcast Sunday in mid-December. The logical assumption was that no one was at home – or else that Rory and her husband lived in that house as if it were a cave, guarding themselves against the glare of natural light, fending off the impingements of the outside world, the sole members of a society of two. There was no doorbell, so I knocked. When nothing happened, I knocked again. Ever since Rory had left her message on Tom's machine, we had been expecting her to call back. But no more had been heard from her, and now that I was standing in front of what appeared to be an empty house, I was beginning to suspect that she no longer lived there. All sorts of gruesome thoughts jumped around in my head as I knocked for the third time. What if she had tried to run away, I asked myself, and Minor had caught up with her? What if he had taken her to another city, another state, and we had lost track of her forever? What if he had struck her down and accidentally killed her? What if the end had already come, and I was too late to help her, too late to carry her back to the world she belonged to?

The door opened, and there was Minor in the flesh, a tall, good-looking man of about forty, with dark, neatly combed hair and gentle blue eyes. I had built him up into such a monster over the past months, I was shocked to discover how unthreatening he looked, how *normal*. If there was anything strange about him, it was the fact that he was wearing a long-sleeved white shirt and a blue necktie knotted tightly at the collar. What kind of man walked around the house in a white shirt and tie? I wondered. It took a moment for me to come up with the answer. A man who had been to church, I said to myself. A man who observed the Sabbath and took his religion seriously.

'Yes?' he asked. 'What can I do for you?'

'I'm Rory's uncle,' I said. 'Nathan Glass. I happened to be in the neighborhood and thought I'd drop by to see her.'

'Oh? Is she expecting you?'

'Not that I'm aware of. As I understand it, you don't have a telephone.'

'That's correct. We don't believe in them. They encourage too much chatter and idle talk. We prefer to save our words for more essential things.'

'Very interesting . . . Mr . . . Mr . . .'

'Minor. David Minor. I'm Aurora's husband.'

'That's what I thought. But I didn't want to presume.'

'Come in, Mr. Glass. Unfortunately, Aurora isn't feeling well today. She's upstairs taking a nap, but you're more than welcome to come in. We're very open-minded in this neck of the woods. Even when others don't share our faith, we make every effort to treat them with dignity and respect. It's one of God's holy commandments.'

I smiled but said nothing. He had a pleasant enough manner, but already he was talking like a fanatic, and the last thing I needed was to tangle with him over theological issues. Give him his God and his church, I said to myself. The only reason I was there was to confirm whether Rory was in danger or not – and if she was, to get her out of that house as quickly as I could.

Based on the condition of the exterior (peeling paint, disintegrating shutters, weeds sprouting from the concrete steps), I was prepared to find some squalid assortment of broken, mismatched furniture cluttering the rooms within, but the place turned out to be more than presentable. Rory had inherited June's talent for doing much with little, and she had fashioned the living room into an austere but attractive environment, decorated with potted plants, handmade gingham curtains, and a large poster advertising a Giacometti museum show on the opposite wall. Minor gestured for me to take a seat on the couch, and I sat. He settled into a chair on the other side of the glass coffee table, and for the next few moments neither one of us said a word. I was tempted to plunge in at full tilt – demanding to go upstairs and talk to Aurora, grilling him with questions about Lucy, forcing him to explain why his wife was too scared to call her own brother – but I realized that this approach would probably backfire on me, and so I tiptoed into the conversation as delicately as I could.

'North Carolina,' I began. 'The last we heard, you were living with your mother in Philadelphia. What brought you down here?'

'Several things,' Minor said. 'My sister and her husband live in the area, and they found a good job for me. That job led to an even better job, and now I'm assistant manager at the True Value Hardware Store over at the Camelback Mall. It might not sound like much to you, but it's honest work, and I make a decent living. When I think about what I was like seven or eight years ago, it's a miracle I've come this far. I was a sinner, Mr. Glass. I was a drug addict and a fornicator, a liar and a petty criminal, a betrayer of everyone who loved me. Then I found peace in the Lord, and my life was saved. I know it's hard for a Jewish person like yourself to understand us, but we're not just another sect of Bible-thumping, fire-and-brimstone Christians. We don't believe in the apocalypse and the Day of Judgment; we don't believe in the Rapture or the End of Time. We prepare ourselves for life in heaven by living good lives on earth.'

'When you say *we*, who are you talking about?'

'Our church. The Temple of the Holy Word. We're a small group. Our congregation has just sixty members, but the Reverend Bob is an inspired leader, and he's taught us many things. "In the beginning was the Word, and the Word was with God, and the Word was God."'

'The Gospel according to Saint John. Chapter one, verse one.'

'So you're familiar with the Book.'

'To some extent. For a Jew who doesn't believe in God, more than most.'

'Are you telling me you're an atheist?'

'All Jews are atheists. Except for the ones who aren't, of course. But I don't have much to do with them.'

'You're not making fun of me, are you, Mr. Glass?'

'No, Mr. Minor, I'm not making fun of you. I wouldn't dream of it.'

'Because if you're making fun of me, I'll have to ask you to leave.'

'I'm interested in the Reverend Bob. I want to know what makes his church different from the others.'

'He understands what it means to sacrifice. If the Word is God, then the words of men mean nothing. They're no more significant than the grunts of animals or the cries of birds. To breathe God into us and absorb His Word, the reverend instructs us to refrain from indulging in the vanity of human speech. That's the sacrifice. One day out of seven, every member of the congregation must maintain a full and unbroken silence for twenty-four straight hours.'

'That must be very difficult.'

'It is at first. But then you begin to adjust, and your days of silence become the most beautiful and fulfilling moments of the week. You can actually feel the presence of God within you.'

'And what happens when someone breaks the silence?'

'He has to begin all over again the next day.'

'And if your child is sick, and you have to call the doctor on your day of silence, what happens then?'

'Married couples are never silent on the same day. You get your spouse to make the call.'

'But how can you call if you don't have a phone?'

'You go to the nearest pay phone.'

'And what about children? Do they have days of silence as well?'

'No, children are exempt. They don't enter the fold until the age of fourteen.'

'Your Reverend Bob has it all figured out, doesn't he?'

'He's a brilliant man, and his teachings make life better and simpler for us. We're a happy flock, Mr. Glass. Every day, I get down on my knees and thank Jesus for sending us to North Carolina. If we hadn't come here, we never would have known the joys of belonging to the Temple of the Holy Word.'

As Minor talked, I had the impression that he would have been satisfied to go on extolling the virtues of the Reverend Bob for another six or ten hours, but I found it curious to see how carefully he avoided mentioning the names of his wife and adopted daughter. I hadn't traveled all the way down from New York to shoot the breeze about True Value Hardware and crackpot temples of God. Now that we had spent some time together and he was beginning to feel a bit less nervous in my company, I figured the moment had come to change the subject.

'I'm surprised you haven't asked me about Lucy,' I said.

'Lucy?' he replied, looking genuinely taken aback. 'Do you know her?'

'Of course I know her. She's living with Aurora's brother and his new wife. I see her almost every day.'

'I thought you were out of touch with the family. Aurora said you lived in the suburbs somewhere, and no one had seen you in years.'

'That changed about six months ago. I'm back in touch. I'm in touch all the time.'

Minor gave me a short, wistful grin. 'How's the little one doing?'

'Do you care?'

'Of course I care.'

'Then why did you send her away?'

'It wasn't my decision. Aurora didn't want her anymore, and there was nothing I could do to stop her.'

'I don't believe you.'

'You don't know Aurora, Mr. Glass. She's not all there in the head. I do everything I can to help and support her, but she shows no gratitude. I pulled her out of the depths of hell and saved her life, but she still won't give in. She still won't believe.'

'Is there any law that says she has to believe what you believe?'

'She's my wife. A wife should follow her husband. It's her duty to follow her husband in all things.'

It was difficult to know where we were headed now. The conversation was branching off in several directions at once, and my instincts were beginning to fail me. Minor's calm, soft-spoken question about Lucy seemed to demonstrate a sincere regard for her well being, and unless he was a ferociously gifted liar, a man who wouldn't hesitate to distort the truth whenever it served his purpose, I found myself in the awkward position of feeling a little sorry for him. At least for a few moments I did, and that sudden, unexpected rush of sympathy caught me with my guard down, turning what was supposed to be a naked clash of wills into something far more complex, far more human. But then he had started bad-mouthing Rory, blaming her for abandoning her own daughter, accusing her of mental instability, and then, even worse, had come out with that idiotic, reactionary pronouncement about marriage. Still, certain facts were nevertheless undeniable. He had rescued her from drugs and fallen in love with her, and based on Rory's past history, who was to say she wasn't prone to fits of irrational behavior, that she wasn't an impossible person to live with, that she wasn't partially out of her mind? On the other hand, perhaps the entire conflict could be boiled down to a single irresolvable point: Minor believed in the teachings of the Reverend Bob, and Rory didn't. And because she refused to believe, he had gradually come to hate her.

From where I was sitting on the couch, I had a clear view of the staircase that led to the second floor. As I pondered what to say next, I looked past Minor's left shoulder in that direction, momentarily distracted by something I'd seen out of the corner of my eye – a small, dark object that appeared for less than a second, then vanished before I could identify what it was. Minor began talking again, reiterating his ideas on what constituted a good and proper marriage, but he no longer had my full attention. I was looking at the stairs, belatedly understanding that the thing I had seen was probably the tip of a shoe – no doubt Aurora's shoe – and if that was the case, I hoped she'd been standing there for some time, eavesdropping on us since the start of my visit. Minor was so wrapped up in what he was saying, he still hadn't noticed that I wasn't looking directly at him. Fuck it, I said to myself. Enough cat and mouse. Enough beating around the bush. It's time to pull up the curtain on the second act.

'Come on down, Rory,' I said. 'It's your old Uncle Nat, and I'm not going to leave this house until I've talked with you.'

I jumped from the couch and skirted past Minor to the foot of the stairs, moving quickly on the off chance that he would try to stop me from going to her.

'She's asleep,' I heard him say behind me, just as I caught my first glimpse of Aurora's legs at the top of the stairs. 'She's been fighting the flu since Thursday and has a high fever. Come back in the middle of the week. You can talk to her then.'

'No, David,' my niece called out as she descended the stairs. 'I'm all right.'

She was wearing a pair of black jeans and an old gray sweatshirt, and it was true that she looked under the weather, not at all in good form. Pale and thin, with dark circles under her eyes, she had to clutch the banister as she slowly made her way toward me, but in spite of the effects of flu and fever, she was smiling, smiling the great, luminous smile of the little Laughing Girl she had been so many years before.

'Uncle Nat,' she said, opening her arms to me. 'My knight in shining armor.' She threw herself against my body and hugged me with all her strength. 'How's my baby?' she whispered. 'Is my little girl all right?'

'She's fine,' I said. 'She can't wait to see you again, but she's doing fine.'

Minor was standing next to us by then, looking none too pleased by this display of family affection. 'Sweetheart,' he said. 'You really should go back upstairs and lie down. You were a hundred and one just half an hour ago, and it isn't good to walk around with a fever like that.'

'This is my Uncle Nat,' Rory said, still holding on to me for dear life. 'My mother's only brother. I haven't seen him in a long, long time.'

'I know that,' Minor said. 'But he can come back in a couple of days – as soon as you're feeling better.'

'You know what's best, don't you, David?' Rory said. 'You always know what's best. Silly me to come downstairs without your approval.'

'Don't go if you don't want to,' I said to her. 'You're not going to die if you stay here for a few more minutes.'

'Oh yes, I will,' she said, making no effort to hide her sarcasm. 'David thinks I'll die if I don't do everything he says. Isn't that right, David?'

'Calm down, Aurora,' her husband said. 'Not in front of your uncle.'

'Why not?' she answered. 'Why the goddamn fucking not?'

'Watch your tongue,' Minor reprimanded her. 'We don't talk like that in this house.'

'Oh, we don't, do we?' she said. 'Then maybe it's time for me to leave this goddamn fucking house. Maybe it's time for the vermin to clear out so you can be left alone with your pure thoughts and your pure tongue and your silent fucking God. This is it, Mr. Holy. The goddamn moment of truth. My lucky day has finally come, and now Uncle Nat is going to get me out of here. Isn't that right, Uncle Nat? We're going to drive away in your car, and before the sun comes up tomorrow morning, I'll be with my Lucy again.'

'Just say the word,' I answered, 'and I'll take you wherever you want to go.'

'I'm saying it, Uncle Nat. I'm saying it now.'

Minor was so flabbergasted, he didn't know what to do. I was expecting him to make a lunge for her, to do everything he could to stop us from walking out of there, but the confrontation had erupted so quickly, so fiercely, that he didn't even say a word. I put my arm around Aurora, and before her husband knew what had hit him, we were already in my car, backing out of the driveway and leaving Hawthorne Street behind us for good.

Flying North

Aurora was in no condition to travel, but when I suggested that we check into a hotel somewhere and wait for her fever to come down, she shook her head and insisted that we get on the next plane to New York.

'David's smart,' she said. 'If we hang around here for just a few hours, he's bound to find us. Just pump me full of Advil or something, and I'll be okay.'

So I bought her the Advil, wrapped her in my overcoat, turned up the heat in the car, and drove straight to the airport. I had landed in Greensboro that morning, but since Minor would surely go looking for us there, Rory thought our best bet was to leave by way of Raleigh-Durham. It was a hundred-mile drive, and she slept for the full two hours we were on the road. After four Advils and the long nap, she woke up feeling better. Still wan, still a bit drained, but the fever had apparently broken, and after another dose of pills and two glasses of orange juice at the airport, she was strong enough to talk – which was precisely what we did for the next several hours: from the moment we took our seats at the departure gate to the moment we stepped out of a yellow cab in front of my house in Brooklyn that night.

'It's all my fault,' she said. 'I saw it coming a long time ago, but I was too weak to stand up for myself, too nervous to fight back. That's what happens when you think the other person is better than you are. You stop thinking for yourself, and pretty soon you don't own your own life anymore. You don't even realize it, Uncle Nat, but you're fucked. You're absolutely fucked . . .

'The first mistake was turning my back on Tom. After I got out of rehab, David and I left California and came east with Lucy. We lived with his mother in Philadelphia for six months, and things were good, about as good as any time I can remember. I was crazy in love with him. No man had ever been so nice to me, and I walked around with this incredible feeling that I was protected, that this smart, decent person actually knew who I was. We were both survivors. The two of us had been through so much, and there we were after all our ups and downs, standing on our feet together, about to get married . . .

709

'One day, I went to New York to see Tom, and I have to admit I found it a little depressing. He'd put on all this weight, he'd quit school and was driving a cab, and he was kind of testy with me, at least in the beginning. Not that I blamed him. I'd been out of touch for so long, why shouldn't he have resented me for it? There was no excuse. I'd been running around California all that time, slowly going to the dogs, and I just couldn't bring myself to pick up the phone and call. I tried to explain, but it didn't do much good. But Tom was still my big brother, and now that I was getting married, I wanted him to walk me down the aisle and give me away – just like what you did with Mom when she got married. He said he'd be glad to do it, and all of a sudden it was like old times again, and I really started feeling happy. I had my brother back. I was marrying David, and Lucy, my amazing little Lucy, was living with her mother again – her dumb kid mother who was finally beginning to grow up. What else could I ask for? I had everything I wanted, Uncle Nat. Everything . . .

'Then I took the bus back to Philadelphia, and when I told David about inviting Tom to the wedding, he said it was impossible, out of the question. He'd been thinking about it the whole time I was in New York, and he'd decided that my brother was a bad influence on me. If I wanted to go ahead with the marriage, I would have to cut all ties to my past. Not just friends, but everyone in my family too. What are you talking about? I asked him. I love my brother. He's the best person in the world. But David didn't want to discuss it. We were starting a new life together, he said, and unless I made a clean break with everything that had corrupted me in the past, I would eventually slip back into my old ways. I had to choose. It was all or nothing, he said. An act of faith or an act of rebellion. Life with God or life without God. Marriage or no marriage. Husband or brother. David or Tom. A hopeful future or a miserable return to the past . . .

'I should have put my foot down. I should have told him I wasn't swallowing that horseshit, and if he thought he could marry me without inviting Tom to the wedding, there wasn't going to be any wedding – period. But I didn't do that. I didn't fight back, and when I let him have his way like that, it was already the beginning of the end. You can't give up power over yourself, not even when you believe in the other person, not even when you think the other person knows what's best. That's what did me in. It was more than just being scared of losing David. The really scary thing was that I thought he was probably right. I loved

Tommy, but what had I ever done for him except cause a lot of trouble and heartache? Maybe it would be better if I cut the tie and left him alone. Maybe he would be better off if he never saw me again . . .

'No, David never hit me. He never hit Lucy, and he never hit me. He's not a violent person. His game is talk. Talk, talk, talk. And then more talk. He wears you down with his arguments, and because his voice is so kind and reasonable, because he expresses himself so well, he sort of sucks you into his brain – almost as if he's hypnotizing you. That's what saved me at the rehab clinic in Berkeley. The way he kept on talking to me, looking into my eyes with that caring expression on his face and that soft, steady voice of his. It's hard to resist him, Uncle Nat. He gets inside your head, and after a while you start to think he can never be wrong about anything . . .

'I know Tom was worried. He was afraid I was going to turn into one of those born-again holy rollers, but I'm not cut out for that kind of stuff. David kept working on me, but I only pretended to go along. If he wants to believe in that crap – fine, I don't care. It makes him happy, and I'm never going to be against anything that makes a person happy. I heard him talking to you in the house before, and what he said was true. He isn't into all that fundamentalist ranting and raving. He believes in Jesus and the afterlife, but compared to some of the things other people believe in, it isn't too heavy. His problem is that he thinks he can be a saint. He wants to be perfect . . .

'So yeah, I went to church with him every Sunday. I didn't have much choice, did I? But it wasn't all bad, at least not when we were in Philadelphia. I sang in the choir there, and you know how much I love to sing. Those hymns are some of the sappiest tunes ever written, but at least I got a chance to exercise my lungs once a week, and as long as David didn't push too hard on shoving Jesus down my throat, I wasn't what you'd call an unhappy camper. I sometimes think that if we hadn't left Philadelphia, everything would have worked out. But we both had trouble finding decent jobs. I had a part-time gig as a waitress in some sleazoid diner, and the best David could do after months of looking was night watchman in an office building on Market Street. We went to our N.A. meetings; we kept ourselves sober; Lucy liked her school; David's mom was a little nuts but basically all right – but we just couldn't earn enough money in that town. Then an opening turned up in North Carolina, and David jumped at the chance. True Value Hardware. Things got better after that, and then, about a year and a half ago, David met the Reverend Bob, and all of a sudden they got a whole lot worse . . .

'David was only seven when his father died. I'm not saying it's his fault, but I think he's been looking for a substitute father ever since. An authority figure. Someone strong enough to take him under his wing and guide him through life. That's probably why he joined the marines after high school instead of going to college. You know, take your orders from Big Daddy America, and Big Daddy will take care of you. Big Daddy took care of him all right. Shipped him out to Desert Storm and did a major number on his head. Fucked him up bad. David goes downhill for a bunch of years and ends up on horse. You already know that. I heard him tell you about it today, but the interesting thing to me is how he finally kicked it. Not with that A.A. line about trusting in a higher power – but with real religion. He goes all the way to the top and gets the biggest father of them all. Mr. God. Mr. goddamn God, the ruler of the universe. But still, maybe that isn't enough. You can talk to your God and hope he listens to you, but unless your brain is tuned to the twenty-four-hour Schizophrenia Network, he isn't going to talk back. Pray all you want, but you won't hear a peep from Dad. You can study his words in the Bible, but the Bible is just a book, and books don't talk, do they? But the Reverend Bob talks, and once you start listening to him, you know you've found your man. He's the father you've been looking for, an actual flesh-and-blood human father, and every time he opens his mouth, you're convinced he's getting it straight from the big boss himself. God talks through this guy, and whenever he tells you to do something, you'd better do it or else . . .

'He's fifty-something years old, I guess. Tall and skinny, with a long nose and a fat cow of a wife named Darlene. I don't know when he started the Temple of the Holy Word, but it isn't a normal church like the one we went to in Philadelphia. The reverend calls himself a Christian, but he never says what kind, and I'm not even sure he gives a rat's ass about religion. It's all about controlling other people, about getting them to do weird, self-destructive things and make them believe they're serving the will of God. I think he's a fraud, a scam artist from the word go, but he has his followers in the palm of his hand, and they love him, they all love him, and David more than anyone else. What gets them so excited is the way he keeps coming up with new ideas, keeps changing his message. One Sunday it's about the evils of materialism and how we should shun worldly possessions and live in sacred poverty like the son of our dear Lord. The next Sunday it's about hard work and how we should earn as much money as we can. I told David I thought he was nuts and didn't want to expose Lucy to any more of that drivel. But David was a true convert by then, and he wouldn't listen to me. Two or three months later, the Reverend Bob suddenly decides that singing should be banned from the Sunday services. It's an offense against the ears of God, he says, and from now on we should worship him in silence. As far as I was concerned, that was the last straw. I told David that Lucy and I were quitting the church. He could keep on going as long as he liked, but we were never setting foot inside that place again. It was the first time I'd spoken up for myself since we were married – and it didn't do me an ounce of good. He pretended to be sympathetic, but the rules were that all families of the congregation had to attend services together every Sunday. If I dropped out, he would be excommunicated. Well, I said, just tell them that Lucy and I are sick, that we have a fatal disease and can't get out of bed. David gave me one of his sad, patronizing smiles. Prevarication is a sin, he said. If we don't speak the truth at all times, our souls will be barred at the gates of heaven and cast down into the jaws of hell . . .

'So we kept on going every week, and about a month after that the Reverend Bob came up with his next big idea. Secular culture was destroying America, he said, and the only way we could undo the damage was to reject everything it offered us. That was when he started issuing his so-called Sunday Edicts. First, everyone had to get rid of their television sets. Then it was radios. Then it was books – every book in the house except the Bible. Then it was telephones. Then it was computers. Then it was CDs, tapes, and records. Can you imagine? No more music, Uncle Nat, no more novels, no more poems. Then we had to cancel our magazine subscriptions. Then it was newspapers. Then we weren't allowed to go to the movies anymore. The idiot was on a rampage, but the more sacrifices he demanded of the congregation, the more they seemed to like it. As far as I know, not one family left . . .

'Finally, there weren't any more things to get rid of. The reverend stopped his attacks on the culture and media business and started hammering away at what he called "the gut issues." Every time we talked, we drowned out the voice of God. Every time we listened to the words of men, we neglected the words of God. From now on, he said, every member of the church above the age of fourteen would spend one day a week in total silence. In that way, we would be able to restore our connection with God, to hear him speaking within our souls. After all the other stunts he'd pulled on us, this seemed like a pretty mild demand . . .

'David works from Monday to Friday, so he chose Saturday as his day of silence. Mine was Thursday, but since no one was around until Lucy came home from school, I could do whatever I damn pleased. I sang songs, I talked to myself, I shouted curses at the almighty Reverend Bob. But once Lucy and David walked through the door, I had to put on an act. I served them dinner in silence, I tucked Lucy into bed in silence, I kissed David good-night in silence. No big deal. Then, after about a month of this routine, Lucy got it into her head to follow my example. She was just nine years old. Not even the Reverend Bob was asking children to join in, but my little girl loved me so much, she wanted to do everything I did. For three Saturdays in a row, she didn't say a word. No matter how much I begged her not to do it, she refused to stop. She's such a smart kid, Uncle Nat, but you know how stubborn she can be. You've had the same treatment yourself, and once she makes up her mind, it's like trying to push over a building to get her to back down. Incredibly enough, David took my side, but I think a part of him was so proud of her for acting like an adult, he wasn't very forceful or convincing. Anyway, it had nothing to do with him. It was about me. About me and her. I told David that I had to talk to the Reverend Bob. If he would release me from my Thursday silences, it would take the burden off Lucy, and then she'd start acting like herself again . . .

'David wanted to come to the meeting with me, but I said no, I had to see the reverend alone. To make sure he wouldn't butt in, I set up the appointment for a Saturday, the day when David wasn't allowed to talk. Just drive me to the house, I said, and wait outside in the car. It shouldn't take too long . . .

'The Reverend Bob was sitting at the desk in his study, putting the final touches on the sermon he was supposed to deliver the next morning. Sit down, my child, he said, and tell me what the problem is. I explained about Lucy and why I thought he would be doing us a great service if he released me from my Thursday silences. Hmmm, he said. Hmmm. I have to think it over. I'll give you my decision by the end of next week. He was looking straight at me, and every time he spoke, his bushy eyebrows did this funny little twitching thing. Thank you, I said. I believe you're a wise man, and I know you'll see it in your heart to bend the rules in order to help a young child. I wasn't going to tell him

what I really thought. Like it or not, I was a member of his fucking congregation, and I had to play along as if I meant what I was saying. I figured our business was over then, but when I stood up to go, he
stretched out his right arm and waved me back into my seat. I've been
watching you, woman, he said, and I want you to know that you get
high marks on all fronts. You and Brother Minor are among the pillars
of our community, and I'm certain I can depend on you to follow me in
all matters, both sacred and profane. Profane? I said. What do you mean
by *profane*? As you probably know, the reverend said, my wife Darlene
was unable to bear children. Now that I've reached a certain age, I've
begun to think about my legacy, and I find it tragic to contemplate leaving this earth without having produced an heir. You could always
adopt, I said. No, he said, that's not good enough. I have to make a child
out of my own flesh, a descendant of my own blood to carry on with the
work I've started here. I've been watching you, woman, and of all the
souls in my flock, you're the only one worthy to carry my seed. What
are you talking about? I said. I'm married to someone else. I love my
husband. Yes, I know that, he said, but for the sake of the Temple of the
Holy Word, I'm asking you to divorce him and marry me. But you have
a wife, I said. No one's allowed to have two wives, Reverend Bob, not
even you. No, of course not, he said. Needless to say, I'll file for divorce
as well. Let me think it over, I said. Everything's happening so fast, I
don't know what to say. My head's spinning, my hands are shaking,
and I'm completely confused. Don't worry, my child, the reverend said.
Take all the time you need. But just so you understand the sorts of pleasures that await you, there's something I want you to see. The reverend
stood up from his chair, came around to the front of the desk, and
unzipped his fly. He was standing right in front of me, and that
unzipped fly wasn't two feet from my face. Look at this, he said, and
then he pulled out his cock and showed it to me. To be honest, it was a
fairly huge cock – much bigger than what you'd expect to find hanging
between the legs of a scrawny guy like that. I've seen a lot of naked men
in my time, and for sheer length and girth, I'd have to put the reverend's
unit up there in the top ten percent. A porn-sized cock, if you know
what I mean, but not the least bit attractive to my eyes. It was stiff and
purplish red, but the hard-on made it all veiny, and at full extension it
also curved to the left. A big cock, but also a disgusting one, and the
man it belonged to disgusted me even more. I suppose I could have
jumped up and run out of the house, but somewhere way off in the back

of my mind I knew this asshole was offering me a priceless opportunity, and in exchange for a few repulsive moments, I could free us all from the morons of that church . . .

'This is the holy bone, the reverend said, holding the erection in his hand and wagging it in my face. God gave me this glorious gift, and the jism that spurts from it can engender the lives of angels. Take it in your hand, Sister Aurora, and feel the fire coursing through its veins. Put it in your mouth and taste the flesh our good Lord saw fit to endow me with . . .

'I did what he wanted, Uncle Nat. I closed my eyes and shoved that big veiny corncob into my mouth, and little by little I sucked him off. It was nasty. My poor nose rubbing up against his smelly crotch, my poor stomach churning around inside me, but I knew what I was doing, and I was glad. Just as he was about to come, I took him out of my mouth and finished the job with my hand, making sure his precious jism squirted all over my blouse. That was my evidence, the one thing I needed to bring the son-of-a-bitch down. Remember Monica and Bill? Remember the dress? Well, now I had my blouse, and it was as good as a weapon, as good as a loaded gun . . .

'When I got into the car, I was crying. I don't know if they were real tears or fake tears, but I was crying. I told David to start up the engine and head for home. He looked upset, but since he wasn't allowed to talk until the next morning, he couldn't ask me any questions. That was when I realized the thing could go in either one of two ways. I was about to tell him that the Reverend Bob had raped me. If David talked then, it would mean that he cared more about me than the goddamn Temple of the Holy Word. We could hand the blouse over to the cops, have it tested for DNA, and the reverend would be cooked in a vat of burning oil. But what if David didn't talk? It would mean that I was nothing to him, that he was sticking with old Bob the Father to the bitter end. There wasn't going to be much time to act. If David let me down, I would have to stop thinking about myself. Lucy was the one who had to be saved, and the only way to do that was to get her out of North Carolina. Not tomorrow or next week, but now, this minute, on the first bus leaving for New York . . .

'After we had gone about a hundred yards, I told him. The bastard raped me, I said. Look at my blouse, David. That's the Reverend Bob's semen. He pinned me down and wouldn't let go. He forced himself on me, and I wasn't strong enough to push him off. David pulled the car over to the side of the road and stopped. For a little while, I thought he was with me, and I felt bad that I'd doubted him, ashamed that I hadn't been willing to trust him. He reached out his hand and touched my face, and he had that sweet, soulful look in his eyes, the same beautiful, tender look that made me fall for him back in California. This is the man I married, I said to myself, and he still loves me. But I was wrong. He might have felt sorry for me, but he wasn't about to interrupt his silence and disobey the Reverend Bob's holy command. Talk to me, I said. Please, David, open your mouth and talk to me. He shook his head. He shook his head, and I started to cry again, and this time it was for real . . .

'We got back on the road, and after a minute or two I managed to pull myself together enough to tell him that we were sending Lucy up north to my brother Tom in Brooklyn. If he didn't do exactly what I told him to do, I would take the blouse to the police, press charges against the Reverend Bob, and our marriage would be over. You still want to be married to me, don't you? I asked. David nodded. All right, I said, then this is the deal. First, we pick up Lucy at the house. Then we drive to the A.T.M. at City Federal and withdraw two hundred dollars in cash. Then we go to the bus depot and you buy her a one-way ticket to New York with your MasterCard. Then we give her the money, put her on the bus, and kiss her good-bye. That's what you're going to do for me. What I'm going to do for you is this: the moment the bus leaves the terminal, I'll give you the blouse with your hero's cum stains on it, and you can destroy the evidence to save his ass. I'll also promise to stay with you, but only on one condition: that I never have to go near that church again. If you try to drag me back there, I'm gone from your life, gone from your life forever . . .

'I don't want to talk about saying good-bye to Lucy. It hurts too much to think about it. I said good-bye to her when I went into rehab, but this was different. This felt like the end of the world, and all I could do was hug her, and try not to crack up, and remind her to tell everyone that I was doing okay. I'm sorry she lost the letter I wrote Tom. I explained a lot in that letter, and it must have seemed awfully peculiar when she showed up empty-handed like that. I also tried to call Tom from the terminal, but everything was so rushed, and since I didn't have enough coins on me, I had to call collect. He wasn't home, but at least I knew he was still at his old address. I might have been acting crazy that day, but not crazy enough to send Lucy to New York without knowing exactly where Tom lived . . .

717

'I don't understand this Carolina Carolina business. I never told her not to say where I was. Why would I do that? I was sending her to Tom – and it never occurred to me that she wouldn't tell him about Winston-Salem. The poor kid. What I said to her was: Just let him know that I'm okay, that I'm doing fine. I should have known better. Lucy takes things so literally, she probably thought that when I used the word *just*, I meant that was the only thing I wanted her to say. She's always been like that. When she was three, I sent her to day care for a couple of hours every morning. After a few weeks, the teacher called me and said that she was worried about Lucy. When it was time for the children to have their milk, Lucy would always hang back until all the other kids had taken a carton before she'd take one for herself. The teacher didn't understand. Go get your milk, she'd say to Lucy, but Lucy would always wait around until there was just one carton left. It took a while for me to figure it out. Lucy didn't know which carton was supposed to be *her milk*. She thought all the other kids knew which ones were theirs, and if she waited until there was only one carton in the box, that one had to be hers. Do you see what I'm talking about, Uncle Nat? She's a little weird – but intelligent weird, if you know what I mean. Not like anyone else. If I hadn't used the word *just*, you would have known where I was all along . . .

'Why didn't I call again? Because I couldn't. No, not because we didn't have a phone in the house – because I was trapped. I'd promised David that I wouldn't leave him, but he didn't trust me anymore. The minute we got home from the bus terminal, he took me upstairs to Lucy's room and locked me in. Yes, Uncle Nat, he locked me in and kept me there for the rest of the day and all that night. When he started talking again the next morning, he told me that I had to be punished for lying about the Reverend Bob. Lying? I said. What the hell did that mean? There hadn't been any rape, he said. The only reason I'd insisted on going into the house alone was because I'd been planning to seduce him – and the poor man hadn't been able to resist my charms. Thank you, David, I said. Thank you for believing in me and understanding what a good wife I've been to you . . .

'Later that day, he boarded up the windows in the room. I mean, what's the use of a jail if the prisoner can crawl out the window, right? Then, very kindly, my dear husband carried up all the things we had put downstairs in the cellar after the Reverend Bob's Sunday Edicts. The television set, the radio, the CD player, the books. Isn't that against the

718

rules? I asked. Yes, David said, but I talked to the reverend after services this morning, and he's given me a special dispensation. I want to make things as comfortable as possible for you, Aurora. Gee, I said, why are you so nice to me? Because I love you, David said. You did a wicked thing yesterday, but that doesn't mean I don't love you. To show the purity of that love, he came back a minute later with a big stew pot so I wouldn't have to piss and shit on the floor. By the way, he said, you'll be happy to learn that you've been excommunicated from the Temple. You're out, but I'm still in. I'm crushed, I said. I think this is the saddest day of my life . . .

'I don't know what was wrong with me, but the whole thing felt like a joke, and I couldn't take it seriously. I figured it would go on for just a few days, and then I'd split. Promise or no promise, I wasn't going to hang around there a minute longer than I had to . . .

'But the days became weeks, and then the weeks became months. David understood what I was thinking, and he wasn't about to let me go. He'd let me out of the room when he came home from work, but what chance did I have to get away? He was always watching me. If I tried to run for the door, how far could I have gone? About two steps, maybe. He's bigger and stronger than I am, and all he had to do was run after me and drag me back. The keys to the car were in his pocket, his money was in his pocket, and the only money I had was a bunch of change I'd found in one of Lucy's bureau drawers. I kept waiting and hoping, but I only managed to slip out of the house once. That was when I tried to call Tom. You remember that, don't you? By some miracle, David dozed off in the living room after dinner. There's a pay phone about a mile and a half down the road, and I ran down that road as fast as I could. If only I'd had the balls to put my hand in David's pocket and steal the car key. But I couldn't risk waking him up, so I went down that road on foot. David must have opened his eyes about ten minutes after I left, and needless to say, he went down that road in the car. What a fiasco. I didn't even have time to finish the damn message . . .

'Now you know why I look so pale, so worn out. I was locked up in that room for six months, Uncle Nat. Locked up like an animal in my own house for half a year. I watched television, I read books, I listened to music, but mostly what I did was think about how to kill myself. If I didn't go ahead with it, it's because I promised Lucy that I was going to come back for her one day, that one day we would live together again. But Christ, it wasn't easy, it wasn't easy at all. If you hadn't come for me this afternoon, I don't know how much longer I could have taken it. I probably would have died in that house. It's that simple, Uncle Nat. I would have died in that house, and then my husband and the good Reverend Bob would have carried me out in the middle of the night and dumped my body in an unmarked grave.'

A New Life

Because of my friendship with Joyce Mazzucchelli, who owned the house on Carroll Street that she shared with her B.P.M. daughter and two grandchildren, I was able to find new digs for Aurora and Lucy. There was an empty room on the third floor of the brownstone. In former times, it had served as a multipurpose workshop-studio for Jimmy Joyce, but now that Nancy's Foley walker ex-husband was gone, why couldn't they live there? I asked. Rory had no money and no job, but I would be willing to pay the rent until she got back on her feet, and now that Lucy was old enough to lend an occasional hand with Nancy's kids, it might work out to everyone's advantage.

'Forget about the rent, Nathan,' Joyce said. 'Nancy needs an assistant for her jewelry business, and if Aurora doesn't mind helping out with the cleaning and cooking, she can have the room for free.'

Good old Joyce. We had been monkeying around together for almost six months by then, and even though we lived in separate places, it was the rare week when we didn't spend at least two or three nights in the same bed – hers or mine, depending on what the mood and circumstances dictated. She was a couple of years younger than I was, which made her something of an old broad, but at fifty-eight, fifty-nine, she still had enough moves to keep things interesting.

Sex among aging people can have its embarrassments and comical longueurs, but there is also a tenderness to it that often eludes the young. Your breasts might sag, your cock might droop, but your skin is still your skin, and when someone you care about reaches out and touches you, or holds you in her arms, or kisses you on the mouth, you can still melt in the same way you did when you thought you would live forever. Joyce and I hadn't reached the December of our lives, but there was no question that May was well behind us. What we were together was an afternoon in mid- to late October, one of those bright fall days with a vivid blue sky above, a gusty nip in the air, and a million leaves still clinging to the branches – most of them brown, but with enough golds and reds and yellows left to make you want to stay outdoors as long as you can.

721

No, she wasn't the beauty her daughter was, and based on the early photographs I'd seen of her, she never had been. Joyce attributed Nancy's physical appearance to her late husband, Tony, a building contractor who had died of a heart attack in 1993. 'He was the handsomest man I ever met,' she once told me. 'The spitting image of Victor Mature.' With her strong Brooklyn accent, the actor's name emerged from her mouth sounding something like *Victa Machuah*, as if the letter *r* had atrophied to such a degree that it had been expunged from the English alphabet. I loved that earthy, proletarian voice. It made me feel on safe ground with her, and as much as any of the other qualities she possessed, it told you that this was a woman without pretension, a woman who believed in who and what she was. She was the mother of the Beautiful Perfect Mother, after all, and how could she have raised a girl like Nancy if she hadn't known what she was about?

On the surface, we had almost nothing in common. Our backgrounds were entirely different (city Catholic, suburban Jew), and our interests diverged on nearly every point. Joyce had no patience for books and was a strict nonreader, whereas I shunned all physical exertion, striving for immobility as the ne plus ultra of the good life. For Joyce, exercise was more than just a duty, it was a pleasure, and her preferred weekend activity was getting up at six o'clock on Sunday morning and riding her bike through Prospect Park. She still worked, and I was retired. She was an optimist, and I was a cynic. She had been happily married, and my marriage – but enough about that. She paid little or no attention to the news, and I read the paper carefully every day. Back when we were children, she had rooted for the Dodgers, and I had rooted for the Giants. She was a fish and pasta person, and I was a meat and potatoes man. And yet – and what can be more mysterious about human life than this *yet*? – we got along like gangbusters. I had felt an immediate attraction the morning we were introduced (out on Seventh Avenue with Nancy), but it wasn't until we had our first long talk at Harry's funeral that I understood there might be a spark between us. In a fit of shyness, I had put off calling her, but then one day the following week she invited me to the house for dinner, and so the flirtation began.

Did I love her? Yes, I probably loved her. To the extent that I was capable of loving anyone, Joyce was the woman for me, the only candidate on my list. And even if it wasn't the full-blown, one hundred percent passion that supposedly defines the word *love*, it was something that fell just short of it – but so close to the mark as to render the distinction meaningless. She made me laugh a lot, which medical experts claim is good for one's mental and physical health. She tolerated my foibles and inconsistencies, endured my black funks, stayed calm during my blistering rants against the G.O.P., the C.I.A., and Rudolph Giuliani. She tickled me with her rabid devotion to the Mets. She astonished me with her encyclopedic knowledge of old Hollywood films and her talent for identifying every minor and forgotten actor who flitted across the screen. *(Look, Nathan, there's Franklin Pangborn . . . there's Una Merkel . . . there's C. Aubrey Smith.)* I admired her for having the courage to let me read to her from *The Book of Human Folly*, and then, in her good-natured ignorance, how she treated my piddling stories as literature of the first rank. Yes, I loved her to the full extent allowed by law (the law of my nature), but was I prepared to settle down and spend the rest of my life with her? Did I want to see her every day of the week? Was I mad enough about her to pop the big question? I wasn't sure. After the long disaster with Name Deleted, I was understandably hesitant to consider another stab at matrimony. But Joyce was a woman, and since the vast preponderance of women seem to prefer couplehood to singledom, I figured I owed it to her to prove that I meant business. In one of the darkest moments of that fall – two days after Rachel suffered a miscarriage, four days after Bush was illegally handed the election, and twelve days before Henry Peoples managed to zero in on the missing Aurora – I broke down and did it. To my immense surprise, the marriage proposal was greeted with hoots of raucous laughter. 'Oh, Nathan,' Joyce said, 'don't be such a nitwit. We're doing just fine the way we are. Why rock the boat and start making trouble for ourselves? Marriage is for young people, for kids who want to have babies. We've already done that. We're free. We can screw around like a pair of teenagers, and we're never going to get pregnant. Just whistle, pal, and my big Italian ass is yours, okay? You get my ass, and I get your nice Yiddish you-know-what. You're my first Jew, Nathan, and now that you've parked yourself on my doorstep, I'm not about to give you up. I'm yours, baby. But forget about this marriage stuff. I don't want to be a wife anymore, and the fact is, my sweet, funny man, you'd make a terrible husband . . .'

In spite of these tough words, she started crying a moment later – suddenly overwrought, losing control of her emotions for the first time since I'd known her. I assumed that she was thinking about her dead Tony, remembering the man she had said yes to when she was hardly older than a girl, the husband she had lost when he was only fifty-nine, the love of her life. That might have been the case, but what she said to me was something entirely different. 'Don't think I don't appreciate it, Nathan. You're the best thing that's happened to me in a long time, and now this, now you give me this. I'm never going to forget it, angel. An old bag like me getting proposed to. I don't mean to blubber, but boy, boy oh boy, knowing you care that much hits me right where I live.'

I was relieved to know that I had touched her enough to produce those tears. It meant that there was something solid between us, a connection that wasn't going to be broken any time soon. But I also have to admit that I felt relieved that Joyce had turned me down. I had made my big gesture, but in all honesty I had been of two minds about it, and she knew me well enough to understand that yes, I would have made a terrible husband, and neither one of us had any business getting married. And so, to paraphrase the words of the immortal Dr. Pangloss, everything turned out for the best – and for the first time in my life, I got to have my cake and eat it too.

Joyce dried her tears, and two weeks later Aurora and Lucy were living in her house. It was a sensible arrangement for all concerned, but even if logic demanded that mother and daughter should be reunited, one mustn't forget how difficult it was for Tom and Honey to let go of their young charge. They had been taking care of Lucy for months by then, and over the course of time the threesome had solidified into a close little family. I had felt a similar pang when I relinquished her to them back in the summer, and she had lived with me for only a few weeks. When I thought of the five and a half months they had spent with her, I couldn't help sympathizing with them – no matter how happy we all were that Aurora had landed safely in Brooklyn. 'She has to live with her mother,' I said to Tom, trying to be philosophical about it. 'But a part of Lucy still belongs to us, to each one of us. She's our girl, too, and nothing will ever change that.'

Hard as it was for them to lose her, their brief foray into parenthood had convinced Tom and Honey that they wanted children of their own. For the moment, they were preoccupied by a multitude of practical concerns – negotiating the sale of Harry's building, looking for a new apartment, applying for teaching jobs around the city – but once those chores were dispensed with, Honey threw away her diaphragm, and the two of them got down to the nightly business of attempting to start a family. In March of 2001, they moved into a co-op on Third Street between Sixth and Seventh Avenues: an airy, light-filled place on the fourth floor with a sizable living room in front, a modest kitchen and dining room in the center, and a narrow hallway that led to three small bedrooms in the back (one of which Tom converted into a study). By the time they set up house in that apartment, Brightman's Attic was no more. As one of the conditions for completing the sale of the building, the buyer had insisted that the books be removed from the premises, which had compelled Tom to spend a frantic period at the start of the year liquidating the entire stock of Harry's old business. Paperbacks were sold for five and ten cents, hardcovers were listed at three for a dollar, and the volumes that didn't sell by February first were shipped off to hospitals, charity organizations, and merchant seamen libraries. I helped out with these lugubrious tasks, and while the rare books and first editions on the second floor brought in a considerable amount of money (even at the rock-bottom prices Tom was willing to accept in order to transfer the whole collection to a single dealer in Great Barrington, Massachusetts), it was no fun taking part in the demolition of Harry's empire – especially when I learned what the new owner was planning to do with the space after it was empty. Books were giving way to women's shoes and handbags, and the top three floors were being converted into expensive co-op apartments. Real estate is the official religion of New York, and its god wears a gray pin-striped suit and goes by the name of Cash, Mr. More-and-More Cash. If there was any consolation for me in this grim turn of events, it was the knowledge that Tom and Rufus would never be hard up again. For the two hundredth time since his death, my thoughts turned to Harry – and his vast swan dive into eternal greatness.

On a Thursday evening in early June, Honey announced that she was pregnant. Tom put his arm around her, then leaned across the dinner table and asked me if I would be the godfather. 'You're our only choice,' he said. 'For services rendered, Nathan, above and beyond the call of duty. For outstanding courage in the heat of battle. For risking life and limb to rescue your wounded comrade under intense fire. For prodding that same comrade to stand on his feet again and enter into this conjugal union. In recognition of these heroic acts, and for the benefit of our future offspring, you deserve to wear a title more fitting to your role than that of great-uncle. Therefore, I dub thee godfather – if thou wilt accept our humble supplication to assume the mantle of that burden.

What shall it be, good sir? We await thine answer with pounding hearts.' The answer was yes. A yes followed by a long string of mumbled words, none of which I can remember now. Then I raised my glass to them, and unaccountably my eyes filled with tears.

Three days later, Rachel and Terrence drove in from New Jersey for Sunday brunch at my apartment. Joyce helped me prepare the spread, and as the four of us sat in the back garden eating our bagels and lox, I noticed that my daughter looked lovelier and happier than at any time in recent months. Her miscarriage in the fall had been a brutal disappointment, and she had been on shaky ground ever since – covering up her sadness by working too hard at her job, cooking elaborate gourmet meals for Terrence to prove that she was a worthy spouse in spite of her failure to bear a child, exhausting herself at every turn. But that day in the garden, the old luster was shining in her eyes again, and though she was normally reserved in company, she more than held her own in the four-way conversation, talking as much and as often as the rest of us. At one point, Terrence excused himself to go to the bathroom inside, and a moment later Joyce dashed off to the kitchen to fetch a new pot of coffee. Rachel and I were alone. I kissed her on the cheek and told her how beautiful she looked, and she responded to the compliment by returning the kiss and then leaning her head against my shoulder. 'I'm pregnant again,' she said. 'I took the test this morning, and the results were positive. There's a baby growing inside me, Dad, and this time it's going to live. I promise. I'm going to make you a grandfather, even if I have to stay in bed for the next seven months.'

For the second time in less than seventy-two hours, my eyes unexpectedly filled with tears.

Pregnant women were sprouting up all around me, and I was turning into something of a woman myself: a person who wept at the mere mention of babies, a lachrymose saphead who needed to walk around with a box of emergency tissues so as not to embarrass myself in public. Perhaps the house on Carroll Street was partly to blame for these lapses of manly decorum. I spent a good deal of time there, and now that Nancy's husband had been replaced by Aurora and Lucy, the household had become an entirely feminine universe. Its only male member was Sam, Nancy's three-year-old son, but as he could barely talk, his influence over its operations was severely limited. Otherwise, it was all girls, three generations of girls, with Joyce at the top, Nancy and Aurora in the middle, and the ten-year-old Lucy and the five-year-old Devon at the bottom. The interior of the brownstone was a living museum of female artifacts, with galleries devoted to the display of bras and panties, blow-dryers and tampons, makeup jars and lipstick tubes, dolls and jump ropes, nighties and bobby pins, curling irons and facial creams and endless, endless pairs of shoes. To go there was like visiting a foreign country, but since I adored every person who lived in that house, it was the single place on earth I preferred above all others.

In the months that followed Aurora's escape from North Carolina, a number of curious things happened chez Joyce. Because the door was always open to me, I was in a position to observe these dramas at close hand, and I watched in a state of perpetual wonder and surprise. With Lucy, for example, all bets were suddenly off. During her time with Tom and Honey, I had been apprehensive, expecting trouble to break out at any minute. Not only had she threatened to become 'the baddest, meanest, cussingest little girl in the whole of God's creation,' but it seemed inevitable to me that her mother's continued absence would eventually wear her down, turning her into a mopish, angry, disgruntled kid. But no. She had thrived in that apartment above Harry's old store, and her adjustment to her new surroundings had continued at a remarkable pace. By the time I brought Rory back to Brooklyn with me, Lucy's southern accent was gone, she had shot up at least four or five inches, and she was one of the best students in her class. Yes, she had often cried for her mother at night, but now that her mother had returned, one would assume our girl would have felt her prayers had been answered. No again. There was an early rush of happiness immediately following the reunion, but after a while resentments and hostilities began to surface, and by the end of their first month together, our smart, energetic, wisecracking child had turned herself into a royal pain in the ass. Doors slammed; polite requests were greeted with sour derision; belligerent shouts resounded from the third floor; grumps devolved into sulks, sulks devolved into storms, storms devolved into tears; the words *no, stupid, shut up,* and *mind your own business* became an integral part of the daily discourse. With everyone else, Lucy's conduct was unchanged. Only her mother was subjected to these assaults, and as time went on, they became more and more relentless.

Demoralizing as this behavior was on the fragile Aurora, I began to see it as a necessary purge, a sign that Lucy was actively fighting for her life. The question of love wasn't at issue. Lucy loved her mother, but that same beloved mother had also thrown her onto a bus one hectic, crazy afternoon and shipped her off to New York, and for the next six months the girl had been abandoned. How can a little person absorb such a perplexing turn of events without feeling at least partially to blame? Why would the mother get rid of the child unless the child was bad, a creature unworthy of the mother's love? Through no fault of her own, the mother had slashed a wound across her daughter's soul, and how can the wound ever heal if the daughter doesn't cry out at the top of her lungs and announce to the world: I'm in pain; I can't stand it anymore; help me? The household would have been a more tranquil place if Lucy had kept quiet, but bottling up that scream would have caused her no end of trouble in the long run. She had to let it out. There was no other way to stop the bleeding.

I made an effort to see Aurora as often as I could, especially in those first difficult months when she was still struggling to find her bearings. The North Carolina horrors had marked her for life, and we both knew she would never fully recover from them, that no matter how well she managed to cope in the future, the past would always be with her. I offered to pay for regular sessions with a therapist if she thought they would help, but she said no, she'd rather just talk to me. Me. The bitter, solitary man who had crept home to Brooklyn less than a year earlier, the burnout who had convinced himself there was nothing left to live for – knuckleheaded me, Nathan the Unwise, who could think of nothing better to do than quietly wait to drop dead, now transformed into a confidant and counselor, a lover of randy widows, and a knight-errant who rescued damsels in distress. Aurora chose to talk to me because I was the one who had gone down to North Carolina and saved her, and even if we had been out of contact for many years prior to that afternoon, I was nevertheless her uncle, her mother's only brother, and she knew that she could trust me. So we got together for lunch several times a week and talked, just the two of us, sitting at a back table in the New Purity Diner on Seventh Avenue, and little by little we became friends, in the same way her brother and I had become friends, and now that both of June's children were back in my life, it was as if my baby sister had come alive in me again, and because she was the ghost who continued to haunt me, her children had now become my children.

The one thing Aurora had never shared with her mother, her brother, or anyone else in the family was the name of Lucy's father. She had guarded that secret for so many years by then, it seemed futile to broach the question anymore, but at one of our lunches in early April, without any prompting from me, the answer accidentally slipped out.

It all began when I asked her if she still had her tattoo. Rory put down her fork, broke into a big smile, and said, 'How do you know about that?'

'Tom told me. A big eagle on your shoulder, right? We wondered if you'd had it taken off, but Lucy wouldn't tell us.'

'It's still there. As big and pretty as ever.'

'And David was all right with that?'

'Not really. He saw it as a symbol of my fucked-up past and wanted me to get rid of it. I was willing to go along with him, but it turned out to be too expensive. When he realized we couldn't afford it, David did a one-hundred-and-eighty-degree about-face. That gives you a good idea of how he thinks, of why I could never win an argument against him. Maybe it's a good thing, he said. We'll leave the tattoo where it is, and every time we look at it, we'll remember how far you've come from the dark days of your youth. That's typical David for you: *the dark days of my youth.* He said it would be an amulet that I wore on my own skin, and it would protect me from further harm and suffering. An amulet. I had no idea what that was, so I looked it up in the dictionary. A charm for warding off evil spirits. Okay, I can buy that. It didn't do much for me when I was with David, but maybe it will help now.'

'I'm glad you still have it. I don't know why I'm glad, but I am.'

'Me too. I'm kind of attached to that stupid thing. I had it done in the East Village eleven years ago. To celebrate getting pregnant with Lucy. The same morning the nurse at the clinic told me I'd tested positive, I rushed out and got my tattoo.'

'A strange way to celebrate, no?'

'I'm a strange girl, Uncle Nat. And that was probably the strangest time of my life. I was renting some rathole apartment off Avenue C with two guys, Billy and Greg. Billy played the guitar, Greg played the fiddle, and I sang. We weren't too bad, really, considering how young we were. Most of the time, we'd perform out in Washington Square Park. Or else in the Times Square subway station. I loved the echoes in those underground halls, belting out my songs as people dropped their coins and dollars into Greg's fiddle case. Sometimes I sang stoned, and Billy would call me his floozy, woozy, boozy girl. Sometimes I sang sober, and Greg would call me the Queen of Planet X. Jesus Christ. Those were good times, Uncle Nat. When we couldn't earn enough playing our music, I'd go into stores and shoplift. They called me Fearless Fosdick. Rumbling down the aisles of a supermarket, stuffing steaks and chickens under my coat. Nothing was serious back then. One week I was in love with Greg. The next week I was in love with Billy. I slept with both of them, and then I wound up pregnant. I never knew which one was the father, and since neither one of them *wanted* to be the father, I kicked them both out.'

'So that's why you never told June. You didn't know.'

'Shit. I can't believe how dumb I am. Shit, shit, shit. I swore to myself I'd never tell anyone, and now I've gone ahead and done it.'

'It doesn't matter, Rory. Greg and Billy are just names to me. Don't say another word if you don't want to.'

'Greg died of an overdose about two years after Lucy was born. And Billy just kind of vanished. I don't know what happened to him. Somebody once told me that he went back home, finished college, and teaches music in some high school out in the Midwest. But who knows if it's the same Billy Finch? It could be someone else.'

Even after she arrived in Brooklyn, it was far from certain that Aurora had seen the last of David Minor. My name and address were in the telephone book, and it wouldn't have been difficult for him to track her down through me. I cringed at the thought of another confrontation with that self-righteous turd, but I kept my fears to myself and said nothing to Rory. Minor was such a painful subject for her, she could barely bring herself to talk about him, and I didn't want to stir up any new anxieties that would add to the problems she already had to contend with. As the months went by, I began to feel more hopeful, but it wasn't until late June that I was finally able to stop worrying and put the matter to rest. A thick white envelope appeared in my mailbox one morning, and because I carelessly failed to notice that the letter had not been addressed to Nathan Glass but to Aurora Wood in care of Nathan Glass, I opened it before I realized my mistake. The brief, handwritten cover note read as follows:

> *Dear One,*
> *It's better this way.*
> *Good luck – and may God ever be merciful to you.*
> *David*

The note was attached to a seven-page document, which turned out to be a divorce decree from Saint Clair County in the State of Alabama, dissolving the marriage between David Wilcox Minor and Aurora Wood Minor on the grounds of desertion.

That day at lunch, I apologized to Rory for having opened her mail, and then I handed her the letter.

'What is it?' she asked.

'A note from your ex,' I said. 'Along with a bunch of official papers.'

'My ex? What does that mean?'

'Open it up and find out.'

As I watched her read the note and scan the document, I was struck by how little her expression changed. I had thought she would smile, perhaps even let out a laugh or two, but her face registered almost nothing. A slight flicker of some buried, enigmatic feeling, but it was impossible to know what the feeling was.

'Well,' she said at last. 'I guess that's that.'

'You're free, Rory. If you wanted to, you could marry someone else tomorrow.'

'I'm never going to let another man touch me for the rest of my life.'

'That's what you say now. Eventually, someone new will come along, and you'll start thinking about marriage again.'

'No, I mean it, Nathan. That part of my life is over and done with. When David locked me in that room, I said to myself: This is it, no more falling for men. Not a single good thing ever came of it. And nothing ever will.'

'You're forgetting Lucy.'

'Okay, one thing. But I already have my kid, and I don't need another.'

'Is everything all right? You sound awfully down on yourself.'

'I'm fine. I've never felt better.'

'You've been here for six months now. You live in Joyce's house, you work for Nancy, you take care of your girl, but maybe it's time to think about the next step. You know, start making plans.'

'What kind of plans?'

'It's not for me to say. Whatever you want.'

'But I like things the way they are.'

'What about singing? Aren't you tempted to get back into it?'

'Sometimes. But I don't want a career anymore. I wouldn't mind doing some weekend stuff around the neighborhood, but no more traveling, no more big ambitions. It's not worth it.'

'Are you happy making jewelry? Is it enough to satisfy you?'

'More than enough. I get to be with Nancy every day, and what can be better than that? There's no one like her in the whole world. I love her to pieces.'

'We all love her.'

'No, you don't understand. I mean, I *really* love her. And she loves me back.'

'Of course she does. Nancy is one of the most affectionate people I've ever known.'

'You still don't get it. What I'm trying to say is that we're *in love*. Nancy and I are lovers.'

'. . .'

'You should see your face, Uncle Nat. You look like you've swallowed a typewriter.'

'I'm sorry. It's just that I didn't know. I could see that you two hit it off. I could see that you liked each other, but . . . but I hadn't realized that it had gone that far. How long has it been going on?'

'Since March. It started about three months after I moved in.'

'Why didn't you tell me before?'

'I was afraid you'd tell Joyce. And Nancy doesn't want her to know. She thinks her mother will flip out.'

'So why tell me now?'

'Because I decided that you can keep a secret. You're not going to let me down, are you?'

'No, I'm not going to let you down. If you don't want Joyce to know, I won't tell her.'

'And you're not disappointed in me?'

'Of course not. If you and Nancy are happy, more power to you.'

'We have so much in common, you see. It's like we're sisters, and our minds are on the same wavelength. We always know what the other one is thinking and feeling. The men I've been with, it was always about words – talking, explaining, arguing, yacking all the time. With us, I just have to look at her, and she's inside my skin. I've never had that with anyone before. Nancy calls it a magic bond – but I just call it love, pure and simple. The real deal.'

'Just like Tony'

I kept my promise and didn't say anything to Joyce, but holding on to
the secret had as much to do with protecting myself as it did with helping out the girls. If and when Joyce discovered the truth, I had no idea
how she would react. I suspected that it wouldn't be calmly, and if that
turned out to be so, then one possible result of her ire would be to look
for someone to blame. And who better to cast in the role of fall guy than
Aurora's uncle, the bungling moocher who had wrangled his unbal-
anced, corrupting niece into the heart of the Mazzucchelli household,
whereupon she had connived to turn the innocent Nancy into a flam-
ing, passionate lesbian? I imagined that Joyce would kick Rory and
Lucy out of the house, and in the family mayhem that followed, I would
be put in the position of having to defend my sister's daughter, which
would so alienate Joyce from me that I would be booted out as well. We
had been together for a year by then, and God knows that was the last
thing I wanted to happen.

On a warm, quiet Sunday just after the end of summer vacation, she
joined me at my apartment for an evening of movie watching and Thai
food. After we had phoned in our order to the restaurant, she turned to
me and said, 'You won't believe what they've been up to.'

'Who are we talking about?' I asked.

'Nancy and Aurora.'

'I don't know. Making and selling jewelry. Looking after their kids.
The usual grind.'

'They're sleeping together, Nathan. They're having an affair.'

'How do you know?'

'I caught them. I stayed here Thursday night, remember? I got up
early the next morning, and instead of going straight to work, I went
back home to change my dress. The plumber was supposed to come that
afternoon, and I went upstairs to remind Nancy about the appointment.
I opened the door of her bedroom, and there they were, the two of them
lying naked on top of the covers, fast asleep in each other's arms.'

'Did they wake up?'

'No. I closed the door as softly as I could, and then I tiptoed down the stairs. What am I going to do? I'm so devastated, I feel like slitting my wrists. Poor Tony. For the first time since he left me, I'm glad he's dead. I'm glad he isn't around to see this . . . this *awful thing*. It would have broken his heart. His own daughter sleeping with another woman. It makes me want to throw up every time I think about it.'

'There's not a lot you can do, Joyce. Nancy is a grown woman, and she can sleep with any person she wants. The same with Aurora. They've both been through rough times. They've both had marriages break up on them, and they're both probably a little sick of men. It doesn't mean they're gay, and it doesn't mean it will last forever. If they can find some comfort in each other for the time being, where's the harm?'

'The harm is that it's disgusting and unnatural. I don't see how you can be so cool about it, Nathan, I really don't. It's like you don't even care.'

'People feel what they feel. Who am I to tell them they're wrong?'

'You sound like a gay rights activist. Pretty soon, you'll be telling me you've had affairs with men.'

'I'd rather cut off my right arm than go to bed with a man.'

'Then why defend Nancy and Aurora?'

'Because they're not me, for one thing. And because they're women.'

'What's that supposed to mean?'

'I'm not sure. I'm so attracted to women myself, I guess I can understand why a woman would be attracted to another woman.'

'You're a pig, Nathan. It turns you on, doesn't it?'

'I didn't say that.'

'Is that what you do when you're alone? Sit around here at night watching lesbo porn movies?'

'Hmmm. I never thought of that. It might be more fun than typing up my stupid book.'

'Don't make jokes. Here I am on the brink of a nervous breakdown, and you're cracking jokes.'

'Because it's none of our business, that's why.'

'Nancy's my daughter . . .'

'And Rory's my niece. So what? They don't belong to us. We just have them on loan.'

'What am I going to do, Nathan?'

'You can pretend you don't know anything about it and leave them in peace. Or else you can give them your blessing. You don't have to like it, but those are your only two choices.'

'I could throw them out of the house, couldn't I?'

'Yes, I suppose you could. And you'd wind up regretting it every day for the rest of your life. Don't go there, Joyce. Try to roll with the punches. Keep your chin up. Don't take any wooden nickels. Vote Democrat in every election. Ride your bike in the park. Dream about my perfect, golden body. Take your vitamins. Drink eight glasses of water a day. Pull for the Mets. Watch a lot of movies. Don't work too hard at your job. Take a trip to Paris with me. Come to the hospital when Rachel has her baby and hold my grandchild in your arms. Brush your teeth after every meal. Don't cross the street on a red light. Defend the little guy. Stick up for yourself. Remember how beautiful you are. Remember how much I love you. Drink one Scotch on the rocks every day. Breathe deeply. Keep your eyes open. Stay away from fatty foods. Sleep the sleep of the just. Remember how much I love you.'

Her reaction to the news was more or less as I had predicted, but at least she hadn't held me accountable for Rory's actions, which was all I was concerned about just then. I was sorry she had opened that door, sorry the facts had been revealed to her in such a shocking, indelible way, but eventually she would have to come to terms with the situation, whether she liked it or not. The meal came, and for the next little while we stopped talking about Nancy and Aurora and concentrated on our food. I remember feeling exceptionally hungry that night, and I bolted down my appetizers and spicy shrimp with basil in just a few minutes. Then we turned on the TV and started watching a film called *The Outriders*, a Western from 1950 starring Joel McCrea. At one point, the cowboys were sitting around a campfire chewing the fat, and the old geezer of the bunch (played by James Whitmore, I believe) delivered a line that got a loud guffaw from me. 'I kind of relish getting old,' he said. 'It takes the bother out of living.' I kissed Joyce on the cheek and whispered, 'That fathead doesn't know what he's talking about,' and for the first time that night, my still-rattled, unhappy darling laughed as well.

Ten minutes after Joyce emitted that laugh, my own life was coming to an end. We were sitting on the sofa watching the film, and suddenly I felt a pain in my chest. At first, I took it for heartburn, indigestion brought on by the food I had eaten, but the pain continued to grow, spreading across my upper body as if my insides had caught fire, as if I had swallowed a gallon of hot molten lead, and before long my left arm had gone numb and my jaw was tingling with the pinpricks of a thousand invisible needles. I had read enough about heart attacks to know that these were the classic symptoms, and since the pain kept building, kept climbing to ever more unbearable stages of intensity, I figured my moment had come. I tried to stand up, but after two steps I fell down and began writhing around on the floor. I was clutching my chest with both hands, I was struggling for breath, and Joyce was holding me in her arms, looking down at my face and telling me to hang in there. Somewhere in the distance, I heard her say, 'Oh, my God. Oh, my God, it's just like Tony,' and then she wasn't there anymore, and I heard her shouting at someone, telling him to send an ambulance to First Street. Remarkably enough, I wasn't scared. The attack had carried me into another zone, and questions of life and death were of no importance in that place. You merely accepted. You merely took what you were given, and if death was what I had been given that night, I was prepared to accept it. As the paramedics lifted me into the ambulance, I noticed that Joyce was there again, standing next to me with tears pouring down her face. If I remember correctly, I think I managed to smile at her. 'Don't die on me, baby,' she said. 'Please, Nathan, don't die on me.' Then the doors closed, and a moment later I was gone.

Inspiration

I didn't die. As it turned out, I didn't even have a heart attack. An inflamed esophagus was the cause of my agony, but no one knew that at the time, and for the rest of the night and the bulk of the following day, I was convinced my life was over.

The ambulance took me to Methodist Hospital at Sixth Street and Seventh Avenue, and because all the beds on the upper floors were full just then, they put me in one of the small cubicles reserved for cardiac patients in the Emergency Room downstairs. A thin green curtain divided me from the main desk (when the nurses remembered to close it), and except for an early visit to the X-ray Unit down the hall, I did nothing but lie on a narrow bed the whole time I was there. My body was hooked up to a heart monitor, and with an IV needle planted in my arm and plastic oxygen tubes stuck into my nostrils, I had no choice but to remain on my back. Blood was drawn from me every four hours. If a coronary had taken place, small bits of damaged tissue would have broken loose from the heart and filtered into the bloodstream, and eventually those bits would begin showing up in the tests. A nurse explained that it would be twenty-four hours before they knew for certain. In the meantime, I had to lie there and wait it out, alone with my fear and morbid imagination as my blood gradually told the story of what had or hadn't happened to me.

Paramedics kept wheeling in new patients, and one by one they passed before me with their epileptic seizures and intestinal blockages, their knife wounds and heroin overdoses, their fractured arms and bloody heads. Voices called out, telephones rang, food carts clattered along the floor. These things were happening no more than a body's length from the tips of my feet, and yet for all the effect they had on me, they might have been happening in another world. I don't think I've ever been more numb to my surroundings than I was that night, more locked into myself, more absent. Nothing felt real to me except my own body, and as I lay there wallowing in my brokenness, I became fixated on trying to visualize the circuits of veins and arteries that criss-crossed below my chest, the dense inner network of glop and blood. I was in

there with myself, rooting around with a kind of scrambled desperation, but I was also far away, floating above the bed, above the ceiling,
above the roof of the hospital. I know it doesn't make any sense, but
lying in that boxed-in enclosure with the beeping machines and the
wires clamped to my skin was the closest I have come to being nowhere,
to being inside myself and outside myself at the same time.

That's what happens to you when you land in a hospital. They take
off your clothes, put you in one of those humiliating gowns, and suddenly you stop being yourself. You become the person who inhabits
your body, and what you are now is the sum total of that body's failures. To be diminished in such a way is to lose all right to privacy.
When the doctors and nurses come in and ask you questions, you have
to answer them. They want to keep you alive, and only a person who
didn't want to live would give them false answers. If you happen to be
in a small cubicle, and just three feet to your right another person is
being questioned by a doctor or a nurse, you can't help overhearing
what that person says. It's not that you necessarily want to know the
answers, but you find yourself in a position that makes it impossible
not to know them. That was how I was introduced to Omar Hassim-
Ali, a fifty-three-year-old Egyptian-born car-service driver with a wife,
four children, and six grandchildren. He entered the cubicle a little past
one in the morning after experiencing chest pains while chauffeuring a
fare across the Brooklyn Bridge. Within a matter of minutes, I had
learned that he took pills for his high blood pressure, that he still
smoked a pack a day but was trying to cut down, that he suffered from
hemorrhoids and occasional bouts of dizziness, and that he had been
living in America since 1980. After the doctor left, Omar Hassim-Ali
and I talked for close to an hour. It didn't matter that we were
strangers. When a man thinks he's about to die, he talks to anyone who
will listen.

I slept very little that night – a couple of catnaps of ten or fifteen minutes each – but an hour or so after dawn, I drifted off in earnest. At eight
o'clock, a nurse came in to take my temperature, and when I looked
over to my right, I saw that my roommate's bed was empty. I asked her
what had happened to Mr. Hassim-Ali, but she couldn't give me an
answer. Her shift had just come on duty, she said, and she didn't know
anything about it.

Every four hours, the blood tests came back negative. There were
morning visits from Joyce, from Tom and Honey, and from Aurora and

Nancy – but no one was allowed to stay for more than a few minutes. In the early afternoon, Rachel showed up as well. They all began by asking the same question – *How was I feeling?* – and I gave them all the same answer: Fine, fine, fine, don't worry about me. The pain had vanished by then, and I was starting to feel more confident about my chances of getting out of there in one piece. I said, I didn't live through cancer in order to die from some dumb-ass coronary infarction. It was an absurd statement, but as the day wore on and the blood tests continued to come in negative, I clung to it as logical proof that the gods had decided to spare me, that the attack of the previous night had been no more than a demonstration of their power to control my fate. Yes, I could die at any moment – and yes, I had been certain that I was about to die as I lay in Joyce's arms on the living room floor. If there was anything to be learned from this brush with mortality, it was that my life, in the narrowest sense of the term, was no longer my own. I had only to remember the pain that had ripped through me during the terrible siege of fire to understand that every breath that filled my lungs was a gift from those capricious gods, that from now on every tick of my heart would be granted to me through an arbitrary act of grace.

By ten-thirty, the empty bed was occupied by Rodney Grant, a thirty-nine-year-old roofer who had passed out while climbing a flight of stairs earlier that morning. His co-workers had called for an ambulance, and there he was in his skimpy hospital gown, a burly, large-muscled black man with the face of a young boy, looking positively frightened out of his wits. After his interview with the doctor, he turned to me and said that he was dying for a smoke. Did I think he would get into trouble if he went to the men's room and lit up a cigarette? You won't know until you try, I said, and off he went, unhooking himself from the heart monitor and wheeling his IV line down the hall. When he returned a few minutes later, he smiled at me and said, 'Mission accomplished.' At two o'clock, a nurse opened the curtain and informed him that he was being transferred to the Cardiac Unit upstairs. Never having fainted before, never having been diagnosed with anything more worrisome than chicken pox and a mild case of hay fever, the young man was confused. 'It looks pretty serious, Mr. Grant,' the nurse said. 'I know you're feeling better now, but the doctor needs to run some tests.'

I wished him luck when he left, and then I was alone in the cubicle again. I thought about Omar Hassim-Ali, trying to remember the names of his various children, and wondered if he hadn't been transferred to the upstairs unit as well. It was a reasonable supposition, but as I looked over at the empty cot to my right, I couldn't help imagining that he was dead. I didn't have a single scrap of evidence to confirm that hypothesis, but now that Rodney Grant had been escorted to his uncertain future, the bare bed seemed to be haunted by some mysterious force of erasure, blotting out the men who had lain on it and ushering them into a realm of darkness and oblivion. The empty bed signified death, whether that death was real or imagined, and as I pondered the implications of this idea, another idea gradually took hold of me, which overwhelmed all thoughts about everything else. By the time I saw where I was going, I understood that I had come up with the single most important idea I had ever had, an idea big enough to keep me occupied every hour of every day for the rest of my life.

I was no one. Rodney Grant was no one. Omar Hassim-Ali was no one. Javier Rodriguez – the seventy-eight-year-old retired carpenter who took over the bed at four o'clock – was no one. Eventually, we would all die, and when our bodies were carried off and buried in the ground, only our friends and families would know we were gone. Our deaths wouldn't be announced on radio or television. There wouldn't be any obituaries in the *New York Times*. No books would be written about us. That is an honor reserved for the powerful and famous, for the exceptionally talented, but who bothers to publish biographies of the ordinary, the unsung, the workaday people we pass on the street and barely take the trouble to notice?

Most lives vanish. A person dies, and little by little all traces of that life disappear. An inventor survives in his inventions, an architect survives in his buildings, but most people leave behind no monuments or lasting achievements: a shelf of photograph albums, a fifth-grade report card, a bowling trophy, an ashtray filched from a Florida hotel room on the final morning of some dimly remembered vacation. A few objects, a few documents, and a smattering of impressions made on other people. Those people invariably tell stories about the dead person, but more often than not dates are scrambled, facts are left out, and the truth becomes increasingly distorted, and when those people die in their turn, most of the stories vanish with them.

My idea was this: to form a company that would publish books about the forgotten ones, to rescue the stories and facts and documents before they disappeared – and shape them into a continuous narrative, the narrative of a life.

The biographies would be commissioned by friends and relatives of the subject, and the books would be printed in small, private editions – anywhere from fifty to three or four hundred copies. I imagined writing the books myself, but if demand ever became too heavy, I could always hire others to help with the work: struggling poets and novelists, ex-journalists, unemployed academics, perhaps even Tom. The cost of writing and publishing such books would be steep, but I didn't want my biographies to be an indulgence affordable only by the rich. For families of lesser means, I envisioned a new type of insurance policy whereby a certain negligible sum would be set aside each month or quarter to defray the expenses of the book. Not home insurance or life insurance – but biography insurance.

Was I crazy to dream that I could make something of this far-fetched project? I didn't think so. What young woman wouldn't want to read the definitive biography of her father – even if that father had been no more than a factory worker or the assistant manager of a rural bank? What mother wouldn't want to read the life story of her policeman son who was shot down in the line of duty at age thirty-four? In every case, it would have to be a question of love. A wife or a husband, a son or a daughter, a parent, a brother or a sister – only the strongest attachments. They would come to me six months or a year after the subject had died. They would have absorbed the death by then, but they still wouldn't be over it, and now that everyday life had started for them again, they would understand that they would never be over it. They would want to bring their loved one back to life, and I would do everything humanly possible to grant their wish. I would resurrect that person in words, and once the pages had been printed and the story had been bound between covers, they would have something to hold on to for the rest of their lives. Not only that, but something that would outlive them, that would outlive us all.

One should never underestimate the power of books.

X Marks the Spot

The results of the final blood test came in just after midnight. It was too late to discharge me from the hospital, so I stayed on until morning, feverishly planning the structure of my new company as I watched the exhausted Javier Rodriguez doze in the opposite bed. I thought of various names that would capture the spirit of the work that lay before me, and in the end I hit upon the neutral but descriptive *Bios Unlimited*. About an hour after that, I decided that my first move would be to contact Bette Dombrowski in Chicago and ask her if she would be interested in commissioning me to write a biography of her ex-husband. It seemed appropriate that the first book in the collection should be about Harry.

Then they let me go. I stepped out into the cool morning air, and I felt so glad to be alive, I wanted to scream. Overhead, the sky was the bluest of pure deep blues. If I walked quickly enough, I would be able to get to Carroll Street before Joyce left for work. We would sit down in the kitchen and have a cup of coffee together, watching the kids run around like chipmunks as their mothers got them ready for school. Then I would walk Joyce to the subway, put my arms around her, and kiss her good-bye.

It was eight o'clock when I stepped out onto the street, eight o'clock on the morning of September 11, 2001 – just forty-six minutes before the first plane crashed into the North Tower of the World Trade Center. Just two hours after that, the smoke of three thousand incinerated bodies would drift over toward Brooklyn and come pouring down on us in a white cloud of ashes and death.

But for now it was still eight o'clock, and as I walked along the avenue under that brilliant blue sky, I was happy, my friends, as happy as any man who had ever lived.

2003–2004